MIRROR SIGHT

KRISTEN BRITAIN

GOLLANCZ
LONDON

The right of Kristen Britain to be identified as the author of this
work has been asserted by her in accordance with the
Copyright, Designs and Patents Act 1988.

First published in Great Britain in 2014 by Gollancz
An imprint of the Orion Publishing Group
Orion House, 5 Upper St Martin's Lane, London WC2H 9EA
An Hachette UK Company

A CIP catalogue record for this book is available
from the British Library

ISBN 978 0 575 09968 5

1 3 5 7 9 10 8 6 4 2

Printed in Great Britain by
Clays Ltd, St Ives plc

The Orion Publishing Group's policy is to use papers
that are natural, renewable and recyclable products and made
from wood grown in sustainable forests. The logging and
manufacturing processes are expected to conform to the
environmental regulations of the country of origin.

www.kristenbritain.com
www.orionbooks.co.uk
www.gollancz.co.uk

ENTOMBED

She lay entombed in stone and dark. Light did not exist here, the blackness snuffing out whatever memory of sunshine and moonglow she carried within her, as surely as the thinning air stole her breath and suffocated her. She kicked and pummeled the close walls of her prison again and again, heedless of causing even more harm to injuries she had suffered in Blackveil.

But no one heard her. No one came to her rescue and opened her tomb. Spent by her efforts, she fell limp and lay gasping in the dark.

Karigan G'ladheon wondered what she had done to deserve such a death. The last she remembered was having been in Blackveil—Castle Argenthyne. She'd shattered the looking mask to prevent Mornhavon the Black from possessing it and then dreamed or imagined she'd fallen through the heavens. Perhaps it had been no dream. Otherwise, how had she ended up here, wherever *here* was?

She found no difference in the darkness when she closed her eyes. She was tired, her mind dulled from lack of air, and she wished to just keep her eyes closed and sleep, but then she remembered her moonstone and pulled it out of her pocket. Its light was a dim, sputtering orange as if the darkness of her tomb were too great, was killing it, too. It cast just enough light to confirm what she felt and sensed: she was trapped in a rectangular stone box like a sarcophagus. She was seized by a new wave of panic that sent tremors coursing through her body, but this time she was too weak to kick or scream.

Instead, she grew listless in the wan glow of the moonstone, caring little about hands bloodied from pounding on unyielding stone, or that the arrow shafts that splinted her broken wrist had shifted in their bindings. Shards of silver protruding from her flesh and glinting in the light, the remnants of the looking mask, elicited only faint interest.

Her bonewood cane, she observed, had also made the journey with her, and lay beside her reminding her of how warriors were often buried with their weapons.

As she lay weakening and starved for breath, none of it seemed to matter anymore. Her hand fell slack and the moonstone rolled off her fingers, extinguishing immediately. She faded, faded away into darkness . . .

Crack.

Scrape, scrape.

Dirt showered Karigan's face. It was a distant sensation. She hadn't the energy to wipe it away.

Scrape, scrape.

Her nose tickled. A faint freshening of the air. Music seeped in, almost as if she were hearing it from under water. A graying of the dark, a crack forming around the lid of her tomb. The tip of a tool pried into the crack, widening it further.

"Help!" she cried, but it came out only as a harsh whisper. Someone must have heard her pounding, after all. She was going to be rescued. She would be free of this death box.

The tool nosed farther in, more light penetrating the dark, the brassy music growing louder. A second tool was shoved into the crack.

Karigan's heart thudded, and she tried to push up on the lid, but she hadn't the strength.

The tools paused their work and the music faded. Light shifted. "No," Karigan moaned. "Don't stop—keep going! Please . . ."

A thrum vibrated through the stone and rose in intensity until she realized it was drumming, a fast rolling rhythm.

The tools went back to work, the crack widening and widening until the lid teetered on one edge and then scraped over the side, thudding to the ground. Karigan wiped grit out of her eyes and took a deep breath, relieved at no longer having to strain to fill her lungs. The drums silenced and an expectant hush suffused the air. A pair of shadowed faces peered into her tomb, then jerked away as if startled.

Guess they weren't expecting me.

Another deep inhalation took in a mixture of scents—soil, horses, sweat, smoke, cooked foods . . . She sat up, head spinning, and was blinded by light that beamed into her face. She heard a collective gasp from a large crowd of people surrounding her, but at a distance. She groped after her moonstone, and with the aid of the bonewood cane, she stood. Screams and murmurs greeted her rising.

Definitely not expecting me.

She squinted against the light, held her hand up to shade her eyes, but discerned little, only that she seemed to be in the middle of a sort of arena, with many people seated around its circumference.

"Behold the marvels of the underworld!" a man's voice boomed. "The dead walk again!" The announcement was followed by stuttered applause, which grew into thunderous approval.

Where am I? Karigan wondered again.

The brassy music started up once more and the light swept away revealing men in white face and motley, tumbling, juggling and battling one another with wobbly swords. One rose up from the ground, arms stretched out before him, walking as if asleep or aroused from the dead. Mimicking her? Their antics were met with clapping and laughter by the audience.

Clowns? A circus? Karigan was trying to put together the notion of a circus with her tomblike entrapment—and when she glanced behind herself she saw it was indeed a sarcophagus with a weathered crescent moon and some script on its side—into some coherent form, when both of her arms were grabbed by a pair of strong clowns with snarling demon visages on their faces. Maybe she was actually dead and this was one of the five hells.

The clowns hauled her across the arena and through a curtain into the back. She cried out in pain as they pushed and shoved her, jarring her injuries. She grayed out, and they dragged her. She barely perceived gaudy performers warming up, a prancing white horse, rigging, platforms, and balance beams cluttering the space.

The clowns threw her into an alcove formed by trunks and crates. Before she could get her bearings and sit up, a third man thrust his way between the clowns and glared at her. He pointed a riding crop in her face. "Who are you?" he demanded. "Who put you up to this?"

He was a small, round man in dark business attire, though in a cut she had not seen before, and his hair carefully trimmed. His cheeks and nose flushed pink.

Karigan rose to her elbow. "Where am—?"

The crop snapped down at her. She raised her arm just in time to avoid being struck across her face. It was her broken wrist that caught the blow. The splint mostly protected her, but pain burned up her forearm and she cried out.

"I ask the questions. Was it Josston who put you up to this? Hmm? He is ever wanting to ruin me, embarrass me."

"Dunno, boss," one of the clowns said. "Crowd liked it. Walking dead and all."

"Thanks to the ringmaster's quick thinking," the man growled. He turned his anger back on Karigan. "What did you do with the goodies inside—keep 'em for yourself, eh?"

Goodies? What was he talking about? With a great deal of effort, she rose to her feet. The man raised the crop again.

"You should not assault a king's messen—"

This time when the crop descended, she broke the blow with the bonewood.

"Try that again and you shall be sorry," Karigan said, hoping it would be enough.

"Insolence! I will not have it!"

She pressed the trigger embedded in the shaft of the bonewood and extended it from cane length to staff length with a shake. When the crop lashed at her again, she thrust the butt of her staff into the man's belly. The wind *oofed* out of him and he crumpled away. The clowns caught his arms before he hit the ground. Karigan took her chance and shoved by them, looking for the nearest way out.

"Stop her!" the man cried.

In her condition, she'd never outrun the man's henchmen.

Henchclowns? She kicked over a bucket of soapy water behind her and pulled down a tower of empty packing crates. The soapy water merely soaked into the dirt and sawdust floor, but the crates impeded them. She rushed for an opening in the tent as fast as her limping gait allowed, dashing past a bear attached to a chain, and a contortionist bent over backward, watching Karigan from between her knees.

Karigan shook her muddled head and escaped into the dark of night.

EXCAVATIONS

Karigan fled from the big tent, her injured leg slowing her little in her desperation. She passed smaller, billowing tents, and cages filled with roaring lions. She dodged past performers and lingerers, and veered away from tough looking circus jacks and roustabouts. When she left the circus behind, she found herself skittering down unfamiliar streets of flagstone and brick paving, walled by faceless, brick buildings that rose sharply into the night sky.

Where am I? she wondered not for the first time.

The circus boss had sounded Sacoridian, but she did not recognize this place. Steady, bright light welled beneath plain, wrought iron lampposts—much brighter than what she was accustomed to in her own Sacor City. She avoided the light, pausing in an alleyway to rest and think.

The air she inhaled tasted acrid, smoky, leaving an ache in the back of her throat. The moon above the tall buildings looked smudged by soot. She had not seen the moon since the eve of the spring equinox, before she and her companions had crossed over the D'Yer Wall and into Blackveil—unless one counted the silver full moon that had hung over Castle Argenthyne back through a piece of time.

And her companions, what of them? Had they survived the shattering of the looking mask? She prayed it was so, refused to consider the alternative. If they indeed survived, had the force of the mask's destruction cast them from Blackveil, or did they remain, even now, in the nexus of Castle Argenthyne wondering where she was?

Her body trembled in exhaustion. If her friends had ended

up here, wherever here was, she needed to help herself before she could help them. She did not know how much longer she could go on. In fact, taking a nap in the alley did not sound unappealing.

No, need help. Need to find out where I am.

She peered out into the street and when she saw no clowns in pursuit, she limped away from the alley. The only sign of life she spotted was a pale cat darting down another street. No lights shone in the tiny, regular windows lining the brick walls. She was alone.

She turned down another street. Each ran straight and precise—she'd never encountered anything like it, and it was a sharp contrast to the winding ways of the Eletian roads she'd so recently wandered along in the ruins of Argenthyne. This street ended at a smaller building, constructed not of brick but of clapboard, light spilling from windows and a pair of doors left open and welcoming.

Karigan proceeded cautiously. This city was strange, and not knowing the customs of the people here, she did not wish to rush headlong into trouble. Leaning heavily on the bone-wood, she limped toward the lit building. As she approached, she heard voices within, mostly that of one man droning on and on. When Karigan reached the doors, she peered inside. On the far end a man stood on a stage pointing at a large map with a long slender stick. On a table next to him were a number of jumbled, dirt-encrusted items, including a rusty long-sword and a cracked earthenware pitcher. There were several smaller objects she could not identify.

An audience of ladies and gentlemen filled the chairs in the large room watching the man intently. A few gentlemen stood along the walls, also watching. Like the circus boss, their clothing was of an unfamiliar cut, and mostly in conservative darks and grays. Arms and necks were not left bare. Most of the men wore beards, some with long drooping mustaches and bushy side whiskers. The ladies wore their hair tucked beneath hats and bonnets, and, most startling, gauzy veils draped their faces.

"So we have initiated our excavations in quadrant seven," the man on the stage said in his monotonous voice as he tapped the map, "which has shown much promise."

A man in the audience raised his hand.

"Yes?"

"It seems to me you shall only find more minor burials."

"But there is much to learn from even minor burials about—"

"Like you learned from the Big Mounds?"

There was some snickering in the audience. The man on stage frowned, then jabbed his pointer at the map again. "We excavated those mounds east of the Old City to put to rest all speculation they were not the burial sites of ancient kings, but simply deposits of sand and gravel shaped by the glaciers thousands of years ago. We have wanted nothing but to be exacting in our methods."

Could it be he was talking about the Scangly Mounds? Karigan wondered. She peered harder at the map. The bright hissing lamps helped her make out the lines and shadings. The landforms looked vaguely like the area around Sacor City, and the Big Mounds he pointed out certainly corresponded to where one would find the Scangly Mounds upon which she'd so enjoyed riding her Condor. The landmass in the center of the map, divided into a grid by precise intersecting lines, could very well be Sacor City, but . . .

Then a gentleman along the wall caught her eye. He stared at her. Karigan's heart leaped. She realized she'd been drawn almost across the threshold of the building, to get a better view of the map, and could be plainly seen by anyone who bothered to look.

The gentleman, whose gray-speckled brown hair swept luxuriantly across his brow, twitched his mouth, which wiggled his bushy mustache. He had full side whiskers, too. He touched the shoulder of a younger man beside him. When the second man turned to look, Karigan ducked from the lit doorway, shaking.

She did not know these people, this place. She was not ready to trust anyone until she learned more. She ran-limped away. Did she hear footsteps running after her, or was it her own that echoed against the canyons of brick walls?

She turned into another alley, breathing hard, sweat slicking down her sides. She decided to call on her fading ability, and in this way she could survey the city, town, or whatever this place was, without being observed. But when she touched the winged horse brooch clasped to her greatcoat, she felt no change. She glanced at her hands and down at her body. She remained solid—she had not faded out. She tried again, and nothing.

"What . . . ?" What had the looking mask done to her?

A scent of putrid, decaying matter wafted to her. She glanced down the alley. She thought she detected movement, but the alley was too shrouded in darkness. Hesitating but a moment, she withdrew her moonstone from her pocket, but it emitted only a weak, dying glow as it had in the sarcophagus.

Magic does not work here, Karigan thought. *At least not much.*

The moonstone emitted enough light to sketch out a heap of rubbish at the other end of the alley. There was more movement. A cat? An oversized rat looking for food scraps?

But then the heap stood and the low gleam of the moonstone caught in the whites of its—his—eyes . . . and on the metallic sheen of a knife.

Karigan gasped and pocketed her moonstone, intending to flee, but when she turned, her escape was blocked by two hulking figures.

She found herself wishing, absurdly, she was back in Blackveil. She raised the bonewood staff to a defensive position, thankful it had made the journey with her, but regretting the loss of her saber, which had served her so well since she became a Green Rider, and F'ryan Coblebay before her. Lost forever, she suspected, in the deeps of Castle Argenthyne.

Even as the two at the open end of the alley rushed her, so did the one with the knife from behind. Karigan did not think, she moved. With her right hand all but useless, she swept the staff at the two forward assailants relying on the strength of her left. She smashed the closest one in the chin. As he staggered away, she rammed the butt of the staff backward catching the knife-bearing assailant in the gut. He fell back with a grunt of pain.

She thrust the staff forward again, battering the metal handle into the bridge of the third assailant's nose. She felt warm splatters across her face, and he reeled away clutching at his bleeding nose.

Not bad, Karigan thought, for being one-handed and pretty much one-legged.

She made to retreat from the alley, only to find half a dozen more figures blocking her way.

MORPHIA

Karigan backed away as the thugs advanced on her. One of her original assailants recovered enough to grab her from behind. She smashed the heel of her boot into his instep, and he hopped away howling. The others paused as one as if reassessing their prey, indistinct in their ragged cloaks. She held her staff in a defensive position, keeping an ear open to anyone creeping up on her from behind. Mostly she heard whimpering from that quarter.

Her limbs quivered from having expended so much of her energy in Blackveil, as well as in the streets of this nameless city. Her mauled leg was likely to give out at any time now, and truly she wanted nothing more than to drop where she stood, but that would mean worse consequences.

"Put down yer stick, girlie," one of the thugs said, "and we won't hurt ya. Real gentlemen we are, ain't we, boys?"

The others answered with affirmative grunts.

"Let me go, and I won't hurt *you*," she said, her dry throat making her voice harsh.

"Got ya some sass, eh? There's them that'd pay good for the likes of you."

Karigan did not wait for them to make the first move. She charged into them with a guttural yell, staff humming as the metal handle thudded into the leader's skull. She had hoped they'd scatter after that, but they grabbed for her, their rags rancid with filth. The staff became entangled in their arms, and when one kicked her injured leg, she sank with a moan, and they descended on her as predators on wounded prey.

Karigan momentarily blanked out beneath their vile

stench as they tore at her greatcoat, tried to force the staff from her hand, groped her. It would be so easy to let go, to give up. . . .

In another moment they were inexplicably off her. She shook her head, the air freshened around her. The predators scattered as a new presence swung a club and threw them aside.

She couldn't move. She lay on the paving only able to watch as the last thug loped away, the one who had fought them off looming over her, a man, she observed, from the silhouette of his profile. The shadows of his hood obscured his features, but she felt his gaze upon her. Was he her savior or a new danger?

He tossed the club aside, and it clattered loudly on the paving. He knelt beside her and helped her sit up. He produced a nondescript cloak from nowhere and tossed it around her shoulders.

"It is foolish to be out here at this hour unescorted," he said.

"Who are you?" she asked.

He did not answer but helped her to stand. She'd kept a death grip on her staff and did not loosen it now.

"Can you walk?" he asked.

"Not very well."

"Lean on me, then."

She did not. "Who are you, and where are we going?"

He made an impatient noise from beneath his hood. "I am the one who drove off your attackers. I am taking you to safety."

Karigan wanted to trust him, to pass the responsibility of her safety on to someone else, but could she trust this man? Really, at this point, how much of a choice did she have? With all her injuries, the lapse in her ability to fade, and not knowing this city and its ways, her choices had diminished significantly. So far the man had only aided her. Coming to a decision, she allowed him to put his arm around her so he could bear some of her weight. At least he did not smell offensive.

He led her toward the alley's outlet and paused to peer

both ways down the street. He hissed and suddenly pulled her back into the concealment of the shadows.

"What is it?" she asked.

"Shhh. You ask too many questions."

She had a sharp retort on her tongue but held it when she heard footsteps out on the street and a curious metallic *click-click-click* sound. When the footsteps paused so did the clicking, which was replaced by an odd purring hum. Light flowed down the alley, but Karigan and her rescuer were pressed hard enough against the brick wall that the light did not touch them. It focused on a trio of thugs left moaning on the pavement.

"What is it?" a man's voice asked.

"Dregs is all," another answered. "Rubbish collectors'll pick 'em up later. C'mon."

The footsteps continued on, and there was an odd toot, and the *click-click-click* started again.

Her rescuer waited at length before peeling away from the wall.

"Who were they?" she demanded.

The man sighed in irritation. "Inspectors. Now come. We don't want to be caught out."

Inspectors? she wondered. What were they inspecting? They had not cared about the men lying in the alley, and her rescuer certainly did not like them.

Karigan hated relying on this stranger's strength. He was not gentle, she thought, as they moved out into the empty street. It wasn't, she suspected, that he was intentionally being rough, but that he was being more vigilant of their surroundings than of her comfort. And perhaps he did not realize the extent of her various hurts.

"Ow!" she cried, when he bumped her bad leg.

"Silence," he whispered. "There could be more thugs about, or Inspectors."

"Then be more careful," she said.

"I am very sorry, but I've a job to do."

Karigan halted, planted herself on the street. If he wanted to move forward, he'd have to drag her.

"What do you mean job?" she asked, darkening with suspicion. "Are you one of those clowns?"

"What? Clowns?" His voice held a tone of incredulity. She still could not see his face beneath the shadow of his hood, but his eyes glinted in the lamplight.

"Then who are you? Where in the name of the gods am I? You sound Sacoridian, but this is like no place in Sacoridia I've ever seen."

He did not answer, just stared at her.

"I'm very sorry," he said finally, "but you do ask too many questions, and this is not the time or place."

Before Karigan could reply, he withdrew a cloth from beneath his cloak and thrust it into her face, pressing it over her mouth and nose, overpowering her with its sickly sweet stench. At first she fought, but he held her fast, and her strength, the little that remained to her, leaked out of her. Her knees gave way, the stranger supporting her as she spiraled into oblivion.

The face belonged to a balding man who peered down at her out of the haze. "Well, hello there, young lady. How are we feeling?"

At first she felt numb, but all her various pains were intensifying with every moment. She appeared to be, however, comfortably situated in a huge bed with a downy mattress and warm blankets pulled up to her chest.

"Who are you? Where am I?" It seemed to take a great deal of strength just to speak.

"I am Mender Samuels, and you are safe and sound in your uncle's house."

"Uncle? What uncle?"

Mender Samuels turned away to address someone behind him. "A little disorientation is not unusual, considering what you said about her time in the asylum, which must have been most distressing."

Asylum? Karigan's heart thudded. She tried to sit up, but the pain took her breath away, and she fell back into her pillows.

"There, there, young lady," the mender cooed. "We've reset your broken wrist, pulled shards of a mirror from your flesh, and tended the ghastly wounds on your leg. You have been through quite an ordeal, it seems, and now you can rest." To someone else he said, "The syringe, please."

An assistant in the shadows handed him a long, sharp needle, which protruded from a glass tube filled with fluid.

This could not be good. "What—what is that?" Karigan asked, feeling like a trapped animal. She glanced around the dim room—too many people hovering in the shadows and standing between her and the door.

"It is only morphia," the mender said. "It shall ease your pain and help you rest." He pressed a plunger on the end of the tube and a small amount of fluid squirted out of the tip of the needle.

Karigan had to get away. She threw her blankets aside and lunged forward to leap out of bed, but she was caught by strong hands that pressed her back into the pillows and did not let her go. The needle descended and stabbed into the meat of her upper arm. She yelped.

"Why?" she asked plaintively. "Why are you doing this to me?"

"Do not worry, my dear," the mender replied with a shadowed smile. "It is for your own good."

BRANDY

The morphia had been, Karigan thought, really quite pleasant, vanquishing her pain for the first time in what felt like forever. One never really knew just how taxing pain was till one was free of it and could feel the difference. She'd given herself over to the lulling, floating quality of the morphia and slept, slept the sleep of tombs, vacant of dreams and visions.

But when the pain began to nag at her again, she found herself surfacing from the depths of slumber. Perhaps in the wakening world she'd find more morphia to once again release her from the pain that ached throughout her body with growing intensity.

Her eyes cracked open to an amber glow, like the dawning light that filtered through her window at Rider barracks and onto the wooden floor.

Rider barracks. Was she there? Was she home after some seriously awful adventures? The barracks burning down and everything that had followed, could they have been dreams?

A shifting inside her. A dislocation. Nothing had really changed, not the light, her pain, the bed. But a brief light-headedness spun her round and when it settled, she knew she was not home, that this was not Rider barracks. Barracks was gone forever, had been gone for some time, just ashes and ruins. A tear formed in the corner of her eye, the grief fresh all over again.

I am not supposed to be here, she thought, though she still did not know where "here" was.

She heard soft footsteps on floorboards—someone was in the room with her. A young woman folding sheets, her back

toward Karigan. Her long skirts rustled as she worked. She
wore a scarf about her head, concealing her hair. One last
sheet was folded, and the young woman, who must be a
household maid, placed the sheets in a cabinet. She cast a
quick glance at Karigan, who closed her eyes and pretended
to still sleep. The maid then strode from the room, softly
clicking the door shut behind her.

Karigan lay there, feeling the full brunt of returning pain.
Her wrist especially, and when she lifted it, it felt much
heavier than it should. She discovered it was immobilized in
a hardened plaster. Much more clever, she thought, than the
wood and linen affairs the menders at home used. Those
tended to loosen and slip, and often bones did not knit back
together properly. Wherever she was, the menders here were
much more advanced.

Gazing beneath her blankets, she inspected herself further
and found she'd been garbed in a very fine linen sleeping
gown; so tightly and perfectly woven that she'd never seen
anything of like quality, which was saying something for a
textile merchant's daughter. And the sheets, too. Her attention moved to her mauled leg and dozens of smaller wounds —
from the shattered looking mask? All had been bandaged.
However she had gotten here, by her own will or not, she'd
been well tended.

Her room was large and airy with a high ceiling. The furnishings, though spare of ornamentation, appeared to her
merchant's eye to have been crafted by masters, and they
gleamed with a high polish. On the walls, paintings of bowls
of fruit broke up the busy, flowery pattern of wall coverings.

She found a hand bell on her bedside table. If she rang it,
she supposed someone would attend her, perhaps bring food
and drink, which was tempting because she was hungry and
thirsty. She could also demand answers from whomever answered her summons. But first things first. She eased out of
bed, her body trembling and weak, and pulled a chamber pot
out from beneath the bed.

That necessity accomplished, she crossed the room to peer
out the only window, espying dull sunlight and the brick wall
of a neighboring building. She began to explore her room

further and, to her dismay, found no sign of her uniform or the bonewood. She limped over to a wardrobe but found nothing inside except for a lonely shawl. Not only had she been disarmed, but they, whoever *they* were, possessed her brooch and moonstone. It did not matter her magic was not working here, those items were important to her and not intended for the idle hands of others.

She wanted her things back. She needed answers. She returned to the wardrobe and removed the shawl of soft lamb's wool and placed it around her shoulders. Then she went to the door, cracked it open, and listened. The tones of male voices in heated discussion drifted to her from somewhere else in the house.

She peered out into the corridor and, upon seeing no one, she stepped out onto a plush runner with an intricate floral pattern, which muted her limping footsteps. She crept past imposing behemoths of mismatched furniture—a few Second Age pieces and several lesser examples from the Third; and busts on pillars, portraits of stern personages in garb of unknown style, and statuettes of young shepherds and milkmaids cast in gaudy gilt. Definitely not to her own taste. There appeared to be no set scheme to the décor, and it had more the look of the jumbled accumulation of a collector who lacked focus. Or discernment.

She came to the top of a curving flight of stairs with a handsome banister of deep mahogany. Under different circumstances she'd enjoy sliding down it to the bright foyer at the bottom. The voices came to her more loudly now, and one she immediately recognized as the circus boss. He must have figured out she was here. As she could not see either of the speakers, she determined they must be meeting in a room—a parlor, perhaps?—just off the foyer.

"I want you to keep your nose out of my business," the circus boss declared. "No more hoaxes."

"I am sure I've no idea of what you are talking about," replied the other man in a milder tone. "You have come into my home accusing me of the most ridiculous—"

"I've five hundred witnesses who saw it, some girl, a *live* girl, stepped out of the sarcophagus."

"I am still mystified as to why you believe I've anything to do with this."

"Who put her in there?" the circus boss demanded. "Eh, Professor? Who put her in there? You are the one constantly attacking me with your libelous detractions."

"I do not care for your tone, sir," the one referred to as the professor replied, "or your accusations."

"I want to know where the coffin is, and the old bones that were supposed to be in it. I want them back and with all the goodies intact."

There was a moment of heavy silence before the professor responded. "Mr. Hadley, I had no part in this hoax of yours. Perhaps you should speak to your *supplier* before heaping groundless accusations upon me." Karigan detected the distaste in the professor's voice.

"Groundless? You are the one always speaking against me, calling me a desecrator. How is that any different from you, hmm?"

"I do not open the resting places of the dead for entertainment, and then sell their burial goods for profit."

"They're dead," Mr. Hadley said, "and they don't care. What you do is not so different, opening tombs for your own audiences. Why shouldn't I profit from it, too?"

"My audience, as you call it, consists of other archeologists and scientists. We do so to study our ancestors, and in dignity, not to entertain the crass multitudes."

Mr. Hadley laughed. "Sure, sure, whatever you say."

"I think this interview is quite over, Mr. Hadley, and I will thank you not to return. You are not welcome here. If you've any commentary to make, take it to my solicitor. Grott! See Mr. Hadley out, please."

A man in domestic livery stepped into the foyer with a brimmed, bowl-shaped hat in his hands and waited. Mr. Hadley, the circus boss, entered the foyer from the opposite direction, grabbed the hat from Grott, and clapped it on his head. He turned toward the room he'd just left. "If I discover you had anything to do with the other night, I will not be back, but I will send Inspectors in my stead and you can answer to *them*. Your solicitor be damned."

Grott opened the door, and Mr. Hadley stomped out into the glare of the street. The butler wasted no time in closing the door after him.

The professor emitted a long, thunderous sigh. "Grott," he said, "I need a brandy."

"Yes, sir." The butler left the foyer in measured steps.

Karigan watched in fascination as the man whose house this must be, the man who either sheltered her or held her prisoner, emerged in the foyer. She remembered him. She'd seen him in the . . . had it been a lecture? The one with the drooping mustache who had spotted her hovering on the building's threshold.

He paused before a mirror, fussing with his cravat and grumbling to himself about bloody-minded grave robbers, and then said to his reflected image, "A little early for brandy, old man, but Hadley does that to you, doesn't he." He chuckled, then patted his cravat and turned when Grott appeared with a glass on a silver tray.

Perhaps catching Karigan in the corner of his eye, or sensing her gaze on him, he glanced up the flight of stairs and found her. Karigan wanted to flee, for she'd become accustomed to running and hiding, but resolutely she held her ground and stared unflinchingly back at him. She would not be afraid, and she would demand answers.

"Grott," the professor said removing his brandy from the tray, his own gaze not leaving Karigan. "I believe we'll need another."

UNCLE

A door at the far end of the corridor burst open, making Karigan jump. An imposing woman, all swishing skirts and matronly bulk, charged through the doorway and down the corridor toward her. Karigan tensed to flee.

"Don't you trouble yourself, Professor," the woman boomed. "I'll deal with her."

Karigan glanced down at the professor, who held his brandy frozen halfway to his mouth, a bemused expression on his face.

Then, before Karigan could utter a protest, the woman swooped down on her, took hold of her good arm, and swept her down the corridor. "You should not be out of bed, missy."

"But—"

"Mender Samuels ordered bed rest, and bed rest it shall be."

"But—"

The woman's expression brooked no argument, and Karigan held her tongue. In moments they were back in her room, and the woman helped her into bed, her assistance gentle in contrast to her brusque manner. As Karigan sank into the mattress, she had to admit it was good to be off her bad leg.

"I don't know what they did to you at the asylum or why," the woman said, clucking as she observed Karigan's bandaged wounds. "One hears such horrid stories. But you are safe now, free of that wretched institution."

"But *where* am I?"

The woman paused with the covers in her hand and raised an eyebrow. Her hair, streaked with gray, was bundled on top of her head, and a monocle hung from a silver chain around her neck.

"Dear, dear," the woman said. "I thought you knew, but the mender said you'd be disoriented. You are in your uncle's house in Mill City. I am his housekeeper, Mirriam."

Karigan had never heard of Mill City, and why did they insist she had an uncle here? "Where are my things?"

"Things? What things?"

"That came with me."

"I could not say."

As Mirriam busied herself with tucking Karigan in, Karigan realized she was not likely to get much in the way of answers from the housekeeper. Either she did not know the answers, or she'd been ordered to reveal nothing. In that case, Karigan needed to see her "uncle," whom she assumed to be the professor. That was another question: why would this stranger claim to be her uncle?

"Now, will you be needing more morphia?" Mirriam asked. "Mender Samuels showed me how to administer it."

Karigan closed her eyes, remembering how the morphia had vanquished her pain, made everything so pleasant she did not care about where she was or why. She'd be able to rest without worry, allow her hurts to mend. She almost craved it. Yet she wished to remain alert, not muddle-brained, and discover exactly where she was and figure out how she was to get home and report to her king and the captain. There was much she wished to tell them about Blackveil, the most troubling being the return of Mornhavon. She hoped once more that her companions had not been harmed by the shattering of the looking mask and were making their way home even now. The morphia *was* a tempting escape, but she could not allow herself to be seduced by it. No, she needed answers first.

"No, no morphia," she finally replied. Was that a look of approval on Mirriam's face?

"Then tea with extract of willow ought to do you," she replied. "Are you hungry? I can have breakfast brought up."

Karigan was, but she said, "I'd like to see my—my uncle."

"You will see him when he wishes you to," Mirriam said,

hands on hips. "He is a very busy man. Meanwhile I'll send Lorine up with your breakfast." She glanced under the bed. "And if you can walk, you can use the privy two doors down, eh? But don't let me find you wandering the halls. Mender Samuels would not approve."

Karigan nodded, and when Mirriam strode from the room, she exhaled in relief. Mirriam seemed to take up a lot of space and air.

Karigan would have to be patient and go along with whatever game these people were playing. They appeared to be concerned with her well-being, and the rest couldn't but help her body, which had been so abused in Blackveil. Another point in their favor, at least in Mirriam's, was that the morphia had not been forced upon her. Considering the lethargic quality it produced, it would be an easy way to control her. Instead, she'd simply been urged not to wander the hallways, an admonition she'd likely ignore if she wanted to learn more about this world and its people, and locate her belongings. She'd just have to make sure she wasn't caught in the process. Mirriam did not strike her as a woman who would easily forgive disobedience.

She gazed at the sunlight falling through her window and wondered what her fellow Riders were up to, if anyone missed her. Specifically, she wondered if King Zachary noticed her absence, and then she shook her head in an effort to reject such painful, yearning thoughts.

Her door opened slowly as the maid she'd seen earlier backed in with a tray laden with covered dishes. In contrast to Mirriam, the young woman moved softly. Her name, Mirriam had said, was Lorine. She brought the tray over and helped settle it across Karigan's lap.

"Your breakfast, miss."

Lorine removed the covers from the dishes and steam rose, the scents of bacon and eggs making Karigan's stomach rumble. And there was toast slathered with jam, a pot of tea, and a generous scoop of butter melting into a mound of fried potatoes.

"If you need anything else, miss, just ring the bell."

Karigan glanced up and noted that the headscarf did more

than just cover Lorine's hair, it concealed scarring that puckered at her temple.

"Thank you," Karigan murmured. "I'm hungry enough that I may eat the dishes and tray, too."

But Lorine was already on her way out of the room. Karigan sighed and ate as she had not eaten since the equinox when she crossed the wall into Blackveil. Hardtack this was not.

As starved as she'd been, though, she did not even come close to eating the dishes or tray. She'd subsisted on so little for so long that it did not take much to fill her stomach. She gazed at the remaining food with regret, but did not think she could possibly handle another mouthful without bursting, so she rang the bell and sipped her tea.

It was not, to her surprise, Lorine, or even Mirriam, who answered her summons. When the door opened, it was the professor who peered in at her, then stepped inside. He was halfway across the room and looked like he was about to speak when Lorine appeared in the doorway behind him.

"Sir? I—" Lorine's eyes were wide and her voice quavered.

The professor turned to her. "Not to worry, my dear, I happened to be almost at the door when I heard the bell ring. You were very prompt."

Lorine curtsied, but looked flustered, especially when the professor handed Karigan's tray to her. It was clear the maid was not accustomed to her employer helping her.

"Do you require more tea?" he asked Karigan.

She shook her head.

"Very well. Off with you, Lorine. If we've need, we shall call."

Lorine bowed her way out of the room, tray in hand. The professor watched after her for a moment. "Poor thing is still nervous after all these years that she might make a mistake," he said. "She was a mill slave before I brought her here, you know, and mistakes aren't tolerated in the mills."

Karigan's mouth gaped open. Mill slaves? Slavery was outlawed in Sacoridia. What a strange place this was, and what a horrifying institution it permitted. She wondered what was being milled that it required slave labor.

The professor dragged a chair to her bedside. Closer up, there was a wolfish aspect to his appearance, his coarse hair shot through with salt and pepper strands, his piercing eyes and direct gaze.

"Are you rested well enough for some company?" he asked.

"Yes!"

He smiled beneath his mustache at her emphatic answer. "I believe we've much to talk about, and it has not been easy waiting these three days as you slept."

Three days, Karigan thought, glad that she had declined another dose of the morphia, though she thought the healing sleep had probably done her much good.

"Are you the one who is supposed to be my uncle?" she asked.

His smile grew even broader. "I am indeed your uncle," he said, "at least for the purpose of keeping you safe."

GOODGRAVE

"Allow me to introduce myself properly."
The professor rose and with a half-bow,
said, "I am Bryce Lowell Josston, adjunct professor of licensed archeology to the Imperial
University." And he sat once again.

Archeology. The term was not well known in Karigan's
world, but she had visited enough museums to recognize it.
"You dig up old things."

"That is quite right, my dear, and study the artifacts so my
colleagues and I may understand the past."

"I'm afraid I have not heard of your Imperial University,"
Karigan replied. "In fact, all I know about where I am is that
this place is called Mill City."

"What is your name and from where do you hail?" the
professor asked, his gaze on her sharpening.

Karigan returned his gaze no less keenly. She wanted to
trust but was not sure how much. Still, she was a Green Rider
whose embassy made her a representative of the king, which
meant she should not hide but declare herself, especially in
the presence of someone who seemed intent on helping her.

"My name is Karigan G'ladheon. I am a king's messenger,
a Green Rider, from the realm of Sacoridia. I noticed you
have some furnishings in your house that are from Sacoridia,
which tells me you are not unfamiliar with my country."

When she had said her name, he leaned forward staring
right into her eyes, squinting as if to divine something about
her, and then opened his mouth to speak. But instead, he
clamped it shut and rose abruptly from his chair to pace as
though deeply unsettled.

Karigan watched as he walked furrows across the floorboards, his hands clasped behind his back, his posture stooped. He spoke as if to himself. "Delusional. Delusional is the only rational explanation. But the objects. Those appear to be authentic." He paused once more, pivoting toward her. "The objects. How did you come by them?"

"If you are referring to my belongings," she replied, her irritation flaring, "the crystal I inherited from my mother, and the walking cane was a gift. I would like them back, please, and my uniform, too."

"You do not claim the winged horse brooch?"

He could see it? Another indication magic was not working here. Rider brooches had spells of concealment on them so that only other Riders could see them.

"The brooch is my badge of office."

He leaned over her, the friendly smile absent from his face. "Do not lie to me, girl. You are playing a very dangerous game. Where did you acquire those artifacts?"

"Who is the one playing games here, I wonder. I am telling you the truth." If he actually reached out to shake her, which it looked like he wanted to do, she would break his nose. "I demand you return my belongings to me, and that you present me to an authority of your government."

"You would not want me to do that," he said, backing off without touching her. "Tell me," he continued, "who is the king you serve?"

"Zachary Hillander."

"Zachary the first, or the second?"

"There is only one Zachary."

"And his queen?"

Karigan raised her eyebrow. Did he believe there was more than one Zachary, or was he testing her? "He is not married, though he is betrothed to Lady Estora Coutre."

"Coutre," the professor murmured, looking as if he might faint. Then he grew sharp and intense all over again. "Where did you learn this information? Who told you?"

"I am a Green Rider," Karigan said through gritted teeth. "I serve Zachary, the king of Sacoridia. The betrothal is general knowledge."

The professor slid weakly into his chair, all intensity vanishing. "My dear, King Zachary and Queen Estora have not reigned for one hundred and eighty-six years."

Karigan's mouth dropped open. "One hundred . . . ?"

"And eighty-six," the professor supplied, nodding. "I can only conclude you are a very disturbed young woman, delusional as I said. But how you acquired information and artifacts of our history that are forbidden is another matter entirely."

"This is Sacoridia—the mask brought me forward," Karigan said with a start but maybe less surprised than she might have been, for she had traveled in time before, though never this far forward. Considering the involvement of the looking mask in all this, she shouldn't be surprised at all. Still, discovering oneself in a future time was a bit of a jolt. But how far forward had she come? When had the reign of Zachary ended relative to her entering Blackveil and smashing the looking mask?

"There was no mask among your items," the professor said, "and how one would . . . *bring you forward* is a notion I do not understand."

Karigan didn't understand it herself, but the mask had been an object of great power. She said no more of it, however, and would not speak of her ability to cross thresholds, to step into other times. He'd only think her more mad than he already did. If this future was without magic, then how would he believe her anyway? Not to mention, Rider abilities were not discussed outside the messenger service.

"You are correct," the professor continued. "This is Sacoridia, though it is no longer called such, and it would be best if you did not say any of these names to anyone. The land that was once called Sacoridia has been incorporated into the Serpentine Empire." His gaze searched her face. "I'd say you were a ghost, but you are all too real. I've seen the wounds of your flesh." He pointed at her plaster encased wrist. "Ghosts don't wear casts. You must be a scholar, then, of secret history, to know these things. Rare for a woman to be of a scholarly bent, but not unheard of. A scholar then, with a sickness of the mind. It appears my claim that I'd removed you from the asylum is rather apt."

There were times, Karigan thought, that she wouldn't argue with the idea that she'd a "sickness of the mind," but this was not one of them. "I want my things back," she said. And somehow she'd have to discover a way to return to her own time. Traveling to the future explained both the strangeness of this world and its similarities with her own, but it looked to be a dangerous future. And the empire? Did this mean Mornhavon had overcome all to conquer her homeland?

"I have placed your artifacts in safe keeping," the professor said. "It would not be prudent to leave them lying around. I am shocked no one found you before we did, elsewise you'd be in Inspector custody, or in the hands of Adherents." He shuddered. "Good thing about the asylum story. Now no one will take your ravings about Green Riders or the old realm seriously, though I warn you not to speak of it at all. The emperor forbids that aspect of history, and he has spies everywhere."

As Karigan tried to digest his words, another thought occurred to her. "You are not the person who stole me off the street."

"No, not personally, but a friend did so at my request," he replied. "And I'd rather not say *stole,* but brought to safety. I do have a reputation for helping unfortunates."

Especially those garbed in historic Green Rider uniforms, she thought. "I am not an . . . unfortunate, and I'd like to be released. You've no right to hold me here."

"Yes, I can see you are a proud one, but trust me, my dear, you do not wish to find yourself on the street again. We shall care for you as Mender Samuels has decreed. In the meantime, I hope you will tell me how you came by those artifacts and learned your history."

"I will leave of my own accord then," she said, tossing her covers aside to do just that.

"Where will you go attired in only your nightgown?"

"Darden!" she snapped.

The professor blinked in surprise, clearly not knowing what she was talking about, and shook his head. "Please rest. Mirriam informed me you turned down a dose of morphia. Perhaps I should have her administer one anyway?"

Karigan heard the inherent threat in his words. "You'll find yourself seriously injured if you try," she said, tensing, ready to spring into action, but he did not move.

"I do not doubt it," he replied. "My friend said you'd fought admirably against those Dregs the other night, which is also curious. No genteel lady would have managed it, had the skill."

"I am no genteel lady. I am a Green Rider."

"So be it. I will not force you to stay, Karigan G'ladheon, or whatever your real name may be, but I hope my hospitality will suffice to keep you peaceably abed until your wounds heal. Just know that the outer world would not be so kind. But perhaps you are beginning to understand that." He rose and gave her a curt bow. "I've no wish to see you come to harm."

He strode across the room, but paused at the door. "Another thing. The name you have given me would incite too many questions from the wrong people. Do not speak it again. We shall use another name. Let us call you Kari Goodgrave. Several Goodgraves have married into the Josston family out east, so it makes sense my niece should be one, too."

After he left, Karigan stared at the door for a long time trying to digest it all. It was forbidden, at least dangerous, to speak of the past—her own present. What had been Sacoridia was now part of an empire, and she could only conclude that Mornhavon the Black had defeated her people. She needed to learn details about how this occurred so she could take word of it home and tell the king. Maybe some advantage could be gained in advance warning.

And just how would she get home? The looking mask had brought her forward, but she hadn't even the shards that had stuck in her flesh.

Her thoughts returned to the professor. If knowledge of the past was forbidden, or at least certain parts of it, then how had he acquired it, even as an archeologist? And how was it that archeology was permitted under such conditions in the first place? She did not understand the contradiction. In any case, she guessed that one reason for holding her here was to prevent her revealing his knowledge of this secret history to others, thus endangering him. And then there was the issue of her name. He had not wanted her to use it—her name was known in the forbidden history.

Why would the empire repress the true history, and what stories did it promote instead? No doubt those that glorified Mornhavon and made the queens and kings of Sacoridia's past appear terrible tyrants. Anything to ensure the populace saw their circumstances as better than what had come before.

She shook her head. Too many questions and too few answers. It was all giving her a headache.

Then she barked a laugh. "Goodgrave!" Of all the possible names. How very appropriate.

RUINS

Lhean Lifeson, child of leaf and wind, born beneath the verdant eaves of the *Vane-ealdar,* the forest of Eletia, now found himself curled in a crevice of tumbled rock and earth. A shaft of daylight plunged through the narrow opening overhead. It occurred to him that this must be what the graves of the mortal dead were like—deep, desolate, though infinitely darker than this.

How did the mortal humans stand it, knowing their lives were so short, spanning but a mere breath of an Eletian's eternal life? That this was where it would end for them, deep in the earth, fodder for worms? And how they struggled to fill that brief life with all the passions humankind could muster. They struggled, struggled as the salmon swimming upstream, only to end, to end forever in nothingness. He did not understand why they did not just collapse in despair, but perhaps he could better appreciate why they clung to myths of their gods and an afterlife—these beliefs of theirs, false or not, gave them hope, allowed them to continue on.

Lhean shook his head. One day, perhaps, he would discuss the peculiarities of mortals with Ealdaen or maybe Telagioth. He never used to care, but now that he had traveled among and with humans, he'd become curious and taken an interest. But that was for another time; at the moment, it appeared he had a problem.

The rupture force of the shattering of the looking mask had thrust him—and likely his other companions—out of Blackveil. One moment he'd been standing in the dying remains of Castle Argenthyne, and the next he'd found himself in this crevice somewhere else. He uncurled himself to climb up, mindful of loose rock that tumbled clattering down if he misplaced his weight. When he reached the rim, he peered cautiously over it, observing only more rocky rubble awash in thin sunlight and stunted scrub trees growing from between black-flecked, gray granite blocks. The air smelled poorly and unclean, of acrid smoke that burned the back of his throat.

He pulled himself the rest of the way out, noting that this upheaved terrain was not just a rending of the land, but the obliteration of some great human work, for the edges of the rubble had not been formed by nature, but by tools. There was also evidence of some great conflagration, for soot adhered to the bottoms and fissures of rock not exposed to weathering.

He turned and found a face of stone staring back at him, its sculpted planes cracked and stained, its beard crumbled away, the remnants of a crown about its temple. The rest was lost beneath the rubble. Despite the ruins and the ill air of the place, it confirmed he was no longer in Blackveil. He knew this place, and he did not. The etherea was nearly gone, sick, dying. A being infused with etherea, as all Eletians were, he could sense inside himself its waning light. It was not just that it was tainted, but that it was almost *gone* from the land, from existence.

And so it was with his home. No matter where an Eletian may be he could always sense Eletia, the water running through the Alluvium, life throbbing through root and leaf, the spirit of his people. Even in the depths of Blackveil he had felt Eletia as a strong presence within.

He placed a trembling hand on his breast plate, over his heart, seeking but failing to feel a stronger awareness of his people. So alone, so bereft, the despair almost broke him to weeping.

Instead he turned his attention to the devastation around him, the jutting angles of hand-cut stone, rotting, sooty timbers. The ruin was upon a high hill, and more stretched all the way to its base where a city, a human city, stood. It was all symmetrically laid out, long rectangular buildings set in precise rows, their huge chimneys spewing filth into the sky. False streams glinted among them, too perfect to be made by nature. Humans called them canals.

He made out streets straight as swords, and more buildings of varying size and shape but still precisely placed. There was little green among the structures and nothing of nature in the design, no curves, no turnings, which made it all so foreign to Lhean's Eletian eyes, so difficult to reconcile in his mind. It was an injury to the land, and the injury extended even beyond his long sight, for the city had beat back the forest that once stood there and much of the farmland, as well.

A clacking of rocks started him to caution again, and he crouched, tugging his gray cloak around his shoulders to conceal the brightness of his armor. He scanned the ruins and discerned two men encumbered with tools, making their way uphill over piles of rubble. They were some distance away, but Lhean's keen hearing was good enough, he could pick up every word they spoke.

"—thought I saw someone up there," said a fellow wearing a brimmed hat.

"Some of the stones look like people and, depending on the light, looks like they're moving."

"Still . . ." the first trailed off, his breath ragged from the effort of climbing over treacherous ground.

"Could be Ghouls," the other replied, "hunting for relics."

"Could be, though they'd be in big trouble if they got caught without a license."

"Enough'll take the chance if they think they'll find something good."

The man in the brimmed hat paused to catch his breath and mop his brow with his sleeve. His companion also stopped, removing an implement from his shoulder and leaning it against a block of granite. He arched his back and kneaded the small of it with his knuckles.

The man in the hat took a long look up the slope. "Sometimes," he said quietly, "I think there are real ghouls in these ruins."

His companion laughed. "You're letting all the old stones get to you, friend. Come, if we don't finish the survey today, we'll be the ones in trouble, especially if we're the cause of a delay for getting that drill emplaced."

His friend shuddered, and they began making their painstaking way, wobbling on loose rocks, sending debris skidding down the hill behind them.

Lhean slid back into his crevice and huddled at the bottom with his knees drawn to his chest. He knew with certainty where he was: these were the ruins of Sacor City, and the one structure in the city that had created so much of the rubble on the crown of the hill was the king's castle.

The force capable of tearing it down must have been terrible beyond imagination, for the strength of the castle was not merely in stone but subtle touches of magic, far less than what was used in the crafting of the D'Yer Wall, but enough to reinforce it. He'd felt the will to endure in the stone when he'd visited King Zachary with Graelalea and Telagioth at the end of winter. He'd felt the castle's confidence and pride even though it was several centuries old. He was also certain the humans who inhabited it, worked and lived within its walls, were entirely deaf to the life in it.

But now it was gone, the castle dead, echoes of memory.

Since Eletians did not see time as necessarily linear, Lhean was not surprised he had traveled forward. He could not sense Ealdaen or Telagioth, so either they had not come here with him, or they lay dead. As for the others, his human companions? He could not say.

It did not matter. He must find some way of returning to the time he'd left behind. Otherwise, in this land where etherea had dwindled to almost nothing, he too, would sicken and fade until he was no more.

In the Present:
YOLANDHE'S ISLAND

The waves rolled Yap onto the pebbly beach. He dug his fingers between the pebbles into silt and sediment to keep the ocean from dragging him back into the deathly deeps. The retreating waves pulled relentlessly on him, hissing over stone and sand, pebbles clicking together. Yap scrabbled forward so he would not lose ground, even while retching all the sea water he had inadvertently drunk.

He managed to reach the crest in the beach that marked the high tide line, and he lay there atop knots of dead rockweed, panting and resting, relieved to have made it to land.

Not food for the fishes today, he thought, as he had often thought after surviving a bad storm on the *Mermaid,* a pirate ship on which he'd served.

Despite having spent much of his life aboard ships, he had never learned to swim. Most mariners never did. Why, learning to swim was bad luck for a sailor. It was like inviting the gods to send disaster, a wave to sweep you overboard or sink the ship.

Somehow he'd made it to land without knowing how to swim. He bet if he knew how, the currents wouldn't have been favorable, and he'd have drowned. The storm and breaking up of the gig notwithstanding, fortune was smiling on old Yap and had brought him ashore alive.

He groaned. But how his head and lungs hurt, and how exhausted he was from his ordeal. He spared a thought for his master. Lord Amberhill was a landsman—surely he did not know how to swim either. Yap hoped it was so. He hoped that fortune had pulled Lord Amberhill ashore, too.

Yap lay there on the stones, oblivious as a hermit crab scuttled by his fingers. He closed salt-rimed eyes against the brightness of the sun uncloaked by the parting of storm clouds.

Later, Yap awoke with a start. His belly ached badly, very badly. He shivered. His back was dry from the sun, but his front wet from lying prone. Waves tickled his toes, which meant the tide was on its way back in. He rubbed his eyes, knocking his specs askew. Somehow they'd stayed with him through the disaster. He tried to polish the residue of salt water from them with his shirt, but when he put them back on, he found he'd only smeared them. It was then, when he looked up to see his surroundings, he realized he was not alone.

First he saw her bare feet and ankles, then he looked up her long legs to the simple kilt of seagrass green. She wore a necklace of pearls and sea glass. Her long hair tousled away from a face he'd seen before. A tremor of fear ran through him, threatening to disgorge the contents of his already upset gut. He writhed on the ground and floundered about in an attempt to crawl away. He'd crawl back into the ocean if he had to.

"Where do you go, small man?" she asked.

Yap squeezed his eyes shut, wanted to clap his hands over his ears, but he knew it was no good, her voice held such power, for she was the sea witch, Yolandhe. She had long, long ago cursed him and his crew to be held stranded on a windless sea, trapped in a bottle for all time until someone had dropped it, releasing the spell. Oddly, the *Mermaid* had materialized in a house nestled deep in the forest, far away from the sea. Yap was the last of his crew who lived.

"I believe," she said, her voice the calming rush of the tide combing the shore, "you took something that is not yours when last you were upon my island."

"N-no," he croaked.

"Give. It. Back." She did not shout, but the command had the power of a storm in it, the crashing waves, the shrieking winds.

An upwelling in Yap's gut caused him to vomit, first only salty fluid, but then more came up, a viscous mass of globules that, when deposited on the ground, was a small pile of pearls slimed with bile. More heaving produced coins of silver and gold, an emerald, a pair of rings, a necklace of gold links, more pearls, a brooch of a dragon, and worst of all, a long dagger with a gold hilt and ruby pommel. He thought it would slice his insides as it came, that it would choke the life out of him as it caught in his throat. When the hilt reached his mouth, he pulled it out and tossed it aside, and yet more pearls gushed out. When it seemed he was finished, he lay there shivering.

Yolandhe did not move. She waited.

Waited for what? Sweat poured down Yap's face. His belly ached, but this time it was from all the heaving. Then he hiccupped and a diamond pendant popped out of his mouth.

Yolandhe nodded. She walked on as if he were no more than driftwood. She didn't even pick up any of the precious objects he'd spewed at her feet. Perhaps that they had been returned to the island was enough.

He rose shakily to his knees, feeling much, much lighter. "Wait!" he called. "Have ya seen my master? We was wrecked in the storm!"

Yolandhe paused, the sea breeze tossing her hair back. She spoke softly, almost delicately, but the breeze carried her words to Yap with no difficulty.

"Yes," she said. "I have found him. He has returned to me."

PLUMBING

Karigan decided she was not a good patient. Not a *patient* patient. Following her conversation with the professor, she was up and down, pacing despite the pain lancing through her leg. She windmilled her good arm and stretched her back. Too much time in bed and her muscles would grow weak and limp. Arms Master Drent would never approve.

She further occupied herself by seeking out the privy Mirriam had mentioned. When she found it, she paused in awe, gawking at the shiny porcelain bowl supported by four bronze mermaids, its seatback fashioned into the shape of a breeching whale.

"Oh, my," Karigan murmured. She peered into the bowl and saw that it contained still water. This was different than the privies she was accustomed to. There'd been shacks with holes and finer closets with aqueducts of actual running water coursing beneath. Selium had a fine system of piped water to deal with the unmentionable.

A brass lever, filigreed with twining seaweeds and periwinkles, jutted from the floor adjacent to the bowl, reaching to the height of her hips. It was not clear to her exactly what the lever was for, but its proximity to the bowl suggested it was integral to its functioning. There was only one way to find out. She pulled on the lever.

It drew back with a *clack-clack-clack-clack* that emanated from some hidden mechanism beneath the floor. When she pulled it back as far as it would go, she released it and the roar of water made her jump. She'd expected *something* to happen, but it still surprised her when it did. She watched in fascination as the water in the bowl whirled out of existence in a forceful vortex through a hole in the bottom.

As the lever slowly returned to its starting position, with additional muffled clicking and clacking, a trap door opened from above the seatback and a brass fish emerged. A stream of water spouted from its mouth and cascaded neatly into the bowl until it was refilled. Then the fish backed into the wall, and the trap door slammed shut.

One would need to be standing when one pulled the lever, she thought, or get all wet. Or, perhaps this was how the people here cleaned themselves?

So enchanted was Karigan, that she pulled the lever again just to watch the fish emerge. And again. And again.

After entertaining herself with the bowl, she discovered an adjoining room with a magnificent tub, also supported by brass mermaids, pairs of fish spouts poised on the edge of the tub, and higher above on the wall. So, one did not have to clean oneself while sitting on the bowl! There was a complicated looking array of levers around the tub. Karigan pulled on one, and again there was the mechanical clattering from beneath the floor and behind the wall, and a rush of water flowed from one of the fish. To her wonder, the water was hot. Perhaps they'd found hot springs to tap into, as in Selium? She guessed its companion spout must produce cold water, and without pumping or dragging in heavy buckets!

She was about to strip off her sleeping gown and fill the tub. She'd not had a bath since before leaving Sacor City— *her* Sacor City—and heading into Blackveil. How wonderful it would be to soak in such—

"There you are!"

Karigan almost fell into the tub as Mirriam burst into the bathing room.

"Are you the one playing with the water?" the housekeeper demanded. "The pressure is off in the kitchen, and Cook is most displeased. In quite a state, actually."

"Uh . . ." Karigan began. "I—I was hoping to take a bath."

"You must not use the tub. If you get your cast wet, you shall ruin it, and then where would we be? I'm afraid it's sponge baths for you until your wrist heals."

Karigan grimaced. "Sponge baths? Isn't there a way to—"

"Mender's orders."

Karigan was beginning to resent the strict dictates of Mender Samuels.

"Speaking of which," Mirriam continued, "you should be in bed."

"I, um, need to use—" and Karigan pointed into the room with the amazing porcelain bowl.

"Land sakes, child, then use it, but no playing with the plumbing. I shall await you in the hallway and see you back to bed directly."

Karigan sighed as Mirriam stepped outside. It was not going to be as easy to sneak around the house as she hoped, with the housekeeper patrolling the halls like a guard dog.

Back in her room, Karigan planted her fists on her hips and stood her ground. "I do not wish to get back in bed." Before Mirriam could utter another of Mender Samuels' proclamations, she added, "I'm restless. I can't just sit here and do nothing."

Mirriam's pose mirrored Karigan's, and the two stared at one another for several moments. "You are right handed?" the housekeeper asked.

Karigan raised her plastered wrist as if it were a foreign object. "Yes."

"Then needle work is likely out."

Thank the gods for small favors, Karigan thought.

"Can you read?"

"Yes, yes I can."

"Good to know that that part of your education has not been neglected. I shall see what I can do." Then Mirriam glanced disapprovingly at Karigan's bare feet. "And I shall find slippers for you. Going without is quite inappropriate."

Karigan glanced at her offending feet and wiggled her toes.

"You get back to bed," Mirriam said.

This time Karigan obeyed, knowing the housekeeper would refuse to leave otherwise. She pulled up the covers, and Mirriam grunted in satisfaction and left, closing the door behind her. From the hallway, Karigan heard a muffled query about "the patient," from someone and Mirriam's caustic reply: "She has an apparent fascination with the plumbing, as if she's never used it before. Did they not have any at the asylum? She's—" Mirriam's voice faded with her footsteps.

Karigan leaned back into her pillows, a little surprised by how weary her explorations had left her, and before she knew it, she had dozed off, only to be awakened sometime later by the clangor of bells from deep within the city. Though she might bristle at being forced to rest, she had to admit her body had been through much and obviously needed at least some.

Drawn by the bells, she swung her legs out of bed and padded to the window. The light against the brick wall opposite had changed its slant, reinforcing the sense of time's passing since last she had looked. Did these bells signify time as they did in her own Sacor City? Did they call worshippers to prayer in local chapels of the moon? If so, they were not particularly beautiful sounding bells but dull and heavy.

Perhaps if she stuck her head out the window she might be able to see more. She struggled with the latch and tried to lift the sash. It was painted closed. She tapped it with the heel of her hand and forced, best as she could even with her broken wrist, to push it upward. The window screeched as it shifted, after no small amount of concerted effort. Had anyone raised it in the last hundred years? No doubt the noise would bring Mirriam running. *Let her come,* Karigan thought, *but not before I have a look.*

She edged the window open wider, enough for her to stick her head out. She craned her neck, looking both left and right. She did not see much, but to the right, between this house and the adjacent building, there was an opening that led to the street. It was just enough for her to observe people, and horses and carriages rushing to and fro. Soon the bells stopped ringing, their leaden tones dying. The activity on the street also diminished. The warm air reminded her of mid- to late spring. She had lost track of time in Blackveil, but they'd entered the forest on the spring equinox. She could not say for sure, but it appeared she'd arrived in the future in the same season she'd left in the past.

"MISS GOODGRAVE!"

Karigan knocked her head on the sash. "Ow!" She backed away from it rubbing the back of her head and turned to gaze on Mirriam and Lorine gaping behind her.

Mirriam was the first to move, setting a pile of books on Karigan's bedside table and storming across to the window to slam it shut. Karigan winced. She decided Mirriam was not good for the nerves of convalescing patients.

"Miss Goodgrave," Mirriam admonished, "the air is not healthy. You must keep the window shut."

The air did have that unpleasant acrid tang to it, but Karigan was definitely tired of hearing what she could and could not do, no matter how much these people were trying to help her.

"I was curious," she said. "All I can see is that brick wall."

"You shall find that curiosity has no place in this household. Now, Lorine has your midday meal and I've brought you some books." She looked at Karigan's feet again and rolled her eyes. "And there shall be slippers, and no more window opening foolishness, do you understand?"

Karigan nodded, and Mirriam marched from the room muttering to herself. Karigan and Lorine exchanged glances, neither of them willing to risk a move lest the slightest breath called the storm back down upon them.

Finally Karigan cleared her throat, and that appeared to be a signal for Lorine to carry the tray to the bed. Karigan hauled herself into bed quickly, observing the tray looked heavy.

"Don't you mind Mirriam, miss," Lorine said as she gently rested the tray on Karigan's lap. "She doesn't like her routine upset."

"What's wrong with the air?"

Lorine shrugged. "It's the way it's always been. Dirty and bad for the weak and elderly. Sometimes better, sometimes worse, depending on what's coming out the stacks and which way the wind is blowing." Then she leaned close and whispered, "Ill humors roam the night air." She held her grave expression for several seconds before nodding and adding in normal tones, "I hear it is better in the countryside."

She removed the lid from the main dish on the tray, and Karigan recoiled at the pungent steam that plumed from the contents. Boiled dinner! Just like her aunts used to make. Boiled cabbage, corned beef, and potatoes. She tried to conceal her revulsion.

"Call me if you need anything," Lorine said, and left.

Karigan stared at the pale, limp offerings on her plate. Ill humors, indeed, she thought, wishing she could reopen the window.

PHOSPHORENE

After Lorine removed the almost untouched meal, the scents of fresh paper and ink replaced the stench of boiled cabbage as Karigan flipped through the books Mirriam had brought. The pages were crisp and the bindings unbent— clearly new-bought. She marveled at the clean print; very little bleeding of ink, the type neat and precise. Though her own time boasted printing presses, none produced such a fine product.

For all that, the illustrations inside were black and white etchings, not nearly as beautiful as the hand-colored renderings she was accustomed to. *Something gained, something lost,* she thought. The illustrations were generally of young men and young women strolling with arms linked, or a man kneeling before his lady. The title of the first she looked at was, *Clara May's Day to Remember.* Another was *A Pretty Proposal.* The books were, quite plainly, stories of courtship and romance, of girls seemingly beset by hardship only to be rescued by gentlemen of means. All stories Mirriam must have deemed suitable for a young lady.

Karigan sighed. Not that she didn't enjoy a good romance, but the idea it was the only sort of book she'd be interested in annoyed her. She supposed, however, she might actually learn something about the mores and expectations of this world, so she picked one at random, *Saucy Sera and Mister Chaunce.*

Saucy Sera, apparently, had a wild streak, rebelling against what was normally expected of girls. She ran and played and climbed trees, and when she was punished for doing what girls should not, she dressed up as a boy and ran away so she could do as she wished, including ride horses. Karigan's heart was with spirited Sera as she strove for freedom, but naturally her plan fell to pieces when Mister Chaunce rescued her from a dire situation in which her true gender was about to be exposed in a humiliating and public manner. Her character underwent complete metamorphosis as she fell immediately in love with Mister Chaunce. Her wild ways quickly faded, and she became a proper young lady interested only in fashion and pleasing Mister Chaunce. Sera's reward? A grand wedding day in which she married the gentleman who had saved her from herself.

Karigan thought a happier ending would have been Sera finding a way to stay free and independent, but, she surmised, this was not what the girls were taught here and probably not what they fantasized about. Who wouldn't want some hero to rescue them and shoulder all responsibilities? And, she wondered wistfully, who wouldn't desire falling in true love? It was all very seductive.

By the time she finished Sera's story, the light in the room had dimmed, and the bells clanged again. As if on cue, Lorine arrived with supper. Much to Karigan's relief, there was no cabbage or corned beef in sight, boiled or otherwise.

"Mirriam says you must eat up," Lorine said in her soft voice. "You must regain your strength and put some flesh on your bones."

Karigan didn't think eating up would be a problem when she poked her fork through the pastry of a meat pie oozing with savory juices.

"Lorine," Karigan said, causing the maid to halt on her way out. She wanted to know for sure what the bells represented. "Why do the bells ring? Is it to tell the time?"

Lorine gazed at Karigan as if puzzled, then smiled. "I keep forgetting you were not raised in the city. Yes. The bells tell us the time. But most importantly for the mill managers, it tells the slaves when they must work, when they may stop for meals, and when they are done for the day."

"Was this their last bell? Have they been dismissed for the day?"

"No, miss. It was the supper bell. After supper, they will work while there is still daylight. From sunrise to sunset they labor."

"Like farmers," Karigan murmured.

"I think farming might be . . ." Lorine broke off, staring toward the window, lost in thought.

"Might be what?" Karigan prompted.

"More bearable." Lorine shook her head as if dazed. "Nothing to trouble yourself about, miss. Is there anything else?"

"No," Karigan replied. Lorine curtsied and was gone, leaving Karigan to reflect on Lorine's words and wonder about what her experiences as a mill slave had been like.

After she ate her fill, she needed to be up and out of bed again, so she crept out into the hallway and again heard male voices from somewhere downstairs. She picked out the professor's tones, as well as two or three others. Unlike the visit from Mr. Hadley, the circus boss, this gathering sounded more sociable with occasional laughter. She was thinking about sneaking down the hall to at least take a peek when a throat was cleared behind her.

"Is there something you need?" Mirriam asked.

Karigan slowly turned round. Of course Mirriam would discover her in the hall. Where else would she possibly be? "No," she replied. "On my way to the privy."

"I trust you remember where it is?"

Karigan nodded.

"Good. I shall await you here."

"Damnation," Karigan muttered to herself when she entered the privy and shut the door. This was much worse than her days as a schoolgirl in Selium, where it seemed every adult had been peering over her shoulder. She couldn't even enjoy the emergence of the fish spout from the wall when she pulled the lever, knowing Mirriam awaited her outside. When she finished, she was duly escorted back to her room.

Once more ensconced in bed, she picked through the books again. This time a piece of paper that appeared to be torn from a larger sheet slipped out of one of the books. It was filled with type and a couple of pictures. It was entitled,

"Excavations of the Old City," and in the top etching appeared the profile of "Professor Bryce Lowell Josston, Licensed Practitioner of Archeology."

> *Professor Josston of Mill City, Known for His Studies of Ancient Sea King Relics, Has Turned His Erudite Attentions to His Own Neighborhood.*
>
> *"The ruins of the Old City have always captivated my imagination as I grew up beneath their brooding visage," the professor said. "And now I have been given permission to excavate in the ruins to seek further links to the legacy of the first Sea Kings."*
>
> *The professor is a scion of a Preferred Family that made its fortune in the manufacture of cotton textiles. It is said he has eschewed industry in favor of scholarly pursuits and sold his majority interest in the Josston Mills. The Imperial Grant to Excavate, the professor believes, will endow him with a lifetime of potential discoveries.*
>
> *"There is nothing better to me than learning about how those of the past lived," he said.*
>
> *Professor Josston joins several others in pursuit of artifacts on the Emperor's behalf, including the notable Doctor Ezra Stirling Silk, Special Consul to the Emperor on Antiquities and True History, who has conducted remarkable excavations along the east coast and in the Northern Sea Archipelago.*

The second etching illustrated a broad knife with an entwined pair of dragons forming the hilt. The caption read, *Bronze knife believed to be Sea King relic, unearthed by Professor Josston in the Bealing Harbor dig.*

Bealing Harbor was in Hillander Province, or what used to be Hillander. To Karigan, the sea kings were but a curiosity of far ancient times, lost in the shadows preceding the Black Ages. She knew little of them except that they'd been violent marauders, pillaging and battling the tribal people who had roamed the region that she knew as Sacoridia. They had subdued the people and ruled for scores of years, especially along the coast. Likely their blood still ran through the veins of many Sacoridians. The sea kings had left abruptly, just simply got up and left, sailing their fleets of ships east. If there was any reason for their sudden departure, it was lost to time.

In any case, it appeared the sea kings were an approved topic of history, perhaps because it was so distant as to be deemed harmless. She wondered if the clipping had been slipped to her purposely, and if so, by whom? Why not just hand it to her? She shook out all of the books, but no other loose papers fell out.

Probably just as well. She'd had enough mysteries and revelations for one day. As the light in her room waned, the bells clanged a final time, and Karigan imagined workers filing out of the mills, weary and relieved another day had finished. Where did they go? If they were slaves, she could not expect they'd be returning to very comfortable accommodations.

My father managed to make his fortune in textiles, she thought, *even though his suppliers did not rely on slave labor.*

If Professor Josston's family had made its fortune with cotton mills, she had to assume slaves were involved. The professor's apparent removal from the business, and his rescue of Lorine, softened her harsh assessment of him. But he was obviously very well off and had profited from slave labor. She wondered what life was like for other people who were not the scions of Preferred families.

The door creaked open and Mirriam strode in, the last of day's light glancing on the monocle hanging from her neck.

"You aren't going to read in the dark, are you?" she demanded. She bustled over to Karigan's bedside table where a globe sat on a bronze pedestal. She twisted a key in its base and at once the globe filled with a bright, steady light.

"Like magic," Karigan murmured.

"There is no magic in this world, young lady," Mirriam said, "but modern wonders gleaned from the ingenuity of men."

To Karigan's chagrin, there was truth in the housekeeper's words about the magic. "Is it whale oil?" she asked.

Mirriam laughed. "Now where are we going to find a whale to make oil? Not enough of them left to supply the needs of the city, much less the empire. It's phosphorene that gives off the light. Surely they weren't still using candles in the asylum . . . ?"

Karigan swallowed, not wanting to reveal just how ignorant she truly was, but she had little choice. "How do you extinguish the light?"

Mirriam muttered something to herself in a tone of disbelief and then added, not without pity, "I am shocked the Goodgraves put you in such an institution lacking modern amenities. Why, it's barbaric! No wonder the professor brought you here. Now watch." Mirriam simply turned the key in the opposite direction and the room darkened.

It was amazing, so simple, Karigan thought. No fires that needed to be started and kept burning. No flint and steel, just the turn of that key.

Mirriam twisted the key once more and light filled the room. Despite the lack of magic, this world was filled with wonders. What else Karigan might discover, she could scarcely imagine.

"In the morning," Mirriam announced, "there shall be bathing and a change of bandages. Mender Samuels will stop by to see how you are doing." With that, the housekeeper left her.

Karigan sighed. Whatever discoveries she made about this world, they would have to be made at night, as the household slept. Did Mirriam sleep? Maybe she'd ask Lorine. In any case, she'd learn the rhythms of the house's occupants and discover what she could.

She yawned and reached for one of the novels. She'd bide her time as evening wore on and begin her investigations once the house fell into somnolence. But before she was four pages into the book, her head nestled in the pillow, and she drifted away once again into the healing sleep her body so desperately needed, unaware of when Lorine came in later and removed the book from her hands, pulled the covers up, and turned off the light.

APPARITIONS

A *scritching* sound irritated Karigan to wakefulness, an incessant noise that scraped at her nerves. She blinked in the predawn gray, once more having to orient herself to where she was and *when.* She rubbed her eyes and yawned, wondering what caused the noise that had awakened her.

Scritch-scritch-scritch, like a pen rapidly stroking across paper.

She raised herself to her elbows. "Hello?" she queried, searching into the shadows spilling across her room.

She discerned nothing, but she pinpointed the noise emanating from a particularly dark corner. She stared hard, perceived movement. A trick of her eyes?

"Hello?" she said again, a slight quaver in her voice, and again there was no response. The scritching did not sound mousey, and it had a sort of rhythm to it.

I'm becoming just as mad as they think I am.

She tossed aside her covers and stood on the rug beside her bed. She took tentative steps toward the dark corner. The scritching grew a little louder as she approached. She made out the frame of the one chair in her room. She thought to turn back and ignite her lamp when she caught a faint flutter of movement around the chair, like pale moth wings in the night. Transfixed, she drew closer. Spectral smoke wafted and drifted above the chair until it resolved into a vaguely human figure.

A wave of cold rippled through Karigan's flesh lifting the hairs on her arms. She licked her lips. She dared not step any closer to the apparition lest it vanish. Its features were so blurred she could not even tell whether it was male or female. It sat bent over a flat object on its lap.

"Who are you?" she whispered. Perhaps, she thought, Who *were* you? was the more appropriate question. In any case, she received no reply.

The gray of her room began to lighten, the puddles of black retreating. The faint apparition faded even more.

"Can you see me?" Karigan whispered, but the hunched figure remained intent on whatever was on its lap, even as it faded to a wisp of smoke.

Scritch-scratch.

Was it writing?

The city bell clanged and, startled, Karigan glanced at the window, which had brightened with the dawn. The bell to call the mill slaves to work. Between tollings, she heard no scritching, and when she glanced at the chair, the apparition had vanished.

Either she had indeed gone mad, or apparitions could appear even in a world deprived of magic. Not that spirits of the dead should have to rely on magic to exist, but it still surprised her.

Why had it appeared to her? She'd enough experience with the supernatural to know such meetings did not usually occur by chance.

She stood there staring at the empty chair for several moments, then shook her head. She gave some thought to using the early hour to sneak around the house, but she heard footsteps in the hallway and other sounds of life elsewhere in the house, bringing to an end any such notion. At least now she knew the household began to awaken with the first bell, which was more than she'd known before.

She sighed and limped back to bed to await the day.

After breakfast Karigan suffered through the humiliation of the sponge bath, protesting all the while there must be a way to take a regular bath without getting her cast wet, and couldn't she do this herself, please. Mirriam was as immovable as a granite pillar and informed Karigan this was not her first sponge bath. Karigan had known someone cleaned her up upon her arrival to the professor's house, though she'd not been conscious. Being awake and aware of it was a whole different level of embarrassment.

"Stop your fussing," Mirriam ordered as she scrubbed Karigan's back. "You're just making it take longer."

After the sponge bath, Karigan had to admit she felt better, especially when Mirriam and Lorine set to work washing her hair in the bathing room sink, which was shaped like a giant clam shell. Mirriam deftly shifted the various levers to make the water temperature just right while Lorine's nimble fingers massaged Karigan's scalp. Afterward, Lorine put much care into detangling and brushing Karigan's hair. The strokes of the brush felt marvelous.

"I wish my hair was half so lovely as yours," Lorine murmured. "Long and thick."

Karigan had not yet seen Lorine's hair for it was always wrapped beneath her scarf.

Lorine expertly braided Karigan's hair, then helped her back to her room, where Mirriam and Mender Samuels awaited with fresh bandages. Karigan withheld cries of pain as crusty scabs were yanked off with the old bandages, the one around her leg hurting the worst by far. The mender bent over her leg and took a long whiff of the wound.

"I smell no putrefaction, and the flesh appears to be healing," he pronounced. "If all continues this way, I shall remove the sutures very soon." He listened to Karigan's heart through a conical tube apparatus, the wide end placed on her chest, his ear listening at the narrow end. Like a small speaking trumpet, Karigan decided. The mender inquired of Mirriam about Karigan's diet. After a favorable response, he asked, "No ill humors, fever, or the like?"

"None that I've detected," Mirriam replied. "Seems eager to get into mischief. But beyond that, only the illness of her mind."

Karigan glowered.

"You say she will take no morphia?"

"I am right here and able to answer for myself," Karigan said. "I will take no morphia."

"My dear," the mender said in a condescending tone, "you've nothing to prove. The morphia is only to benefit you by subduing your pain."

And *me,* she thought. "I do not need morphia."

The mender gave her a testy frown as though he preferred his patients drowsy and malleable. "Very well, but I shall bring it up with your uncle. Most young ladies would desire relief."

Karigan held her tongue, but it was not easy.

"Her mental frailties," the mender told Mirriam, "do not make her fit to speak for herself."

The housekeeper escorted him to the door. She paused and gave Karigan an enigmatic look and then was gone. What was in that look? Approval? Disapproval? Something more complex? Karigan could not tell.

"I just want to go home," she murmured. Now that she was once again alone in her room, it hit her. She wanted away from these strange people and their ways. She profoundly missed her Condor, her fellow Riders, and the way the world worked in her own time. She missed Ghost Kitty curling up beside her on her pillow and purring her to sleep.

She would find a way home; she would learn how Mornhavon had defeated Sacoridia, and she would take that information with her. Until she figured out these matters, she must remain patient and accept the professor's protection so she could rebuild her strength.

If she couldn't get past Mirriam, she would use the window. She'd enough bed sheets to tie together . . . Karigan considered plans and counter plans until the midday bell rang, and Lorine appeared with a meal. Karigan steeled herself for more boiled dinner, when Lorine lifted the lid off the main dish and there was only barley soup. Karigan did not think her sigh of relief went unnoticed.

She thought to question Lorine about Mirriam's habits and schedule but dismissed the idea as too obvious. She'd have to observe on her own. The maid curtsied and departed, leaving Karigan to thoughtfully spoon soup—carefully blowing on it first—into her mouth. Perhaps if she made herself sleep all day, then she'd stay awake long enough in the night to commence her prowling. It was ridiculous, really, that she, a Green Rider, was cooped up like this. She—

Karigan paused with a spoon of steaming soup halfway to

her lips, when she felt someone's gaze on her. Had her ghost returned, here in the brightness of day? Slowly she turned her head, seeking any sign of that filmy presence. She did not see it, but when her gaze fell across the window, and she discovered a pair of golden eyes staring unblinkingly in at her, she screamed, and barley soup cascaded across the room, the bowl smashing on the floor.

Mirriam burst in almost immediately, with Lorine on her heels. "Miss Goodgrave! What on Earth? How dare you fling the professor's porcelain!"

Karigan hissed as the burning hot soup soaked through her nightgown, and she plucked the fabric away from her skin. "I saw a pair of eyes! In the window." Now for certain, she'd utterly convinced them of her insanity.

Mirriam stomped over to the window, gazed up, gazed down, and gazed all around. "I see nothing," she replied, whirling around to stare at Karigan, her hands on her hips.

Karigan was not surprised, and as her wits settled back into their proper place, she belatedly realized that whiskers, and white and pale gray fur had accompanied the eyes before her scream had scared the poor cat off her window ledge. She laughed at herself.

"Miss Goodgrave, stop this instant." Mirriam raised her hand as if to slap her.

Just as quickly Karigan raised her arm to block it. "I am not hysterical," she said, no laughter in her voice now. "I was laughing because I'm just realizing I was startled by a cat. A cat at my window." Karigan did not add that her sighting of an apparition in the early morning hours had put her on edge.

Mirriam's posture relaxed, and her upraised hand fell to her side. Her expression, however, revealed she was not entirely convinced.

"There has been a cat hanging about the back garden lately," Lorine said.

"White with gray?" Karigan asked.

Lorine nodded.

"No one had better be feeding it," Mirriam replied. "Filthy creatures."

Lorine clasped her hands in front of her and glanced down

at the floor, but Mirriam did not observe it for she was gazing intently at Karigan.

"Just after we've cleaned and put fresh bedding on," Mirriam said. "Now we'll have to do it all over again."

"I'm sorry," Karigan said with a grimace. "I was just really startled."

"See that it does not happen again."

A clean nightgown and bedding were brought in, and after Karigan changed, she was ordered to sit in the chair while the bed was made anew, soup was sopped up from the floor, and broken porcelain swept away. In addition, the butler arrived with a little table, Mirriam directing where it should be placed. *Not* next to the window, she ordered the butler.

"From now on," she informed Karigan, "you shall dine at this table. You are obviously well enough to sit up, and I won't have you flinging the professor's porcelain."

"I did not—"

"And slippers!" Mirriam threw her hands into the air. "Why do I see no slippers? That girl never remembers anything I tell her, and I must do it myself." She turned on Lorine who had a rag bunched in her hand from wiping up stray droplets of soup. "I am off to Copley's for slippers and perhaps a few other shops while I'm out."

With that, Mirriam marched out of the room, and both Karigan and Lorine sighed simultaneously. Lorine smiled shyly at Karigan.

"Is there . . . is there really a cat in the back garden?" Karigan asked.

"Oh, yes, miss. We do give him leavings now and then, but please don't tell Mirriam—he does no harm."

"I certainly will not tell Mirriam," Karigan said with more feeling than she intended.

"Thank you, miss. Like I said, we just give him leavings. He'd like to come in, but, well, as you saw, Mirriam wouldn't have it. He lets us near enough to pet him sometimes. Well, I must be off to begin laundry now."

"I'm sorry," Karigan said again as Lorine loaded her arms with sheets, cleaning rags, and Karigan's soup-stained nightgown.

"No trouble, miss," Lorine replied, voice muffled by linens as she headed out the door.

Karigan sat back in her chair wondering if she'd made enough trouble for one day. *Not by far,* she decided. Mirriam had left the house to go shopping, which meant she could poke around without her watchdog pouncing on her the moment she stepped out of her room.

MOTIVES

Karigan snuck out into the empty hallway. She had no illusions about getting very far before someone caught her, since it was full day and everyone was up and about, but her chances of success were better with Mirriam absent.

She was deciding how to proceed when she heard voices once again coming from the foyer, so she crept down the hallway to the top of the staircase and crouched, hiding behind the newel post and balusters. A man in a red uniform stood just inside the doorway, peaked cap on his head and, girded around his waist, a black belt that held stubby tools or weapons of some sort. Behind him, through the open door, an object like a large metallic ball, glinted in the sun, but she could not discern it clearly. It made her inexplicably nervous. She sensed a roving eye watching, judging, seeking. Seeking what? Or who?

The professor strode into the foyer. "Inspector Gant," he said with great ebullience. "How kind of you to stop by. What a surprise to see you! May I offer you a brandy?"

"No thank you, Professor Josston." The Inspector had the squared shoulders and crisp demeanor of a soldier. "I'm on duty and here on official business. There has been word you're sheltering an undocumented person in your house."

"Undocumented? That's not very likely now, is it? The emperor knows I respect his laws to the utmost."

The Inspector proffered a slight bow of acknowledgment. "Even so, I am required to check. You did take in a young woman recently, did you not?"

Karigan stiffened, but the professor laughed. "My dear

Gant, I've made no secret of it. Indeed I have taken in a young woman—my poor niece—so she may live in better circumstances than she left."

"I understand," the Inspector said, clearly unmoved, "but all the same, I must see her documents."

"Documents. Of course." The professor cast about himself as if they'd appear out of thin air. "One moment, please, Inspector, while I return to my office to retrieve them." And he strode out of view.

The Inspector remained where he stood with hands clasped behind his back. There was a querying chirp from behind him, and he glanced over his shoulder. "Yes," he said.

This was followed by several more chirps and hoots. They did not sound like anything Karigan had heard before—not at all like birds. Sharper, more tinny. Not at all like any living creature she knew of.

"Of course," the Inspector replied to the chirps. "He is highly favored and has a habit of taking in strays."

There was a soft whistle and Karigan had an impression of the whatever-it-was expressing doubt.

"He bought that slave's freedom, legal and documented. He does not have a history of harboring runaways. Now, silence."

There was a rude *blatt* from behind, and the Inspector raised an eyebrow.

The professor emerged into the foyer with a sheaf of papers in his hand, which he passed immediately to the Inspector. The Inspector scrutinized the papers, taking time with each page.

"So you say she is your niece," the Inspector murmured. "Several Goodgraves have married into your family as I recall."

"Indeed," the professor replied. "Historically and currently. A bit too much intermarrying with that branch if you know what I mean. Some ill-conceived notions of pure bloodlines and the like, leading, shall we say, to unfortunate frailties in the offspring." He tapped his temple in emphasis.

"Yes, I see you had your niece released from an asylum in the northeast."

"They left her to rot in terrible conditions," the professor said full of indignation, "and it's not her fault she's a bit touched. They are very uncivilized in that region. Mender Samuels can attest to her condition, mental and physical."

"I've heard that asylum has an unsavory reputation," the Inspector said. "There has been some agitation to close it down."

"And so it should be closed down and the administrators condemned by the Imperial Council." The professor's righteous zeal was very convincing. Karigan thought he put to shame any actor of The Royal Magnificent Theater with his performance. "My poor niece. She is a pretty thing, and I'd a thought to marrying her off to some nice young man not concerned about the disarranged state of her mental faculties, but after such trauma? I doubt anyone would have her."

Not to mention his performance was making her feel pathetic.

The Inspector made sympathetic noises. "I must check the seal," he said, and he stepped outside with the papers. Shortly an ominous whine emitted from without. Did she discern a tensing of the professor's posture as he watched through the doorway?

The Inspector returned and handed the documents back to the professor. "Everything checks out," he said. "It's a fine thing you are doing, helping family."

"Well, unlike you, Inspector, I've not been blessed with children of my own, so I guess I find a way to compensate. Speaking of which, how many do you have now? Last I heard, eight?"

The Inspector grinned. "We've a ninth coming along."

"My word! Good man!" The professor clapped him on the shoulder. "Wait till I tell Mirriam."

The two said their good-byes, the Inspector politely doffing his hat and saying, "Sorry to have troubled you, sir." When the door closed behind him, the professor sagged against the wall, mopping his brow with a handkerchief.

"Everything all right, Professor?" a male voice asked from the room off the foyer. The voice sounded vaguely familiar, but the speaker did not reveal himself.

"A close one, that," the professor replied. "I'd only received these documents yesterday."

"Rasper does good work."

"Yes. Good enough to fool an Inspector and his mechanical. Thankfully it was Gant this time — he's more, shall we say, reasonable than some of the others. But don't give Rasper any idea of how good he is or he'll start demanding that I pay him more."

The two laughed, and the professor moved into the room, drawing a pair of doors closed behind him. Karigan sat where she was, dumbfounded that her patron had gone to such lengths to protect her. Obviously he'd be in trouble if he was found out. How odd this world was that everything must be approved and documented.

The idea that the Inspector had a mechanical something-or-other to help him made her shiver. The concept of "mechanicals" was not unknown to her or to others of her time. Mornhavon the Black had brought them to these shores in his conquest of the New Lands. Her ancestor, Hadriax el Fex, had referenced them in his journal. But none of her contemporaries, not even the scholars, seemed to know what the mechanicals looked like or how they operated, except that some incorporated etherea in their workings. They were part machine and part magic, but if magic was absent from this time, perhaps the Inspector's device was purely mechanical. The future, it appeared, held many marvels both useful and frightening.

Encouraged by having witnessed this much. Karigan decided to try and learn more. She crept down the stairs, her bare feet silent on the carpeted treads. At the bottom, she glanced all around her. There was, as she thought, a formal parlor to her right, and the closed doors of the room the professor and his companion had entered to her left. A grand hall went deeper into the house from the foyer. No one else was about. She limped over to the closed doors and pressed her ear against one of them. She heard voices within.

"It's downright strange, I tell you," she heard the professor proclaim.

His companion made a muffled response.

"Both Samuels and Mirriam observed the wounds on her body as unusual," the professor said, "the old ones and the fresh ones. The old ones, Samuels said, are like stab wounds from . . . from edged weapons." He sounded disturbed. If he had believed she were a Green Rider, then perhaps he wouldn't be so surprised, but it appeared there were no Green Riders in this time and no memory of them. To think all their bravery and efforts came to this, unremembered and disbelieved.

"Mirriam thought her muscles unseemly for a girl, too, even one who might have labored in the mills," the professor mused. "Maybe a field hand? No lash marks, though. Her wounds, combined with the artifacts lead me to only one conclusion."

Karigan did not get to hear what it was because someone said, *"Psst,"* behind her. She jumped.

"Miss," Lorine said, "you must go back to your room."

"I'm tired of my room." Oops, that sounded a tad more petulant than Karigan intended.

Lorine gently took her arm and turned her toward the staircase. "Please. Mirriam will be home soon, and if she or anyone else sees you down here . . ."

Karigan heard the implication that if mad Miss Goodgrave were discovered wandering around, the fault would fall on Lorine, who'd be in a great deal of trouble. Not wishing to cause Lorine problems, Karigan started up the stairway compliantly, but was vexed not to have heard the rest of the professor's statement. Midway up, she stopped, thinking to go back down, fling those doors open, and confront the professor. But Lorine anxiously tugged on her sleeve. With a sigh, Karigan continued her upward climb.

When they reached the top landing, the double doors opened, and Karigan paused to look back down. A man strode out into the foyer with books beneath his arm.

"Don't forget I need those papers tomorrow morning," the professor called from the adjoining room.

The man halted and turned. "The Hudson Study?"

"That's the one."

When Karigan saw the man's profile, it took only a moment

for her to recognize him. He'd been standing next to the professor in that lecture hall the night of her arrival. His voice also matched that of the man who'd helped her fight off the assailants in the alley and brought her to the professor's house.

She ignored Lorine's pulling on her arm. "Who is he?" Karigan asked in a whisper.

Whether the man heard her or some other impulse caused him to glance up the stairs, she did not know, but he did, and he stared hard at her, his face unreadable, brows drawn together. He was in his mid-twenties, she thought, very trim in his plain longcoat, but beneath his scrutiny she felt naked, as if he could see past her nightgown, through her skin, and right into her being.

Then it was all over. He turned curtly on his heel. "I'll have the Hudson Study for you first thing, Professor."

"Good man!"

And he swept out the front door.

"Who was he?" Karigan asked Lorine again.

"One of the professor's students. It's not proper for you to be seen like this." She fussed and pulled till Karigan followed her down the hallway.

Karigan assumed "not proper" meant the professor's mad niece should not be seen by anyone from outside the household, especially when she was wearing nothing but a nightgown. "Does he have a name?" Karigan persisted.

"A name?" Lorine's nervous disposition made her seem just about to quiver apart.

"Yes, a name."

"Mr. Cade Harlowe." Lorine spoke breathlessly, and when Karigan espied the pink in her cheeks, she thought she knew why.

"Does he come here often?"

Lorine nodded. "He assists the professor. To help pay his tuition, as I understand it."

They were about halfway to Karigan's room when another door at the far end of the hallway opened and a girl of about eight in servants garb stepped out. She stared openly at Karigan.

"Arhys!" Lorine said. "What are you doing? Mirriam is not pleased with you. She had to go to Copley's after Miss Goodgrave's slippers."

The girl tossed her head. "Mirriam is never pleased about anything."

That was for sure, Karigan thought.

"And mind your manners," Lorine said. "This is the professor's niece, Miss Goodgrave."

"I know," the girl said. She boldly walked up to Karigan and gave her a flippant curtsy as though she were above such things. Karigan almost snorted with laughter. This Arhys was no docile servant—she had cheek. Once she grew out of the round contours of childhood, Karigan predicted she'd be a great beauty with hair that varied in the light from deep amber to sunshine gold.

"I must dust the parlor," Arhys announced as if she were bestowing a great favor upon the world. She skipped down the hallway toward the stairs.

"That girl," Lorine grumbled. Then, "I apologize for her lack of manners. The professor dotes on her and has made her vain. I suspect she may be a little jealous."

"Of me?"

Lorine nodded. "His attention has been diverted from her since your arrival. Though she has no call to be jealous. She is an orphan the professor took in as a servant, and he employs Mr. Harlowe to tutor her. Otherwise she'd have been taken to the orphanage." Lorine shuddered. "Or she might have ended up living on the streets with the Dregs. She should show a little more gratitude, if you ask me."

"The professor—my uncle—seems to help a lot of people," Karigan said as they entered her room.

"Yes," Lorine replied. "He helps when no one else will lift a finger. He's a good man."

A good man . . . Karigan wondered if he were simply altruistic, or if he had some other, hidden, agenda. The fact that he was willing to forge documents on her behalf and lie to an official suggested to her suspicious mind that perhaps he possessed motives beyond those that benefited her personal welfare.

PROWLING

It still took Karigan by surprise how the need for sleep dropped her so unexpectedly and with such immediacy. After her excursion down the stairs to spy on the professor, she'd been overcome as soon as she returned to her room. One minute she was alert and wide awake, and the next Lorine was rousing her for supper. Her healing body continued to demand its due.

It interfered with her plans to learn the schedules and habits of the household, and no matter how much she slept during the day, she couldn't stay awake at night to prowl.

When she was awake, she restlessly paced, scuffing the soles of her new fur-lined slippers along the floorboards, wishing for some way to vent her energy. Instead of reading the novels Mirriam had brought her, she lifted them to keep her good arm limber, now and then adding a book to the pile to increase the weight. She practiced the various forms she'd learned in arms training, only without a practice sword, and while trying to remain silent so no one would come scold her and discover what she was up to—which was an exercise in itself. She came to know exactly which floorboards creaked, and which did not.

She eventually convinced Lorine to provide her with a broom by saying she wanted to keep her already immaculate room tidy. Lorine looked at her like she was mad, then probably remembered that Karigan was supposed to be, and relented, hoping it would keep her happy.

Working with a broom handle was not nearly as good as using a properly balanced practice sword, or a real blade for that matter. She of course had to use her left hand because of her broken wrist, but it was not as hard as it might have been since she was trained to use her non-dominant side after a previous elbow injury. Grateful as she was just to have the broom, she wished she at least had her bonewood, and planned to request it of the professor citing her bad leg, but she never saw him, which was hugely irritating. When she asked Mirriam where he was, the housekeeper informed her it was none of her concern, but let it slip later he was out at the "dig site" with his students.

The only people she continued to see were Lorine and Mirriam. If she had her way, that would soon change if only she could stay awake. There weren't even any visitations from the ghost—none that she was aware of at any rate.

To make matters worse, beneath her cast the flesh itched so much it drove her wild. She had nothing to slide beneath the cast to probe the itches, and she was sorely tempted to go to the bathing room and soak it in water to dissolve it off. Instead, she furiously scratched at the cast itself as if she could somehow transcend the plaster and reach her skin to find release.

When next Mender Samuels appeared to check on her and remove the sutures from various wounds, she demanded, "When is this cast coming off?"

"Three or four more weeks, I should think."

Karigan perceived the hint of a malignant smile as he said it, like he enjoyed telling her bad news. She wanted to scream her frustration but would not give him the satisfaction.

"You do want it to heal correctly, don't you?" he asked, while tugging out another stitch.

Karigan grunted and said no more.

Finally a day came when she felt more herself. The combination of good food and sleep infused her with most of her old energy. Her wrist still ached and itched in its cast, and she still limped, but on the whole, she was ready to take on the world, or at least the part of it that contained the household of Professor Bryce Lowell Josston.

She'd made her plans, so now it was a matter of waiting for the night. She took her mind off the coming excursion by sneaking into the bathing room to attend to her own ablutions. She filled the tub with hot water, and just as she sank into it, settling her broken wrist safely on the rim, Mirriam barged right in.

"You get out this instant!" she ordered.

"I will not," Karigan replied. "You will have to lift me if you want me out."

Mirriam paced in agitation, perhaps considering her options. "I could ask the gardeners to help . . ."

Karigan did not reply, guessing she was bluffing.

After some moments, Mirriam jabbed her finger in Karigan's direction. "You will not get your cast wet, and we shall speak when you are done."

When the housekeeper left, the tension eased out of Karigan's body, and she took a glorious, long hot soak and a thorough scrub, not getting her cast wet in the process, thank you very much. Afterward, while she dried off in her room, she endured Mirriam's scolding with equanimity.

"As you can see," Karigan said, brandishing her cast before Mirriam's face, "no harm has been done. It's obvious I'm capable of bathing myself, though Lorine will still need to help me with my hair." Karigan thought she heard giggles from the hallway in response to Mirriam's being bested. Arhys, perhaps?

Mirriam pursed her lips. A muscle twitched in her cheek, but she nodded curtly and left. When the door shut behind her, Karigan spun around in a little dance of victory.

And then she saw the cat watching her through the window, that same pair of golden eyes, the white and light gray fur. He appeared neither scrawny nor scruffy, so perhaps he was a well-fed neighborhood cat. Since she'd already defied Mirriam once today, it did not seem a great leap to do so again. She went to the window and started to lift the sash, but at the first hint of a squeal, the cat jumped. She looked down, but could not see where he went. She shrugged and decided she would have to find some grease with which to ease the window.

Karigan busied herself the rest of the day practicing sword forms and was pleased by the increasing strength and precision of her left arm. When she finished, she gazed out the window. The sky was heavy, deepening with rain clouds. By late afternoon showers fell, accompanied by rumbles of thunder, and kept falling as the household settled into night and eventually into sleep, until only one soul remained awake, or so Karigan hoped. The constant patter of rain on the roof would help cover up the sound of her movements.

Wrapping the shawl around her shoulders, her feet clad in slippers, she tiptoed to her door, opened it, and peered out into the hallway. At night time, she discovered, the hallways were kept dimly illumined by phosphorene lamps at low glow. Some were made to look like tapers in candle holders, the glass flame bright, but false in that it did not flicker like a real candle. These, unlike the larger lamps, could be carried with ease. She picked one up from its place on a small marble-top table and moved down the hall toward the stairs, followed by her own monstrous shadow.

She hadn't the nerve to open the doors along the hallway, figuring they could very well be inhabited. She suspected Mirriam slept only a couple doors away from her. No, her goal was to look around on the lower level, where the professor's business took place. If she were to find out anything of interest, it would be downstairs.

She carefully descended, her shadow exaggerating her steps. When she reached the bottom landing, she ignored the parlor—one glance the other day had shown her an impersonal room of overstuffed furniture and the requisite portraits of important ancestors. It was enough to tell her the room was rarely used and that she would find nothing of interest there. It seemed to her parlors had not changed much since her own time.

She went straight for the room across the hallway, the one with the double doors. She pushed one door open and stepped inside. Her taper revealed walls of books, gold gilt titles on the bindings winking in the light. A library, then. A long heavy table gleamed in the middle of the room, stacked with a few volumes, and a fireplace yawned black and sooty on the far wall. Rain pelted at heavily draped windows.

She glanced at a few titles: *The Complete Compendium of Archeological Implements, Pride of Empire,* and *The Wonder-*

ful Realm of Abstract Mathematical Intangibilities. She supposed if she looked further, she'd find history books on the
empire, but they'd probably be propaganda from all she'd
heard about the "true history" so far. They might be interesting, but probably would not illuminate what had really happened to *her* Sacoridia and the free lands.

As tempting as it was to linger and look through books,
she thought her time would be better spent prowling. She
backed out of the library, softly closing the door. Back in the
foyer, she paused, listening. Except for the distant sound of
falling rain, the house remained sepulchral in demeanor.

She forged ahead, trying to shake off comparisons with
tombs, and almost immediately found a privy just as extravagant as the one upstairs, but this one had a bird's nest theme.
The bowl looked like a nest, supported by branches of brass.
Tempted though she was, she did not pull the lever to learn
what came out from the trap door above to fill the bowl with
water.

She hastened on and found a dining room that attached to
the parlor through a doorway. A crystal chandelier glinted in
her light above the immense, polished table. She found a pantry and stuck her head into the kitchen but did not investigate.

Down an austere side passage, she found storage rooms
full of draped furniture, chests, and lamps missing shades. She
hoped not to accidentally open a door to the servants quarters. Mirriam, who was exalted above all as head housekeeper,
got a room in the plush upstairs. The rest of the servants
would be housed in more utilitarian quarters. Still, she did not
have a sense of anyone sleeping or otherwise inhabiting this
corridor.

The next door she opened proved more interesting, for
she found a very messy and cluttered office. She stepped inside and marveled at the piles of paper and stacks of books
rising like columns almost to the ceiling. There was something
of a path to a chair and desk, likewise buried in paper and
books. The black eye sockets of a horse's skull peeked out
from a shelf crowded with books and rolled documents. A
rusted dagger sat on a pile like a paperweight. Here and there

shovels and pick axes leaned against a bookstack. Some were buried up to their handles. She saw no sign of her own belongings, but there was no way to tell if they were buried anywhere in this clutter.

Karigan thought that if the professor wished to conduct archeological excavations, he should begin with his own office. She dared not touch anything for fear it would all come crashing down on her. Across his desk a map lay unrolled, but she could not make sense of it with its gridwork of numbers, transects, and layers.

She froze when she heard a door open and close somewhere else in the house. She wondered what to do—hide, or stay where she was? What if it was the professor coming to work late in his office?

She hastily lowered the light of the taper to a dim glow. She headed for the door, brushed against a stack of books, and watched in horror as they listed precariously. She gritted her teeth and tried to steady them so they would not topple, but the stack was over-balanced and fell, taking out the stack behind it, and another.

The noise was like thunder, and she flung herself out of the room, across the hall, and into one of the storage rooms. So much for her stealthy sojourn. If they discovered her, she'd be banned from leaving her room *ever*. Not that she'd let them stop her.

Hurried footsteps came down the corridor. She extinguished the taper entirely so no hint of light leaked through the crack at the bottom of the door. There was a second set of footsteps, and she opened the door just the tiniest bit. She saw the professor's back, and Mirriam's, each of them holding a taper.

"What in the world?" Mirriam demanded. She wore a plaid housecoat over her nightgown and a bonnet over her hair. The professor was attired in what looked like formal evening wear, as if he'd just returned from a party.

"It appears," he said, "one of my bookstacks gave way, leading to a chain reaction."

"I've warned you many times, Professor, that it is dangerous in there—a death trap! A whisper could've knocked

those books over. What if you'd been in there? We'd be sending for Mender Samuels is what."

"Then a good thing I was not."

"I guess we'll have to set it right in the morning, then,"
Mirriam said with a mournful note in her voice.

"No, no," the professor said. "I'll let the boys handle it.
What are first year students for anyway? You go back to bed
and don't worry one iota about it."

"If you're sure . . ."

"I'm sure. Go back to bed."

Dismissed, Mirriam retreated down the hall. The professor continued gazing at the mess in his office, tugging at his
bushy side whiskers.

"And my night's just beginning," he grumbled, and he
shook his head.

Karigan expected him to make some attempt at straightening his office, but he turned and walked away. She did not
hesitate but slipped out of the storage room to follow him,
keeping to the darkness, away from the halo of light emitted
by his taper.

He swept past the kitchen and pantry area, past the dining
room, and veered into the library, leaving one of the double
doors ajar. By the time Karigan reached the doors and peered
inside, she discovered he'd left his taper at dim glow on the
main table, but he was gone. Vanished.

She stepped boldly into the library, but he was nowhere to
be seen. She had observed him entering the library, hadn't
she? Here was his taper as proof. Vanishing was usually *her*
trick and the absurdity made her want to chuckle, but she
swallowed it back.

She hid herself behind a big leather armchair in a dark
corner to see if Professor Josston reappeared, but she'd barely
gotten herself situated when she heard what must be the
house's front door opening and closing. She'd made a serious
miscalculation about the amount of night time activity in the
house.

She dared not leave her hiding spot, and was glad she
hadn't when someone entered the library. She peered around
the chair, and in the dim light took in the wide shoulders and

serious expression of Mr. Cade Harlowe, his face etched in shadows. He glanced over his shoulder as if to ensure he had not been followed, then did something very curious. He stepped over to one of the bookcases and reached up to a dragon sculpture on one of the shelves. He twisted its tail. This was followed by a distinct *snick*. He then pushed the bookcase, and it swung open silently on well-greased hinges and tracks. He stepped through the opening and the bookcase moved smoothly back into place leaving no evidence of his passing except for a stray wisp of air current. Now she knew how the professor had vanished. A hidden room or corridor behind the bookcase.

Just what were he and his student up to?

She smiled. There was only one way to find out.

UNDERGROUND

Karigan allowed several minutes to pass before she left her concealment. She made right for the dragon sculpture, its bronze surface aged to a dark patina. It crouched with wings partially unfurled and sinuous neck curving so that it seemed to gaze directly at her with shadowed eyes, almost daring her to touch it.

She took a deep breath, reached for the tail, and turned it as she'd seen Cade Harlowe do. The *snick* made her jump. It sounded so much louder when she did it that she feared it would awaken the entire household and bring Mirriam running. It did not, but she understood Cade Harlowe's impulse to check over his shoulder.

A gentle push of the bookcase was all it took to swing it open. The space beyond was dimly lit with a wall lamp, but she took her taper with her just in case and passed through the opening into a cupboard of a space just large enough for the bookcase to move and for her to stand in. When the bookcase swept closed behind her, her heart pounded—it was difficult to breathe—too like the sarcophagus in which she'd so recently been sealed.

She steadied herself with deep inhalations. There was no lack of air, just nerves too tautly strung in this tiny, closed space. How would she get back out? She saw no mechanism for unlocking the bookcase. She shrugged, telling herself she was going forward, anyway, not retreating, and the way forward was clear, a door outlined by the lamplight.

She lifted the latch and opened it, cool air exhaling into the little room. The lamp sketched out stone steps descending into blackness. Three unlit tapers sat on the top step, but she bypassed them and ignited hers. Closing the door behind her, she began a spiraling journey downward.

She plunged down and down on rough cut stone steps, the air growing increasingly damp. She felt she must surpass even the house's foundation before she reached the bottom, her bad leg quivering from the strain of bearing her own weight with each step down.

In a small chamber at the bottom she found another door, this one much older-looking and ironbound, yet when she tried it, it opened as easily as the others with no groan of ancient hinges. Hoping she'd finally found where the professor and Cade Harlowe had snuck away to, she stepped boldly across the threshold into a dark space dense with silence of which she could make no sense.

She brightened her taper, and even then the scene mystified her. The path before her was like a cobblestone street, and along its sides were dusty shop fronts, hitching posts, troughs. Rubble filled the spaces between and behind the buildings. Hefty beams and brick and masonry arches supported the earthen ceiling above.

"Gods," she murmured, her voice clamorous in the silent world.

Mill City must have been built right over the remains of this old city, she thought, or at least part of it. These stone and timber structures were more like what she was accustomed to in her own time than the brick of Mill City. She limped over to one shop front, her slippers raising puffs of dust, and used the tail end of her shawl to rub grime from the rippled glass. Her light revealed little of the interior but the rough plank floor riddled with debris and a table with a chair pulled slightly away as if its occupant might return at any moment. A plate and tankard draped in cobwebs also waited.

Karigan shivered and backed away. A sign hung askew from one hook over the door, drawing her eye. The sign of the Cock and Hen.

The Cock and . . . ? No! She almost dropped her taper. This could not be possible. The Cock and Hen was in the lower quarter of Sacor City. But there could be no mistake—

this was *the* Cock and Hen, a disreputable inn in a rough
neighborhood that nevertheless brewed the finest darkest ale
in the city. She knew the sign—and the ale—well, and now
she began to recognize the rest of the exterior, even as out of
place as it looked underground.

Mill City had been built on top of Sacor City, or at least
part of it. That was the only conclusion she could come to.
The street she now stood on was the Winding Way. The revelation that her city lay buried beneath the foundations of another sent her reeling. She sat on the edge of a trough,
oblivious to the dirt smudging her nightgown. "I can't be seeing this." Passing her hand over her eyes did nothing to
change the scene before her.

Was all of Sacor City buried? How had this come to pass?
And when? She had to keep reminding herself she was in the
future, but she could not draw herself away from the enormity of it, the sense of loss. Her time, her world, was hidden,
literally buried. She shook her head and released a rattling
breath.

The only one who could explain it to her was down here
somewhere in this strange, but familiar, muted world, and
now she was more eager than ever to find him. The way was
not difficult, for footprints over the dirty, dusty cobblestones
had made a clear path she could follow.

She passed buildings she recognized, though sometimes she
had to think about which one was which, because of their new
setting and the damage to otherwise familiar facades. There
was the harness shop that made the special lightweight saddles
of the Green Riders. It was next to a blacksmith's shop. She
peered through the cracked window and spotted an anvil and
forge still intact. If ghosts wished to visit her, she thought, this
was the appropriate time and place, but not one so much as
whispered past her ear or fluttered among the ruins.

More buildings were crushed beneath rubble, actually cutting off the Winding Way. The footprints veered off to a gaping doorway. There was not much inside the building to
suggest what it had once been, but some broken shards of
pottery littered the floor. Karigan racked her brain but could
not remember.

Plain wooden stairs ascended to an upper level. They were not old, these stairs, but of a more recent construction and covered with dirty footprints. She followed them, climbing into an upper story and landing in a room that could have once been a bed chamber. She discovered another set of stairs that led into the attic. Up she went again and, once in the attic, discovered steep, narrow stairs that rose through a square cut in the roof, through which faint light trickled.

She gathered herself and climbed again, clutching a rope that served as a handrail, and rose through the roof, the roof of the old city, as she thought of it, and for several lengths through a vertical shaft of stone and rubble braced with cross beams. Eventually she emerged into a long chamber of bricks with barrel-arched ceilings. The room smelled dank, of wet stone. Her light fell across hulking metal contraptions that shone with a dull green gleam, rust eating painted surfaces. They'd valves and levers and gears, and she had no idea what they were supposed to be used for.

The faint light she'd seen had not originated here but spilled down the shaft of a stairwell behind her. *Got to keep going.* She entered the stairwell, took a deep breath, and climbed again, her feet ringing dully on wrought iron steps, the handrail clammy to her touch. When she spiraled up to the top of the first flight, she found a lamp at low glow and a door hanging open. She stepped out onto a wooden floor splotched with dark stains, the air thick with dust and a metallic, oily tang.

Even at full brightness, her taper could not begin to illuminate the vast space. She couldn't tell how far the long room extended, but support beams marched down its length like lines of soldiers before vanishing into the dark. Shafts were attached to the ceiling, and wide belts of looping leather dangling down from pulleys swayed in subtle air currents like beckoning nooses. She shuddered.

Deeper in the room, her light glinted on square-framed skeletons of steel heaped in a jumble of parts: rollers embedded with fine metal tines, toothy beveled gears the size of cart wheels, rods and pipes and chains, and many other unidentifiable pieces. She could not fathom their purpose or how they might all fit together—an impossible puzzle. The building groaned and complained with settling noises, and its listless air currents stirred loose tendrils of her hair.

To Karigan it was as if the building echoed the energy, activity that it must have once known; that something of it remained captured here, restless, contained by boarded up windows and disuse.

She shuddered again and backed into the stairwell. No one was in that darkened room of derelict mechanicals. More light shone from above, so she climbed up the spiraling stairs yet one more level, and when she stepped through the door into the dazzling light, she stood blinking some time before her eyes adjusted. When they did, she could see the actual proportions of the room. It was longer than even the king's throne room, and wider, too.

Chandeliers, half a dozen of them, hung down the center of the room between whatever shafts were still attached to the ceiling. The floor, unlike the rough one below, shone to a high polish, and it was almost like standing in a ballroom, though the battered support beams and brick walls were clues to the room's more utilitarian past. The windows were not simply boarded up, but were hung with heavy velvet draperies. Lamp sconces provided additional light.

She was not alone.

About halfway down the room and to the left, Cade Harlowe, stripped down to his trousers and quite unaware of her, punched at a heavy oblong bag hanging from the ceiling, the sweat gleaming on his muscles. The wall near him held racks of swords, pikes, staffs, and other weapons. Weights were lined up along the wall, as well.

Standing near him was the professor, watching his student as critically as any arms master, still dressed in his fancy attire. He noticed Karigan first, his gaze alighting on her. Then Cade Harlowe paused what he was doing and followed the professor's gaze. The three of them stood frozen like that for a long time, just staring at one another, then the professor broke the spell by striding toward her with his arms outstretched.

"How very good to see you up and about, my dear," he said, his voice ringing out across the large space. "I see your curiosity finally got the better of you."

SANCTUARY

Karigan waited as the professor crossed the long space between them, followed by Cade Harlowe, who grabbed a towel along the way to mop his face. Would she get any answers from them, including one to explain what this building was all about? Or would her "uncle" continue to play the mysterious professor and try to put her off. When they reached her, he was all smiles beneath his mustache, but Cade Harlowe's expression was one of suspicion, which must, she thought, match her own.

"I told you she would come looking sooner or later, didn't I, Cade?"

"Yes, Professor." Cade's tone was bland.

"And I would bet all my sweet, old auntie's finest gems — she had seven husbands, you know — that our young lady is the one who caused the disarray in my office tonight."

Karigan chose not to respond one way or the other.

"Well, I suppose it was not unexpected," the professor said as if to himself.

She wondered if he meant the shambles of his office or her causing it.

The professor came back to himself, his gaze turning to one of concern. "I'd hazard you've had a tiring journey to find us, my dear. Shall we retire to someplace more comfortable?" He extended his arm.

Her leg *was* sore after all the stairs. Cade relieved her of her taper, and she took the professor's arm. The professor walked slowly to accommodate her limp, and she was grateful to be able to lean on him.

"How do you like my little sanctuary?" he asked, waving his arm at their surroundings.

"It's . . . it's not little—it's huge! What is this place?"

"It is what remains of the original Josston Mills complex, number four," he replied. His smile faltered slightly. "Five floors of industry in this one building alone. This floor was once the spinning room."

Karigan tried to imagine how many spinners and spinning wheels it would take to fill the place but found she couldn't quite. The professor continued to smile down at her as if he guessed just what she was thinking. She shook her head.

"Nowadays, it is believed this building is but a shell I occasionally use for storage."

"Is it?"

"I do use it for storage," he replied, "though it is not precisely a shell."

As they crossed the great length of the room, her wonder grew. The far end appeared to be an opulent sitting area and library with stout furniture upholstered in rich leather. The wood of furnishings and shelves was dark, burnished with brass fittings. An old Durnesian carpet covered the floor. It was not old in that it looked worn or faded, but that its dyed weavings were of a texture and deepened tint that suggested age. Only the most masterfully made Durnesian carpets aged so well. It also featured the "homestead pattern" that had belonged to a clan of the most revered of makers.

A chipped and hairlined marble sculpture of the god Aeryc cradling the crescent moon stood beside a handsome desk. At first she took the sculpture for granted because she was used to seeing such iconography in her own Sacoridia, but then it occurred to her she'd heard no reference to Aeryc or Aeryon or any other gods since her arrival in this time. She remembered Mornhavon the Black and his Arcosians had worshipped only one god and thought the Sacoridians heathens for supporting an entire pantheon.

As if one god could take care of an entire world's needs, she thought with derision.

Did Mornhavon require his empire's citizens to worship the one god, or did he allow them to choose? She couldn't imagine he would allow choice in religion or in any other matter of importance.

She released the professor's arm and limped to the shelves which rose from floor to ceiling, with a rolling ladder to reach the uppermost heights. Unlike the library in the house, she found some titles she recognized, such as *Lint's Wordage* and *The Journeys of Gilan Wylloland,* the latter an old favorite of hers. She pulled down another book, *The Sealender Legacy,* and found the book largely charred. In fact most of the books she checked were damaged and had the look of age upon them. Unlike the carpet she stood on, they had not done well through time, though it looked like someone had taken care to clean and mend them as much as was feasible.

These were all Sacoridian titles, at least as far as she could see, including its history and fictional works. She even spotted several volumes of census reports. She turned around trying to take it all in — the extensive library of damaged books, the huge mill building, the Durnesian carpet, and a professor in formal evening attire.

"Ah," Professor Josston said. "Here is Cade with some tea."

The professor had allowed her time to try and absorb it all, but now Cade strode toward them bearing a silver tray service from the opposite corner where a small kitchen was set up with a stove, cupboards, and table. He'd since put on a white shirt and waistcoat, but he still wasn't quite up to gentlemanly standards with his sleeves rolled up and his collarless shirt unbuttoned at his throat. He set the tray down on a low table and stepped back.

"Shall we sit?" the professor asked. He gestured at a chair and Karigan sat, glad to get off her leg.

"You, too, Cade."

The younger man's arms were folded across his chest, and he opened his mouth as if to protest, but the professor cut him off.
"*Sit.*"

Cade sat. He did not look very happy. He continued to look unhappy while the professor served tea and poppy seed muffins. Karigan thought it an odd time for tea, as she reckoned it must be past the midnight hour, but she welcomed it nonetheless. Tea made everything better.

The professor seemed to agree. "Nothing like tea," he said, "when in unfamiliar or confusing circumstances, eh?"

He did not sit behind the big desk, which, Karigan noted, was immaculate. There were no piles or stacks or mess here. Everything was neatly arranged. Instead, he sat with them around the small table and its tea service.

"Ah, yes," he said, "tea warms the spirit, does it not?"

She and Cade nodded.

"I would guess, my dear, you have many questions. But first, I need you to tell Cade your name—the name you gave me. Not the one *I* gave you."

Karigan narrowed her eyebrows. "Why? You believe I'm mad."

"It was the only rational explanation I could accept at the time."

"But now you believe that I am who I said I am?"

"I believe that I do believe so," the professor replied. "I do not know how it is possible, or why you've come to be here, but the evidence supports your . . . assertion. I told Cade who I believe you to be, but I'd like him to hear it from you."

Karigan glanced at the glowering Cade, now unsure if she wanted them to believe her, to know her true identity. Still the professor had gone to some lengths to protect her.

"I am Karigan G'ladheon," she said, challenging Cade with her gaze.

"*Rider Sir* Karigan G'ladheon," the professor added.

Cade lowered his cup, slowly and with control, until it settled gently onto its saucer with a soft *clink,* as though he was suppressing an outburst of denial.

"It cannot be true." He swept his hand through his hair. "It is not possible. You can't make me believe that a historical person is sitting in this room *now.*" It did not sound like the first time they'd had this particular discussion.

"Like I said," the professor replied, "I don't know how it's possible that someone from so long ago could be here now, living and breathing among us, but the evidence . . . from her clothing to the brooch she wore. The textiles were of a time when cloth was hand-woven."

Early on in this world, Karigan had noticed the extremely

fine, almost perfect weave of her nightgown and bed clothes. Not even the best textiles her father traded in were so intricately woven. She had wondered how it was accomplished, and now the professor implied it was not by hand.

"The details were right," the professor said, his gaze settling on Karigan. "The dye of the green, the embroidered gold winged horse on coat and shirtsleeve. But Cade asks a legitimate question. *How* did you get here to this time? In our first conversation, you mentioned something about a mask bringing you forward. Can you explain this?" Both men sat there staring hard at her, waiting.

"I—I don't know exactly how or why it happened," she replied. "We were in Blackveil and—"

The professor blanched. Cade raised an eyebrow, his large hands gripping the armrests of his chair until Karigan thought he'd puncture the leather.

"What did I say?" Karigan asked.

"Blackveil," the professor murmured. "It is not spoken of. We are unaccustomed to hearing it named."

Karigan sighed. Here they go again, she thought, with the secret histories versus "true history."

"We did not mean to interrupt, my dear," the professor said. "Please continue."

She did and found herself explaining how she and a party of Sacoridians and Eletians crossed the D'Yer Wall into Blackveil to observe the status of the forest after a thousand years of being closed off from the rest of the world and subject to the influence of Mornhavon the Black. Eventually they found themselves at the forest's heart, in the deserted Castle Argenthyne, legendary bastion of the Eletians who were conquered by Mornhavon long ago. She did not speak in great detail of the trials she and her companions endured, for it would require more than one night in the telling, but she told enough that Cade's and the professor's expressions were rapt and suffused with amazement.

When she reached the part about finding the looking mask in the nexus of Castle Argenthyne, she said, "It was a true object of magic. Beyond magic even." A thing of the gods, she thought with a shudder, remembering how she'd raised the mask to her face and looked through it and saw the strands of time and the heavens intersecting, diverging; weaving and unraveling. She'd held a million, million possibilities in her hands, the power to manipulate the fabric of the universe. She'd rejected that power and smashed the mask on the floor to prevent Mornhavon the Black from seizing it, and the next thing she knew, she found herself trapped in a sarcophagus at a circus, from which she escaped into Mill City and Cade Harlowe's hands.

"So that's why you asked me if I was one of those clowns," Cade said.

"And it enlightens me as to how Rudman Hadley ended up with a live body in his sarcophagus," the professor mused, "which he accused me of planting to discredit him, by the way."

The two men quieted, seemed lost in their own reveries, perhaps trying to digest Karigan's story. She plucked nervously at the hem of her nightgown awaiting a more definitive response.

Cade was the first to react. He turned to the professor and said, "You can't possibly believe all this."

"Part of me finds it extremely difficult," the professor admitted. "But the past was filled with wonders that defy rational explanation."

Cade snorted. "And you believe this thing about the mask?"

"Looking masks are part of our heritage, Cade, perhaps trivialized in the latter part of Sacoridia's history but derived from ancient rituals when magic was as rife in the land as water in the ocean. Who is to say that true looking masks did not hold power? And as you may recall, we found all those broken pieces of a mirror embedded in our young lady's flesh when she arrived."

"Which could have been just an ordinary broken mirror," Cade said. "It's not proof."

Karigan's heart pounded, hearing of the shards. Had they saved any? If so, would any power remain in them? Then she dismissed the idea, remembering that magic did not seem to work in this time.

"Perhaps not," the professor said, "but like the uniform, the brooch, it all supports what she says. I'm pretty good at detecting liars, and I don't think she has fabricated this story. There are too many precise details, and she did not bungle them, trip herself up, as a liar would have."

Karigan was not sure it mattered if they believed her—she would find some means of reaching home one way or the other. But if they did believe her, it would ease the way for her to find out the information she wished to take back to King Zachary about the defeat of Sacoridia and the rise of the empire. On inspiration, she said, "Test me."

"What?" Cade asked.

"Test me. Ask me questions that only someone who lived during my time, or scholars like yourselves, would know."

Cade wasted no time and jumped in with the first question. "What is the Order of Black Shields?"

"Easy. They guard the royal family, living and dead. Usually we just call them Weapons."

Cade sat back, rubbing his chin. "Perhaps easy for someone who studies history, but not generally known. What was the succession of Clan Hillander on the throne?"

Karigan started with the Clan Wars and Smidhe Hillander, down the line of succession to King Zachary. Thus began an exhaustive period of eager questioning by both Cade and the professor about Sacoridian history, as well as facets of everyday life. Early on, they tried to slip her up with false or very specific questions. She could not answer all they asked.

"Who was Lady Amalya Whitewren?" Cade asked.

"I have no idea," Karigan replied.

"She was only one of the most popular poets of your time."

Karigan shrugged. She'd never heard of this person, but it wasn't surprising since she did not follow what was happening in poetry.

The professor cleared his throat. "Cade, if I'm not mistaken, Lady Amalya came into prominence after Karigan G'ladheon left for Blackveil."

"That could be," Cade said, nodding thoughtfully. "Then tell me—"

And so the questioning went on. At times the two men seemed to forget they were testing her, more interested in confirming or debunking theories about customs, dress, architecture, arts, and politics. Karigan had to sip her cooling tea to moisten her throat.

"Enough," the professor finally said. "For now, anyway." He smiled. "Are you satisfied, Cade?"

"Either she is unusually well-tutored and a good actress, or she is speaking truth." He sighed heavily. "I concede that by some miracle, whether by this magical mask or other means, she has come to us through time. The evidence supports her."

"But you still doubt?" the professor persisted.

"You know me, Professor, I always question."

"That's a fine attribute in an archeologist." The professor turned back to Karigan. "My dear, despite my own doubts, I began to believe you rather early on, after our initial chat. I had come across the name of 'Karigan G'ladheon' in some of my books. One mentions how you saved King Zachary's throne from his usurper brother."

Karigan squirmed in her chair, thinking it very odd to be mentioned in any book.

"I'd also seen your name listed in various roll calls that have survived to this day, and the one in which you suddenly became Rider Sir Karigan G'ladheon rather than just Rider G'ladheon. There is an account of how a Rider G'ladheon had rescued King Zachary's betrothed, though the telling of it is maddeningly lacking in details. In any case, if I am correct, it is after this rescue that you were anointed to knighthood."

Karigan nodded, squirming some more.

"I hope you will tell me that story sometime, yourself, but not tonight as we've already asked much of you."

She sighed in relief and relaxed.

"There is another G'ladheon mentioned in passing in some of the histories, a prominent merchant."

"Yes," Karigan said, "my father."

The professor brightened. "Ah, I had hoped so. It's just so very exciting to make connections. I mention all this because after your arrival, I sought to confirm your identity, or at least that of whom you claimed to be, so I took to doing research on the G'ladheon name. I once again came across those references I mentioned before, and found new ones, including a roster of those Sacoridians going on the expedition to Blackveil. It included details about how the expedition was provisioned and outfitted, which I found very interesting. You see, one little detail had nagged me about the garb you were wearing when you arrived here. Everything was right but the boots. You were not wearing riding boots as a Green Rider ought."

"No," Karigan agreed. "We were issued infantry boots because we'd be on foot in Blackveil, not riding."

"Exactly! And it was the detail of those infantry boots that clinched it, that made me believe absolutely that you are who you say you are. They matched the roster. How could you have known such a fine detail if you hadn't been there, or read the reference only I own, which is stored here in my secret library?"

"You did not tell me any of this," Cade said, and now he looked at Karigan with perhaps more belief in his eyes.

"I am telling you now. I've kept you busy watching the students while I researched." He gestured with an expression of pride at his shelves of books. "I did find something intriguing, my dear," he said, turning back to Karigan, "and about Blackveil. It seems you entered the forest and never returned. And if I may leap to a conclusion, you never returned because you ended up here."

Karigan now found herself gripping her armrests. "You mean I never returned home? Not even from here?"

"The records, scant as they are, reveal nothing."

A scream of despair welled up in Karigan's chest.

MISSING

**"I**t does not mean you never returned," the professor said, his expression kindly. "It just means I never found a record of it." He stood and started scouring the bookshelves, muttering to himself.

For Karigan, it was as if a trapdoor had flung open beneath her, revealing a yawning chasm. She did not want to be stuck here—she wanted to go home to her friends and family, the world she knew. His pronouncement had defeated any hope that she would find a way back. She squeezed her eyes shut trying to recall the words the Berry sisters once told her about the future . . . *It is not set in stone.* That's what they had said. Even the looking mask had shown her the infinite possibilities, the variations of the world's time threads. But if she were already *in the future,* could her past now be set in stone?

When she opened her eyes again, the professor was rolling the ladder along the bookshelves until he found whatever section he wanted and climbed. He reached for a volume on the top shelf. "Ah, yes," he said muttering to himself. "This one."

Cade Harlowe simply stared at her, immovable. She stared back, refusing to be intimidated.

"Here we are," the professor said. He clambered back down and handed Karigan the book before retreating to his chair. "The last evidence."

She examined it. It was ledger size, bound in plain leather, so like the many others she had handled; but the leather was worn and damaged by moisture, and the pages within as delicate as fallen autumn leaves. She carefully flipped through a few of the pages, gazed at the precise handwriting within, set in columns listing payroll by the week. Some of the ink was smeared, some pages torn or too stained to read, but she knew this ledger, had handled it in a different age. And she knew the handwriting well, for it was her own.

She caressed the familiar names listed in the columns: Mara Brennyn, Ty Newland, Alton D'Yer, Osric M'Grew . . . A few more pages in, and she saw where she had written, *Deceased* next to Osric's name, and the time-in-service pay he had not lived to collect. A notation showed that the pay, and a death benefit, had been forwarded to his mother. She wiped a tear from her cheek before it could besmirch the ledger.

She had not been happy to take on the duty of keeping the Rider accounts, but with her merchant background, Captain Mapstone had thought her the best one to handle them, and rightly so. Maintaining the ledgers for the business ventures of Clan G'ladheon had been her least favorite duty when she worked with her father, but she'd been good at it. She'd thought it a terrible irony when she ended up having to do it for the Green Riders.

Now as she looked upon those names, no few marked *Deceased* as Osric's had been, she realized it had been an honor to keep the ledgers. And what a marvel to have such a connection to her own time, something as mundane as this. It was almost like, she thought, peering out of one's own grave. No, better to think of it as a window to her own time.

She continued looking, oblivious to the two men who watched her intently. Of course she saw her own name listed and rate of pay. There was that snarl she'd made of Rider accounts at the end of winter. Well, the end of winter back in her own time. She smiled, remembering the mess, spending such long hours trying to untangle it that she'd forgotten the payroll. Here her handwriting grew less tidy, as though she'd been frantic to fill in names and numbers in record time. Unpaid Riders were unhappy Riders.

Pages rustled as she turned them. Abruptly her own handwriting ended, and the equally neat but distinctive hand of Daro Cooper began. The captain had thought it wise that another Rider be trained to handle the accounts during Karigan's absences, and Daro assumed that duty when Karigan left for Blackveil.

"How did you ever . . . ?" Karigan began. She glanced up at the professor. "How did you ever find this ledger?" She was surprised something so mundane had survived the years as well as the presumed purging of such records by the empire.

"It was not easy. Occasionally one in my work stumbles upon such relics from the time before the emperor. I am duty bound to hand over anything of particular interest to the emperor. Not all of it, of course, comes into his hands. And there are others who . . . scavenge . . . beneath the emperor's notice. There is quite a healthy black market for relics. I purchased the ledger from one such dealer. Indirectly, of course. Wouldn't do to leave a trail for the Inspectors to follow."

"Black market . . ." Karigan murmured, her gaze drawn once more to the book. She turned the pages, everything looking right and orderly, until abruptly she came to Yates Cardell's name and the word, *Deceased.* A sob caught in her throat, and her eyes blurred the matter-of-fact statement that his accrued pay and benefits were to go to a cousin in D'Ivary Province. Had Daro cried when she made the entry, as Karigan had when she recorded the deaths of Osric M'Grew and others?

With another glance she saw that Lynx's name remained with no additional statement. Lynx must have made it—made it home—and reported Yates' death.

Oh, Yates . . . She had feared it was so, that he'd died in the nexus of Castle Argenthyne, deep in the heart of Blackveil. How could he have survived the presence of Mornhavon in his body, burning him from the inside out? And when she had smashed the looking mask at his feet, she thought she might have destroyed *all* her companions, including the Eletians. Their names threaded through her mind in a subconscious whisper: *Ealdaen, Telagioth, Lhean.*

Despite her fears, she'd held out hope; hope for dear, funny Yates. Yates, who'd had so much of a future ahead of him. Yates, her friend. He'd kept her going when the two of them had become separated from the others in Blackveil, had helped each other survive.

She did not notice when the professor stood and crossed over to her chair, but there he was at her elbow proffering a handkerchief. She took it gratefully, dried her eyes and blew her nose.

He must have seen how her fingers rested on Yates' name because he said, "One of your companions who went into Blackveil with you. A good friend?"

"Yes," she replied. "They all were."

She found her own name several lines beneath Yates'. She was listed as *Missing*.

Missing, not deceased.

"Is this what you wanted me to see?" she asked the professor, pointing at the entry.

"Er, keep looking."

She did. Over the weeks of entries that followed, Daro continued to list her as *Missing*. Pay was set aside for her. Weeks turned into months when finally she came to the entry, *G'ladheon, Sir Karigan, presumed dead. Accrued pay and benefits to father in Corsa, L'Petrie Province.*

She glanced through the last few pages of the ledger, but did not see her name again. "They thought I died in Blackveil."

"It is the only evidence of your fate we possess," the professor said, "other than your sitting here at this moment in this very chair."

"I never returned."

"Who is to say? They presumed you dead, but you are not. You got here somehow so who is to say it's impossible for you to return? But that said, I'm afraid we've never found anything to suggest that you made it back."

Karigan reread the simple words in Daro's neat script, so toneless and without emotion. How had her father taken the news? Her aunts? How long did it take her friends to forget about her and move on with their lives? Not very long, she figured. Green Riders were always kept busy with duties to fulfill, more dangers to face. They could not afford to dwell on the death of any single Rider.

Her beloved Condor would have been partnered with another Rider. They'd been in need of many more horses. Who was chosen? Karigan had not been his first Rider. He, too, would move on.

And King Zachary? What would he feel? He was to be married on the summer solstice—Day of Aeryon—of that year. He, too, would have his attention drawn elsewhere.

As it should be.

She closed the ledger with a thump, this familiar, yet at the same time strange, book, this artifact that tied her to her home. She handed it back to the professor, who reverently laid it on his desk.

"I can't imagine how odd it must be to see that." He shook his head. "No, I cannot. Makes me shiver to think of it. Makes me shiver to see you sitting here before me, a living artifact."

Karigan bristled with anger. "Should I place myself on one of your shelves then?"

The professor winced. "Sorry, my dear. Forgive me. It was my archeological bent speaking. Here you are, torn from your own time and home, and I spoke without thinking."

"Don't mind the professor." Cade Harlowe's voice was so unexpected that it startled Karigan. His expression had lost its intensity and had softened into compassion. "The professor," Cade continued with a bit of a drawl, "sometimes forgets we're not all artifacts."

"I'm not that bad, Old Button," the professor said.

Old Button? she wondered. The two men laughed as at a familiar joke, and Karigan's anger bled away.

"Do I have your forgiveness?" the professor asked.

Karigan nodded and he responded with a courtly bow.

"Good, because I have more to show you and the night grows short."

SHARDS

"**I** would like to have my things back," Karigan said. "The things I had with me, on me, when I arrived."

"I shall show them to you," the professor said, "and you will see that I've kept them safe."

Cade excused himself to resume his training. The professor led Karigan toward the nearest end of the room, where another stairway corkscrewed up its shaft into the dark. By the time the professor found and lit a taper, Karigan saw with a glance over her shoulder that Cade had picked up a practice sword and was moving through a series of forms.

He does all right, she thought, but found herself critical of how he seemed to focus more on correct posture than execution. His posture did look good, very good—picturesque, even, but picturesque would not help him dispatch an opponent. His balance, though, was solid and would hold him in good stead. Though she studied Cade from a professional point of view, all her seasons of sparring with swordmaster trainees in various states of undress and at the peak of their physical form did not leave her immune from appreciating the aesthetic charms of a pleasing figure of manhood in action.

"This way," the professor said.

Karigan tore her gaze away from Cade with some regret and followed the professor into the stairwell, keeping close to his light.

"The upper floors were once the weave rooms," the professor was saying, their feet ringing on wrought iron stairs as they climbed. "They were filled with looms and workers and the clatter of machinery, but no more."

When they reached the landing, the professor stepped into the dark room and fumbled around a bit, muttering to himself, while Karigan peered into the vast, black space, discerning nothing. Just the rough, scraped floor in their immediate halo of light, pocked with small holes where very heavy objects must once have been bolted down. It was so quiet, she could not imagine the noise the professor spoke of.

"Ah, here it is," he said. "Usually I enter from the other end." He pushed up a lever embedded in a box in the wall, and the room exploded with light.

Karigan blinked until her eyes adjusted. Many plain phosphorene globes hung from the ceiling rafters, revealing row upon row of crates stacked high, shelves with articles covered by sheets, numerous freestanding statues and urns and pieces of decorative scrollwork; gargoyles, and columns. A portion of one wall was lined with imposing cabinets.

The professor set his taper aside and gestured grandly. "Behold my treasure trove. All artifacts that have passed into my care, and many that I, myself, have found or otherwise acquired." He beamed proudly like a father looking upon his offspring.

"All of this? And you've kept it hidden from the emperor?" Karigan looked doubtfully at some of the larger statues, trying to imagine how one of those could have been concealed and brought here.

"I've been tireless in preserving our rightful heritage. If the emperor caught wind of my collection, well, I and everyone I know would be in very serious trouble. You do understand, do you not, that you are to speak to no one, absolutely no one, about this building or its contents? Not even Mirriam or Lorine. Not even Cade or me outside of this mill building unless I raise the subject first. I am placing great trust in you that you will not expose the secret. I've gone to great pains to keep *you* secret, as well, for your safety."

Karigan studied him long and hard, his expression almost beseeching. "Why is the emperor so afraid? He's in charge isn't he?"

Professor Josston nodded, setting off toward the shelves, his hands clasped behind his back. Karigan limped behind

him. "Yes, he runs his empire like a machine. Unfeeling, relentless, productive, and people believe it's the way it has always been. Always the emperor, always the empire. That's
what makes our real history so dangerous—it would inspire
hope in the populace, and he can't allow that to happen." He
paused beside a shelf that held bottles of all sizes and colors,
many cracked and broken, placed next to pieces of gold jewelry. He fingered a brooch of the crescent moon, tilting it so
that it flared in the light.

"These objects," he continued, "are not just old things, but
symbols of what could have been, what should be. What we
were before the emperor said we were nothing without him."
He set the brooch aside and faced Karigan, his expression
intense. "My artifacts are the spark of a fire, a fire that will
burn down the empire. Rebellion, my dear. This mill building
and its contents are an act of war."

In that moment, he reminded Karigan of the Anti-
Monarchy Society and its leader. What was her name? Lorilie. Lorilie Dorran. She'd been eager, full of the fervor of her
beliefs. She had plans to change the world, or at least how
Sacoridia was governed, but nothing had ever come of them.

"Why keep it secret?" Karigan asked. "Why not reveal all
this to the people and let them rebel?"

"Oh, we will, but not all the pieces are in place yet. If we
act prematurely, we will be crushed." He abruptly turned and
continued to walk alongside the shelving. As Karigan followed, she glimpsed an ivory comb set with rubies. It had
been placed next to the ruin of leather boots. Rotting chunks
of wood that once could have been tools sat next to fine porcelain dishes. The mundane and the exquisite, all lined up one
next to the other, a wagon wheel as prized as a pair of golden
goblets.

"Truthfully," the professor said, "the rebellion has been
going on for some time, an unspoken war brewing beneath
the polite workings of society. Our battlefields have been
charity balls and banquets and evenings at the opera."

Karigan considered the formal attire he currently wore
and wondered if he'd been engaged in battle this evening.

"The opposition has been in play for as long as there has

been the emperor," the professor said. "The kings and queens of the past had a pact, a trust, to protect their people, not abuse them as chattel. The emperor keeps no such pact, only keeps his machine well oiled and productive, wearing out the spirit of the people." He halted beside the worm-eaten figurehead of a swan propped against the shelving, pausing to allow her to weigh his words, before finally asking, "So, will you keep our secret?"

She regarded him carefully, his earnest expression, for she knew Mornhavon's evil first hand. She had no argument with Professor Josston regarding the emperor. and, the professor, in turn, must have known how the Green Riders had opposed Mornhavon from the very beginning, which, she assumed, prompted him to take her into his confidence. She had no illusions, however, that if she ever posed a threat to his secrets, he would make her disappear as easily and quickly as she'd come into his life, no matter to what lengths he'd already gone to keep her safe. His secret was much more powerful, much more important to him than her life, intrigued though he might be by her passage through time and the part of her that was a living artifact. If the conditions in the empire were as bad as they seemed to be, she could not blame him.

Her silence must have made him nervous. "If I cannot convince you with my words," he said, "perhaps over the coming days I can show you what the empire has turned my land—*our land*—into."

By offering her another chance to keep his secret, it was clear he preferred not to harm her if he didn't have to. "I do not need to be convinced of the emperor's evil," she said. "I'm quite familiar with it. Your secret will not be exposed by me."

The professor relaxed perceptibly and smiled. "I had hoped you would see our common purpose."

Common purpose? She wasn't too sure about that. Her goal was to get home, to take back any information to King Zachary about how the empire overcame Sacoridia—not to become involved in this time's problems, its intrigues. Besides, with the information she obtained here, she might actually improve the situation in *this* time, from the past. Meanwhile, she needed the professor's protection and knowledge, and in this regard they were allies.

He had already moved off, once again strolling down the aisle between shelves. "I thought you could tell me what some of the objects are that have been a mystery to me," he said over his shoulder. "If they're from your time, maybe you know their purpose." He lifted a moldering wooden rod with rectangular slots along its length. "Do you know what this is?"

"I have no idea," Karigan replied.

Undeterred, he picked up a rusted iron hook dangling from chains. He raised a querying brow.

"Looks like a pot hook," Karigan told him.

"For over a hearth?"

She nodded.

"But of course! I thought maybe it was something more nefarious, a tool of torture, perhaps." He chuckled as he set it back down. "Cooking tools always throw me. I'm not even allowed in my own kitchen."

He showed her a few more items she could not identify, except for a coin balance, which any merchant would know—at least, any merchant of her own time. She demonstrated its use by stabbing its spiked end into a wooden shelf to make it stand erect, then pivoted open the weighing appendage.

"Have you a coin?" she asked.

He reached into his pocket and produced a silver piece. Karigan placed it into the slot of the weighing appendage, which dipped down. It was difficult to determine its value because the measures inscribed on the device were nearly worn away.

"Ah," the professor said, smiling. "Not that the emperor's coin requires weighing, as it's very precisely minted."

"Currency is—was—fairly precise in my time, too," Karigan said, "but there were still some very old coins in circulation, not to mention less accurate coinage from other realms." She removed the coin, gazing at the image of a man's profile on it, struck in relief. It was more clear, more perfect than the imprint on any coin from her own time. There was something familiar about the man's profile, too, the high forehead and strong chin.

"This would be our dear emperor," the professor said,

piquing Karigan's interest. So this was how Mornhavon looked now. He'd long been capable of using the bodies of others. To whom had this one belonged?

The professor turned the coin over on her palm. "And this would be the emperor's dragon sigil."

The dragon was curled round on itself, with its tail wrapped around its neck. She didn't recall Mornhavon using a dragon sigil, but a dead tree. Perhaps with his victory over Sacoridia, he'd chosen a new emblem for his empire. Now that she thought about it, she remembered the professor referring to the empire as the "Serpentine Empire."

"Why a dragon?" she asked.

The professor shrugged. "Some say it has to do with some great weapon the emperor used against his enemies." He paused, taking a reflective stance. "I did some research and have determined it came into use about two and a half years after you went into Blackveil. In fact," and now he lowered his voice as if it was not just the two of them there, "it's something we've been investigating for years, this weapon, but whatever it is or was, it is well concealed."

"Hmm." Karigan rolled the coin onto the professor's palm, then unstuck the coin balance from the shelf and folded it before handing it to him. Only two and a half years after she had gone into Blackveil? "What did this weapon do?"

"It's said it wiped out all the realm's important defenses, that it was devastating. We see evidence of it at many of our dig sites."

She had been hoping for an easy answer to take back to the king, but it appeared there wasn't one, at least concerning this weapon, although now she had a timeframe to work with.

The professor deposited the coin in his pocket and set the coin balance in its place. Without explaining further, he set off down the aisle once again, continuing along at some length before pausing. He drew another object off one of the shelves that Karigan recognized immediately.

"My—my walking cane!" she cried.

The professor did not hand it over to her. "No, actually it's *my* walking cane." He pressed the trigger, shook the cane, and it extended into a staff.

"But—"

"Look closely," he said. "It is the same as yours, and it is not."

Karigan took it into her hands, feeling the familiar weight and the smooth black lacquer on the bonewood. But the professor was right—this one had acquired scars—scrapes and dints that hers never had. The handle was not leather-wrapped iron, but silver. Silver concealed its iron core. And there was a piece missing on the shaft. She ran her finger over the slight depression. Someone had painted it with lacquer, but it did not quite match the perfect midnight hue of the rest of the staff.

"The shield is missing," Karigan said. It would have been a small, plain black shield representing the Order of the Black Shields, the Weapons.

"One of my predecessors decided he could not take a chance of the symbol being recognized," the professor said, "so he carved it off. Alas, he did not save the piece. Not that I know of, at any rate."

"So they made more than one."

The professor nodded, seeming to know who "they" were. "I was quite astonished to see yours. I had assumed there'd been others, but I believed them destroyed or lost."

Karigan returned the cane to the professor, wondering where and how his "predecessor" had found it, but before she could ask him, he set it back on its shelf and moved down the aisle for several strides, stopping when he came upon a work table situated between two shelving units. She hurried to catch up, and there she saw her uniform laid out on a length of linen with utmost care, no matter it was ragged and dirty and blood-splattered by her travails in Blackveil. Her winged horse brooch gleamed golden in the phosphorene glow and she reached out to caress it. It felt as it always had—oily smooth and cool. There were her muddy boots, too, and belt, and the white feather of the winter owl, and of course her own bonewood cane.

Her mother's moonstone sat nested in crumpled purple velvet. She picked it up, but it still emitted only a feeble dying light.

"Is that really . . . ?" the professor began in awe. "Not just a legend?"

"If you are thinking it's an Eletian moonstone, you'd be correct." Karigan replaced it, hesitant to hold it too long as if her touch would use up its remaining magic. When the light winked out, the professor's expression fell.

"So many things we have lost with the empire," he murmured. "So many wonders."

The professor had even kept the broken Eletian arrow shafts that had been used to splint Karigan's broken wrist, and beside them, she was pleased to see, the mirror shards that had been removed from her flesh, still hazed with her blood. They were laid out on the velvet.

"I would like my belongings back," she said.

"I have deemed it safer to keep these objects well out of sight," the professor said. "I'm sorry, but I cannot permit them inside my home. I would not wish them to be found either by accident or by prying eyes."

"What about this building? How safe is it?"

"It is watched, and if it's breached, it's quite easy to destroy the evidence, though the loss of these objects that are so priceless to me would be extreme, to say the least."

Karigan's eyebrows scrunched together, his reference to destruction not reassuring her. "*I* breached the building."

The professor smiled enigmatically. "If that's the way you'd like to think of it."

Karigan scowled. So they had been expecting her. "I'd at least like my walking cane back—to support my bad leg." She would take it even if he said no. Her hand twitched as she resisted the urge to just grab it.

"Bad leg, indeed. It's done magnificently with all the stairs you used to get here. No, my dear, I understand completely the desire to have a weapon close to hand, but I can't take the chance of anyone seeing that symbol on it, no matter how subtle."

Karigan was about to argue, but the professor's raised hand forestalled her. "I shall lend you mine. People have seen me use it now and again and won't think twice at my niece's having it, especially with her very delicate leg."

"What about you? You won't be able to use it."

"Oh, I have several walking canes to choose from, my dear, and all of them quite as lethal, if not more so, than your own." He winked and brushed past her, heading back down the aisle, presumably to retrieve his bonewood cane for her.

She turned to follow with one last glance at her belongings. Her reflection fell fractured and distorted on the mirror shards. One eye, part of her mouth, and the tip of her nose. The reflections rippled and changed, and instead of revealing parts of her own visage, she saw, like a kaleidoscope scene, a tiny image of Captain Mapstone walking in a rough stone corridor in each fragment, all featuring a different angle, a different distance. Karigan almost called out to the captain, who glanced over her shoulder.

"What's this?" Professor Josston exclaimed, and Karigan started, darting her gaze at him down the aisle. He knelt, peering intently at the floor. "Tsk, tsk," he said. "Mouse droppings. I shall need Cade to set more traps."

Karigan exhaled a breath she had not known she was holding. A glance revealed the images of Captain Mapstone were gone, and the shards were back to reflecting her own face. Without hesitation she grabbed the largest mirror shard, which fit in the palm of her hand, and concealed it in her shawl.

The looking mask may have been shattered into hundreds of pieces, but even in this future where magic failed, something of its power remained.

In the present: Captain Mapstone

The flickering lamps along the rough stone walls of the corridor barely pushed back the dark that perpetually suffused this part of the castle. It was always noticeably cooler in these lower regions, as well. Laren Mapstone shivered, but not from the cold. These corridors she walked, on her way to the records room in the administrative wing, were among the oldest in the castle, and she often sensed she was not alone; the lateness of the hour only contributed to the feeling. She glanced over her shoulder as if someone's gaze touched her. It was not the first time the sensation had come over her, and of course no one was there. She hastened her step.

The records room had a certain reputation for being haunted. In fact, in the past, ghosts had made the life of the recordskeeper, Dakrias Brown, miserable. The ghosts had constantly left the vast chamber in a state of disarray, forcing Dakrias to clean up and reorganize repeatedly. Apparently he and the ghosts had come to some accord over time, for now the records room remained as peaceful as any other part of the castle. Or mostly, anyway. It did not mean the ghosts had actually left.

Laren paused, still feeling that gaze on her. She whipped around, but as usual, no one, or no *thing,* was there. She broke out in a cold sweat. Yes, she'd encountered ghosts before, and perhaps stranger phenomena in her long career as a Green Rider, but experience didn't make it easier for her. Dead spirits, she thought, ought to be dead and off to the heavens, not spying on and spooking the living.

The sensation of being watched vanished all at once, and she shook herself. Probably just her imagination living up to the reputation of these corridors. It was certainly easy enough down here, she mused, as she passed the gaping black maw of an abandoned corridor that branched off to her left.

Finally she entered the records room and breathed a sigh of relief to find Dakrias dictating to two of his clerks. A whole wing was devoted to administration, but when Dakrias was made chief of administration, he chose to remain in the records room rather than occupy his predecessor's large and well-appointed office a couple of levels above. It was quieter down here, he said. Fewer people to pester him. He left the daily operations of administration to an able deputy, who loved the big office and the authority, while Dakrias dealt with only the most pressing matters, and the records room, of course.

Laren was grateful he'd agreed to meet her so late at night, but it was the only time she had to spare. He'd said it was no trouble, that he often worked after hours. Apparently that meant his assistants did, too. Usually she found him poking through some old crate of documents or poring over old tomes. Whether they were an account of grain production from a hundred years ago, or a tally of how many loaves of bread the castle kitchen served per month, it all seemed to fascinate Dakrias. The records room contained all manner of the realm's statistical arcana, from maps to financial accounts, and when a Rider ledger was filled up from front cover to back, it was sent here to be archived, along with any other paperwork that covered the administrative workings of the messenger service.

While Laren waited for Dakrias to conclude his dictation, she gazed toward the high ceiling. She couldn't help but look all the way up, high beyond the uppermost shelves, seeking a glint of glass, but the ceiling was so high that light could not reach it. Had the original ceiling, a dome of stained glass, not been built over, in daylight she would have seen scenes from the Long War and the part the First Rider played in it.

"Ah, Captain," Dakrias said, clapping his hands. "You've come to find out what we've discovered, eh?"

"The question is, did you find anything at all?"

"Come and see." He led her to a table filled to capacity with books, sheaves of paper tied with ribbon, scrolls of faded parchment, and ledgers. The table appeared to bow beneath all the weight.

"All of this?" she asked incredulously. She had requested that Dakrias track down any records pertaining to Green Riders and warfare, including provisioning, tactics, special uses . . . any wisdom that her predecessors might have left behind that would aid her when it finally came to war with Second Empire. Historical records of the Riders were scarce, so the amount of documents burdening the table surprised her more than just a little.

Dakrias nodded and grinned. "There may be more. We're still looking. But I'll warn you that most of these contain but passing or oblique references to the Riders."

She touched the brittle binding of one book. It was so old it looked apt to fall apart if she opened it.

"We even pulled files and accounts of actions against the Darrow Raiders," Dakrias said, "though I know you were intimately acquainted with some of that."

She noticed his gaze shift. He was looking at her neck scar, which he must assume she had acquired during battle with the Raiders, but the injury that had caused it had in fact occurred at a later time. When he realized what he was doing, he cleared his throat and looked away.

"Elgin might be interested in those," she said. He'd been Chief Rider back then. Now in retirement, he'd returned to the castle to help train up new Riders.

Dakrias went through the piles explaining to her what was in which, as if the records were old friends of his. It was clear this was going to be more than a one-person task, sorting through what looked, to her, to be an overwhelming mess. She'd thought Dakrias might find a few items that she could go through in a spare moment, but she hadn't time to deal with this treasure trove. She'd assign one or two of her more studious Riders to assist Elgin.

As Dakrias grew more enthusiastic about his finds, Laren found her attention drifting toward the ceiling again. After a while, she realized Dakrias had silenced and followed her gaze.

"Do you see something?" he whispered, as if he didn't want ghosts to hear him.

"I don't, but if you don't mind, I'd like to go up above and take a look at the glass."

"Don't mind at all, and if you don't object, I should like to accompany you to make sure my junior clerks are minding their duty."

Laren had heard that Dakrias sent wayward clerks up to clear dust and cobwebs from the stained glass as punishment for their transgressions, meanwhile providing them with some educational insight into the darker times of Sacoridia's history and how the realm had emerged victorious. It was something she wished to be reminded of, as well.

She welcomed Dakrias' presence. Not that she feared the dark of the corridor and steep stairs that led to the dome, but, well, having a companion made it more palatable.

Dakrias located and lit a pair of lanterns, and as he led the way out of the records room, he asked, "Any word from, er, Blackveil?"

"No," Laren replied. She tried to tell herself it was much

too soon to hope for any news, but there was never a waking moment that some part of her brain didn't worry about her Riders and the success of the expedition.

"You used to send Rider G'ladheon over here quite a lot," Dakrias said. "I miss her. She understood about . . . well, you know."

The ghosts.

They entered the low-ceilinged chamber that covered the dome of glass that rose from the floor like an iridescent bubble. Their lights rippled on color and movement, bringing to life battle and victory, the defeat of the enemy. Laren slowly walked around the dome, her lantern animating Riders on prancing steeds, brandishing their weapons at the cowering army. She could almost hear the snorts of horses and their pounding hooves, the cries of triumphant Riders and the ring of swords on scabbards. Leading them was Lil Ambrioth, the First Rider, founder of the Green Riders. She stood tall and commanding in her stirrups atop a fiery, red steed, the silk standard of the gold winged horse unfurled behind her. The enemy retreated before Lil, threw itself to the ground in front of her, or lay slain all around her and her Riders.

While the Riders and the background of the forest and mountains were vibrant, the enemy was depicted in drab grays, black, and crimson.

Laren worked her way past another scene in which Lil knelt before a moon priest with King Jonaeus looking on. There'd been some debate among the Riders about what this scene actually depicted. Was Lil receiving a blessing on behalf of the gods that she do well in battle, or did it occur after the battle, and she was being recognized for her heroism? Perhaps they'd never know.

The third scene showed the Eletian king, Santanara, giving Lil the winged horse banner that was now a cherished artifact of the Riders. The apex of the dome was illustrated with constellations and the god Aeryc looking down on the mortals beneath him, but from her vantage point Laren could see very little of it. Beside her, Dakrias produced a white cloth and wiped it across a glass panel. When he withdrew the cloth, he inspected it in his light.

"They are doing a good job," he pronounced.

Laren wondered if it was wise to have just any clerk clean the fragile glass, but she had to admit, there was no dust or cobwebs in evidence, unlike the first few times she'd come up here. And if she wasn't mistaken, the color in the glass looked even more vibrant.

"One of my senior clerks comes from a glassworking family," Dakrias said, "that has created stained glass windows for many chapels of the moon, as well as private commissions. He trains and supervises the clerks who do the cleaning."

"I see," Laren replied, much relieved. "So he knows how to care for this *properly*." She gestured at the dome.

"He does. Very much so."

Laren slowly walked around the dome again, not sure what called to her. Just restless, perhaps, tired of talk of oncoming conflict, worried for her Riders, both in Blackveil and those carrying out their duties elsewhere.

As she came back again to the scene of a triumphant Lil Ambrioth standing in her stirrups, a detail caught her eye that she hadn't seen before. It was in the receding storm clouds, blended in so that it almost disappeared, a symbol, more silver than the gray of the clouds. She leaned closer.

"Captain?" Dakrias asked.

"Look here." She pointed it out to him.

Dakrias also leaned in, adjusting his specs. "I say, you are correct. Looks like . . . looks like the threefold leaf symbol of the League, but if I'm not mistaken, it's got four leaves."

The threefold leaf had been taken by the League to represent the unity of its member nations: Sacoridia, Rhovanny, and Eletia. She had never seen the fourfold leaf before. What did it mean? Was there a fourth ally that history forgot? Or a fourth ally that history purposely chose not to remember?

"Dakrias," she said, "do your clerks ever clean the underside of the dome?"

"Er, why no. It had not occurred to me to have them do so. It would be a complicated undertaking requiring lots of scaffolding and such. I think we'd need people accustomed to working at those heights to do it."

"Hmm. I imagine with all the years of lamp smoke beneath the dome that it's quite dirty, and that maybe there are other details we're not seeing."

Dakrias stood there thoughtfully for a while. "I will look through the castle's maintenance budget to see if there are any funds available for a proper cleaning by master glaziers." He smiled. "If there isn't, I'll apportion the funds from elsewhere."

Laren was pleased. If the stained glass dome hid any stories of the past that might help them in the present, she wanted to see them.

DIRT

Karigan emerged onto the main floor of the mill building gripping the bonewood walking cane, pleased to have the professor's in hand if not her own. In her time as a Green Rider, she'd grown accustomed to bearing sidearms and felt naked without any within reach. She still regretted the loss of her saber in Castle Argenthyne, and she would take what she could get. The day would come, she vowed to herself, when she reclaimed her own bonewood and all her other belongings, and took them home with her.

"It would probably be wise to return you to your chamber," the professor said. "The night is waning. Wouldn't mind a little sleep myself before the full of day begins."

They found Cade going through cooling down exercises. He flicked his gaze at the bonewood in Karigan's hands. "Is that wise?" he asked the professor.

"Her bad leg requires support."

Cade arched an eyebrow.

Karigan wondered if he thought her incompetent in its handling, or just didn't trust her. No, he wouldn't think her incompetent, for he'd seen her use hers in the alley that first night. She could not resist a jibe: "Are you afraid of me?"

He scowled, but to his credit did not rise to her bait.

"Well," she said in the face of his silence, "considering what I've seen of your moves so far, you should be." With that she walked away, not waiting for either of the men, the tip of the bonewood tapping on the floor as she went.

She heard some angry, hushed mutters from Cade behind

her, and she smiled. The professor responded in a calm voice with, "We shall discuss it later, Old Button."

Before Karigan had gotten very far, the professor caught up with her. "I've your taper," he said, "and will carry it since you've the bonewood to hold onto."

She was relieved, because she also had that shard of mirror closed in her fist beneath her shawl and, with her broken wrist, would not have been able to carry another thing.

"Cade will follow in a little while. He'll close up behind us."

Karigan glanced back and observed as he put away his practice weapons, shoving them with more force than necessary. Yes, she had irked him. Her smile deepened.

They traveled down, down, down, back into the earth, which proved more tiresome to Karigan and harder on her leg than going up had been. The professor tried to assist her where he could, but on the narrow stairs she was pretty much on her own. When finally they reached the very bottom stair, which ended on the first floor of the building in the underground city, they paused to catch their breath. Karigan was really tired now. Her days in bed had sapped her strength and endurance, despite her efforts to remain limber and in condition.

The light of the taper cast sharp, intersecting shadows of the support beams across the walls and ceiling. It gleamed dully on broken pieces of pottery scattered across the floor.

"Is all of Sacor City underground?" she asked. Her own voice sounded close, damped down.

"Er, no," the professor replied. "In the coming days I'll show you what remains above ground. It's mainly the lower parts of the south side that are buried."

Abruptly he left the building, puffs of dust rising in his wake. Karigan hastened after him before the cage of shadows closed in on her. The professor stopped in the middle of what had once been the Winding Way, gazing at the facades of buildings.

"It was a stroke of luck, really, finding this place," he told her when she reached him. "I knew, of course, that parts of old Sacor City lay beneath Mill City, so I did some test digs looking for artifacts, surreptitiously, mind. Found the occa-sional pot or horse shoe, a copper coin or two. Whenever any-thing is built over the old remains, objects are found, old walls and chimneys, a few interesting objects here and there. But nothing like this with buildings intact."

"Did you find this with one of your test digs?"

"I had excavated to a certain level through all manner of rock and rubble and was resting at the bottom of my pit when I felt a breath of air from the earth. It had that unmistakable dank odor of wet stone and dirt. I found the hole and tapped my shovel round it, and the ground crumbled beneath my feet, and I fell through." He laughed hard, and the sound seemed to raise dust. "By whatever graces still exist in the heavens, the fall did not kill me, nor was I buried alive."

They started walking along the street. Their reflections in clouded windows startled Karigan, as if she saw ghosts who inhabited the ruins.

"Naturally I explored," the professor said, "and was aston-ished this pocket of preserved city appeared to extend as far as the Josston Mills Complex, number four. That's when I decided to build my house adjacent to the hole I'd fallen through. I needed to be able to do an extensive study of the site, and I thought it might prove useful in other ways, which it has."

"As a secret corridor to the mill."

"Exactly. The elite of the Capital think me exceedingly strange for living out here among those of lesser status. Most of the Preferred would not even consider it, but then again, they've thought me eccentric from the beginning. But tell me, do you recognize any of this?"

Karigan nodded, pointing out the saddlery shop with the smithy beside it. She explained how the lower city tended to be occupied by rougher neighborhoods.

"The nobility and wealthier classes were closer to the cas-tle," she said. The professor nodded as if he knew this.

When they reached the Cock and Hen, she sighed. "This place was known for its ale, but it was also well known for its brawls and the unsavory characters who frequented it."

"Fascinating," the professor replied, gazing up at the tilted sign. "If you were to enter the building and descend to the cellar, you'd still find intact kegs of ale. It's rather turned at this point, I fear." He puckered his face from what appeared to be an unpleasant memory. "I should have liked to have tried it when it was freshly tapped."

They continued on until they reached the rough door that opened to the stairwell that led up to the professor's house. Before they proceeded, he placed his hand on Karigan's arm. It was warm through her sleeve.

"Please, I must remind you to speak of this to no one. Not any of it. And do not attempt to return unless I say otherwise."

Karigan nodded and followed him along, up the spiraling stairs and into the house. By the time she reached her room, she was stumbling tired. Before dropping into bed, she carefully leaned the bonewood in a corner and hid the mirror shard in one of her slippers, which she tucked under the bed. She pulled the sheets over her and fell into a deep sleep full of dark passageways with only a dying moonstone to light the way . . .

. . . and was abruptly awakened by daylight beaming through her window. She squinted, taking in the silhouette of Mirriam opening the curtains, then turning round to face her with hands on her hips.

"Have we relapsed?" the housekeeper demanded, her abrasive voice making Karigan cringe.

"Relapsed?"

"It is eleven hour. Well past breakfast, so you will have to do without."

Karigan sat up with a yawn. This was certainly a change of routine. Usually she was allowed all the rest she desired and was served breakfast no matter when she woke up.

"Your uncle deemed you well enough on in your recuperation that it was time you began fitting into the routine of this household. The dressmaker will be here after the midday meal."

"Dressmaker?" Karigan still was not awake and found herself in need of a pot of strong tea.

"You don't expect to spend the rest of your life in a nightgown, do you?"

"Well, I—"

Then Mirriam bent toward Karigan, drawing her monocle to her eye. Her frown deepened as she scrutinized Karigan's nightgown. Her glance swerved to the bonewood cane leaning in the corner, then back to Karigan.

"Miss Goodgrave, have you been rolling around in a dirt pile?"

"I—" Karigan glanced down at her nightgown and saw it was smudged with dirt, and no wonder after the previous night's wanderings through underground cities and old mill buildings.

The monocle dropped to the end of its chain, and Mirriam straightened. "Oh, never mind. Nothing a good washing can't fix." And she rolled her eyes.

Karigan was surprised Mirriam did not pursue the matter and wondered if the woman was simply too overcome by the sheer offense of all the dirt, or maybe it was that she *knew* where Karigan had been.

Mirriam steered her into the bathing room where the tub brimmed with steaming water. As Karigan eased into its warming depths, maneuvering carefully to keep her cast dry, she realized that from now on she would constantly wonder who in the household knew what, and how much, and which ones were supposed to remain ignorant. To keep the professor's secret, she'd have to be on her guard. He'd seemed to think his enemies were everywhere.

DRESSED

After Karigan bathed and ate a midday meal, she had no time to worry about who knew what, or to think about old mills and underground cities, for a Mistress dela Enfande, accompanied by a coterie of young, stylishly attired assistants, invaded her chamber and instructed her to stand on a stool for her measurements to be taken. And measure her they did, her every dimension.

"She will need everything," Mirriam informed Mistress dela Enfande, "including the intimate basics."

There was much clucking of tongues among the assistants and pitying looks. Karigan hugged her nightgown to her. They were unable to conceal how appalled they were that she hadn't even any undergarments, but Mistress dela Enfande's expression was fierce.

"All the better," she declared. "We shall not have to build upon someone else's inferior work. She's a blank canvas. We shall create perfection from the foundation up; from the most private garment to the most public."

"That is why the professor desired *you* to take on this challenge," Mirriam said.

Mistress dela Enfande discussed inseams and bust lines and hems with her young ladies, and patterns and colors and fabrics. Two of the young women took notes, while still others sketched pictures Karigan was not privy to. She sighed in resignation, the object of their attention but an object only, and listened to Mistress dela Enfande's sing-song voice. Her accent sounded Rhovan, and Karigan almost asked her about it before remembering, just in time, that Rhovanny was proba-

111

bly just another part of the empire, and no longer known by
its old name.

Now and then, she was instructed to turn around or stretch
out her arms. She was pinched and prodded and then measured again until, after what seemed like hours, she was allowed to step down from the stool as Mistress dela Enfande
and her assistants flittered from the room. She flopped onto
her bed with a groan of exhaustion.

"You will have one of the finest wardrobes in all Mill City,"
Mirriam told her, "suited to a young lady of your station.
Your uncle is being very generous."

"Yes, of course," Karigan replied, though all she wished
for was the simplicity and comfort of her Green Rider uniform. "I'm tired is all."

"I shouldn't wonder why," Mirriam murmured before
leaving.

Karigan watched after Mirriam, wondering herself . . .

Once she was sure Mirriam was gone, she retrieved her mirror shard. She'd hidden it behind the headboard of her bed after
she'd nearly crushed it when stepping into her slippers earlier.

She sat back on her bed and polished the shard with one of
the sheets. It was two-sided—the looking mask had been mirrored on both the inside and the outside. When she gazed into it,
she hoped to see Captain Mapstone again, or any sign of her
friends, but all she saw was a small fragment of her face in the
now. Even when she flipped the shard over, there was no change,
just in the distortion from concave to convex. The looking mask
had been made in a contoured form to fit over a person's head.
Made? she wondered. Who could have made such a thing?

Frustrated, she wrapped the shard in a handkerchief and
returned it to its hiding place behind the headboard.

Over the ensuing days, she saw nothing of the professor or
Cade, but much of Mistress dela Enfande and her assistants
with their arms full of fabric and rough-cut garments. Karigan
was relegated to the stool once again as hems and superfluous fabric were pinned up and the seamstress consulted with
her assistants on the fit.

Karigan was amazed to see so much progress so quickly,
and said so.

"Our empire is a modern wonder, is it not?" Mistress dela Enfande said. "Yards and yards of fabric rolling off the looms in mere minutes, and treadle machines that save our fingers in the sewing room. Can you believe it was once all done by hand?"

Karigan opened her mouth, then closed it again, not sure what to say without giving away her ignorance. Yards and yards of fabric in mere minutes? What would her father, the textile merchant, make of such a miracle?

By the end of the week, boxes began to arrive: hat boxes, shoe boxes, glove boxes, undergarment boxes, and a couple of dress boxes. There was more to come, Mirriam told her. Mistress dela Enfande and her assistants were working at a terrific rate, all so Karigan could appear appropriately attired in the public sphere.

Arhys came into the room to observe each box as it was opened, her eyes nearly popping out of her head. "These are sooo pretty. You'll be a princess!"

"You would do well to remember there are no princesses in our empire," Mirriam scolded.

Karigan had to admit the new clothing was very fine, but compared to her own time, very modest and subdued. Even veils draped from the hats to conceal the face of the wearer. She was not going to complain, however, if the clothing allowed her to finally leave the house.

"Why can't I have dresses like these?" Arhys asked, lifting a deep sapphire dress from its box.

"Because, if you will recall," Mirriam said, "you are a servant. You are not a member of the Preferred set."

"Wish I was," Arhys said, pouting. She carelessly dropped the dress back into its box. "I'm just as good as anyone."

"Arhys!" Mirriam said in warning.

Without another word, the girl stomped out of Karigan's room, still pouting.

"That girl," Mirriam muttered. "I don't know what I'll do as she gets older. I can't expect her to come to her senses and know her place, what with the professor spoiling her. She's been jealous of you since you arrived, and this—" she pointed at all the boxes "—can't be helping."

Karigan felt only pity for Arhys; just because the class system of this world made her a servant, she'd never be treated to an entirely new wardrobe. For Karigan, all of this—the dresses, everything—was a fluke of circumstance.

The next morning, she was roused by Lorine as the morning bells rang in the distance.

"You must ready yourself for breakfast, miss," the servant told her with an anxious expression. "Your uncle asks that you join him downstairs. I will help you dress."

One thing that had not changed since her own time, Karigan discovered, was corsets, though now they were no longer structured with whale bone, but with wire. Karigan begged Lorine not to cinch it too tightly and the young woman obeyed. Lorine then added the other layers with the necessary hooks and lacing. The dress itself was a subdued green that buttoned all the way up to her neck and covered her arms all the way down to her wrists. At least it was green! Even the shoes laced up to above her ankles.

Lorine made several braids of Karigan's hair and pinned them up, then brought in a mirror so Karigan could see the result. She was not sure she recognized herself.

"It is so good to see you out of that nightgown, if I may say so, miss."

She smiled feebly at Lorine. It wasn't that she disliked dressing well—in fact if she hadn't heard the Rider call and remained a merchant, she'd often be garbed in the latest and best—but she missed the freedom of her Rider uniform, which had become as natural to her as a second skin. That was the crux of it. She felt trapped in these clothes, consigned to a role of what was appropriate, a prisoner to the professor's good graces.

She needed to stem that line of thought. Instead she must think of the new clothes as freedom, for now she could escape the confines of the house.

Before leaving her room, Karigan grabbed the bonewood. If she was going to create the pretense of needing it to support her leg, she'd better get accustomed to using it in that fashion.

As she descended the stairs with Lorine, mouthwatering

aromas and the clatter of dishes rose up to meet them. It was clear that breakfast was already underway. When she reached the dining room, she paused in the doorway, Lorine halting meekly behind her.

The professor sat at the far end of the table, with Cade to his right. Four other young men sat with them, carving into steak, or sipping from teacups. One had a book open beside his plate.

The professor was the first to notice her presence. He dabbed his mouth with a napkin and rose. "Good morning, my dear! So good to see you up and about."

There was a scraping of chairs as all the others hastily stood and regarded her with unabashed curiosity. The professor rounded the table and took her by the elbow, guiding her toward the chair at the closest end of the table.

"Gentlemen," he said, "allow me to introduce my niece, Miss Kari Goodgrave."

This was followed by a polite chorus of "good morning" and "delighted to make your acquaintance."

The professor pushed her chair in and proceeded to his end of the table. Once ensconced, he said, "Kari, these gentlemen are my students. You've met Mr. Harlowe, of course."

She glanced at Cade. He did not smile or scowl, just kept his expression neutral. Karigan rested the bonewood against the table, the silver handle clinking against wood. This faint sound produced a subtle twitch in Cade's cheek. She thought, perhaps, she should amuse herself by finding ways to irritate him. He almost reminded her of a Weapon the way he remained stoic, keeping his countenance cool and stony.

The professor introduced the others. If she were any judge, she guessed they were her age or just slightly younger. They nodded politely in each one's turn, their relaxed demeanors, fine dress, and seeming careless confidence not so very different from other young men she'd known from her own time.

She hesitated, unsure of whether or not she was expected to carry on a conversation. What if they started asking questions? What if they wanted to know something about her past? Did they know that she'd supposedly been rescued from an asylum? Would the professor share what must be such a stigma with his students? Did he tell any of them who she really was?

Gratefully she accepted a plate of steak and eggs from Lorine, with a stack of toast. She spread jam on a slice and sipped at tea Lorine poured for her. As she applied herself to breakfast, she observed the students trying to glance at her without her noticing, even as the professor told them the day's assignments.

"More digging and sifting," the stoutest of the four grumbled, helping himself to another slab of steak. His name was Mr. Stockwell.

"What did you think archeology was?" another, Mr. Ribbs, asked.

Mr. Stockwell muttered something and sawed into his steak. Karigan had a nice tender bite on its way to her mouth when one of the young men boldly looked down her way. He was, perhaps, the most nattily dressed of the students, his forelock neatly draped along the side of his head in a way she was sure that many young ladies admired.

"So, Miss Goodgrave," he said, his tone both casual and cocky, "we are to understand you've recently arrived from the east coast to find good health in your uncle's house. How do you find Mill City?"

She observed Cade tensing as the professor watched her with interest.

"I wish I could tell you, Mr.—Mr. Card, was it?"

The young man nodded.

"Yes, well, I have yet to see the city."

"We have kept her confined," the professor explained, "until we were certain her constitution was strong enough to endure the city's environs." He then smiled beneath his mustache. "But that is all about to change, for she is well and the air without is tolerable today. Do you feel up to an outing today, Niece?"

Karigan nearly jumped out of her chair to shout a hurrah, but she kept demurely to her seat and gently set her teacup on its saucer.

"Yes, Uncle. I think I should enjoy an outing today."

AN OUTING

At that moment, Arhys darted into the room, throwing herself at the professor's chair.

"An outing?" she cried. "I may go, mayn't I? And we can stop at the sweets shop! I could wear my new coat!"

The students appeared unfazed by Arhys' abrupt appearance and outburst, though Cade frowned.

The professor tousled Arhys' hair. "But you've already had several outings this week, dear child, and I know Mr. Harlowe has your lessons all ready for you."

"I don't want to do my lessons! I want to go out—"

"Another time, perhaps."

"But I want to go NOW."

"Arhys, child, I need to spend some time with Miss Goodgrave and introduce her to the city. You've your lessons with Mr. Harlowe to attend to, and when Mirriam returns from her errands, she'll have a list of tasks for you."

"No, I want—"

"Arhys!" The professor's voice, which had been mild, turned sharp. "I have spoken. That is enough."

The girl pouted, then pointed at Karigan. "I never get to do anything nice since you got here. I hate you." And she stomped from the room.

The professor looked bemused as he watched the girl.

Cade stood. "I'll see to her, sir," he said. He dropped his napkin on the table and left.

"Don't envy that," Mr. Stockwell said in a low voice.

"My pardon," the professor said gazing at Karigan. "Usually the girl is cheerful and biddable—I've never had to raise my voice with her. I guess I shall have to give her a talking to about her behavior."

Karigan nodded, but he struck her as the sort of man who'd rather avoid such a confrontation and would likely forget about it.

The rest of breakfast proceeded quietly enough, with the students discussing their day's work or joking among themselves. They did not seem to know what to say to Karigan and so did not address her. She, herself, had no idea of what to say, so it was a relief.

Eventually the students finished and one by one stood and bowed to her with a polite, "Miss," and departed. Grott, the butler, appeared, bearing a thick roll of papers on a silver tray, along with a steaming mug. Karigan caught a whiff of the rich aroma of kauv.

"Ah, very good, Grott. The morning rag." The professor removed both mug and papers from the tray and sipped at the kauv appreciatively. "Dark and brisk, just the way I like it." He unrolled the papers—they were densely printed with type and pictures.

"What is that?" Karigan asked after the butler left the dining room.

"Kauv. Would you care for some?"

"Er, no. I mean the papers."

"Oh. The daily news, such as it is. Mainly the emperor's propaganda, I daresay. What new laws have been enacted that we must follow, the latest fire in town, and the emperor's patronage to various ceremonies and events. That sort of thing. Now my dear, when you are finished with your meal, Lorine will help you prepare for our excursion into the city."

"I—I'm not prepared?" Karigan glanced down at herself as if to once more find herself in her nightgown.

"Women's dress is beyond me," he said with an absent wave of his hand, "but I understand there are certain protocols to follow if a woman is to be considered properly stylish. Lorine will know what to do." He rolled his eyes and attended to his papers.

Karigan stood, and Lorine came to her at once. Upstairs, she helped Karigan change out of the green dress into the sapphire. Evidently the green was her morning dress and the sapphire was an outing dress. Her shoes were changed to a stiffer and more polished black pair, and this time she was equipped with matching gloves, cloak, and brimmed hat adorned with a silk ribbon and a fine veil of netting that fell over her face. Karigan tried to blow it away, causing Lorine to laugh.

"You must wear the veil," she said.

"Why? It's ridiculous, and it tickles my nose."

"It is proper. And it may protect you from the ill humors in the air. Now this color suits you, doesn't it." She straightened Karigan's cloak with a satisfied expression on her face.

Ill humors, Karigan thought acerbically. The veil itself was giving her ill humors. She did not understand the reasoning behind how hiding her face was supposed to be more proper.

Once more downstairs, she said as much to the professor while they waited in the foyer for the carriage to be brought around. He replied, "The emperor came up with the guidelines for what is acceptable. He has certain notions of how a true woman should behave and appear." He shrugged. "It is all we've ever known and are accustomed to it. Best you pretend to be, as well." He leaned down and whispered, "I've always thought the women have a certain advantage with their veils, because the rest of us can never tell what they are thinking."

"Are the women here even allowed to think?" She assumed he'd have no trouble in detecting the sarcasm in her voice.

The professor gave her a startled glance, then said, his voice very low, "The emperor would prefer none of us to think very much."

With that pronouncement, a carriage drawn by a smart pair of white horses pulled up front, and the professor escorted her out into the open air of spring. It was damp and cool, and as she inhaled deeply, she tasted the now familiar acrid tang that permeated the city. The professor handed her up into the cab, and as she settled onto a cushioned leather seat, he paused outside to give the driver instructions before joining her, taking the seat across from her. When the carriage rolled forward, she observed that the sleek vehicle rode much more smoothly than those she was accustomed to.

"Almost like home, but not quite," she murmured, before gazing out the window to take in the sameness of rows of brick houses.

The professor sighed, leaning back in his seat. "I'm afraid the horse and carriage have not changed very much in the last two hundred years. You would think with all the ingenuity of the machine men and engineers they'd have invented some other form of less tedious conveyance."

"Why haven't they?"

"The emperor likes horses. Machine replacements are not permitted."

Karigan didn't know what to say to that. She didn't recall Mornhavon the Black having any special affinity for horses. In fact, she didn't think he'd had an affinity for anything but cruelty and violence.

The veil clouded her vision, so she pulled it aside to continue watching out the window, noting that other women along the street also wore hats with veils of one kind or another, whether or not they appeared by their dress to be of an upper or lower class. Then she saw a young woman with neither hat nor veil, her gaze cast down and her garb very plain, burdened by several parcels and following behind another woman.

"Professor," Karigan said, touching his sleeve and pointing. "*She* hasn't a veil."

"Probably a slave," he said, as if that explained everything. "Household slave, I'd hazard."

"Slaves don't wear veils?"

The professor shook his head. "No, they are beneath consideration by society, not people."

Appalled, Karigan watched the young woman disappear from view, the irony that slaves were free to bare their faces, while non-slaves were not, was not lost on her.

As happy as Karigan had been to be allowed out of the house, the yellow, gray haze in the sky, the cheerless brick facades of the buildings, and seeing her first slave, weighed down her spirits. She asked the professor what his students knew about her.

"Not much," he replied. "That you were confined to an institution, and I brought you here to regain your health. They'll draw their own conclusions from that."

The carriage turned down another street before resuming its rhythmic sway. The clip-clop of the horse's hooves was familiar and soothing.

"We've left my neighborhood," the professor said, "which is, if I may say so, the best you will find in the city. Dregs by the standards of those who live in the Capital, but extremely nice by Mill City standards. Now we are heading toward the commercial district."

Brick houses changed into brick storefronts, the main variation the signs that hung out front and big windows to display wares. They passed a grocery, a lens maker, a barber, a baker . . . The sidewalks were crowded with men and women intent on reaching their destinations. A couple of brawny men, with brands on their cheeks and ankles shackled, loaded heavy-looking crates into the back of a wagon. They were overseen by a stern-looking man holding a whip.

"More slaves?" Karigan asked quietly.

The professor nodded. "Some masters are crueler than others and brand their slaves as boldly as they would live-stock. There are those who protest such treatment, but the majority believe, as they've been taught, that slaves are indeed the equivalent of livestock. Of course, few raise their voices in protest, as it draws unwanted attention from the Capital, and dissenters have a way of disappearing."

They drew past the pedestal of a statue, but from Karigan's vantage, she could see only the statue's boots.

"Our emperor," the professor said in a flat voice. "Statues of him are in every city, town, and village."

The carriage slowed down and eventually came to a standstill, the street growing more congested with people and vehicles and horses. The professor swung open the door and leaned out. "What's going on, Luke?"

Karigan could not hear the driver's response.

"Well, then circle round, man," the professor called, and he pulled himself back inside.

"What is it?" Karigan asked.

"Horse market," he replied. "I'd seen it announced in the news, but forgot entirely. So Luke will take us by another route."

"Where are we going?"

"I thought you'd like to see what remains of the Old City, and get a feel for the new along the way."

Karigan thought she already had a pretty good feel for the new city: hard, gloomy, heartless.

The carriage barely moved.

"We'd get farther along on foot," the professor grumbled.

"Then why don't we? Go on foot, I mean."

The professor looked at her in surprise. "I—well—usually ladies don't . . ."

"I'm not a lady," she said.

"I know, I know," he replied and then whispered, "you're a Green Rider."

"Is it improper for us to walk?"

"Er, not necessarily. It's just most ladies of a certain status would not, is all."

Karigan was darkly amused. She'd never been overly fond of the aristocracy, and here she was pretending to be part of the elite class that must pass for the aristocracy in this time.

The professor helped her out of the carriage, and she leaned on the bonewood cane while he gave instructions to the driver where to meet them. She took in the pigeons fluttering to rooftops, folk trying to make way through the crowds. Most fixed their gazes ahead, intent on where they were going. Many carriages, carts, and wagons stood immobile like the professor's. Somewhere up ahead a horse screamed a challenge, sending a shiver through Karigan.

"Shall we?" the professor asked, and he extended his arm. Karigan smiled beneath her veil and slipped her arm through his.

"The horse market is ahead. Usually it does not cause such a back up."

As they proceeded, men bowed their heads to them, and a few of the better dressed gentlemen greeted the professor, flicking curious glances at Karigan.

The professor leaned close. "Some word of your condition may have gotten around."

"My madness, you mean."

"Precisely, and usually those with such a condition are locked out of sight. I am flaunting what is generally considered unacceptable, but then, my eccentricities are well known."

In Karigan's own time, it was the same. The insane were either locked away or cast out to wander the streets dressed in rags and gabbling to themselves, left to survive as they could. No one wanted to be near them, as if their madness was catching, though some moon priests did try to help them.

As they continued, the crush grew worse, though some gave way to the professor and his niece. They were getting close to the source of the problem, when a horse reared up above the heads and hats of onlookers. A whip lashed out and the horse screamed again. The scream resonated all the way through Karigan's body, to her very nerve endings, shaking her where she stood. The stallion called to her, drew her forth. She tore out of the professor's grasp and rushed ahead, compelled to answer an urgent summons.

DR. SILK

Karigan pushed and squeezed past bystand-ers, fighting her way through the crowd to reach the horse.

"What is going on?" she heard the professor ask from behind.

A man laughed and replied, "Handler can't control his horse and get it inside the market. He's a wild one."

Karigan stumbled free of the press and into a cleared space where horse and handler struggled with one another. The horse, a huge bay stallion, was so dark he was almost black with subtle ebon dappling on his hindquarters. He'd a star on his forehead and a chip of white on his nose, his mane long and full. He quivered in terror, or maybe defiance, showing the whites of his eyes. He tossed his head, the lather of sweat, mixed with blood, flying off his strong arched neck onto the cobbled street.

The handler's assistant held a twitch, which he could have used to restrain the stallion, but he seemed afraid to draw near enough to the horse's head and flailing hooves to make use of the device.

He should have employed it *before* the horse went berserk, Karigan thought.

A red-uniformed Inspector also stood nearby, his hands on his hips. She almost forgot the horse when she spotted the bizarre mechanical crouched beside the Inspector, a metal orb about the diameter of a large barrel, with brass fittings and six spiderlike legs, an oily ichor oozing around its joints and staining the metal like blood. A spyglass eye lengthened and retracted as though to focus on the scene before it. Karigan staggered back into the professor.

"What is that thing?" she asked him.

"An Enforcer. Most Inspectors work with one."

Karigan's knees weakened, and she was glad to have the bonewood cane to support her.

"They are some of the most advanced machines in the empire," the professor explained with a shudder. "Avoid them at all costs."

Karigan did not have to be told. Her shudder echoed the professor's as the Enforcer lifted one of its long, jointed legs and stretched it forward as if to sense something in the air. Steam puffed from a short pipe that protruded from the top of the orb. It was a nightmare, she thought, such as only Mornhavon the Black could devise.

The horse reared, and the assistant with the twitch retreated again, eliciting laughter from the audience.

"If you cannot control that horse," the Inspector shouted, "I will shoot it. You are disrupting traffic." He settled his hand on what Karigan took to be a tool sheathed on his belt.

"What does it mean he'll shoot the horse?" Karigan asked the professor desperately.

"He will fire his gun at the horse to kill it."

Fire? Gun? But Karigan did not ask for an explanation. Knowing it meant the horse would be killed was enough. The poor beast was simply enraged by, and fearful of, the whip, and the commotion of the crowd was not helping.

The bay scraped his hoof on the cobbled street. The Inspector grasped the handle of his tool—gun—whatever to pull it from its sheath.

"No!" she cried.

The professor gripped her arm hard as if to silence her, but it was too late. The Inspector darted his gaze at her, and so did many others, including the horse whose ears went to point. The dark molasses brown of his eye caught hers. She was fixed by his gaze to the exclusion of all else. She became oblivious to the shouting of the handler and the Inspector drawing his weapon, the murmur of the crowd, the Enforcer riveting its telescoping eye on her.

The bay lifted his nose to the sky to scent the air, still

watching her. Something passed between them, a warmth, an understanding.

Suddenly the horse half-reared and surged toward her, dragging his handler behind him. In her peripheral vision, she saw the Inspector raise his odd weapon and aim it at the horse.

"Nooo!" she screamed.

The professor tried to pull her away, but she'd the strength to resist.

"Don't shoot!" cried an authoritative voice. "The horse is mine, and I'll deal with it."

The Inspector paused, then lowered his weapon. After that, Karigan heard no more, for the bay had reached her, halted, and placed his velvety nose in her hands. He blew gentle breaths into her palms, and she saw herself mirrored in his eye. The handler jerked on the lead rope.

"Give that to me!" Karigan snatched it right out of his grasp. He waggled his whip. "If you raise that whip again," she told him, "I shall take it from you as well and break it."

The man paused, seeming to debate the level of threat she posed. The professor stepped between them. Karigan concentrated on stroking the bay's sweat-slicked neck.

"Good boy," she said in soothing tones. "Good, good boy." The horse's eyelids drooped, and his ears flickered as he listened to her. Then everything stilled for her and the image of immense black wings brushed through her mind, the echo of distant hoofbeats. "Raven," she murmured. "Your name is Raven." She did not know how she knew this, but she did with a firm certainty.

"Actually," said the owner of the authoritative voice who'd stopped the Inspector from using his weapon, "his name is Samson, and he belongs to me."

The professor groaned beside her and whispered to her, "Now you've done it. Let me do all the talking."

Karigan looked up. The crowd had begun to disperse, the Inspector shooing people along, his Enforcer prodding them with the tip of one sleek leg. Again she couldn't help a shudder of revulsion. Traffic began to move around them, and Samson's owner stood before them, his arms folded across his chest.

He wore a finely tailored gray suit and the tall style of hat that seemed so popular here. His cravat was a matching silk, and diamond cufflinks winked in the sun. He wore a gold brooch shaped in the emblem of the empire on his lapel—the dragon with tail wrapped around its neck. Tucked beneath his elbow he carried a slim and elegant walking cane topped by a golden knob. Even as she took in these details, one above all others caught her attention: his specs. The lenses were a smoky dark that hid his eyes.

The three of them and the bay became an island in the traffic, the Inspector directing carriages, wagons, carts, and pedestrians to flow around them. They were not asked to relocate, all else was required to move around them. It spoke to the man's importance.

The bay remained calm beside Karigan despite the activity on all sides However, if any of his handlers attempted to approach, he laid his ears back and stomped.

"Samson likes you, young lady," the man with the dark specs said, "and I did not think him capable of liking anyone."

Before Karigan could reply, the professor intervened. "Kari, this is Dr. Silk, a *colleague* of mine in the field of archeology." The way he said the word "colleague" made it sound like an epithet.

"And I trust this is your niece, Miss Goodgrave, who has so recently joined your household."

"It is."

Dr. Silk extended a black-gloved hand to her. It rotated unnaturally on his wrist, emitting a low whirring sound, then came to a stop with a distinct *snick*. The stallion tossed his head, and it took all Karigan had not to recoil from the man. Instead, she turned to the horse to quiet him, but still, Dr. Silk's hand remained extended. He raised a silver gray eyebrow over the rim of one of his lenses, the darkness of the glass seeming to billow like storm clouds or a swirling void.

The professor passed her an imploring look. Reluctantly she placed her hand in Dr. Silk's. Although his grasp was firm, it did not feel unlike any other hand she'd ever held. Perhaps she'd only imagined the unnatural motion, the noise.

Dr. Silk bowed over their clasped hands. "It is a pleasure

to meet you." He smiled and released her, and the moment passed.

The two men stared at one another like cats, though the professor was probably at a disadvantage, unable to see Dr. Silk's eyes. Karigan absently stroked the bay's neck, his flesh quivering beneath her touch.

"Kari," the professor said, without averting his gaze, "give the lead rope to Dr. Silk."

Karigan felt her hackles rise. The bay snorted. She could not let this horse back into the possession of those who would abuse him. Karigan was about to argue, when Dr. Silk spoke.

"Perhaps we can come to some accord. I have brought Samson to market because he's unmanageable. He's already killed one of my hostlers. I thought perhaps if no one else would buy him today, maybe the meat men would. A pity, for he is a fine specimen of a horse."

"Knackers?" Karigan demanded, her hand tightening on the lead rope.

"Precisely." A faint smile fluttered on his lips. "A terrible shame."

Karigan found herself staring at her own reflection in his specs, though the cloudy darkness of the glass seemed to swallow it.

He returned his gaze to the professor, and Karigan exhaled in relief. "Seeing as your niece and Samson have taken to one another, perhaps he need not face slaughter after all."

"What are you saying?" the professor demanded. "That I buy this beast from you?"

"For a very reasonable price."

"I don't need—"

"Uncle," she said hastily. She grabbed his arm, squeezing it to make sure she had his full attention. "Please, this horse, he's *special.*"

"Kari, he's killed a man."

"You wouldn't know by looking at him now," Dr. Silk said. "Harmless as a kitten in your niece's hands."

The bay watched the exchange with ears perked, head lowered beside Karigan so she could pet him. Nothing about him indicated danger.

"In fact," Dr. Silk continued, "your niece appears to have a calming effect on him. It'd be a waste to send him to slaughter, but if that is what I must do, that's what I'll do. You are the one who will have to contend with your niece's broken heart."

Karigan would use the bonewood on anyone who tried to take the horse away from her, even if it meant ending the whole charade and losing the professor's protection. This horse, he was not ordinary, in fact . . . Well, she couldn't swear on it, but . . . "He's *special*," she said again to the professor, trying to impress it upon him with all her will.

"See? She's already attached," Dr. Silk said. "And my price is reasonable."

The professor stared hard at Karigan. She tried to gaze meaningfully at him through her veil. He frowned, made a noise of exasperation, then nodded to himself as if coming to some conclusion and began negotiating.

She sighed in relief. The connection she felt with this horse was so like the one she shared with her own Condor, the quiet intelligence that went beyond an ordinary horse. She could only conclude that the big bay stallion was of the same lineage as all Green Rider horses, and that maybe magic was not completely dead in the world after all.

WATER POWER

It was clear to Karigan from the outset that the two men were enemies, or at the very least, rivals, as she watched them dicker over the price of Raven. If the professor had hackles, they'd be standing right up. Dr. Silk remained cool even as the professor smoldered. The image of a pair of predators came to mind, pacing around each other, snapping and growling in a dominance display, for all that they spoke in polite terms and behaved cordially.

"I will accept four gold dragons," Dr. Silk said suddenly.

The tension eased in the professor's shoulders.

"I will accept four gold dragons and one other thing."

The professor instantly tensed again. "What? Four gold dragons is absolute thievery for a problem horse. What else could you possibly want?"

Dr. Silk turned his gaze on Karigan, a tight smile on his lips, the sun flashing on the rims of his specs. "Why, a promise that you'll bring your delightful niece around for a visit. That, or the horse goes to the meat men."

Karigan watched the professor struggle with himself. The restraints of this society likely did not permit an outright refusal, and she had a notion of him trying to find an adequately polite way out and to suffer defeat without losing face. He would let Raven go to the knackers after all, just to prevent her from calling on Dr. Silk. She tightened her grip on Raven's lead rope. She could not allow that to happen.

"I would be delighted," she said before the professor could speak, "to pay you a visit, Doctor."

"Niece!" Now the professor attempted to mask his horror.

"Uncle," she said calmly, "surely it is but a trifle in exchange for this fine horse, and I should like to get to know the people of Mill City better."

"Dr. Silk is not of Mill City," the professor replied in a flat voice.

"I am for a time," Dr. Silk said, his grin one of triumph. "I hail from Gossham, in the Capital," he told Karigan, "but have lodgings here while I oversee my latest project."

The professor muttered under his breath.

Dr. Silk once more took Karigan's hand and bowed over it. "A pleasure to meet you, Miss Goodgrave. I hope Samson does not cause you harm. Do be wary of him."

"I shall send my man-of-business around with the payment," the professor said.

"Partial payment, you mean," Dr. Silk replied with a lingering glance at Karigan, her tiny reflection looking back at her in each lens of his specs.

Polite conduct continued as the two men shook hands, but even this seemed some sort of contest, the professor's features rigid as he gazed directly into Dr. Silk's specs.

"Good day to you," the doctor said, and in a moment released the professor's hand and walked away. An Inspector parted the traffic for him.

Professor Josston watched after him for some moments brushing his hands off on his coat as if to wipe away any residue of Dr. Silk's touch, despite the fact both men wore gloves.

"Come," he told Karigan, taking her arm and glancing over his shoulder. "We must get off the street."

Karigan tugged on Raven's lead and the stallion followed obediently behind. They found that during the negotiations, Luke had come around with the carriage.

"Raven needs some attention," Karigan said, looking at the lash marks on his hide.

"Should've let him go to the knackers," the professor muttered. Raven laid back his ears and snapped at him. "See what I mean? And you have no idea what a hornet's nest you've walked into with—"

"That's a fine beast," Luke said, jumping down from the driver's seat of the carriage. He produced a jar from his coat pocket. "I've some salve that might do for those lashes. If you keep him quiet, miss, I'll put some on."

Raven watched Luke with ears half down, but Karigan spoke softly to him and he relaxed, tolerating Luke's touch as he smeared salve on the wounds. Meanwhile, the professor stood there beside her, fuming, his wolfish eyebrows drawn down low over his eyes.

"Would've been a shame to see this one turned into meat and glue," Luke muttered, patting Raven soundly on the neck, "but some see horses as no more than machines, easy to replace when they don't work right."

He tied Raven's lead to the back of the carriage and held the door open for Karigan and the professor to climb into the cab.

"We shall continue our tour," the professor instructed his driver, and he added to Karigan, "and there will be no more buying of horses."

Karigan smiled behind her veil. She was tempted to tell him she thought Raven to be of the stock once used to mount Green Riders, very special horses, more intelligent than ordinary ones, but she decided to hold onto that particular thought for now. She wished to get to know the stallion better to ensure she was not mistaken. And she feared the professor would see Raven as just another artifact. She did not know what that would mean for the poor horse who had already been so ill-used.

"Of all the men you could come to the attention of," the professor said, breaking into her thoughts and still glowering. "Dr. Ezra Stirling Silk. Have you any idea?"

The carriage bumped along the street, and Karigan shook her head. "No. How would I?"

Her response seemed to take the steam out of him, and his features eased. "You are correct. There is no way you could have known." He reached over and patted her knee. "I'm sorry to have sounded so harsh, my dear, but I worry so."

"Why does Dr. Silk worry you so much?"

"His father is one of the most important men in the whole of the empire, and Dr. Silk is just as entwined in the upper echelons of imperial authority. My dear, if ever you wanted the attention of the emperor brought down upon you, you just succeeded. The one thing you—we—do not want is the emperor's attention."

"I thought Dr. Silk was an archeologist."

"He is. We trained together at the same school. We're both of Preferred families and so also engaged socially. We became quite close, actually. But his father, as the Minister of the Interior, is responsible for repressing the truth of the empire and our heritage. You might say that Silk and I had a parting of philosophies, though I never openly expressed my true bent. He continues to pander to the empire, while I am more or less considered outcast for not actively seeking favor for myself. I'm considered odd, and it suits my purposes."

The carriage rumbled on, taking several turns, the clip clop of Raven's hooves coming from behind like an echo. Karigan saw another Inspector strolling the street with a mechanical beside him, its legs propelling it in spiderlike fashion. It made Karigan shudder all over again.

"What do they do?" she asked.

"Hmmm?" the professor asked.

"The mechanicals—what do they do?"

"The Enforcers are so called because they enforce the empire's laws."

"But what do they *do?*"

"Well, as you can see here, they patrol with Inspectors, keep order, that sort of thing. They watch and report everything and anything deemed suspicious, looking for anti-empire agitators and the like."

"I do not like them."

"As you should not, my dear. You should know, and never forget, that they are armed and do not hesitate to use their weapons. They have no capacity for compassion or mercy and will shed blood based on suspicion alone, without regard to possible innocence. They are made to protect the empire, and not its citizens, no matter what the propaganda says."

Karigan liked this future she found herself in less and less.

As the carriage moved along, they turned, leaving the business district behind, and entered a section walled by mill buildings with a narrow canal running in front of them, up against their foundations and . . . through them? There were arches in the foundations, of which she could only see the tops, the rest submerged in the canal. The water reflected in ripples in the tall windows of the mills.

The professor followed her gaze. "Ah, yes. We've entered the heart of industry. This is Canal Street."

"Canals—" Karigan began.

"They power the industry. They deliver water to turbines, which set the machines in motion. Water power, my dear. Certainly you had mills in your . . ." He hesitated, then whispered, *"in your time."*

Karigan nodded, though she didn't know what a turbine was. She knew water wheels, knew them on the outsides of wooden barnlike structures situated along streams and rivers. Not these imposing brick buildings.

"The Amber River feeds the canal," the professor continued. "You, er, would not know the river. The final battle that marked the ascension of the empire altered the topography around the Old City. It was the force of . . . the force of those unknown weapons I mentioned before. Anyway, the Amber River runs down from the north and splits north and west of the city. So the canal you see right here flows beneath the mills and empties out behind into the north branch of the Amber. Remarkable engineering, really."

Karigan didn't care about the engineering. The professor had gripped her with the idea of the river and how the force of battle had changed the landscape, had caused a river to flow where there had not been one before. A stream, yes. But not a river, here, in Sacor City. It spoke of magic to her, of vast power. She shuddered. These weapons of Mornhavon's had been magic, or something magical. No wonder the Sacoridians had been overcome.

"Closer to the Capital," the professor continued, oblivious to her disquiet, "they've other means of powering machines, but in a blighted backwater such as this, we rely on old technology. Water, I think, is elegant in its simplicity. Perfectly suitable. Men like Silk do not appreciate that line of thinking. For them, it is always what and who they can twist and destroy for their own benefit."

The professor seemed to forget Karigan as the identical brick facades rolled past the carriage's window. Lost in some reverie, he brushed his long mustache with his forefinger. Karigan felt just plain *lost,* not liking the future her land and its people had found themselves in. Inside those impersonal brick walls, slaves labored over machines. She could not see them, but she knew they were in there. And, while she did not know what their labor was like or what the conditions inside the mills were, she could not imagine any of it was pleasant. As for the transformation of the countryside into this city? It was not an improvement. From all that she could tell, the empire was not about its people, but about the machines and what they produced. She sighed, feeling homesick and alien.

A pall settled over the interior of the carriage, Karigan with her own grim thoughts, and the professor gazing out his window, chin resting on his hand. Karigan followed his gaze and saw that the scene had changed from orderly brick buildings to burned out mills, a grouping of them with a central courtyard scattered with debris and choked with weeds. Remnants of blackened brick walls looked like jagged teeth. Only one building in the grouping stood unburned, yet forlorn, its windows boarded up.

"Do you know that cotton is very flammable?" the professor asked.

Karigan nodded. She was the daughter of a textile merchant, after all.

"All those fibers clouding the air inside the mills. The dryness, a spark. Who knows how the fire truly started, but that's all it would have taken."

A rusted wrought iron gate guarded the bridge that crossed the canal to the ruins. Arching above the gate in scrolling ironwork were the words, "Josston Mills Complex 4." The sun glinted on flecks of gold as though the letters had once been painted in gilt.

"Complex number four," Karigan said with a start. "This is where—"

"Yes," he replied, cutting her off. "This is where the one building you visited stands. Miraculously. The fire was terrible, ferocious, and consumed the others in the complex without mercy. I could see the flames from the house."

The professor had hidden his secret cache of historical artifacts in plain sight, in this one remaining mill building. And she

had accessed it from underground. She gazed at the floor of the
carriage as if she could see into the passages of lost Sacor City.

The professor guessed her thoughts. "Yes, the house is
about two blocks that way." He pointed at the opposite window, away from the mill complex. "This street runs parallel to
the neighborhood. The whole city is set up on a grid pattern."

The burned out complex fell out of sight as they traveled
on, but a profound sadness remained in the professor's eyes.
The wrought iron gate had indicated that the whole complex,
not just the one surviving building, had been his: *Josston Mills
Complex 4*. She did not think it was so much the loss of the
buildings and industry that saddened him—he'd turned his
back on it after all, to pursue archeology.

"People died in that fire, didn't they," she murmured.

"It is the practice to nail the windows shut, lock the doors,
and chain the slaves to their looms. They hadn't a chance.
Hundreds of them died."

Horrified, Karigan could only stare at him, but he dropped
his face into his hands as if to blind himself against the memories. He must relive them every time he passed the complex.

"That is when I devoted myself entirely to archeology.
And the cause," he said, his voice muffled. Karigan recalled
the slip of paper, the article, she had found tucked into a
novel Mirriam had given her. It had mentioned the professor's giving up industry for archeology, but said nothing of
the fire. Either it was a small grace for the professor, or the
deaths of hundreds of slaves was not noteworthy to this society. She rather thought the latter.

Sunlight flickered across the professor's haunted features.
"Sometimes I suspect it was arson, someone who knew my
leanings trying to tear me down, but there was never any evidence despite thorough investigations. Though the investiga-
tors were the emperor's men, of course."

They sat in silence for some time, the carriage rumbling along,
and Karigan wondered how Raven fared as he followed behind.

"Where are we headed now?" Karigan asked to break the
silence and the pall that had settled over them.

The professor gave her a bleak smile. "To see even more
devastation."

TWO OUT OF TIME

The carriage surged forward past more mill complexes before it turned north and crossed a bridge over the canal and then a second bridge, traversing the glistening strip of blue that was the north branch of the Amber River. Karigan shook her head not seeing anything that reminded her of her own Sacor City. If she hadn't seen the section that lay underground, she might not believe this was the same place at all.

Even more devastation? She pondered the professor's words as the carriage thudded and jolted over rougher ground. She shuddered with foreboding, beginning to guess what he was going to show her.

The carriage began to rise, the road growing more bumpy. Raven whinnied and snorted behind them as they climbed. Gradually the well-ordered city gave way to ramshackle wooden buildings, rundown houses, and shanties with squatters sitting outside on steps and old crates, watching their passage with hostile eyes. Was this the devastation he meant to show her?

"Dregs," the professor muttered. "So low on the ladder they scavenge the city's leavings but not low enough to be slaves. They exist in forgotten places, the abandoned buildings and hidden alleys, and here on the edge of devastation. The Inspectors round them up now and then, and there's been talk of burning them out of here, but they always come back and find a place. A good many of them are the ones who dig up illicit artifacts and sell them off to the likes of Rudman Hadley for his circus. Ghouls, we call them, those who dig up the dead."

As they continued to climb, all habitation fell away, and the landscape was strewn with rock and rubble, through which poked scrub brush and stunted trees. To one side of the carriage, a rocky escarpment sloped down until it met the river, and beyond it lay Mill City with its regular angles of buildings and streets and the shimmering network of canals, like veins of blue, stemming from the west branch of the river.

The professor pointed out gatehouses and dams along the river, and locks on the canals, and explained at great length how they controlled the force of water flowing into the mills to power the turbines, which in turn powered the machines. Karigan barely listened, her attention pulled to the view on the other side of the carriage, to the great immense mount of talus and scrub that rose high beyond what she could see through her window.

When the carriage halted, the professor stepped out and extended his hand to help her down. Her feet prickled when they touched ground. The sensation traveled up her legs and into her spine as if the land were trying to send her a message, or was screaming. Her sense of foreboding intensified. Her breath caught in her throat. Her mouth grew dry.

"Do you know what this is?" the professor asked, gesturing to the mount.

She could not see its summit even from outside the carriage. She was too close. The sloping uneven terrain was cluttered with . . . She looked closer to hand, just off the rutted track the carriage had followed. Rotted, half-burned timbers. Piles of rock shaped not by nature, but the tools of men. As her gaze sought details, she found patterns—the foundations of walls, a well hole, a half-toppled chimney. The land jabbed at her feet as though it knew her, reached out to her.

"Sacor City," she whispered.

"Yes," the professor replied. "What remains."

Karigan wailed and dropped to her knees, oblivious to the professor at her side and Luke looking down in alarm from his perch on the carriage. On her many travels she'd seen the ruins of ancient habitations, not least of which had been the lands of lost Argenthyne. She'd seen what abandonment, time, and nature had done there, leaving a once-great civilization in ruin. She, however, never expected to see her own city in such a state.

Not just ruin, but purposeful destruction. This wasn't just the work of time and nature on an abandoned city. Sacor City had been defeated and systematically obliterated. She could see it before her, walls being torn down by unimaginable forces, fires raging, people scrambling in terror. She closed her eyes, trembling. What forces could have leveled the city? Altered the landscape enough to divert a river? What of the people? Her friends? The king? Perhaps that is what the land remembered: the echo of all those souls.

As her own cries faded away, Raven's whinnies broke through to her, resonating through her grief. He sensed her distress. She rose unsteadily to her feet, brushing away the professor's solicitous hands. She staggered to where Raven stomped and tossed his head behind the carriage. Instinctively she threw her arms around his arched neck, pressed her cheek against the warmth of hide and muscle. He calmed with her contact. Her own breathing slowed, she stopped trembling. She could almost imagine it was her own Condor she hugged.

"She's, er, just having a fit," she heard the professor telling Luke in reassuring tones. "Nothing to be alarmed about."

Then closer to her, speaking softly, he said, "I'm sorry, my dear. I wasn't thinking of the shock this would give you. It's abstract to me, you know, this history. I'm used to seeing these ruins, and it did not occur to me what it would do to you. I've been terribly callous, and I hope you'll forgive me."

Karigan pulled away from Raven and scrubbed a tear from her cheek. "You need to tell me what happened here. All that you know."

The professor glanced from side to side as if to ensure no one eavesdropped. "Not here. I do not trust that no one can hear."

The caw of a crow shattered the silence around them. It bobbed on a limb of crooked sumac, beak open, its cries raucous. But there hadn't been true silence, Karigan realized. The mournful sigh of a breeze among the ruins brought to them the distant sounds of pounding and scraping, of tools thudding on rock. She gazed past the professor, up the side of the mount, and espied the movement of small figures hard at work, wielding tools that glinted in the sunlight.

"What's going on up there?" she asked.

The professor followed her gaze. "Silk's project, I daresay. Those aren't archeologists on a dig, but a gang of slaves clearing a road."

"A road?" Nothing of the old Winding Way or other streets of Sacor City was visible to her eye. It appeared the slaves were simply building over and through the ruins. It felt like a desecration. "Dr. Silk's project is a road?"

"No," the professor said. "The road will lead to the project site. An ambitious excavation."

Karigan watched the laborers in the distance, their pickaxes rising and falling. The mount, the ruins of Sacor City, were draped in a dull gray gleam. She turned back to Raven, stroking his dark neck, and it occurred to her she was meant to come to this time, to see this. She'd been . . . brought? It was still all too hazy to her. Westrion, god of death . . . as she plummeted through the infinite universe after smashing the looking mask, had he really caught her and left her here? The only thing that would interest Westrion in what had become of Sacor City and the realm was the souls he could collect. He wouldn't care about the politics of mortals or their strivings, so why bring her here? She could only wait for the answer to unfold on its own, for the ways of the gods were mysterious, but no matter what it was, no matter what the death god wanted of her, she would do what she could to reshape this future, and she would do it from the past. Somehow she would return home, to her own time, and make all this better.

"This was once a thriving city," she said, the words catching in her throat.

"I know, my dear," the professor replied. "I know. And I imagine you've seen enough for one day. A pot of Mirriam's tea, or brandy if you prefer, would do us both good about now. Shall we return to the house?"

Karigan gave Raven one last pat and, as she prepared to enter the carriage, she glanced once more at the ruins. A glint of white high up caught the corner of her eye, and when she looked full on, it was gone. She blinked, wondering if she had imagined it. No doubt just the sun glancing off a piece of metal or broken glass.

Moving about the ruins was dangerous, no matter how light-footed an Eletian was. Mostly Lhean kept still during the day, hiding in crevices and depressions, fearing discovery. He spent his long days of stillness meditating, trying to make sense of this world he'd ended up in. Periodically, however, he rose to scout and take stock of what was happening to his surroundings. He'd first been roused by the sounds of tools hammering on stone a few days ago. It was not difficult to espy the laborers down below, one chained to the other, thin, wretched creatures of humanity, in rags, flogged by those who supervised them when they lagged, or as whim struck.

As if to demonstrate the danger of moving among the ruins, on the first day the slaves began work, their efforts caused a small avalanche of rock and debris to tumble on them. Three did not survive, but they were replaced on the second day.

Another group worked on the summit where King Zachary's castle once stood. They dug and dug as if seeking the very foundations of the Earth. It was an enormous challenge to move the rubble of the castle, and derricks and booms had been raised to lift the debris the slaves could not. Here, too, accidents happened; a slab crushed a pair of workers. It was as if the castle, even in its ruin, resisted the invaders.

Lhean did not know what they sought and assumed they dug for treasure. Mortals had an insatiable appetite for precious things, and certainly the castle would have contained many. It did not matter to him, only that he needed to see what was happening around him.

He was still undecided about what to do, stranded here in this harsh land, the silence of what had been Eletia grieved him. He slaked his thirst on the acrid runoff of dew or rain that trickled from unnaturally-shaped rocks, and ate sparingly of the stores that remained from his journey into Blackveil. Very shortly those would run out, and he would truly weaken. Already his armor had begun to dim, looking neglected, its inner light fading. He'd have to make a decision about what to do soon, but where in this blighted land would he be safe?

He was about to creep into a shadowed recess when something pulled at him, a twinge, something familiar that, like him, did not belong in this world. He took a great risk and hoisted himself up on a promontory of rock in naked sunlight. He was fairly high up on the mount, and the feeling came from down below. He took a quick look, his sharp, farseeing eyes sweeping across the vista below him in an instant, then he dropped flat to reduce chances of his being spied.

Down near the base of the mount he'd spotted a carriage drawn by two white horses, with a bay tied to the back. The bay had its own special aura, but that was not what had caught his attention. There were three people with the carriage—the driver who sat on his bench, a man who held the door open, and the young woman to whom he gave his hand to help her climb in.

The young woman was out of place and time. Lhean had not arrived here alone after all.

SILK

Dr. Ezra Stirling Silk gazed at the large sheets of bridge schematics strewn across the drafting table while, outside the rough office, the machine shop clattered and rang with metallic resonance, the air dense with the fumes of oil and burning. Here the machines that made Mill City hum—the looms, turbines, governors, steam engines, and more—were designed and fabricated by skilled laborers. The work was not trusted to dull-witted slaves, who were suitable only for lift-and-carry work and other menial tasks.

Across the empire, engineers were revered for their genius, even if not of Preferred families. They opened the gates to the empire's modernization, economy, and, most importantly, its power. Many of the engineers were descended from the First Empire's artificers, but the great makers who long ago melded machines with etherea were long gone. Those few who retained such singular skills worked in the Capital, mainly in the emperor's palace. Ordinary engineers must rely solely on their intellect and craftsmanship.

The chief of Mill City's engineers now lumbered into the office. Large in girth and stature, he did not merely draw the designs for machines, but helped in their building and implementation. Heward Moody pulled off his goggles and carelessly tossed them atop the papers on his drafting table. Silk's sight made it difficult for him to perceive the details of Moody's appearance, though the aura of life outlining his body shone clearly. Silk's mind painted in the stained leather apron, the heavy gloves that protected Moody's hands up to his elbows, a cap covering sparse hair atop his head.

The engineer untied a scarf from around his neck and used it to mop sweat and soot off his face. "Well, Dr. Silk," Moody said in his gravelly voice, "come to badger me about your drill again?"

"Badger you, Mr. Moody? Your shop is receiving exorbitant payment for the efficient production of the drill. I am here to see that the empire's funds are not being misused."

"As I've said time and again, you cannot rush precision. If it's not precision you want, black powder would do the job for you some quick."

Silk grimaced. Blasting was not an option. He needed that precision, the drill was to be a surgical instrument in his excavation. He had no wish to destroy that which he sought. "Let's see it then."

The partially assembled drill was too long to fit in any of the machine shop's bays, so it was situated in a neighboring warehouse, laid on its side on supports. The steel gleam of its spiral contours burned in Silk's eyes while all else in the warehouse's depths fell into shadow. Moody polished it with a rag. Despite his grumbles about Silk's badgering, he was justifiably proud of his creation. No drill of this length had ever been created before.

The bit, not yet attached, rested on its own table. It had the ridges of a molar, but unlike a tooth, these were angular, symmetrical, and perfect, and embedded with diamond dust. It would chew through granite bedrock with ease.

"We'll check the calibration one more time," Moody said, "then it'll be ready for a test. If the test is successful, you can haul it up to the site, and we'll connect the engine."

"How long before you test?"

Moody's face cracked into a grin. "Oh, a few days give or take. We'll have to assemble the components here to see how she goes." He indicated the steam engine, its valves, piston rod, and flywheel in shiny brass.

Not as elegant as an etherea engine, but it would do.

"In the meantime," Moody continued, "you might want to speed up construction of the drill house. Fast enough for you?"

Silk tapped the tip of his walking stick on the stone floor.

Very fast, he thought. He'd have to assign more slaves to clearing the site and building the road. "You exceed expectations, Mr. Moody."

Moody doffed his cap and bowed. "My pleasure to serve the empire. Now if I could have me one of those etherea engines, I'm sure the work could be completed even faster."

"You know that is the province of the Capital and cannot be . . . exported to the out regions." Indeed not. There was not enough etherea in the world to execute mundane functions outside the Capital. It must be protected and sustained for the Preferred. After all, it was a precious resource that did not renew itself fast enough for the empire's needs, and supplies were dwindling steadily.

His waistcoat pocket chimed. Well-aware of Moody's scrutiny, Silk pulled out his chronosphere, attached to his waistcoat by a gold chain and fob of carved ivory. The sphere split in half and delicate leaves of metal unfolded into a miniature emerald hummingbird with a ruby throat. The other sphere half contained two circles of glyphs carved from mother-of-pearl. The outer ring of larger glyphs represented the hours of the day, while the inner ring designated the minutes. The tiny mechanical chirped, then cocked its head, tapping first the hour with its beak tip, and then the minute. With a final chirp, it folded back up and withdrew into its own half of the sphere. Silk snapped the device shut and deposited it in his pocket. He smiled. Only those closest to the emperor possessed time pieces. Owning time was not just a perk of power, it *was* power, power he held over those beneath him.

Alas, the chronosphere would not continue to work outside the Capital without its daily winding and an infusion of etherea, but it was worth using just to taunt people like Moody, and remind them of just who ranked over them.

"I will return on the morrow to inspect your progress," Silk said. "But now I've another appointment to attend." He turned on his heel and twirled his walking stick into a neat tuck beneath his arm, strolling past the magnificent drill without another glance.

He did not really have another appointment but it was tea time, and he had a dinner party to plan, during which he'd

extract the second part of his payment from Bryce Lowell
Josston for the stallion. Long ago an accident had left Silk's
sight less than adequate, and bright light caused his eyes pain.
But the accident had also enhanced his vision in some ways,
allowed him to see *more,* and what he saw of Miss Kari Goodgrave indicated there was more to her than ordinary sight
might perceive.

IN THE SHARD OF THE LOOKING MASK

Mirriam stormed into the stable, and Luke and his stable lads slunk into the shadows like chastened cats. She glowered at Karigan, who was in the center aisle of the stable currying Raven's neck, but Mirriam directed her fury at the professor. "Professor Josston! You know better."

"I—I do?" He stepped backward and fiddled with the brim of his hat, which he held in his hands.

"The stable is not a suitable place for a young lady."

"Oh, well, I—"

"And Miss Goodgrave!"

Karigan paused her currying.

"Step away from the horse," Mirriam commanded.

Karigan did no such thing, but thrust her veil out of her face to glare back at Mirriam. "Why? This is my new horse."

Mirriam's gaze flashed again to the professor, who took another step back. "New horse?"

"It's . . . it's true. We, uh, acquired him on our outing."

Mirriam gazed hard in turn at Raven, who perked his ears at her.

"You bought the young lady an . . . an . . . *intact* stallion?"

The professor glanced at Raven's nether regions as if to confirm Mirriam's observation. "It does appear that way," he replied.

"His name is Raven," Karigan said.

"It's unseemly. Thoroughly unseemly. Young lady, you come to the house this instant before you ruin that fine dress. Or your shoes. Mind the droppings." Mirriam turned and marched from the stables, apparently expecting Karigan to obediently follow behind her.

"You'd best go, my dear," the professor said anxiously. "Best not to incur Mirriam's wrath, or she will not allow you out of her sight ever again."

"Don't worry, miss," Luke said, coming out of hiding. "We'll settle Raven in. I think he'll let us handle him now."

Karigan ran her hand down the stallion's nose, and he nickered. "You behave. I'll be back, no matter what Mirriam says."

He bowed his head as if to acquiesce, and Karigan departed. Once out of the stable and in the sunlight, she gazed in guilt at the horse sweat, dirt, and hair soiling her fine gloves. The front of her dress had not fared much better. Mirriam was definitely going to be displeased.

When Karigan reached the house, Mirriam was that and more. She paced about Karigan's room and snatched parts of the outing dress as they came off.

"What was the professor thinking?" she demanded. "A horse! A stallion, no less!"

"I will need clothes suitable for riding," Karigan said quietly.

"*Riding?* Proper young ladies do not *ride*. They especially do not ride stallions. Proper young ladies are conveyed in a carriage with an appropriate chaperone in attendance."

Karigan sighed. The professor had said as much. With Mirriam around, getting to spend time with Raven was going to be a more difficult challenge than she had anticipated.

"I know you are from the country where people are . . . different, so I don't really blame you, Miss Goodgrave. But here where young ladies are under the scrutiny of fashionable society, it's just not acceptable. It would cause a scandalous stir here in the city. I'm afraid your station is above the crassness of such things as riding."

Above the *crassness?* Well then, Karigan would have to cause a stir, which was not a good plan if she didn't wish to draw the notice of the imperial authorities. Such a strange world she'd stumbled into. She tried to imagine Mirriam's reaction if the housekeeper could travel to the past, Karigan's own time, with women on horseback and doing so many things that would not be considered ladylike in Mill City. Mirriam would be appalled, Karigan decided. Ironically, for all of her bluster, Mirriam was strong in nature the way she reigned over the household and commanded all who dwelled there, including the professor. She was the antithesis of the delicate, wilting flower the empire appeared to desire of its women. Karigan decided not to point it out and considered that perhaps the delicate, wilting flower thing did not apply to servants anyway.

Karigan wrapped herself in a puffy robe, and Mirriam propelled her down the corridor toward the bathing room.

"What could he have been thinking?" Mirriam muttered for the nth time.

Karigan made no attempt to answer but entered the bathing room, closed Mirriam on the other side of the door, and headed for the tub, eager to wash away the grime of the city that clung to her like a second skin. Just having been out in the open air had made it so, and if this was a good day, she was not anxious to find out what a bad day would be like.

As she soaked, her cast-bound wrist safely on the edge of the tub, she heard a flurry of movement in the hallway. A furious sounding Arhys proclaimed, "I want a horse, too! If she gets one, I get one, too!" This was followed by stomping and the slamming of a door, and an exasperated cry of, "Arhys!" that sounded like it came from Lorine. Karigan winced. She was sorry that by rescuing Raven she caused Arhys to become even more jealous and difficult, but better that than allowing the stallion to be given over to the knackers.

Afterward, attired in a "day dress" of creamy yellow, she joined the professor in the parlor for tea and the midday meal. The professor had changed as well, into less formal tweed and boots.

"I must check on the dig," he explained, "and make sure the boys are not slacking off."

"What are you digging up?" Karigan asked, looking over a cranberry-nut muffin before taking a bite.

"We've come upon the ruins of a modest house in the lower regions of the Old City. Nothing we haven't seen before—shards of crockery, buttons, clay pipes, and the like. Gives us a good idea of how people lived."

Karigan yearned to discuss what had become of her city, but though she sat with her back to the doorway she observed the professor's eyes tracking the comings and goings of servants. They could not speak freely.

"Have you ever found remains? Human?" she asked.

"Not much were left behind, though a few of my colleagues have uncovered cemeteries. Unfortunately, the sites are usually quickly looted for burial goods. People back then placed valuables like amulets and coins and jewelry with the dead."

Karigan nodded. She knew, for she was from *back then*. It was the custom to bury the dead with something to offer the gods for safe deliverance into the heavens. Even the poor usually managed a coin or two. The professor grimaced. He must have forgotten her origins and just realized what he'd said.

He cleared his throat. "After a while the graves weren't looted solely for burial goods, but entire caskets with their remains inside started disappearing, and sometimes whole sarcophagi from wealthier sites." He snorted. "I'd like to see how the Ghouls manage that. The best sarcophagi are made of stone! What a job it would be to remove one of those from the Old City." Then he sighed. "But they've managed it somehow.

"Usually the remains have been sold to that despicable circus, or to the Preferred set for parties. Remove the shroud and see what's inside." He shook his head. "A shame we'll never know what valuable pieces of the historical record have been lost as a result, not to mention the distasteful desecration of the dead." He leaned forward over his tea and said in conspiratorial tones, "When I die, I aim to be cremated. No digging up my old bones!"

Karigan thought it a curious sentiment from an archeologist who reveled in finding clues to the past. Wouldn't he rather be exhumed with all kinds of objects that would benefit future archeologists?

She didn't have the opportunity to ask more because he then said in a very low voice, "Meet me in the library tonight once the household is abed." He set his teacup aside and rose.

Without another word to her, he strode from the parlor calling for Grott to bring him his hat and coat. "It is time I checked on those sluggard students of mine," he declared.

Karigan contemplated her muffin once more. She had to admit the professor had a point about the desecration aspect of being buried as opposed to cremated. She had been, after all, revealed in a tomb before a large audience at the circus. Happily, she was alive when it occurred, but she would have hated for her own Earthly remains to have become part of some macabre entertainment to be stared at and giggled over. Violated.

Tombs, burials, and cremations aside, it was not going to be easy to remain patient until late night when she was to meet the professor in the library. He must be planning to take her to the old mill to answer her questions.

The afternoon did draw long for Karigan, forbidden as she was to go to the stables and visit Raven. That was something else she needed to address with the professor—how she was going to get to spend time with the stallion. So, she did as she was accustomed. She returned to her room where she worked with her bonewood, fully extended to staff length, to practice forms and keep herself limber. It was not so easy in her dress, but she considered it useful practice, too. Chances were, if she needed to fight with the staff in this world, she'd be in a dress, not her more practical Rider uniform.

Sometime later she spilled onto her bed puffing and sweating. Her left arm was getting a good amount of work, but when the cast came off her right wrist, it would be alarmingly weak. Well, she'd just have to work it till it was back to its old strength. That's what Arms Master Drent would make her do.

Arms Master Drent. She was riddled with sudden pangs of homesickness.

Of all the people to miss. She shook her head.

Yes, she actually missed Drent with his abrasive manner and the abuse he heaped on his trainees. She would welcome seeing even a glimpse of him in her shard of the looking mask.

Thinking of it, she sprang from the bed and retrieved it from its hiding place behind the headboard. Sitting once more on the bed, with pillows propped up behind her, she unwrapped the mirror fragment and gazed into it. When no visions immediately appeared, she flipped it over, but saw only her own reflection.

Maybe she just needed to be patient. It wasn't like she didn't have the time. She'd hours till supper. So she settled in, gazing at the mirror shard, occasionally turning it over to see if it made a difference which side she looked at. It did not. She yawned and nodded off, the piece of looking mask loosely cradled in her hand.

She dreamed of her friend Estral scribbling madly on a slate with a piece of chalk. Or was it a dream? She shook her muzzy head and the dream, or vision, or whatever it was, continued. In it, Estral held the slate up for someone — Alton? — to see. At first Karigan could not read the writing, as if it was formed in arcane symbols her dreaming eye forbade her to understand, but she concentrated, and the words blurred and came into focus: *Have they found my father yet?*

After a pause, Estral lowered her slate to the table, gazing as if listening to a speaker Karigan could not see or hear. Then Estral wiped the slate clean with a rag and started writing madly again, worry creased across her forehead. When she raised the slate once more, Karigan had no trouble reading the words, and it was then she realized she was no longer dreaming and that the scene was playing out on the mirror shard.

Yes, he wanders, Estral had written, *but he always returns to Selium in time for the spring convocation.* Estral seemed to listen to some response, then dropped the slate and turned away, placing her face in her hands. The scene vanished, leaving Karigan staring slack-jawed at her own reflection.

She shook herself to make sure she was awake. What was that scene about? Why was Estral writing on a slate to communicate? It couldn't have been for Karigan's benefit, because Estral seemed unaware of her looking in. Some singers went to great lengths to protect their voices, but Estral wasn't like that. Perhaps she simply had a sore throat or laryngitis. And why did she seem to need her father, the Golden Guardian of Selium, so urgently? She had looked so worried. And she was right, he never missed the spring convocation when journeymen minstrels were raised to masters and awarded their gold knots.

Karigan was happy the looking mask shard had finally revealed one of her friends to her, but the scene had not been at all reassuring.

In the present: Alton D'Yer

Alton slipped out of his tent, fists clenched and ready to batter something hard, like the D'Yer Wall, but he didn't do that anymore and hadn't for a long while. But how was he to vent his frustration on Estral's behalf? For the loss of her voice, the voice that had begun to mend the cracks in the wall? He, himself, tried to coax the guardians of the wall along with song, but his voice lacked the magic Estral's held. Or had held.

The guardians had grown dispirited without her. The cracks stopped mending. Thank the gods the established repairs hadn't reversed themselves.

The worst part was how powerless he felt in the face of Estral's despair. Voice, song, music were as integral to her as the blood flowing in her veins. He did his best to soothe her, hold her, love her. Estral had once written out on her slate for him, that without music, she'd rather die. The spell that had stolen her voice had taken more: her very musicality. She no longer knew how to play her lute, and reading musical notation was like trying to read a foreign language.

If he ever found the caster of that spell, he'd crush the life out of him with his bare hands. He balled his fists compulsively and scowled at nothing but the air in front of him. The other tents, the trees, were all a blur, the sounds of the encampment far away. He had very strong hands, a stoneworker's hands. He smiled grimly, savoring what he'd do to that spellcaster.

It did not help that Estral's father, Lord Aaron Fiori, the Golden Guardian, seemed to have gone missing. He was known for his penchant for traveling anonymously, as an ordinary minstrel, but Estral insisted he was actually missing, that it was not like him to overlook certain events. They'd sent messages hoping to call him down to the wall so he could help Estral, and perhaps his voice would revive the interest of the guardians and the mending could continue, but the only word they'd received was that no one knew the where-abouts of the Golden Guardian. Last that was heard of him was that he'd been somewhere in the north of Adolind Province. The north was dangerous, what with all the Second Empire activity in that general direction.

"I promised to write the king," Alton murmured. He'd promised Estral he would ask King Zachary to investigate the Golden Guardian's disappearance. From what Alton gathered from some of Estral's scribblings, Lord Fiori, along with some of his capable master minstrels, often made informal observations of what was happening in the realm and shared that information with the king as necessary. It did not take much imagination to conclude he'd gotten into trouble. Alton would also request that Captain Mapstone alert her Riders for any sign of the Golden Guardian.

The tent flap rustled open behind him, and he stepped aside so Leese, the encampment's chief mender, could stand beside him.

"I've given Estral a draught to help her sleep," Leese said. "But we can't just keep dosing her."

"I don't know what to do," Alton replied, gazing at his feet.

"Keep doing what you've been doing. Be with her, comfort her. She needs you right now. But, for all that love is a miraculous thing, you need to persuade her to eat when she wakes up, even if it's a weak broth. I don't like seeing her grow so thin so fast."

"I know, I know."

Leese placed her hand on his shoulder and squeezed it before moving off among the tents with her mender's satchel slung over her shoulder.

Alton took a deep breath and plunged back into the dim interior of the tent. Estral lay on the cot on her side, the peace of sleep erasing the torment and worry from her features. He sat on the stool next to the cot and caressed her hair back from her face, the hands that had been so ready to kill just moments ago now gentle.

He would find her answers. They would get her voice back—they had to. He wasn't sure if, even with all the love in the world, she'd care to live without the ability to sing.

Maybe if the Blackveil expedition returned—Karigan was Estral's best friend. Maybe Karigan's return would brighten Estral. But they'd had no sign from the expedition. Alton worried for Karigan. Stepping into Blackveil was placing oneself in mortal danger, and she'd been in there since the spring equinox. He loved Karigan, but his feelings had gone in a different direction than they had with Estral. *Come back, Karigan,* he thought. *Estral needs you, and so do I.*

He leaned over and kissed Estral's cheek. She did not stir, and her soft, deep breaths indicated she was well asleep and would be for a while. It was time for Alton to attend to his duties, so he left Estral to her peace. He would check in often, and when she woke, he would get her to take broth as Leese instructed, and if love could heal, he would give her as much as was possible. He'd give her everything.

YOLANDHE'S ISLAND

Yap was left to his own devices as Yolandhe the sea witch tended Lord Amberhill in the cave. Yap did not stray far, meaning to keep an eye and ear open for any change in his master's condition, or for any harm Yolandhe might tender him. So far, however, Lord Amberhill remained unresponsive, and all Yolandhe seemed to do was sing to him in wordless tunes and rearrange the furs spread over him to keep him warm.

So Yap roamed the shore looking for driftwood with which to make fires—not just for warmth and cooking but to signal passing ships. Not that any ships came close enough to Yolandhe's island, thanks to the currents and superstitions surrounding the place, though he was sure she could sing them in if she wished. That was part of her power, drawing in the unwary to crash upon her shore.

He searched for flotsam and found pieces of their own ruined gig rolling in with the tide that also brought in lost fishing gear and an empty bottle or two. His rumbling stomach also kept him busy. He liked his vittles as well as any other fellow, but after he'd retched up Yolandhe's treasure, it had left a yawning pit in his belly waiting to be filled. So he sharpened a branch with his belt knife. The branch he turned into a spear, and he attempted to stab fish in the shallows.

If there was land flesh to be had on the interior of the island, he had no idea. He didn't know how to go about hunting, and he dared not abandon watch on his master. So he fruitlessly stabbed the water, nearly impaling his own foot in the process. It looked like he'd be eating dulse and mussels and snails again, which was getting a little old. It was more than he'd eaten, however, when he and his shipmates aboard the *Mermaid* had been trapped in the dead calm of Yoland-he's spell for untold years.

When his spear failed once again, he was startled to see the sea witch's reflection rippling beside his own. He glanced up. She looked outward, seemingly to gaze beyond the horizon. She stretched her hand out before her, fingers splayed, and she spoke-sang.

Yap prepared to run to take cover, for this looked like witchery, but he was too transfixed to move.

Waves roiled up before Yolandhe. Not huge, but larger than the others, and definitely not natural. They just hung there stationary. Then she jerked her hand back and a fish flipped out of the wave and smacked Yap in the face. He was too stupefied to catch it, but when he realized what was happening, he was ready to catch the next, and the next, and the next. Many others landed on the shore. It wasn't that the fish were jumping out of the water, but that they were being *spit* out of the waves.

When Yolandhe released the waves, the fish stopped flying. She turned to Yap. "You will watch over your master tonight. I must cleanse myself in the moonlight." And she walked away across a beach alive with flapping, silvery bodies.

"I'll need to dry 'em," Yap murmured. He may have a yawning pit of a belly to fill, but even he could not eat so much in a single sitting. Unfortunately, he had no salt.

Yolandhe paused. As if she knew Yap's thoughts, she said, "There is a barrel of salt near the back of the cave." With that, she vanished into the forest.

Yap set to work, immediately impounding as many fish as he could in a tide pool, and then gutting and boning the rest and spreading them to dry on makeshift racks of driftwood, even hanging them over the silvered branches of a still-standing, dead tree. He must work fast before the incoming tide reclaimed the tidepool and most of his bounty.

Hours later, he stumbled into the cave covered in sticky scales and viscera. In the back of the cave, fingers of the setting sun revealed a clutter of objects—wreckage, chairs, a chest, casks and barrels, coils of rope, and even a ship's figurehead of an armored knight. Other items were lost among dusky shadows.

Instead of searching for the salt right away, he knelt beside his master who slept peacefully beneath his furs. Yap did not know what injury plagued Lord Amberhill, just that he did not wake. There was no wound Yap could see, but he knew not all wounds could be seen. Sometimes they were on the inside. They'd both been knocked around in the stormy waves after their boat had failed them.

Lord Amberhill's hands lay across his breast atop the furs. On his thin, pale finger was the dragon ring with the ruby eye. The dragon's tail wrapped around its neck, forming the ring part. The ruby, though, *that* caught the eye. Yap did not know if it was how the sun glowed upon it, or if it was some innate quality of the gem itself, but it flickered with blood-red intensity.

"Sir," Yap said in a hushed voice, hoping against hope that Lord Amberhill could somehow hear him. "Sir, you've gotta wake up. This is the sea witch's island. Y'know, the one that kept me and the other lads of the *Mermaid* trapped in the bottle. We gotta find a way out of here before she curses us, or worse."

Initially there was no response. Then Lord Amberhill's hands struck out and grabbed Yap's shirt and pulled him down as Yap cried out in surprise. Lord Amberhill's eyelids peeled back, and his irises, usually a striking light gray, were clouded, smoky.

"You do not command me!" His voice was strange, lower, harsher, not at all the refined manner Yap remembered. "Do you hear me?" Lord Amberhill demanded.

"Aye, sir! I hear ya!"

As quickly as the outburst had come, it dissipated. Lord Amberhill's hands dropped back down to his chest, and his eyes closed, and once again he rested at peace.

He saw the man standing over him in wavery ripples. It was like looking through water.

But Amberhill was not in water. He was pretty sure about

that. He had been, but his present existence felt warm and dry. He reached out and felt a rough fur blanketing him. He closed his eyes thinking he should know the man. One part of him thought so, anyway, and another part said, "stranger." He wasn't sure if he remembered who he was himself—king or serf, farmer or fisherman.

Beneath the surface of wakefulness, it was not all dark, nor was he alone. Not far off were the slumbering shadows of those whose dreams leaked into his own. Dreams of soaring high above the land and swimming the depths of the sea. Of burrowing into the earth. Their desires became his, and he sensed their great power, their strength and ferocity, they, the changers of worlds. He felt himself drawn to reach out to them, to touch them, though he feared them. But they slept, and so must he.

He drifted until he settled into the still of dark.

BRIMMING WITH SECRETS

Karigan kept gazing into the shard of the looking mask in hopes of seeing something of her own time, but try as she might, she saw no new visions.

She concealed the fragment beneath her pillow when Lorine knocked on the door to help her prepare for supper. Supper entailed another change of clothes into a more formal black and gray affair. It seemed a waste when she realized she'd be dining alone at the big table, with only the company of the servants waiting on her. The professor, apparently, was still out and attending to his duties. She felt conspicuous and out of place, and ate as quickly as good manners permitted, retreating to her room when she finished.

She changed into her comfortable nightgown, doomed to wait again till it was time to meet the professor. She did so, pacing as dark gathered outside her window. Mirriam poked her head in to check on her and to ensure she was ready for bed. Karigan obediently climbed in beneath the covers and turned off her lamp. Mirriam made a grunt of approval and left.

Just like when I was a child being raised by my aunts, Karigan thought a little resentfully. It was difficult enough to lose her freedom as a female, much less as an adult, but it was the façade she must maintain for now.

And so she waited for the house to quiet down, her eyelids drooping. She kept shaking herself awake, and eventually crept to her door and listened as the household settled down for the night. This time when she slipped out, shawl once more draped across her shoulders and bonewood in hand, she had a much better feel for the layout of the house, and in the dim light, picked her way down to the library without hesitation.

She found the professor sitting in the glow of the low lamplight, a book open on the table before him. He glanced up as she entered.

"Ah, good evening," he said in a quiet voice. "My apologies for missing supper, but I had some details to attend to at the university. Are you ready?"

Karigan nodded, and he closed the book. He extinguished the lamp and, taking up a taper, gave the dragon statuette on its shelf a twist of its tail, opening the secret passage. Neither of them spoke until they were securely through the second door and on the spiral stairs winding their way downward.

"Er, you have nothing else to wear down here than your nightgown and slippers?"

"The dresses you had made for me are very fine," Karigan said, "but too fine. Mirriam would have a fit if I got dirt on them. The nightgown is bad enough."

"I see," the professor said. "I had not thought of that. She is, you see, accustomed to dirt on me." His chuckle was muffled in the close confines of the shaft that contained the stairway. The taper he carried, bobbing up and down, cast weird shadows on the rough stone walls.

"Which brings up something else," Karigan said. "Mirriam will not tolerate my visiting Raven at the stables, and she especially won't tolerate my riding him."

"Do you know that Arhys now demands a stallion of her own?"

"I . . . heard something about that," Karigan replied, recalling the ruckus outside the bathing room earlier in the day. "I need to spend time with Raven, even if it causes trouble. I hate to draw attention, but I will if I have to."

"Yes, yes, I do not doubt it. I have gathered there is a certain willfulness of character about you. And yet it does not come from a spoiled place as it does with Arhys. I grasp that Green Riders were great horsemen and that it in part came from love of their steeds."

Were. She tugged her shawl more closely against the chill

of the stairwell. She still could not think of her friends in the past tense. They remained alive to her, robust and carrying on their duties as Riders. To her it was more like they were some-*where* rather than some*when*.

"Let me think on it, my dear, and see if we can't come up with a solution that won't tax poor Mirriam's propriety or draw unnecessary attention to you or my household."

"Thank you," Karigan said. She'd have to be satisfied with his response for now but promised herself that even if he found no acceptable solution, she'd find one of her own. And, she thought, if the professor gave her enough information tonight about what had happened to Sacor City, she could work harder at finding a way to deliver that information home to her own time. It might mean that fitting in with this world would eventually become unnecessary.

Finding home would be the hard part, she thought with a sigh. All the other occasions she had transcended time had been with the aid of some supernatural force like the ghost of the First Rider, or Laurelyn, queen of Argenthyne. She had not achieved it on her own, but there had to be a way.

Their descent down the stairs seemed to go much faster than her last journey into the underground. Their feet thudded almost rhythmically on the stone steps. The bonewood kept her from straining her leg too much.

When they reached the bottom of the stairs, passed through the door at the landing, and entered the underground, its existence still shocked her. Even though she knew it was there, had seen it herself and pictured it in her mind since, she still could not believe it. She shied from her reflection in dusty, cracked windows. Mourned once again for the city, her home, that was no more.

The professor watched her, his taper casting a half-shadow across his face. "Yes, no matter how often I travel this way, I, too, feel unsettled."

They continued on past the facades of buildings that were familiar, but were not. Walking in the underground oppressed Karigan as though all the weight of the earth that covered it also bore down on her shoulders.

"I also fear," the professor said, "that some day some catastrophe could do the same to Mill City. It is not the most beautiful of places, but it is my home."

That, she could understand. They went on, saying no more as if afraid to break the melancholy silence of the underground. She tried to remember this section of the city as daylit and full of travelers afoot and on horseback, riding in carriages and wagons, the traffic streaming up and down the street as shoppers paused to peer into windows, but she could not quite get past the deadness of it all.

Eventually they came to the building that contained the stairs that led into the bowels of the mill. They climbed and climbed, and kept climbing until they alighted on the landing of the second floor where the professor kept his library and Cade Harlowe had practiced his fighting technique. This time, however, Cade was absent, and all was dark except for the professor's taper, which was no more than a firefly glow in the vast space. In moments he raised a lever that ignited the phosphorene lights, leaving the pair of them blinking for several moments.

The professor shed his somber mood and strode across the floor. Karigan hurried after him, once again amazed by the grand scale of the room with its velvet draperies, polished floor, and fine furniture occupying an otherwise rough interior. She glanced at Cade's wall of practice weapons with some longing. Staves, swords, knives, axes, and daggers she understood; the cabinet with a few of the snub-nosed weapons—the guns like that which the Inspector had brandished earlier in the day, she did not.

When they arrived at the professor's sitting area with his desk and shelves of books, he turned to her. "You have questions about the rise of the empire. I will tell you what I have discerned from accounts that were long ago outlawed. There is so much that remains unanswered, but I will tell you what I know. Perhaps you'll be able to answer a few things in exchange."

At that moment, Karigan did not see the sometimes preoccupied professor, befuddled by women and the dictates of society. She didn't even see the man made solemn by memories of the fire that had destroyed the other mill buildings of this complex and killed hundreds of workers. No, she saw a man with a canny eye and a sharp wit, the man who had been able to hide his anti-empire activities and cache of artifacts from imperial authorities for a very long time. She saw a man brimming with secrets.

"I need to know," she said. "How did Sacoridia fall?"

THE FALL OF SACORIDIA

The professor gestured for Karigan to take a seat on one of the overstuffed leather chairs while he remained standing, his hands clasped behind his back as if he was about to deliver a lecture before his students.

"You are aware of the dissidents that called themselves Second Empire?" he asked.

"Very," she replied.

"They built up their army by conventional and . . . magical means, enough to actually challenge King Zachary's forces."

"The king has been working to counteract them."

"He failed."

The words fell as a blow that would have knocked her to her knees had she been standing. Rationally she'd known King Zachary must have failed for his realm to have come to this end, but hearing it spoken so baldly? She closed her eyes wishing it was not so but knew wishing would change nothing.

"By whatever means," the professor continued, "the forces of Second Empire grew to be a serious threat. Battles were won and lost, but the fiercest and bloodiest happened right here." He flung his arms wide to encompass the area around them. "Mill City not only stands on parts of the Old City, but also on a battlefield. The last battle took place before the Old City's gates. It is said the conflict raged for months with Second Empire seeking to breach the city walls." He paused, as if deep in thought, then added, "They don't make walls like that anymore, do they. Clan D'Yer's work, if I'm not mistaken?"

"You're not," Karigan replied. Clan D'Yer, renowned masons, had also built the vast wall that separated Sacoridia from Blackveil Forest; a wall that had withstood the forces of nature and magic for a thousand years. There had been no better stoneworkers than Clan D'Yer, and yet, as she had seen today, Sacor City's walls, and the castle itself, had been more than breached—they'd been pulverized. "How did . . . how did they overcome the walls?"

"I've the diary of one named Seften, a guard at the gate who witnessed the final battle. His words are better than mine." He raised a finger, indicating that she should hold her questions, and dashed over to his shelves, scanning his collection of damaged books. He hummed tunelessly as he ran his fingers across creased and tortured spines, finally pulling out a small volume with a cry of triumph. It was, Karigan saw, half-charred, the remaining pages stained and stiff from water damage . . . and something darker.

"The diary of Seften," the professor said. "Sadly, little of it survived." He thumbed through brittle pages, then paused for some time, his eyes darting across the lines. "Here's what I want. Seften writes: . . . *after so many months of striving for victory, the king led a final charge onto the field, splendidly arrayed as always in his armor and the regalia of Sacoridia. We cheered as he led his elite Weapons and the reserve forces behind him. The enemy quailed and . . . and . . .*" The professor muttered and squinted. "Much of this is muddled, I fear. Oh, I see. He says, *and the troops on the field rallied, forcing the enemy's host back, verging on retreat.*" The professor flipped through some torn pages as Karigan dug her nails into her chair's leather armrests.

"I lose it until this," the professor said. "*Then the enemy unleashed its great weapons, and it was like all five hells bared as one and all its mightiest demons came unleashed. We hadn't a chance . . . So terrible they could not be of this Earth.*" He paused, scanning the page for more legible parts, then cleared his throat. "*When the clouds and rage and fire settled, I espied the king as he fell to the bloodied field, his Weapons slain in a black circle around him, his standards limp on the ground.*"

Karigan squeezed her eyes shut. "No . . . ," she murmured. But what had she expected? She'd seen the ruin of Sacor City, saw how an empire had risen up. And the king, she knew, would have laid his life down for his realm. He would not let the enemy overcome it while he still lived. He would not have hidden in the castle. *I should have been there.* Her presence wouldn't have changed the tide of battle, but she ought to have been there with her people, even if it meant dying with them.

When she opened her eyes, she found the professor kneeling before her, the diary in one hand and a handkerchief extended in the other. "I seem to be causing you quite a bit of distress today."

Only then did Karigan feel the hot stream of tears on her cheeks. She accepted the handkerchief.

"It's clear you believe King Zachary was a good leader," the professor said.

"He *is* a good leader," Karigan said. *And more than that. Much more.*

The professor lifted his chin as if she'd only confirmed his own thoughts on the matter. He patted her knee, his expression compassionate. "I have found nothing in my research to dispute it," he said. "And it is grand to hear one of his own servants corroborate it. Now, there is just a little left in Seften's diary that is legible. Can you bear it?"

She nodded.

The professor solemnly returned her nod and remained on his knees. It appeared to Karigan that he skipped paragraphs. Perhaps he was trying to spare her from some further unpleasantness. It did not take much imagination to guess what an enemy would do to a fallen monarch's corpse, especially with no bodyguards left to defend it.

"Here it is," the professor said. "Seften writes: *The king's death stole the courage of our soldiers. We were lost after that. The demon beasts descended on us, crushing the city walls and all within as if they were nothing, destroying, destroying . . . No one was safe. There was nowhere to go. We were lost, Sacoridia was lost.*"

After a long pause, Karigan asked, "That's all?"

"I'm afraid so." Professor Josston rose, closing the diary. "The rest is illegible or destroyed. Elsewhere, we find tantalizing mentions of the weapon or weapons that destroyed the city, often referred to as demons or hell beasts. In some accounts it is said that Second Empire raised the beasts from its one hell. In others, it is said that the Sacoridians drew the beasts out of their five, but the beasts turned on them."

Beasts, weapons . . . Karigan shook her head. "What of Rhovanny? The Eletians?" she demanded, thinking of Sacoridia's allies of old. "Did no one come to our aid?"

"Rhovanny sent help, but they were also under attack. Of Eletia?" He shrugged. "It appears the Eletians did not come. It did not prevent the empire from seeking out Eletia, however, and capturing it along with every other country on this continent. But Eletia, it seems to me, suffered the most."

"How so?" she asked, thinking everything she had done, everything the king and her fellow Riders had tried to do, was worthless. If this was the outcome despite everything they tried, what had been the point of their effort? She clenched her hands as despair darkened her thoughts.

"Any Eletians that were taken captive were hauled off to the Capital," the professor replied. "You see, my dear, long ago, in their own land, the Arcosians learned to draw etherea out of the air, the earth, the water, and . . . out of those with inherent magic, all for the pleasure and use of the emperor of Arcosia and those he favored. It is why the Arcosians first came here—they depleted their own sources of etherea. By all accounts, Eletia and its inhabitants have been sucked dry."

That would explain why her special ability and her moonstone had not worked.

"Our emperor is always seeking new sources, for one day even the Preserve will run dry."

"The Preserve?"

"You know it as the Blackveil Forest."

"But it's tainted."

"Those who harvest it, the emperor's artificers, claim they purify it through a filtration system. They process it somehow. Turn it into forms they can use it in—liquids, solids. As we use rivers and canals to power the machines of Mill City, so the emperor uses etherea to mold the Capital into whatever form he desires. It is said he uses it to make himself and his most special servants immortal."

"Like Eletians."

"Yes, like Eletians."

One of Karigan's ancestors, Hadriax el Fex, had been Mornhavon the Black's closest companion, and she'd read his journal, which had survived the centuries hidden in the archives of Selium. She gathered from his writings that Mornhavon had been obsessed with the Eletians. He was both in awe of them and resented them. Hadriax had written of grotesque experiments Mornhavon performed on them to learn the source of their immortality and magical nature. It sounded as if he had achieved that goal.

"The world is much poorer for its lack of etherea," the professor said. "Ever since your arrival, I have wondered how things might have been different."

"Even in my time," Karigan replied, "magic was scarce, or at least the magic users were. Very few survived the Long War and the Scourge that followed." She believed that Green Riders survived simply because their abilities were so minor and only worked if amplified by devices like their Rider brooches. During the Scourge, the brooches were supposed to be destroyed, but the Riders of the distant past hid them by placing a spell of invisibility on them. She touched the empty place where her brooch should have been pinned, feeling only the warmth of her own flesh through her nightgown. The Riders continued to keep the secret, and it was so ingrained in Karigan to do so that she did not speak of Rider abilities to the professor. He obviously knew something of the brooches, because he had recognized what hers was, if nothing more than a symbol of the messenger service.

"Still," the professor said, "you lived in a time and place where there were still Eletians and some magic. Magic that was not used to subjugate the populace. Wonders still existed—it wasn't all machines. There were forests and clear lakes, fresh air to breathe."

It was not perfect in her own world, and she thought some of Mill City's machines a vast improvement compared to what she had in her time—the accoutrements of the privy and bathing room coming immediately to mind—but she agreed that this bleak future lacked all the richness and beauty of her time. It was drab, hard. Depressing.

"Believe me when I say," the professor continued, "that Mill City is a paradise compared to other parts of the empire. The city magistrate does not tender abuse upon his populace to the degree it is done in other places, and the lands about us are not torn asunder and stripped for coal or silver or other minerals. Of course, the true paradise is the Capital, as artificially contrived as it is."

"Where *is* the Capital?" She kept hearing about it, but if it wasn't Sacor City, where was it?

"Let me show you." The professor returned to his library shelves, gently sliding the diary of Seften into its slot and humming again as he gazed along the bottom shelves. Eventually he tugged out a large volume with red leather covers. In contrast to the others, it did not show damage. He laid it on his desk with a thump and beckoned Karigan to his side. They leaned over the volume shoulder to shoulder, he smelling faintly, though not unpleasantly, of earth.

"This is an atlas of the empire," he said. "I have one in the library at the house, too, for reference." He opened it near the beginning, and there, displayed in vibrant color, lay the Serpentine Empire occupying the continent that had once been home to several countries. She saw that those countries had become subject territories, or protectorates, of the empire. Borders were, in some cases, altered. Hura-desh, for instance, had been combined with the Under Kingdoms to form the Under Territories. Eletia was gone completely from the map, and the empire claimed even the Northern Wastes and the harsh, dry lands to the southwest of Durnesia that Karigan had known as the Unclaimed Territories, inhabited only by non-aligned tribes, and visited only by the hardiest of travelers. They were now simply labeled, "Imperial lands."

As for Sacoridia, it was renamed "Imperial Seat." Sacoridia's neighbor to the west was no longer Rhovanny, but the Rhove Protectorate.

Though Karigan saw it all laid out there before her, she still couldn't quite believe it. It was like a map drawn from some tale of fantasy, not real life.

The professor seemed to pick up on her disbelief. "It is said," he told her, "the empire's forces were an irresistible tide that swept the continent, all enemies falling before it. Durnesia and Bince capitulated before they could be crushed. Tallitre has never been fully subjugated and most slaves now come from those periodic uprisings as the bounty of war."

He turned pages that showed detailed maps of each of the protectorates and opened up to the Imperial Seat. Sacoridia's borders remained very much the same, but gone were the twelve provinces and their names, their boundaries redrawn in straight lines, and the areas numbered. Karigan's home province of L'Petrie, or what was roughly L'Petrie, was now squared off and labeled "Section 1, the Capital," and painted in gold leaf. She glanced at the Blackveil Peninsula, colored a bright blue, and simply labeled, "Imperial Preserve." A city had grown about where the breach was, called, "Etherium Plantation."

"Etherium Plantation?" she asked, glancing at the professor.

"A huge industrial complex where they acquire and process etherea from the Preserve. Er, Blackveil."

Karigan shuddered, thinking about what effect tainted etherea from Blackveil had on those exposed to it, filtered or not. She did not believe it could be *purified*.

"Mornhavon must revel in it," she muttered.

The professor gave her a sideways look. "Eh? Who?"

"Mornhavon—the emperor."

The professor gazed at her aghast. "My dear girl, Mornhavon the Black is long gone. He is not our emperor."

It was Karigan's turn to be taken aback. "He's . . . I've believed . . . If he is not the emperor, then who is?"

The professor flipped the pages of the atlas to the very front of the book where the portrait of a man, framed by the sigil of the dragon with its tail wrapped around its neck, occupied a full page. It looked as if a child had scribbled on the picture, adding a large curling mustache to the man's upper lip and giving him a pointy beard and very shaggy eyebrows.

"Arhys," he said, rolling his eyes. "You can see why I can't have this copy in the house's library. If the wrong person saw this image of the emperor defaced, if even by an innocent child, there could be unspeakable consequences."

A sick feeling bubbled in Karigan's belly as she gazed at the picture, for even with the childish scribbles partially obscuring the man's image, he looked familiar, his well-chiseled cheeks and chin, his dark hair swept away from his face, and the gray eyes staring out from the page. When she realized who the picture depicted, she gasped.

THE SEA KING REBORN

"It was not the Arcosians who conquered all the lands," the professor said, "but the return of the sea kings. I apologize if I misled you."

This had to be some dream, or even a joke, but to Karigan, the professor looked all too serious as he regarded her with a twitch of his mustache.

She glanced back at the portrait, and there it was in fine script beneath his picture, his name: *His Excellency Xandis I, Supreme Emperor.*

Unable to contain herself, she blurted, "What in five hells is *he* doing here?"

Her voice echoed across the expanse of the mill floor, and the professor glanced around fearfully as if expecting someone or something to leap out of the shadows.

"You . . . you know the emperor?"

"I know him not as an emperor, but as a minor aristocrat distantly related to the king. A very irritating man."

"I—I beg your pardon?" Clearly the professor had never heard anyone speak about his all-powerful emperor in such a way before.

"Xandis Pierce Amberhill," she muttered.

"Yes, that is his name in full," the professor replied with a puzzled expression.

"But is it really him?" Karigan mused. "He'd have died by now." And then a mad laugh burbled out—she shouldn't be here either, so why not him, too? But how? He had been nowhere near the looking mask when it broke, nowhere near Blackveil for all she knew.

"He is, er, undying," the professor said.

173

"Undying?"

"The etherea. One would assume that the rumors about him learning how to prolong his life are correct."

"Could it be a descendent?" Karigan murmured.

The professor shook his head. "Any offspring he's begotten has been slain to prevent competition for his throne."

It had to be the same Amberhill. She would know his face anywhere. She'd also seen stranger things during her time as a Green Rider, so why not an eternally lived Amberhill who was emperor of all the lands? She took one last look at the portrait, at Amberhill's expression of smug self-confidence, even with the childish scribbles on his face, and she stumbled back to her chair, falling heavily into it and pressing her hand against her forehead. And she laughed some more. She could not help laughing. The professor watched her aghast.

Lord Amberhill, the annoying, arrogant aristocrat . . . But really, how much had she known about him? She knew he'd attempted to rescue Lady Estora when she was abducted by Mirwellian thugs working on behalf of Second Empire. He'd ended up helping Karigan, allowing her to escape from those very same thugs. He had seemed to know something about her special ability and had always taunted her about being the "vanishing lady." Before she had left on the Blackveil expedition, she'd heard something about him leaving Sacor City, but not why or where he was going. She didn't really care at the time. The last she'd seen of him was at the king's masquerade ball, and he'd been full of his usual swagger.

How had he come to dominate Sacoridia and build an empire? Why had he chosen to oppress his own people and revive slavery? If he were the conqueror, that meant he was responsible for the death of King Zachary and probably most of her friends, as well. Her laughter ended abruptly and was replaced by a burning anger.

"How?" she demanded. "How did he become emperor?"

The professor, who had been gazing at her in incredulity, clasped his hands once more behind his back.

"He is the Sea King Reborn. He commanded the weapons that destroyed the Old City and caused the fall of all these nations."

"Sea King Reborn? Amberhill? The sea kings are old history, gone a long time. Why would he think himself one?"

The professor shrugged. "I dedicated the first decade of my archeological research to the sea kings, trying to discover the answers to this and many other mysteries, and found almost nothing. Very few artifacts remain. Why the emperor should fancy himself the Sea King Reborn, I never discovered, but he had the power behind him. I was hoping by redirecting my research to more recent times in the ruins of the Old City that I could learn more, especially about these weapons he commanded and how they might be counteracted. With that power in our hands, we might be able to reclaim our sovereignty, our heritage."

"I could ask him about it," Karigan said on inspiration. "He knows me."

The professor gripped the back of his chair to steady himself. "My dear, that would be suicide! Whatever you once knew of the man he was, he is not as he was. He does not negotiate, and past acquaintances are little safer in his presence than opponents. His temper is mercurial. Besides, he is not due to awaken for another three years."

"Awaken?"

"Every ten years. I am not sure he actually sleeps, mind you, but he is at least sequestered during that time."

"Then who is ruling the empire?"

"His inner circle of Adherents, at his sufferance. They take care of the day-to-day running of the empire. When the emperor rises, that's when they receive his instructions, and he reviews what has happened during his sleep." The professor shuddered. "We never look forward to the emperor's rising."

"Why?"

"That is when he makes a point of reminding his subjects of his authority. Examples are made to the populace—the streets run with blood. Criminals, dissidents, and innocents alike are purged."

Karigan frowned. That didn't sound like Amberhill, but she had not known him well. She suddenly felt very tired, the phosphorene lamps seemed barely able to hold the suffocating dark of night at bay. She watched as dust settled in the streams of light. She thought once again about why she'd been brought here, why the god of death had seen fit to intervene, and she couldn't help but still believe that whatever had become of Sacoridia, and Amberhill's involvement, was beneath Westrion's notice. She'd been brought here for some other cause that had not yet been revealed to her.

Regardless of the death god's plans for her, she knew that if she was able to find a way home to her own time, she would do whatever it took to stop Amberhill, to stop him from using his weapons, whatever they were, to conquer Sacoridia. She could not allow him to destroy everything—and everyone—she loved.

The professor stepped around his chair and sat with a creak. They gazed at one another, mirroring grim expressions.

"I have opposed the emperor in my own small way for most of my adult years," the professor said, "but never have I felt such hope as when I came to believe that you are what you say you are. By whatever the miracle wrought by this looking mask of yours, or the old gods, that brought you to me, it is like a sign, and now that you say you knew the emperor when he was just a mortal man, I can only feel that the time has come."

"For what?"

"To resist in earnest. It is time. And you shall help."

Karigan shifted uncomfortably in her chair. She had not wanted to become involved in this world's problems. Her duty was to get home with information. "How?"

"There must be things you know about the castle complex, its grounds. How it was all laid out."

"Yes," she said cautiously.

The professor leaned forward, now eager. "Earlier today on the outing you asked about Silk's excavation. What he's up to. Well, I'll tell you. He plans to excavate the castle to its very foundations."

Karigan stilled. A prickling ran up her arms.

"He will make some pretense at finding artifacts along the way, but I believe I know what he is truly after."

"And that is?"

The professor slowly grinned beneath his mustache. It was

a feral grin. "He seeks objects of an arcane nature, of course, in the very lowest regions of the castle. One in particular."

Lowest regions of the castle. Karigan's frown deepened.

"It is said," the professor continued, "that there were arcane devices, magical objects, stored in the royal tombs. Would you know anything about this?"

Karigan kept still. Tried to keep her expression neutral. "No, not really," she lied. She still felt that need, that desire, that obligation to protect that which one did not openly discuss in her own time. "One hears the occasional rumor. The tombs themselves aren't talked about. I suppose the king's Weapons don't want to deal with thieves trying to break in to steal valuables." It sounded like a plausible answer to her, and not that far from the truth. She just didn't admit how much she really knew and that she'd actually been in the tombs.

The professor stroked his mustache as if deciding how much to say and question. "There is a very good chance the tombs survived the destruction of the castle," he said, "considering how deep beneath the ground they were placed. The only entrance we know of was through the royal chapel."

Karigan nodded. "That is what I've heard." She did not tell him she'd actually been through those doors.

"Have you ever heard of there being other entrances?"

Karigan paused, pretending to consider the question, then shook her head, unwilling to divulge such secrets. The professor looked disappointed.

"What is this arcane object Silk is after?"

The professor did not answer for they both started at a thudding sound echoing from somewhere deep in the mill building.

"I was not expecting Cade this evening," the professor said tersely, and he slipped over to his desk and opened a drawer. From it he withdrew a gun weapon. Karigan shook her walking cane to staff length. In unspoken assent, they moved stealthily, but swiftly, across the floor to the entrance where they paused and listened. Footsteps clanged on the wrought iron steps as their intruder climbed.

Karigan adjusted her grip on the bonewood, and the professor pulled back a mechanism on his gun with a quiet click.

As Karigan gazed at the gun, her eyes blurred. She looked away, blinking rapidly, and everything fell back into focus, but when she looked directly at the gun, it blurred again. She found she could look at it in general, or see it on the periphery of her vision, but she could not see it clearly when she looked directly at it.

She let the oddness pass as the footsteps grew nearer, louder, then paused.

"Professor?" a voice called.

"It is Cade," the professor said in obvious relief, his hand that held the gun falling to his side. Karigan relaxed, but kept the bonewood at full length. "Come up, Old Button!"

Cade did, blinking in the light as he joined them. He set aside his taper and raised an eyebrow when he noted their weapons.

"I wasn't expecting anyone to be here," Cade said. "I couldn't sleep, so I thought I'd come and do some training."

The professor chuckled. "We were not, as you can see, expecting you either. I would not have come tonight, but Miss Goodgrave needed some things explained to her, and I in turn have discovered some startling information from her. She knows—or knew—our emperor personally."

Cade glanced at Karigan in surprise, and the professor explained as the three of them strolled to the library sitting area. When they reached the big desk, Cade said, "It is difficult to envision the emperor as an ordinary, mortal man."

"Clearly not ordinary if he became our emperor," the professor said.

Karigan silently agreed. She'd known the swaggering nobleman, but there had to have been more to him that she hadn't been able to see.

"I was just about to tell our Miss Goodgrave about what Silk is after."

"I will make some tea." Cade moved off to the kitchen area in the opposite corner, and Karigan resumed her seat, rolling the bonewood in her fingers, watching as Cade lit the tiny stove and placed a kettle of water on it, his movements calm, unhurried.

The professor did not wait for tea, and after returning his gun to its drawer, he began to explain.

ANSCHILDE'S HEIRLOOM

 "**N**aturally it comes back to the sea kings," the professor said. "As you pointed out, they were long gone from here during your time, and one of the enduring historical mysteries is why they left, and why so suddenly. A major focus of my research was trying to figure out the answers, and I eventually discovered some tantalizing clues."

Cade joined them while he waited for the tea water to boil. "Perhaps, you should have asked why they came in the first place."

The professor waved his hand dismissively through the air. "Oh, the usual. Land, resources, the fishing. A people to dominate. Why they left is of more importance to the opposition so we may learn something from it. Did our ancient ancestors somehow banish the sea kings? Or did the sea kings leave of their own volition?"

The professor gazed intently at Karigan like a storyteller relishing the build up to a dramatic point. "On the far east coast of what you knew as Coutre Province, I found a possible answer chipped into a rock ledge, submerged by the sea at high tide. It was almost worn away by the constant surf, and it was miraculous I found it. I would not have but for a local fisherman who knew the shore well. One of my finest discoveries!"

"If the fisherman knew of it, it wasn't precisely a discovery now, was it, Professor?" Cade asked. Karigan espied a mischievous glint in his eye.

The professor *harrumphed*. "Semantics! To him it was nothing. To those of us searching for the stories of the past, it was a breakthrough. Now make yourself useful, student, and fetch my journal."

"Yes, Professor. I am your obedient servant." Cade bowed with an affectionate smile for his teacher and headed for the desk.

"Cheeky lad," the professor said good-naturedly.

Cade rummaged through various drawers before producing a worn leather book tied with a string. The professor said nothing until Cade placed the journal in his hands, leaving Karigan to wait in suspense. The whistle of the tea kettle pierced the silence, and Cade sauntered off to attend to it.

The professor untied the journal and rested it on his knees. As he flipped through the pages. Karigan caught images of diagrams and sketches, and copious writing. It brought to mind the memory of Yates' sketching in his own journal as they sat in camp so many nights in Blackveil. His duty had been to map and document their journey, and she'd seen some of his beautiful drawings of other members of the company, as well as that of the flora and fauna there. She closed her eyes trying to push the images away, for they were suffused with sorrow and loss.

By the time Cade returned with a tea tray and poured, the professor had found the page he was looking for. He turned the journal so Karigan could see it right side up. His drawing showed the figure of a man with some sort of helm or headdress who held a shield and an oblong object like a sword or rod. Three ships with triangular sails and curled bows and sterns, with lines dashed through the hulls that must have been oars, seemed to sail away on surging waves from the male figure. Beneath the picture the professor had written in a strange script.

"This is what I found chipped into that rock ledge," he said. "The script is a primitive form of Old Sacoridian and it says, *Anschilde, son of Ansofil, chief of men, bearer of the erangol.* Erangol roughly translates to 'dragonfly.' The rest of the inscription has weathered away."

Bearer of the dragonfly? Karigan wondered.

"However," the professor continued, "the Second Age historian, Havoness, relates the legend of Anschilde, who banished the sea kings by using his 'dragonfly device,' perhaps a weapon with arcane qualities. Anschilde was considered a great leader and was something of a king of his day after his defeat of the sea kings. The few historical references I can access disagree about whether or not armies and battles were involved or if it was just Anschilde and his dragonfly device. I was lucky to find that unpurged volume of Havoness." He glanced fondly at his library of damaged books.

"What does this have to do with the tombs?" she asked.

The professor slapped his journal shut, and Karigan jumped, almost spilling her tea. "Patience, my dear, I am getting there. Now, there are other elusive references to this incident with Anschilde, but most interesting is what's handed down orally in the east about him and his weapon. Stories are passed down, despite suppression by the empire, and tell how the dragonfly device became a revered heirloom of Anschilde's line, later known as Clan Sealender. No one after Anschilde knew how to use it or even what it was capable of—if anything—besides sending away the sea kings.

"Oral tradition holds that the heirloom was hidden away during the Scourge after the Long War so it would not be destroyed, and then brought to Sacor City when the Sealenders ascended the throne. Then it vanished altogether about the time the first Sealender king died. One concludes it was interred with him in the royal tombs."

"Ah," she said, "so this is what Silk is after. This heirloom, this dragonfly device." It seemed more than plausible to her such an object would be hidden in the tombs, if it really existed in the first place.

"Yes," the professor replied. "You see, he too, did much research into the sea kings, trying to excavate along the coast. Back then we were still on friendly terms, sharing in our discoveries, so he, too, knew of Anschilde's device. In fact, I suspect he may know more." He glowered. "Little did I realize he was just using me back then, on top of his access to a library of forbidden books hidden away in the emperor's palace. Naturally, as the scion of one of the emperor's inner circle, Silk would seek ways to further the empire for his own benefit, to be rewarded with immortality as his father had been. Finding the dragonfly device would be a coup because by handing it over to the emperor, Silk would insure that the emperor could not be threatened by it. We, the opposition, of course, desire it in case the old stories are true. We would like to banish the Sea King Reborn. You were my best hope, my dear, for helping us to find another way into the tombs, a way to get there before Silk."

She sat and stared at the steam rising from the teacup warming her hands. The vapor twisted and drifted in a ghostly dance, dissipating long before it reached the high ceiling. Was there a way to help the professor without giving away the secrets of the tombs? Could she do so while minimizing her entanglements in this world's problems? If Silk was going to excavate his way into the tombs—and she could not imagine how he'd get through all the rubble and solid granite bedrock—wouldn't she rather the professor reach them first? But if the tombs remained intact and contained powerful relics of the past, she preferred that no one enter them.

She found it interesting how forcefully the taboo concerning the tombs kept her silence. Few were permitted entrance: only royalty, the Weapons who guarded the dead, and the caretakers who tended the tombs. Rules had been bent to allow Karigan to enter and then leave again. Interlopers were not usually permitted to see the living sun ever again, and were doomed to live out their lives in the tombs assisting the caretakers.

If the tombs had survived the devastation of Sacor City, they were the last bastion of old Sacoridia remaining in this time, and she was reluctant to see them overrun and defeated as the rest of the realm had been.

"How does Dr. Silk plan to reach the tombs?" she asked. "How can he excavate through all the rock?"

Cade and the professor exchanged glances.

"A drill," the professor replied.

"A drill?" Karigan was incredulous, trying to imagine workers pounding and pounding on iron hand drills. Even with a multitude of drills and workers, it would take decades to reach the tombs. The thought eased her mind until the professor explained.

"My dear, do not forget this is the modern age, the age of machines. Silk's drill is not the simple tool of your era, but a gigantic instrument powered by a steam engine. Once the site is made ready and all is set in place, it will take no time at all for the drill to work through the castle ruins and bedrock. Weeks. A couple of months at the most."

His words shook her, the idea of such inhuman power.

"Which is another reason why," the professor said, "it is time to step up the opposition."

"You must destroy the drill!" Karigan said.

"Even if it can be destroyed," Cade said, "it can be re-made."

"Machines can be tampered with," the professor said, rubbing his hands together in anticipation, "and work sites compromised. Even if Silk can remake the drill, it would slow him down, buy us time. Unfortunately, the warehouse it resides in is too well guarded."

"The work site will be, too," Cade said.

"Perhaps, but Silk's men can't possibly secure the entire mount. We shall see, we shall see . . . I will have to consult with our brethren to find out what they know of such things, so we can prepare."

He left the armchair for his desk. He sat and searched through drawers, producing paper, pen, and ink, and then writing furiously and with such focus that Karigan and Cade might as well not have existed. Cade shrugged, collected the empty teacups on a tray, and carried them away to the kitchen.

As Karigan watched the professor work, she wondered just exactly what had been set in motion.

THE TRAINING OF CADE HARLOWE

Neither Cade nor the professor paid Karigan any mind. The professor stayed at his desk scribbling away on papers, and after Cade deposited the tea tray in the kitchen, he proceeded to the training area without a glance in her direction.

She switched chairs so she could watch Cade work. First he removed his suit coat, and then his waistcoat, hanging them on a brass hook on the wall. Perhaps conscious of her gaze, this time he did not remove his shirt. He next looked over the weapons arrayed before him on wall mounts, and after some consideration, chose a longsword. He stood with it at his side for some time, his eyes closed and head bowed, chest rising with slow, deep breaths.

Karigan waited and waited, while he stood there breathing, wondering when he would begin. If he were one of Drent's students, he'd have been pounded into the ground already, solely for standing there, with Drent screaming in his face. Sword fighting was not about peaceful contemplation but acting, and Drent never let his trainees forget it, for in a real-life fight, hesitation meant death. Enemies did not wait for an opponent to be ready.

Finally, Cade moved slowly and deliberately into some warm-up exercises, stretching his limbs and torso. This, too, went on for far longer than Drent would have ever permitted, and Karigan found herself tapping her fingers on the armrest of her chair.

She settled in when he finally, and swiftly, transitioned to forms, the sword arcing through the air with a bright silver gleam. He began with simple, beginner moves, gradually progressing to intermediate and more advanced forms. It was much as she had observed before—his posture and balance were very good, but his execution lacked finesse. Some of his transitions were rough, and a couple of the forms were plainly incorrect. Drent, she thought, would have enjoyed tearing Cade Harlowe apart.

After he tried to sweep from Crayman's Circle into Aspen Leaf—very advanced moves—and executed them so poorly, she could stand it no longer. Before she knew it, she was on her feet and crossing over to the training area with her bonewood in hand. She halted before him, but he seemed determined to ignore her, and she had to admire his focus, though the longer she stood there, the more his movements became jerky, less clean, her proximity having some effect on him. No, Drent would not approve.

He fumbled with the simple but elegant Deer Hunt form in such a way that he was inviting an opponent to impale him. Karigan decided to oblige. With a single swift thrust of the bonewood, she knocked the sword out of his hand, then jabbed him in the belly. The clang of steel on the wooden floor echoed through the vast room. He staggered back, hunched over and clutching his belly, gasping for air, while simultaneously shaking out his sword hand. Karigan watched faintly amused while he tried to regain enough breath to swear.

"What in damnation was that for?" he roared.

It was a pleasant surprise to see the usually stoic Cade show some anger. "Your sloppy technique provoked me."

"What do *you* know about it?"

"Enough to disarm you, evidently."

"You could have caused me to injure you by interfering like that."

"You're more likely to injure yourself," Karigan observed.

Cade's face reddened as he fought to stifle his anger. He swiped his sword off the floor. "How do you know? Girls may have played at carrying swords back in your day, but they could hardly fight men."

His pronouncement irked her, but she could hardly blame him for the teachings of his world. The empire had reduced the roles of women significantly from what she'd been accustomed to in her own. Women couldn't even bare their faces in public and were relegated to passivity, systematically made powerless by the rules of the empire. If this was all Cade had ever known, she could not expect to change his attitude about "girls" in one evening, but she could try.

"Apparently you do not have all the facts of your history correct." The bonewood hummed toward his face and he barely blocked it in time. The blood now drained from his cheeks. If she'd the use of her dominant hand, she might very well have bashed in his face had she so desired. As it was, she easily disarmed him again by catching the crossguard of his sword with the bonewood and yanking it right out of his hand.

He bent once again to retrieve his sword, rage building in his expression, but she stepped on the blade and jabbed the tip of the bonewood into his neck. He stilled. "I'm a sword-master initiate," she said, "as were other *girls* of my time, as were so many who came before me over the generations. You forget that the armies of the Long War were filled with fe-males because so many of the men had died, and many *were* children when they took up arms. You forget that *girls* were swordmasters and Weapons. Even female Green Riders, who never trained for swordmastery as I have, are very handy with swords and are taught to fight men as well as other *girls*. If this bonewood were a sword, and we were enemies, I'd have killed you at least three times already."

She removed her foot from his sword blade and withdrew the bonewood from his neck. It left a red mark on his skin. He stood, sword in hand, once again trying to master his anger. "We don't fight with swords here," he snapped. "We use other weapons."

"Like your guns?" She gestured at the cabinet with sev-eral of the objects displayed behind glass.

"Like the guns," he replied with a curt nod.

She still did not understand exactly what the guns did, but she understood swords. "If you don't use swords, why bother to train with them?"

"For discipline. To master the techniques of . . . of the past. Of the Bl—swordmasters."

Karigan narrowed her eyes at him. It had sounded like he

almost said, "Black Shields." His demeanor had reminded her of the Weapons she knew. Her suspicions were roused, but she chose not to pursue them at the moment. "If you are going to work with swords, even if just for discipline, you should do so correctly to properly honor those who perfected the techniques. To do otherwise shows disrespect."

Cade started to protest, but the professor cleared his throat, startling Karigan who had been so intent on Cade that she hadn't heard his approach.

"You would do well to listen to her, Cade," the professor said. "The king would not have anointed her a knight without cause, especially since there had been no knights for two hundred years previous." To Karigan he explained, "I train Cade in the techniques as they were handed down to me, and as they've been handed down in secret since the rise of the empire, but as you can see, we've remembered them imperfectly. Cade, I believe you have a new teacher."

Cade's mouth dropped open. It would be, Karigan thought, a huge challenge for him to accept her as a teacher, but she relished the thought of actual arms practice and not just sneaking through forms with the bonewood in her bedroom.

"I am returning to the house now," the professor said. "See that Miss Goodgrave is also returned before dawn."

Cade nodded.

"Good night, then," the professor said, and he strolled away from them across the mill floor.

Karigan and Cade watched him until he disappeared through the door, and then they glanced uncertainly at one another. Unable to hold her gaze, Cade paced restlessly, testing the heft of his sword. Would he accept her instruction, even when told to do so by the professor? Or would he prove obstinate, too stuck in the ways of the empire?

He paused, and without looking at her, he said, "This all seems very improper. Females do not teach. They bear children and keep the home. They certainly do not teach sword fighting."

Karigan sighed, thinking that any discussion between them would deteriorate rapidly into philosophical arguments, but Cade continued, "However, I know things were once different, and if we are to defeat the emperor, we must shed the ways of thinking he has shackled us with. Teach me what you can."

She nodded, guessing how humbling a concession this was for Cade to make. With renewed respect, she said, "Why don't you show me all the forms the professor has taught you, one at a time, beginning with the most basic."

Cade complied, and as he performed one form after another, Karigan commented and corrected as necessary. When she had to, she stopped him to demonstrate the proper execution of a form, using her bonewood as her sword. Occasionally she had to position Cade, placing her hands on him, to move his shoulders or arms or legs. Initially he flinched at her touch, but as they went on, he relaxed. She could only imagine what Arms Master Drent would think of his least-favored student teaching another.

"I want to show you that Crayman's Circle into Aspen Leaf you had trouble with before," she said, "so you know what it's supposed to look like."

Cade rested his sword tip on the floor and placed his other hand on his hip, waiting as if he were simply indulging her. Karigan dropped her shawl to the floor and pushed it aside with her foot. She inhaled deeply and settled into her starting stance, but unlike Cade, she allowed no time to pass. She released her breath and began.

Although she was not in top form and relying on her left hand did not come as naturally to her, the movement felt good. So good that she did not stop with Aspen Leaf, but flowed into a series of forms that was one continuous progression, a dance ascending and falling to accompaniment of the silent tempo so ingrained in her that it beat through her whole being. She twisted and turned, the bonewood carving the air. Unleashed from her burdens, unhindered by the fear of someone discovering her secret practices, she lost herself in the freedom of motion. Her body awoke to the dance stretching, flexing, blood surging, her hair flowing about her shoulders, her nightgown billowing. Her slippers flew off as she leaped and whirled, shoulders rotating and hips following. She landed lightly on bare feet only to surge seamlessly into the next form.

She became unconscious of her surroundings, of her exile here from her own time, of Cade's gaze. Though most forms demanded restraint and minimal movement, she felt as though she soared, choosing to repeat those forms that required the big leaps, the long-reaching strokes. Then showing the utmost control, she stopped. Simply came to a standstill, back erect, the point of the bonewood coming to rest on the floor. Her hair brushed across her shoulders and settled. She panted a little, felt how her nightgown clung to the perspiration on her skin. Cade just stared. She could not read him. She shrugged and slid her feet back into her discarded slippers, and retrieved her shawl. And still he stared.

"Well?" she demanded.

"You—you are a swordmaster . . . ?"

"No," she replied acerbically, thinking he was going to launch into criticism. "I am a swordmaster *initiate*. I may never make swordmaster." She definitely would not if she couldn't find her way home to resume training. "Swordmasters are the best of the best."

"I—I can't believe there are any better than what you just showed me."

A tart reply formed on Karigan's tongue, accustomed as she was to the criticism and sarcasm that she always received from Drent and her fellow trainees, but then she saw the awe forming in Cade's eyes.

"I have never seen anything like that," he said. "Such beauty . . ."

Taken aback, she did not know what to say, especially when Cade knelt before her as if in obeisance.

"You can teach me how to . . . how to do as you did?" he asked.

"Um . . ." His tone was so humble, his reaction so unexpected that it took her a moment to regain equilibrium. "I think so. It'll take some work though." She smiled tentatively.

Cade seemed to collect himself then. "Good. I had no idea what . . . I just had no idea." He bowed his head, then stood.

Karigan wasn't sure whether he meant he'd had no idea of what she was capable, or what the forms were supposed to look like when executed properly.

"It's fortunate you are left handed," he said, indicating her right wrist in its cast.

"I'm not. I'm right handed."

Cade stared once again.

His discomfiture both pleased and amused Karigan. "I was made to train my left side after a previous injury to my right elbow. Swordmasters, especially those who become Weapons, are trained to be capable fighters using their whole bodies."

Cade shook himself. "Seems I've a ways to go." He turned and placed his sword on its wall mount, and stood there in silence for a moment before striding over to the closest window. Behind the drapes it was boarded over, but there was a minute crack he peered through. "It is nearly dawn," he announced, "so we'd better head back."

As he dressed, she glanced at the cabinet of guns once more.

"Tell you what," she said, "if I help you with the sword work, you can teach me how to fight with your gun weapons."

Cade cocked an eyebrow. "I will have to ask the professor, but I will do so if he permits it."

"Good," Karigan said. It occurred to her that if she learned the use of advanced weaponry from this time, she might be able to reproduce and use it in her own, bringing Sacoridia an advantage over its enemies. It could change everything.

A CAT, THE GHOST,
AND RAVEN

On their return journey to the house, Cade rarely spoke, but treated Karigan with deference. She caught him stealing surreptitious glances at her as they walked through the underground. His awe made her uncomfortable enough to wish he'd go back to his former dismissive self. What would he have thought of her performance if she'd been in top form?

Before they entered the library, he lightly touched her arm as if to reassure himself she was real. "You will teach me more?" he whispered.

"Yes. Of course."

He nodded gravely, and then they emerged into the library, as the shelves that concealed the secret passage closed behind them. They made their way to the foyer, and Cade quietly let himself out through the front door. She wondered where he lived that he could sneak around at odd hours. Then she shrugged and returned to her bedroom. The first thing she noticed when she got there was that the window was open, the curtains billowing in a cool breeze that curled into the room.

"What . . . ?"

She hurried over to the window wondering who had opened it and how it had been done without rousing Mirriam. She inspected the window finding nothing amiss, but when she touched the inner edges of the frame, her fingers came away greasy. Someone had oiled the window so it wouldn't screech when opened. It was not entirely the cool air that gave her a chill.

The second thing she noticed in the pre-dawn dusk filtering into her room was a cat sitting on her bed, watching her. It was the stray that had come to her window before.

"Hello," Karigan said, glancing around her room to make sure there were no other surprises awaiting her. "Did you open the window?"

The cat just yawned and flopped, rolling from side to side, rubbing his whole body into the comforter. Lorine had referred to the stray as a "he," and Karigan saw she'd gotten his gender correct. Karigan sat beside him and stroked his cheek. Before she knew it, he was bumping against her and purring so loudly she was sure it would cause Mirriam to come storming into her room.

"You're a nice kitty, very friendly," Karigan murmured. He certainly wasn't skittish as many strays were. "Maybe you're not a stray at all, but just like to visit other houses."

She lay down on the bed, spreading her shawl over her like a throw, and the cat walked up her legs, sat on her belly, and started kneading her chest. "Ow!" she said as claws pricked her skin.

A short time later he curled up on her stomach, his purrs vibrating through her body as she petted him.

"Nice kitty," she murmured, fading into sleep. "I think I'll call you Cloudy." His white and light gray fur made the name apt, and without worrying about who had opened the window, and content with a soft purring cat to soothe her, she fell into a deep slumber.

Pat-pat. Pat-pat.

Karigan groaned. Despite her efforts to keep in condition, sword practice with Cade had left her whole body aching, and there was an uncomfortable weight on her chest.

Pat-pat.

She fluttered her eyes open to find the cat staring into her face, his paw raised to tap her cheek again.

"Oh, Cloudy," she murmured, remembering. She stroked his head, but he turned away and walked down her body, tail twitching. He crouched at the foot of the bed and stared off into the darkness of the far corner. His tail thumped on the comforter.

Gray morning cast irregular shadows in the room and the

curtains rustled listlessly. Karigan rose up on her elbows to see what the cat watched. At first she saw nothing, then she detected movement. Disregarding her aches and pains, she sat all the way up and stared. A filmy figure was seated in her chair facing away from her, seeming to write or draw on something on its lap. Faintly she could hear the scritching of its—*his*—pen.

She swung her legs off the bed and stood. She took halting steps forward and paused just behind chair and ghost. He was still filmy, translucent, but better defined this time. His garb appeared familiar, looked like . . . looked like the uniform of a Green Rider. *Who?* she wondered. Someone she'd known? She could not see his face from behind, so she slowly started to circle around him fearing that any sudden move would cause him to vanish. She glanced at his drawing.

It was a drawing of himself, from the same perspective she'd had of seeing him from behind. As he drew, his ghostly shape grew more solid, more defined, as if the act of drawing himself helped him materialize more fully. Faint green began to tint his uniform.

As Karigan circled him, his profile grew more familiar. She knelt before him, now able to look into his face that was so intent on the drawing, and she knew.

"Yates!" It came out as a throttled cry.

He paused his sketching, and without looking at her, raised his forefinger to his lips. And vanished.

A faint green afterglow wavered where he had sat, and then dissipated. Karigan knelt there hugging herself, fresh tears washing down her face, grief that she'd been unable to express before. She grieved for Yates, she grieved for all those who she'd known and were now dead. From the perspective of this time, all of them were gone.

The cat came to her with a questioning *Prrrt?* and then rubbed against her leg. It quieted her enough to hear the strains of a distressed whinny come through her open window.

"Oh, no!" She swiped tears from her face with her sleeve, feeling Raven's urgency, his need, ringing through her. She ran from her room with neither her shawl nor slippers. She pelted down the corridor, one door opening in her wake. Mirriam called after her. Karigan ignored her and charged down the stairs, and then to the back of the house past bleary-eyed servants just beginning their day.

She threw open the back door and raced across the yard toward the stables, her healing leg hindering her not at all. Raven's sharp whinnies called to her, and when she entered the stables, she found him rearing in the center aisle, only one cross-tie secured to his halter, and she had no doubt he'd rip it out of the wall, bolt and all, at any moment. Standing before him, with a carriage whip in her hand, was Arhys, a small figure in contrast to the huge stallion. Trapped beyond Raven, just out of range of deadly hooves, stood Luke and his stable boys still in night dress, unable to get around the horse to stop Arhys.

What did the girl think she was doing? Did she have no sense of the danger she placed herself in?

Arhys laid the whip back, preparing to lash Raven. "Stupid horse!" she cried.

Raven reared again, bellowing, hooves thrashing. He would kill Arhys.

"No!" Karigan cried, and she lunged forward and grabbed Arhys. The danger of the moment gave her the surge of strength she needed to heave the girl out of the way. Karigan, however, lost her footing and fell prone beneath descending hooves. She scrunched her eyes closed and gritted her teeth against the pummeling that could crush her.

And felt a whiffling against her ear instead. She rolled to her side and saw that by some miracle, or quick reflex and wit of Raven's, that his front legs had not crushed her, but straddled her body instead. He nickered at her questioningly. She reached with a shaking hand to pat his nose.

"*Bad* horse!" a little girl's voice cried.

Raven jerked his head up and snorted. Luke shouted. A quick glance revealed Arhys back up on her feet coming toward them with whip ready. Karigan hauled herself out from between Raven's legs and intercepted the girl. She snatched the whip out of her hands and tossed it aside, then grabbed Arhys' wrist.

"Lemme go!" the girl cried.

"Don't. You. Ever. Go near that horse again. Do you hear me?" Anger made Karigan's voice harsh.

"Lemme go!" Arhys started kicking her and screaming.

Karigan dragged her out of the stable, the girl wild in her hand, and a specially well-aimed kick brought Karigan to one knee. Arhys seized the opportunity to pull her hair and scratch at her face. It was almost as bad as fighting one of the tainted Sleepers in Blackveil.

"What's going on here? Release the girl!"

Karigan looked up to see the professor, Mirriam, and half the household staff running across the yard.

"I hate her and her stupid horse!" Arhys screamed.

Before Karigan could retort, Arhys smacked her in the face and surprise made her release the girl. She felt blood trickle from her nose. She wiped it and smeared blood across her wrist. When she looked up, Arhys was folded in the professor's arms, her angel's face pressed against his chest, everyone staring at Karigan in condemnation.

"Miss Goodgrave!" Mirriam cried. "What were you doing to the child?"

Karigan looked to the professor, but even his gaze was accusing, his hold on Arhys protective. What did they see in the girl? She was nothing but a spoiled brat.

"Yes," the professor said, his voice the flat, low growl of a dog preparing to attack. "What were you doing to Arhys? Speak!"

Karigan's mouth dropped open. The professor had a look in his eye, the one suggesting he'd kill her if she didn't say the right thing. The contrast from the congenial man she'd grown to know shocked her.

Then suddenly Luke was at her side and the stable boys behind him. Somehow they'd gotten around the upset Raven to reach her. Luke held out his hand and helped her stagger to her feet. "Raven's much calmer now," he reassured her.

To the professor, he said, "Sir, Miss Goodgrave saved the lass's life." He went on to describe how he was roused by the stallion's whinnies, and when he came to see what the matter was, he'd found Arhys taunting and lashing at the stallion with the carriage whip. Luke's quarters were in the rear of the stable, and he and his boys had been trapped behind Raven, unable to reach Arhys.

"A blessing Miss Goodgrave came when she did," Luke continued, "or Arhys would've been done for."

"Is this true?" the professor asked of no one in particular.

"Liar! Big fat liar!" Arhys cried.

"It's true," the stable boys chorused in counterpoint. "We saw it."

"I told you that horse was dangerous," Mirriam said. "He almost killed Arhys."

Enough anger had built in Karigan that she stepped toward Mirriam and pointed at her. "The horse was a danger to Arhys only because she put herself there. Any horse can be dangerous if it's tormented enough."

"Miss Goodgrave!" Mirriam snapped. "I—"

"Silence!" the professor bellowed. "Arhys, you've been a very naughty girl. Very foolish."

"But you didn't get me a horse! Why should *she* have one?"

"We will talk about this," he said, "but right now, Mirriam is going to take you to your room and there you shall remain until I say so."

"No!"

"Do as I say."

Mirriam dragged the shrieking child away and ordered the servants back to the house. Luke and his lads returned to the stable, leaving Karigan alone with the professor.

"I am sorry, my dear." He produced a fresh handkerchief and offered it to her.

She pressed it to her nose, but discovered the blood was already drying.

"Arhys is headstrong and spoiled, and I'm overprotective."

"I'd—I'd best see to Raven." She turned to go, but he touched her arm.

A tick pulsed in his cheek as though he struggled over what he wanted to say. "I need to thank you. I'm indebted to you. You not only saved the life of an innocent child—troublesome though she might be—but also that of the heir to the throne."

Karigan was not sure she'd heard correctly. "Throne? What throne? The emperor's?"

"No. As I told you, he assassinates all his offspring. No, Arhys is heir to the throne of Sacoridia. She is directly descended from the king you served, and his queen."

AN EXCHANGE OF
SECRETS

Karigan shook herself, not sure she'd heard him right. He had spoken barely above a whisper, though the yard was empty of potential eavesdroppers.

"That—" She was about to say "brat," but caught herself in time. "Arhys is a direct . . . ? A descendent of . . . ?"

The professor nodded. The brightening morning revealed the seriousness etched into his features. "We, the opposition, have preserved the bloodline. It's been so very dangerous. The heirs were always hunted by the emperor. The general belief is that the line was wiped out when a boy, who would have been Arhys' uncle, was slain. We managed to keep his younger sister separate and safe, her identity hidden. Arhys' mother. She died in childbirth, however."

"So King Zachary and Estora . . ."

"Had a son. When Sacor City fell, the queen escaped with her son and went into hiding. They were hunted ceaselessly, and it is said only the queen's courage kept them alive."

Karigan wanted to sit down. This was one revelation too many on too little sleep.

"You should get inside," the professor said, "warm up."

"I'm not cold," she replied, though she was, and had wrapped her arms around herself to ward off a chill. "Does Arhys know what she is?"

The professor gave a throaty chuckle. "Can you imagine what she'd be like if we told her she was to be queen?"

Karigan shuddered at the thought.

"No, for her safety, and ours, she will not know till she comes of age. So now, perhaps, you understand why I coddle her a little too much. I really must learn another approach—it would not do to have a spoiled brat on the throne." He hesitated, then said, "I expect that you, as a Green Rider, will guard this secret with your life. You will, won't you?" His tone was both pleading and tinged with the inherent threat that if she did not comply, her own existence was forfeit. The professor would protect his royal heir at whatever the cost, and no matter how much he might regret it.

Arhys was Zachary's many-great granddaughter. How could Karigan not guard such a secret? Besides, she would never let harm befall the girl, no matter who she was, or how foolish. "You have my oath," she replied, "as a royal messenger of the king."

"Thank you." He bowed formally and looked wistful. "I should have liked to have met your king, he who instills such loyalty. Now, perhaps we should go in?"

"I need to check on Raven."

"Mirriam may be right," he mused.

"About Raven?"

He nodded. "Too dangerous to keep."

Anger rose in Karigan once again. "He was provoked. Keep Arhys away, and he'll be all right."

"I don't know . . ."

"You just told me an important secret," she said, "so I'll tell you one in return. Raven is a Green Rider horse. A *true* Green Rider horse, and if you know anything of your history, you'll know that Green Rider horses are exceptional." She did not await an answer but turned and strode for the stables.

She found all four horses, housed in the stables, including Raven, each in their stalls munching on hay. Raven spared her just a passing glance before returning to his fodder.

Luke joined her at the stall door. "He calmed down just as soon as you got Arhys out of here," he remarked. "Can't decide if it was brave or crazy of you to pull Arhys out of his way. Er . . ." He looked chagrined, as if suddenly remembering she was supposed to be crazy. "So, is the professor gonna get rid of Raven?"

"I don't think so," Karigan replied, hoping that her shared secret was enough to convince him of Raven's value.

"Good," Luke said with emphasis. "None of it's his fault if he doesn't like getting teased." That said, he sauntered off to attend to his other duties.

Satisfied that Raven was content, she left the stable for the house, limping a little from the strain of running and the previous night's swordplay, but not as much as she might have guessed. She was truly healing, and it was only a matter of time before the cast, which had begun to look rather grimy of late, came off her wrist.

When she entered the house, the servants regarded her with silence, and she hastened her step. After she climbed the stairs and headed down the corridor to her bedroom, she was not surprised to hear Mirriam bustling behind her. Indeed, the head housekeeper, now fully dressed, followed Karigan right into her bedroom. Karigan rolled her eyes at the expected, "Miss Goodgrave!"

But then Mirriam froze as she took in the open window and Cloudy the cat sitting on the bed. She screamed and went for the broom with which Karigan had been practicing forms before acquiring the bonewood.

"Cat!" Mirriam cried in horror. With astonishing speed, she slammed the broom on the bed, but Cloudy was already out the window. Mirriam scrambled to the window, holding the broom as a shield, and looked this way and that for some moments before slamming the sash shut. She turned her back to it and sagged, her hand on her heaving chest.

Karigan waited for the inevitable upbraiding to come. She said nothing while Mirriam caught her breath and collected herself.

"We have been over this," Mirriam finally said, pointing at Karigan. "No open windows! I shall have it nailed shut if I must."

"That won't be necessary," Karigan replied.

"I should hope not. But if it comes to it—"

"I doubt my uncle would permit it, in case there was a fire or something."

Mirriam blanched, revealing she knew exactly to what Karigan referred.

"The window shall remain closed regardless," Mirriam

said. "And the vermin! I will see that one of the gardeners destroys it!"

That was it. Karigan had had it. She was tired of this strange world, she missed her home and her friends, and she'd been awake far too long hearing the most incredible—and terrible—tales of what had become of her world. Mirriam's imperious ways were like the spark to an explosion. Karigan stepped right up to her. "You will do no such thing. If you so much as harm a hair on his body, I will—" Karigan thought hard for a suitable threat. "I will draw such attention to this house that you will want to wither in shame, and my uncle will have no choice but to dismiss you."

"How dare you!"

"No, how dare *you*." The rage was on her now, and she could not help but lash out, somehow maintaining enough control to uphold her guise as Kari Goodgrave, the privileged niece of Bryce Lowell Josston. "I think you forget your place, Mirriam. You are a servant in the employ of Professor Josston, and I am Professor Josston's niece. I do not answer to you as the servants do. It is rather the other way around."

"You have a sickness of the mind. You—"

"I am not so sick that I don't know the place of servants." All of Karigan's frustrations about her situation, and all that had happened to her since arriving in this house, enflamed her words.

Mirriam's mouth worked but nothing came out for once. Obviously no one had ever stood up to her before, and Karigan could almost see the woman's brain trying to realign her understanding of her place in the world.

After a time, she smoothed her skirts and drew on a neutral expression. "Very well. Might I suggest Miss Goodgrave bathe and leave her dirty nightgown out so it might be laundered?"

"You know," Karigan said, as if she hadn't just heard Mirriam, "I believe I shall take a bath." It was like twisting the dagger, and strangely satisfying. "And I think this nightgown ought to be laundered."

Mirriam visibly fought with herself, trying to suppress a rebuke, but she swallowed and said in a constricted voice, "As you wish, Miss Goodgrave." And she left Karigan just standing there.

Karigan, too tired to feel victorious, wanted to flop in bed and catch up on sleep, but she could just as easily nap in the tub, which would also relieve her aching muscles. She plucked at her nightgown, soiled with dirt, sweat, blood, and maybe a bit of horse manure. At least her confrontation with Arhys at the stables would explain any dirt picked up from her time at the mill.

"What a day," she murmured, gazing at the morning light pouring into her room. And it had hardly even begun.

A long soak was just the thing, though Karigan's mind, too filled with all the revelations acquired since last night, would not allow her to doze off. The emperor was Lord Amberhill? Maybe it was because she was so tired, but the thought produced a latent chortle that sent ripples across the surface of the bath water. The revelation that followed, however, that Dr. Silk wished to acquire this dragonfly device, was far less shocking. But the idea that machines existed—machines that could drill through all the bedrock into the tombs—caused her to tremble, rippling the bath water once again.

And then there was Arhys. It was not the little girl being the heir that so staggered Karigan, but that she was directly descended from King Zachary and Estora. Queen Estora. She'd known the two would marry, and that offspring was inevitable. That was why royals married after all—to maintain the line of succession and the stability of the realm. No, these things were not unexpected, but the girl was a living, breathing extension of Zachary, a connection to Karigan's own life, a link to Zachary himself.

Painful as it was, she thought she would always love him, no matter that he had to marry Estora, but Karigan's feelings were tempered by her situation, that she now lived so many years—almost two centuries—after his death. Maybe she was better off in this time. Knowing he was entirely out of her reach, she would not be tempted to . . . she shook her head and splashed water on her face.

Even if she were back in her home time, even though she

knew and understood the reality, she would continue to love him in her own way. She would always fight to protect him, and if that meant helping to protect Arhys? There was no question that she'd do so with all her being.

With that, she sighed and rose from the now lukewarm water to see what the rest of the day held for her.

Apparently it held obsequious servants. Lorine awaited in Karigan's bed chamber and curtsied when she entered. Lorine had been quiet, respectful, and efficient before, but now there was a distance as she helped Karigan into her morning dress; no cheerful conversation, just silence. Fewer smiles. When she finished the stays on Karigan's dress, she backed away, curtsied again, and asked, "Would Miss Goodgrave like me to help her with her hair?"

There had never been any question before—Karigan had always welcomed Lorine's help with her hair, especially since her broken wrist made everything more complicated. She nodded and sat in her chair so Lorine could begin. Lorine had always seemed to enjoy brushing out Karigan's long hair, and then either braiding it, or pinning it up. Today, as the horsehair brush worked through her locks, she detected no enjoyment from Lorine, and shifted uncomfortably.

When her hair was done, she left her room to attend breakfast. Lorine followed at a polite, subservient distance. When she reached the dining room, the professor's butler, Grott, bowed to her and pulled out her chair.

"Good morning!" the professor called cheerfully to her from his end of the table. One would never know from his present demeanor the disaster that had almost struck earlier this morning.

Beside him, Cade nodded his greeting, quickly averting his gaze. The other students were absent.

"Good morning," she murmured.

Ham, eggs, sweet buns, and tea were brought to her by bowing servants. They even spread butter and strawberry preserves on her toast for her. The professor watched with a glint of amusement in his eyes.

Karigan had the dreadful feeling that whatever she'd said

to Mirriam, who was nowhere in sight, had trickled down through the rest of the staff. She barely tasted her food, regretting having lost her patience with the woman, yet she had enough of being endlessly badgered. At times Mirriam was worse than all four of her aunts together. Still, she feared losing possible allies among the staff, and she needed allies in this hostile world. She sighed heavily.

"That was certainly heartfelt," the professor said.

She looked up in surprise. The professor was already into his kauv and paper of news. Cade had slipped away unnoticed.

"A little preoccupied, my dear?"

"It's been a long day," she replied.

"Already?" He chuckled, then said, "You should know that it has been made clear to this household that only you, Luke, and Luke's lads are allowed to go anywhere near Raven. It's also been made clear that you will visit Raven as you wish and that no one is to discourage you from doing so."

Karigan wanted to cheer. At least something positive had come of this morning's events.

"Luke has, of course, been notified as well. You may trust him with . . . whatever may be required."

Did this mean Luke was aware of the professor's opposition to the emperor and his various secrets? She could not ask openly and could not come up with a discreet way of asking. In any case, she would proceed cautiously.

"How is Arhys?" she asked. She noted a slight quickening of interest from the servants.

"She has already endured one lecture from me this morning." A slight smile formed beneath his mustache. "She is confined to her room for the day so she can contemplate her actions of this morning."

Probably deepening her hatred for me, Karigan thought, but at least the staff knew that Arhys had been the one in the wrong, that she had misbehaved and endangered herself and that Karigan had not been hurting her but saving her life. Karigan did not want the entire household turned against her. Arhys was ostensibly one of them, and who was Karigan but some stranger who had arrived out of nowhere, now living in relative luxury beneath her "uncle's" roof?

"If there is anything I can do to help—" she began.

"Er, I think it best we all keep our distance from her for the time being."

With that the professor returned to his paper, and Karigan picked at what was left on her plate. No more words passed between them until he stood to leave. He paused by her chair on his way out to say, "What you did this morning, as I hear it from Luke and the lads, was very bravely done. You saved Arhys by putting yourself at great personal risk. I'm not sure if that ungrateful girl will ever understand, but I wholeheartedly thank you."

Humbled, Karigan could only stare at her plate.

"Go ahead and look in on Raven when you're done here. I'm sure you would enjoy that." He gave her a quick smile and was gone.

She did not wait. She left her napkin and unfinished breakfast on the table and strode through the house to the back door. No one stopped her. Mirriam did not rush to intercept her. Feeling a new surge of freedom, she hurried across the yard toward the stables. With no one to hinder her, maybe now she would find her way home.

RAVEN AND RYDER

 **W**hen Karigan stepped into the stables, Luke looked up from a length of harness he was oiling and grinned. "The professor left something in the tack room for you," he said.

Curious, Karigan lifted the hem of her skirts, careful not to drag them through dirt and manure to prevent further antagonizing Mirriam, and crossed over the threshold into the tack room. The scents of leather and saddle soap pervaded the small room. Buckles and bits gleamed in the light of a small dusty window. She caressed the seat of a well-used, but equally well-tended saddle mounted on a wooden horse. Despite all the changes wrought in this future, some things had not changed at all.

She discovered a package wrapped in brown paper and string on a small, worn table. A piece of paper with her initials was propped on it. She unfolded the paper and the note inside read: *Wear these for riding. You are my new part-time stable boy, by the name of Tam Ryder, retained to exercise Raven for my niece.* Karigan could almost hear the professor chuckling at the pun he made of her new alias. *Luke will tell you more if need be.* It was signed, *B.L.J.*

Karigan tore the package open and shirt, jacket, trousers, and a cap spilled out. She gazed at them in astonishment. They were worn and patched, and carefully mended, but clean.

"Professor asked if I might have some old clothes to lend," Luke said from the doorway, a bucket of water in his hand. "These belonged to my son, Luke, Jr. We used to call him Little Luke, but he's grown into a big strapping man. He's a farrier now in mid-town. Why don't you give me that note."

Karigan passed it to him, and he immediately submerged it in the bucket. "One quick way to destroy the evidence," Luke explained. "Clean the ink off. Now, if you like, you can change so we can see how Raven does under saddle, eh?"

He showed her a cedar cabinet where he stored his formal coachman's livery. In there, he explained, she could leave her dress and "female things" while riding. When not playing the part of Tam Ryder, she could leave her riding clothes in there.

"Got some boots, too." Luke indicated a pair of scuffed, dusty boots bent at the ankles, next to a pair of tall, black shiny boots that must be part of his livery. "Professor got your shoe measurements off the bills he received from the shoe-maker."

"You've both been busy," she remarked.

Luke just smiled. "The sooner you change, the sooner we can get to Raven."

"I have a bit of a problem," Karigan said.

Luke paused uncertainly.

"I need help with, er, my dress." She could not reach the stays in back.

Understanding dawned on Luke's face without a sign of embarrassment. "Oh, I help the missus deal with such things all the time, and my daughters when need be. I will help you if you wish it."

Karigan nodded and he closed the tack room door and proceeded to undo the stays on the back of Karigan's dress. He'd have to help her again when she changed back into it. The deed was accomplished with some grumbling from Luke about how much more complicated Karigan's dress was, and then he stepped out of the tack room so she could take care of the rest. It proved to be a battle with Karigan drowning in superfluous fabric, and she appreciated anew Lorine's assis-tance when dressing and undressing. She hung it all as neatly as possible in the cabinet beside Luke's livery and set to work turning herself into a boy.

When will I just be able to be me? she wondered.

The clothing was baggy, which was probably just as well to hide her feminine shape. Fortunately the trousers came with suspenders. The boots, in contrast, were well-broken in and fit perfectly. There was also a pair of gloves with flared cuffs, not unlike her old Rider gauntlets, which would help hide the cast on her wrist. She modified what Lorine had done with her hair, pinning it tighter to her head. When she finished, she put on the oversized cap and gazed at the mirror on the inside of the cabinet door. She determined that if no one was expecting to see a young woman, all they'd see was a scrawny boy. It was an effective disguise.

When she exited the tack room, Luke greeted her with an appraising look, then nodded his approval.

"Now, a couple things about Tam Ryder," he said. "Tam's of the Dregs, no folks, and he scrounges on the outskirts of the city. I discovered Tam had a way with horses one day in town and told the professor about it. The professor thought maybe Tam could manage his niece's new horse and pays him to exercise it. The professor, being of the generous sort he is, also thinks this will keep Tam out of the way of the Inspectors and out of trouble. Tam doesn't talk much. In fact, when we go out in public, you'll let me do all the talking, eh?"

Karigan nodded.

"Here in the stables your disguise is safe. But you are not to speak of this to anyone in the house. Understand?"

"Yes."

"Good then. I found a saddle that looks like it'll fit Raven. I suspect he's been used hard on the mouth so we'll try some different bits and see what suits."

Raven whickered in greeting at her approach. There was no disguising herself from him. She laughed and stroked his neck. He seemed none the worse from his encounter with Arhys earlier in the morning and stood calmly while she brushed him down, burnishing the gold and mahogany dapples on his rump. However, when she took the bridle Luke handed her, she could almost feel Raven's suspicious regard, how he tensed up, but he tolerated her sliding the bit into his mouth and buckling on the bridle. He chewed on the bit and shook his head, but did not rebel further.

"He wouldn't have let me or the boys do that," Luke mused. "He trusts you, maybe because you're not male, and it would've been males who mishandled him."

The professor must not have told Luke that Raven was truly a Green Rider horse nor Karigan a Green Rider, which would have explained why Raven was so receptive to her.

"Let's see how he likes the saddle," Luke said.

It was an ordinary saddle, larger and heavier than those used by Green Riders, who tried to minimize the weight their horses must carry while on message errands. She set pad and saddle on Raven's back as gently as she could, praising him softly the whole time. His flesh quivered, and his ears darted back and forth as he listened. He stamped his hoof quite profoundly when she pulled the girth around his belly. He shifted and snorted when she tightened it, and curved his neck around to get a good look at what she was doing.

Luke pressed some pieces of carrot in her hand. "Give him these. He's being good."

She did, and Raven daintily lipped them off her palm. The carrots took his mind off the tack.

"Let's take him out and see how the pair of you do," Luke said. He led them out of the stables into the paddock. The paddock was necessarily small because of the way the buildings in Mill City were packed together. It was a sign of the professor's status that he had space for one at all.

"Now the professor tells me you're an experienced rider," Luke said. "That true?"

She nodded.

"Good. Thought so. You seem competent around horses anyway. Not common in girls."

Karigan frowned but put the comment aside to focus on preparing to mount. She felt no small trepidation. She hadn't much direct experience with stallions—mostly geldings and mares—and there was no telling how Raven would react to a rider on his back no matter their bond. She and Luke had no way of knowing his exact origins or how long or deeply he'd been abused. It may be that he was entirely unrideable or that it would take a very long period of gentle retraining to make him accept a rider. Even the intelligent Green Rider horses were animals of instinct first. It might come down to how he'd been treated and trained by owners prior to Dr. Silk.

The last thing Karigan wanted to do was convey her nervousness to the stallion, but she knew mounting up could prove very painful in the end for her, and it was difficult to quell her anxiety.

"Leg up?" Luke asked.

She took a deep breath and nodded, and up she went, landing lightly in the saddle. Raven flicked his ears, then looked back at her as if to see her for himself. He didn't even flinch, and her nervousness faded, replaced by joy to be on horseback once again.

"Walk him around a bit," Luke said. "See how he does."

Karigan adjusted the stirrup leathers then squeezed him into a walk. There was a good deal of head tossing and prancing, a buck or two, which only increased when she attempted to correct him with the reins.

Luke scratched his head. "Let's change out the bit to something milder." As it turned out, they tried three different bits before Raven settled sufficiently. In the meantime, he got used to Karigan mounting and dismounting, and riding on his back.

With the new bit, he had quite a bounce to his gait, and he tossed his head though this time not in discomfort. Karigan had some trouble holding him in, and when she finally allowed him to trot, he arched his neck as if to show just how handsome he was.

Luke laughed in pleasure from his place at the fence. "He's a proud one, that one. Give us a canter, will you?"

From the way Raven responded to her commands, Karigan could tell he'd once been a well-trained saddle horse. He'd not always been abused.

"Responds better to a light touch than the whip," Luke observed. "Something those louts of Dr. Silk's never understood. There are all kinds in my work, and more than half of them ought not to go anywhere near the beasts."

Raven's canter was smooth, as comfortable as her Condor's had ever been. Thinking of her horse almost two centuries in the past brought on a wave of guilt. Was she betraying Condor by bonding with Raven? Eventually those concerns dissolved, replaced by the sheer joy of riding once again.

When she returned Raven to a walk, Luke said, "He's doing much better than I thought he would. In fact, I'm thinking he's doing good enough to take him out for a bit of a hack. What say we get out of the city so we can really take him through his paces?"

"Yes," Karigan said eagerly.

"All right, you stay out here and keep getting used to him while I tack up Gallant."

She circled Raven around the paddock at a posting trot, getting a feel for his surging muscles, his barely contained power. He kept trying to break into a canter and pranced and sidestepped every time she pulled him back. He was testing her will, thinking to master her. He broke into a canter again, and she sat back and adjusted the reins. He half-reared, and she began to wonder if taking him outside the paddock, much less into the city, was such a good idea. But the horse did need exercise and maybe that would help calm him.

When next Raven acted up, Karigan recalled Luke's words about using a light touch, and kept her commands firm but quiet. Combining the two was not necessarily easy and took subtle skill, but he responded with much less fuss. When she observed Luke watching by the gate, Gallant's reins in his hands, she brought Raven to a walk and then a halt.

"Normally I might suggest a riding crop and spurs as aids," he said, "but with him I don't think it's such a good idea."

It wasn't, Karigan agreed. Raven still had fresh whip lashes healing on his flanks, and she wanted to live, thank you very much.

Luke opened the gate for Karigan and Raven to exit the paddock. She felt the stallion bunch up, preparing for a bolt for freedom, but she managed to hold him in. He tossed his head in protest, almost yanking the reins out of her hands. The weakness of her right hand, due to her broken wrist, did not help.

Luke mounted up. Gallant was the professor's saddle horse, a handsome steel gray gelding of twelve years. According to Luke, the professor rarely rode anywhere, preferring his carriage, so Luke saw that the gelding received adequate exercise.

"Be interesting to see how Raven does on the city streets," Luke commented.

Interesting, right.

As if he'd heard her thought, Luke chuckled. "He'll be fine, and he likes Gallant. As long as Gallant stays calm, which he will, Raven will, too."

They followed the drive out onto the street, which was thankfully quiet. Raven engaged in looking here and there, ears flickering, hooves clopping along at a lively walk. He sidestepped at a passing carriage, and spooked once at who-knew-what, but Gallant, who was accustomed to the city, was a steadying presence, almost bored in demeanor.

As they departed the professor's neighborhood and entered busier streets, Luke served as Karigan's steadying influence, talking her through it when Raven acted up. Karigan considered herself a very good equestrian. Working with horses came naturally to her, but she knew Luke had years more experience, especially with stallions, which sometimes seemed like an entirely different species.

Riding Raven took all her concentration. It was tiring keeping up with him—she couldn't be a passive rider with him at all. The last time she'd been on horseback was the day she entered Blackveil, the spring equinox, and where were they now? Just a couple weeks from the summer solstice, Day of Aeryon? If the seasons of her past and this future ran parallel, as she believed, it had been quite some time since she'd been in the saddle. She was going to be sore. Very sore. Could feel it already.

"Hello there, Inspector," Luke said, suddenly projecting his voice ahead of them. "Yes, it is. The new horse the professor got his niece yesterday. A real handful."

Karigan only saw the Inspector and his mechanical Enforcer as blurs. Something about the Enforcer spooked Raven, or maybe Raven was just trying to prove Luke's words true, because he whirled on his haunches almost tossing her from the saddle. She held him best as she could, her cap slipping down over her eye. At least it didn't go flying off in front of the Inspector! She finally got Raven to settle, but foam lathered his neck and his ears lay flat.

Doesn't like the mechanical.

The Enforcer stood still on its metal spider legs, not making any noise or puffing steam. Its eyestalk didn't swivel about, though it was clearly planted on Raven. Perhaps the Inspector ordered it to be still, or it had intelligence enough not to spook the horse further.

"My new lad here, Tam, has a way with horses," Luke was saying. "The stallion will tolerate only him on his back."

Karigan pushed her cap back so she could see better. The Inspector was chuckling. "If young Tam there can stay on his back! I wish him luck."

"Best be on our way," Luke said. "Good day to you, Inspector."

"You, too, Luke."

Luke urged Gallant past the Inspector, Raven dancing close behind. She noticed a subtle easing of Luke's shoulders. She hadn't noticed him being tense around the Inspector, but then she'd been too busy trying to maintain her seat.

As she thought about it, it was probably a good thing she'd been too busy, or else she would have worried about being discovered. What if the cap had flown off? Perhaps they could pass her off as the professor's mad niece going out for a ride, but in disguise so she did not break any social codes of conduct. Maybe that would work, or maybe the Inspector would have grown suspicious and decided on investigating further. In either case, it would have invited more scrutiny than she or the professor desired.

What would happen, she wondered, if imperial officials did, indeed, find out who she really was? She couldn't even appeal to Lord Amberhill because he was "asleep" or whatever, and the professor had shown that Amberhill, as emperor, had grown cruel and unlikely to help her. As a servant of King Zachary from the past, she doubted she'd be treated with much mercy or fairness. No, she did not wish to invite further scrutiny.

PERCUSSION AND POWDER

At Canal Street, Luke reined Gallant in the opposite direction than the professor had taken the day before, away from the Old City. The power canal and rows of mill buildings stretched in this direction as well. They passed a wagon full of cotton bales and a pair of well-dressed men chatting on a bridge that spanned the canal and led to one of the mills.

Karigan tried to imagine again all the industry that must take place in the mill that she could not see with the sun reflecting off the windows. And then the midday bell rang. Raven acted predictably by attempting to bolt. This time it took Luke's help to hold him back.

"Will you settle?" she demanded of Raven.

Raven canted his head as if considering, then shook it. But he settled.

Karigan sighed in relief. When the bells finished tolling and the last tone faded away, she had a moment or more to observe the doors of the nearest mill complex opening. Men with cudgels and whips exited, followed by workers in worn garments with ankles shackled. They shuffled out of the mills, chain links scraping the paving stones, jingling almost musically. The mill slaves were male and female. Many were children, few were old. Many looked Sacoridian, others had the skin tones and features of other nations: Hura-desh, the Under Kingdoms, the Cloud Islands, and even the desert folk of the Unclaimed Territories. Many peoples of many origins had come under the empire's rule, and the empire had not discriminated over who it forced to serve.

"Hurry up!" one of the guards yelled at the slaves. "If ya want yer midday rations, you'll hurry up."

The slaves did not alter their pace. Most just watched their feet to avoid stumbling over the shackles. Some bent double with harsh coughing.

"The brown lung," Luke muttered, following her gaze. "From breathing all the cotton dust."

A guard prodded his group of slaves along none too gently with his cudgel. A boy fell to his knees, looked too tired to stand again. The guard grabbed him by the hair and hauled him to his feet, shouting worse obscenities at him than Karigan had ever heard on the docks of Corsa Harbor.

Karigan touched the sleeve of the jacket she wore. It was used and faded, yes, but was well-made. She thought about how its cloth, and that of all the fine dresses she wore as Kari Goodgrave, were made by the labor of slaves. Slaves dressed in rags. As the line of workers made its way across the canal bridge to the street, one of the guards waved his whip threateningly, causing Raven to sidestep and snort.

"Best that we move on," Luke said. "They're making Raven nervous, and you don't need to see this."

Karigan thought she did. She did not want to see it, but she had to witness what the emperor, Xandis Pierce Amberhill, had wrought, what he'd done to his people, and those of other nations. She couldn't look away from the gaunt faces, misery etched in their expressions, the children looking as defeated as the adults. No, they were not children. The youth had been worked and beaten out of them. They would not know joy or play. But Luke urged Gallant into a trot, and Raven was so eager to follow he burst into a canter. Karigan had no choice but to look away and contend with the stallion.

They passed only one more mill complex, and it was the same scene, with hundreds of exhausted, shackled slaves shambling along the street like some parody of a parade. This was the future, Karigan thought, that she had to change.

The canal dog-legged to the south and the hooves of the horses thudded across a bridge that spanned the dark, quiet water. Only subtle ripples revealed that it flowed with any current. Karigan felt herself ease, breathe more freely, as they left the mills and slaves behind. Luke kept them at a trot, Gallant's tail swishing as though they were finally getting down to business.

The city extended well beyond the canal, breaking up into neighborhoods of small houses and tenements. It was a rather sorry looking area with smashed windows, overgrown gardens, and broken fences. Trash rotted in the street. It was not the tidy, well-kept neighborhood the professor lived in.

"I don't linger in this quarter," Luke told her. "Most folk here aren't bad, but the few who are won't hesitate to murder you for a pair of boots."

And so they trotted on, crossing another bridge over the river, the water here glimmering with a swift current. Once they were across, space opened up between buildings, and eventually habitation became sparse enough that trees grew freely, and the people had small plots of land to farm.

Eventually Luke slowed Gallant to a walk and Karigan did likewise with Raven. While still energetic and eager, the stallion had calmed down quite a bit.

Karigan tried to place the location in the context of her own time, but the land was too changed. They were well east of the city now, that much she knew. "Where are we?" she asked.

"Well, I like to take Gallant out to the Big Mounds where there is a lot of open space," he said. "Good for riding, a breather from the city."

The *Scangly Mounds,* she thought with a thrill. At least this one familiar landmark remained.

But when they reached the mounds, several had been flattened—mined for gravel—and others that Luke pointed out, had been mined for artifacts by archeologists who found only . . . gravel. Karigan used to ride Condor to the Scangly Mounds when she needed to get away from the castle. She was dismayed by the destruction. But even their remnants lent her some comfort, another link to the past, and several of the mounds still stood. She rode Raven up the biggest, which appeared to be more a granite outcrop than a mound. Scrub alder and grasses grew out of its crannies, and lichens studded the nubbly rock. She gazed at the panorama that surrounded her. While the landscape was familiar, something . . . something beyond its current condition was out of place. The mounds couldn't have moved, could they? She scratched her head, puzzled. Maybe she wasn't remembering correctly, or perhaps the forces that had created a river where Sacor City once stood had also changed the topography.

From this vantage, she also had an excellent view of the Old City in the distance. In the past, she used to look back and see the castle rising high and proud over Sacor City. Now it looked like no more than a rocky mount. Only a good spy-glass would allow her to see the details of the ruins, and per-haps that was for the best. Smoky plumes rose from beneath the mount, from Mill City, spreading a grayish-brown haze across the view. A dirty sky—she could never have imagined it. All was quiet here, except for crows that squawked and flew-hopped from brush and scrub.

Luke reined Gallant up beside her. "Grand view, isn't it? Sometimes I try to picture what it looked like in the past when there was a castle up there. A shame everything was destroyed. It must have been amazing."

"It was," Karigan murmured. Then hastily added, "I mean, yes, it must have been."

Luke raised an eyebrow and gave her a sidelong glance. "It leaves a strong impression, those ruins. Growing up be-neath them, I had nightmares. Thought the ghosts of the old ones, the people who lived up there, were going to come down and do terrible things to me. But I was just a boy then. Some will swear there are still ghosts, but I've never seen 'em." They sat in silence for a while, then Luke stood in his stirrups and shielded his eyes from the sun as he gazed into the distance. "If I'm not mistaken, that's Mr. Harlowe coming along. Pro-fessor said he might join us out here."

Cade? She looked where Luke pointed and saw a man driving a mule cart along a dirt track that bypassed the mounds. It could certainly be Cade, but she wasn't sure. He turned off the track and guided the mule toward the mounds.

"Shall we go down to meet him?" Luke asked. Without waiting for an answer, he reined Gallant down the slope of the outcrop. Karigan shrugged and followed.

It turned out to be Cade Harlowe after all, and he took the cart into the mounds as far as was possible without losing a wheel. He hopped off the cart and greeted them, giving Karigan an odd look.

"Afternoon, Miss Goodgrave," he said, "or is it Tam?"

"Kari—" She almost gave her full name, but recalling that Luke did not seem to know everything about her secrets, she stopped just in time. "Just call me Kari for now."

Cade gazed hard at her, and she guessed at what he was thinking—that it was not appropriate to call her by her first name and that her dressing like a boy was extremely improper. He shook his head.

"What are you doing out here?" she asked, thinking this could not be a coincidence.

"Officially? I have an imperial permit to do some test digs. Not that the mounds have not been entirely sifted through by other archeologists."

"Unofficially?"

"Unofficially I am here to show you how to use a gun."

This time it was Luke who frowned and shifted uncomfortably in his saddle. "The professor is allowing this?"

"Yes," Cade replied. "We come out here for target practice sometimes. Civilians aren't supposed to own guns," he told Karigan, "though Inspectors are more lenient with the Preferred families. In any case, we shouldn't be heard out here."

"Heard?"

"Yes. Guns are loud."

Karigan thought it silly that a weapon should be noisy. There was no stealth in noise as there was with an arrow or a dagger.

"I'll go graze the horses and keep watch then," Luke said warily. "No point in inviting trouble."

Karigan dismounted Raven, who was behaving admirably, and handed the reins over to Luke. He rode away, Raven trotting alongside him.

"How much does Luke know? About me?" she asked Cade.

"He knows that the professor is a member of the opposition and holds you in high regard. Luke may have his own suspicions about whether or not you are really the niece of

Bryce Lowell Josston. Though he is loyal, he has not been informed of your true background, that you were a Green Rider from long ago."

"Am."

Cade looked at her quizzically. "Am?"

"I am a Green Rider. Not was."

Cade dismissed her words with a curt nod and began unloading some bales of hay from the mule cart, as well as a target printed on cloth, much like archers used for practice.

She helped him place the bales in front of one of the mounds and drape the target over them. His deference from last night was replaced by his usual stoic and efficient self. They returned to his cart, where he lifted a wooden box out from a false bottom in the cart's floor. Inside the box, nestled in red velvet, lay a gun and a variety of small tools. Karigan blinked hard trying to see it. The metal glared in her eyes, making them water and blur. It was just like when she tried to look at the professor's gun last night. She turned her head so she could see it on the edge of her vision. This was better but not by much. The metal was blued steel, inscribed with some intricate image she could not make out. The wooden handle was stained in deep blue.

"This is a Cobalt-Masters revolver," Cade said, sounding very instructorial. "It's the firearm of choice for mounted units and Inspectors, only theirs aren't so fancy. This one was *acquired* from an Adherent."

Karigan wondered who "acquired" it and how, but Cade didn't say and went on to describe, instead, the parts of the weapon. Trying to see it all was bringing on a headache, or maybe it was her lack of sleep getting to her. She tried to listen closely knowing this was important information to take back to her own time, but there was a buzzing, like a whole hive of hornets in her ears, that competed with Cade's words. She could not concentrate, and only heard bits and pieces about caliber and percussion and powder.

Then he broke the gun in half. She squinted. No, not broken. The device opened on hinges.

"The cartridges breech load," he explained.

From a satchel at his waist, Cade withdrew brass cylinders

and started pushing them into holes in the halved gun. Karigan closed her eyes to cut the glare and relieve the headache. It helped, but she still couldn't hear Cade clearly until he asked. "Is something wrong?"

She opened her eyes and made a point of looking at his face and not the gun. "Keep going. I'm fine."

He hesitated, then nodded. "I need to make sure you are listening. These weapons can be dangerous if misused."

"Weapons are supposed to be dangerous," she said.

"Which only accentuates my point." He snapped the two halves of the gun back together. She heard it and saw his movement more than witnessed the two pieces joining. "I am going to demonstrate the firing of the Cobalt. Here is how you sight the target."

His words once again competed with the hive of hornets exploding in her ears. He raised the weapon, arm outstretched with elbow slightly bent. She watched his face and not the Cobalt, how his brow furrowed and eyes squinted at the target, his head slightly tilted. His intensity reminded her of an archer.

"I'm exceptionally good at fifteen yards," he said, "and proficient at twenty-five. Long-arms are more accurate at greater distances. Now I cock the hammer like this. The trigger will release it and the percussion will . . ."

His words were drowned by the buzzing. His gaze never left the target. Karigan's gaze never left his face. Thunder blasted beside her and nearly knocked her off her feet. She cried out, heart pounding wildly.

Cade lowered the gun, blue smoke drifting from the tip of it. Slowly he turned his gaze to her. "Told you it was loud."

This time it wasn't the buzzing that muffled her ears, but the shock of the blast. She shook her head trying to clear it.

"What is the advantage of the noise?" she demanded. "To deafen your comrades?"

"Can't help the noise, but the reach and force of the weapon is its value. In your day, such a weapon would pierce the stoutest armor better than any arrow. Come see."

He strode toward the target, and she hurried after him. She saw a hole in the center circle.

"Your gun did this?"

"Haven't you been listening?"

Even though she'd had such a hard time hearing and observing his demonstration, she put it together that the gun had sent a small projectile through the target. She looked beneath the target and saw that the projectile had traveled through the bales of hay and into the mound behind. If only she could take knowledge of such weaponry home with her!

It's a concussive, she suddenly thought. *Or something like.* The Arcosian Empire had used weapons called concussives in its attempt to conquer the New Lands. Did the mechanicals and guns of this time represent a natural progression of invention over the generations, or had Amberhill somehow acquired the information to create such tools from some unknown documentation of Arcosian engineering?

She kicked her heel at the dirt around the hole where the projectile had entered the mound, and found it not too deeply buried. She tried to pick it up, the small chunk of lead, but it scorched her fingers.

"Ow!"

"Bullet still warm, eh?" Cade asked, a bit of a smile on his lips. Karigan scowled. He started to walk away, and then paused. "Want to give it a try?"

Karigan nodded, though she did not know how it would go with her unable to see the gun or hear Cade's instructions.

"We'll start at ten yards," he said.

He paused some distance from the target and waited for her. She joined him, fingers still stinging. When he passed her the gun, she did not look at it. Just held her hand out to receive it. When the metal touched her palm, it seared, burning all the way up her arm, lightning flashing through her head. She screamed, the ground rushing toward her, the gun tumbling from her hand.

THE WILL OF THE GODS

Karigan curled into a fetal position when she hit the ground. She groaned. Her outstretched hand felt like it was on fire.

"Miss Goodgrave?" Cade patted her cheek and alternately sprinkled water from a canteen on her face.

"My hand!" she shouted. "Pour it on my hand!"

"It's burned red," he murmured.

She sighed as cool water flowed over burning flesh. The sensation eased, as did the throbbing in her head. When the canteen was emptied, Cade helped prop her into a sitting position.

"What happened?" he asked anxiously.

"Not sure. The gods. I don't think they want me to know about guns." She gazed at her hand to see the angry red color quickly fading, along with the pain, to a more normal shade.

"What? What do you mean the gods?"

"What else could it be?" It had been the shattering of the looking mask that had propelled her into the universe, but it was Westrion, god of death who had delivered her to this time. She could only conclude that the gods were blocking her and did not want her to bring the knowledge of such powerful weapons back home with her. In one way, it was a hopeful premise, because maybe they expected her to find a way home. In another, it was unfortunate they did not wish Sacoridia to obtain an advantage in weaponry over its enemies.

"We were forced to give up the gods over a century ago," Cade said. "It was a very bloody episode in our more recent history. We were forced to worship the emperor and his machines."

Perhaps that was the crux of it, the gods did not want their people on Earth rejecting them for machines. Yet, hadn't she touched other marvels of this time, such as the plumbing and lighting? She'd seen machines, or at least pieces of them, in the professor's mill, and the ominous mechanicals of the Inspectors. So far she'd experienced no ill effects from them. What was the difference?

Cade settled down beside her with the Cobalt in his lap. She did not look directly at it as he emptied the unused cartridges and began to clean it. "Whatever it is that is causing your, uh, problem," he said, "maybe it's for the best. Guns, well, they can cause harm in the wrong hands. Even be turned against the user." His head was bent down as he worked. "It is also said that guns and machines have hastened the loss of etherea from the world."

She glanced at her hand. It was now back to its natural color, no blistering, no sign of injury. If what Cade said was true, maybe it was for the best she did not take the knowledge of firearms home. She had the general gist of what they did but not the how. And come to think of it, she did not have the "how" of the plumbing or phosphorene lighting, either. What would happen if she tried to understand how *they* worked?

As for guns, that knowledge seemed to be particularly forbidden to her since she could barely even look at them. She clenched her hand closed. What would have happened had she held onto the gun and not dropped it? Could she have overcome the will of the gods or would they have destroyed her? She rather thought the latter.

"I must admit I was very sure I knew the way the world worked," Cade said. He was now oiling the moving parts of the gun, suffusing the air with a heavy, metallic scent. "And then you arrived. I thought there was no place for magic in this world, but how else could someone from the past come to be here? I am learning there is much more to the world than can be plainly seen."

Karigan knew the truth of that. Hadn't she seen the ghost of Yates Cardell that very morning? She'd dealt with ghosts since becoming a Rider, but how they existed, why they appeared to *her*, remained a mystery.

The thud of hooves announced the return of Luke. Gallant and Raven were mildly damp with sweat, revealing they'd had some exercise.

"Heard only one shot," Luke said, "then nothing. That all you're doing today?"

Cade placed the Cobalt in its velvet lined box and closed it. "It is."

Luke hitched the horses to the back of the cart, and the three of them disassembled the target. Cade's pouch of cartridges, and the box with the Cobalt in it, were concealed in the false bottom of the cart, along with the actual target. Cade slid the cover of the false bottom in place, which was in turn concealed by the bales of hay. Then he pushed aside a variety of digging tools and removed a picnic basket.

"I took the liberty of bringing along a midday meal," he said.

Karigan, Luke, and Cade lounged on a blanket to eat the simple meal of cold meats, cheese, and bread, and sip cool tea sweetened with honey. They spoke little, and when they finished, Cade collected the remnants into his basket. "I must return to the city."

When Luke went to the horses, Cade turned to Karigan and said, "The professor told me all about what you did for Arhys this morning. Thank you. She can be trying at times, but she is worth protecting, even if it means protecting her from herself."

Worth protecting. It was an odd way of putting it. Did Cade see himself primarily as Arhys' protector? And then it dawned on her: That was precisely what he was.

"You're her Weapon," she whispered.

"Apparently not a very good one."

Karigan was pleased she had guessed right and that he didn't bother to deny it.

"I wasn't even there to save her this morning," Cade continued, "and you have shown me how deficient my fighting skills are."

"But not with the gun."

"No, not with the gun."

And that was the end of their exchange. Cade climbed up into the driver's seat of the cart and wished them a good day before whistling his mule on. As Karigan watched him guide the cart along the bumpy ground, she thought a child like Arhys needed more than one Weapon to keep an eye on her. Several more.

Luke handed her Raven's reins. "I think this one is ready for a nice strenuous workout. I've but warmed him up."

Karigan mounted. Riding Raven, truly riding him, was a dream. He was tireless, moving effortlessly between gaits, attentive to her commands. Someone had trained him well before he came into Silk's hands. They ran up and down the mounds as once she had done with Condor, Raven as smooth as a sloop cutting through calm waters. For a while she forgot about being in a different time, and the oddness of not being able to look at a gun, much less handle it.

Though Raven showed no signs of tiring, she slowed him to a walk and joined Luke and Gallant near where they'd picnicked.

"Looks like you're getting some good paces out of him," Luke said.

"He's wonderful."

"Well, sorry to say, but we best head back."

Karigan wondered if Raven detected her disappointment because he pulled on the reins and turned as if he wanted to run up and over the nearest mound. She corrected him. "Sorry, boy, but we'll do this again."

"Of course you will," Luke said cheerfully, "but it wouldn't do to keep Miss Goodgrave out all day. Her absence might become too noticeable."

As they rode away from the Scangly Mounds, Karigan took one more glance toward where the castle once stood in the distance. The smoke and haze had settled more heavily over the Old City than when she'd first viewed it. The clouds looked to suffocate all that was left. She turned her gaze away with a sigh that carried all the tiredness and sorrow she felt, and watched the path ahead.

The haze hovered over the mount like a poisonous fog. It shortened Lhean's breath and burned his eyes. From its rim, he dropped down into his crevice and sat with his back against compressed rock and debris, a dim shaft of light falling on him. He closed his eyes, wondering why the people here allowed themselves to be exposed to such filth. He could only guess that they did not care they were shortening their already short, mortal lives.

He'd tried leaving the mount to search for the Galadheon, whom he sensed to be somewhere down in the city. He'd gone at night and only got as far as the river. The aura of misery, of cold brick and machine, had been too much for him, and he retreated to the remains of the Old City, back into hiding where he could consider his next move.

And now, another day was passing. He'd die here in these ruins just as surely as he would in the city below. His armor had turned a shade of gray, and not just from dirt. It had begun to flake and it ached. Ached all over his body. How long before it perished, and he must shed it? The armor mirrored his overall well-being. If he could not get home, or at least get off this mount and find proper nourishment, he too would perish, cease to exist.

He gathered a few edible wild herbs and roots growing among the ruins, but they were sparse and stunted, poisoned by the same air and water as he himself, and it was not enough to sustain him. He had one precious nugget of chocolate left in his pack. The maker of the chocolate called the variety Dragon Droppings. Eating it would revive Lhean's spirit and vitality for a while, but he'd been reserving it for a time of dire need. As he weakened, he realized the need was nearly upon him. There would be a point after which even chocolate would not aid him.

He cracked his eyes open to gaze at the gray sky drifting past the craggy rim of his hiding place. If he ate the chocolate, he would have to take advantage of its benefits and enter the city to find the Galadheon. She was no Eletian, but she was his only link to home, and perhaps between the two of them they could find a way back. After all, it was the Galadheon who caused them to be here, wasn't it? She who could cross thresholds . . .

He would do it under cover of darkness, of course. During

the day the mount was too busy with slaves and their masters making the road and erecting a wood-framed structure at the summit. Fortunately his excellent sense of hearing had not deserted him, and even now he heard voices in conversation. They were not very close, and he was not in any present danger of being discovered.

"I'm telling ya," one man said, "it's got some of the slaves spooked, and their overseers, too."

"These ruins are full of ghost stories," a second man said.

"Yeah, but it's slowin' down work and making the boss none too happy. They say they see a figure all in white standing there, then the next moment it's gone."

Lhean frowned. Though he'd been careful in his scouting, he must have been seen. How else could he find out what was happening in the world if he did not scout? Just as well he was mistaken for a ghost—these ruins lent themselves to mortal superstitions very well.

The second man laughed. "Tell you what. If we see a ghost, I'll shoot it, and then we'll see whether or not it bleeds. Eh?"

The rest of the conversation faded as the two men moved out of range. Lhean would have to be more careful than ever to avoid discovery. The men he saw on the mount—men other than the poor slaves—carried weapons. Not bows and arrows, or swords, but devices that reeked of death and made him almost ill to look at. He'd seen them use the weapons, taking aim at the occasional hare or rodent. He'd covered his ears at the terrible noise they made, his eyes stinging from the quick gouts of flame that burst from the devices. The men usually missed their targets, but Lhean had seen how forceful the weapons were, how deadly they could be. He could be taken down long before he ever got within sword's length of one of these shooters.

He'd heard of "concussives" used in the days of Mornhavon the Black, weapons that had helped defeat Argenthyne. What he saw of these shooting weapons sounded like the concussives of old. Had time bent round on itself?

He shook himself, trying to replace the images of these weapons, this place, by recalling memories of home, of Eletia, spring green and rattling aspen leaves, the slender white boughs of birches entwining overhead; of the music of water flowing through a lush glen and the myriad voices of song-birds. He faded into the memories, whispering a song of home, the ruins and gray air vanishing from waking thought.

The stars of Avrath, moon to rise, guide me, guide me home, he sang in his own tongue, *for I am a mariner lost, a mariner lost on the misty sea . . .*

AN INVITATION

On the ride home, Raven grew more skittish the closer they got to the city, but Karigan now knew what to expect, and so they reached the professor's stables without incident. Upon their arrival, however, Luke received a message from one of his lads.

"You'd best get changed," he told Karigan. "The boys will take care of Raven. You've got a guest."

"A guest?"

Luke nodded. "Apparently someone of importance. It was conveyed that I should urge you to hurry."

The boys provided her a bucket of clean water and a towel to wash the dust off herself in the tack room. Luke once again assisted her with her dress and stashed her boy clothes in the big cabinet. She gave herself a look in the mirror and spared a couple minutes to primp her hair, which had been mashed down by the cap, and to ensure that everything was in its proper place. Satisfied, she rushed across the yard and through the back door of the house. Mirriam nearly pounced on her.

"Finally! You've a guest waiting on you. He has been visiting with the professor this last half hour."

"Who?" Karigan asked, but she could guess. She'd met only one other person outside the immediate household.

Mirriam did not answer but thrust a hat and veil on Karigan's head and ushered her down the corridor as if herding baby ducklings. When they reached the parlor, Karigan paused in the doorway and smoothed her skirts.

"It was the most amazing discovery of eating utensils

ever," the professor said with enthusiasm to the guest, a teacup and saucer balanced on his knee. "Whole place settings!"

With a certain amount of unease, Karigan saw she had guessed right. Her visitor was none other than Dr. Ezra Stirling Silk, who looked politely bored as the professor regaled him about each pewter fork, knife, and spoon found at his current dig site. A hulking man, well-dressed, stood against the wall behind Silk. A servant, or a bodyguard, or both.

Mirriam discreetly cleared her throat. "Sir, Miss Goodgrave."

"There you are, my dear," the professor said. Both men rose at Karigan's entrance, but before Silk could take her hand again to bow over it, the professor guided her over to the sofa so she could sit next to him. In this case, she did not mind him being overprotective.

When all were seated, the professor poured her a tea. It was less hot than she liked, and bitter, indicating it had been steeping for a while. She glanced over the rim of her cup at Dr. Silk. Even inside he wore his dark specs. Did he wear them as an affectation, or did he have some disease of the eyes?

"I am to understand that you are quite taken with Samson. I mean, Raven." Dr. Silk smiled.

"She can't bear to be apart from him," the professor said. "Must run in the family. I had a cousin with a great affection for animals, too. He took in strays, fed birds from his hands, trained dogs. He was a Goodgrave as well. In any case, we're trying a lad named Tam to exercise Raven. The two seem to get on well, and he has my niece's approval, doesn't he my dear?"

Karigan played along and nodded.

"A high-tempered stallion needs his exercise," Dr. Silk said amiably. "I hope your lad works out."

"Luke speaks highly of him," the professor said.

Karigan focused on her tea, sipping beneath her veil, hoping the two men would simply carry on the conversation without her, but it was not to be so. Dr. Silk turned his gaze on her, and she caught her twin reflections in the lenses of his specs.

"I am grateful for your uncle's swift payment—the first half—for Raven, but I am now here for the second half." He gestured, and his servant removed an envelope from an inner pocket of his coat. He crossed the room in three strides and presented it to Karigan. The fine paper and flowing ink made it look suspiciously like an invitation. "Normally I'd send Mr. Howser around with invitations, but I was so charmed to meet you yesterday, Miss Goodgrave, and anxious to hear how you were getting on with the horse, that I decided I must come myself."

Mr. Howser resumed his station behind Dr. Silk. Karigan glanced at the professor, who did not look very happy.

"Now, now, Bryce," Dr. Silk said. It was odd to hear anyone call the professor by his first name. "Try not to look so glum. It's a party, not an inquisition, and you haven't been to one of my affairs in, oh, *years,* and I can guarantee this one will be very interesting. But now that I've made my delivery, duty calls and I must be off."

Dr. Silk rose and bowed in Karigan's direction. "I look forward to seeing you again very soon, Miss Goodgrave."

While the professor saw Dr. Silk and his attendant out the door, Karigan flipped the veil out of her face and cracked the gold wax seal on the invitation. She and a companion, it said, were invited to an evening of dinner and entertainments hosted by the Honorable Dr. Ezra Stirling Silk. The party was to be the next week at seven hour, but no location was listed—it was intended as a surprise. A carriage would come promptly on the evening to deliver her and her companion to the affair.

When the professor rejoined her, she passed him the invitation.

He scowled as he read it. "I don't like it," he told her. "I don't like that he does not disclose the location or that we cannot use our own carriage."

Karigan agreed that it sounded all very mysterious. "Wouldn't all his guests have to do the same?"

"If there are others."

"You suspect a trap?"

The professor stroked his mustache, deep in thought. "It

does not seem subtle enough for Silk. Still, there is no way I am going to trust him. I'll make some careful inquiries to see if anyone else has been invited, and whom, but I'm rather disposed to decline the invitation."

"We can't decline," Karigan said. "It's part payment for Raven."

"I know, I know. I'll see what I can find out, but no matter how innocuous a dinner party may seem, Silk's motives never are."

Karigan returned to her bed chamber with nothing to do, and she welcomed the respite. Everything that had happened, all the revelations over the last twenty-four hours, had left her numb. She tossed her hat and veil aside, sprawled on her bed, and stared at the ceiling. She worked everything through her mind once more: Arhys, Amberhill . . . If—*when*—she returned home, the first thing she'd tell King Zachary about was Amberhill. He must not trust his cousin.

She wondered about the ghost of Yates. She wondered why he had appeared to her. She'd had enough experience with ghosts to know that they did not appear without reason. What would compel him to come across time and the veil of death to her?

If there was one facet of her day that made her smile, it was learning about Cade's aspirations to be Arhys' Weapon. He was beginning to show depths that she had not expected, and she looked forward to their next training session. Still, all that she had learned since she'd been in this time did nothing to reveal the purpose of the gods. Why was she here? Maybe there was no purpose, maybe she was arbitrarily deposited here, but she did not think so. There was too much connecting to the past, *her* past, for it to be a coincidence.

Karigan could only ponder these things over the following days, which were, essentially, quiet and left her to brooding. She saw little of the professor or Cade and received no invitations to join them in the old mill. She spent hours with Raven, grooming him and tending the healing lash wounds on his hide. The air was too noxious, Luke explained, for even the horses to go for a run. And it was true—a cloud had settled over the city, and she was not at all disposed to open the window in her room. The sulfurous air made her cough and her eyes water. Cloudy, the cat, had not appeared at her window for a visit anyway.

Some of her time was taken up by a visit from Mistress Ilsa dela Enfande and her coterie, there to create an evening gown for her attendance at Dr. Silk's dinner party.

"It shall be my latest, most daring design," Mistress dela Enfande declared. "Dr. Silk is known for inviting only the most fashionable of the Preferred to his engagements."

Karigan could only sigh. She had no choice in the matter so she gave in to her fate, as well as to the capable talents of Mistress dela Enfande.

She managed to avoid Arhys for the most part, although during the assault of Mistress dela Enfande's assistants and their measuring tapes, she caught Arhys peering through her cracked door, scowling. Likewise Mirriam kept her distance and remained aloof. It was mostly Lorine who attended Karigan, and she'd gone from formal back to her former quiet but friendly self.

One afternoon while Karigan sat by her window, boredly gazing at another day's vaporous clouds—hazing even the wall of the neighboring house—Lorine came in with clean linens, which she proceeded to store in the wardrobe.

"How often is it like this?" Karigan asked. Unable to ride, unable to do much of anything, she felt like a landlocked sailor in a storm.

"We once had a full month of it that I can remember," Lorine said thoughtfully, a folded sheet forgotten in her arms. "That was when I was still . . ." She trailed off, gazing into space.

"You were still what?" Karigan asked quietly.

"I was still a slave in the mill. The air in the mills can be bad enough with all the cotton fibers flying about, but the smoky days made everything worse. The weak among us would sicken, even die. We still had to work, you see, no matter what the air was like. But that was just one of a thousand hazards in the mill."

And here Karigan had been going mad confined to the indoors to avoid the bad air. "I'm sorry," she said.

Lorine shrugged. "For what? You did not make slavery."

Karigan had not made slavery, but she'd done nothing to stop it either. It was easy to forget, in the comfort of the professor's house, how hard others labored. "Do all the mills use slaves to do the work?"

"As far as I know, miss. I heard that many years ago there were small shops that made cloth goods, owned and run by free folk, but they couldn't compete with the big mills that came in, so they went out of business."

Lorine finished what she was doing and closed the wardrobe doors. She prepared to leave, but Karigan called her back.

"Yes, miss?"

"How was it you came to work for the prof—er, my uncle? You don't have to answer if you don't want," she added hastily.

"It's all right," Lorine replied. "I don't mind telling you." She cleared her throat before continuing. "I—I'd had an accident at the mill." She touched the ever-present scarf covering her hair. "I wore my hair back, always, but it didn't always stay tied. A bunch of it got caught up in the belting attached to one of the looms I tended. Tore out a large piece of my scalp."

At Karigan's sharp intake of breath, Lorine said, "I'm sorry, miss. It's indelicate of me. I shouldn't have said anything."

"Please, don't stop. I'm sorry—you must have suffered terribly."

"The mill I belonged to, if you could not work, you were disposed of one way or another, sold off, or thrown out like garbage. I lost a lot of blood and was insensible. They left me out to die among the day's corpses, to be picked up later by the rubbish cart. I guess my master did not want to waste money or time on my healing."

Karigan shuddered, not able to even imagine what Lorine must have gone through as a slave in such conditions.

"I don't know what chance brought the professor to that spot on that day," Lorine continued, "but he found me. It's all hazy to me, a little dreamlike, but he took me from there and brought me here. I was tended till I healed, and then he presented me with legal papers declaring me a free and sovereign citizen of the empire. I couldn't read them, of course. I also don't know what it cost him to buy those papers, but I know it wasn't just a little." A smile flickered at distant memory. "I begged him to let me serve him. Despite the papers, I thought I'd be sent back to the mills or sold off, but he just laughed and said that if I stayed, that we'd have to work out an agreeable wage. Not only did he save my life and bring me into his household, but he paid me. I live in luxury, miss! I am so happy here. To top everything off, he and Mr. Harlowe have taught me to read and write, too. I can read my own papers, now."

Although Karigan had glimpsed slaves out on Mill City's streets, Lorine's story brought another dimension to it, made it all too real. "There should be no slavery," she said.

"It is the way that it is," Lorine replied with a shrug. "Some come to it from family that've been enslaved for generations, as I did. When the emperor came, he made slaves of his enemies. It has been this way always."

No, Karigan thought, it had not always been so. But much of the empire's populace would not know there was any history prior to the emperor.

"You have a kind heart," Lorine said, "but it is safest not to speak those things aloud. People who are against slavery and speak of it, well, they tend to disappear."

On that sober note, Lorine left Karigan to her ruminations. As she watched the smoky air waft outside her window, she thought about what Lorine had said about the emperor enslaving his enemies after his rise to power. She wondered about her friends, so many who must have died in the war with Second Empire, and then during the destruction of Sacor City. If any had survived, they may have been enslaved. What had become of her father and aunts? The aftermath of the war and all the destruction must have been tumultuous. People must have known great fear.

She leaned her head against the window frame. Did she really wish to know what had become of her friends? Of her family?

It was too painful to contemplate, so she tried to dash those thoughts with a renewed determination to get home and prevent any of this from happening in the first place.

SEEING CONDOR

It wasn't until the following day that Karigan was invited to return to the old Josston mill, although this time it was Cade who asked and not the professor. It was during breakfast, and the professor was busily going over schedules and duties with his students, all except for Cade who, it appeared, was senior in ranking to the others. Instead Cade finished his breakfast and stood to leave. On his way out he paused by her chair.

"Have a pleasant day, Miss Goodgrave," he said, and then mouthed, *"Tonight."*

She took his meaning immediately and nodded. She didn't think anyone else noticed their exchange, although Lorine watched Cade leave. Was that longing in her eyes? Briefly Lorine's gaze met Karigan's, and Karigan looked away, focusing on her plate of eggs.

The day could not pass quickly enough. Brownish-gray clouds still billowed overhead, and upon Karigan's visit to Raven, Luke voiced his hope that they'd get some rain in the night and maybe that'd clear the air.

"The horses need a good run," he told her, "but I won't hurt their lungs out in that filth." He jabbed his finger out the stable doorway at the sky.

Karigan tended Raven till once again he shone, and she even took to pulling his mane, which had grown bushy. He didn't like it much and told her so with a trumpeting whinny and an authoritative stomp of his hoof. She settled for only minimal thinning. When she did all she could for Raven, she returned to the house and to her room.

What was keeping her, she wondered, from simply saddling up Raven and just leaving? From finding her way home? She'd amassed some significant information about how the world had turned out . . . She paced in front of her window, arms crossed. She only came to the same conclusion as she had on other occasions: Nothing was preventing her except the fact that the professor kept her safe, clothed, and fed. If she ventured out into the world without a plan, there would be no escaping the empire. It claimed the entire continent. How long could she hide? If she was busy hiding, how could she find a way back to her own time?

She needed to figure out how to get home while under the professor's protection rather than while out in the world trying to fend for herself. The problem was, she had no idea how to proceed. She'd not done much to find her way home because she didn't know what to do. It was almost as if she'd been awaiting some sign, some miraculous indication to direct her actions. She'd thought that, maybe, if the gods had put her here, they'd show her the way home, but nothing seemed forthcoming. Not even a hint. Maybe the gods intended for her to stay in this time forever, though she couldn't imagine why, just as she could not fathom why they'd brought her here in the first place.

"Bloody damnation," she muttered. She was supposed to have the ability to cross thresholds, to pass through the layers of the world, which somehow included time, but she could not do so in a world lacking magic, and there had always been something drawing her into the past, like wild magic and the First Rider, or Queen Laurelyn of lost Argenthyne. Would any of the "pieces of time" of the Eletians have survived? Even if she could find one of the moondial devices, either by re-entering Blackveil and searching for one, or by going to conquered Eletia, without knowing what remained of that country, she wouldn't know how to use it. Not precisely, anyway. She could end up any*when.*

She didn't even have a looking mask to smash, and she didn't think trying to crush the few remnant shards that had come with her would have the same effect of launching her through time.

Frustration made her feel like smashing *something,* her

window, maybe. There had to be a way home. Thinking of the looking mask made her remember her shard hidden behind the headboard of her bed. This time she propped her chair against the door to prevent anyone from unexpectedly entering, then she retrieved the shard and settled atop her bed.

She expected her mirror gazing to prove fruitless. She was prepared to sit for a long time and see nothing but her own reflection, so she was surprised when an image appeared almost immediately. At first it was abstract—all mottled greens, all blurred—but slowly it focused, and she found herself looking through leaves at a path down below, as if she were a bird perched on a branch. She felt a throb rising through the fingers holding the shard, through her arm and pulsing through her blood, the rhythm of hoofbeats like the Rider call.

She nearly cried out when two horses and a Green Rider appeared trotting along the path. Her vision swooped down from the birches to keep pace with them. There was her friend Dale Littlepage riding her mare, Plover, and ponying Condor alongside.

"Condor," Karigan whispered in a shaky voice.

The shard allowed her to examine him from nose to tail, the dullness of his chestnut coat, his ribs more prominent than they ought to be. It was not from neglect, she knew, for her friends would never disregard his care. She'd left Condor under Dale's stewardship, and she appeared to be exercising him. Did Condor pine for his Rider? Was he off his feed because she'd gone missing? She wanted to run her hand down his neck, but her finger only tapped on mirror.

"Condor, I am here," she said in an anguished whisper.

Condor stopped short, and whirled, snapping the lead out of Dale's hand. He did not bolt, he looked. Dale wheeled Plover around, expression perplexed. She spoke words Karigan could not hear.

Condor kept looking until he seemed to fix her with his eye, staring back at her through time, through the mirror shard.

"Can you see me, boy?" Karigan asked, wishing it were true. Something she'd heard before more than once came to her now: *Sometimes the mirror goes both ways.*

His eye filled the shard, the liquid brown, the pinpoint pupil. "Do you see me?" she asked again, but then the mirror reflected her own eyes as his melted away until he was entirely gone.

Karigan tried to summon back the vision, tried and tried but failed. She curled up atop the bed hugging a pillow and pressed her face into it, missing her horse and home terribly. Had he really seen her? Whether or not he had, she needed to believe it.

In the present: Dale and Condor

The lead rope snapped out of Dale's hand. If not for her glove, it would have left a nasty rope burn across her palm. "Condor!" she cried.

She pivoted Plover around expecting to have to chase Karigan's horse into the woods. She'd made a promise to care for Condor so he'd be in top condition for his Rider's return, but Karigan's fate remained unknown, and Condor was off his feed, his spirit discernibly low. He'd gotten thin, and no matter how much Dale groomed him, his coat repeatedly lost its usual vibrant chestnut sheen.

Normally he followed compliantly along on these exercise runs. Dale perceived that he did not care one way or another if he came along with her and Plover. She couldn't make him care, but she could at least prevent him from declining into a worse state. So it surprised her, almost cheered her, that he was showing some sign of spunk.

She was further surprised when he hadn't run off, and she and Plover didn't have to chase him down. He whirled, and faced the opposite direction they'd been headed, his lead rope dangling from his halter to the path. He stared, angling his head this way and that, ears twitching. What did he see? Dale looked but identified only the usual forest sounds and signs—squirrels railing in the branches, a woodpecker chipping at a rotting tree. Insects clouded in the light, and on the forest floor, patches of sunshine wove patterns of golden green and shadow. Dale sensed nothing unusual or dangerous afoot or in the air.

"Something out there, Condor? What do you see?"

She knew animals sensed their surroundings differently than people, but Condor did not act alarmed—just vigilant. She was just glad he acted interested in *something*.

Yates' horse Phoebe was even worse off. She'd colicked, almost died. The Riders at the wall encampment gave her what attention they could, and it appeared to Dale the other Rider horses lent support as well. What Phoebe needed was to return to Sacor City to find a new Rider. Yates was gone. They'd received the news through Trace's psychic rapport with Connly: Lynx had returned from Blackveil, but Yates had not survived. Humans mourned, and so did their horses. Phoebe needed a new Rider, and the Riders needed seasoned messenger horses. Conflict was brewing with Second Empire, and though Damian Frost was due to deliver new horses to Captain Mapstone, they'd be young, untried, and untrained, and definitely not ready for message errands much less battle.

Phoebe needed to return to Sacor City as much for her own sake as that of the Riders. And Lynx needed his horse, Owl, so Alton decided that tomorrow, Fergal would pony Phoebe, Owl, and Condor back to the city. It was all very depressing—a pall hung over the encampment at the news of Yates' death, and hope dwindled daily with no word of Karigan. The mood did not help Estral any, who remained without her voice, and her father's disappearance still a mystery.

Dale gently sidled Plover up alongside Condor and took up the dangling lead rope.

"What's got your attention, boy?" Dale murmured.

Condor shook his mane and blew gently through his nostrils as though suddenly waking up. He allowed her to lead him away as docilely as ever.

The poor horse had lost his first Rider, F'ryan Coblebay, but Karigan had been right on the spot to claim him. Where was Karigan now? Had she died in Blackveil? It was difficult to tell from Condor's demeanor if he knew. Perhaps, Dale thought morosely, it was time for Condor, like Phoebe, to claim a new Rider.

CENTERING AND
FOOTWORK

After the house settled down for the night, Karigan, with bonewood in hand, met Cade in the library. He opened the bookcase and ushered her into the antechamber beyond. When the bookcase slid back into place, she noticed something new: a stool and a row of hooks on the wall. Hanging from the hooks was some clothing.

"The professor left these clothes for you," Cade whispered. "You are to wear them when you come to the mill, so Mirriam doesn't become irritated about the state of your nightgown." He ignited one of the extra phosphorene tapers and pushed the door open to the stairway that led to the underground. "I'll wait for you on the stairs."

He stepped into the stairwell and shut the door behind him, leaving Karigan alone in the antechamber to examine the clothes: a pair of black trousers with a fine leather belt, and a black shirt with the billowing sleeves favored by swordfighters. There were also stockings and a pair of supple shoes, all black.

"I am not a Weapon," Karigan murmured. She thought the professor was taking liberties, but she set aside the bonewood and changed. Everything fit well, even though the pieces were obviously made for men. The shirt buttons were on the wrong side, and the trousers gaped slightly at her waist. Tightening the belt more or less solved that problem. She wondered if the professor had gotten her measurements off an invoice from Mistress dela Enfande as he had for the Tam Ryder outfit.

She had no way of assessing how she looked, but when she

stepped from the antechamber and into the stairwell, Cade's raised eyebrows told her enough. Only after she closed the door to the antechamber did he speak.

"It is not proper, and yet it's entirely appropriate." He shook his head, and turned abruptly—too abruptly—to lead the way down the stairs.

Karigan thought she understood. She challenged Cade's preconceptions of a proper woman as defined by the empire, leaving him conflicted. In the mindset of the empire, this garb on a female reeked of impropriety, yet he struggled to adjust his way of thinking because he opposed the empire.

The clothes felt good as she descended the stairs, much better than the nightgown that had always left her feeling exposed and vulnerable. The clothes made her feel more like her old self, for all they were not green. Her Tam Ryder outfit was comfortable enough, but it was a disguise, and she was not herself when wearing it.

Cade remained his reticent self even as they traversed the underground then climbed up into the bowels of the mill. It was just as well. Since seeing Condor in her mirror shard, Karigan had little desire to talk. She'd remained uncommunicative all through supper despite the professor's efforts to engage her in conversation. Though she'd been looking forward to sparring with Cade, she would have been just as happy to stay in bed, alone with her morose thoughts.

"You're quiet tonight," Cade said as they climbed the final set of stairs.

"So are you."

After a pause, Cade said, "I'm always quiet."

True enough, Karigan thought, but was he also implying she was never quiet?

Finally they reached the floor with the professor's secret library. Cade threw the lever for the lights and they crossed over to his practice area.

"I was wondering," he said, as he removed his suit coat, "if your looking at the guns here would afflict you the same way as the Cobalt did at the Big Mounds."

"I don't think this sort of thing just goes away," she replied, but she walked over to the cabinet displaying several of the weapons, including some that were as long as a sword. It was these Cade must have been referring to when he spoke of "longarms."

She suffered no ill effects when looking from a distance, but then again, she couldn't see the details. When she approached more closely, the glare of the weapons made her avert her gaze and step back from the cabinet as though physically repulsed.

Cade's head was tilted as he watched her. "Curious," he said. "I guess we'll have to stick with swords." He removed a longsword from its wall mount. He took up a relaxed stance and closed his eyes. He breathed deeply. It was as Karigan had seen him do the last time.

"What are you doing?" she asked.

"Centering myself," he replied, without opening his eyes.

Karigan watched the rise and fall of his chest. There was something to that, she knew, and Arms Master Drent made sure his trainees learned how to use their breath while exerting themselves in a fight. It not only steadied their hearts and conserved energy, but allowed them to focus, or as Cade put it, center themselves. However, centering happened while *doing* in Drent's world.

"So in a real combat situation you expect the enemy to politely wait around while you center yourself?" Karigan asked.

"I would not meditate when in combat." Cade's voice held an edge of irritation.

"Then why do you do so now? Combat can happen unexpectedly, with no time for . . . meditating. Practicing this centering thing could make you reliant on it and throw you when you don't have time for it in an unexpected fight."

Cade bristled and opened his eyes, plainly annoyed. "I'll be using a gun on the battlefield."

"Look," Karigan said, "you wanted my help. I am trying to teach you as I've been taught, and I've been taught by a true swordmaster, the man who chooses who becomes the king's Weapons. His way is common sense and practicality. We do not have guns. We use swords. These methods work for us."

"Very well. I did agree to this."

Agreed to it? He'd practically begged her to instruct him.

She ran him through some quick warm up exercises—much quicker than he would have done on his own—and she began to teach him how to use his breaths to maintain focus. She then had him go through the forms he'd worked on before. They were much improved.

"You've been practicing without me." She wasn't displeased he'd been practicing, just annoyed he hadn't invited her along.

A blush colored Cade's cheeks. "I did not wish to embarrass myself again." That alleviated her annoyance some, until he added, "I learn fast and am getting quite good if I say so myself." There was a certain amount of smugness in his voice that irritated her. She tapped the tip of the bonewood on the floor, thinking.

"Give me the Heron Stance," she said.

He did, and she nudged his feet into better positions with the bonewood.

She then rattled off a series of forms that required intricate footwork, which was to conclude on Heron Stance. He stumbled over his own feet as he tried to make his way through the series.

She crossed her arms and shook her head.

"What?" Cade demanded.

"Your footwork," she said.

"Yes?"

"You're mincing about like you're standing on hot coals. I'm guessing you are something of a clumsy dancer."

"I am not!" he burst out.

"We need horse hobbles," she murmured, recalling some memorable training sessions with Drent. Cade stared at her aghast. "I'm going to go through the same set of forms," she announced. "Watch my feet."

She was intentionally goading him so she could in turn humble him. Overconfidence was another path to an early demise when it came to swordfighting. She then started in surprise when she realized that was exactly what Drent had been doing to her all this time—mocking and criticizing her so she wouldn't get too arrogant and be killed as a result. It was a good thing to keep in mind for herself: that by trying to prevent Cade from getting dangerously overconfident, she didn't do so herself.

So, instead of going through the forms at full speed, as she had planned to do in order to impress him, she went very slowly. When she finished, she asked, "Did you watch my feet?"

He nodded, his brow furrowed in thought. "Your feet moved, but they didn't."

"Yes," Karigan said. "Swordmasters are spare in their movement, using their feet only as necessary to maintain balance, position, rhythm, and to aid the force of their blade-work."

"Dancing without dancing," he said thoughtfully.

She guided him slowly through the same forms, helping him with his footing, which meant adjustments to the rest of his body.

When they'd gone through it twice, he said, "I think I understand how it's supposed to feel, how the power, the force, is connected through my whole body, from my feet to my sword hand."

Karigan nodded, gratified he understood, maybe comprehending better than she ever had herself.

"Can you show me what it looks like at normal speed?" he asked.

Karigan smiled. She thought he'd never ask.

SPARRING

When Karigan ended on the Heron Stance, she found Cade looking thoughtful. It was an improvement over the near worship he'd exhibited the first time she'd demonstrated what she could do, and in a way, it was not. At least some acknowledgment of her performance, with its speed and intricate footwork, wouldn't be remiss.

Instead, Cade diligently paced himself through the forms again, trying to emulate her. He did well, much better than before, but he still stumbled.

"I suggest you keep practicing," Karigan said. "Change up the order, as well, so your body doesn't get too used to one particular flow. You want to be able to respond to change, according to whatever situation you're in."

He nodded. "What now?"

Karigan thought for a few moments, then asked, "Do you ever get to spar with the professor?"

"Rarely. Very rarely. He's much too busy."

That was unfortunate. In fact, it was downright unacceptable. Training by one's self was in no way adequate. Learning the forms was important, but putting them into use by practicing with an opponent was imperative. Then she remembered he would not be depending on swords as his weapon. However, he'd asked for proper training, and he was going to get it.

"We'll use practice swords," she said, striding over to the weapons wall. The battered wooden swords were crudely made and piled on the floor, appearing rather neglected.

"You aren't going to use a real sword?" Cade asked, surprised.

"Neither of us are. Only swordmasters train with steel, and you're not a swordmaster. Nor am I."

She searched through the wooden blades until she found one that felt adequately balanced. It was a poor substitute for a real sword, she admitted, but one could be more aggressive, truly work the forms, when there was no danger of killing one's sparring partner. She leaned the bonewood against the wall and waited as Cade hung up his longsword and started sorting through wooden blades.

"Does the professor spar with steel?" Karigan asked.

"No, no. I just thought you probably did, being as well trained as you are."

"I only use steel when necessary to—" She faltered.

Cade nodded. "When necessary to kill. That's how it is with guns. Although there is no substitute for target practice with anything but an actual gun."

When finally Cade chose a wooden sword to his satisfaction, they touched blades and began. Karigan kept the pace slow and steady, offering commentary as she went and pointing out his mistakes, as well as what he did correctly. Steadily, she increased speed and spoke less, enjoying the work and how her puffy sleeves billowed with each stroke and thrust.

Cade grew in confidence, turning on the offensive. Karigan let him, parrying and blocking in a steady rhythm as the clack of wooden swords echoed through the cavernous room. She let the rhythm lull him and gave him no reason to doubt his confidence. She even let him score a touch on her arm that normally, she'd deflect. When she saw the slight smile on his lips, felt the aggression increase in his attack, and saw he was about to go for kill point, she simply allowed him to put all his force into a single scything swing. Before his blow landed, she lithely pivoted out of the way. The momentum of his effort unbalanced him, and he stumbled forward. She jabbed the blunt tip of her blade into his back.

"You are dead," she said, and explained where he had gone wrong. "Now again."

She lulled and goaded him enough times like this that she could tell he was growing both frustrated and mistrustful. Being wary of an opponent was good. Not being able to trust oneself, not so good. When he fell for yet another trap, and she sent his sword flying across the floor, she could tell by his sharp movements and glower that he'd become angry. He stomped away to pick up his sword.

When he returned, she said, "A couple of important things—there must be balance between instinct and technique. Your technique is getting better. However, I've been tricking you, and it's making you question yourself. I think you should assume that a genuine opponent will do whatever it takes to defeat you, including deception. Your instincts will grow with practice. You'll be able to sniff out trickery. Also, if you're angry, you are prone to make more mistakes."

Her words did not appear to mollify him much. He still glowered. Karigan needed to be extra aware in their next bout, as fighting angry opponents could be dangerous. They became unpredictable, and trainees were apt to make painful errors in judgment.

In Cade, the anger worked to his advantage, sharpened his reactions and made him more calculating in his offensive moves. She thought she was goading him into another trap, but he pulled a reversal, and to her surprise he passed through her defenses and got kill point with a hard smack to her ribs.

"Bloody hell!" She doubled over in pain. When she caught her breath, she tentatively probed her rib cage to see if he'd broken or cracked something, but it didn't seem like it. She'd have a good bruise, though.

Cade's sword clattered to the floor, and he rushed to her side. "Did I—did I injure you?"

"I'm fine," Karigan said breathlessly, gratified by his concern. "Just smarts."

"Let me see—"

She pushed his hand away.

"I just want to see if I broke your ribs," he said.

"With that technique? Not even close."

"I do not trust your bold words," he replied.

When he reached for her again, she slapped his hand away. He grabbed her wrist. She hooked her leg around his and swept him off his feet. He fell on his back, and his head thunked on the floor. He lay there unmoving.

"Hells!" Karigan knelt down beside him. "Cade? Are you all right?"

His eyes fluttered open. "What are all these stars I see?"

"Let me check the back of your head for—"

As she reached for him, he grabbed her wrist and pulled her close. "Not till I check your ribs."

They were nearly nose to nose. The end of Karigan's braid brushed his cheek. They glared at one another. Warmth rushed through Karigan's body. Driven by some impulse she did not know she'd been harboring, she closed the gap between them and kissed him. He jerked beneath her. If he'd been standing and not on the floor he would have pulled back. But he couldn't, and after the initial shock of the kiss, he relaxed and gave into it, and gave back.

What was she doing? Karigan's blood rushed, and she shivered. His grip on her wrist had loosened, and his hand was traveling up her arm. She broke off the kiss and hopped to her feet.

"Ha!" she cried as if it had all been some grand joke. She was all at once giddy and triumphant for both kissing and besting him, and embarrassed she'd let her guard down, for revealing herself that way. And the sudden move had pulled painfully at her sore ribs. She embraced the pain, which edged out certain other sensations but not the regret for having broken off the kiss. Cade still lay down there looking bewildered. Perhaps . . . perhaps she should kiss him again?

He sat up, rubbing the back of his head and wincing. She knelt again beside him, concerned. His gaze was steady and clear, not unfocused the way it would be if he had a bad head injury. Definitely not unfocused. As he reached for her, she suddenly felt shy and looked away, only to glimpse the professor standing just a few paces away, watching them. They'd been so preoccupied with one another they hadn't heard his entrance.

"Am I interrupting anything interesting?" the professor asked.

Cade staggered to his feet and swayed. Karigan leaped up to steady him, a small cry of pain escaping her lips before she could prevent it. The professor looked from one to the other.

"I'd rather the two of you be circumspect in the injuring of one another," he said at last. "Makes it hard to explain away such things." Giving Karigan a long, appraising look, he added, "You look stunning in black, my dear, and you have some very good moves."

How long had he been watching? Karigan wondered. And he *was* referring to her sword work, right?

He strode off toward the library, and Cade and Karigan nearly tripped over themselves in their haste to follow.

"Don't stop doing whatever it was you were doing on my account," the professor said.

"Miss Goodgrave—I hurt her ribs," Cade said.

"Cade banged his head," Karigan said.

The professor turned on his heel to face them once more. "Are these life-threatening injuries?"

"Miss Goodgrave won't allow me to see her ribs."

The professor crooked a bushy eyebrow.

Cade blushed and started to stammer.

"I'm fine," Karigan interrupted. "We both are. Really. I think . . ."

"Hmm." With that, the professor continued on his way to the library.

Cade glanced at her, but Karigan could not meet his gaze.

AT TWO HOUR

Karigan and Cade hovered just a little too anxiously over the professor's desk as he searched through various drawers. He paused to give them an all-too-knowing look before reaching into a drawer with an, "Ah ha!" He withdrew a gold sphere with a delicate chain dangling from it. It was etched with decorative whorls and ornate script. Initials, perhaps? It fit neatly into the palm of his hand.

"What is that?" Karigan asked.

"This, my dear, is a very rare item. A chronosphere."

"A what?"

"A timepiece," Cade supplied. "Shows time down to the minute. The finest can show time to the second with great accuracy."

"To the second?" she asked "In that little thing?" She thought of her world's few huge water clocks, used to synchronize the bells in the chapels of the moon. There were other modes of time telling, of course: candles, sundials, hour glasses, and on the coast, posts that marked time with the rise and fall of the tides. But the general population listened for the bells if they needed to know the hour, just as they did here.

The professor thumbed open a clasp and the sphere sprang open on hinges, revealing two halves. Karigan peered closely. In the center of one half, a tiny mechanical figure of a man with a tall hat and cane straightened up from a bowed position. He was deftly detailed and colored with enamel paint, his elbow chipped. He pivoted on a rotating disk and extended his cane to the other half of the sphere, which con-

250

tained two rings of numerical glyphs carved in yellowed ivory. The numbers of the outer ring were larger, and the mechanical man bowed so that the tip of his cane clicked on the glyph for the number one. Then he straightened and pivoted again with a distinct whirring noise and tapped on a glyph of the inner ring.

"It is ten till two hour in the morning," the professor announced. When the mechanical man returned to his starting position, the professor snapped the chronosphere shut.

To Karigan, the device was almost as impressive as the plumbing, and the gods had permitted her to see it, which meant she probably couldn't hope to understand how it worked. When the professor placed it back in his drawer, she asked, "Why do you leave it in your desk? If I had something like that to tell me the time, I'd carry it everywhere."

"I'd like to do so," he replied, "but only the emperor's elite, his most favored, are allowed to have one. It's one more thing that elevates them over everyone else. Having such immediate access to the time is a form of power. And of course, it is they who control when the bells ring."

Karigan saw the advantage immediately. If someone wanted the mills to be more productive, they could stretch the hours by changing the time the bells rang. Ordinary people might feel something was off, but they'd have no other way of verifying it, and must rely on the bells—controlled by the empire's leadership—for the time, correct or not.

"Fortunately the empire rarely manipulates the bells," the professor said, "though it has happened. Another reason I don't use the chronosphere regularly is that winding the mechanisms is not enough to make it function forever. They rely on etherea, and I fear this one is running very low, so I must be conservative in its use."

"If only the most favored receive these timepieces," Karigan said, "how did you get this one? Did you *acquire* it like you did the Cobalt gun?"

The professor chuckled. "No, my dear. This was different. It was my grandfather's."

"You inherited it."

"No, they can't be inherited as other goods can be. It's not allowed. It was supposed to be buried with my grandfather when he passed. I'd been so fascinated by it, and he'd often show it to me to amuse me."

"So you acquired it before he was buried."

The professor paused. Then said, "After."

"You . . . ?"

"You could call it my first archeological excavation."

Karigan exchanged glances with Cade. She could not tell how he felt about that particular detail. Undoubtedly he'd known.

"Funny," the professor murmured, "but I despise grave robbers and don't hide the fact. Yet, it's how I began. Stealing from the grave of my own grandfather." He cleared his throat. "We've ten minutes—less now—to make it to the roof. Let us hurry."

"What's going on?" Cade asked.

The professor laughed. "The opposition is making its move."

There was no time to ask questions. The professor sprinted off across the mill floor, and if she wanted answers, she had to follow. Cade looked just as perplexed as she felt.

They hurried after him, Karigan glad of the distraction the professor presented, a reprieve from dwelling on the . . . on the kiss. Just thinking of it warmed her cheeks. At the stairwell they each grabbed a taper and ran up the stairs, their feet clattering on the steps like a platoon of soldiers. They passed the landing that led to the artifact room, continued up past another landing with the door yawning open to who-knew-what. She had never explored beyond the third floor and was curious, but the professor's pace did not waver. When they reached the fifth floor, the professor dove through the doorway, and Karigan found herself pursuing his shadow.

They emerged into another expansive mill floor, largely empty but for a few chests and crates piled in the center of the room. The professor walked over to a rope that dangled from the ceiling. He waited for Karigan and Cade to join him.

"We need to extinguish all but one of the tapers," he said, "and the one will stay here on the floor at dimmest glow."

When this was done, he said, "I don't believe I need to

remind you to remain silent, but I will anyway. Most likely we'd not be heard, but sound can carry in odd ways, and I'd rather not take a chance."

He pulled down on the rope hanging from the ceiling and a ladder descended, unfolding to full length as it came. It must have been well-oiled for it did not make a single creak or groan. It seemed to Karigan another clever innovation of this time.

At the top of the ladder there was a trap door. The professor climbed, worked a mechanism in the door and carefully pushed it open. Again, it moved silently. Damp, cool air curled down through the opening. The professor beckoned Karigan and Cade to follow.

Karigan left behind the dim amber light pooling on the floor beneath her and climbed more by feel than sight. When she reached the opening and poked her head out, she saw the dirty skies had cleared enough to permit moonlight to guide her. She crawled onto the roof, rusted metal hard and rough on her hands and knees.

Rising to her feet, she patted dust off her trousers. Despite the professor's urgency, all was quiet. What was supposed to happen at two hour? Karigan was distracted by the unusual vantage point the roof presented. She observed first not the sea of stars overhead, but the rivers of misty street lamps below, their glow spread and warped by the fog that snaked along at ground level. She was drawn toward the edge of the roof. At first she'd thought it flat, but it had a subtle slant, perhaps to shed rainfall and snowmelt into the canal below.

The reflection of street lamps glimmered in the canals. Other lights spread far out into the night and there was beauty in it. Beauty in a city where she'd found so little. The inventions of these people—her descendents—were almost like magic, able to do marvelous things, like the city streets lit up at night, or the mechanical man in the professor's chronosphere. Some of it *was* magic. Harnessed etherea, as in the chronosphere. Somehow the empire had learned to meld magic and machine.

A dog bayed in the distance and Cade came up beside her. He took her arm and drew her away from the edge.

"Someone might see your silhouette against the stars," he whispered, his lips almost brushing her ear. She trembled.

He released her. She steadied herself with a deep breath, and silently berated herself for her carelessness. She should know better, but the city seemed, for all its light, asleep, abandoned. Who would be up so late to chance sighting her?

Inspectors, she answered herself, and the view of those hundreds of street lamps burning away the dark of night became much less enchanting than they had been just a moment ago.

The professor gazed off in the direction of what she guessed to be the Old City. There were few lights in that direction, only tiny dots of illumination that gleamed across the river, but mostly it was dark. She discerned the mount as a hulk rising against the starscape of the sky.

What was the professor waiting for? What did he expect to happen?

The clanging of bells made her jump. From the many towers of the mill complexes, the hour pealed out. Two tollings for two hour. Karigan yawned as the bells reminded her she was up well past bedtime.

Even after the resonance of the bells lingered on the air and then faded out, the professor waited, head cocked, but nothing changed. Eventually he shrugged and indicated they should climb back down into the mill. No one spoke until the professor, last on the ladder, closed the trap door after him and descended to the mill floor.

"What did you expect to see?" Cade asked, brightening each taper.

"I wasn't sure I expected to see anything or hear anything. Actually, I hoped to hear nothing, because it was supposed to happen at two, right on the bell."

"What was supposed to happen at two?" Cade asked, an edge to his voice.

Karigan thought it interesting the professor kept things even from Cade.

"Oh, we've done a little something—or at least I hope we have—to slow down Silk's drill project. If we have succeeded, I am sure it will be the talk of town tomorrow. You'll hear the rumors."

"You know that whatever you've done, Silk will retaliate," Cade said.

"I do know."

"He'll punish innocent people, unless your men were careless enough to get caught. What if they are and they give away secrets?"

"Sacrifice for the cause is necessary." The professor's voice had grown very quiet. The light accentuated the crags and lines on his face. "All involved know the dangers they face. They will not betray us in the unlikely circumstance they are captured."

"And the innocents Silk will punish in their stead?"

"This is war, Cade. In every war there is collateral damage."

A chill caught hold of Karigan. Every time she thought she knew the professor, some new facet of him surfaced. Every time she was lulled by his kindness and humor, she saw another side. This one was cold, dispassionate. One had to be willing to sacrifice for one's ideals, but cold-bloodedly and willingly give up the lives of innocents? She averted her gaze, wondering how that made him any different from Silk or the emperor.

"If Silk or his cohorts should ever learn our secrets," the professor continued, deadly calm, "you know what to do."

"I do," Cade said.

Hide and protect Arhys, Karigan thought. As a Weapon, that would be his primary objective. She studied his face. His expression was both determined and . . . disturbed. Was he as disturbed as she by the professor's willingness to accept the deaths of innocents?

As if the world were once again daylit and sunny, the professor's whole posture and demeanor changed, and he strode off before they could ask more questions. "Come, you two," he called over his shoulder. "We must have a look at Cade's social calendar."

Back down in the library section of the second floor, the professor explained, his chair tilted back and his feet propped on his desk.

"Silk has scored a point against us," he said. "He has skill-fully found a way to cut me from attending his dinner party as Miss Goodgrave's escort and chaperone."

"What did he do?" Cade asked.

The professor tapped an ornate letter opener against his knee that looked like it could do much damage to more than just a letter. "He ensured a mandatory meeting with the board was called at the university, to review my projects and ensure they are worth funding. No funding and the opposition, I'm afraid to say, loses its front." At Karigan's quizzical expres-sion, he explained, "The shield behind which the opposition hides much of its activities."

Karigan thought she understood. The university gave the professor contacts through a range of societal levels, allowed him to keep watch on Dr. Silk and dabble in research and excavations, secretly, of course, that were outside the param-eters of his official projects. Adding to his collection on the third floor, for instance.

"Dr. Silk will take Raven away if we don't go," Karigan said.

"I know, my dear, but that's only if *you* don't go. You are the important one. It's you he wishes to see, not me. He thinks if he parts us, you are unprotected and vulnerable to his de-signs. That is why I'm sending Cade in my stead. You must prepare your best suit, Old Button."

Cade gawped from his chair. "Me? B-but—!"

"You did not seem to object to being in Miss Goodgrave's presence before."

Cade's cheeks flooded with red. Karigan felt herself warm again.

"Besides," the professor said, "it's about time you started delving into the social intrigues and not just your books and weapons, eh?"

Cade cast about himself as if looking for some excuse to present itself. "But I am nothing to those people—they will just look down on me."

"Exactly!" The professor pointed the letter opener at him. "They will underestimate you. Yes, they will know you are my protégé, but because of your lower status, they will dismiss you at the same time. You will use that to listen and observe in a way that I cannot. They will treat you like a servant, forget that you've eyes and ears, and you will bring your observations back to me. You will also keep a sharp eye on Miss Goodgrave here and ensure she isn't beguiled into any missteps by Silk's charm."

Cade did not protest. He said nothing at all, his gaze projected straight ahead. Karigan did not think he'd make a very good spy—he was much too transparent in his thoughts, but she believed the professor had it right about the upper class guests regarding him as no more than a servant. They'd ignore him.

"I haven't got a good enough suit," Cade said finally. "No evening wear."

"All the better," the professor replied. "It will just reinforce your low status."

Now Cade stared at the ceiling as if trying to suppress further argument.

"I haven't got the full list of guests," the professor said, "but I know the city master and his wife are invited, along with some of the elite of this city and the Capital."

"The Capital?" Cade's voice was tight.

"Yes, my boy. They'll be even less informed about the lower class, since they are not exposed to it in the same way they would be if they lived in Mill City. They'll find you quaint. Perhaps mildly exotic."

Cade swallowed, said nothing. Karigan almost laughed at the idea of him as mildly exotic. And she had kissed him!

It was not the distant clamor of the bells that roused Lhean from the deep meditations that left him adrift in memories of verdant Eletia. No, many bells had come and gone without his notice, but this time there was something underlying the metallic clamor, like thunder in the earth. The minutest tremor reverberated through his body, so subtle that, besides himself, perhaps only burrowing creatures could feel it. Fine dust stirred in the air. A thread of unrest rattled through the rubble of the old castle.

Lhean sharpened his awareness, and when the second tolling came, he heard beneath it the subdued thunder, three separate blasts of it, that broke apart earth and rock, a power like
the great magicks of old, which he was too young to have
witnessed.

But etherea was gone from here. He climbed out of his
crevice and in the night saw nothing amiss, but on the air
drifted a hint of burning powder like that which he'd smelled
after the firing of the shooting devices. In time, the scent became more pronounced.

He must not slip into his dream-memories again. They'd
sustained him for now, but something new was afoot, and he
must keep watch.

SILK

"I don't care if we have to empty all the mills of slaves to find enough labor," Silk told the construction boss. "I will have the road repaired by this afternoon, at three hour at the latest."

"B-but—"

"If you cannot see that it is done," Silk said, leaning down from his saddle and pointing his riding crop at the man, "I shall appoint someone else, and you can join the slave gang in their work."

"Yes, sir. Three hour."

Silk nodded, and after a swift bow, the man ran off to make his arrangements. Silk sat erect once again in his saddle. Even now his household slaves were raising a canopy for his comfort while he waited.

Down the slope of the Old City's mount, the morning light shone on his caravan where it waited at a standstill on the winding road. It consisted of Moody and his assistants from the machine shop, guards, laborers, and a long, specially constructed wagon hauled by a team of mules. It was laden with his precious drill, all covered in canvas. Even so, a steely glow permeated the cloth. Silk wondered if others saw it or if it was just an effect of his own peculiar sight.

He wrenched his stallion around and gazed up the road where a swarm of slaves were already at work repairing the first crater that had been blasted by the opposition. It had been a nasty surprise to find the first one, and even nastier to learn there'd been five others. He'd posted guards up at the drillhouse on the summit, but he hadn't thought to cover the road. After all, the drillhouse and steam engine would be the more obvious targets, wouldn't they? But they hadn't been touched.

The guards had been killed stealthily, with knives driven into their backs. Silk tapped his crop on the toe of his boot. Why hadn't the insurgents blasted the steam engine or the drillhouse? If they'd really wanted to slow him down, that's what they should have done. Perhaps they feared his reaction?

It was true that if the steam engine were harmed, he would have butchered every inhabitant of this sorry city if he had to in order to find the culprits. So the opposition had moderated its crime hoping to escape the worst of his wrath. *Spineless.* A wasted opportunity on their part.

Still, there was some logic in their choice, if their desire was to preserve lives. Yes, undoubtedly some would die as a result of his inquiry into the blasting of his road, but there would be no bloodbath. Not today, anyway. He'd immediately tasked the chief of the Inspector force here in the city with the investigation. Clearly, the perpetrators knew how to use black powder and had some access to it. That gave the Inspectors a starting point.

In contrast, Silk reflected, the emperor would have commanded his troops to haul people out of their houses and stores and slaughter them, heedless of their guilt or innocence, to send a message to his enemies. In theory, it would turn the populace against the opposition for giving the emperor cause to shed the blood of so many. Sometimes such demonstrations worked to bring the insurgents out of hiding, to sacrifice themselves to prevent further killing, but more often than not, Silk thought, it just caused them to go to ground. And for all the emperor's demonstrations over the decades, there was still an opposition that refused to learn his lessons.

They struck in such a way to expect a more moderate response, Silk thought. *So fine, I will give them that. I will take a more surgical route. They will drop their guard, and if we can catch even just one of the scoundrels, we can extract useful information from him. Maybe get him to give up his fellows. Then we exterminate the opposition once and for all.*

He absently watched the dim shapes of slaves moving

rocks and debris. His horse stamped its hoof as a fly tried to settle on its wither.

If, Silk thought, his approach proved successful and led to the fall of the opposition, it could only bring him closer to the emperor's inner circle, and immortality.

An hour later found Silk properly situated in a comfortable reclining armchair beneath a canopy, his feet propped on a cushioned footstool. Even with his dark specs, the light made his head ache. One of his servants refilled his crystal glass with lemonade. Another wielded a large fan to keep him cool and prevent insects from alighting on him. Farther up the slope, slaves toiled to repair the road, their numbers supplemented by workers pulled from one of the Churlyn Mills. He'd no doubt Churlyn himself was furious, but he was barely of Preferred status and had no recourse against the likes of Silk. Churlyn would not make his day's production quota. Silk shrugged, unconcerned, and sipped his drink.

The fringe of the canopy flapped listlessly in the breeze. There was the clatter of slaves pounding on rocks, the shouts of overseers, and the snorts and neighs of beasts.

Every thirty minutes, one of the Inspectors offered an update on their investigation. Little, of course, had been achieved in so short a time, but the Inspectors were diligently rounding up men in the city known to work with black powder or who otherwise dealt in it, for questioning. As Adherent Minister of the Interior, Silk's father was in charge of the Inspector force, so it was only natural that the members of the force would defer to the powerful minister's son. As the current thirty minutes lapsed, an Inspector came forward with a filthy man whose wrists were manacled and attached with chains to an Enforcer. The Enforcer dragged him along until he stumbled to a stop in front of Silk.

Delicate blue-white bolts of energy arced and danced around the central sphere of the Enforcer, and up and down its spindly, metallic legs, intensifying with the movement of each limb. It amazed Silk that no one else saw it, or at least not anyone he'd ever asked. It was, he thought, like being able to see the soul of the machine.

The Inspector bowed.

"What have you brought me?" Silk asked.

"This *Dreg,*" the Inspector replied, with obvious distaste, "who has confessed to being here in the Old City last night around two hour."

"Out for an evening stroll, were you?" Silk asked the man.

When he didn't supply an immediate answer, the Inspector snapped, "Answer!" A pulse of energy arced down the manacles from the Enforcer, emphasizing the Inspector's orders.

The Dreg cried out in pain, his knees wobbling. "Y-yes, sir. A walk. I was out for a walk."

Silk chuckled. "Out looking for a little treasure, I expect."

"No, sir! Never!"

"Do you have papers sanctioning the seeking of artifacts, Mr . . . ?"

"Calls himself Biggs," the Inspector supplied.

"Mr. Biggs?"

"No. I mean, I'd never look for treasure, sir, not without the emperor's permission."

Silk set his glass aside on a table. A puff of air from the fan wafted through his hair. "I do not suppose that while you were on your evening walk, Mr. Biggs, that you saw anything out of the ordinary?"

Biggs, it turned out, was eager to talk, no doubt hoping his captors would overlook the fact he'd been prowling around the Old City. He'd seen silhouettes up against the summit doing he didn't-know-what, but figuring they were Silk's own men, he kept his distance.

"Then the bell rang for two hour, sir," Biggs continued, "and I heard the blasts and felt the ground shake a little, and those men, they scattered quick as could be."

"Did you see their faces? Hear names or anything?"

"No, sir. It was dark, and I was too far off."

"Beyond learning the hour of the attack," Silk told the Inspector, "this is not useful."

Biggs glanced nervously at the Inspector.

"He is the only witness we've found so far, Dr. Silk."

"Can you at least tell us how many of the men you saw?" Silk asked Biggs.

Biggs raised his hands as if to scratch his scalp, but the manacles held them down. "Five, six, or so," he replied.

"You are sure?"

Biggs nodded eagerly, as if encouraging his captors to believe he'd been helpful.

"Enforcer," Silk said.

The mechanical chirped and seemed to straighten to attention. It was an oddly human response.

"Enforcer," Silk said once more, "this man in your custody, Biggs, is guilty of unsanctioned artifact hunting and possibly grave robbing."

Biggs' eyes widened, and his mouth dropped open. "But—but I'm no Ghoul, sir! I'd never—I'd never dig up the dead. I'd—"

"Then just the artifact hunting. That's stealing from the emperor, Mr. Biggs."

The man fell to his knees. "Please, sir, mercy! I'll pay the emperor back. I'll give him the things."

Silk did not listen. Instead, he said, "Enforcer, this man admits his guilt. Render justice."

The mechanical trundled off, dragging the crying Biggs away to a polite distance, the Inspector trailing behind. Biggs babbled and begged for mercy all the way, but Silk was as indifferent as the mechanical to the pleas of a useless, statusless Dreg.

The Enforcer halted with a puff of steam from its stack. It lifted one of its spidery legs and retracted it. Silk watched in fascination as the arcing energies concentrated around the leg. Then, without warning, the Enforcer punched its leg through Biggs's chest, penetrating his back.

It was not out of perversity that Silk watched the Dreg's death. No, he watched to observe the life energy that surrounded Biggs's form, in this case, the color of rusted iron or old blood. It flickered, then faded out. He saw no separation of body and spirit, no lifting of the soul to the heavens as in the old theology the emperor had outlawed. No, he simply saw life extinguished.

Some of his more philosophical friends debated what came after death. It was difficult to conceive of a life, of a consciousness full of experience and learning, not continuing on, but Silk knew the depressing truth, courtesy of his peculiar vision. He'd watched his mother slowly expire on her deathbed, as well as the results of countless executions. Just as the gods of old were a complete fiction, so was the idea of something beyond death. There was nothing. The life energy went out like a phosphorene lamp permanently switched off. A waste.

Silk did not avert his gaze from the hapless Biggs as the Enforcer yanked its blood-smeared leg from the corpse's torso. There was nothing to suggest Biggs's life energy had moved on.

The Inspector gathered a couple of slaves to carry the body to a nearby cart. It would be donated to the university's College of Mending, as were all executed criminals, no matter the wishes of the family. *Let the menders figure out how to prolong life*, Silk thought, *since it is all we have. This one life.*

It made him all the more determined to become a favorite of the emperor, to enter his inner circle and be rewarded with that rare gift of an endless life. Destroying the opposition, and finding the dragonfly device, and any other treasures the royal tombs might contain, were keys to his success.

He clasped his glass of lemonade once more in his gloved, mechanical hand and sipped. His gaze strayed to the ridge of the mount with its toothy ruins, toward the summit where the ancient castle had once stood. He would have liked to see it in all its grandeur, but if the castle and its king had not fallen, the emperor would not have arisen to greatness. Would that have been so bad? The empire's teaching would have it that the people would have suffered privation under the rule of the despot king. They'd all be his slaves.

Perhaps not so different from the empire, after all. The import-ant thing was his family's position within the empire. Who knew what it would have been had the old king prevailed?

A flame of color amidst the ruins near the summit caught his eye, a flame like a figure burning in blues and greens. Silk sat up and almost spilled from his chair in excitement. The glass crushed in his hand.

"Howser!" he cried.

His manservant was at his side in an instant. "Sir?"

Silk pointed. "Do you see . . . anything up there? There's an outcrop surrounded by scrub."

Howser remained silent, and Silk could almost feel the big man trying to see.

"Use your spyglass, idiot!" he snapped.

Howser turned away, fumbled about, and returned with the telescoping device. He aimed it where Silk pointed.

"Well?" he demanded.

"Sorry, sir, I can't seem to find it."

The colorful figure of fire had died in Silk's vision. He sighed. "It is gone." Had he truly seen it? Something so magnificent and—and magical? In this day and age?

"Howser," he said, "you and your men are to go hunting up there. But you will not kill, no matter what it is you find. Do you understand? Capture only."

"Yes, sir."

Silk sat back in his chair as Howser hurried off. Already his servants had swept away the broken shards of crystal and were pouring him a fresh glass of lemonade.

His day had just gotten very interesting, and if Howser successfully captured his quarry, it would more than make up for any damage caused by the opposition.

From a distance, Lhean had studied the craters created by the exploding powder. By the time dawn broke, lines of workers were shambling up the roadway. Far back in the procession was an object shrouded in cloth and carried in the bed of a wagon, modified to support its impossible length and apparent great weight. Lhean did not like the metallic feel that it all but radiated. It was, no doubt, another soul-destroying mechanical creation the people of this time seemed to worship.

The whole procession came to a halt when it encountered the first crater. The humans investigated and set slaves to work to repair the road.

Lhean watched it all from his perch on an outcrop, protected from view by a boulder and thicket of scrub oak. He massaged his forearm. It was tender, the flesh almost raw beneath the membrane cloth, which was sodden with ichor. The wrist guard of his armor had blackened, died, and shed itself during the night. Soon the other segments of the armor would follow, and he'd be completely exposed to the elements and to weapons. He would be unable to regenerate new armor unless he returned to his own time, to Eletia.

He glanced toward the city. The Galadheon was out there, somewhere, but so far he'd failed to penetrate the city. It repelled him, turned him around every time. But now time was running out.

Lhean watched the Important Man beneath the canopy take his leisure while others toiled. He saw the prisoner executed by the terrible long-legged mechanical. How could the humans allow mechanicals the power? The power to take lives? They were soulless fabrications only, falsely alive. He could see it was animated with etherea, a perversion of nature. That the people of this time had learned to manipulate etherea as Mornhavon had once done was more disturbing than surprising. That this world still contained some etherea should have given him hope, but it only sickened him to see it so defiled.

The Important Man down below had some peculiarities that suggested that small parts of him were not . . . real. Like the mechanical orb with the spindly legs, the man's not-real parts—his hand, for instance—emitted a tainted ethereal gleam.

The man's gaze turned in Lhean's direction. It was difficult to determine what the man saw because of the dark specs he wore, but his sudden reaction, one of surprise, told Lhean he'd been spotted.

Lhean scrambled from the outcrop into deeper cover. If there was any time he needed to eat that last piece of chocolate he'd been holding in reserve, that time was now. He could not allow himself to be seen again. So far the people who had glimpsed him thought him a phantom. He couldn't say why, but he suspected the Important Man saw him differently.

THE WITCH HAS SPOKEN

Hard-soled shoes struck the white marble floor of the colonnaded great corridor, the sound echoing up into the vaulted heights of the ceiling where the life and greatness of the emperor was exalted in a series of fresco murals. They had been painted by the master, Adolfi Fyre, who had made the ceilings of the imperial palace his life's work. He'd died well over a hundred years ago and a succession of artists had carried on the great endeavor, expanding into other areas of the palace. The current master was focusing on the ceiling of the ballroom.

But Webster Ezmund Silk's goal was not the ballroom, nor did he seek to admire the art to which he'd become so accustomed over his long years. His goal, in fact, was not any of the great rooms or corridors found in the palace. At least, not those found above ground. No, he sought the dark places of the palace down below, untouched by art, beauty, or natural light.

Webster Ezmund Silk, Adherent Minister of the Interior, and personally highly favored by His Imperial Eminence the emperor, turned on his heel into a side corridor. While still lavishly ornamented and grand, the ceiling was perceptibly lower. His brisk stride unerring, he did not pause or even slow down as he perceived the rapid, uneven footfalls of someone hurrying to catch up with him. He did not have to look to know it was Paulson Gladstone, Minister of True Education in the emperor's circle of Adherents.

"Is it true?" Gladstone gasped from a few strides behind. "Is it true the witch has spoken? The timing—it's most irregular."

Gladstone's breathing was ragged as he fought to keep pace. He was a nervous man who had a habit of tugging at the cuffs of his coat as though the sleeves would roll up his arms of their own accord. Webster did not spare Gladstone a glance. He knew the man's characteristics well, had watched him grow from a boy into an old man. He'd never borne enough favor with the emperor to receive the Gift.

Webster had. He was over a century old, but exactly how old he didn't bother to remember. He let his secretary keep track of such tedious details. No matter his age, he would remain eternally a man in his early prime, strong, steady, his hair untouched by gray, his face unmarked by the years. At this point, his son, Ezra, looked more like his father.

Webster had married several times through the years and fathered many children. When his last wife died, he hadn't bothered to remarry. All his children, except Ezra, had grown up, become old, and died. He'd gotten used to it, watching his children age and die. There was no need to rush into another marriage. If there was one thing he had, it was time.

Time. The word echoed in his mind. Something was out of kilter with time. He felt it like an itch he could not reach, a tingle in his nerves.

"The witch!" Gladstone whined beside him. "Has she spoken?"

Webster halted at a tall oak door, ornately carved with a dragon. A soldier in the red of the palace guard drew it open for him. Without turning to Gladstone, he answered the old man's question.

"The Scarlet Guard has said it is so. I am going down to confirm it."

Without another pause, he strode through the door and into the lift that, through a series of flywheels, belts, cranks, and cables would lower him to the roots of the palace. As he turned to work the brass levers that would set the machinery in motion and initiate his descent, he finally looked upon Gladstone and saw the aged man's pallor and how unbearably fragile and careworn he appeared.

For all of Webster Ezmund Silk's enduring youth and vigor, he thought he knew how Gladstone felt.

*   *   *

Far below the palace there were no crypts, no tombs cared for in perpetuity to honor kings and queens as Ezra claimed there had been in the castle of the old realm. The emperor, immortal in name and body, had no use for tombs.

When the lift juddered to a stop and Webster opened the door, the contrast to the light, airy regions above couldn't have been more stark. Bare phosphorene bulbs were strung along the ceiling of the corridor, their glow sickly against the dark that collected at these depths. The corridor was narrow, made of stone, some of it granite bedrock that served as rough, natural walls. They glistened with seepage, and somewhere in the distance he could hear the plink of dripping water.

At this low level, the churning of great turbines spinning beneath the palace, fifteen of them, each as large as a small house, throbbed through the floor and the soles of his feet. They pulsed, the empire's heart of power, circulating waterborne etherea throughout the palace and into the Capital. The roar of water was muffled, but everpresent and unrelenting. He did not doubt the constant throbbing, pulsing, and roaring had contributed to the witch's insanity as much as anything else.

He was greeted by two masked members of the Scarlet Guard, soldiers he'd handpicked, whose sole duty was to guard the witch. Even though he had chosen the men himself, he could not identify them behind the scarlet masks that hid their faces wholly. The masks had the unsettling effect of making the guards inhuman in demeanor. Webster almost caught himself in a shudder.

Silently they turned and led him down the corridor, their feet grinding on gravel and bedrock. The muffled sound of their footfalls seemed to come from all directions at once. Step by step they led him toward the prison. A prison with only one cell and one inmate.

The corridor ended in an antechamber where the Scarlet Guard stood watch. There were half a dozen on duty at any one time, so four waited at attention, not acknowledging him or their two brethren who escorted him. Behind a steel door with several locks to secure it lay the cell.

One of his escorts peered through the sliding peep hole, then proceeded to insert an array of keys into a series of locks, his movements almost ceremonial, rhythmic. The unlocking produced a cold musicality as tumblers rotated and internal mechanisms clicked, tripped, and sprang open. The door was several inches thick and mounted on reinforced hinges. When the unlocking was finished, it took both escorts to haul the door open.

Perhaps it was overkill, but the depth of the prison and the thickness of the door lessened the chance of any etherea present in the palace reaching the witch.

A fetid odor of damp, decay, and excrement oozed through the doorway. The cell was black within. They did not waste phosphorene on one who did not need light.

One of his escorts retrieved a taper, for *they* needed light, and led the way into the chamber of the witch. Webster followed next, and he was in turn followed by his second escort. The guards' brethren shut the door behind them with a damning thud.

The taper was almost nothing in this black place. Shadow was layered upon shadow. He could see the pale grime of the witch's naked flesh, the oily sheen of long, snarled hair that tumbled down her shoulders. The light glinted on the chains that held her upright in a spread-eagle position. But the rest of the details were lost to the dark. He knew them though, intimately, for he had overseen the creation of the cell and her imprisonment—the reinforced chains with cuffs that did not encircle her wrists, but ringed each finger with prongs that were buried into the flesh to the bone. A collar around her neck, also pronged, was attached with a taut length of chain to the ceiling, restraining her from moving her head or upper body much. Spikes had been driven through each foot and bolted to the floor.

Once in a while all the restraints were removed and she was cared for until she healed. It was not out of compassion they did this, however. They did it so she would not become inured to the pain. When she healed and they chained her once more, the pain was renewed.

The wretched creature snuffled, could shift her head just

enough so that it seemed she looked right at him. Webster's polished shoe scuffed on the edge of sawdust bedding that was thrown on the floor to absorb her waste. He should not be so disturbed for she could not see. He knew this well—he'd been the one who had burned out her eyes with a red hot poker.

"I smell you, Silk," she croaked in a broken voice. They'd had to damage her vocal chords, too, for the sweetness of her song had snared many an unwary man in the past. No more. "You smell pretty, Silk, very pretty."

The witch had been tortured, abused, and imprisoned for over a century, but she remained unbroken. She carried some internal fire that retained a modicum of power. It infuriated Webster he'd been unable to break her entirely, and even more so that she aroused a primal fear in him.

"Pretty perfume," she grated. "Have you come to romance me, Silk? Have you come to sate yourself in me with your feeble prick?"

Webster frowned, his gorge rising. In the early years he and the guards used her, enjoyed doing to her whatever they wished, for having one chained and helpless was very sweet, very seductive, very gratifying. Like a tree carved with the initials of lovers, her body was etched with a spider web of scarred initials sliced into her flesh by the guards who had pleasured themselves with her over the years.

Shadows upon shadows, scars upon scars.

The filth of her disgusted him now, the sockets of burned out eyes, and her ravaged lips. Ribs and hip bones protruded. There were rarely fresh initials carved on her body nowadays. Even so, he felt a rising pressure against the crotch of his trousers.

The witch laughed as if she knew. It was a dry, breathy rasp.

"You know why I'm here," he said, thankful his voice remained steady.

She made smooching noises at him and laughed again.

She was not, he had concluded long ago, quite sane.

"You know why I am here," he repeated through gritted teeth. "Are you toying with us, or is it true? Ten years have not yet passed."

She stilled and every muscle in Webster's body tensed.

"I do not toy." Her tone no longer mocked but was cold and full of menace. *"My beloved rises."*

Her pronouncement was like a thunderclap. Without another word, he turned to face the door, suddenly overwhelmed and claustrophobic, barely able to contain himself while he waited for the guards to open it. He could not escape her presence soon enough. When the door opened, he hastened out, not awaiting his escort, not pausing in the antechamber. He made straight for the corridor and the lift.

Before the great steel door could close behind him, however, her rasping voice reached him. "Webster Ezmund Silk! My beloved rises, and he will make you eat your own entrails!" The door slammed on her hysterical laughter.

Webster closed his eyes and clenched his fists at his side. No matter how many times he'd heard her repeat this threat, cold dread slid through his gut like a serpent.

He shook himself and entered the lift. He threw the appropriate levers and the car lurched upward, leaving behind the gloom and the constant drubbing of the turbines. Once he was above, he'd bathe and order the clothes he was wearing burned. He could not tolerate the stench of her that clung to him, so overpowering that it almost suffocated him in the small space of the lift. Afterward, he would meet with his fellow ministers and plan for the emperor's awakening, whether it was time or not, for the witch had spoken.

No, he thought after some reflection, not just a witch, but a goddess. A goddess of a far more ancient and earthly pantheon than the ones the old realm had worshipped. As Aeryc and Aeryon and their cadre of fellow gods rose to primacy, the ancient goddess and her sisters fell and were denigrated to the level of mere witches, relics of a forgotten past. But to believe she was less than a goddess, and an insane one at that, was a fatal error that Webster did not intend to make. It was why he kept her so elaborately imprisoned. Not to mention that she was, unfortunately, inextricably linked to the emperor.

As the lift chugged upward, its mechanisms clacking and whining comfortingly, he recalled her name, somehow extracting it from the dusty regions of his mind among other discarded memories. *Yolandhe. Yolandhe of the sea.*

In the Present:
YOLANDHE'S ISLAND

"I remember when I first set foot upon your shore," Amberhill told Yolandhe as they lay together beneath the furs in the cave. "The climes were colder. There was more of a sharpness in the air."

"That was very long ago, love, when much was different, but I've not changed and my island remains."

"Foolish and arrogant was I to be sailing among those islands alone," he said.

"But then you would not have found me."

Amberhill chuckled. "No, then I would not have crashed upon your shore. I remember Tolmarth was always fond of saying to me . . ." Who was Tolmarth? Had he known a Tolmarth? And if so, what had he been fond of saying?

Amberhill blinked in confusion. He'd been recovering well from the injuries suffered when the gig broke up during the storm, but he still tended to have these lapses. Sometimes he forgot himself and recalled memories he could not have possibly experienced. His head must have got a worse rattling than any of them thought.

Yolandhe did not push or request him to complete his sentence. What had he been speaking of, anyway? It did not matter, as Yolandhe now pressed herself against him and kissed him. Memories did not matter, only the present.

Yap paused at the cave entrance only to hear the familiar sounds of Yolandhe and his master rutting. His master had

273

recovered—that much was abundantly clear as a lusty cry issued from the cave's mouth. When rare opportunities came for Yap to address their situation with him, he put him off, promising to think on it and then returning to Yolandhe's arms. There were times, Yap suspected, that his master forgot he existed.

So Yap continued to catch fish, collect clams and mussels, and steal seabird eggs from rocky nests. He built himself a rickety lean-to along the tree line using driftwood, timbers, sails, and rope from the wreck of their gig. He soon investigated farther afield, the bottoms of his bare feet as tough as they had ever been during his pirate days. He even explored into the interior of the island, overcoming his fear of ferocious beasts, but only startled birds from brush to branch. If there were any other animals, he was sure his clumsy stumbling about scared them off. But maybe, he thought, there weren't any because it was a long swim from the mainland.

It took Yap one day to cross the island, and even when he paused somewhere in its middle he could hear the incessant heave of waves, smell the brine. Rather than grating on his nerves, it was reassuring as his feet sank into deep moss and trod across the knuckled roots of evergreens.

He found a stream trickling down from a rise, and after scooping some handfuls of water to his mouth, he decided to climb up the rise to see what he could see. There were a few such small mounts on the island. He vaguely remembered seeing bumps on the island from sea, aboard the *Mermaid*.

For years, Captain Bonnet had followed a trail of rumors of sea king treasure. Mounds of gold and jewels, it was said, and the captain's persistence paid off. They'd found an unbelievable cache of treasure entombed on the island, much to their woe. It had been hidden beneath one of the mounts. This one? He could not remember, it had been so long ago. But he was no longer seeking tombs. He must not.

Ferns and brush snagged his legs as he approached the base of the mount. He started to circle it, looking for a way to climb to the top. He stumbled out of a prickly patch of brambles onto soft moss, hissing at the bloody scratches on his legs and ankles. It took him a moment to realize he'd come to a path. A lightly traversed path, but a path all the same. It was overgrown and narrow, but it led up the hill, which was his goal.

The path wound up, at first gently, then over a boulder field, where his bare feet grasped at granite. Yolandhe had probably made it. If not her, who? He hadn't encountered anyone else on the island. At one point he had to scrabble up a ledge, and when he succeeded, he sat on it panting and rubbing sweat out of his eyes. He had risen enough that he could see the ocean through the tops of trees that sloped away below him.

When he caught his breath, he pushed himself up to resume his climb. To his surprise and trepidation, the path led through a cleft of rock and into a large cavern. A shaft of sunlight poured in from behind him, and he groaned when he realized what he had found: the tomb of the sea king.

His first impulse was to run away. He and his crewmates had been severely punished for disturbing this tomb once before, and he was not anxious to raise Yolandhe's ire again. Yet, he could not help but stare. The light that streamed past him sketched out the mid-section of the intact ship, but the stern and bow fell into darkness. He remembered the bow particularly, with its dragon's head and red painted eyes. Chests and barrels and pots gleamed with treasure. Across the chamber, other fainter shafts of sunlight poked through the earth, revealing yet more offerings to the dead king. One of the holes must have been the one Eardog fell through, the one they had used to haul out all the treasure.

Stairs of carved stone plunged into the cavern gloom below. Their natural appearance must have camouflaged them from pirate eyes the last time.

Before he even realized it, he was descending down, down, down the stairs, drawn instinctively to treasure. Either his eyes had adjusted to the gloom, or ghost light now limned the shapes of chests and barrels and precious cargo. And of course, the ship of the dead one.

When he reached the bottom step, he marveled, as he had the first time, that a ship had been either magically brought into the cavern, or brought in piece by piece by hand to be reassembled. To his mind, either method was an impressive feat.

He was pulled to a nearby chest overflowing with coins and jewels and strings of pearls. A giddy feeling burbled in his throat as he sorted through the booty. He was overcome by a sense of madness he hadn't felt in many a year, and he laughed. He laughed until a gold dagger with a ruby on its pommel came into his hand. One he recognized. One he had drawn out of his mouth on Yolandhe's beach. He shuddered and allowed the dagger to clatter upon the other treasure. He wiped cold sweat from his brow and blew out a rattled breath. "No, no, this stuff's not for old Yap," he told himself.

He resolved to turn around and march back up those stairs without giving the cavern and its treasures a second look, but just then, a voice thundered from above filling every crevice, every alcove of the cavern: "Are you going to plunder my treasure again, Pirate?"

Yap whimpered, thinking the dead king had come to life. He slowly rotated and looked up. There, at the top of the stairs, shafts of sunlight streaming past him and half-blinding Yap, stood Lord Amberhill and beside him, Yolandhe.

"Well?" Lord Amberhill demanded, his voice once again filling the cavern. "Speak now or suffer judgment."

"No! No, sir!" Yap cried. Then he wondered about Lord Amberhill claiming the treasure as his own. "It's cursed, sir."

Yolandhe's light silver laugh trickled down to him. "Leave the small man be, my love," she told Lord Amberhill. "He has repented. He returned the treasure he had taken."

Repented? Is that what she called it?

"Yap, what are you doing here?" Lord Amberhill asked in his normal voice.

"I was just lookin' round and came to the opening. I swear! I had no idea it was right here. What are *you* doing here, sir?"

"Yolandhe tells me I've an inheritance here, and I must say this is most unexpected."

Inheritance?

"Not just an inheritance," Yolandhe proclaimed. "You are the sea king reborn!"

In the Present:

YOLANDHE'S ISLAND

 **"T**he sea king reborn?" Amberhill asked. "Is that what you said?" Whatever caused his frequent episodes of confusion might have also impaired his hearing and comprehension.

"It is what I said," Yolandhe replied, and with a subtle gesture of her hand, light hissed to life throughout the cavern—dirty stubs of beeswax candles and dry reed torches flared along the cavern walls, clam shells filled with rancid oil and crude lanterns shielded by tarnished punched bronze flickered with tentative flame. The light allowed Amberhill to see the enormity of the cavern and his "inheritance," as well as the size of the ship with its gleaming red eyes. At the bottom of the steps, Yap had fallen to his knees and flung his arm over his face as if to ward off a blow.

It was the first show of real power Amberhill had seen from Yolandhe. Yap had called her a sea witch, and now Amberhill could see it was no exaggeration. He had great discomfort with any woman who held such power. Discomfort mixed with intrigue by the danger of it. He gazed at Yolandhe anew. She was neither beautiful nor homely but deceptively average. Back in Sacor City, he would not have given her a second glance, but . . . It was all in the way she held herself. Her manner. He could not quite put a finger on it, but there was something terribly hypnotic and arousing about her, something he felt with his entire body, especially when she sang. When she sang, he lost himself in her.

She took his hand and led him down the stone steps to where Yap knelt. Was Amberhill mistaken, or was the pirate fighting back tears?

He is truly afraid. But Amberhill did not dwell on his servant's state of mind, for it was as if he stood among constellations, the way the lights shone in the vastness of the cavern. They revealed the riches all around him. From a chest, he plucked a silver coin impressed with a ship on one side and a dragon on the other, its tail wrapped around its neck just like his ring. The silver was icy smooth between his thumb and finger.

"Did you say this is my inheritance?" Amberhill asked Yolandhe, still in disbelief. In all his widest ranging avaricious dreams, he could not have imagined so much treasure collected in one place. It made him light-headed. To think, as the Raven Mask, he had plucked a brooch here, a necklace there, from the possessions of the wealthy just to retain his estate, and all this time this hoard was sitting here waiting for him.

"I did," Yolandhe replied. "It is your birthright."

"I still don't understand."

Yolandhe sighed as though tired of explaining to a child, and the cavern echoed with it as if exhaling its own breath.

"You are descended down the line of kings," she said, and she pointed at the ship. "*His* blood runs thick in your veins. You are Akarion incarnate."

"Huh." Once just low level nobility and just this side of poverty, Amberhill was now descended from kings and richer than some nations. He almost laughed wondering what he was going to do with it all. Where would he stash it? *I will fix the estate and then some,* he thought. He could create his own kingdom.

The ruby eye of his ring winked in the light. The gold slithered around his finger. He found himself drawn to the ship. Yolandhe did not stop him. Yap sobbed. There was a ladder nearby, rickety with age, but he leaned it against the ancient hull between two of the oar ports. The oars jutted from the sides of the ship symmetrically positioned as though those who manned them had heeded the commands of the coxswain to the last.

The decking bowed and creaked beneath Amberhill's feet. The bier of the dead king stood just behind the mast with its ragged sail still unfurled though listless. The king's bones

were layered in moth-eaten furs. A helm with intricate geometric patterns protected his leathery skull. Thick braided
hair and beard of faded red bristled from beneath the helm
and wreathed the skull. At his feet lay a shield and a pitted
iron sword.

"So lies Akarion," Yolandhe said.

Amberhill had not heard her climb aboard.

"And so stands Akarion," she added, gazing at him.

"I am not he," Amberhill replied.

She did not answer.

"I am Xandis Pierce Amberhill of Sacoridia. An aristocrat,
thief, and the owner of a fine if unintelligent stallion named
Goss that will be the foundation of my breeding farm. I am
not this Akarion."

"I know who you are," Yolandhe replied. "You wear his
ring."

"A pirate wore this ring before me. Did that make him
Akarion reborn, too?"

"No. It rejected him and found you."

Amberhill struggled between the gratification of learning
that he had royal blood, and the need to remain his own man.
He gazed at the ring, the facets of the ruby afire, lively in the
wavering light. He could claim all this treasure and his birthright, but such possessions, and such status, required a great
deal of responsibility.

Without it, Amberhill could remain the master of his own
desires, free to go where he wished, do as whim dictated, even
scale walls to steal the jewelry of noblewomen. As a king, he
could never be so free. He'd be collared by duty.

He noticed Yap had drawn closer to the ship. "What say
you, Yap?" he called down. "Am I the sea king reborn?"

"I dunno, sir, but all this treasure is cursed. Keeping it can
come to no good."

"Even if it is mine by birthright?"

"I wouldn't touch it, sir." Yap shuddered.

"Those memories I get," Amberhill said to Yolandhe,
"those false memories belong to Akarion, don't they."

"They are not false."

He noted she did not deny to whom they belonged. Amberhill did not like another wielding such influence over him, especially from *within,* never mind from without. The invasiveness of it irritated him. He could not believe it of himself: to be considering whether to reject all that treasure, he who had purloined the wealth of others for so long to rebuild his estate. But no amount of treasure was worth allowing another to alter his memories or gain control over him in any way.

"Akarion can have his ring back," Amberhill said, sure this would prove to be the solution. He took one last look at the treasure he was giving up and slipped the dragon ring off his finger. Akarion's skeletal hands lay across his breast. One finger looked disjointed as though someone had tampered with it, no doubt Yap's old captain who had stolen the ring. Without another moment's hesitation, he pushed the ring onto Akarion's finger, gold clicking against bone.

To his surprise, Yolandhe did not object. Yap, in contrast, looked jubilant.

"Well done, sir! The right thing. I am sure of it!"

Amberhill thought so, too. He felt no different, though, just pleased with himself for making the decision to stay free and unencumbered. Until he realized he was twisting a ring around on his finger, as had been his habit. He glanced at his hand, then Akarion's. Akarion's boney finger was bare. Amberhill's finger of living flesh was not.

"No," he whispered.

Yap wailed.

"It is your birthright," Yolandhe said, "and your inheritance. It is a gift of greatness."

NEWS

As tired as Karigan was, she spent the remainder of the night twisting and turning in bed, speculating about whatever the professor and the opposition had set in motion, and about Cade. Mostly about Cade, as it turned out. What had possessed her to kiss him?

Well, he certainly wasn't hideous to look at or anything, and they'd been so close, actually in contact on the floor. How could she resist? Was it so wrong for her to crave the touch of another? She had been denied it for so long. The man she loved was unattainable. King Zachary had offered her the opportunity to become his mistress, a practice that was more or less an institution in aristocratic circles, but she had refused him. Soundly and without regret. She thought better of herself than that, than being used by any man. She still loved him, though. Couldn't help it.

When last she'd seen Alton just before heading into Blackveil, she'd hoped for . . . What? They'd pick up where they'd once left off? Companionship? Love? Something to fill the loneliness gnawing at her? Only to be rejected because he'd found Estral.

I am *lonely,* she thought, her eyes moist. She pressed her face into her pillow.

She'd been snatched away from family and friends and everything that was familiar. She wasn't even in her own time. Raven's presence helped, but it was not the same as that human touch. Lorine was almost a friend, but that barrier between servant and the served could not be breached. Karigan certainly could not confide in her. There was no one else. Not even the professor, who was too caught up in his opposition movement. He had little time to spare for her.

But Cade seemed to accept her company, want it even. He knew her true identity, and she could be herself with him. He had responded to her kiss.

Karigan sighed, and with that, she finally fell asleep, only to be awakened what felt like just seconds later by Lorine.

"Time to get ready for breakfast, miss."

Karigan peered blearily at her from beneath the covers. "Are you sure?"

"Very. The bell for seven hour rang just a short while ago. Are you ill?"

"No, no."

Karigan forced herself out of bed, grimacing at the soreness of her ribs, and got on with her morning ablutions. Residual memories of the kiss made her smile, and then, while Lorine brushed her hair out, Karigan thought about whatever it was the professor had said was supposed to have happened at two hour in the morning. He'd said that if the opposition succeeded, they'd hear news and rumors of it in the morning.

Karigan opened her mouth to ask Lorine if she'd heard anything but stopped herself in time realizing she'd never before asked such a question of her, and it would be too obvious if something had, in fact, happened. She did not believe Lorine an operative of the empire, but a wrong word to the wrong person could prove disastrous.

So while Lorine stroked the brush through her hair, Karigan sat in quiet suspense, hoping Lorine would mention any unusual news without prompting. She did not.

It was not until Karigan presented herself at breakfast that she began to get some inkling. The professor and his students rose to greet her, Cade barely looking her way. When all were seated once again and served breakfast, it was as though she'd ceased to exist. It wasn't just the food that claimed the attention of the young men but an undercurrent of excitement, their voices a little too loud requesting the pepper to be passed, their movements sharp, and they appeared to wolf down the food without even tasting it. Then there was the conversation, seemingly picked up midstream by Mr. Stockwell.

"I say it's some kind of drill."

"That much is obvious," Mr. Card replied. "That structure up on the summit looks like a drillhouse, and I hear there is an engine to power it."

The professor hid behind his paper of news. Karigan wondered if it reported whatever the opposition was supposed to have done.

"Not your usual archeological tool, a big drill like that. A bit heavy-handed."

"Figured that out by yourself, did you?"

Mr. Stockwell ignored the jibe. "If it's not for an archeological dig, what is it for? Why, it could damage all kinds of relics."

The question was met with gravid silence.

The usually quiet Mr. Philips looked up from a book he was studying and asked, "Why did the rebels blast the road? If they wanted to do real damage, they should have blown up the drillhouse or engine."

Karigan waited, transfixed, for an answer.

Mr. Card deliberately stabbed a piece of ham with his fork and examined it. "How angry would *you* want to make Dr. Silk?"

Silence fell once again as the students considered.

The professor had indicated that the opposition could slow down Dr. Silk's excavation by attacking the worksite, which it sounded like they had done by putting holes in the road. The drill itself, he and Cade had said, would have been too well protected. These other things, the drillhouse and engine, sounded like they would have been excellent targets, but not destroyed because the opposition feared reprisal. Extreme reprisal. Despite the professor's chilling words about "sacrifice" and "collateral damage" last night, it appeared he did not wish to spark the annihilation of innocents.

The professor still held his paper taut before him. Cade's gaze was fixed on his breakfast.

"I heard the Inspectors have rounded up just about every blastman in the city for questioning," Mr. Ribbs said.

The others nodded as if they'd heard the same thing.

"Professor," Mr. Stockwell said, "do you have any idea why the rebels would try to ruin Dr. Silk's road? And what's he after with a drill that big?"

The professor slowly lowered his paper, his eyes shadowed by his bushy brows. "Of the latter, it is no doubt the emperor's business Dr. Silk is about. I'm sure all will be revealed in time and in proper scholarly fashion, or not, as the emperor wishes. As for the former, I haven't the faintest."

After a pause, he added, "It is best for all of you boys to keep your thoughts and speculations to yourselves, and to remember that Dr. Silk is an esteemed leader in our chosen field of archeology. Gossiping about his intentions is not becoming of young gentlemen like yourselves. Especially for those of you who wish to make your names in the field. Never forget that Dr. Silk can make or break you."

Karigan shuddered at the double warning in that last sentence.

"Do I make myself clear?" the professor asked.

There were muttered, "Yes, sirs" around the table and the professor hid himself once again behind his paper.

Mr. Stockwell moved his food around on his plate with his fork until finally venturing, "Professor, aren't you the least bit curious about it all?"

"Of course I am, but I am also patient and have my own business to attend to, as you have your studies. And if I'm not mistaken, exams are in two weeks, and I think preparing for them ought to be your primary concern, especially considering everyone's marks to date."

At this response, all the students looked glum, and breakfast became a subdued affair with the earlier agitation of the students now worn off. Karigan shook herself when she realized she'd been so engrossed by the conversation that she hadn't touched her breakfast. She rectified the matter before anyone noticed.

As each student finished his meal, he excused himself and left the table, giving her a quiet, "Good day, Miss Goodgrave." When Cade stood to leave, he did not meet her gaze and barely gave her a nod.

What was that about? she wondered. Did he suddenly decide she was nothing to him? Was he embarrassed? Or, she thought more hopefully, was he trying to make sure none of the servants became suspicious of the two of them behaving in too familiar a way? Whatever Cade's reasons, she found herself vexed. There was no invitation for her to meet him for an evening in the mill. When would she be able to be with him again, and alone?

"My dear," the professor said from his end of the table, startling her. He gazed at her with intent eyes, and she wondered if he guessed at where her thoughts traveled.

"Yes, Uncle?" she asked.

"I was wondering what plans you have for the day."

Plans? Since when did she ever have plans? "I've nothing scheduled," she replied. "Nothing I'm aware of, at any rate."

"Good," he said. "As you may have perceived, there is some unrest in the city—lots of Inspectors in the streets looking for those who did the appalling damage to Dr. Silk's road. I'd like you to remain home and out of their way until the criminals are apprehended and the city is quiet again. Er, work on your needlepoint or whatever it is you young ladies do."

Needlepoint? Karigan almost laughed out loud. He'd forgotten about her broken wrist, and he had no way of knowing what a disaster she was with needle and thread. However, she gave him credit for a performance well done, delivered for the benefit of the staff who attended them. He never forgot they had ears.

His admonition for her to stay home was clear enough. She would not be riding Raven today, not even disguised as Tam Ryder. Even if she'd been born of this time and place and was really the professor's niece, heading out onto streets full of Inspectors and their unnatural Enforcers did not sound palatable.

"I will . . . stay home," she said, the disappointment in her voice unfeigned.

"Very good, my dear. It is for the best. Now I must catch up with those students of mine. There will be no digging today. The Old City is off-limits for the time being, so I shall have to come up with an assignment with which to keep them busy."

He bade her farewell, and only Karigan remained with her tea. The professor, she noted, had left behind his paper. Usually he took it with him. No, not usually, but always. He'd left it on purpose. For her. Servants moved in to start clearing dishes. When one reached for the professor's paper, she forestalled him.

"May I have it, please?"

He nodded and brought it to her.

"Thank you." She had no idea if it was deemed proper for young ladies to read the paper, but she didn't care. Besides, the servant hadn't shown any surprise, hadn't even flinched, when she requested it. She hadn't thought much about the professor's papers before because he'd downplayed their importance. "Rags," he had called them. "Propaganda" for the empire.

Curious, she unfolded the paper and saw that its title, in bold fancy lettering, was *The Mill City Imperial Sun*. A quick look over the front page showed her what she was looking for, a story with the heading: "Traitors Sabotage Archeological Endeavor."

It amazed Karigan that the publisher of this paper could produce and distribute an article so quickly about an incident that had happened just hours ago. The presses of this time must fly compared to those of her own.

The article told of how Dr. Silk's imperially sanctioned archeological project in the Old City had been attacked in the deep of night. There was no mention of the goals of this project, just that the doctor sought items of "great antiquity." Karigan was not surprised by the omission since the paper was a mouthpiece of the empire and could reveal or conceal information as the empire wished. The article stated that Dr. Silk's watchmen had been cold-bloodedly murdered, and that portions of the road that had been so carefully laid out and built with imperial funds had been purposefully damaged.

These traitors to the Empire used black powder to render the road impassable for Dr. Silk's equipment. Dr. Silk states that his project will go on as scheduled. "My work is important to all citizens," he told The Sun, *"and I shall be tireless in my efforts to see it through." The doctor requests that if any of the good citizens of Mill City have any information or suspicions about who committed this crime, or aided and abetted it, please report it to the nearest Inspector Station immediately.*

Nothing like using citizens to inform against one another, Karigan thought. If kept in discord, they were less likely to unite against the emperor. The rest of the paper did little to diminish this impression, even in its reporting of mill productivity, proclaiming those named on the low end "a disappointment" to the "shining ideals of the Empire."

Lesser stories covered house fires and the unveiling of the latest statue of the emperor. Nothing terribly enlightening. There were some advertisements, and she gazed at these with interest. There was hair cream for "gentlemen of discernment," guaranteed to grow back a full head of hair within a month. Rudman Hadley's Great Imperial Circus occupied a quarter of a page, but the black and white etching of clowns and the big top tent did not look terribly jolly. "Coffin Openings at every evening performance!" The advertisement proclaimed. "See the mysteries of death revealed!"

The people here had a strange idea of entertainment. It did not help that she'd been unwittingly made a participant in that entertainment.

Beneath the advertisement for the circus was a notice for a slave auction for later in the week. "Strong males and females of all ages. Good, fertile breeding stock." Her gorge rose, threatening to spew her as yet undigested breakfast. She shoved the paper down the table in revulsion. A servant glanced curiously at her, then collected the paper along with a stack of teacups and saucers, and left the room.

This world, Karigan thought in despair. The professor was right to oppose the empire.

She was roused by the rush of skirts that announced the entrance of Mirriam into the dining room. "There you are!"

Karigan steeled herself against whatever she was going to be accused of this time.

"Lingering over breakfast, are we?"

Karigan glanced at her plate as though the leftover crumbs of her meal proved her guilt.

"Miss Goodgrave! Have you lost your tongue?"

"Um, no."

"Well, it is time to get moving."

"Get moving?" Karigan asked, bewildered. "Get moving to where?"

"Why, to your bed chamber. Mender Samuels is due here any moment."

"Mender Samuels?"

"Honestly. Doesn't your uncle tell you anything?"

"No," Karigan said, with feeling.

Mirriam actually chuckled, unexpectedly easing the strain between the two that had been present ever since Karigan had stood up to Mirriam about Cloudy the cat and other matters. "Well," the housekeeper conceded, "the professor can be rather forgetful. Come, child."

Karigan rose and, grabbing the bonewood, followed Mirriam out of the dining room. "What does Mender Samuels want with me? I'm not sick."

Mirriam glanced at her in surprise. "No, I daresay you are not. In fact, I'd even say you are . . . robust. It is unseemly in a refined young woman of your status. I can only guess it comes of your being reared in the countryside."

Karigan tried to digest the housekeeper's skewed logic. Should she try to be more sickly in order to fit in? Would being "robust" somehow reveal her true identity? "Then why is Mender Samuels coming to see me?"

"Miss Goodgrave," Mirriam said as they began to mount the stairs to the second floor, "you did not expect to be wearing that cast on your wrist to the end of your days, did you?"

TIME

Karigan gazed at Mender Samuels with trepidation and tightened her grip on the bonewood.

"Put that down, silly girl," he admonished her as he polished what looked like the blade of a bone saw.

"You are not coming near me with that," she informed him.

He paid her no heed and simply checked his blade gleaming in the sunlight that filtered through her window.

Mirriam heaved an exasperated sigh. "He isn't going to saw your arm off, Miss Goodgrave, just the cast."

Karigan raised a skeptical eyebrow.

"Put your stick down and come sit at the table so I may do my work," the mender said.

She reluctantly set the bonewood aside, figuring it was just as well the mender did not know how lethal her "stick" could be. She sat at the little table as he directed and placed her forearm on top, pulling up her sleeve to reveal the cast.

The mender looked at it in dismay, wrinkling his nose. "Have you been dragging your arm through a pig sty, Miss Goodgrave?"

Mirriam loosed another great sigh. Karigan knew she had been Mirriam's very trying responsibility, and perhaps she found some vindication in the mender's recognition of her ward's incorrigibility.

Karigan watched closely as the mender sawed through her cast, plaster dust collecting beneath her forearm on the table. When he removed the cast in sections, her relief that he hadn't even nicked her skin, was replaced by repugnance at the odor that rose up reminding her of dead fish. She saw, for the first time in several weeks, the pale thin thing that had once been her forearm. A current of cool air rippled across flesh that hadn't felt a breeze for a month or more, and she sighed then, to have it finally free and in the open.

And now she could satisfy her urge to scratch, which she did furiously, raising flakes of dead skin and plaster dust.

Mender Samuels slapped the back of her hand. "None of that," he said. "I have a jar of cream to relieve the itch."

He took her forearm into his hands, prodded it, and bent the wrist, while Mirriam at his side observed through her monocle. He then asked Karigan to bend it on her own, and rotate her hand, and wiggle her fingers. Her wrist felt dull and weak, but it worked. Mender Samuels grunted with satisfaction and turned to Mirriam.

"See that Miss Goodgrave does not do too much at first, that she uses it gently. It is still fragile. Gradually she may increase its use."

"Yes, Master Samuels."

Karigan held her tongue despite the fact that the mender did not address her directly.

"By the way, why is she using that cane?" he demanded. "I've heard no complaints of her leg injury worsening."

Mirriam raised an eyebrow at Karigan. "Has your injury been bothering you, Miss Goodgrave?"

Karigan didn't know what to say, fearing to be caught in a lie and not wanting the bonewood to be taken away from her.

"Let me see your leg," the mender said.

Karigan's heart sank, but she hitched up the hem of her dress and rolled down her stocking so he could see the well-healed injury.

"Hmm," he said. "This looks good. I see no reason for the walking cane."

To Karigan's surprise, Mirriam came to her defense. "Her uncle gave it to her. I expect she's attached to it."

Karigan nodded eagerly. "It was a gift."

The mender stopped his probing. "There is no medical purpose for it, but if her guardian approves?" He shrugged and told Mirriam he'd be back in a week to check on Miss

Goodgrave's wrist. Then he collected his satchel filled with tools and devices and departed, Mirriam escorting him out.

Karigan wasted no time in bathing her wrist and slathering it with the cream he had left behind, then she gazed at her forearm, acknowledging it would take some work and time to bring it back to its former condition. But she smiled and whirled across her floor in a little dance of pleasure at having it free of the unlamented cast that lay in pieces on her table.

Over the next couple of days, she was frustrated that neither the professor nor Cade invited her to the mill where she could fully work on strengthening her wrist. She thought to ask the professor if she could go on her own, but a safe, private moment to do so never presented itself, since she saw him so rarely. She supposed she could always sneak over to the mill on her own, but doing so felt like it would violate the professor's trust, and that was one thing she could not afford to lose. She could not say for sure, but she did not believe Cade and the professor ventured to the mill either. Perhaps with all the unrest following the sabotage on Dr. Silk's road in the Old City, the professor did not want to be caught engaging in perilous behavior should any suspicion be flung in his direction.

It was hard for her to know exactly what was going on outside the house, except for whatever Luke told her when she visited Raven. Close to a hundred men, he told her, had been rounded up for questioning, and rumor had it that an Inquisitor had arrived from Gossham to lead the interrogations. The number of Inspectors and their Enforcers patrolling the streets, he added, remained uncommonly high.

The professor told her nothing, let on nothing, but he was quieter than usual during the rare times she saw him at meals, indicating to her the level of his concern. Of Cade, she saw only glimpses.

There was nothing she could do about it, so in the privacy of her bed chamber she practiced with her bonewood and bided her time gazing into her mirror shard, but to no avail. She spent hours in the professor's library poring over his atlas of the empire, this one free of Arhys' scribbles. Viewing her own world redrawn and transformed once again exacerbated her feelings of loneliness and sorrow, but she resisted caving in to them, reminding herself she'd find a way home and change this future from the past.

She could not help but stare at the portrait of Amberhill at the front of the book, with his aristocratic face rendered in flattering detail. How did he come to be emperor? she wondered over and over. How could he betray his king? She had never cared for his haughty ways, and while every aristocrat she had ever met vied and schemed for power, she had never sensed in Amberhill the monster who would wreck so much of what was good in Sacoridia to create this empire of his.

When she got home, she'd destroy him if she had to, to prevent him from bringing about this future. If she didn't make it back? Then she'd make him answer for it in the here and now. She'd avenge her family, her friends, and the realm. Yes, she would.

She glanced up from Amberhill's portrait, startled to see Arhys one step into the library and staring at her.

"What are you doing?" the girl demanded.

Karigan considered telling her to go away and mind her own business, but she thought maybe this would be an opportunity to make peace. "I'm looking at the atlas of the empire," she replied.

"You're just looking at pictures. I bet you can't even read."

"You'd lose." Karigan proved it to her by reading from the preface.

The girl sniffed and tossed her golden hair. "I can read very well. Mr. Harlowe says so. I can write, too."

"I'm sure he's correct."

"Bet I can write better than you."

"Perhaps you can."

Frustrated that Karigan didn't challenge her, the girl stomped and declared, "You're ugly."

Just then Lorine paused by the doorway and looked in. "There you are, Arhys. Cook needs you in the kitchen."

Arhys gave Karigan one last contemptuous look that would have rivaled even one of Amberhill's, and flounced out of the room.

Lorine rolled her eyes, then seemed to note what Karigan was looking at. "Ah, I used to spend much time gazing at the atlas, dreaming of far off lands," she said with a smile. "I've never been outside the city."

Karigan found it hard to believe, for she had traveled often, whether with one of her father's merchant trains or as a Green Rider. She could not imagine being confined to one city.

"Then I figured out that all the lands, the whole continent, and lots of islands besides, belong to the emperor, and I stopped dreaming."

"Really?" Karigan asked in surprise. "Why?"

"I figured that since it was all the empire it would be just like Mill City. I wouldn't mind seeing the Capital, though. It is supposed to be wondrous."

There was a knocking on the front door of the house, followed by the even footsteps of Grott the butler as he went to answer it.

"I came to tell you," Lorine said, "that I saw Mistress dela Enfande's carriage drawing up. She's come for the final fitting of your gown for the party."

The gown the seamstress had made for Karigan this time was midnight blue, with threaded silver stars on the front panel of the bodice and sleeves that glimmered in the light. Mistress dela Enfande had said that this would be her most daring design yet. Karigan wasn't sure what made it more daring—it fit much the same as her other dresses—and she could not yet judge how stylish it was in regard to this time. Maybe the neckline was lower, her throat revealed, and that was what was considered "daring." Regardless, the gown was exquisite and lent her, she thought, an air of maturity.

Mistress dela Enfande, however, was not satisfied, and she clucked her tongue over the right sleeve. It was sized, Karigan realized, to fit around her cast. The sleeves were made to be more snug around the forearms with lace spilling from the cuffs like foam.

"I shall have to refit the sleeve, and the right glove as well."

Karigan stood patiently as the seamstress' assistants took measurements, and tweaked and adjusted the fabric with pins.

"I shall have the dress and its accoutrements delivered in

the morning," Mistress dela Enfande told Karigan and Mirriam. Then her gaze turned on Karigan alone. "You, Miss Goodgrave, shall tell me how the design is received, especially by those from the Capital, and you will tell me what *they* are wearing, every detail. Yes?"

"Um, yes," Karigan replied. She had a good eye for such things, having grown up a textile merchant's daughter, but thought she might be focused on other matters at Dr. Silk's party, such as portraying Professor Josston's mad niece and not compromising her true identity.

Mistress dela Enfande and her young ladies took their leave, Mirriam hustling them out of Karigan's room. Karigan closed the door after them and sprawled on her bed. She was of the decided opinion that these fittings were more exhausting than a sword training session with Arms Master Drent.

Her eyelids grew heavy, drooped, and finally closed. She drifted to sleep and dreamed of exquisitely attired cats dancing . . . or was it people dressed as exquisitely attired cats? They swept around a ballroom beneath a chandelier of shattered mirror shards that reflected fragmented light upon the dancers. A chronosphere appeared in her hand. It popped open, and the mechanical man inside, who resembled the professor, swiveled back and forth on his rotating disk tapping out random numbers with his cane.

Tap, tap, tap.

Karigan sensed time racing. Time, she was running out of it.

Tap, tap.

She sat up with a start, groggy and disoriented. She looked about, her gaze settling on the window where Cloudy the cat sat on the sill outside. He raised his paw and tapped the glass.

Oh, Karigan thought with a chuckle, *the source of my dream.*

She was going to let the cat in, but at that moment Mirriam entered her room, and Cloudy leaped out of sight.

"Miss Goodgrave," Mirriam said, "you are late!"

Karigan raised her eyebrows. *Late?* Was she still dreaming?

"For what?" she asked with a yawn.

"Why, the midday meal. Didn't you hear the bells?"

No, she had not. "I'll be down in a moment."

Mirriam nodded, giving Karigan an assessing look that said much without her having to actually say a word. Then she left.

Karigan shook her muddled head. What had she been dreaming about? Something about cats. And running out of time. She laughed.

It was too bad Mirriam had arrived when she had, Karigan would have liked to have invited Cloudy in for a scritch. Hopefully the housekeeper hadn't permanently scared him off.

At last she rose, stretched, and left her room before Mirriam could return and scold her for being late.

CARRIAGE RIDE

The hired carriage sent by Dr. Silk arrived precisely as the city bells pealed out seven hour. Lorine ushered Karigan from her bed chamber. Clad in her midnight blue gown, Karigan attempted to peer beneath the bottom fringe of her veil so she would not miss a step as she descended the staircase. She steadied herself with one velvet gloved hand on the railing, and her bonewood clasped in the other.

No, she was not leaving the bonewood behind. Even if Mender Samuels knew she didn't need it, the other attendees at the party wouldn't know. At least she did not have to fuss with a purse. It was considered crass, she learned, for a woman of Preferred status to carry one, and it was left to her escort, whether a servant or a gentleman, to handle the lady's purse.

It was, Karigan thought, just another way for the empire to constrain its women. In her case, she possessed no coins so the point was moot. However she felt about the empire's controlling even the use of purses by its women, it was a relief not to have to tote around a useless accessory all evening.

There appeared to be a small reception committee waiting for her at the bottom of the stairs, consisting of Mirriam, Grott, the professor, and Cade. Cade looked ill at ease in a stiff woolen suit. It appeared to be a faded brown, and too bulky on him as though acquired second hand. It did not flatter him. He cast her nervous glances, but refused to hold her gaze. Not that doing so was easy with her gauzy veil between them.

"Well, well!" the professor exclaimed in a jovial tone. He, in contrast, cut a dashing figure in a well-tailored suit of deep gray. "You look lovely tonight, my dear, brighter than the stars, doesn't she, Cade."

Cade mumbled something unintelligible.

The professor turned to his staff. "I need a moment alone with my niece and protégé."

"But Dr. Silk's carriage awaits," Mirriam protested.

"And it can continue to wait. Now shoo." He did not speak again until only he, Karigan, and Cade remained in the foyer. In a low voice he told Karigan, "Remember, you are my niece from the asylum. You won't even have to act insane for them to believe it. They've heard it, it is your reputation, and that is enough. If in the unlikely event it is not, and you find yourself in an awkward situation? Then . . . act mad."

"But how?"

The professor shrugged. "Be creative, my dear. And be alert. As I mentioned before, Silk is wily and may try to extract information of one kind or another from you. Cade will be your constant companion and will divert Silk as necessary. He will look after you."

Karigan flicked her gaze at Cade. Really? He was having enough trouble just looking at her now.

"By the way," the professor added, "try not to break any heads with that bonewood. I should hate to have to answer to the Inspectors, especially when they've been so suspicious." He started to turn away, then paused. "One more thing. Luke will follow behind you with my carriage, should you need to leave early, and to keep an eye on things from the outside of wherever this dinner party is being held should anything untoward happen." In a louder voice, his joviality back on display, he said, "And you two shall have an enjoyable evening, eh?" He clapped Cade on the shoulder and left them alone in the foyer.

Shortly Grott returned to place Karigan's matching cloak over her shoulders and to see them to the carriage.

"Huh," Cade said as they stepped through the front door.

"What is it?" Karigan asked, startled just to hear him speak.

"I guess I should not be surprised, but Dr. Silk hasn't sent just any cab to pick us up."

"No, indeed, sir," Grott said in awe. "This is from the Hastings Livery Company, all the way from the Capital."

Karigan, of course, did not know the Hastings Livery Company from any other, but she noted that the coats on the matched pair of standardbreds gleamed in the light of the streetlamp, the silver on their harness shimmering. The carriage itself was a spotless lacquered black with a filigreed "H" on the door. Three coachmen in uniform accompanied the carriage, one up front driving, the other two riding the footboard at the rear. One of the attendants stepped down to open the carriage door as Karigan and Cade approached. He expertly handed Karigan up into the carriage, and she found herself in a commodious cab of shining brass, gold burnished oak, and deep red brushed velvet. A crystal lamp cast a warm glow. She sank into one of the luxuriant cushioned seats, as Cade sat opposite. She had never ridden in anything quite this elegant.

"Would the gentleman and the lady care for some refreshment?" the coachman asked.

"No," Cade said definitively.

Karigan opened her mouth to protest but stopped, remembering she was supposed to be Miss Goodgrave, not Rider G'ladheon.

"Very well, sir," the coachman said, and he closed the door.

"What if *I* wanted something?" Karigan demanded.

"Invariably what they'd offer is wine or brandy or something like that. We need to avoid drink."

When the carriage started forward, Karigan marveled at how distant, almost faint, the hoof beats and the grind of the wheels sounded outside. Little noise seemed to permeate the interior of the cab. "It's so quiet," she remarked.

"It's a hallmark of a Hastings. The cab is almost impervious to noise inside and out. Just as very little sound comes in from outside, conversations inside are not overheard from without. This is why Hastings is the vehicle preferred by those in the Capital seeking discretion. Those who are wealthy enough to hire one, that is."

"So they cannot hear us?" Karigan asked, vaguely gesturing to indicate the coachmen.

"Not likely, but . . ."

"Dr. Silk sent it," she said in a low voice.

Cade nodded. "Most likely he just wishes to impress his guests with his wealth." He leaned toward her and spoke softly. "If word got out that guests were overheard in a Hastings, it would be a tremendous breach of trust, and it would ruin the company's reputation. Not only that, but it would put Dr. Silk in ill odor among his peers. Still . . ."

"It's Dr. Silk," Karigan finished for him in a whisper.

He nodded, and sat back in his seat. He pushed the drape away from the window of frosted glass and squinted, trying to peer through it. "Looks like Luke is following right behind us. I suppose it's better to be obvious than have him sneaking around and looking suspicious."

How did one sneak around in a carriage anyway? Karigan wondered.

Not only was the cab quiet, but the carriage itself rode very solidly with no jarring bumps or thuds. No doubt as much attention had been paid to the engineering of its workings as to the luxurious passenger compartment.

The carriage made several turns, and Karigan was entirely disoriented, able to see little through the frosted glass. "Can you tell where we're going?" she asked.

"I haven't the faintest," Cade replied. "I lost track a few turns ago."

Even though Karigan had known their destination was supposed to be a mystery, and even though she knew Luke followed behind, trepidation of the unknown gnawed at her. She did not like having so little control, and she gripped the handle of the bonewood more firmly. At least she had this weapon, if nothing else.

It further displeased her that Cade continued to avoid looking at her or initiating conversation. It was as if nothing had happened between them that night in the mill. As if—as if she were naught to him.

She thumped him soundly on the leg with her bonewood.

"Ow! What was that for?" He rubbed his calf where she'd struck him.

Karigan smiled beneath her veil. Not only had she roused his attention, but she'd forced him to look at her.

"You've been avoiding me," she said. "I thought—I thought after . . ." Now she found herself at a loss. Why did things never go well for her when it came to men? She shook herself and flipped the annoying veil out of her face so there was no barrier between them. Did Cade actually flinch upon seeing her face bared? "I thought," she now said with resolve, "that after that night when we . . . well, that you might be a little more . . . that you'd at least talk to me."

The light of passing street lamps flashed across his face. He squirmed in his seat and stared at his knees.

"You can't even look at me," she said, her voice higher in pitch from frustration.

"It's not appropriate," he quietly replied, balling his hands together on his lap.

"Looking at me is not appropriate?"

"No. I mean, none of it. I shouldn't have . . ." He shuddered.

She leaned forward and spoke in a whisper in case Dr. Silk had chosen to breach the trust of his peers and the Hastings Livery Company by finding a way to eavesdrop. "Is it because I'm not like the empire's women, obedient and modest?"

"No, no!" he said hastily. "Nothing like that. On the contrary. I . . ." And now he also leaned forward and whispered. "I like that about you, that you are different. I find it . . . stimulating." He actually blushed. Karigan said nothing and waited for him to go on, which only seemed to add to his discomfort. "Well, it's inappropriate."

"Why, because the empire likes to hide its women behind veils and cloth and treat them like children?"

"No." He paused, then, "Like children? Really? Is that what you think?"

She fixed him with a stony glare.

"All right, I guess I can see that," he mumbled. "But no, that is not the basis of my feelings of impropriety."

The carriage gently rocked as it rounded another corner. Improper. Impropriety. She was getting sick of those words. "Then what is the problem?"

"Something I thought you of all people would respect," he replied.

"And what is that?"

He licked his lips, moved in even closer so he could whisper directly into her ear. "My aspiration to be a Weapon, a true Weapon." His breath was warm against her cheek. "To protect Arhys without distraction."

"But I've helped you with your training. I wouldn't call that a distraction."

"I am to be celibate." He'd whispered it so softly she almost didn't hear him. "I must be so I can focus on my duty alone."

Celibate, she thought, and then realized that it insinuated he'd considered its opposite. With her. She did not know whether to laugh or be pleased that the idea had entered his mind. They were cheek to cheek, nearly touching. Her neck and face warmed. She felt that urge to kiss him coming over her again.

"Weapons do not marry," Cade continued. "You must know this. They commit themselves wholly to those whom they serve."

Karigan thought maybe he was reading too much into one kiss to be worrying about marriage.

"It's true, Weapons do not marry," she whispered, all too conscious of his pleasant musky scent, of the heat he radiated from so intimate a proximity, "but it does not mean they are celibates."

"You know this for certain?"

The Order of the Black Shields was secretive and there had been plenty of speculation among her friends as to what actually went on in the private lives of the Weapons. Although the Weapons had allowed her into their world more than any other outsider she knew of, it wasn't like she'd casually chatted with them about the state of their private congresses, or lack thereof. "No," she admitted, "I don't know for certain."

"For me," Cade said, "it is assumed."

This time it was Karigan who looked away, suddenly tired and defeated. She wrenched herself away from him, sliding back in her seat, and pulled the veil down over her face. She'd done it once again, opened herself to someone, exposed herself only to be rebuffed. She was glad she could hide her humiliation behind her veil.

I should stay celibate myself, she thought. *Forget about men, period.* Probably it was all for the best, wasn't it? That he didn't want her? It would be less messy that way when it came time for her to leave.

Cade took her hand into his. "Look, Miss Goodgrave . . . Karigan . . . I—"

She snatched her hand away. "Forget I brought any of this up. Just forget it."

"But . . ." The word hung in the air for a while, then Cade gave up and leaned back into his seat, his posture rigid, and a painful silence followed. It engulfed the cab, and the space felt too close, stifling.

"I am sure you will find a proper gentleman to settle down with," Cade said eventually.

"What? Settle down? *Here?*" she whispered harshly and then laughed. It was a bitter sound. "If you think I'm staying here, you are most profoundly mistaken."

"Where will you go?"

"Home. Back where and *when* I belong."

Cade looked like he'd been punched. It was a mixture of surprise and hurt. "How?" He mouthed it more than whispered it.

She did not answer him for she did not know the answer. A moment later, the carriage eased to a halt. She was relieved when a gentleman in a long-tailed serge coat, with a tall silk hat atop his head, opened the door. He smiled at them, and she found her relief short lived when she realized who he was.

"Welcome," said the ringmaster of Rudman Hadley's Imperial Circus. "Dr. Silk awaits you in the big top."

INTO THE BIG TOP

"The circus?" Cade demanded after he jumped out of the carriage, landing beside Karigan.

"Yes, sir, the finest entertainments you will find in the whole empire." The ringmaster removed his tall hat and extended it toward the big top with a flourish. The walkway was lit with torchlight. "The most amazing, the magnificent, the original, Imperial Circus lays before you!"

Acrobats came tumbling out of the dark. A man appeared before them and inserted a torch into his mouth, then expelled a fiery breath. Karigan and Cade slowly made their way along the path, dazzled by contortionists, jugglers, a woman wound up in a bloated snake.

Karigan was not sure which was worse in the flickering torchlight—the snake or the clowns with their pale faces and false expressions. Whether their painted masks were jolly or grotesque, they all seemed to leer at her even as they cavorted around her.

"If there is all this before we even enter the tent," Cade said, "I wonder what we shall find inside."

She had no idea and wasn't sure she wished to know. From outside they could hear the strains of music, fulsome, metallic tones different than anything she'd ever heard before. It was closer to horns than strings, and deep and powerful.

A harlequin in motley with a half red and half black face bowed them into the tent. All the activity and clamor, the light and color, was too much to take in all at once, and Karigan was glad to have her veil to filter some of the visual assault. Footlights surrounded the entire center ring and were augmented by crystal chandeliers suspended from rigging up above, sending shattered light twinkling across the red and white diamond pattern of the tent ceiling and walls. The tent reminded her of the costume she'd worn to the king's masquerade. How long ago had that been?

Up above, a tightrope walker balanced her way across a wire. Like Karigan, many guests turned their faces up to watch. She wondered if the men enjoyed the novelty of being able to gaze openly at scantily clad females who didn't even conceal their faces with veils.

The source of the music was at the far end of the tent. A man sat at a keyboard contraption with four levels of keys and several pipes that rose up into the heights of the big top, spewing periodic hissing clouds of steam. The man operating it not only had his fingers dashing across the keys and pulling levers and knobs, but also his feet never stopped pumping treadles.

"What is that thing?" Karigan pointed it out to Cade. When the man hit the low notes, it made her bones rattle.

"A music steamer," Cade said. "It can make all the sounds of a band. It means Hadley doesn't have to pay a whole lot of musicians for the same effect, although it doesn't sound as good to my ear."

He did not appear terribly impressed by it, but then he had lived his whole life in this time where mechanicals were commonplace. Karigan wondered fleetingly what Estral would make of the music steamer.

"Hello, hello," a man said, striding right up to them. Karigan recognized him as the circus boss. "Welcome to the Imperial Circus. I am Rudman Hadley. I don't believe we've had the pleasure . . . ?"

Karigan started to speak, but Cade cleared his throat and passed her a warning look. "I am Cade Harlowe, and I'm escorting Miss Kari Goodgrave this evening, niece of Professor Bryce Lowell Josston."

"How interesting," Hadley said, giving Karigan a second look. Once again she was glad of the veil. What if he recognized her as the "corpse" that had "risen" from his sarcophagus the night she arrived? "Professor Josston's mysterious niece. Your custodian has managed to keep you sequestered it would seem. Is this truly your first evening out since your arrival?"

She nodded.

"Very good. Enjoy all that Dr. Silk offers tonight—the entertainment, the food, the exhibits."

He gave a slight bow and moved on to other guests. Karigan thought she and Cade both exhaled in relief at the same time. "Now what?" she asked.

"I guess we do as Hadley suggests—enjoy what's here."

Nearby, a burly man in a black mask hurled knives at a woman splayed against a wooden board behind her. The knives thunked into wood, outlining her figure with a precision Karigan could only admire. When he finished, he bowed to a smattering of applause. To Karigan, the one who deserved most of the acclaim was the woman who had stood unflinching as sharp blades flew at her.

Servants passed among the guests with glasses of wine. Cade demurred for both of them. "No spirits for us tonight. Perhaps there is punch somewhere."

They drifted on past the next attraction, a caged lion with full tawny mane, padding around in circles. Nearby, another cage, this one tall and domed, was draped and guarded. Some of the guests tried to get the guards to tell them what was hidden beneath, but the guards only smiled and told them it was a surprise of Dr. Silk's.

"Not sure if I like the sound of that," Cade murmured.

A goodly number of guests filled the circus ring, supplemented by entertainers and servants. It was odd to be among so many women with their faces blanked by veils, but a few wore veils that barely reached their rouged upper lips. They wore gorgeous gowns that bared more of their necks and revealed more of their curves than any attire she'd seen thus far. Jewels glittered on their fingers, hung from their necks and wrists. All the other women, Karigan included, looked staid in comparison. If Mistress dela Enfande had been hoping for Karigan's gown to make a statement of daring, she had fallen short.

"These women of the Capital," Cade muttered, following her gaze, "no modesty at all."

Karigan raised her eyebrow. There was something about these women. They were less reserved. They laughed more loudly and wore the most dramatic colors—vivid reds, and blues, and golds. The Mill City women were almost like mourners haunting a side show with their quiet demeanors and comparatively drab clothing and lack of baubles.

"What about the circus women?" Karigan asked him.

"Huh?"

"The circus women. How is their modesty level?"

"That's different. They don't count."

"Really? Why not?"

"They're circus performers," he said, as if that should explain all.

"So it's all right for them not to cover themselves with veils?"

"It is the way it is," he said gruffly.

Some of the so-called modest women were giving Cade studied second looks through their veils as they passed by. If they only knew he wanted nothing to do with the opposite gender.

Something caught his attention and without warning he angled off across the ring. Karigan hurried to catch up. Fortunately the sawdust of the ring had been removed and replaced with wood flooring, otherwise her skirts would have raised quite a cloud and all the fine attire of the guests would be coated in a layer of dust.

Cade halted before one of the exhibits Hadley had mentioned. It was a life-sized sculpture of a p'ehdrose—part man, part moose—and enormous. The moose part looked authentic, as if the neck and head of a real moose had been removed, the body stuffed by a taxidermist, and the torso of an oversized man inserted into the shoulders and chest of the moose. The human part was not quite so well rendered, the skin looking like the texture and color of parchment, and puckered, the hair of his beard and head strawlike. The figure held a bow with arrow nocked, as if about to loose it.

"I've read about this," Cade said, an expression of wonder on his face. "It's part of the emperor's private collection."

Karigan had thought Amberhill had better taste than this.

The figure was, she thought, grotesque. Then she read the inscription on the brass plaque on the platform that held the figure: *This, the last known p'ehdrose in the world, the chieftain, Ghallos, was hunted and slain by the emperor in the first year of his reign.*

"Ghallos's mate must still be at the palace," Cade said.

"Mate?" A horrible feeling came over Karigan.

"Yes, her name was Edessa. The emperor hunted all their people to extinction."

"They're real?" Karigan clapped her hand over her mouth to prevent further outbursts. As it was, Cade wasn't the only one giving her peculiar looks.

"Of course they were real," Cade said. "You see the evidence before you."

Karigan was glad she hadn't had any wine for she suddenly felt ill. The figure before her was not just an artistic rendering of a p'ehdrose, but an actual p'ehdrose. A taxidermied p'ehdrose.

No one in her own time had ever seen one, in fact no one had in known history. They were legends, just like Eletians had been, until the Eletians decided to make themselves known to the world again. It was said that the horn carried by the First Rider had been given to her by a p'ehdrose, but that had been a *story.*

She could hardly believe it. The p'ehdrose were *real.* She was both appalled and fascinated by the stuffed specimen and could not help but stare at it, the human part muscular and powerful, the head positioned in a proud tilt, glass eyes shining in the light.

"Admiring old Ghallos, are we?" It was Dr. Silk, and before Karigan knew it, he was bowing over her hand.

"I've always wished to see him," Cade said, "and his mate."

"Ghallos is on loan for this one special evening," Dr. Silk replied. "Alas, we left Edessa at the palace as insurance that should some accident befall Ghallos, at least one specimen would remain. He is in good condition, is he not? When he was mounted, though, the technique for preserving the human part of his flesh had not been perfected. A tricky thing, that, the preservation of human flesh."

Karigan felt even more nauseated and turned her back to the display, unable to look any longer at poor Ghallos. She was thrilled that the p'ehdrose were real, but now they were extinct. Why had Amberhill done that? Why had he destroyed everything?

"I'm sorry, is it too much, the display of this beast?" Dr. Silk asked her. "I know you have, er, delicate sensibilities."

Cade stepped between the two of them. "Are you all right, Miss Goodgrave?"

Now he decided to pay her attention?

"They stuffed a p'ehdrose," she murmured, still incredulous.

"Miss Goodgrave?" He peered at her as if trying to see through her veil.

She shook herself remembering who she was and who stood nearby. "I wish to see something else."

"I have just the thing," Dr. Silk said, pushing Cade aside. He hooked his arm around hers and led her away.

At first Karigan stiffened at his touch, but she forced herself to relax. It was a perfectly acceptable and gentlemanly gesture, though in her time she would have been asked for her approval first.

Cade followed so closely he practically stepped on her heels.

"I am sorry your uncle could not join us this evening," Dr. Silk said.

She doubted that very much, but she nodded as if accepting his apology. "He is busy with work tonight."

"I'm sure he is," Dr. Silk said in a voice like a purr. "He is often busy. And what is my esteemed colleague working on these days?"

Karigan narrowed her eyes. Was he hoping to attain some unguarded information from her? In answer, she shrugged, and said very carefully, "Old forks and spoons, I think. Mr. Harlowe would know the particulars."

"That would be about it," Cade said, striding alongside them almost too eagerly, Karigan thought. Unlike Dr. Silk, Cade lacked subtlety. "With the Old City closed off to excavations due to . . . due to the recent incident, the students are learning to catalog the artifacts we already have."

Their host chuckled. "Industry to keep idle hands from finding trouble. I approve."

He greeted other guests as he led her along, pointedly ignoring Cade. He introduced her to an elderly man, hard of hearing. "This is Josston's niece, Miss Goodgrave."

"Good for the grave, you say?" the old man asked, cupping his ear.

"No, this is Miss Goodgrave," Dr. Silk said in an elevated voice. "Josston's niece."

"Ooh." The old man chortled. "Josston's niece. I thought you were sending me off to an early grave, young man." He patted Dr. Silk on the shoulder and moved on in halting steps, chuckling to himself.

"An early grave?" Dr. Silk laughed softly himself. "Wills Barrow is nearly ninety-five years old."

As Dr. Silk and Karigan approached a display in a glass case, other guests deferentially made space for them.

"Some of my better archeological finds," he said.

Karigan gazed into the case with interest at corroded pieces of bronze that must have once been daggers and pieces of swords. They had no guards, and nothing remained of the hilts.

"Black Age weapons," Dr. Silk said. "Or earlier. It's a very hard time about which to make conclusions."

"The Black Ages were before the emperor?" Karigan knew when the Black Ages had been. They'd led into the period of Mornhavon and the Long War, but she thought she ought to ask questions as Miss Goodgrave would.

Dr. Silk smiled. "Very good. Yes, my dear, long before the emperor came and provided salvation for our people from despot rulers."

Karigan tried not to bristle at the insinuation of King Zachary being a "despot." He'd been—still was—a just and fair ruler.

Other artifacts included metalwork pendants and sigils with rough depictions of lizards or dragons, some deteriorated almost beyond recognition.

"These," Dr. Silk said, "are works by the emperor's very early ancestors."

Amberhill's ancestors? That would explain the dragon sigil used by the empire, Karigan thought. "Is this also from the Black Ages?"

"Have you ever heard of the sea kings?"

"Very little," she replied truthfully.

"They once ruled these lands, and their blood runs through many of our people, perhaps yours, too."

So, Karigan wondered, did Amberhill fancy himself a conquering sea king? What in the five bloody hells would have put that notion into his head?

"The sea king's people worshipped the sea dragon, and dragons in general," Dr. Silk explained. "It shows up as a recurring motif in much of their handiwork. Does your uncle show you any of his findings?"

Not an innocent question, she surmised, and wouldn't he like to know the truth. She was not about to reveal the professor's secret treasure trove, so she replied, "Not really. His office is quite a mess."

Dr. Silk appeared to think about her answer for a moment as if trying to divine a hidden meaning, before moving onto the next series of artifacts, pairs of rusted spurs, their leather straps rotted away. He did not question her further.

There were several more artifacts in the case, of varying antiquity and condition, but the gleam of a bright blade caught the corner of Karigan's eye, and disregarding the other artifacts, she moved down the case, her heart thudding faster and faster.

Dr. Silk saw her interest and said, "Ah. A more recent piece, maybe only two hundred years old. I found it in a very unusual site."

He had to have, Karigan thought, for it was her very own saber that she had lost in Castle Argenthyne, in the heart of Blackveil Forest. She would know it anywhere.

THE IMAGE TRAPPER

Karigan knew each scratch and nick of the finely honed blade, the feel of the leather-wrapped hilt against her palm. She was so startled, so overwhelmed to see it here, she backed into the stolid person of Cade, who grabbed her shoulders to steady her. Dr. Silk appeared not to notice her reaction. He was bent over the case, the saber gleaming in the lenses of his specs.

Cade looked at Karigan. What could she tell him? *How* could she tell him this was her sword? She flexed her hand, yearning to grasp the hilt.

"A very unusual find, indeed," Dr. Silk murmured. "Not that we haven't found plenty of swords like this. They were favored by the mounted units of the last despot king."

"What makes it so unusual?" Karigan asked, her voice quavering. Although she knew where it must have been found, maybe this would be a way of communicating to Cade its importance without having to say it herself.

"We found it completely out of context in a place you would not expect to find one. We've dug up a number in the Old City, and a handful have been found scattered across the empire. This one was found in the Imperial Preserve, which was once known as the Blackveil Forest, inside the castle of an ancient civilization. There were a few other artifacts out of place there, but I chose this particular piece for display because I like the old weapons."

"I've read most of your papers on your various discoveries," Cade said.

"I should hope so, Mr. Harlowe, as it is your field of study, after all."

"Yes, sir, but I don't recall mention of any discoveries like this in the Imperial Preserve. I know there had been surveys, but . . ."

"I had not written about this because disclosure was not permitted at the time. We needed to study the problem further."

"And your conclusions?" Cade asked.

"Simply that some poor, brave wretches had entered what we know as the Imperial Preserve, most likely sent against their wills by the king of that time. One sees references to rumors of such an expedition, but though I've looked tirelessly, I've never been able to find definitive documentation." He sighed and shook his head. "It will be one of those mysteries to plague future generations of archeologists, I imagine."

Karigan saw realization spread across Cade's face as he connected the sword to her. She was glad Professor Josston had obtained the documentation that Silk could not find. She could only imagine what would happen if he knew that it did, indeed, exist, and that one of the "poor, brave wretches" stood there beside him.

She had thought she would never see her sword again, that it would lay abandoned forever in the depths of Castle Argenthyne. She certainly could not have imagined seeing it on display in this fashion. It was so close. All she need do is break the glass case and reach in, but she couldn't do that. No, not now, not even as someone who was supposed to be insane. They'd just take it away from her and ask too many questions.

She wrenched her gaze from it, walked determinedly away as if she weren't very interested. In a daze, she drifted past a dog act, a little mongrel leaping through a hoop to the delighted applause of onlookers. Both Cade and Dr. Silk caught up with her. She halted when suddenly confronted with a great gray eagle, its wings outspread, the feathers glistening in multi-hued brilliance in the fragmented light of the big top. He was magnificent, his beak as sharp as a dagger and his talons powerful and sharp enough to deeply score the massive branch he perched on. He was as majestic as the one gray eagle she had once met, but inanimate. Dead. He was another stuffed specimen with glass eyes lacking the fire of life.

"Another excellent kill by the emperor," Dr. Silk said. "It is rather fearsome, isn't it?"

Karigan wanted to say it was tragic, and that his emperor was a murderer, but Cade pulled her, unresisting, past the display, perhaps sensing her sorrow and the fury that had been building toward Amberhill.

"Perhaps it is too fearsome," Dr. Silk mused. "My apologies to the lady. Perhaps Miss Goodgrave would like to see one of our modern marvels rather than dusty old relics of the past?"

Without waiting for an answer, he once again took Karigan's arm and led her off across the ring, Cade staying resolutely at her side. Being tugged this way and that by the two men was getting annoying. Cade, she thought, was only trying to be Weaponly, but she was tiring of this subordinate role she must play.

Dr. Silk took them to a small covered wagon which stood parked next to a curtained area. A cluster of guests milled around it. Fancy lettering on the wooden-sided wagon proclaimed: *Fine Image Trapping by T.C. Stamwell.*

"An image trapper?" Cade asked in surprise. "I've read about image trapping but haven't seen it done."

"You are a studious boy," Dr. Silk said, and Karigan felt Cade bristle beside her at the jibe. "Now you may see it for yourself," Dr. Silk went on. "The process has been simplified, so I believe it will spread across the empire."

"What is image trapping?" she asked. It sounded dangerous.

"In this case, portraiture."

Hanging from a wire strung along the side of the wagon were small framed pictures. They were all black and white portraits of gentlemen with serious expressions and stiff postures. They had not been drawn or painted as far as she could tell. She could not identify the medium that had captured such realism.

"Would you like to try?" Dr. Silk asked her.

"Er, try what?"

"Having your portrait made."

She was dubious and found Dr. Silk's motives highly suspect, still having no idea what the procedure entailed. "Won't it take very long?" And then she gestured at the portraits. "And isn't it just for men?"

"No on both counts. It takes less than a minute, and only the faces of gentlemen are revealed publicly, as is appropriate. You may take your portrait home and give it to your uncle to display as he wishes."

"I don't think—" Cade began.

"Now, now, Mr. Harlowe," Dr. Silk said, forestalling him with a black gloved hand. "I have been through the process a few times myself and it is entirely harmless."

"I don't know." Cade visibly struggled with himself, at once eager to try the image trapping and reluctant to comply with Dr. Silk's wishes.

"We'll do you first then, and when you see how easy it is, there shall be no question. Now come, come." Dr. Silk cut through the line of waiting patrons. They moved respectfully out of his way, and the man at the head of the line ceded his place.

Karigan suspected that propriety compelled Cade to follow and play along. One did not refuse the wishes of one of the empire's most important men at his own party, and that doing so would have only drawn unwanted attention and questions.

A man in an apron with his sleeves rolled up emerged from the back of the wagon. He pushed his specs up on his nose and took in the line that had formed. "Dear me," he said. "I should have brought an assistant."

He dismounted the steps of the wagon and bowed to Dr. Silk. "You are wishing another portrait, sir?"

"No, T.C., but this boy and this lady wish to have theirs done."

"Oh, very good. Together, or singly?" He gazed at Karigan and Cade as if attempting to establish their relationship.

"Singly," Dr. Silk replied. "The boy first, so the lady can see that it is painless."

T.C. Stamwell clapped. "Ah, new to image trapping, are

we? Come with me then. It is a fascinating process that preserves the captured image forever." He prattled on about wet plates, emulsion, and salt solutions as he led them behind the curtained area. There, they discovered a small stage set with a painted pastoral scene as a backdrop. An empty chair stood in the center of the stage.

A wooden box sat propped atop a three-legged apparatus in front of the stage, a spyglass-like protrusion aimed at the chair. T.C. Stamwell directed Cade to sit in the chair and adjusted his pose, using an armature with a neck brace and headrest behind to hold him still.

"The key, Mr. Harlowe, is to maintain that pose without moving. Keep your face relaxed. Do not speak, laugh, or sneeze. But you can be easy for a minute more while I get ready."

Cade looked nervous, Karigan thought. She still did not understand what was supposed to happen.

Stamwell aimed three bright phosphorene lamps at Cade, who squinted in the light.

"What is the light for?" she asked.

"It brightens his image so we may capture it," Stamwell replied. "You see, we are painting with light and shadow."

His reply did little to answer her question. Perhaps if she'd been born of this time she would understand.

"Now, Mr. Harlowe, please hold your position as we discussed. Tilt your chin up. That's it." Stamwell gazed through a hole in his wooden box, then lowered it a little by winding a wheel crank on the apparatus that supported it, and twisted the spyglass protrusion he referred to as the lens. When he was done, he said, "I am going to begin image trapping *now*." He removed a cap from the lens and flipped an hourglass on a nearby table.

Karigan fingered the handle of the bonewood, waiting for something to happen. If the image trapping showed signs of endangering Cade in any way, she'd make short work of that wooden box and T.C. Stamwell. But nothing happened. Absolutely nothing. Cade sat there stiffly, unmoving, his face expressionless. She found herself holding her breath along with him.

"Hold steady, Mr. Harlowe, you are doing just fine."

Karigan's muscles tensed as if she were the one who had been told to remain still. When all the sand emptied into the bottom half of the hourglass, she guessed only half a minute had elapsed, but it had felt much longer.

Stamwell covered the lens with the cap and said, "All right, Mr. Harlowe, we are done. I will take the plate into the wagon where the chemicals will quicken your image and preserve it."

Cade sighed loudly in relief, and Stamwell chuckled as he removed the "plate" from a slot in the side of the wooden box and headed up the steps into his wagon.

That was it? Karigan wondered. That was how an image was trapped? It did not seem so bad. Did the image trapper hold captive some essence of a person? She gave Cade a sideways glance, but he appeared wholly unaffected. She examined Stamwell's wooden box. There was not much to see, but when she gazed through the viewing hole from behind, she discovered the now vacated chair and stage were upside down. She jerked back in surprise and saw that outside of the box, the world remained upright.

"You see?" Dr. Silk said. "Perfectly harmless. A mirror within turns the view upside down."

She gazed through it once more and started again. Not because everything was upside down—no, she was expecting that—but because the dim form of Yates the ghost sat in the chair sketching away. She took in a hard breath, choking back his name lest she shout it aloud in Silk's presence. Then he simply faded from her vision. She stepped back from the wooden box, shaking. She hid her hands behind her back so the men would not see them trembling.

Cade, unaware of her distress, examined the box. "A modern wonder," he murmured.

"Exactly," Silk said. "I believe the emperor will be most intrigued by it when he next awakens."

Karigan shook herself. It was not the first time Yates had appeared to her, but it was so unexpected to see him here. *Yates, what are you trying to tell me?* He did not look alarmed or agitated in anyway. He'd shown no awareness of her—just kept sketching. Perhaps she would never know. Perhaps his spirit was just as restless as he had been in life.

Stamwell returned wiping his hands with a towel. "The image came out very well, and now it is fixing."

Fixing what? Karigan wondered.

"Miss Goodgrave," Stamwell said, "it is your turn."

"Miss Goodgrave is a modest lady," Cade said. "I do not think she will wish to remove her veil in front of a gentleman who is not family."

"T.C. Stamwell is an imperially licensed image trapper," Dr. Silk said, "and he is legally permitted to trap the faces of ladies as well as gentlemen."

Dr. Silk, Karigan thought, seemed a little too eager to see what her veil concealed. If she allowed her image to be trapped, who would see it besides Stamwell? Dr. Silk? Mr. Hadley? Dr. Silk would then know her face and perhaps somehow use it to his advantage, and Mr. Hadley might recognize her as the animated corpse that had stepped out of his sarcophagus, and cause trouble.

"I do not wish to try," she said. "I do not wish to have my image . . . trapped."

"Come, come, Miss Goodgrave," Dr. Silk said in a cajoling voice. "It is harmless. No one will view it except Mr. Stamwell, unless you wish it."

"When it is done, I will wrap it so no one else can see it," Stamwell said.

"If she does not wish it, she does not wish it," Cade said.

"As your host, I insist you indulge me." Dr. Silk said it while smiling, but his smile was underlain with threat.

"She does not—" Cade began.

"The other ladies have enjoyed having their portraits made and have shown gratitude," Dr. Silk said.

Karigan sensed Cade's increasing tension, and that the conversation was about to escalate into an argument. She placed her hand on his arm to still him. Arguing with Dr. Silk would not end well. He was an important man, a dangerous man, and already the professor's enemy. And the professor's student, a young man of low status, could be harmed in many ways by someone of the doctor's ilk. She suspected that the very least damage he could inflict on Cade was to disrupt his education at the university, although

Dr. Silk was capable of doing far worse to anyone who displeased him.

It was also possible that strenuous refusals—whether from
her or on her behalf—would only rouse the doctor's suspicions further. When it came down to it, making him angry
seemed more dangerous than revealing her face. As for Mr.
Hadley? Well, he was nowhere in sight, and in any case, the
professor could handle him.

She glanced at the wooden box with the lens. On a whole
other level, she couldn't help but be curious about this image-
trapping business, and she wondered what her portrait might
look like. "You promise not to show my image to any other?"
she asked Stamwell. Not that she would wholeheartedly believe any such promise, but she had to keep up pretenses.

"As you wish, Miss Goodgrave," he said and bowed.

"Very well, I will allow it."

"But Miss Goodgrave—" Cade began.

"I have made up my mind, Mr. Harlowe."

His expression turned stony, but he did not argue further.

"I am delighted," Dr. Silk said with an air of victory. "You
will not be disappointed."

"Miss Goodgrave, please be seated," Stamwell said.

"Will I feel anything?" Karigan asked.

"No, nothing at all. Now, if you would be so kind as to remove your veil."

"Just a moment," Cade said. "Dr. Silk?"

Dr. Silk raised his eyebrows expectantly.

"As Miss Goodgrave is about to remove her veil, I ask, as
her chaperone, entrusted by her uncle, that you please step
outside."

Anger flickered across Dr. Silk's face, and then it was gone.
He was clearly unused to being told what to do, but he did not
protest. He simply bowed and slipped out between the curtains. The fact that he did not argue indicated to Karigan that
he intended to see the portrait later.

She sat through the process as Cade had, wondering if
Yates were nearby. Perhaps she was sitting on him? Would
she know? Not a reassuring thought. Although she must remain still for only half a minute, her nose tickled, and it was

difficult to resist rubbing it or shifting her position. The neck brace kept her from moving her head, which just made her want to move it more. She could have sworn she felt a cold touch on her shoulder—Yates? These, however, were the only discomforts she experienced. She did not feel any of her essence being drawn out to be trapped in Stamwell's box. She felt nothing at all, just as he promised. When it was done, Stamwell assured them he'd have the portraits prepared for them before their departure.

They thanked him, and before leaving the curtained area Karigan once more dropped her veil over her face. Outside, Dr. Silk was nowhere to be seen. The clamor of the music steamer faded away, and its absence left behind a deafening silence. On a high daïs in the center of the ring, a brawny man in balloon trousers and a feathered headdress swung a mallet against a gong. The chatter of guests died away as the tone of the gong reverberated throughout the big top. The ringmaster mounted the daïs and shouted in his well-practiced voice through a speaking horn, "Ladies and gentlemen, dinner is served!"

Karigan saw no food, no tables, no chairs. Where were they supposed to dine if not here in the big top? But then tables did appear. They trundled in through the main entrance, covered with white cloths and all set with plates and silver. That was to say, she saw them trundle in by themselves, rolling in on iron wheels under their own power, and without anyone to guide them.

PERFORMANCES OF
DESECRATION

 murmur arose among the guests. Even they, the people of this time, were surprised and astonished by this display of apparently autonomous tables. *Click-clack-click-clack.* They kept rolling in until they arranged themselves into two straight lines across the ring. When they halted, servants swooped in with chairs and helped seat guests. No few of them peeked under the tablecloths to discover the secret of the tables.

"How'd they do that?" Karigan whispered to Cade as they were seated.

"I'm not sure," Cade said, his forehead creased, but others were murmuring about etherea and etherea engines.

She peeked under the tablecloth but saw nothing more than the undercarriage and wheels.

"Etherea," she muttered. But magic was dead here, wasn't it?

"A tremendous waste of it," Cade whispered. "Just to impress us lowly citizens of Mill City."

If etherea, the natural element that allowed magic to occur, had powered the tables, why hadn't she been able to touch it with her brooch? Could it be isolated, contained so it did not spread out into the environment?

Without her brooch, she could not test it. Etherea was invisible, inaudible, without odor or taste. Perhaps those in the past who were more magically gifted, such as Great Mages, could sense etherea, but there had been no one that strong for centuries, probably not since the Long War.

"Silk is showing off his wealth and power by using etherea frivolously," Cade muttered. "As if the rest of this is not enough." He gestured to take in the whole of the big top.

The wonder of the tables appeared to wear off among the guests as servants brought out steaming platters, but Karigan thought she heard their table chuff. Maybe she was hearing things, but the sound, subtle as it was, seemed to come from beneath the table, and it hadn't sounded mechanical. The table then quivered, causing water, jellies, and sauces to ripple, and dinnerware to clatter. The other guests chattered on as if nothing was amiss, but Karigan couldn't help but glance under the table again. She didn't see anything she hadn't seen before. Was it . . . alive? Surely not. It did not move again or make any noises.

A string quartet started playing, not quite filling the void of sound left behind by the music steamer, but far more pleasant. Still, the whiney sawing of the strings grated on her nerves.

The chair to her left remained unoccupied, even as the first course, bowls of clawfish bisque, were placed before the guests. She wondered how she was supposed to eat it from beneath her veil. She'd never eaten while veiled in the professor's house. The women of the Capital with their stylishly short veils had no problem, but the women of Mill City only seemed to pretend to eat, dipping their spoons into the bisque, stirring it a little, but never attempting to bring it under their veils to their lips.

It smelled wonderful, and Cade slurped his beside her. Karigan considered trying to actually eat some. If she broke some code of acceptable behavior, the proper people could always put it down to her not knowing better after her stint in the asylum. But she did not wish to draw attention to herself. She sighed, dipped her spoon, and stirred.

Shortly after the servants collected the bisque bowls, Dr. Silk reappeared and seated himself beside her. She frowned and sensed Cade straightening in his chair. A quick glance revealed a tightening of his features. Even the table creaked subtly as though its wood was contracting.

"Seems I missed the opening course," Dr. Silk said cheerfully. He snapped out a napkin and let it float to his lap. "How was it?"

Karigan wished she knew. But as it turned out, she didn't

have to supply an answer. A man with a gold-rimmed monocle across the table said, "Delicious bisque. Positively delightful."

The servants brought out a meat course next. The men sawed into the beef and conversed gregariously. The short-veiled women were more delicate, cutting tiny pieces to eat, chatting animatedly with their neighbors. The long-veiled women cut dainty pieces, too, and arranged them around their plates, but none of it made it beneath their veils to their mouths.

Of all the idiotic things, Karigan fumed, her stomach growling at all the tantalizing scents. She was going to have to ask for something from the kitchen when she got home, and when she did, there wouldn't be any of this useless *picking.*

She tried listening to the conversations going on around her, but they were unrevealing unless she wanted to know about a dear uncle's gout or the "tiresome habits" of servants. The wise, she guessed, did not discuss sabotage and the rounding up of a hundred men for questioning at a dinner party hosted by one of the very Preferred of the emperor, especially when he was within earshot.

"I trust you are finding the evening entertaining?" Dr. Silk asked.

"Um, yes," she said quickly to cover the rumble of her belly.

Dr. Silk smiled and focused on his meal. Sitting beside him, she could study his profile. She could almost see behind the lenses of his specs, and she tried to, surreptitiously, without seeming to stare. She could not see his eyes, but his eyelashes were white.

Odd, she thought. There might be silver and gray in his hair but no white.

He caught her gazing at him, and she turned away, pretending to eat.

"Tell me, Miss Goodgrave, what do you do to amuse yourself in your uncle's house?" he asked.

Another seemingly innocuous question. Was he testing her again? "Oh, the usual things," she replied airily. "I've been given a few books to read, and I visit Raven."

"Ah, that troublesome horse, but I am actually grateful to

him since it was he who allowed us to meet. Very fortuitous, don't you think? How else do you use your time?"

Karigan stared at the untouched meat on her plate. "The use of my time would not interest a gentleman."

"I wouldn't be so sure about that. Everything about you interests me, my dear."

Was it politeness, or too intense a regard? She shifted uncomfortably in her chair. Cade's expression had gone all stony again. Dr. Silk appeared older than her father. She had to remind herself that he was not so much expressing admiration for her as digging for information.

"Tell me—" he began, but he was interrupted by a man on his other side. He made a barely perceptible noise of annoyance but turned to the man and engaged in conversation. Karigan nearly wilted in relief to have his attention directed elsewhere.

A fish course came and as a bread basket was offered to her, she could not help herself. She snatched a still warm, doughy roll, tore it in half and slathered it with butter. She broke it into smaller pieces, slipped them up under her veil, and popped them into her mouth.

The titter of laughter drifted from across the table. Two short-veiled women of the Capital seemed to be watching her and laughing. With the music and noise of other conversations swirling around she caught only a few of the words they shared with one another: *bumpkin, unstylish,* and *insane.*

Let them laugh and talk about me, Karigan thought. Having Dr. Silk sitting next to her probably had aroused their attention even more than her "background." She didn't care one way or the other. She was starving, so when chocolate truffles were presented to her, she was not bashful. At first the Mill City women shook their heads in disapproval, their long veils swaying, but then a few decided to follow her example and actually ate the truffles, not just moved them around on their plates. Karigan smiled. Was it a groundswell of insurrection she'd just started? Probably not, but at least a few of these women got to enjoy chocolate this evening.

Dr. Silk showed no particular concern at her small rebellion. Either he had not noticed, or he accepted it as one of her mad eccentricities.

"You were going to tell me how you spend your days," he said to her.

Taken off guard, she almost swallowed a truffle whole. Trying not to choke, she turned the question back at him. "How do you spend *your* days, Dr. Silk?"

He smiled, like a cat pleased to be playing with a mouse. "The use of my time would not interest a lady."

Fair turnabout, she thought.

Dr. Silk laughed softly in delight. "Now now, my dear. I simply tease. My days are fully occupied by work on my latest project. Except for tonight, of course."

"What is your project?"

"Unearthing old things, just like your uncle."

"Surely you're not digging up just forks and spoons."

"Indeed, not." But he offered no more. It appeared they were at something of an impasse. He sipped his wine and then asked, "What do you hear of your parents? You are so very far away from them."

Cade tensed beside her, a truffle poised halfway to his mouth. The professor had supplied her with an extensive false background filled with enough details for a book. Even with her good memory, it was impossible to memorize the names of all her supposed relations, where they lived, where her false father had been schooled and where he worked as an overseer at a large imperial farm. Perhaps, she thought, simplicity would be the better approach. She'd be less likely to make a mistake, and she could shut down Dr. Silk's line of questioning at the same time.

Dr. Silk waited, just as Cade waited, for her response.

"I do not wish to think of them," she said finally. "They put me in an asylum. My uncle is now my guardian."

Dr. Silk remained quiet. Karigan stared at her hands folded on the table. Cade popped his truffle into his mouth and chewed mechanically.

"Please accept my apology," Dr. Silk said at last, "for broaching an obviously difficult topic. I did not wish to distress you."

Karigan doubted he was at all apologetic, but she nodded in acceptance.

Before they could continue the awkward conversation, a note chimed from somewhere on Dr. Silk's person. He pulled a chronosphere from his waistcoat pocket. Karigan was not the only one who stared in curiosity as he opened the device and a tiny mechanical hummingbird picked out the time.

After a mere glance he snapped it shut and announced, "Now you must forgive me once again as I must leave your side, with much regret, to attend to more entertainments." He stood and bowed deeply to her and left. She felt, more than saw, the table sag as though it was relieved Dr. Silk had departed. If so, she could relate—Dr. Silk's presence had left her as exhausted as a long, hard run.

Cade leaned toward her. "You did well," he whispered.

Glasses of wine were refilled, plates removed and replaced with fruit and cheese plates. She was pleased. Fruit and cheese she could nibble on without making a mess. Some of the long-veiled women once again followed her example. She'd start a revolution yet.

They did not see Dr. Silk again until the eating and drinking waned. He mounted the daïs at center ring. Quickly, conversation diminished.

"I trust everyone enjoyed their dinner?" There were affirmative responses, few of them female, and Dr. Silk beamed. "I will ask now that you turn your chairs toward me, ensuring your legs do not impede the movement of the tables as they leave."

Karigan could not help but lightly pat the table top. Was it her imagination, or did the wood hum with a purr? It was overridden by the mechanisms creaking as the tables were set in motion with no visible person or method of control in view. Most of them moved at a sedate pace toward the big top entrance, but her own raced away, scattering crockery and silver overboard and crashing onto the floor, its tablecloth whipping behind it. Guests and servants alike peeled out of its way. One man who was not fast enough screamed as one of the wheels ran over his foot.

Good heavens, Karigan thought as she watched after her unruly table, but it made it out of the big top without further casualties.

Beside her, Cade sat with his arms crossed and a scowl plastered on his face, probably displeased once more by the frivolous use of etherea. She elbowed him.

"What was that for?" he demanded.

"You are radiating your disapproval," she quietly scolded.

He shifted in his chair, his expression struggling toward neutrality.

"I've a few more surprises for you tonight," Dr. Silk announced, "entertainments I'm sure you won't soon forget." He gestured and six men in white face rolled out a stone sarcophagus, balanced on a hand wagon, and placed it in front of the daïs.

Karigan groaned.

"From within the Capital, I bring you a box of mysteries, the sarcophagus of a prominent person who lived long ago."

Karigan tensed. The Capital, she remembered, was essentially her home province of L'Petrie. She was too far away to make out the glyphs carved in the stone of the sarcophagus.

"What treasures were buried with this man?" Dr. Silk asked. "He was, after all, an affluent merchant of Corsa."

Karigan stiffened even more and, as Dr. Silk took a dramatic pause, her fear grew with the pairing of the words "merchant" and "Corsa."

"Open it!" some of the guests called out. "Let us see!"

"You want to know what has lain asleep for so long?" Dr. Silk's question was followed by choruses of, "Yes! Open it now!"

"It is a good thing the professor is not here," Cade grumbled to Karigan, unaware of her growing horror. "He cannot abide these performances of desecration."

"Open it!" the guests cried out.

Dr. Silk clapped once and the servants in white face returned with tools. While they worked levers beneath the heavy cover, Karigan sent up a prayer that no one from her time was in that coffin, no one she knew. A merchant of Corsa? It couldn't possibly be her father, could it? There had been many affluent merchants in Corsa throughout the centuries. Even if the chances were miniscule, she could not help but think it.

To her, her father still lived, carried on, if in another time. She could not help but wonder what had become of him. How would he have responded to her never returning from Blackveil? He would not have remained idle while Amberhill ravaged Sacoridia. No, he would not have stood for it. Had he been lost in the turmoil as many of her friends must have been? Or had he died of sickness or old age?

Surely Dr. Silk knew nothing of her true identity. He couldn't have found out, could he? Was he doing this to torture her? Anything was possible in this strange world, but she did not think he'd allow her to walk freely if he knew who she really was. The coffin of a Corsa merchant was quite a coincidence, though.

She swallowed hard, wishing to be someplace else, anywhere, but she could not tear her gaze away from the servants levering the cover off the sarcophagus. Stone grated against stone and the cover teetered on edge, finally sliding to the floor with a thunderous boom. Dust rose from the open sarcophagus, and Dr. Silk gazed down into it from his perch on the daïs.

"Ah, yes, a nicely carved coffin lies within." He gestured, and the servants reached down into the sarcophagus and lifted. "Gold handles. *Very* nice."

Karigan chewed on her bottom lip. She would skewer Dr. Silk if this were her father, and then they could desecrate *his* grave.

The servants hoisted a coffin of dark wood out and rested it crosswise atop the sarcophagus. The handles did appear to be gold. Would her father have demanded gold handles on his coffin? Would he have been so frivolous? Not her father, no, but her aunts might have done so for their younger brother.

"There is an inscription on the lid," Dr. Silk said. *"Here sleeps the greatest merchant of all Corsa . . ."*

DR. SILK'S EXHIBITION OF BONES AND BLOOD

K arigan closed her eyes, waiting.
"He is," Dr. Silk said, "Orhald Fallows, gold merchant."

A breath of relief gusted from Karigan's lungs, her veil fluttered in front of her lips. Not her father, but yes, she'd heard of Orhald Fallows, who, it was rumored, had had Breyan's touch for gold. From his shop came all sorts of fabulous objects, including a gold and bejeweled bathtub for the last Sealender king. That put him at two hundred years earlier than her father's time. She was surprised his entire coffin was not made of gold, but perhaps he was humbler than legend made him out to be.

Dr. Silk also seemed to know Orhald Fallows' history, and Karigan felt the excitement build in the audience as he tantalized them with whatever incredible artifacts might have been buried with the gold merchant. He gestured again, and his servants lifted the lid off the coffin. She was not close enough to smell the immediate fetid air that would have risen from it, but she could imagine the stink of old rot, of bones that had lain undisturbed for about four centuries. The servants paused before reaching into the coffin.

"Careful now," Dr. Silk instructed them.

While everyone's attention was riveted on the coffin, additional servants placed a table on the daïs next to Dr. Silk. The shrouded form of Orhald Fallows was then lifted out and carried up to the table.

Dr. Silk explored the winding sheets, cutting them away with a knife layer by layer, seeking burial items and tokens as he went. He found a stoppered gold flask that would have been filled with wine or brandy that served as a common ritual offering to the gods. There were unformed gold nuggets scattered throughout and a scale bundled at Orhald's feet. Sheaves of parchment were found between the wrappings, prayers for the departed written by the family. Dr. Silk ignored such mundane items, digging for gold. At last he cut away the final sheet, and there lay Orhald Fallows's skeletal form, exposed, with a full head of white hair and garbed in faded red velvet robes.

"Well this is curious," Dr. Silk said, peering closely at the skull. "One would expect gold coins to close his eyes, but I see copper."

He searched Orhald further and found a purse, but it was empty. He frowned. The only other piece of gold he found was Orhald's wedding ring. Dr. Silk looked dismayed, but Karigan understood. The merchant had been fabulously wealthy, but he'd tried to appease the gods with his humility. Yes, there had been offerings of gold, but if he'd offered *too much*, he would have appeared not virtuous but arrogant. While his coffin was fine enough to impress those left behind, it wasn't garish. He'd played both sides—enough gifts to please the gods, but not enough to anger them by flaunting his excess. It was well known that entrance to the heavens could not be bought by wealth alone. Moral character counted as well.

And, Karigan thought, if Orhald Fallows was anything like her father, he'd been too practical to allow too much gold to be buried away where it could not be useful to his heirs.

Dr. Silk was plainly unimpressed, and he laughed. "Well, old Orhald has played a joke on us. He took little of his gold to the grave."

"He ignores all the artifacts," Cade murmured to Karigan in disgust. "The merchant's clothing, the coffin itself, the parchments. Those are more valuable than gold."

And that, Karigan thought, was what made the professor and Cade different from Dr. Silk. The former were actually interested in the past, and the latter was simply a gold miner. A tomb thief.

"Take this away," Dr. Silk told his servants.

They bundled the remains of Orhald Fallows into his windings, carelessly dropped him into the coffin with a clatter, and carried him away.

"Let us not be dismayed by the scarcity of Orhald Fallows," Dr. Silk said. "I've more diverting entertainments for you than a bundle of old bones."

At his command, the draped, domed cage Karigan and Cade had seen earlier was wheeled forth. A slave, marked by a brand on his cheek, herded a large sow into the big top. The audience laughed, but Dr. Silk smiled enigmatically.

"This show has gone to the pigs," a man joked, and the audience laughed again.

"Come, gather around so you can see," Dr. Silk said.

The guests left their chairs to stand around the domed cage, leaving ample passage for the sow and herder to approach.

"I have brought some of my pets all the way from Gossham for you to see," Dr. Silk said.

"You're keeping pigs now?" the wag called out.

Dr. Silk chuckled and signaled with his hand. The covering was pulled off the cage revealing gilt bars. A filament of fine mesh netting, almost invisible depending on the angle of light, filled the spaces between the bars.

"I don't see anything inside," Cade said. "Just some plants."

Karigan didn't see anything either, but trees and shrubs in planters, and a mini-fountain in the center spouting water. It was a little like an oversized terrarium with bars instead of glass. It looked pleasant enough, but a sense of foreboding came over her, and after all the various surprises she'd already endured this evening, she wasn't sure she could take much more.

The slave led the sow up a ramp right to the door of the cage. He opened the door and chivvied her inside into a small antechamber and slammed it behind her. He then hoisted the inner gate with a rope and pulley system. The sow ambled into the main chamber, attracted to a trough of feed, and the gate was lowered behind her.

A loud buzz emanated from the cage, the buzzing sound of furious tiny wings Karigan remembered all too well. With a sickening, sinking feeling, she realized that the cage was an aviary.

The sow, who until this point had behaved complacently enough snuffling at the trough, squealed and cowered against the bars of the cage.

"Oh, gods, no," Karigan murmured.

A cloud of tiny, iridescent hummingbirds, heretofore unseen among leaves and branches, rose from the vegetation and hovered in the air, wings flickering too fast to see.

"Oh, how beautiful," a woman nearby said. "They are so quick and dainty. Look how their feathers shine."

The few bits of food Karigan had nibbled burned in her chest. The sow squealed again and dug at the door, seeking escape. Hummingbirds darted and hovered, darted and hovered, the thrum of their wings rising in a crescendo.

"I love hummingbirds," another woman said, "but they are so rare."

One flashed downward, skimming across the sow's back, chased closely by a second. They whizzed around the aviary, fighting over the sow, defending her as territory and chasing off interlopers. This went on for several minutes until some unknown, invisible signal released the entire furious cloud of birds, and they dove as one, their beaks plunging into the sow.

Members of the audience gasped. Karigan closed her eyes, knowing how it would play out, the sharp beaks, a hundred times over, stabbing into the sow's flesh, frantic wings driving them deeper and deeper so they could get at the blood. Karigan knew how the scarlet patches on the birds' throats would glow as they consumed the blood, how they'd become engorged with it. Murmurs of fear and fascination rippled through the audience. A couple of ladies fainted and had to be carried out.

"Interesting pets you keep, Silk," a man said, no humor in his voice.

"From the Imperial Preserve," Dr. Silk replied over the cries of the sow.

Karigan's hands clenched at the sounds of the sow's distress. She had seen such hummingbirds suck the life out of a man.

Eventually the sow's cries and the sounds of her struggles weakened, and the collective wingbeats of the hummingbirds subsided to a drone. Even then, when Karigan finally opened her eyes again, she did not look in the aviary, but stared at the shoulders of the man in front of her. The show over, the guests applauded. They actually applauded! This was entertainment, this exhibition of slaughter, Dr. Silk's show of bones and blood. She shuddered.

Dr. Silk ordered the cage to be covered and taken away, much to Karigan's relief. After all she had seen tonight, the p'ehdrose, her sword, the eagle, Orhald Fallows, and now this, she wished to take action, to tear down the empire. But what could she do? She was only one person. She would not get far, although giving Silk a good whack with the bonewood would provide her with a strong sense of satisfaction. She was not helpless, but she felt it, immobilized by not knowing what to do, not knowing how to reach her own time where she could, perhaps, do the most good.

"How can I top that, eh?" Dr. Silk asked his guests. "The best of the night is yet to come, even more exotic than feral hummingbirds from the Imperial Preserve, something not even the emperor has seen since his rise to power almost two hundred years ago. A sight so rare you will not believe your eyes!"

Oh gods, what now?

A pair of white horses, red plumes rising from their head-stalls, trotted into the big top drawing a garish circus wagon behind them. The wooden sides were painted with fierce lions and bears, and concealed whatever might lie within. The lights of the big top lowered dramatically, except for a pair that shone directly on the wagon as the horses came to a halt.

"Here is something you will likely never see again," Dr. Silk told his guests.

Dramatic notes thundered out of the pipes of the music steamer causing more than a few people to jump and laugh nervously. They watched the spotlighted wagon with rapt gazes.

"Are you ready?" Dr. Silk asked.

His guests shouted, "Yes!" back at him and clapped.

He nodded to the circus men at the wagon, and they dropped a painted side down to reveal a cage. The wagon was probably used to transport and exhibit large, dangerous animals, but Karigan did not see an animal. What she did see so shocked her that she could only whisper: *"Lhean."*

"An Eletian, ladies and gentlemen!" Dr. Silk announced to more applause and *oohs* and *aahs*. "A genuine living, breathing Eletian."

Lhean's face was turned away from the glare of lights, his hands clenched around the bars of his cage. Segments of his armor had gone missing, revealing black cloth underneath, glistening as though wet and oozing. His remaining armor was dull, not at all the almost glowing pearlescence Karigan remembered. He looked weak, the vibrancy that was him dimmed like his armor. And yet . . .

And yet, he shone, and it was not just the lights on him, but the innate power of what he was: an Eletian, a being of etherea. The crowd, gawking at him in awe, could see it, too.

Cade, however, was watching her. She turned to him when he placed his hand on her shoulder.

"It's Lhean," she said, stricken.

He raised his finger to his lips. "Shhh . . ."

"He needs—we need to—"

"Shhh . . ."

Her every nerve prickled with energy, with urgency. Cade stared at her calmly, sternly, steadying her.

She turned back to Lhean, who looked lost and alone. Slowly he peered into the light, his gaze sweeping across the audience, and then it alighted on her. She felt it, knew it, that he had picked her out from all the assembled. He thrust his arm between the bars, reaching out to her. The startled guests exclaimed and laughed. Karigan could not hear him speak, but she saw his lips form the word: *Galad-heon.*

"It is time to leave," Cade said. He took her arm and began to lead her through the crowd.

"But I've got to help him," she said, stumbling alongside.

"Not here, not now," Cade replied tersely.

"I can't leave him here!"

Cade drew her up close. "You must. You cannot help him

now. We must leave before people realize he's reaching for *you*."

Fortunately the music steamer had started up again, drowning out their voices.

Cade was right. People were glancing about to see who or what the Eletian wanted, and it would be dangerous for Silk, in particular, to connect the two of them. Cade was also right that trying to save Lhean at this moment would fail, and she'd end up in even less of a position to help him. So she followed Cade, but could not stop looking at Lhean, his forehead now pressed against the bars.

Oh, Lhean.

It took what felt like an eternity to make it to the big top's entrance, and it was a relief to step out into the open night air. There were no performers to greet them, just a couple of watchful guards. The torches still hissed along the pathway as Karigan and Cade hastened on.

A carriage drew up. It wasn't a Hastings, but the professor's. Luke must have spied them right off. He hopped down from the bench to open the door and assist Karigan inside the cab.

"Take us home at a good clip," Cade instructed Luke, "but not so fast as to be too obvious."

"As you wish, Mr. Harlowe."

After the carriage lurched forward and the big top fell behind, Cade said, "That was an Eletian? An actual Eletian?"

Karigan nodded. Cade had not seemed unsettled in the big top, but he was now.

"You know him?"

Karigan nodded again. "Yes, Lhean. He was one of my companions in Blackveil." She felt an impulse to leap out of the carriage and run back to the big top—she couldn't abandon him! She had a terrible image of Dr. Silk taking him to a taxidermist to be stuffed and exhibited with the p'ehdrose and eagle.

"So he must have come with you somehow." Cade shook his head as if disbelieving his own words.

"Yes," she replied. "Somehow." Or, had he been here all along through time? He was, after all, eternally lived, and

Eletians did not appear to age. But she did not think so. The scarcity of etherea in this mechanical world was antithetical to the existence of Eletians. She'd assumed they'd vanished, died out for good thanks to Amberhill. Besides, Lhean looked like he was suffering. Could he have sustained his life for almost two hundred years in this condition? There was much she did not know about Eletians, but instinct told her he had arrived in the future when she did.

Why was she only seeing him now? Why had they not arrived together? The breaking of the looking mask had sent her cascading through the universe, and Westrion had brought her here. That was what she now believed. But why Lhean? Were any of her other companions at large in this time, or another? Were they, too, held captive by Dr. Silk? What was Westrion's intent? Was there an intent? She had many questions but no answers.

Cade tapped his fingers on the seat beside him to the rhythm of the trotting carriage horses, his expression pensive. "I hope the professor is home. He will want to hear about this right away."

"We need to rescue Lhean."

"I do not doubt that, but I need to talk to the professor. Any rescue requires planning."

He was right, but would the professor actually help?

"There is one thing I hope," Cade said.

Karigan waited. "Well?"

"I hope that Silk did not see that the Eletian sought *you*."

SILK

Silk bade good-bye to the last of his guests as they funneled out of the big top entrance. Already workers swept the floor and removed his exhibits. The operator of the music steamer had played his final note and was now lowering the lids over the keyboards.

It had been, on the whole, a successful evening. His guests had been impressed by his offerings. The Eletian, especially, caused a sensation, and all of Mill City and beyond would talk about it for weeks to come. Hadley had approached him about using the Eletian as part of his sideshow, which would no doubt fill circus coffers, but Silk needed to get the Eletian to Gossham to be examined by his father and other members of the emperor's inner circle. He would deliver the creature himself to ensure he received proper credit for its capture. One day, he hoped to personally present the Eletian to the emperor as a gift.

Silk gazed at the diminishing crowd searching for Miss Goodgrave and her escort, but in vain. They must have slipped out early, which annoyed him. He'd ask Howser if he'd seen them leave, and if not, tell him to ask around. Discreetly, of course. There was something about that young lady, something much more than was hidden behind the veil. He'd known this since the first time he'd looked upon her. The vibrancy of life energy that pulsed around her—favoring green hues—had intrigued him, had roused his interest enough that he needed to know more. Tonight it had been much the same, but . . . At one point as they sat at dinner, a wavering of her aura caught the edge of his vision, like the downsweep of vast, dark wings. He fought to conceal his surprise, and soon wondered if he'd actually imagined it all, for it did not happen again. An enigma was Miss Goodgrave.

He had noted, of course, how careful she'd been answering his questions, almost shrewd in her responses. She did not seem insane to him, but she mystified him with contradictions. In many ways she carried herself in a confident manner, and in others, less so, such as when confronted by the taxidermy specimens from the Imperial Museum. Clearly she was intelligent but appeared naïve, as if she did not know the customs of society. The latter, he thought, could be due to her confinement to the asylum and life in the country. And insanity did not necessarily negate intelligence. It disappointed him she'd shown little interest in the artifacts he'd so carefully displayed. She did not fit easily into a puzzle.

And then, he could not swear to it, because he'd been more focused on the reaction of his guests to the Eletian, but he thought he'd seen the Eletian reach out to her, speak to her . . . He'd ask Howser about that, too, and also question the creature later. Not that the creature would cooperate—it refused to respond to the common tongue and spoke only in Eltish gibberish when it spoke at all.

Silk espied T.C. Stamwell dismantling his curtained image trapping space, and on impulse Silk set off across the ring. When he arrived, Stamwell paused what he was doing and bowed.

"How may I help you, Dr. Silk?"

"Miss Goodgrave . . . Did she pick up her portrait before she left?"

A strange expression fell over Stamwell's face. "No, sir, she did not, nor did Mr. Harlowe. It's probably just as well."

"Explain."

"Her image, well, it came out poorly. The young man's quickened just fine, and so did every other portrait I trapped tonight, but not hers."

"How so?"

"Let me show you." Stamwell climbed up into his wagon and rummaged around. He soon returned with a small portrait in each hand. "This is Mr. Harlowe's."

Silk took it and gazed hard at the image of Josston's
protégé. In Silk's vision, the image was dim, but Cade Harlowe was defined well enough for him to make it out, and the
image probably appeared as it should to people with normal
vision. He discerned a strong, if disapproving, face. Harlowe
was still young and inexperienced, but Silk did not doubt he'd
be a force to be reckoned with one day, considering who his
mentor was.

Stamwell then handed him Miss Goodgrave's portrait. He
could not make it out. Her dress and shape appeared defined
well enough, but her face . . . He squinted. He perceived little
of her features, like they were rubbed out.

"What happened?" he demanded.

"I wish I knew. She did not move during the exposure, I'd
swear to it, and it's not as if her face is blurred. It's more like
it's, well, mostly faded out."

"Some flaw of your image trapper or the quickening process."

"I don't think so, sir. I handled her portrait as I have every
other this night. It's . . . it's an anomaly. And there is something else."

"What is it?"

Stamwell shifted uncomfortably and produced a magnifying glass from his pocket. "Look there, look real close at her
shoulder."

Silk took the magnifying glass and moved beneath one of
the lamps Stamwell had not yet removed. He gazed at the
picture from top to bottom. Miss Goodgrave's dress remained
solid but not her face.

"I can see the backdrop through her face," Silk said in
surprise.

"Yes, sir."

Silk scrutinized her shoulder. It was grainy, and very light,
but he could make out what looked like a ghostly hand resting there, where her likeness was most faded, as if that hand
had absorbed her image so it could not be captured by Stamwell's box. He glanced again at Harlowe's portrait, and saw
no sign of anything unusual.

"Very strange," he murmured. "It must be your equipment. Some mistake. Such things happen with image trapping, do they not?"

"Yes, sir, images can be superimposed if you use the same plate, but that was not the case here."

Stamwell knew better than to argue with him beyond that point. Silk returned Cade Harlowe's portrait, but decided to hold onto Miss Goodgrave's. He had truly wanted to see what she looked like, but all he'd gotten was a ghost. Stamwell had botched her portrait. Or had he?

As Silk crossed the circus ring once again, it occurred to him that the image trapper had actually managed to capture some true aspect of Miss Goodgrave. It was an interesting notion, one that he'd toyed with for some time, but just then Howser entered the big top and strode rapidly toward him, really almost at a trot. Seldom did the big man move that fast. Silk wondered what urgency propelled him.

"What is it?" he asked when Howser reached him.

Howser, in too fine a physical form to be out of breath, replied, "A message, sir." He pulled an envelope from an inner pocket of his coat and passed it to Silk. "A courier from the palace just brought it."

Silk immediately recognized the handwriting on the envelope as that of his father's secretary. He tore it open and removed the missive inside. There was no salutation, no niceties. His father had long ago abandoned wasting effort on his short-lived issue. The simple fact he'd sent any message at all showed that he held at least some esteem for his son, if no affection.

The letter contained only three words carefully inscribed by his father's secretary: *She has spoken.* At the bottom was his father's official seal.

Silk calmly folded the note and slipped it back into the envelope. He knew exactly what the three words meant, and they evoked both fear and opportunity.

The last time the emperor had awakened, he'd purged much of the empire's governing body. That event was remembered as the "Bloody Session," for it had been done right in the main council chamber and much actual blood had been shed. Silk imagined that, as the news spread, politicians and bureaucrats alike would be shaking. Resignation would not preserve them from the emperor's wrath if he decided to repeat the "Bloody Session."

He tucked the envelope into his pocket. With the emperor awakening early, opportunity had come early. He would start working the drill in the Old City all day and night. He would commandeer more slaves if he had to. And he could present the Eletian to the emperor all that much sooner with less chance of someone, like his father, stealing all the credit.

His footsteps sounded hollow on the wooden floor as he exited the ring past animal keepers rolling the caged lion away and slaves moving chairs. The emperor's awakening was a time to fear, but Silk's mind filled with plans and possibilities. This was his opportunity to find favor with the emperor, to be offered eternity, just as his father had once been. But why, why was the emperor awakening early? It had never happened before. It was as odd as — as discovering an Eletian in a world where there were none. He halted. Coincidence? Had something in the world altered? Were they on the verge of some great change?

On impulse he glanced at the portrait of Miss Kari Goodgrave. Her image remained as transparent as when he'd first looked at it. Was it a coincidence she had suddenly appeared in Josston's household?

He shook his head, smiled, and resumed his walk, at last passing from the big top and into the night. He did not have answers, but he was fond of puzzles.

A WAR OF SECRETS

The professor was home by the time Karigan and Cade arrived, and between his greeting and asking about their evening in jovial tones, he indicated, through a series of whispers and gestures, that they should meet in the library for an excursion to the old mill at one hour.

In the intervening time, Cade presumably headed home, wherever that was, the professor retreated to his office, and Karigan ate leftover chicken and biscuits in her room. Lorine asked about the evening while she helped Karigan change into her nightgown, and Karigan was just as glad to tell her about it to keep her mind busy so she did not dwell on Lhean's plight.

"Was there dancing?" Lorine asked, carefully folding Karigan's gloves and laying them in their box.

"Dancing?"

"Yes. Did . . . did you and Mr. Harlowe dance?"

Karigan flashed not to the party, but to their sword practice sessions, which was dancing of a sort, and lingered in her memory causing a half smile to form on her lips. Recalling herself, she removed the smile from her face and cleared her throat. "Er, there was no dancing. I can't imagine dancing to that awful music steamer, anyway." She could not quite read the look on Lorine's face. Hope? Did she wish to ask questions of her mistress that one of her class was not permitted? If Cade remained steadfast in his desire to be a celibate Weapon, Lorine's interest in him would only lead to disappointment.

Karigan went on to describe some of the circus performers and exhibits, but Lorine seemed only mildly interested unless Cade's name came up.

When all was done and Lorine left, Karigan lay in bed waiting for the bell to ring out one hour, haunted by the specter that had been Lhean. Where had he been hiding all this time? Had he known she was here, too? If so, why hadn't he come to her? Had it really been him? Yes, Cade had seen him. *Everyone* had seen him.

The tolling of one hour startled her awake. Somehow, despite the events of the evening and her concern for Lhean, she had managed to doze off. She made her stealthy way to the library where the professor and Cade awaited her. As they began their descent into the underground, she lingered behind to change into her black swordswoman's garb and then hastened down the steps to catch up with them.

As they walked through the underground, each of them bearing a taper through the dark passage, Karigan and Cade told the professor about their evening, their voices ringing against the deserted storefronts and buildings of the Old City preserved beneath the foundations of the new.

"That's remarkable," the professor said when he heard about Karigan's sword on exhibit. "I knew about the survey of the Imperial Preserve, but very little was ever disclosed about it."

Cade related the part about the image trapper. "We left in a hurry," he said, "and failed to retrieve the portraits."

"That is unfortunate," the professor said, "but probably not a significant problem. Silk already knows what *you* look like, Old Button, and I cannot imagine there is much he will gain from seeing our Miss Goodgrave's image. It will but sate his curiosity about her appearance. You were better off appeasing him rather than intensifying his suspicions."

It was much as Karigan had thought, but it was a relief to hear the professor thinking along the same lines.

They continued their description of their evening, and when they mentioned the hummingbirds, the professor's expression darkened. "Yes, Silk has always been drawn to the rare and exotic, and has accrued a collection I can only guess at. I'd warrant he doesn't feed just pig's blood to those birds."

Karigan shuddered.

By the time they reached the second floor of the mill, they had gotten to the part about Lhean.

"My word!" The professor halted in the middle of the room. "An Eletian? In this day and age? I'd heard Silk was hunting a ghost in the Old City, but I never imagined . . . My word."

"He was one of my companions on the Blackveil expedition," Karigan said.

"One of your companions? He came through time with you? I think I need to sit down."

So they moved on to the library sitting area, the professor sinking into one of the armchairs rather than sitting behind his desk. Karigan remained standing.

"To see an Eletian, a real Eletian. How fantastic. And you saw him, too, Cade?"

Cade nodded.

"He needs help—to be rescued," Karigan said, "before Silk—before Silk has him stuffed or something."

The professor shook his head. "No, no, my dear, he wouldn't do that. The Eletian is a great find, a creature of etherea. Much too valuable to be sacrificed as a specimen for the Imperial Museum. No, Silk will use him to his advantage."

Karigan folded her arms and shifted her stance. That did not sound much better. "How?"

The professor shrugged. "Take him to Gossham, I suppose, where he can be shown off, and Silk can impress the Adherents. It would help remove him from his father's shadow."

Karigan paced rapidly back and forth, back and forth, then halted. "He and I have to find a way home. I mean to go home, and I'm not leaving him behind."

At first the professor looked confused, then he said softly, "You mean, return to your own time."

Karigan nodded.

"Well, now, how do you propose to accomplish that?"

"I do not know," she admitted, "but I feel Lhean is part of the answer. You must help us—*please.*"

"I was thinking this was your home now. That's why I was a little taken aback."

"You have been very kind to me," Karigan said. "You've kept me hidden, but my home is in the past."

"I see."

Did he? Did he understand what it was to be ripped away from everything you knew, everyone you loved? And there had been so much left undone. The professor's features sagged. She hadn't meant for her words to sadden him, and she hadn't meant to blurt out her intention, but best he hear it now so there would be no surprises later. She would, she knew, miss him, as it appeared he would her.

Cade stared off in the distance, his gaze unfixed. Was he sorry she wanted to leave?

"Will you help me?" Karigan asked the professor. "Help me free Lhean?"

The professor's bushy eyebrows shadowed his eyes. "What you ask is difficult—it could bring down the opposition. As much as I long to see an Eletian for myself, stealing Silk's prize would provoke retaliation on a grand scale. I need to consider it, think about the consequences and how they might be avoided. I must consider if his rescue is even achievable. I'm afraid it may already be too late."

"What do you mean?"

"Well, depending how soon Silk sends the Eletian to the Capital, once he is there, he is beyond our reach."

"Then we must help him *now*."

"No." The forcefulness of the professor's voice stilled Karigan. "You must promise me you will not go off on your own. This requires thought and planning."

"But—"

"You requested my assistance," the professor said sharply. "I have not granted it, but I may. I definitely will not help if you don't allow me to consider the problem in my own time. That is my final word on the matter." Then he softened his voice. "I realize you fear for your friend and are homesick, my dear, but please realize that there is much more at stake here. I need at least a couple of days to mull it over, to gather information."

Karigan knew that pushing him would not help, but to wait would be agonizing. Rescuing Lhean on her own would be difficult—she knew so little of this world—and if she made the attempt without the professor's leave, he would see it as a betrayal of his trust, and she could lose his protection. He would never allow her to endanger the opposition. She dropped into one of the chairs with a heavy sigh.

"How was your meeting with the board this evening?" Cade asked the professor.

"Not nearly as interesting as Silk's party, apparently." The professor chuckled and something of his jovial self returned. "The board members were brutal in their questioning, but I have secured our funding for another year."

As the two men discussed the affairs of the university, Karigan sank deeper into her chair and rested her head on her hand, wondering how they could go on and on about the inane politics among their fellow scholars at the university when much more important issues were at hand. She thought again about Lhean and decided the consequences of aiding him, even on her own, did not matter. She simply could not allow him to be hauled away for whatever torment awaited him in the Capital. She had to try. He was part of the answer to her way home, she was sure of it. And, he'd been her comrade through all the horrors of Blackveil. They'd been through much together. She was sure he'd aid her if their positions were reversed—not something she could say of all Eletians. It wasn't just a matter of honor but of friendship.

"Lights, eh?" the professor said.

Karigan shook herself back to the present. Had she missed something important?

"Yes, making their way up the road," Cade replied.

"I wonder what he's up to. Perhaps we should take a look."

"Can't imagine we'll see much."

The professor shrugged. "Can't hurt."

The two men rose and Karigan looked uncertainly at them. "What are you doing?"

"Going up on the roof," the professor said. "Cade saw some activity in the Old City when he came over tonight."

"Oh." Karigan rose, too.

"Wait for us here, my dear. I would feel better with fewer of us up top this night. And I should like to speak privately with Cade."

Karigan watched after the two men with a frown. Were they going to discuss Lhean? What didn't the professor want her to hear? Perturbed, she tapped the armrest of her chair. *Well, let them go,* she decided and stood looking around the expanse of the mill room. It was odd being there alone, empty. She wasn't going to idly wait for them, she decided. There was another way she could occupy her time. She strode for one of the stairwells, grabbing a taper as she went.

The lights streaming up the road coalesced on the summit of the Old City at Silk's worksite. In the still of night, the distant sounds of tools and voices carried all the way to the roof of the mill. After watching for some time, the professor signaled that he and Cade should descend back into the mill.

When they had done so, and it was once again safe to ignite a taper and speak, the professor said, "It appears our act of sabotage slowed Silk down even less than I thought. Now he is going at his work at night. I wonder why."

Cade offered no answers, so the professor went on. "Whatever the reason, it can't be good, which means we should probably call a gathering of our brethren. As much as I should like to lay eyes on that Eletian and aid him, I cannot help but think Silk's activities in the Old City are more important to us."

"I'm not so sure," Cade replied.

"Why not?" the professor asked, surprised.

"It is an Eletian. An Eletian here and now when they have been, to our knowledge, extinct for a very long time? The singularity of such an event . . . I don't know, it just seems he is worth putting forth our resources to rescue."

"Bringing the empire's forces down upon us," the professor countered, shaking his head. "I'd rather we prevented Silk from finding that dragonfly device, or that we found it first. To me, that is where we should focus our time and energy, though my niece—I mean, our Green Rider—would not like it."

"No, she would not," Cade agreed, his expression troubled in the light of the taper.

"I have grown fond of her, and she fascinates me when she

speaks of her own time. Professionally speaking, she is a treasure. I had hoped she was feeling at home here, happy even, and willing to settle down. I have certainly enjoyed having her as a member of my little family."

The professor unconsciously twisted a silver button on the cuff of his coat. It occurred to him that if Karigan was able to travel back to her own time, she could change his present. What if, with all the information she had attained here, her return allowed her king to defeat the emperor? That could be a very positive outcome, the professor thought, and then he wondered what his own time would be like if that were the case. Would he and his people be better off? Would the ancestors who created his bloodline meet under the altered circumstances? *Would he even exist?* Who knew what threads of the world her return would realign. Perhaps everything would be better but perhaps not. He was just beginning to see how dangerous this time thing was. As much as he despised the empire, there was comfort in a known evil.

I wish to exist, he thought.

He let go of the tortured button now hanging on a loose thread and, not wishing to give voice to his concerns to Cade about Karigan's altering time, he said, "It has come to mind that our Green Rider has not revealed the extent of her knowledge of the past."

Cade shifted. "You believe she is withholding information?"

The creaks of the restless old building filled in the silence as the professor considered his reply. "She has done nothing to challenge my trust of her—not yet, anyway—but I believe her first loyalty lies with her king and her time, and that if she felt she needed to protect some aspect of the past, she would see fit to withhold information from us." Like an alternate entrance to the tombs, he thought, or knowledge of the dragonfly device. "She is our ally so long as it suits her, but she is an independent spirit. I think, for instance, she would go after the Eletian by herself if I declined the help of the opposition. You've spent time with her, Old Button, what do you think?"

"I believe," Cade replied, head bent in a thoughtful posture, "you are correct. Her independent spirit is something we don't see much of here. Not even among the male population after almost two centuries of being trammeled down by the empire. I would also submit she is a person of honor, honor of another era, a time of great deeds when enemies came face to face in the light of day."

"What is it you are saying?"

"I am saying that Silk's work goes on at a great pace because we, the opposition, are too cautious. We attend parties, go about our routine, and this war of ours, well, it's a war of secrets. Little is actually ever done. It—it is more like a gentleman's club than an active resistance. But Silk, as well as the emperor and his Adherents, are fully committed. They take the active role."

The professor stared at his protégé in disbelief, restraining the impulse to lash out at him—at Cade who had never before spoken a word of criticism against his efforts to lead the opposition, to keep its members safe, and most importantly to protect the royal heir. How could Cade protest that? But it was Cade, after all, a man of few words, his obedient student. That he should speak out at all was enough to stun, and the rarity of it meant the professor needed to take notice, to consider his words.

"Gentleman's club, eh?"

Cade nodded, his serious expression unchanged.

A war of secrets, he had said. The professor knew it. Every time he attended the theater, a dinner party, or a tea, he participated in that war, spying, exchanging veiled barbs with his enemies. It had become a game, albeit a deadly game. He'd been so consumed with protecting the opposition that he'd preserved it like one of his artifacts. He'd stopped it in time. There was no forward momentum, no action, no victories to claim. The emperor and his minions moved ahead as steadily as they ever had, and there were no gains for the opposition.

Feeling drained, the professor wished for a chair to sit on, but there were none on this floor so he leaned against a sturdy pillar.

"Our Green Rider," Cade said, "is a woman of honor. She will respect your request to wait on your decision about the Eletian. I suspect, however, that as a woman of honor, she won't let the Eletian go unrescued no matter your response, and she will do what she believes is necessary."

At least he and Cade agreed on that matter. The professor had identified her fierce spirit early on, but the more he thought about it, the more he began to feel like he'd been sheltering a keg of blasting powder beneath his roof. It was regrettable. If she were a more compliant woman of his own time, he'd have nothing to worry about, but then she wouldn't be the interesting person he'd grown so fond of. Unfortunately, he might have to quell everything that made her who she was.

There were ways to prevent any rash action on her part, he knew. Convenient he'd given her the cover of being mad. It would be easy to withdraw her from society, lock her away, which would also prevent her going back to the past and altering time. He shook his head, sorry to even consider such possibilities. He would do so only if necessary.

He realized he could not confide in Cade these darker thoughts, these contingencies, since it was clear that Karigan G'ladheon had won him over. The professor had seen them kiss, he'd seen the way Cade watched her when she wasn't looking. "Keep an eye on her, Old Button, and let me know if she seems likely to make a move without me. I have much to consider."

Cade nodded, obedient as ever. But how obedient? the professor wondered, in light of his student's countering opinion.

Gah, he thought. *I have spent so much time intriguing that I've become suspicious of everyone. Even Cade, who is like a son to me.*

His shoulders sagged as he led the way toward the stairwell. There was an enemy around every corner ready to reveal him and all he'd worked for. He had to be suspicious, even of his dear Old Button.

LETTERS

K arigan flipped the lever just inside the doorway of the third floor, and light came to life throughout the room. She hadn't asked the professor's permission to see her belongings, and why should she? He'd never said she could not. They were *hers,* after all, and she had no plans to disturb his other artifacts.

She sought the correct aisle, passing draped furniture and a stack of empty, gilt frames. She strode past a rusty kettle balanced atop a birdbath, and turned down the aisle, drawn inexorably on. Though the professor's shelves were packed with all the treasures he'd amassed, she walked right past them, interested only in the objects that had traveled through time with her.

When she reached them, she found them just as she had last seen them, her uniform, her brooch, and the owl feather spread out on plain linen, the moonstone glistening on crumpled velvet. There, too, was her bonewood cane and the shards of the looking mask. She caressed her brooch, but felt nothing other than its smooth texture, no tingling resonance of her special ability, nothing. The moonstone only offered a dim flicker at her touch. She feasted her gaze on the green of her tattered, muddied uniform. Well dried now, the mud crumbled at her touch.

She had come here, she realized, because these items were her only link with home, her own time. She pressed her cheek against a length of green fabric. It had taken on the scent of the dusty mill, displacing any that may have come from her own time, even that of her toil through Blackveil. If only she could take her things back to the professor's house—or at least one item, perhaps her brooch. But she knew the professor was right—her things were safer here. Maybe she could just visit them more often. She feared that the more she grew accustomed to the professor's world, the more she would forget what it was like to traverse a public street unveiled or to carry a sword. She feared her former life would become like the memory of a dream, the details dissipating with every passing day. Already, she thought, she had adjusted to the acrid air of the city. The customs of the people were becoming more familiar to her. Would she forget what it was like to be a well-rounded citizen able to take part in the many spheres of life as she had in her Sacoridia? Would she accept her role here, limited to domesticity and having no say in her own affairs? The women here lived well or poorly based solely on the sufferance of the men who held control over their lives.

While Karigan's Sacoridia had not been perfect, she could not believe it had come to this. How had Amberhill managed to steal the individual power of all the people here, leaving the women—and the slaves—trapped at the bottom of society?

It was the weapon. The weapon the professor said Amberhill had wielded in the decisive battle. Some great weapon, the one that had destroyed Sacor City and the castle. Now Silk was delving for a device that could counteract the emperor's power, trying to reach it before the professor and his opposition could. If only she could get back home, warn the king . . .

The shards of the looking mask flashed when she thought of King Zachary. She jerked back, startled, but when there were no images in the offing, she assumed she had merely caught the light glancing on them at an odd angle.

Then, a few heartbeats later, the images came, revealing a chamber draped with heavy tapestries and shields. In the center of it stood King Zachary who wore a gleaming breastplate. He tugged at it, as if checking the fit. She did not see him as she'd once seen Captain Mapstone—the same image but at different angles in each shard. She saw his image as a mosaic that created a single picture.

She noted how light from an unseen window slanted in on

the king, burnishing his hair and close-cropped beard more red-gold than amber. It glared on his breastplate. He was the same as she remembered, and yet not . . . His cheekbones looked sharper, his eyes shadowed, tired. Despite the sunlight, there was a darkness on him. He turned, as if to examine himself in a mirror from a different angle. His profile looked too thin to her. Had he been sick? She frowned, worried now.

An attendant came forward and also checked the fit of the breastplate, tightening side straps, and then stepped back and out of the image. Karigan wished she could hear what was being said, if anything. Wished she could step through the vision to be there in the chamber with him.

Theirs was a story of two people bound strongly to one another yet forbidden to be together. He was royalty, she was a commoner. He must marry Lady Estora to maintain the unity among Sacoridia's twelve provinces in the face of threats from Second Empire and Blackveil. His taking a commoner as wife would only thrust the country into discord.

Not that Karigan hadn't imagined such a marriage. She laughed at the thought of herself as queen. *I'd be terrible!* A queen would be as confined to that role and to the castle as any woman of the professor's time to the hearth and veil. If she stayed here, it would kill her. The confinement. The rigid and limited expectations. So would the crown. No matter it was the highest rank to which one could ascend—after the king, of course—it was just another kind of prison. Even duty-bound to the messenger service and required to follow orders from her superiors, she was freer as a Rider, as free as anyone could be, which was amusing because she had once believed the opposite.

Despite her feelings on the matter, she could not help but want to be there with the king. No, not the king, but with Zachary, the man. She'd met no other like him and doubted she ever would.

He turned, once again facing her, and looked up, almost as if gazing into her eyes. She inhaled sharply.

"Your Majesty?" she whispered.

He gazed thoughtfully back at her, or so it seemed. She

felt as if she could almost reach out and touch him, but his gaze shifted away suddenly, and it was a sundering that hurt almost physically. Another entered the vision, this time a Green Rider with red hair that could only be Captain Mapstone.

"Karigan?"

The professor's voice echoed through the vast space. Karigan jerked back in shock, and the image in each shard fluttered like a candle flame and then darkened as if snuffed. As King Zachary's image vanished, she cried out, feeling so alone in her exile.

"Well, hello there!" The professor appeared at the end of the aisle, then made his way toward her. "We did not expect to see the lights ignited on this level." He did not sound angry.

Karigan found she could not speak or move, only hold herself and stare at empty mirror shards.

"What is it?" the professor asked as he neared her. "You look troubled."

Troubled was an understatement. She had lost everything, everyone.

The professor glanced at her possessions, then back. "Oh, I see. You are homesick." His voice was gentle. "No doubt the presence of the Eletian has brought thoughts of your home to the fore."

To Karigan's disgust, her eyes brimmed with tears.

"There, there, my dear." At first the professor patted her shoulder, then awkwardly he embraced her. "I am so sorry. It must be unbelievably difficult for you, and it's been a long night, too, eh?"

Karigan leaned into him, actually comforted by his stiff attempt at an embrace, the texture of his tweed coat pressing into her cheek. Then they parted, and she sniffed. She had managed to avoid a blubbering torrent, and for that much she was grateful.

"I'm sorry," she said. "I just needed to—" She waved her arm vaguely at the artifact room to indicate her trespass.

"I understand, my dear. No need to explain. These items are reminders of your home."

She nodded, and let him believe that was all.

"Professor?" Cade called from the end of the aisle. "Is everything all right back there?"

"Everything's just fine," he replied, and he extended his arm to Karigan. "Shall we?"

She nodded and took his arm. They strolled down the aisle, and she did not look back. As they approached Cade, who stood in the shadow of the shelves, she saw him as a Weapon in black, still and silent, and it seemed right, as if this was the way it had always been. For a moment, she forgot where and when she was, just pleased to see the familiar visage of a Weapon. In the next moment her vision cleared, and she saw he was, in fact, not a Weapon but just Cade in his poor student's garb. She shook her head at the trick light and shadow had played on her.

"It's been a long night, Old Button," the professor said, "and I think a little sleep would do each of us a world of good."

Karigan remained silent during their walk through the underground, trying to recall the picture of King Zachary. She wondered what was happening back home. It was vexing to be in the future and not be able to find out from some book of history. So much had been destroyed. She certainly had not found anything useful in the professor's library, and no history book would cover the king's day-to-day existence anyway. What was Zachary doing at this very moment? She'd observed their timelines were no longer concurrent—she'd seen sunlight aglow in the chamber he'd been standing in, but it was still the deep of night here. What could it mean?

When finally they climbed into the house, and she returned to her room, she thought she would look into the shard she kept concealed behind her headboard to see if she could call his image back. But once inside, she discovered, to her surprise, cool air curling into the room through the open window, and Cloudy the cat sitting on her bed. He watched her expectantly.

"What?" she murmured, and she softly closed the door behind her. No one else occupied her room—not even a ghost. None that she could see anyway. She set her taper on the bedside table and sat next to Cloudy. He rubbed into her hand and purred.

"How did you get in?" she whispered. It had happened once before and was a mystery that remained unsolved.

As she caressed him, her fingers trailed across a leather collar. She didn't remember having seen one on him before. It was a plain collar, nothing fancy about it, but attached to it was a cylindrical case like those attached to the legs of messenger pigeons, but larger. He was no stray cat after all.

"Odd," she said.

It got even odder when she opened the case and found a letter within addressed to "Karigan," her name written in familiar and sure strokes.

In the present: Captain Mapstone

When Vasper the royal armorer tightened the side straps on the king's breastplate and then stepped away, Laren noted two important things: The first was that Zachary had not yet recovered much of the weight he had lost since his wounding from the assassin's arrow. His cheeks were more sharply defined making his expression more severe. He had trained away any remaining weakness and excess flesh with Arms Master Drent. She thought, perhaps, he worked too hard. Maybe he thought that by doing so he could erase the past. She did not know if it worked. What she did know is that it left him all sinew and muscle.

The second important thing Laren noticed as he turned to gaze at himself in the mirror, tugging on the breast plate to check its fit, was that this was not his parade armor. This was true battle-worthy steel lacking decorative embellishment. The only ornamentation was the silver etching of the firebrand and the crescent moon across his breast. This was Zachary's war armor.

They'd been slowly readying for conflict with Second Empire, making plans and contingencies. There had been minor skirmishes in the north country, but no out and out battles, no formal declaration of war. Still, she should not have been surprised to find her king preparing here in his private arming chamber on so personal a level for a time when he might have to lead his forces onto the field of battle. She found herself startled on some level. Disturbed.

I pray he has no need to go anywhere near a battlefield, she thought. Second Empire was a people without a country and only a small rebel army. Given time, they'd be brought to heel, but their forces were slippery, very slippery, and were backed by a necromancer. Should Mornhavon reappear and reinforce them . . . No, she did not wish to think of it.

Zachary turned toward Laren, faced her, but gazed thoughtfully into the air somewhere over her head. Where did his thoughts travel? What did he see?

"Your Majesty?" She stepped forward.

Her voice roused him from some reverie. "Yes?"

She bowed. "I—I was wondering if I might have a moment to speak privately with you." She almost hoped he'd refuse her.

"Of course, but let me get this off first."

Vasper came forward and helped the king unbuckle and remove the breastplate, which he set on an armor tree next to other pieces that made up the full suit. On the walls, alongside tapestries depicting battles of old, hung the weaponry and shields that had belonged to past kings, some marred by hacking blades, others pristine pieces of parade armor, gleaming with the heraldry of the clans and the sigil of Sacoridia. Zachary excused Vasper as well as his Weapon, leaving the two of them alone together, the westering sun flowing through the window turning the steel in the room bronze. Laren hesitated, wishing for a way out, but she must not delay any longer.

"What is it, Laren? You look . . . bereft. What is wrong?"

It was not, she thought, so far from the truth. "Zachary," she said very softly. "I . . . I thought you should know. The standard time has elapsed and . . ." She took a deep breath. "It is time to acknowledge that Karigan is not coming home." He stared, his eyes boring into her. There was a smoldering quality to them that had not been there before. Before the arrow. Before the betrayal of some of his closest advisors. Before Karigan had gone missing. The dark gaze did not make her task any easier. "We have removed her from the active duty rolls, and I intend to notify her father myself, in person, since he has been such a good friend to His Majesty and the messenger service." This, she knew, would be as difficult, if not more so, than facing the king. It had been bad enough telling Stevic G'ladheon she'd sent his daughter into Blackveil. "Zachary, it has been too long. She is not coming back."

He turned away from her to face the window. "Her brooch has not returned."

"That is true. When a Rider has passed, his brooch will always find its way home." She clenched her fists. She knew it all too well. "But it does not indicate that she still lives. It may be that Blackveil is too great a barrier for even a Rider brooch to find its way home, or, as has happened historically, it will take years before it returns to us. I believe the record stands at about a hundred years in one instance." She had to convince Zachary Karigan would not be coming back. She had accepted it herself, mostly. A small part of her held out hope, but it had diminished as the days rushed by and there was still no sign or word of Karigan.

She'd watched Condor closely, hoping the horse sensed something about his Rider with that special connection that messengers and their horses shared, but it was difficult. He appeared neither content nor disconsolate. He ate his feed, but *dragged,* heaving long, heavy sighs. Often he just stood in the pasture with head lowered, the picture of dejection. No, he wasn't declining, precisely, but he wasn't thriving either. She could not divine what went on in his horse brain. Each horse handled the passing of its Rider differently.

The time had come to end the limbo, to seek closure. It was time to declare Karigan dead.

"Your Riders will be holding a memorial circle for Karigan tonight should you and the queen wish to attend."

He bowed his head. "I feared it, that this time would come. However, I do not wish to believe it. She has survived other dangerous missions. She has always returned."

Laren did not think she needed to remind him that Karigan's walking into Blackveil Forest had been her most perilous deed of all. And it appeared that, even in death, she had bought them more time against Mornhavon. Lynx said Karigan had wounded Mornhavon, and the forest had lain quiescent ever since.

Zachary strode to the window, placed his hands on the wide stone sill. The lowering sun washed across his face. The window looked out on the west castle grounds where the mounted units, including her Riders, liked to exercise their horses. A barely perceptible smile formed on his lips as he immersed himself in a pleasant memory. He looked so very tired to her, and she did not think it was just the pressures of his kingship.

"It seems I failed," he said.

"Failed? What do you mean?"

He shook himself as if suddenly recalling her presence. As he gazed at her, she saw something of the young boy she'd once known, before he'd grown into a man and become a king, hardened by all its responsibilities.

"I'd made an oath," he said. "To myself. To protect her. And I failed."

Laren's shoulders slumped. His quiet anguish was worse than any display of grief or outrage. When she'd learned of the dangerous mutual attraction between Karigan and Zachary, she'd tried to quell it for the sake of the realm. She'd sent Karigan away on errands, kept them separated, but to no avail. And now there was this. She would never have wished to keep them separate in this manner.

"She is . . . *was* . . . a Green Rider," Laren replied. "If you exerted your will to protect her from all harm, she would not have been able to perform her duty, follow her calling. That surely would have killed her just as readily as her stepping into Blackveil."

"I know it," he said, gaze downcast. "But still, I could have—"

"Stop!" He looked at her, startled by her sharpness. Lost. "There is nothing you could have done. She was the best one to send into Blackveil. I knew it, and you knew it. Yes, I question myself all the time, and the doubts flood in, late at night, in the back of my mind, but I come back to the same conclu-

sion each time. Whenever I assign a Rider to an errand, I
wonder if they'll return, and sometimes they don't. But if I
allow my desire to protect them to get in the way of the
realm's business, nothing would get done. The realm would
not move forward. My Riders—*your* Riders—do their work
willingly because they believe in their country and their monarch. Karigan believed no less than any other."

She reached into the inner pocket of her shortcoat and
pulled out an envelope with "King Zachary" written across it
in Karigan's exacting hand. She had considered not bringing
it to him, thinking it would only deepen his feelings for
Karigan even in her death, and she did not want it to come
between him and his new queen. But, while Laren might act
for the good of the realm, she was also human.

"We've been cleaning out Karigan's room so I can take
her belongings to her father." Laren remembered the few
books, a blue gown that had once been quite gorgeous but
was now in rough shape; hair ribbons and combs, slippers, a
few oddments of jewelry. It might have seemed strange that
there were not many personal items in a Rider's room, but
the nature of the messenger service required that they often
be on the road and rarely home long enough to accumulate
possessions. As for Karigan's cat, Ghost Kitty, he'd taken to
sleeping with Mara, but could still be found hanging about
Karigan's room much of the time.

"As we packed," Laren continued, "we discovered some
letters. It appears she knew there was a good chance she was
not coming home. She left one for her father, which I'll be
taking to him, and one for the Riders, which I'll be reading at
the memorial tonight. And, she left one for you."

She strode over to him, by the window, took his hand in
hers and squeezed it, then pressed Karigan's letter into it. She
excused herself with a bow, but she didn't think he noticed
her departure. A final glance revealed him gazing out the
window, the letter unread in his hand.

They were difficult, these gatherings, but as captain, Laren
must remain strong for her Riders. They'd had too many of
these memorial circles in the past year. Her footsteps rang

hollow in the empty corridor she walked to the records room. She always came ahead of the others to collect her thoughts, to steel herself for the simple ceremony. Afterward was soon enough to give in to emotion. Afterward, when she was alone in her quarters with no one to serve as witness. It made it harder that they hadn't even a body, no idea of precisely what befell Karigan, but it also made this ceremony all the more imperative. It provided the solid ground of ritual and leave-taking, allowed the Riders to acknowledge her passing and to comprehend for themselves the finality of her absence. In this way they could move on.

It was ironic, Laren thought, that it was Karigan for whom they'd be performing the ceremony, since it was Karigan who had brought it back to the Riders of the present from the time of the First Rider. There was a circularity about it that seemed appropriate.

Laren had not hurried, but she arrived at the records room all too soon and now saw that she would not have the chamber to herself to gather her thoughts. The glassworkers — hired to do the special cleaning of the stained glass dome — were still there, clambering about the scaffolding. A fretful Dakrias Brown came to her side.

"I'm sorry, Captain, I told them they needed to be out by now."

"They appear to be packing up," she replied, observing them placing tools in bags. A couple were already descending the scaffolding.

The Weapons Fastion, Ellen, and Willis arrived. They would assist with the ceremony by lighting the stained glass dome from behind. Sadly, the view of the glass would be obstructed by the crisscrossed network of scaffolding high above.

Then to Laren's surprise, more Weapons filed in, Weapons who guarded the king and queen. And still more she recognized from the tombs, led by Brienne Quinn. Arms Master Drent actually brought up the rear, dressed not in his training gear, but in the black of a Weapon.

Fastion, noting Laren's wonder, said, "Rider G'ladheon was our sister-at-arms, an honorary Weapon. Any of us who were not required elsewhere would of course be here."

The Weapons made a ring around the room, a dark honor guard.

The chief glassman ambled up to Laren and Dakrias, a bucket in one hand and a bag of tools in the other.

"A good evening to you, Captain," he said, bushy side whiskers wavering in air currents.

"Master . . ." She fought to remember his name. Dakrias had said he was the finest glassman in Sacoridia. He'd come all the way from the eastern province of Bairdly to work on their dome. "Goodgrave!" she remembered in triumph. "Master Goodgrave. How fares your work?"

"Very fine, Captain, very fine. It is an honor to restore a masterwork such as this. We finished up the first panel this day—wanted to make sure we did so for your ceremony this evening. I think you will appreciate the difference between it and the as yet untouched panels when you light them up, I surely do. The beauty of it will properly honor your fallen comrade. Wish I could have finished the whole dome, but it's exacting work and . . ." He faltered and looked troubled.

"And?" Laren prompted.

Master Goodgrave glanced this way and that, and then in a hushed voice said, "This place, it is haunted. Did you know?"

Both Dakrias and Laren nodded. Yes, they knew.

"My helpers, they keep running off, saying they are being pinched or their tools moved by unseen hands. I keep having to hire and train new ones, and it takes time. But my son-in-law, young Josston there, and I keep at it. We are not letting the, hmm, spirits chase us off."

Laren glanced at the skinny young man he pointed out as his son-in-law. He was busy shifting a ladder.

"Don't you worry," Master Goodgrave said, "we will finish our work. No matter what little jokes those restless shades play on us." He gazed up at the dome and glowered.

"Thank you," Laren replied.

Just as the glassworkers left, Riders filed in and started to form a circle within the ring of Weapons. The circle had grown much larger since the first one they'd held. The influx of new Riders gladdened Laren, but she was also taken aback by how many of them never had the chance to meet Karigan.

Among them, of course, were some of Karigan's old friends: Mara, Tegan, Garth, and Ty. Laren's own friend and former Chief Rider, Elgin, joined them and cast her a reassuring smile. They'd have told the new Riders of Karigan's exploits. Missing from the group, most notably, were Alton and Dale, but they were needed at the wall. Lynx scouted the north woods helping to sniff out Second Empire, and Beryl, well, even Laren wasn't sure where the king had sent Beryl.

Like a star aglow in the gloom, one other entered the records room flanked by an additional Weapon. Queen Estora arrived resplendent in dark blues, her crown shining atop her head. She came directly to Laren.

"Captain," Estora said.

"Your Majesty." Laren and Dakrias bowed. "Thank you for coming. It will—it will ease the hearts of your Riders to have you here." They were after all, not just Zachary's Riders, not anymore.

"It is a difficult reason to be here," Estora replied.

Laren fleetingly thought of Estora's complicated position, of coming between two who had loved one another.

Estora added, almost like an answer to Laren's thoughts, "Karigan was my friend. I would be no other place at this hour. My husband, however, will not attend."

"So he chose not to come," Laren murmured in disappointment before she could stop herself.

"It was not a matter of choosing," Estora replied. "He received unexpected visitors—Eletians."

"Eletians? Should I go—?"

"Your duty, I think, lies here at this time, Captain, with your Riders. They are looking to you to lead them, to give them solace. I am sure my husband and his other advisors will be able to manage the Eletians until you are done here."

His new *advisors*, Laren thought with concern. But Estora was right. Zachary could handle it and no matter the Rider lost, the business of the realm must go on.

Laren excused herself to take her place in the circle, sad but proud to see the Riders and Weapons, not to mention Queen Estora, all assembled here to remember Karigan. Her mind strayed to the news of the Eletians' presence in the castle—what could they want?—but when she cleared her throat, and all the Riders turned their solemn attention to her, she forgot about the Eletians.

She began by welcoming those who had come and by enumerating Karigan's deeds. She made sure they heard about her quieter accomplishments—the expert keeping of Rider accounts and the many successful messages she had delivered—in addition to the more notable and dangerous missions she had undertaken. Laren told of how Karigan became a Green Rider in the first place by completing the errand of a fallen Rider, F'ryan Coblebay, and subsequently helping to protect the king's throne from his brother's coup attempt. Karigan had carried the spirit of Mornhavon the Black into the future, securing time for Sacoridia to prepare for his eventual return. She had done so with the aid of the First Rider—the *First Rider!*—whose brooch she had worn.

Laren did not stint in the telling of how Karigan had helped rescue Sacoridia's then future queen from kidnappers, a deed for which the king awarded her knighthood, the first Sacoridian to be so dubbed in two hundred years. Laren spoke of how Karigan had gone bravely into Blackveil Forest and aided the Eletian "Sleepers" who had been left behind in Argenthyne during the Long War. Once again she had defied the will of Mornhavon the Black and wounded him. Lynx had been unable to tell Laren more than that, for what had become of Karigan was a mystery even to him, and he had been there.

It was all the stuff of legends, and by Laren reiterating Karigan's record here, the Riders would carry those stories on to the next generation of Riders, and out into the greater world, and in that way Karigan's memory would live on.

Laren was about to say as much when from somewhere within the depths of the records room a loud thud made several of the Riders jump and look around uneasily. On the periphery of her vision, Laren saw Dakrias chewing on his nails as he glanced behind in the direction of the noise.

What in the name of the gods *was* that? It sounded like someone slamming a book on the floor. Laren stood there momentarily at a loss. She'd forgotten what she meant to say next. She patted her shortcoat, pulled out Karigan's letter, and cleared her throat. "Uh, Karigan left a letter for the Green Riders. She knew the risk she would be taking when it came to entering Blackveil. She knew she might not return." She broke the seal—she had not read the letter herself, feeling that they should all hear its contents at the same time.

"My dear friends," she began. Karigan's handwriting had always been neat and well-practiced, the result of keeping records and ledgers in meticulous order, and this letter was no exception. *"If you are reading this, it means I have died in Blackveil."*

Thunder boomed somewhere behind Laren, somewhere beyond the nearest shelves, making everyone jump again. She squeezed her eyes shut, feeling about ready to leap out of her skin. It hadn't really been thunder, no, but maybe a whole armload of books hitting the floor with resounding force. When she opened her eyes again, she saw two Weapons peeling away to investigate. A murmur arose from the Riders.

"Don't be troubled," Dakrias said, raising his hands, palms outward. "It's, uh, just the resident spirits making their presence known." There was an aggrieved edge to his voice. It was he and his clerks, after all, who would have to clean up after the mischief.

Laren waited for silence to be restored before she started reading again. *"Most of you know it was never my intention to be a Rider—I had other plans, to follow in my father's footsteps and become a merchant, but the call rang true. I have not regretted a moment of—"*

BAM!

This time, something excessively heavy had fallen. Dakrias put his hand to his head and muttered to himself before dashing off to investigate among the shelves.

The Riders shifted uneasily. Rattled, Laren searched the letter to find where she had left off. *"I have not regretted a moment,"* she read, *"of my service to the king and Sacoridia. It has especially been an honor to serve so fine a captain, and among such courageous and dedicated people."*

From nowhere, papers, many papers, started snowing down on them from the shadowed heights above. Laren watched in disbelief.

Someone snickered.

Laren tore her gaze to her Riders and saw to her amazement, her Chief Rider, Mara, cover her mouth with her hand, her shoulders shaking. As more papers drifted downward, Tegan joined her, and then Garth let out a great guffaw. Ty looked scandalized, and the newer Riders perplexed. What had possessed them?

"Leave it to—" Mara sputtered between laughs. "Leave it to Karigan!"

Laren raised an eyebrow.

"Only at *her* memorial!" Mara then doubled over with the laughter.

Others who had known Karigan started laughing as well, and it spread to the new Riders. There was even a hint of a smile on the queen's lips. At first Laren was taken aback, but then she understood. As serious as many of Karigan's adventures had been, she'd often found herself in ridiculous situations, such as wearing a theatrical costume of Mad Queen Oddacious to the king's masquerade ball. People still talked about the girl who had ridden her horse all the way from Corsa to a busy market in Darden wearing nothing but her own skin. Under the influence of the Rider call, Karigan had actually worn her nightgown, but the story persisted.

So Mara was right. Only at Karigan's memorial would something so ridiculous occur as spirits lobbing books off shelves and tossing papers into the air. It couldn't be just a normal, somber, dignified affair. Laren found herself grinning. Perhaps it was better they all remembered not just the serious parts of Karigan's life, but those that left a lightness in their hearts. Whether the ghosts had intended to do so or not, they'd allowed the Riders to release some of their grief through laughter.

When the flurries of papers settled and the mirth mostly subsided, Laren returned to the letter. Karigan mentioned the Riders with whom she had worked, alive and dead, remembering some small detail about each of them. Some memories were humorous, such as the time Tegan and Dale had dyed Garth's uniform yellow. Others were more serious, such as acknowledging Mara's bravery in facing a deadly wraith in the old Rider barracks, now gone to ashes, its foundation filled in and buried. There was gentle laughter now and again, and tears. Laren herself almost lost control when she read, *"There is no finer leader than Captain Mapstone. She is brave, and fierce in her loyalty to the king and her Riders, and always my mentor, the woman I've admired most. I've tried to emulate her as a messenger and a person, but I fear I've mostly fallen short."*

Karigan, Laren thought, *you have never fallen short.*

She began reading Karigan's final farewell, but was interrupted by a rattling, almost like the sounds of the earth quaking. The ground did not move, however—it was everything else: scaffolding, shelves, Dakrias' desk and table, his piles of books . . .

More objects started to fall from shelves and crash to the floor, and as the rumble intensified, debris also dropped from the scaffolding onto the assembled. The Weapons hustled Estora from the chamber.

"Everyone out!" Laren cried after a plank of wood clattered down next to her.

She waited to ensure everyone else was clear before she exited herself. The rumble had grown into a continuous thundering clamor. As soon as she stepped across the threshold after Dakrias, it all stilled, went silent.

"They've never done *that* before," Dakrias said, bemused, as he gazed back into the chamber.

Nor had the ghosts ever interfered with a memorial circle before. In times past, she'd sensed them as watchful presences, but nothing more.

Everyone milled in the corridor, voices raised in consternation.

"Silence!" Laren bellowed, Karigan's forgotten letter fluttering in her hand as she gestured for attention. She cleared her throat, folded the letter carefully, and inserted it into her pocket for safekeeping. "The memorial circle is postponed for tonight due to . . ." Due to what? Mischievous ghosts? "Well, you saw. In any case, we will conclude the memorial honoring Karigan another evening."

Her pronouncement was followed by the crash of what

sounded like a heavy wooden crate hitting and splitting on the records room floor. Dakrias groaned.

"In the meantime," Laren said between gritted teeth, "you are dismissed to quarters."

As Weapons and Riders filed down the corridor, Arms Master Drent paused before her. "Interesting ceremony, Captain. Can't say as I've seen the like. Fitting, somehow." And then he moved on, his hulking figure shouldering its way through the others.

Laren sighed. Yes, it was fitting. As Mara had said, such madness would happen only at Karigan's memorial.

Queen Estora also stopped to speak with her. "You must inform me when you decide to conclude the ceremony." She glanced into the records room with bright eyes. "I think Karigan would have been overwhelmed by it all and not just by the unusual circumstances."

Laren could not disagree with this, either. Karigan was often surprised when she became the center of attention, and shied from it. The queen bade her goodnight, and Laren bowed. As the corridor emptied, she caught Fastion's arm as he strode by. "Would you mind waiting behind?"

"Not at all, Captain." He sidled to the wall to allow others to pass.

When everyone else had left, Laren found Dakrias in the doorway of the records room peering inward. "Do you think it's safe?" he asked.

"You would know better than anyone," she replied.

Dakrias appeared to steel himself, settling his administrator's gowns about him and straightening the specs on his nose. With a curt nod he stepped into the records room. When nothing ill happened, he took a few more cautious steps. Laren and Fastion followed him, surveying the damage.

"I will assign some Riders to help clean up this mess in the morning," Laren told Dakrias.

"I thank you," he replied, "and my clerks will, too. I've not the faintest idea of what got into the, um, spirits tonight, but it was rude conduct on their part during so solemn an occasion." He projected his voice upward as if to ensure the ghosts heard his remonstration.

Who could know what had stirred up the ghosts? She might have to finish Karigan's memorial elsewhere for safety's sake.

"Fastion," she said, "I'd like to see the glass dome to make sure it hasn't been damaged." Since it was not the actual chamber that had trembled, she was optimistic no damage to the glass had occurred, but she had to make sure.

"Of course. I will light it up for you and check for damage up top, while you inspect it from below." Without another word, he strode from the records room.

Laren waited, hearing muttering from Dakrias who attempted to straighten the mess on his desk. She turned at the sound of footsteps entering the room. It was not a ghost, or one of her Riders, but none other than Zachary, accompanied by a pair of Weapons and three Eletians. After her initial surprise, she bowed to her king.

Zachary looked about, baffled by the mess. "Tell me, Captain, exactly what kind of ceremony is it you conduct here?"

Laren refrained from making a sarcastic reply. "We have decided to conclude our memorial for Rider G'ladheon on another night when there is, er, less turbulence."

The mention of Karigan's name in the same breath as the word "memorial" brought a flash of pain to his eyes, but he revealed no more of his true feelings. As for the Eletians, she had met none of them before, two males and one female, but they held the beauty all Eletians possessed that made it so difficult not to stare at them. One of the men, the younger male, was somehow muted in his looks compared to any other Eletians she had ever met. He was still striking, but his inner light was less intense. There was a more earthly quality about him. But why had they come? And why had Zachary brought them to the records room, of all places?

"Allow me to introduce our guests," Zachary said. "This is the leader of the *tiendan*. His name is Somial."

The foremost Eletian nodded, silvery hair flowing about his shoulders.

"Somial," Laren said. "I have heard that name. Karigan met an Eletian named Somial." It had been before Karigan was officially a Rider, at a time when Eletians were little more than legend.

"Yes," Somial said in a pleasing voice. "We helped her along the road after her most heroic battle with a creature of *Kanmorhan Vane*. It brings us great sorrow that she ..." He paused as if searching for the correct words. "It is difficult for us to know what to say as we deal so little with mortality. Perhaps I should just say we have sorrow that she is not here with us."

"Thank you," Laren said quietly. They hadn't come just to offer condolences, had they? If that were the case, wouldn't their prince have sent one who knew the proper words?

"My companions," Somial said, "Idris—"The woman nodded gravely. "—and Enver."

The young man came forward and presented his hand. When Laren got over her surprise, she clasped it and shook.

"How do you do?" he asked in a practiced cadence.

"Well, thank you. And you?"

He smiled, his eyes alight. "I am fine."

"Enver," Somial explained with an indulgent smile, "has been studying the customs of your people. He is very pleased to use what he has learned."

"Somial and his people have come to us," Zachary said, "at the behest of Prince Jametari. Specifically, they wish to see you."

"Me?" In a night of surprises, this was the biggest.

"Yes, Captain," Somial replied. "He wishes you to send a message."

Laren glanced at Zachary, who shrugged, their purpose as much a mystery to him as it was to her. "Surely Prince Jametari has his own messengers?"

"Yes." Somial looked amused. "We tiendan serve that purpose, but our prince has had a vision. The message must be written in your hand. In fact, three messages."

When Somial told her what she must write and what she must do with the messages, she thought the Eletians and their prince positively mad. Something like hope lit in Zachary's eyes though he attempted to conceal it. Laren thought the scheme not only foolish but also cruel. If nothing came of it, it would only compound and extend their pain at losing Karigan.

Zachary must have sensed her hesitation, because he said, "I order you to do as they say, Captain. I feel that it is right."

"Yes, Your Majesty," she said. She bowed as he left the chamber. It was his final word on the matter.

The three Eletians remained behind and were all looking up. She followed their gazes to the lighted stained glass dome. Even with the scaffolding in the way, she could clearly tell the difference between the panel Master Goodgrave had cleaned and the ones he had not yet gotten to. The colors of Lil Ambrioth kneeling before a moon priest were brilliant, her green cloak never before so vibrant, King Jonaeus' crown no longer dim, but a shining light. The uncleaned panels were subdued by comparison.

"The leaf you seek," Somial said, as if pronouncing a vision of his own, "will be revealed to you in the panel of victorious battle."

"What?"

But he was bowing away, his two companions after him. How did he know? Before she could ask, they were gone.

She gazed back up at the dome—not at the newly cleaned panel, but at the one that depicted Lil and her Riders in an aspect of victory over their enemies, the mountains rising behind them and the storm clouds of war receding. That was where she'd seen the symbol of the four-fold leaf, and it made sense that if more clues were to be found about the League's major ally in the Long War, then it should be in that panel. She would leave a message for Master Goodgrave to clean that one next.

Then she would write the messages as relayed to her by Somial. And commanded by Zachary.

Karigan, I do not know what you would say to all this, she thought. Then revised, *Or perhaps you, of anyone, would.*

She decided to join Fastion up above and inspect the dome from that angle. As she left the records room, of all the oddities this evening had brought, she wondered why Eletians traveled in threes, or multiples of three.

It was one mystery among so many.

THE FIRST MESSAGE

Karigan barely listened as her two visitors prattled on and on about Dr. Silk's dinner party the night before, evaluating the dress of this lady or that.

"And oh, those women of the Capital!" Mrs. Downey exclaimed. "No sense of decency among the lot of them with those short veils of theirs."

Mrs. Greeling nodded in agreement. The two appeared to carry on the conversation quite adequately without the least input from Karigan, which was just fine with her. It had been this way all morning, since just after breakfast—ladies calling on her as if her appearance at Dr. Silk's party had immediately rendered her acceptable to society. She assumed what lured them to the professor's parlor were equal measures of curiosity about his reclusive niece and a desire to inspect her worthiness as a possible match for their sons. A number of callers had looked her up and down most intently, as if judging livestock suitable for breeding.

She thought that it was probably the professor's Preferred status, more than anything else about her, that had drawn Mill City's matrons, but they would want to make sure she was not defective physically and able to produce heirs for their sons. Female mental capacity, she guessed, was not terribly important in the empire. They would look past Kari Goodgrave's madness if it meant aligning with a family as important as the professor's.

Karigan's own thoughts were immersed in the visit of Cloudy the cat in the very early morning hours, and so she became deaf to the indignation of Mrs. Downey and Mrs.

Greeling over short veils and low necklines. Even now, in her mind's eye, she could see the message Cloudy had borne, the loops and curves and angles of the handwriting that was so familiar to her, that of Captain Laren Mapstone. She'd sat there on the bed, stunned, staring at her own name written in faded black ink. The paper was yellowed, coarser in texture than that produced by the empire, indicating it was of some age. How had anyone known to send it to her? How had it come to her over so many years? Was it even real, or had someone forged the message, and if so, to what end?

She became aware of Lorine and Arhys entering the parlor, bringing in more trays of tea cakes and a fresh pot of hot water. Arhys was pouting and glared at Karigan before she tromped out of the room with a toss of her head, apparently jealous of all the attention Karigan was receiving. Most likely, Arhys would have loved sitting in the parlor sipping tea with the matrons of Mill City.

"—and he has co-opted the slaves from mill three of my husband's cotton mills to work on that excavation of his," Mrs. Greeling was saying. At some point the conversation had moved from veils to Dr. Silk's project.

"His and four others," Mrs. Downey replied, "so he can operate the site all day and night."

"I do not know how my husband shall make up for the lost labor," Mrs. Greeling said. "It is setting us back—and the cost to replace the slaves and the time it takes to train them to the work?" She shook her head at the hopelessness of it all.

"It is the emperor's will," Mrs. Downey replied, gazing into her teacup.

They could, Karigan thought, hire *paid* labor, but such a revolutionary idea would reap accusations of sedition. The empire's foundation was built on the backs of its slaves, allowing a very small elite class to live very well, like the two ladies before her. Like the professor. That much was clear. The discussion turned abruptly from that depressing theme back to the less controversial trivialities of the party and its entertainments.

Karigan sank back into her own thoughts. The message had been very direct and very like the captain.

Karigan,

> *Go to the Heroes Portal at midnight.*
>
> *L. Mapstone, Capt., HMMS*

She could almost hear the captain speak the words, see her fold the paper, and still Karigan was assailed by all the questions. How had the captain known she'd receive the message? What did it all mean, and why now? Why not when she'd first arrived? One point she was certain about was that Cloudy could only be a tomb cat, like her friend, Ghost Kitty. Somehow the tombs had survived Amberhill's catastrophic weapon after he'd turned on his own king and country. The tombs had survived with at least some members of its caretaker community intact; enough that someone knew to send Karigan a message in the future.

Karigan had dealt with ghosts, had confronted monsters and Mornhavon the Black. She'd witnessed strange magic and had moved through time before. Still, the simple message from her captain, brought to her somehow through the passage of years, rattled her. Little ripples formed in the cup of tea she held in shaking hands.

It also gave her hope. Someone knew she had not died in Blackveil. Someone knew she had come forward in time. At the Heroes Portal, would someone tell her how to get home?

"Well, it has been very charming to visit with you, Miss Goodgrave," Mrs. Downey said. She and Mrs. Greeling were rising from their chairs and dropping their veils over their faces.

They were leaving at last, thank the gods.

After Grott showed them out, she told him absolutely no more callers. She could not take it anymore. She paced back and forth in the parlor, wondering what to do with herself until midnight, because she had to do *something* or go truly mad.

Decisively she turned on her heel and headed out of the parlor and down the corridor. She would go to the stables to visit Raven. She'd ensure he was ready to go tonight and that her Tam Ryder outfit was in its usual place, and then she'd work out her route.

"Miss Goodgrave!" Mirriam intercepted Karigan at the back door. "Grott says you do not wish to receive any more callers. You should be grateful these ladies are willing to make your acquaintance."

Grateful because I'm supposed to be mad, and they are willing to overlook such an embarrassing deficiency? Karigan wanted to snap that she had better use for her time, but she held her tongue and said, instead, "I am very tired." At least it was true. How could she have slept after Cloudy's visit?

"But several of them have eligible sons, and from Preferred families!"

So she could become breeding stock. "I am not interested."

Mirriam sputtered in astonishment, and before she could say another word, Karigan was out the door and striding across the yard.

Later, at supper, the professor glanced at her more than once. Karigan felt she must exude restless energy. Raven had certainly picked up on it earlier, circling in his stall and digging at his bedding. Now she pushed legumes about her plate. Had Mirriam reported her agitated behavior to the professor? Perhaps he'd put it down to her concern for Lhean.

She had sat still long enough, after seeing Raven, to study the city maps in the professor's library and to select a route for her midnight excursion. No streets or developments appeared to venture near the vicinity of where she remembered the Heroes Portal to lie. The area still seemed to be rural, which no doubt helped maintain the secret of the tombs. This would be her first time heading out into the city—the city and beyond—on her own. The fact she had confronted many frightening situations as a Green Rider, not least of all becoming lost in Blackveil Forest, did not make her any less nervous about sneaking out into hostile territory in the deep of night. Alone. Yes, that was what this future was—hostile territory.

She had considered taking someone into her confidence and asking him to accompany her. Luke? Cade? But she immediately dismissed the idea. This was *her* business and no one else's, and it was her duty to keep the existence of the Heroes Portal a secret.

When Karigan excused herself before she finished supper, the professor asked, "Are you not feeling well, my dear?"

"I'm fine, Uncle, just a little tired."

She returned to her room, and Lorine helped her change into her nightgown early. When left on her own, Karigan took out the mirror shard from its hiding place, along with the note from Captain Mapstone. She stared long and hard at the words and handwriting, confirming for herself once again that this was, in fact, real and not a hoax. It had to be. She had to believe. Even if it was a trap of some kind, she could not ignore the summons. She had to go.

She gazed at the mirror shard, but it produced no vision for her.

When the bell struck ten hour, she swung her legs out of bed and crept to the door. She had to be especially careful—this was an earlier hour than when she usually slipped out to meet the professor to go to the old mill, and there was always the chance someone in the household was awake, notably the professor himself. However, as she made her way, she encountered no one. Light might glow in the crack beneath a bedroom door, but no one emerged.

Once she let herself out the back door, she knew the stable would be the next challenge, for Luke and the stable boys had rooms there. She worked up a few excuses in case she was caught. *I'm sorry, Luke, I couldn't sleep and wanted to see Raven.* Or, *I'm sorry Luke, but it seemed like a good night for a ride* . . . Right. Very convincing.

When she entered the stable with the light of a very dim taper to guide her, Raven whickered sleepily at her.

"Shhh," she admonished him.

She let herself into the tackroom and the wardrobe where her Tam Ryder garb awaited her. She changed quickly, stuffing her braid into the cap. She froze when she thought she heard a door groan open, expecting Luke to come at any moment and demand what she was about. She strained to listen, but heard nothing more than the movements of horses and the settling noises of the building itself. Still, she crept out of the tackroom, looking around carefully. When she saw no one, she went to Raven to groom and tack him. She had groomed him earlier in the day and now only had to brush a light layer of dust off his coat. He was fully awake now and nuzzled her for treats.

"Not now, silly," she whispered, and she set the saddle on his back.

Karigan prayed her luck held. It was one thing if she was caught by Luke, but as she led Raven out of the stable, she knew it would be quite another if she were spotted by an Inspector. She'd brought the bonewood with her but did not think it would be much of a defense against a gun or mechanical.

She led Raven down the drive and mounted. He pranced and tossed his head, full of high spirits. The silver of his tack jingled, and to Karigan it sounded like an alarm ringing in the quiet of night.

"Settle down," she murmured.

Raven whickered.

She leaned down on his neck and whispered to his twitching ear, "Tonight you are a Green Rider horse, and we are on an important mission. Understand?"

He quieted.

Good, Karigan thought, and she squeezed him forward.

He promptly started prancing again, behaving like the energetic young stallion he was, his neck handsomely curved. She sighed, made another short prayer, and they were out on the street. She looked carefully this way and that. A clammy mist hung in the air, turning the glow of streetlamps hazy, droplets turning into sparks and embers as they passed through the light. A little fog would be helpful. If only she had her brooch and her special ability worked. She could disappear and none would note her passage.

She held Raven in, peering down streets at every intersection. There were a few others out—street sweepers, cabs rumbling by at a trot, amorphous shapes in the mist. She followed the route Luke had taken when they'd gone to the Scangly Mounds that one day. When she looked over her shoulder toward the Old City, the light of Silk's worksite at the summit boiled and wavered in the thick air. It would be her beacon and help her keep her bearings as she sought the foundation of the small mount—where the Old City, *her* Sacor City, had been—and searched for the Heroes Portal.

As she continued on her cautious way, Raven's hooves clopping all too loudly on the street, she wondered if, instead of stealth, they should actually move along as if she had business to attend to. The cabs certainly did, as well as other carriages she saw out and about. She paused, thinking it over, and in the silence heard the mechanical *click-clack* of an Enforcer tapping its way down the street on its spindly, metallic legs, accompanied by the footsteps of an Inspector. Karigan backed Raven into an alley and peered around its entrance. A sickly glow hovered around the mechanical, its looking-glass eye rotating on the orb of its body. The Inspector swung a club at his side. The mechanical made a sharp *bleep* and turned down a side street.

Relief settled over Karigan, but Raven mouthed the bit, so she decided they would trot through the city and try to leave it behind as fast as possible, come what may. She was tired of caution, and the message Cloudy had brought made her decide that the time of waiting and inaction was over. They set out at a ground-eating trot.

In the center of town there was a little more traffic, and she felt less conspicuous. She slowed Raven to a jog to accommodate others on the street, even passing another Inspector and his mechanical patrolling shop fronts. The Inspector didn't even glance her way, more interested in the window displays. Once away from the town center, they picked up their pace again along Canal Street, past silent mills with darkened windows. Fog wisped along the surface of the canal's black water. Soon they clattered across the bridge that spanned the canal, then the second that crossed the river, and she urged Raven to a canter through the poor neighborhoods on the other side.

They did not slow down till they were far away from streetlamps and habitation. Karigan circled Raven around more than once to ensure they were not being followed. A couple of times, she could have sworn she heard something behind her, maybe a hoofbeat that was not Raven's or the clacking of a rock, but even with her senses sharply attuned, she found no evidence of pursuit.

They proceeded more slowly now, the density of the dark and the fog challenging her night vision as they traveled the road that bypassed the Scangly Mounds. Eventually they would have to leave the road and rein in toward the base of the Old City's mount, but she was unsure of the terrain, and it was difficult to reconcile the lines of a map with the actual landscape, especially submerged in a night fog. She paused Raven at a lightly trodden track that veered off the road to their right. She thought that this was the one that led to the Scangly Mounds. If this was the correct turning, she must travel farther along it. But how far? After they'd gone some distance, she halted Raven again and sat, indecisive. The summit of the mount she'd seen, ablaze with the lights of Silk's excavation, had vanished from view due to tree growth and the shape of the mount itself. Not that she could make out even basic shapes; the wafting mist made everything indistinct. Though she stood still, the world streamed around her in vaporous currents.

Even had it been clear and sunny, she was not sure she'd be able to find the Heroes Portal. She had been there but once, led by a Weapon and the king, and it was well hidden. It was possible to pass very close by and never know it. She worried that her hesitation would make her late for whatever was supposed to transpire at midnight, but she worried more about becoming lost and not finding it at all.

Raven stamped and pranced, interrupting her thoughts. When she finally got him to settle, she realized they were no longer alone on the road.

Meow, said Cloudy the cat. He sat with his tail wrapped around his feet right in front of them.

Karigan had never been so glad to see a cat.

FOLLOWING THE CAT

 Raven lowered his head to snuffle Cloudy. A puff of air from his nostrils ruffled the cat's whiskers. Cloudy tapped Raven's nose. The stallion jerked his head up and snorted, leaving both horse and cat disgruntled.

"Right," Karigan said. "Now that you've introduced yourselves, what's next?"

Cloudy flicked his tail, rose, and strutted off with an air of righteous disdain for all horsekind. He veered off the road to their left and into some brush. Remembering the last time that she, accompanied by several Weapons, had needed to find a way into the tombs, they'd been led to a secret entrance by Ghost Kitty. Karigan reined Raven after Cloudy. It was utterly ridiculous to even consider following a cat, but what else was she supposed to do?

Maybe, she thought with some perversity, it wasn't the gods who controlled the universe, but cats. Cats who toyed with humans as a puppeteer would a marionette. Ghost Kitty had always manipulated her into feeding him treats and giving him the greater part of her bed.

Raven plodded into the brush after Cloudy.

I am following a cat. One part of Karigan wanted to laugh, and another part of her was resigned to the absurdity. Who was she to judge what was utterly ridiculous after all she'd seen and done and experienced?

Cloudy continued into a thatch of woods and thick undergrowth with his tail erect and crooked at the tip. Branches Karigan could not see almost knocked her off Raven's back, so she dismounted. Cloudy hurried back and rubbed against her legs, then forged onward. She hoped he was not leading her to his favorite mouse hole. She tried to console herself with the fact that the night she and the Weapons had been so desperate to enter the tombs, Ghost Kitty led them true.

The woods only deepened the gloom, and Karigan tripped over rocks and depressions in the earth. Fortunately Cloudy's light coloring made him visible. Occasionally, he paused with a glance back to see if she was still there. She pushed away wet tree limbs and pulled strands of spider webs off her face, wondering how far they had to go. And was this the easiest way for a horse and human to go, or just a path convenient for a cat? With Raven plowing through the woods, snapping branches as he plodded behind her, they certainly were not making a quiet approach. Anyone who might be waiting for her—friend or enemy—would hear her coming.

Karigan felt like she trudged after Cloudy forever. Would she be late? Would someone be there to meet them? She amused herself by imagining a whole glaring of cats awaiting her, led by one Supreme Cat. Such notions took the edge off her nerves. It was better than worrying about walking into a trap.

So immersed was she in her fancies of a feline greeting committee, that it took her several moments to realize the going was easier—less brush, fewer branches grabbing at her. Raven's hooves clopped solidly on stone and the ground grew more even underfoot. Karigan's hopes lifted—there had been the remnant of a granite-paved path leading to the Heroes Portal. If she were able to see the trees that towered overhead, would she find herself passing beneath a grove of hemlocks?

She strained her eyes looking for another sign of where she was and almost missed it. The obelisk had toppled over and broken in two at some point, and only a little of its pale stone shone in the dark. It appeared it was being claimed by the earth, swallowed by moss and leaves and pine needles. They were close now.

She picked up her pace behind Cloudy, her excitement rising, though she also tried to remain alert for trouble. Cloudy jumped up onto a rock and sat to groom himself. No, this was no simple rock. Karigan paused to glide her hand across it. This was a slab of granite shaped by the hands and tools of people. It was pocked by age and covered with forest debris and thick, sodden moss, but it had once been polished smooth. It was a coffin rest. That meant the portal was straight ahead. Not far.

Cloudy leaped down and led her on. After some time, Karigan felt, more than saw, the space closing in on them, that they were coming to a wall of rock. Sound changed as they neared, the thud of Raven's hooves rebounding. The mineral scent of wet stone grew heavy in the air. Water trickled nearby from some height above to the forest floor. Cloudy stepped off the path and jumped onto a fallen log and sat, waiting expectantly. Karigan strained her eyes, peered into the dark, and yes, there was the tall, pale finger of stone, the second obelisk, that marked the entrance to the tombs.

Had she missed the appointed time? Would someone come out to see her, or would she have to knock on the portal? Not that anyone would hear her if she did. She thought she remembered how the door was opened that long ago night—there was a glyph of Westrion on its center. One only had to press it . . .

She took a step forward thinking to do just that. She did not feel like standing there forever in the dark, waiting for something to happen. She was about to take a second step when a low voice issued out of the dark: "Do not move."

She froze, throttling down a scream at the sharp edge of steel suddenly touching her throat. She swallowed slowly, carefully. A trap after all! She had not even seen or heard anyone draw the sword, and now she dared not see who wielded it for fear he would cut her throat.

"Name yourself," said a second male voice behind her.

Karigan had not been around guns very much, but she easily identified the particular *click* of the hammer being drawn back. She could feel the man boring his sight into her.

Beside her, Raven moved his head about, snuffling the scents of the two men. Were there more? He flattened his ears back and whinnied. She gripped the reins tightly.

"Your name," the man with the gun demanded.

Karigan knew she could be giving away everything, but if

these were in fact the people she was supposed to meet and not a pair of villains who'd drawn her here for nefarious purposes, withholding her real name could mean her death.

"I will not ask again," the gunman said.

Karigan opened her mouth to answer, but Raven lunged, knocked the sword away from her throat, and lashed out with his rear hooves. Someone cursed. Karigan whirled, the bonewood extended to fighting length. She stood in a defensive posture, the entrance to the tombs somewhere behind her.

People moved about the woods farther down the trail. It sounded like a brawl had erupted, fists thudding on flesh, branches cracking, grunts of pain and muted shouts. *What in the hells?* Raven snorted beside her and dug at the ground.

Even as the fight continued, Karigan sensed someone angling toward her from the side. She turned to face him but saw little.

"Put the staff down. It is of no use against a gun." When she paused, he added, "I will surely blow a hole through your head if you do not comply."

She believed it. His voice was imbued with layers of threat. Slowly she laid the bonewood on the ground and raised her hands palms outward to show they were empty. Obviously he could see her better than she him.

"Now your name. Your name and that of your accomplice."

Accomplice? "But—"

"Name."

Karigan swallowed hard. Well, if she was going to give her name, she might as well do it right. "I am Rider Sir Karigan G'ladheon of His Majesty's Messenger Service." She'd have bowed, but she feared any sudden movement on her part would cause the man to pull the trigger.

He paused, most likely digesting her name and title. "Who did you bring with you? Name your accomplice."

"I have no accomplice, unless you mean my horse."

"You were followed," he accused.

"I was? But I—"

"We've subdued him," someone called out, this time a female voice.

The sound of the fight was replaced by that of several approaching footsteps.

"Light," someone said.

Lanterns flared to life, and Karigan averted her face, shielding her eyes. After all that time in the dark it was like falling into the sun.

"Is it her?" someone asked.

"Hard to tell."

Karigan blinked, willing her eyes to adjust.

"Watch the horse," another said. "He kicked me."

Karigan squinted at Raven who tensed up at her side again, then she turned her gaze on those who stood arrayed before her. The light was aimed into her face so it was not easy to see past the glare. She guessed there were a half a dozen of them, and they were dressed darkly, probably in black. The cut of their clothes—their *uniforms*—was very familiar. So was the way they held themselves: Weapons.

She wanted to cry out in joy at finding something so familiar in this unfamiliar world, but her reaction was tempered by wariness. Were these Weapons like those of her own time, or had they and their loyalties changed?

Raven bunched up beside her, preparing for another lunge. "No!" she cried, and grabbed the reins. He half-reared, but she coaxed him down.

"We do not attack Weapons," she admonished him.

At this statement, the tension of all concerned diminished a notch. Raven nudged her, seeking reassurance. Absently she patted his neck.

"At least I presume you are Weapons," she told them. "I received a message to be here at midnight."

One of the black-clad warriors stepped forward, lowering the lantern so it would no longer glare in her eyes. Raven tensed again.

"Enough," she told the horse.

The man halted before her. "I am called Joff. Yes, we are of the Order of the Black Shields. If you are not who you say you are, you will not leave this place."

"Never to see the light of the living day again, eh?" she replied.

"It appears you know the law," he murmured, bemused. "I would like to believe you are who you say, but we must make sure. Before we do that, will you identify this man who followed you?"

Two Weapons, not in the immediate group, shoved a figure forward, guns pointed at their captive.

"Cade?" Karigan said in astonishment. "What in five hells?"

He gazed in her direction, looking dazed. Blood trickled from a split lip. "Miss Goodgrave? Are—are you all right?"

"Apparently better than you."

"They jumped me, otherwise I'd have had the upper hand."

Joff gazed harshly at her. "Why does he call you by another name?"

"For my protection," Karigan replied. "To keep me hidden from the empire."

Joff nodded, accepting her explanation. "Who is this Cade to you?"

"He is Cade Harlowe, a student of archeology who studies under the man who shelters me." She would tell no more until she was very sure of these Weapons. It was one thing to give herself away, but Cade and his connection to the opposition? Not yet.

"He will not be permitted to leave," Joff said.

Then there was that, the law of the tombs. The Weapons had their own interests to protect. She would deal with Cade later. Now she had to know why she'd received a message written by her captain telling her to come to this place at the midnight hour.

"We need to have Chelsa come out now," said the female Weapon. "Chelsa can tell us if this person is who she claims."

"Agreed," said Joff. "Dash?"

One of the Weapons strode past Karigan to the rock wall. With the light of the lanterns, she could make out the rocky overhang and the round, iron door embedded into the granite wall with its glyph of Westrion barely visible. It was as she remembered that night of Prince Amilton's coup attempt, the door large enough to admit a coffin and pall bearers.

Dash pressed the glyph and pulled the door open a crack.

It did not creak or groan, nor did it look difficult to move. Again, just as Karigan remembered. She noticed, as he spoke to someone beyond the door, that Dash wore a sword sheathed on one hip and a gun on the other. A quick glanced revealed that Joff and the others were likewise armed. Not all things had stayed the same.

Dash paused in his conversation and opened the door just wide enough to allow a small cloaked and hooded woman to slip out. Karigan could see nothing beyond the door before Dash securely closed it, but she remembered the long, rounded corridor with its smooth granite walls that led to the avenues of the dead.

The woman clutched what looked like a portfolio to her chest. She walked boldly up to Karigan. The light revealed a young face beneath the hood, younger than Karigan, but estimating the age of a caretaker was difficult for they lived out their lives underground, and their faces remained curiously pale and unlined. The light gray cloak the woman wore was as much a uniform marking her as a caretaker, as the black uniforms designated Weapons.

Cloudy pounced off his perch on the log to rub against the caretaker's leg and purr loudly.

"Well, hello, Scruffy. Who have you brought us?"

Scruffy? Cloudy's real name was *Scruffy?* It seemed so undignified.

"I am Chelsa," the young woman said, "chief caretaker. Dash tells me you claim to be Rider Sir Karigan G'ladheon."

"Yes," Karigan said. "I am she."

"I tend to believe it is true due to the circumstances. Who else would know the Heroes Portal? And Scruffy would not have brought the wrong person, but we must be sure."

Chelsa untied the string that bound her portfolio and removed a piece of paper.

"Joff, your light, if you please."

Joff joined her, and the two stared at the paper, then back at Karigan. They did this a few times before Chelsa asked, "Sir Karigan, would you please remove your cap?"

She wondered what they were looking at, but complied, her braid falling back into place between her shoulders.

Chelsa and Joff looked some more.

"What do you think?" Chelsa asked the Weapon.

"It is her."

"I quite agree."

"What is . . . what is that you are looking at?" Karigan asked.

"It is a drawing of you," Chelsa said. "You, or your twin."

She brought it over to Karigan, who understood as soon as she saw it. "Oh, Yates," she murmured.

"Yes," Chelsa said. "The Rider who made this drawing so long ago was Yates Cardell. Buried on the Wanda Plains was he, so far from home." Her voice was wistful.

The pain of his loss lanced Karigan anew. The drawing was a page from the journal Yates had taken into Blackveil. She'd seen some of his other drawings—one of Hana, an Eletian who had not survived the expedition, and one of a *nythling* creature that had taken the life of Grant, another of their companions. She had not known Yates had drawn her. It was a good likeness, she thought. He'd caught her at some unguarded moment, perhaps by the campfire, maybe before they had even crossed over the wall into the forest. He had labeled it with her name, but no date.

"I cannot believe you have this," Karigan said, "from so long ago. My understanding is that most everything from before the empire was destroyed."

"The last king—*your king*—ensured it was preserved in the tombs." Chelsa gave her a penetrating look with a slight cant of her head. Karigan did not know what to make of it. The king had preserved it? This picture of her?

"I—I wasn't even sure the tombs remained intact."

"They do. For now." Chelsa's features darkened.

She worries about Silk's excavation, Karigan thought, *as well she should.*

"But if I may say," Chelsa said more brightly, "we are probably more in awe that you are here in . . . in our time. I confess, I had my doubts about all this, with old messages and whatnot. It is a great honor to meet you, Sir Karigan. You are rather legendary." She bowed, and so did the Weapons.

Karigan's cheeks warmed. "Er, just call me Karigan, please.

The 'sir' is not necessary. It is frankly a relief to see you all. You are not from my time, but you are *of* my time."

"Aptly put," Chelsa replied.

"I would like to know," Cade said, apparently coming out of his daze, "what this place is and who these people are." His eyes were full of questions, and he, too, now regarded Karigan with some awe.

Before Karigan could say a word, one of the Weapons, with a deft flick of his wrist, reversed the gun in his grip and struck the back of Cade's head with the butt. Cade crumpled to the ground.

"Cade!" Karigan cried. She thrust Raven's reins into Joff's hands and raced to Cade's side. She knelt, checking him, lightly patting his cheek, but he was unconscious.

"Was that necessary?" she demanded of the Weapon. "He has been studying the old ways, training to become one of you."

The Weapon did not look remorseful. "He was not expected here. There are things he should not know. As it is, we shall have to keep him in the tombs or kill him."

Karigan stood. "You will have to kill me first."

THE SECOND MESSAGE,
AND THE THIRD

"**P**lease, Sir Karigan," Chelsa said, already forgetting Karigan's request not to use her title. "This is not necessary. No one will be killed."

Karigan looked warily at the Weapons who now encircled her, but none made an aggressive move. Cloudy—no, Scruffy—rubbed against Joff's leg and casually sauntered over to her, first rubbing her knee and purring loudly, then climbing onto Cade's belly and kneading his coat.

"This man came armed," said the Weapon who had struck Cade. "We cannot trust him."

"He was just keeping watch over me," Karigan replied, though she did not know exactly what he'd been up to. But why else would he have come? Whether he had followed her because he didn't want her to come to harm or because the professor had decided he could not trust her, she did not know, but whatever the reason, Cade did not deserve such harsh treatment. She removed her jacket, rolled it up, and placed it gently under his head. Scruffy, curled up now, rose and fell with Cade's deep, even breaths. At least the cat was content.

Karigan stood and placed her hands on her hips, giving the chief caretaker and the Weapons a good, assessing gaze. At first no one moved or said anything.

Eventually Chelsa broke the silence. "I shall ask a death surgeon to attend to your friend."

This might have been an alarming statement had Karigan not been somewhat familiar with the ways of caretakers. In the royal tombs, death surgeons not only prepared the dead for interment but also served as menders among the caretakers. "Thank you," she replied.

Another silence descended on the group. "I was summoned here," Karigan reminded them.

Chelsa shook herself. "Yes, do forgive me. It is not every day we receive a visitor from the long ago past—alive, that is. Shall we go in?"

"You will permit it?" Karigan asked with some surprise. "And you will let me leave after?"

"Yes, of course. It is well documented in the past that you were permitted into the tombs and allowed to leave, although one occasion involved deceiving the chief caretaker of that time."

Karigan nodded. She'd been dressed in the black of the Weapons, by the Weapons, so she could go into the tombs despite the taboo that forbade all from entering except royalty, caretakers, Weapons, and of course, the dead. Many Weapons spent their entire careers guarding the dead, and the other secrets buried in the tombs. Any other unauthorized soul who somehow stumbled his way into the tombs would not be allowed to leave and must spend the rest of his life as a caretaker.

"Come to think of it," Chelsa mused, with a light, impish smile, "Agemon did complain in his log books quite a lot about the mess, as he put it, that you left behind."

Karigan had played ghost, borrowing some royal raiment to scare the Second Empire thugs who had invaded the tombs. There had been a bit of spilled blood, too, that had required clean up. For all of Agemon's complaints, much worse could have happened that night had she not made a "mess."

"Shall we?" Chelsa asked, gesturing toward the Heroes Portal.

With one last look at Cade to ensure he would be all right, Karigan retrieved Raven's reins from Joff and tethered the stallion to a nearby tree. She gave him a sound pat on the neck and told him to behave, then joined Chelsa at the door. Before they entered, Dash presented the bonewood to her with a bow.

"We have only heard about these," he said. "None ever found their way below."

Karigan took it with thanks, shortening it to cane length, and after the round door was opened, she followed Chelsa into the corridor she had never expected to enter again. Joff and the female Weapon accompanied them, leaving the rest to watch over Cade. Their steps thudded around them in the tubelike corridor, and when the iron door shut behind them, the rest of the world ceased to exist. There were no more sounds of small forest animals scurrying in the brush and leaf litter, no breezes rustling through the branches of the woods. Just their footsteps and breaths and the blanketing quiet of the tombs.

Chelsa let out a deep exhalation. "The air is so much better in here. It's always a relief to come in. Outside is so—so fecund and disorderly."

Orderliness appeared to be a desirable trait Chelsa shared with Agemon.

The corridor rose toward a round antechamber, its ceiling low. The top of Joff's head brushed against it. Several corridors spoked off from the chamber, but only one was lit, just as on the night of Prince Amilton's coup attempt. It was, Karigan knew, Heroes Avenue, which led to the resting places of Sacoridia's long dead heroes, including the First Rider, Lil Ambrioth. In the chamber's center, sat a coffin rest carved with funerary glyphs and runes. There was no coffin on it, but a pair of phosphorene lamps that lit the room.

Karigan hugged herself against the heavy cold that penetrated through her damp clothes. She hadn't even her jacket, which remained outside pillowing Cade's head. She shivered.

"Here," Joff said, removing his own heavy cloak and draping it over her shoulders. "This will not be the first time you've worn our black."

"Thank you," she said. "It is not." She wrapped the cloak around her, grateful for its warmth. Yes, she reflected, these people were not from her time, but of it. They knew the past in a way that the professor never would from the bits and pieces of artifacts he dug up. These people *lived* the past.

"Serena," Chelsa said, and the female Weapon stepped forward. "Could you please fetch one of the surgeons to tend Sir Karigan's friend?"

The Weapon nodded, and headed down the lit corridor at a trot. Joff, meanwhile, produced a pair of chairs from down the corridor and brought them to the coffin rest so Karigan and Chelsa could sit. He then posted himself by the wall.

Chelsa placed her portfolio on the coffin rest.

"How have you survived all these years?" Karigan asked as she seated herself.

Chelsa smiled, and when she pushed her hood back, it revealed that she was indeed young looking, and not just on account of the non-wrinkling properties of the tombs. There was a freshness of spirit to her that Karigan did not expect in a caretaker. Not that she was any judge—she'd only met a couple, but she'd expected them all to be like Agemon, every one of them sepulchral in disposition.

"Secrecy, of course," Chelsa replied, "and we've always had Helpers on the outside. From the days of our very origins."

"Even now with the empire?"

"Even so. The bonds with our Helpers are very close, and those who share our secret are very few. Now and then one of our Weapons will venture into the city seeking news and supplies. We watch for any who might come too close, or grow too curious. We have, on occasion, added to our population when we've had cause."

Karigan did not know, even in her own time, how many caretakers lived in the tombs. She had been told there was a "village," and that from time to time the Weapons had tried to transfer families to above, but it rarely proved successful. It went against everything the people had learned about not seeing the living light of day. She could well imagine the shock of moving from the quiet of the tombs to the hectic, thriving world above.

"We live as we always have," Chelsa continued, "governing ourselves and caring for the dead. We are no more, and no less, than we ever were."

"But how have you managed?"

"By honoring our traditions. Traditions allow us to maintain our culture, the stability of our society."

"Yours is a world within a world," Karigan said.

Chelsa nodded. "That is it exactly. We have our traditions and laws. Magicks set in place by the first caretakers ensure that our population remains diverse and at a manageable level, so we don't exceed our capacity, our resources. With the advent of the empire, however, we have had to make some changes."

Karigan, pleasantly warmed by Joff's cloak, was intrigued. Caretaker society was usually as secretive as the tombs themselves. "Such as?"

"Well, we've received no new royal dead in many generations, our last being Prince Amilton from your time period. We were never able to locate King Zachary's remains, and Queen Estora vanished from the world, so some of our people have turned from the funerary arts to other disciplines."

Karigan closed her eyes and tried to steady her breathing. She kept forgetting that, in this time, Zachary was gone and should have been interred here, in the tombs, not so very far from where she sat. She shuddered, not from the penetrating chill of the tombs, but from her sudden image of him, lying dead, his flesh pale and cold. Before she could stop herself, she saw him, in her mind's eye, laid out on this very slab of stone before her, prepared for interment in a sarcophagus long made ready for him.

But the caretakers had not received his remains. He was not here, his body likely desecrated by the enemy, forever lost. Would his death be more real to her if he was here? How could it be worse than her horrible visions of his desecrated corpse?

The difference was reality. A body would have been undeniable proof that he was gone. Dead. Lost to her. As terrible as the thought of desecration was, the absence of his remains made his death more abstract, intangible, left an edge of . . . of what? Hope? An increment of hope despite the damning record that was the diary of Seften, so lovingly preserved in the professor's library?

She passed her hand over her eyes. *He is still alive to me. I can't accept any of it.*

"Sir Karigan, are you all right?" Chelsa asked.

Karigan nodded. She could not allow herself to get caught

up in such thoughts and images, these questions of real and abstract. They would surely defeat her, submerge her in grief. No, she could not allow this to happen, she must go forward. Go forward to return to the past, so she could prevent Zachary's death in battle and the rise of the empire. "I am fine," she said at last. "Please go on."

Chelsa did not appear entirely convinced, but she continued with her explanation of how the caretakers had been getting on. "As for the disciplines our people have been engaged in, history is, as you may guess, a natural. Others have taken on the black of the Weapons since we no longer receive them from the outside, though a Helper or two have joined their ranks through the years. They are trained from within, trained in the same exacting manner as taught to us by the Weapons who had been in the tombs with our people when Sacor City fell."

It explained much, Karigan thought, about how they'd been able to carry on since the rise of the empire. "There are outsiders, archeologists," she said, "who would like to find these tombs."

"And so there are. But I suppose in its own way, the empire has helped keep our secret. Our history, the true history of Sacoridia, is denied. Few learn of it, and the empire restricts who has enough knowledge of it to do archeological work. We watch. We watch very closely, indeed. We, in fact, captured one archeologist who now lives among us. He was terribly excited and actually thanked us for allowing him in. A lifetime of discoveries, he said. A veritable treasure trove. It troubles him not that he can't share it with anyone above. He's too busy looking and discovering." Chelsa chuckled.

"Will you induct Dr. Silk into your community?"

Chelsa's smile faded. "Ezra Stirling Silk and his drill are a serious matter. One that must not be underestimated. But first things first, the matter which brought you here. On the day of my ascension to chief caretaker, just one week ago, I was given many objects in addition to my new responsibilities, among them documents, keys, tools, and secrets. It's overwhelming even though I had apprenticed to my predecessor, Threllis, when I was only nine. She passed to me all her knowledge. She went to the heavens the day before my ascension."

"I am sorry," Karigan said.

"I do miss her, certainly I do, but she has the joy of dancing with the gods while the rest of us labor on in our daily toil."

It was so lightly spoken that Karigan had to remind herself that Chelsa dealt with death constantly. Surrounded by its artifacts and iconography, as well as the husks of the dead, it was not surprising caretakers might have a different outlook on the passing of people important to them.

"Among the secrets revealed to me," Chelsa continued, "was a message from—"

They were interrupted by the return of Serena with a companion darkly cloaked and hooded, a satchel across his shoulder. The death surgeon. The two swept through the chamber without pausing and headed down the entrance corridor.

"Good," Chelsa said, watching after them. "Brunen will take good care of your friend."

"The message," Karigan urged.

"Of course." Chelsa removed a piece of paper from her portfolio. It looked very much like the one Karigan had received—yellowed around the edges, folded the same way. "The instruction in this message read: *To be given to Chelsa, upon her ascension.* And so it, along with accompanying documents—one of which you received—was handed down the generations of chief caretakers and spoken of to no one else. They remained unopened until me. I am the first and only Chelsa to become chief. Since this was kept secret by the chiefs, there was no way my parents would have known that their daughter, whom they named Chelsa, would eventually become chief. It is . . . rather strange to be thought of long before your birth. Long before anyone else knows that you will ever exist."

"I think I can sort of understand," Karigan said.

Chelsa laughed. "And so you, of anyone, could." She unfolded the message. "I was instructed within to send you the summons. It reads, *Dear Chelsa, Please send this first message to summon Rider Sir Karigan G'ladheon to the Heroes Portal.*

The cat will find her. Expect Sir Karigan to arrive at midnight on the Hollow Moon."

"The Hollow Moon?"

"We caretakers keep our own lunar calendar." Chelsa smiled brightly and passed Karigan the paper. "I trust that is your captain's signature?"

Karigan nodded as she looked the message over, a little thrill coursing through her. "Yes, this is her handwriting."

"Good. My predecessors have vouched for its authenticity. Upon your arrival, the message instructs me to give you another. If not for the order to actually give you the message, I might have expected to be receiving your remains, considering the period of time that has elapsed since your disappearance. To tell the truth, we would be delighted to have them."

Karigan was too disconcerted to know how to respond.

"That is not to say we are not very excited to have the living, breathing legend here with us, out of time as she is. It's extraordinary. But do know, we would welcome your remains and care for them diligently."

Karigan smiled weakly. "Er, thank you? I mean, wouldn't that be for the king to decide?"

"Of course, and if he were here, I'm confident he'd want you on Heroes Avenue, at the very least."

The very least?

While Karigan pondered that, Chelsa produced another folded piece of paper and silently offered it to her. It quavered in Karigan's hand. Her name was written on it just like the other, in the captain's style. This one was sealed with green wax imprinted by the winged horse. Just seeing it brought an onrush of emotion, a storm threatening to break. So homesick . . . She cleared her throat, forcing back tears, and broke the seal.

The captain had written:

Dear Karigan,

The scything moon is held captive in the prison of forgotten days. Seek it in the den of the three-faced

reptile, for you are the blade of the shadow cast.
Beware! The longer you linger, the faster we spin apart.

L. Mapstone, Capt., HMMS

Usually the captain was concise and to the point. But this . . . this was downright obscure. Even murky enough to make an Eletian proud. Karigan had hoped for some clear instruction to help her find her way home, but she'd gotten this instead. A riddle.

"Sir Karigan?" Chelsa said tentatively. "Is everything well? You've gone pale."

Karigan wordlessly handed the message to Chelsa.

"Oh, my," Chelsa murmured as she read it. "I take it this is not what you were expecting."

Karigan gave a humorless laugh. "I was expecting explicit directions about how to get home. To my own time. But of course, nothing is ever that easy."

Chelsa returned the message. "I am under the impression, from what I've read of her, your Captain Mapstone was never this cryptic."

"No," Karigan agreed. "This is not . . ." She struggled to find the right words. "This is not her voice."

"But it is her handwriting, yes?"

Karigan nodded.

"In his log books, Agemon spoke of receiving the documents from the captain's own hands. He described her as looking unhappy about it all as she instructed him to keep them secret until he was ready to pass his responsibilities on to his successor."

The captain, Karigan thought, could have been unhappy about any number of things. It told her nothing about why the captain had written such a riddle.

"She obviously meant for you to find meaning in her words," Chelsa said. "Somehow. I thought it remarkable that she knew you'd someday be here to read her words. I assume such pre-cognition is one of the skills Riders are endowed with?"

"Perhaps, but it was not the captain's. I've asked myself how she knew, but have no answers." Karigan was not surprised Chelsa knew of Rider abilities. She shook her head. "All I know is that I just want to go home."

Chelsa reached over and placed her hand on Karigan's arm. The warmth of that touch helped.

"I do not know what it is like to be sundered from home," Chelsa said, "for I was born and raised in these tombs, but I fear I may see its destruction." Her face was clouded with worry.

"What will you do?"

Chelsa shrugged. "We shall do as anyone would do when their home is threatened—defend it. The Weapons wish to stop Silk directly, but they are few and stand no chance against the numbers that can be deployed by the empire."

Karigan gave Joff a sideways glance. He had not left his station by the wall, and gave no indication he had listened to a word of their conversation. A true Weapon.

"If only I knew why Silk has started drilling now, and with such fervor," Chelsa said.

"Do you know of an object called the dragonfly device?" Karigan asked. If Chelsa did, not only would it help the opposition in this time, but if Karigan could solve Captain Mapstone's riddle and get home, she could find the artifact and prevent Amberhill's empire from rising in the first place.

"Dragonfly device? I have not heard of it."

Karigan tried to remember what the professor had said about it. "It was supposedly some sort of magical device used by a forerunner of the Sealender line to run off the sea kings. It disappeared afterward. The professor, the man who shelters me, thinks it may have been interred here with the first Sealender king."

If Chelsa was shocked that some professor knew of the tombs, she did not show it. She gazed thoughtfully into space.

"The professor thinks," Karigan said, "that this device has the power to stop whatever great weapon the emperor has at his disposal. He says Silk would like to get his hands on it to give to the emperor, to gain his esteem. Once in the emperor's own hands, it would no longer be a threat to him. The opposition would like to prevent this from happening and use the device to their own advantage if they could."

"There are many objects down here that have been interred with the royals, with all the heroes," Chelsa said. "Much of it is just the ephemera of lives lived, some of it priceless jewels and gold, some of it not. There are other relics that have been kept secret down here for their more arcane properties. I have to say, your dragonfly device is not one. Or, at least, it is not one I've ever heard of, which is entirely possible. It could even go by another name. The sheer number of objects we keep under our care is more than one person, even the chief caretaker, can know."

Nothing, Karigan thought once again, was ever easy.

"It appears," Chelsa said, "we have both been presented with riddles this night."

OPENING THE DOOR

"**D**id your professor happen to say what manner of object this dragonfly device was?" Chelsa asked.

Karigan felt a subtle change of air currents circulating the cool chamber, which she attributed to the Heroes Portal opening and closing. "He seemed to think it was a sword or rod or something. Maybe a spear." She thought back to the drawing she'd seen in his journal. "All he had to go on was an ancient etching on stone that is being worn away by the sea."

"Well, that is something." Chelsa, however, did not sound optimistic and the two sat in heavy silence for some moments.

Soon the rap of boots on stone preceded the return of Serena, who strode across the chamber to Joff and whispered in his ear. When she finished, Joff stepped forward.

"What is it?" Chelsa asked.

"If you and Sir Karigan have concluded your business, then we should take up the matter of her companion."

"One moment," she told him. "Sir Karigan? Is there anything more we need to discuss?"

There was much more, and nothing. Karigan carried many secrets, not least of all the existence of a royal heir, and as tempted as she might be to unburden herself, to entrust Chelsa with such secrets, honor prevented her. They were not her secrets to tell, just as she had not told the professor what she knew of the tombs.

It was clear Chelsa could not help her understand the captain's riddle, or otherwise tell her how to reach home, so she just said, "I would like a little time to commit the captain's message to memory. I do not wish to chance taking it with me into the outside world."

"Very wise of you," Chelsa said with approval.

So Karigan sat there, snuggled in Joff's cloak, memorizing every word just as she had been trained to do as a messenger. Already her tired mind was trying to unlock the puzzle of the words. Surely the "scything moon" meant the crescent moon that represented Sacoridia and the god Aeryc. But for now, she must put aside meaning and concentrate solely on remembering the words. When she was sure she had it, she returned the written message to Chelsa's keeping.

"I would now ask that you return to the outer world," Chelsa said. "Serena will escort you, and after I hear what she and Joff have to say, we will come out."

Karigan nodded and rose, taking a hard grip on the bonewood. She hoped she would not have to use it in Cade's defense.

Serena proved a silent escort, and when they reached the portal, Karigan unwrapped the cloak from her shoulders and handed it to Serena. "With my thanks to Joff."

Serena accepted it with a bow and pushed the portal open so Karigan could exit the tombs into the damp world outside. Would it be her last time through the Heroes Portal? She glanced over her shoulder. Serena had already disappeared back into the corridor. Dash closed the door. Karigan may not care for the tombs, but being within had felt like the closest to home she'd been since being ejected from Blackveil.

Raven nickered, and she went over to give him a pat on the nose. From the looks of it, he had managed to behave. Nothing looked destroyed, at any rate.

"Miss Goodgrave?"

It was Cade, sitting on a log. A Weapon stood nearby speaking quietly with the death surgeon. The other Weapons must be keeping sentry duty in the woods. Karigan strode over to the log and sat beside Cade. Scruffy purred on his lap.

"How are you?" she asked him.

"Head throbs," he said. Tentatively he touched the back of his head and winced. "I've got a nice lump. The mender gave me medicine for the nausea. I'll live."

"You have to be careful with knocks to the head."

"I know."

"Why were you following me tonight?" she asked.

"The professor asked that I keep watch on you. He was afraid you'd go after the Eletian on your own."

"As you can see, I did not."

"No . . ." An expression of awe came over his face once again. "You're full of surprises. There have been rumors of such an entrance to the tombs, but no one has ever found it. You told the professor you did not know of another entrance."

"It was not my right to tell him otherwise."

"Not even to help the opposition?"

"It is not my place to entrust such knowledge to outsiders."

Cade digested that for a moment, then tried another tack. "I don't suppose you'd tell me what it's like in there?"

"No."

He nodded, and to her surprise, did not press her further. Perhaps he knew there was a very good chance he'd be forced to live out the rest of his days within—for however long that may be. And with Silk's excavation delving ever deeper. She shivered, both from the damp chill and the likelihood of Silk's breaching the tombs. She could only imagine what he'd do with all that he found inside.

"The cat is warming your jacket," Cade said. He tugged it out from beneath the dead weight of the purring Scruffy.

Karigan drew it on. It was not nearly as nice as Joff's cloak, but it would do. "Scruffy has certainly taken a liking to you."

"The others," and he nodded at Dash, "seem to think it has some significance."

Karigan gazed at the content feline. Were tomb cats discerning about the humans they chose to commune with? All cats were, she conceded, but were tomb cats extra particular? If so, what did it mean that Ghost Kitty kept company with her, except that she provided a soft bed and warm body for him to sleep with?

"What was it that brought you here at this hour?" Cade asked. "This night?"

"I was summoned."

"Summoned?"

"By my captain. She knew—or someone knew—I'd be here in this future." Karigan explained how Scruffy had brought her the message, and about the riddle—though not its content—that had awaited her in the tombs.

"You were hoping it would tell you how to return to your own time," Cade guessed.

She nodded. "At least some hint. Instead I've a puzzle to unravel." She had thought it sounded obscure, something like what an Eletian would say, and now it occurred to her that maybe the one person who could help her figure it out was Lhean. If so, that meant it was more important than ever for her to retrieve him from the hands of Dr. Silk.

"Thank you," Cade said.

"What? What for?"

"I am told that while I was unconscious, you were willing to defend me."

Now that Karigan thought of it, it had been rather rash, challenging virtually all those Weapons when she hadn't even the bonewood to hand. "You can return the favor some day," she said, trying to sound light.

"I will," he replied with a fervor that surprised her. He leaned closer to her, their shoulders almost touching. "If you cannot find your way home, I will do my utmost to see you comfortably settled and safe. Not that you can't protect yourself, but our ways here are different, harder for a woman. You understand that a woman here is not allowed to own property?"

Karigan nodded. She had gathered as much.

"That means not even her clothes or any wages she might earn. It all goes to her nearest male relative. Here, you are practically owned by your uncle."

"Who is not really my uncle, but I see your point."

"And if you married—"

"I'd be owned by my husband."

"It is a coarse way to look at it, yes, but it is the emperor's law that it is so. It would be difficult for you on your own. I would see that you were not simply left to fend for yourself."

What exactly was he saying? That he'd be willing to take

her on as his property? "Won't you have your hands full with Arhys?"

There was a fierce glint in his eyes. "Of anyone, you would understand that duty."

"I suppose. But Cade, I intend to reach home or—die trying." And she would not be owned by anyone, not even Cade.

He hung his head, trailing his fingers over Scruffy's fur. "I selfishly wish you would stay. Or fail in your endeavor without dying."

Karigan stared at her knees. "I'm afraid it would kill me to stay." And, she wondered, would he even be allowed to leave the tombs this night? Would he even be there for her in the outside world if she couldn't get home?

"I would hope that I could make it worth living for you."

She gaped at him, but before she could gather her thoughts, the Heroes Portal swung open, and she stood hastily. Maybe too hastily. Cade rose more slowly, depositing Scruffy on the log. When Cade swayed on his feet, she grabbed his arm to steady him.

"I'm fine," he said. Then he whispered, "It would look better to the Weapons if you weren't holding me up."

She let go, wondering if it would look better if he fell flat on his face, but he managed to remain upright. They met Chelsa, Serena, and Joff by the portal, the other Weapons returning from the misty woods to surround them.

Chelsa's hood was up again, but Karigan detected a smile. "This has been a most extraordinary meeting," the caretaker said, "and one that shall be recorded in our histories and be preserved for as long as . . . for as long as the tombs survive." Her smile faltered. "If only the opposition could act to truly halt Silk's excavation." She shook her head.

"I will try to encourage Professor Josston to do so," Cade said, "without giving you away, of course."

Karigan glanced at him in surprise. He had told the Weapons the professor's name, and of his link to the opposition?

"I trust that is so, Mr. Harlowe," Chelsa said. "As a matter of fact, I have just been discussing you with Joff and Serena."

Karigan shifted her grip on the bonewood. Just in case.

"They told me that you claimed some interesting things—

that you are training in the arts of a Weapon under Professor Josston, and why."

Karigan glanced again at Cade, now doubly surprised. He would share the secret of Arhys?

"We had lost hope and believed the royal line had succumbed," Chelsa continued. "We lost track of the line after Queen Estora's escape with her son. It gladdens us to hear that the line is not lost. I do wonder how it is you felt you could trust us with this information."

Karigan wondered, too.

"Because." Cade swept his hand through the air at the portal, at the Weapons. "Because you are who you are. You are of the old realm. The Weapons of the old realm would believe in protecting the royal heir."

"As we discussed earlier," Joff said, "it is more than the royal heir we protect."

"Yes, I know."

Karigan wondered what exactly she had missed while she was inside with Chelsa. She'd always had an inkling that Weapon loyalties were not necessarily tied to the sovereign, but to whatever other secrets they were sworn to keep and protect. From the bits and pieces she had picked up, it had to do with shielding the realm from the misuse of magic. The Order of the Black Shields had originated, after all, during the Long War when such terrible magicks had torn the land apart.

"You have gambled by trusting us," Chelsa insisted.

"A gamble, perhaps, but one with excellent odds," Cade replied. "Miss—Sir Karigan revealed her true identity to you. That, too, was a huge gamble, but you have not threatened her in any way, and you treat her as befitting her station. If you were worthy of her trust, you are worthy of mine. You are of the old realm. I see it, I believe it."

"You are well spoken, Mr. Harlowe. I do not think your trust is misplaced, nor ours with you. Sir Karigan's example goes both ways. If she trusts you, that counts for much, as does Scruffy's regard of you. He is attuned, shall we say, to Black Shields. However, it is not necessarily enough proof for us to release you."

"What will you do?" Karigan asked, stiffening.

"There is a brief test we can administer," Joff said, "and it shall help us determine all is as Mr. Harlowe says." The Weapon then gave what must have been a rare smile. "We've already tested his fighting skills and they are not bad. Not bad at all."

"Let us do this test," Cade said eagerly.

"We must enter the portal. If you fail the test, then you shall never see the outside world again."

"I'm ready."

Was he so keen to give up everything? "Cade," Karigan said, touching his sleeve, "do you know what you are doing?"

"I know enough that if I don't even try, I will have to stay in the tombs anyway. Forever. So it will hurt nothing to undergo this test."

She nodded. He knew.

Joff gestured for Cade to precede him. Karigan moved to follow, but Dash blocked her way. "I am sorry, Sir Karigan, but you must stay back."

"Open the Portal, Mr. Harlowe," Joff instructed. The other Weapons stood in a semi-circle behind him, waiting.

Cade did not hesitate. He strode right up to the door. He must have observed it being opened and closed enough times that it was no mystery. His hands hovered almost reverently over the glyph of Westrion, and then again, without hesitation, he pushed it in. The door released and exposed a handle that rose from its flat iron façade. Cade pulled it open, the cool air of the tombs tumbling out and mixing with the moist world of outside, suffusing him in a vaporous cloud.

"Congratulations, Mr. Harlowe," Joff said. "You have passed the test."

"Opening the door? That's it?" Cade actually sounded disappointed.

"If there were more time, there would be more rigorous testing of your knowledge and physical skills, but as far as ascertaining your suitability to be a Black Shield, thus deserving of our trust, this test was enough."

"You see, Mr. Harlowe," Chelsa explained, "it is usually only Weapons who can open the door. It is said the reigning monarch, and certain others attributed as worthy by the door, can open it. Always the Weapons can, but few others. It *knows* the Weapons."

Attributed as worthy by the door? Karigan shook her head. Would the oddness of the world never end?

Cade glanced at his hands as though they belonged to someone else. "What would have happened if I could not open the door?"

Chelsa shrugged. "The door would have remained locked, exposing you as unworthy to the Order, and we would have had to welcome you into our caretaker community."

"Come," said Joff. "Let us go inside for a short while, and we shall talk a little more."

Joff led Cade, Chelsa, the death surgeon, and most of the Weapons through the Portal. Even Scruffy abandoned Karigan and trotted inside after them. Dash, who remained outside, closed the door after them. Karigan could only stare at the portal in disbelief, feeling a little left out.

Raven whickered a query, and she went over to him and stroked his neck. She wondered what would happen if she tried the door, but she had a strong sense of foreboding, that this was not her time.

Time. It was all about time.

CADE VALIDATED

 **W**hile Karigan waited for Cade to return from the tombs, she felt herself growing stiff where she sat on the log, so she stood and paced and went through some exercises with the bonewood, the mist swirling around her as the staff arced through the air. She ran through the words of the captain's riddle as she worked, again and again, ensuring they were committed to memory.

The scything moon is held captive in the prison of forgotten days. The bonewood hummed in a forceful downsweep that could break an opponent's collar bone.

Seek it in the den of the three-faced reptile, for you are the blade of the shadow cast. She thrust and parried to the rhythm of the words.

Beware! The longer you linger, the faster we spin apart. She flowed through a series of forms, feeling free with the release of movement, and she ended with a backward thrust.

She paused after several repetitions, panting from the exertion, and planted the tip of the staff on the ground.

Dash said, "It is good to see the staff at work. I fear we have come to rely on firearms too much in this day and age."

So deeply focused had Karigan been that she'd forgotten the Weapon at his post by the Heroes Portal. She wiped sweat from her brow with her sleeve.

"I also fear the day," Dash continued, "when our firearms become so accurate that we no longer have to be at close range to see the faces of our foes, their eyes." He shook his head. "Battle, I think, will become far less personal, a matter of business and efficiency, like the mills."

Karigan's cooling body, or perhaps Dash's words, made her shiver. Soldiers as machines, efficient killers. *I must get home. I do not belong here. I do not like it.*

The Portal opened, and finally Cade, led by Chelsa, Joff, and Serena, returned. He appeared well, except for the bruises on his face and swollen lip that had developed from his initial tangle with the Weapons. She slid the bonewood to cane length, and joined them.

"It is time we bade you farewell, Sir Karigan," Chelsa said. "The night grows old and dawn will be upon us all too soon."

"It has been an honor to meet you, Sir Karigan," Joff said. He bowed, and Serena and Dash did likewise. Karigan nodded in return. It felt odd having Weapons bow to her. The three stepped away, leaving just Chelsa with Karigan and Cade.

"I have a feeling your presence has heralded change," Chelsa said.

"Change for the better, I hope," Karigan replied. "I wish you and your people well."

"Thank you. Dr. Silk will find that he will not take the tombs easily. No, he will not. Meanwhile, we shall search diligently for this dragonfly device you mentioned. If we find it, we shall send Scruffy with a message to Mr. Harlowe. From there we shall determine what to do with it."

"Scruffy will find me?" Cade asked in surprise.

Chelsa smiled beneath her hood. "He found Sir Karigan before we knew she was here and needed to be found."

"I wish," Karigan said, "you would just call me Karigan."

"I am sorry," the caretaker replied, "I cannot. You are too . . . large in our history. So many things I would ask you about the old realm and times past, but so little time." She hesitated, her head tilted at a thoughtful angle as though she were making up her mind about something. She said, "There is one question I desire to ask, if you would indulge me."

"Yes?"

"It is impertinent of me to do so when there are much larger matters at stake, but . . . It is a personal curiosity." Chelsa took a deep breath and asked, "In your time, is it so that you met the caretaker named Thursgad? He was not born into the community, but came into it in adulthood."

Karigan stared incredulously at Chelsa. Thursgad? She wanted to know about *Thursgad,* the bumbling Mirwellian outlaw? He'd been among the Second Empire thugs she'd helped catch down in the Halls of Kings and Queens, when they sought the high king's tomb. Karigan had not heard what became of him. Either he'd been executed or inducted into the caretaker community. Of course, if Chelsa was asking about him, it could be for only one reason.

"Are you descended from Thursgad?" Karigan asked.

Chelsa nodded. "My several greats grandfather."

Who would have guessed that one of Thursgad's descendents would one day become chief caretaker? Karigan barely refrained from laughing. "Yes, I knew him in passing, and not under the best of circumstances."

"Ah! So you confirm it." Chelsa clasped her hands before her, clearly delighted.

Cade simply watched the two of them with his own questions in his eyes, but he did not interrupt.

"It is so much more interesting having an ancestor with a, shall we say, colorful past, isn't it?" Chelsa asked. "Now, when I have children, I can pass the story on to them with confidence, and then tell them I got to meet you in a later century."

It felt very odd, Karigan thought, to be considered the stuff of stories.

"Oh, I do so hate to say good-bye," Chelsa said, "but we must. Should you not find your way home, Sir Karigan, do know you are welcome among us in the tombs. We would keep you as safe as we can."

Karigan suppressed a shudder at the idea of living in the tombs, but she was also grateful for the sincerity behind the offer. After the farewells were spoken, she watched with regret as Chelsa and the Weapons entered the Heroes Portal one last time and closed the door behind them.

Karigan blinked, trying to adjust to the absence of lantern light, and maybe also trying to clear the tears that had collected in her eyes. Chelsa and the Weapons were the closest to home she had felt in a long time.

Raven whickered softly, reminding her that she also had

him. She went to him and stroked his neck. The sudden flare of light startled them both.

"Here we go," Cade said. It turned out, that along with the various pistols and knives he'd brought with him—now restored to him by the Weapons—he'd also had the foresight to bring a phosphorene lantern that fit in his hand.

She was relieved, as they didn't even have a cat to lead them out of the woods this time.

He held the light while she untethered Raven, and then lit the way as they walked into the woods. She glanced once more over her shoulder, but already the Heroes Portal had submerged into shadow.

"Did you walk all the way here?" Karigan asked, knowing he couldn't have kept up with her if he had.

"I've one of Widow Hettle's mules," he said. "Tied him up a ways into the woods."

"Widow Hettle?"

"I board at her house in exchange for chores and upkeep."

"You have time for that?"

Cade chuckled. "I make time for it. I am a poor student, and it is a good arrangement. Not to mention, Widow Hettle is in her elder years and nearly blind and deaf, which makes it easier for me to come and go at odd hours."

That, Karigan thought as she stepped through some brush, solved one mystery. They walked on in silence for a while, Cade scrutinizing the way ahead with his lantern.

"So what happened back there?" Karigan asked. "In the tombs?"

Cade paused, casting his light about, mist curling in its beam. "As you could not tell me about the tombs before, there is not much I can tell you now, except that what I saw there, even the little I saw, has left a great impression on me."

The tombs had that effect, Karigan knew.

"Also, I learned more of my responsibilities to the Order of the Black Shields and how I must conduct myself. I am now subject to the justice of the Order should I prove disloyal."

This all should have been quite grim, as Karigan knew how brutal Weapon justice could be, but she detected a frisson of excitement just below his calm exterior. He halted abruptly and turned toward her. Then, before she knew what he was about, he wrapped an arm around her, drew her into him, and kissed her soundly. When he let go, she staggered backward into Raven, who snorted in surprise. She had to throw her arm around the stallion's neck to remain upright.

"What—what was that for?" Not that she had minded.

Cade gingerly touched his swollen lip. "That hurt." He grinned, then winced at the pain *that* caused.

"Well?" Karigan demanded.

"If not for you," he replied in all seriousness, "I would not have met these other Weapons and had my calling answered. They validated the worth of what I am doing and the tradition behind it, all that I've given up to pursue this course. I mean, I know its worth, but now I know it truly. You led me to it."

"Not on purpose," she pointed out. "You followed me."

"You led me in other ways, as well. You have awakened me to the fact there are other possibilities in this world than having to live with oppression. Without you, I would not have realized it, nor would I have come to the tombs and truly become a Black Shield. Thank you." He gave her a courtly bow.

She wished people would stop bowing to her. "I think I preferred the kiss," she murmured.

He smiled enigmatically, then turned back to their path, searching through the woods with his light. They soon came upon Widow Hettle's mule, and Karigan held the light while Cade unbuckled hobbles and tightened the girth. From there they kept walking until the woods fell away and they reached the road. Cade extinguished the lantern.

"We will have to be very careful as we near the city," he said. "It is after curfew. *Well* after, if I'm any judge."

Karigan pulled her cap out of her jacket pocket and placed it on her head, tucking her braid back under. They waited for a few minutes for their eyes to adjust to the dark, then mounted up and rode back in the direction of Mill City.

They rode in companionable silence in the misty dark, Raven prancing in a decorous pirouette now and again to remind her of his stallion-ness. Soon the billowing glow of Dr. Silk's excavation came into view atop the summit of the Old City, his slaves still hard at work in the deep of night. All too soon they came across signs of habitation, and not long after, the lights of Mill City wavered in the mist before them.

"Be watchful," Cade said in a low voice.

He didn't need to tell her.

They entered the poor neighborhood on the east side of the canal bridge. Few streetlamps worked well here, and Cade stayed away from those that did. There were few signs of life at this hour—a stray dog dug through rubbish alongside a ruined building, bats swirled around a sputtering streetlamp. The hooves of horse and mule clattered all too loudly on the street. The neighborhood reminded her of the empty ruins that surrounded Castle Argenthyne, the buildings but corpses of a long ago civilization. But this, this was not a long ago civilization—people lived in these buildings in the here and now.

All remained quiet until the bridge over the canal came into sight. The lamps at both ends of the bridge illuminated a pair of Inspectors chatting in the middle of the span, two Enforcers with them. Cade touched her sleeve and urgently gestured they should head down a side street. It was narrower, darker.

"We'll not be able to cross till dawn," he explained in a low voice.

"What about another bridge?" Karigan asked.

"Too risky to travel that far, and they may be keeping watch on all the bridges. They do that sometimes."

"Well, you have all your weapons, and I bet I could take out both of those Inspectors myself."

"And harming an Inspector or Enforcer would bring the city's entire complement swarming into this section of the city and leave no one alive. Now, let us go and go carefully."

He took her down a series of derelict streets. Twice they spotted Inspectors on patrol with their Enforcers trundling alongside them.

"The Enforcers don't see as well at night," Cade told her, "or at least as far as we can tell."

Who was "we?" she wondered. She assumed Cade and the professor, but perhaps he meant the opposition as a whole.

When they heard a shout and running feet, they slipped behind the ruins of a tenement and into overgrowth. A young man pelted past their hiding place, breathing hard. An Enforcer shot after him stretching its long, spindly legs, moving more swiftly than Karigan could have believed of the mechanicals, the tips of its legs hammering the street cobbles in a menacing *rat-a-tat-rat-a-tat.*

Just as quickly, it skittered to a halt beneath a sputtering street lamp. A hatch on its central orb popped open and disgorged a long metallic tentacle, which lashed out and wound around the man's torso. The Enforcer tugged, and the man fell. It then reeled him in.

Karigan started in her saddle — it had happened so quickly. Cade grabbed her wrist.

"We should—" she began in a whisper.

Cade's grip on her wrist tightened. "Too risky."

She was about to protest when an Inspector jogged up the street huffing and puffing and stopped when he reached the mechanical.

"Got the thief, have we?" he demanded.

"I'm no thief," the man said, struggling in the coils of the tentacle.

"That so."

"Lemme go! I din' do nothing."

The Enforcer made a series of clicking and whirring sounds, a sort of machine speech, maybe.

"He's just trash," the Inspector replied with a shrug.

The Enforcer loosened its tentacle and the man was able to clamber to his feet.

Karigan's apprehension eased. It looked like they were merely going to arrest the man, or maybe even let him go, but before she could finish that thought, the tentacle coils constricted. The man screamed until the tentacles silenced him, followed by the snapping of bones.

She barely contained a scream of her own and looked away feeling like she could vomit. She'd seen horrible things before — gore, death, plenty of blood — but nothing like this.

A glance at Cade showed he'd gone pale and looked likely to be sick himself. His grip on her wrist would leave bruise marks.

Beneath the dimming light of the streetlamp, the Enforcer unraveled its tentacle, dropping the crushed body that flopped like a rag doll in the middle of the street. The Inspector and his mechanical left it behind, discarded, just like the trash the Inspector had proclaimed the man to be.

When they were well away, Karigan said, "Cade—"

"Shhh," he said, and pointed.

Gray forms in rags crept out of the shadows and emerged from rotten doorways.

"Dregs?" Karigan whispered.

"Ghouls."

The Ghouls surrounded the body, picked it up, and carried it away into the night.

"Someone at the university will pay them for that body," Cade said with disgust.

Karigan shuddered. It had all happened so fast.

"I am sorry," Cade said.

"For—for what?"

"We could've helped that man, but I feared the risk to us and the opposition. And I didn't know . . ." He took a moment to collect himself. He licked his lips. "I didn't know they would do that to him. I thought they were just going to arrest him."

As they rode on, moving carefully from their concealment and onto the dark streets, Karigan remembered the professor saying that the Enforcers were incapable of compassion, of mercy. They were, after all, inhuman mechanicals. What was, she wondered, the Inspector's excuse? Then she asked herself: Which was worse? The actions of an unthinking machine, or the inaction of a man devoid of mercy?

The latter, she thought. By far. She now appreciated, on a deeper level, why Cade and the professor dared oppose the empire.

They encountered no more Inspectors. Cade led her to a brick building that stood apart from the others. He looked around carefully, then dismounted and signaled for her to do the same. He opened a door on the front, large enough for him to lead the mule inside. She followed behind with Raven who blew through his nose and chewed on his bit.

Cade hastily drew the door closed behind her, and she heard chains rattling.

"You are locking us in?" The echoing of her voice startled her.

"Yes," Cade replied. "It'll keep out unwanted visitors."

From what Karigan could tell, the building was cavernous and empty. Dim light from streetlamps filtered in through windows up high, silhouetting bars across them and lending a menacing atmosphere to the place. The mule's hooves clopped on the stone floor as Cade led him down the center of the room toward the far end. Karigan followed, her boots crunching on broken glass. Between the barred shadows on the floor she saw other debris scattered about—papers, an old shoe, scraps of wood, bird droppings. When they reached the far end, she made out a railing that stood before a raised stage, and Cade tying the mule to the railing.

Karigan followed his example with Raven, wishing she'd brought some water to offer him. And herself. Cade, who was better prepared, shared some from his canteen. She took a swig for herself, then poured some into her cupped hand for Raven. It wasn't much, but it was something.

"Here," she said, returning the canteen to Cade.

"Shhh, I heard something."

Karigan listened, but all she could hear was horse and mule shifting and settling. Then, in an interlude of silence, she heard the distinct crunching of someone stepping on broken glass just as she had done. It was followed by more silence.

She espied the gleam of a blade as Cade unsheathed a knife. He did not draw one of his guns, perhaps fearing its use would attract too much unwanted attention. She remembered all too well the noise they could make.

In one direction, she heard a stealthy noise, the rustling of cloth. In another, the pad of feet. Karigan and Cade had locked themselves in the building with at least two others. Not Inspectors, she thought. She neither heard nor saw evidence of Enforcers, and she did not think it was their way to skulk in the dark.

Ruffians or vagrants, then.

Raven whickered nervously and Karigan sensed someone creeping toward her from the left. A flurry of movement came from the opposite direction and Cade grappled with an assailant, followed by a shout and grunts, then the thud of two bodies slamming to the hard floor.

Karigan extended her bonewood to staff length, and when the attack came, she was ready.

PENNED IN

Arms Master Drent had devoted some training time to sessions on the art of fighting with one's senses dulled. He'd made his trainees stuff cotton in their ears to muffle their hearing. He'd made them wear helms that blocked their vision in different ways. Karigan had not fared well in those sessions, especially when her opponents were able to fight unhindered.

Here, in the dark building, she and her foes were on even footing. Each possessed all their senses and were submerged in the same murk. How keen was the night vision of her opponents? She couldn't know, but hers had been attuned to a lack of light by a night of rambling about the countryside and keeping to the shadows.

The first attacker came at her wielding a long metallic weapon—not a blade, but something heavy, dull, a bar of some sort. Before he even had a chance to use it, an easy jab with the point of the bonewood to his gut made him double over. His weapon fell to the flagstone floor with a resounding clamor that battered the ears. It cloaked the sounds of her other adversary as he advanced on her, but she was ready for him nevertheless. She whirled, and as the staff cracked into his ribs, he cried out. Then he dropped a jagged piece of glass and fell to his knees hugging himself.

The first attacker barreled toward her. She leaped out of the way, and as he passed her, she whacked the back of his head with the silver handle of the bonewood. He thudded to the floor and did not move.

"Yield!" someone shouted.

Cade's fight appeared to have paused. "Jax, is that you?"

"Cade? Get off me!"

"Hold on."

So, Cade knew these men?

Karigan detected him rising and shuffling over to his mule. He groped through his saddlebag and in a moment he had the phosphorene lantern alight at low glow. When her eyes adjusted, she saw that the one man who had attacked her lay unconscious on the floor. The other remained on his knees, groaning. Cade's opponent rose unsteadily to his feet, blood running from his nose.

All three men wore the work clothes of laborers — formless, dull, and patched, and in deep contrast to the fine wardrobe in which Professor Josston attired himself. It was even worse than Cade's own garb, which had already seen a fight with the Weapons at the Heroes Portal.

The one called Jax wiped at the blood beneath his nose and steadied himself by placing a hand on the mule's haunches. "What in the name of all mercy are you doing here tonight?" he demanded of Cade.

"Hiding from Inspectors."

"And you brought . . . you brought a *stranger?*" Jax's gaze bore into Karigan. She held her offensive position with the staff and would not hesitate to lash out if given cause, whether Cade knew these men or not.

"A trusted person," Cade responded.

"A girl," Jax said with distaste and pointed at her. "That's right, I heard your voice. You are no lad."

"A girl who easily took out your boys," Cade said. "Why don't we go down below and discuss this?"

"Aye, safer. Give me a hand with Thadd and Jonny."

Cade hoisted the unconscious Jonny over his shoulder.

"Stop whining," Jax told Thadd, helping the man to his feet.

"I think my ribs are broke."

"So what if they are? Whining's not gonna help."

Karigan followed behind as they made their way past the stage, and then behind it. In the light of Cade's lantern, she glimpsed a yellowed poster tacked to the wall: *Auction!*

Adults and Youths fit for all needs and types of labor. Healthy breeding stock . . .

The place was an auction house, an auction house for slaves.

A door creaked open ahead, and Cade led them down a set of sagging, wooden steps. The scent of dank earth and rot flowed up and out, and something else that was less a scent than a psychic infusion of fear, agony, torment.

Karigan halted on the last step, wanting to turn back, to ride Raven away regardless of how many Inspectors patrolled the streets. Could the others not feel it? The oppression, ghost voices screaming and moaning, children crying . . .

Cade set Jonny down on the earthen floor, having to move in a stooped position because of the low ceiling. His light glanced off metal chains dangling from the support beams. Rusty and strung with cobwebs, the chains ended in manacles. A couple hundred pairs must hang there. The gorge rose in Karigan's throat.

After Jax settled Thadd onto the floor, he brushed past Karigan to shut the door at the top of the stairs. She closed her eyes as the souls of the tortured wailed at being trapped, confined, enslaved, with no way out.

"Your girl got a problem?" Jax demanded of Cade as he trotted back down the stairs, bumping her out of the way.

"Mind your respect," Cade replied.

"Mind whose respect? You came here unannounced."

"It was not planned, and I'd no choice."

"There are always choices."

"I do not consider being arrested by Inspectors a choice."

Jax sat down beside Thadd. Cade sat opposite him on the dirt floor. Karigan did not know how they could stand it, touching that earth, being down here. She could almost see the captives crowded together out of the light, out of the fresh air, stripped naked and their bodies pressed together, wrists shackled over their heads. She did not sit, she did not leave the wooden step.

"And what brought you out after curfew, eh?" Jax asked.

"My reasons are my own."

Jax snorted and glanced at Karigan. "I'm sure they are."

"I would ask what *you* are doing here," Cade said. Karigan heard the edge of anger in his voice. "It is not a meeting night."

"No, no it isn't, but Thadd, Jonny, and I, we wanted to talk over some business before the next meeting, what with Silk and his machine in the Old City. Went house to house, his Inspectors did, hauling out blastmen for questioning after your professor tried to delay the drilling. Those men that were taken away, well, they haven't been seen again. Their families are wondering when their husbands, poppas, and brothers will be coming home. I don't think they will be. Ever."

"I know," Cade said.

"Your professor mucked it all up."

"He was trying to—"

"Playing at an opposition is not the same as being one. Your professor goes to his parties, plays cards with his enemies. Their only opposition is to see who can be more polite than the other. Meanwhile, the rest of us suffer under the emperor's rule."

Who was this Jax, Karigan wondered, that he knew of the professor and his opposition?

"We have waited for your professor's group to do something, but nothing ever comes of it."

"I know," Cade said again.

"Weeell," drawled Thadd, tearing his attention from his sore ribs to attend to the conversation, "so you finally admit it. Your professor is not gonna change things."

"I have been coming to this conclusion for a while."

"Oh? And what decided you?"

"Various things," Cade replied evasively. "The professor's failed attempt to slow the drill is not least in my mind."

Karigan wondered if his experiences in the tombs had sealed this change in him, given him a resolve that had not been there before. She was relieved that he did not mention the tombs, Weapons, or caretakers. He apparently trusted these men but honored his secrets.

"Then destroying the emperor," Jax said, "comes down to us. As the hard work always does."

So they were another opposition group? Did the professor

know about them as they knew of him, or had Cade been going behind his back? Had he shared his knowledge of Arhys' existence with Jax and his cohorts, or had he honored that secret as well? This furtive activity was fascinating, but very un-Cadelike. Or at least, unlike the Cade she thought she knew, who was utterly devoted to the professor. How much did she really know about this brooding student of archeology, anyway?

She mounted the steps and sat on the top one, trying to distance herself as much as possible from the haunting cellar. She rested her arms on her knees, then her head on her arms. It had been another very long night, and she'd already been short on sleep. She tried to listen as Cade argued with the other men about this plan and that, but her eyes sagged closed. This was not her world, after all, not her war. She had not wanted to get involved in its problems. If she could get home, she'd take care of Amberhill from there before he had a chance to make himself an emperor. Problem solved, just like that. She laughed tiredly to herself.

She drifted into an uneasy sleep filled with images of slaves beseeching her to unlock their manacles. They called out to her for help, and there, across the waves of people in bonds, stood Lord Amberhill. She saw him clearly, large in her vision, his gray eyes now dark, burning holes. He held a cruel looking whip, ready to lash it at the slaves, and the dragon-eye ruby on his ring winked at her.

Cade shook her shoulder. "Tam? Tam Ryder?"

"Tam Ryder who?" she mumbled.

"Tam Ryder you."

Karigan gazed blearily at Cade. "Is it time to go?"

"Dawn is breaking, so we need to get you back."

The murmuring of low voices down below indicated that Jax and his fellows were still there. The sound of a new voice indicated Jonny had regained consciousness.

Cade helped her rise. "I ask that you speak to no one of this. Not least of all the professor."

So the professor did not know about this group. "What's a few more secrets?" she replied.

"That is what I ask myself all the time." He extinguished his lantern before opening the door to the main floor. He peered about before stepping through.

Gray light provided dim illumination through the barred windows high above. As Karigan made her way around the back of the stage after Cade, she saw that the mule and Raven had been dozing, but with her arrival, Raven perked up and whickered.

"Cade," she said, sounding as tired as she felt, "why do you meet in an auction house for slaves?"

"Abandoned auction house," he replied. "It closed years ago, and the trade moved across the canal to the horse market in the center of town. This location, when we use it, reminds us of what we are fighting for."

"To free the slaves?" The dream images of so many terrified people penned up in the cellar to be bought and sold came back to her.

"To free us all."

Karigan checked Raven's girth and untied him from the railing. "And those men downstairs? They are . . . opposition?"

Cade stowed his lantern in a saddlebag. "Yes, but a different opposition. The real folk of the empire, the laborers, the merchants, the Dregs. Not the elite like the professor and his friends, who have gotten nowhere. Jax, Thadd, and Jonny? They see the professor's opposition as a bunch of useless old men, and as much as I love the professor, I'm beginning to agree. Just seems like there is never enough of us, though, or power enough, to oppose the might of the empire. Too many are too scared to go against the empire, as well they should be."

Karigan leaned against the railing while Cade tightened the straps of his mule's gear. The gray light revealed paint peeling off walls and debris strewn across the floor. She imagined the room thronging with people bidding on human livestock.

"I once told you," she said, "how in the Long War women took up weapons to fight Mornhavon the Black because so many of the men had perished in battle."

Cade paused what he was doing. "Yes . . . ?"

"Don't exclude half the empire's population in your efforts. To do so would be very stupid. This is their home, too, and they have, perhaps, more to lose."

"Well, that half of the population isn't entirely unrepresented—"

"Do not underestimate what ingenuity and support they could bring to your opposition. And I'm not just talking about cooking your dinner or darning your socks."

"I don't—"

"Furthermore, don't forget those who may be your most ardent supporters."

Cade stood there just staring at her.

"The slaves," she told him. "Remember? The ones you want to free? They have more to fight for than anyone." *Free us,* the ghost slaves murmured in her mind.

"But they—they don't know how to—"

"How to work?" Karigan snapped. He looked stung by her response. "They may be uneducated, but that doesn't mean they're stupid. And some must know how to fight. If I recall, many are captives from rebellious areas of the empire. Wouldn't some of them have a military background? Don't you think they know how to fight, and willingly, if it's against the empire?"

The gray in the windows lightened subtly. Doves cooed in broken panes of glass.

"It is not so simple," Cade said quietly.

"Perhaps," Karigan replied. "After all, the empire is a powerful state, and it can't be taken down with ease. But you are sounding very like the professor, finding excuses not to act."

Cade glowered at her. "Is that all?"

"Pretty much. It's your rebellion. I'm just observing from the outside. After all, I have my own problems—a riddle to solve, an Eletian to rescue, and a home to find my way back to."

Cade bowed his head, gazing at the reins in his hands. "You are so determined to leave us?"

"If you are asking that question, then you have not heard what I've been telling you. Cade, if I can reach home, maybe there is some way I can—I can affect what has happened here. If I get home, maybe I can help prevent the empire from rising in the first place."

If only, she thought derisively. As if she were so powerful. If she were able to get home, wouldn't the events in this future have changed already? No, she must not think in terms of the paradoxes—it would only drive her mad, make her lose hope.

"Then," Cade said, "perhaps I can come with you."

Karigan's mouth dropped open, but before she could think of something to say, he was leading his mule away toward the other end of the building.

She hurried to follow, Raven bobbing his head eagerly beside her, as ready to leave the deserted building as she.

Would Cade be able to come with her? she wondered. Through time? Give up his own world, everything he knew, for hers?

She'd seen his longing for the old realm at the Heroes Portal, but she thought that, just maybe, she might have something to do with it, too.

A MAP OF THE CAPITAL

Karigan and Cade did not encounter trouble as they, along with many city denizens, moved through the early morning murk. The fog was thicker than ever, and people hurried to and fro on the streets with hoods drawn up or the brims of hats pulled down low. These were the earliest of workers, Cade told her; the ones who opened up shops, lit the lamps, tended the locks on the canal system, and fixed the machines in the mills.

Cade rode with his collar turned up and dark hair lank against his face. He'd a night's growth of beard, a swollen lip and bruises, and he looked more than a little disreputable.

They had hardly spoken once they'd left the old slave market. He was now more the terse, guarded Cade she'd come to know. Silent as a Weapon, she realized, but now he looked like a bedraggled man on a mule. She'd never seen a Weapon ride a mule—until now. Those at the Heroes Portal had validated his status, so yes, he was a *Weapon on a mule*. She was so tired the thought almost made her burst out laughing.

He rode with her as far as the professor's house, but did not rein his mule onto the drive. "I will see you soon," he said.

She did not know what to say. They'd been through much during the night, but no words seemed adequate. Raven danced beneath her, sensing his grain bucket nearby.

"I'll see you," Karigan said quietly, but Cade was already riding Widow Hettle's mule back down the street at a steady jog.

When she led Raven into the stable, Luke nearly pounced on her.

"There you are, there you are! Where have you been?"

"I couldn't sleep," Karigan replied, drawing on the excuse she'd planned earlier.

"Couldn't sleep?" There was a tightness to Luke's voice as though he wanted to scream at her and only protocol restrained him. "Don't you know how dangerous it is to go out on your own and at such hours?"

"I was not alone."

"You weren't . . . ?"

"Mr. Harlowe was with me."

"He was? I thought he knew better than that. I thought he was more sensible."

Karigan smiled at him. "He was lovely." Let Luke make of that statement what he would. Then she decided to build on it, encourage Luke's direction of thought. "Please don't tell my uncle. I—I don't know what he'd think if he found out I was alone with Cade—I mean, Mr. Harlowe—all night."

"Oh, Miss Goodgrave." Luke looked like he wanted to yank all the hair out of his head. "You know I can't lie to the professor."

"You don't have to lie, Luke. Just don't tell him. I can't imagine how he'd react if he found out you let me go out on Raven at so late an hour and didn't stop me."

Luke just stood there shaking his head as Karigan started to remove Raven's tack.

"Oh, Miss Goodgrave," he said. "The Inspectors are thick as a hill of ants in the dark hours. How could you endanger yourself so? How could Mr. Harlowe?"

"We were careful."

He muttered to himself, but when Karigan reached for a curry comb, he grabbed her wrist.

"No," he said. "I'll take care of Raven. We will discuss this again later. But now you change your clothes and go to the house. You get in there before the professor comes down for his breakfast. Hopefully Mirriam is not yet up and about."

Karigan didn't waste another moment and did as Luke told her. He would keep her secret, she was sure, then she shook her head. One more secret to layer on top of all the others.

Inside, the only ones who appeared to be up and about were the cooks, firing up the ovens to prepare breakfast. She hastened past the kitchen and all the way to her room without being seen.

When she reached her room, she threw herself into bed and fell asleep before she could even finish the phrase, *The scything moon is held prisoner in the chamber of forgotten days . . .*

She dreamed she was taking tea with Yates. "Yates," she mumbled.

They sat at a table draped in a lacy white cloth with a silver tea service between them, and plates of fancy tea cakes and scones. Yates paid her no heed for he was intent on sketching in his journal . . .

"What is it you draw?" She was so tired, even in the dream, that it was difficult to make her mouth form words properly. She felt deadened.

He did not reply. It was then she realized their tea table was surrounded by the dusky environs of Blackveil Forest, shadowed limbs writhing around them, and pairs of malicious eyes glowing from behind tree trunks and in the snarled brush.

Why am I here? she wondered.

She reached for the teapot, but it had transformed into a looking mask—not the perfectly smooth oval mask that had encased the tumbler's head at the king's masquerade, no. No, it was riddled with spidery cracks, and when she touched it, it fell to pieces, so many shards glimmering in the middle of the table.

She picked one up and held it to her eye. In it she beheld the universe, stars piercing black emptiness. She traveled, the stars sweeping by, falling ever more distant, racing away. To where was she traveling? Why?

She gripped the table to steady herself, but the shard of the looking mask stayed in her eye so that she still hurtled through nothingness.

Out of her other eye, however, she could still see Yates sketching obliviously in his journal.

"Help me," she told him between gritted teeth. "Make it stop."

He paused, and looked at her with mirror eyes. All the beasts of the forest who had been watching stared at her with mirror eyes.

Karigan sat up in her bed with a muffled scream and clawed at her eye. It took her several seconds to realize she was awake and her vision was normal. It took even longer for her quickened pulse to slow down. "Gods," she murmured. Shaken, she fell back into her pillows and drew her covers back up.

Her room had lightened, and when the bells tolled in the city, they rang six times. She'd been asleep maybe an hour, hour and a half. What had brought on the dream? Why hadn't she dreamed of the tombs or heard the spirit voices of slaves? She thought to pull out her mirror shard and look into it— put it up to her eye—but after the dream, she feared what she'd see. She snuggled beneath the safety and warmth of her blankets, and before she knew it, she became heavy with sleep once more.

It seemed like she'd barely drifted off when she was roused by Lorine's arrival to ready her for breakfast. A good hot bath helped wake her up, but by the time she reached the dining room, breakfast was already underway. The professor and his students all politely stood at her entrance, except Cade who was nowhere to be seen. Where was he? Had he gotten home safely?

"Good morning," she murmured, and took her place at the end of the table opposite the professor. The gentlemen sat, and the professor, his usual aloof self, was quickly nose-deep into his paper of news. The students resumed the conversation she had presumably interrupted, and she turned her attention to the plate of eggs and sausage Lorine brought her. She sipped tea, her reflection in the dark liquid reminding her of mirror eyes. She set it aside hastily and decided to worry about Cade and where he might be, which turned out to do anything but calm unsettled nerves. She did not listen to the students at all, until she caught the word "circus." She looked up and listened attentively.

"Does the paper say anything about it, Professor?" Mr. Card asked.

"Eh?" the professor peered over the top of a page.

"The circus. I heard it's packing up."

"Oh. Yes. The paper only says it's ending its season here and moving on." With that, the professor returned to his reading.

"I heard the Eletian is going to the Capital," Mr. Stockwell said, "to show him off to the people there."

Karigan almost dropped her fork with its piece of sausage impaled on the tines, her attention now focused on the students.

"Wish they'd exhibited him here," Mr. Ribbs said. "Who knows if he's the real thing."

"Oh, he's got to be authentic," Mr. Card replied, "or Dr. Silk wouldn't bother with him. Dr. Silk found him and owns him, so it's not surprising the Eletian would be heading to the Capital. I heard the Eletian will be a gift to the emperor himself."

"Heard Dr. Silk will be accompanying him."

The professor remained glued to his paper, making no indication he was aware of the topic of conversation. Karigan, however, was more than aware. If they were readying to move Lhean, she could no longer wait. She had to find out the professor's decision on whether the opposition would help her rescue Lhean. Whatever the answer, time was running short, and she must act.

The students had moved on to other topics: Who would supervise the excavation in the Old City during Dr. Silk's absence? What artifacts had been found? Nothing notable as yet, it turned out, since the drill destroyed most everything in its way.

"They've got a hundred slaves just to sift the tailings," Mr. Stockwell said.

"I heard fifty," Mr. Card countered.

The two began arguing over numbers.

Would the professor help her rescue Lhean? she wondered again. Would Cade?

"Excuse me," she said. When they did not hear her over their argument, she tried again more loudly. *"Excuse me."* Unaccustomed as the students were to her speaking to them during breakfast, they gazed at her in surprise, as if she had awakened from the sleep of the dead and arisen from one of the circus's sarcophagi. Even the professor peered at her over his paper.

"Where is Mr. Harlowe this morning?" she asked.

Mr. Card shrugged. "Said he had some personal business to attend to and took the morning to do it."

Karigan was so relieved to hear this that she almost missed the young men's snickering about Cade's bruised face and their speculation over how he must have gotten in a drunken brawl last night.

Let them believe it, she thought. Better that than the truth.

Lorine entered the dining room and sidled nervously over to the professor. She whispered in his ear.

"Eh?"

Lorine whispered some more.

The professor tossed his paper on the table and stood abruptly, his brow furrowed. He followed Lorine out of the dining room and down the hall, Karigan and the students watching curiously after him. No one interrupted the professor from his paper without good cause.

A minute later, his roar shook the whole house. "ARHYS!"

Karigan and the students looked at one another stunned. When had the professor ever raised his voice so?

There was a patter of light footfalls down the hall, no doubt Arhys', followed by the professor's angry tones rumbling in an upbraiding, the actual words of which they couldn't quite make out. Arhys' shrill protestations countered the professor, and then there was silence. Lorine reappeared in the dining room.

"Miss Goodgrave? Your uncle would see you now in the library."

What was this about? Karigan wondered, doubly startled. She set down her piece of toast and followed Lorine out and down the hall to the library. Inside, she discovered a red-faced professor staring down at Arhys. The girl turned and pointed at Karigan, a malicious expression on her face.

"She did it! I saw her using the atlas lots. *She* tore it up."

Karigan saw that the object of the argument was on the floor, its pages ripped out and strewn about.

The professor gazed at Karigan. "Is this true?"

Of all the idiotic things. "Yes, I have been looking through the atlas of late. Lorine saw me. It is *not* true that I damaged it. Why would I do so?"

The professor glanced at Arhys. "Why would Miss Goodgrave damage the atlas, girl?"

"Because! Because she wants to get me in trouble! She hates me."

"That's absurd," the professor replied. "It's rather the other way around, I should think."

"You hate me, too! Ever since *she* came!"

"That's not—"

"You give her nice things, and I just got these old, ugly dresses. And you take her places, even secret places. Mr. Harlowe, too."

Both Karigan and the professor stilled. Had the girl witnessed their disappearances through the secret door in the library? Lorine looked on, uncomprehending.

"It's not fair!" In a final bout of rage, Arhys kicked the remains of the atlas, scattering the pages.

The professor snatched her arm. "That is quite enough. You come with me, young lady." He dragged her from the library, she wailing all the way. When she was gone, Lorine and Karigan both sighed.

"It's about time the professor took action," Lorine declared. "That girl has become a little monster."

And not fit to be a queen, Karigan thought. Certainly not until she learned how not to be such a brat.

Lorine knelt to start picking up the pages of the destroyed book. Karigan did so, as well.

"Oh, Miss Goodgrave, you do not have to help."

"I'd like to."

The two worked in silence for a time, until Lorine asked, "What was Arhys getting on about when she mentioned the professor taking you to secret places?"

"If I told you, then it wouldn't be a secret," Karigan replied, trying to make it sound like a joke. To her relief, Lorine did chuckle. "Actually, I haven't the faintest."

Lorine nodded in acceptance. "Who knows what that girl has dreamed up. I can't believe she went so far as to damage one of the professor's precious books. This has gold leaf in it."

"She was looking for attention," Karigan replied.

"Yes, I agree."

When all the pages had been picked up and placed on top of the library table, Lorine said, "I'll leave those for the professor so he can decide what to do with them. He'll know if the atlas is beyond repair or not." And she left to tend to other duties.

Karigan gazed at the pile. On the very top were the pages comprising the map of the Capital—with lettering in gold leaf. It had been a two-page spread, and now had holes ripped out where it had been stitched into the binding. Without a second thought, Karigan snatched the map and folded it up into as small a square as she could make, tucked it into her hand, and headed upstairs where she could study it in private and think.

In the Present:

YOLANDHE'S ISLAND

 A storm came in the night bringing shadows to Amberhill's mind. As waves tossed on-shore and the sky rumbled, he turned restlessly beneath his furs.

The outer turmoil seemed not to affect the shadows. They remained stolid, somnolent forces. Where were they? Just in his head? What or who were they?

Soon his breathing eased, the restlessness fading as though he mirrored the shadows. Beyond the veneer of stillness, he knew, lay ferocity, chaos, and destruction. It should bother him more, even cause him fear, but as the beating of his heart slowed into counterpoint to the storm, it did not.

"What are they?" he asked Yolandhe the next morning.

"I do not know of what you speak, my love." She was re-arranging sea shells on a rock in the cave, something she did from time to time to please herself, as though they were priceless art pieces on display.

Amberhill remained beneath the furs at his ease. How to explain? "The shadows. I sense them in my sleep. They sleep, too. It's not exactly a dream."

Yolandhe turned away from her shells to stare hard at him. After a time, she came to some decision and said, "Let us take a walk."

Amberhill tossed aside his furs and rose. Once out of the cave and on the beach, they passed Yap's lean-to, which had miraculously withstood the storm. The pirate snored within.

They crossed the beach, Yolandhe leading Amberhill along a shoreside trail wet with puddles.

"Where are we going?" he asked.

Ahead of him, Yolandhe shrugged. Her gait was easy and unhurried, but Amberhill felt like he had to rush to keep up, splattering mud in all directions.

"The place has no name," Yolandhe said. "It is just a headland."

Amberhill was not surprised. Yolandhe had not seen fit to name any of the features of her island. In fact, he did not think she had even given the island itself a name. Had a Sacoridian come to take possession of it, the first thing he would do would be to name it after himself.

Amberhill Island. He considered the flavor of it and shook his head. It didn't sound right. This was Yolandhe's Island, and that's how he would always know it.

Even if he should take his treasure and form his own kingdom, naming a realm after himself would sound awkward: Amberhillia, Amberhill Land, New Amberhill. Even while he considered the idea of his own kingdom absurd, a kernel of ambition awakened to the idea.

As he hastened after Yolandhe, his clothes ragged, a scruffy beard on his face, and mud sucking at his feet, he imagined himself upon a throne, his vassals kneeling before him and praising King Xandis. They offered gifts and their loyalty . . . *Now where would I put a kingdom?* he wondered.

A voice inside him that was not his own, replied, *Wherever I am, it is mine to rule.*

The voice belonged to a leader of warriors who raided and sacked settlements wherever he went, incorporating the land, its wealth, and its inhabitants into his own vast holdings. The intrusion of that voice chilled Amberhill, and he tried to extinguish it like stamping out the embers of a fire.

The trail rose on granite ledges, moss and sedges growing in the joints between rock layers, the roots of evergreens fingering across the trail, seeking the barest pockets of sandy soil. Gulls squawked offshore and terns skimmed the waves. As they climbed up, the water fell away below them. Amberhill avoided the edge.

Yolandhe halted at a good lookout point—or it would have been had a veil of fog left behind by the storm not sat offshore obscuring the horizon and just about everything else. Amberhill discerned the cold, white disk of the sun behind the clouds. Perhaps the fog would burn off before long.

Yolandhe sang, more a whispered melody than a fullthroated song. The birds, the trees, the plants all seemed to lean in toward her, and as always, Amberhill's body reacted, this time prickling all over as her power passed into, and through, him. He could not describe the song, except that it was soft and lilting, like aural fog, if fog were a song.

Her song was a command and the fog receded, revealing some of the granite girding the islands of the archipelago, but did not dissipate entirely. The islands farther out remained ghostly behind the veil of mist.

She had command of the elements, Yolandhe did, the power to light fire, and to manipulate the air and water. What could she do with earth? Or did even her power have limits?

Amberhill never ceased to be amazed when he witnessed such power at work. When he found his voice again, he asked, "Why did you bring me here? What does this have to do with my shadows?"

"I brought you here because some of them sleep out there." She swept her arm out toward the water.

What were they? Amberhill wondered. Fishes?

"They are ancient," Yolandhe said. "They were here before Akarion, before even the Eletians, but Akarion learned the command of them, his greatest, his most terrible power. His was a devastating weapon. It made him a king of kings. It is how he and his people came to dominate so much of the lands."

"Well, what are they?" Amberhill felt an inner burble that could only be his "infestation" laughing at his impatience.

"Hold my hand," Yolandhe instructed, and Amberhill did. Though he enjoyed holding Yolandhe's hand, he didn't see what it had to do with anything. Until he did. The presences were suddenly there, slumbering away in his waking mind.

"The ruby is your key to their awakening, to commanding them. But I do not advise it."

"No? Why? Can you at least tell me what they are?"

"Think deep into the heartstone and you will discern their shape."

Heartstone—that is what the Berry sisters had called the ruby on his ring. And he was to think deep into it? He wanted to snap his irritation at Yolandhe for giving him no concrete answers, but he took a deep breath instead and settled. Yolandhe might come at things from an odd angle, but she had not been wrong about arcane matters so far. It was just her way to be abstruse. If she said he should think deep into the ruby to get his answers, well, then he should.

He was not sure how to go about it, but he figured asking Yolandhe would accomplish little, so he took another deep breath and gazed at his ring, at the ruby. He stared at it till his eyes watered. Nothing happened.

Think into it. The words came to him on a breath of air or in a stream of memory, and then something, a knowing, clicked inside him. He fought the urge to resist the knowing, for it came from his infestation. He closed his eyes, and saw red. Red bathed his inner eye, deep and glistening. Before he could repress it, the part of him that was Akarion issued a non-verbal command, more a force of personality, an order for the shadows to awaken.

Glowing, faceted eyes snapped open and stared into Amberhill's mind. He recoiled as a sense of the shadows' raw, primal nature washed over him, their cold intelligence, their anger at his intrusion.

When he opened his eyes, the surface of the water around the nearest islands roiled with waves and counter-waves, for the islands were moving.

BREAKING BONDS

 arigan sat in the chair by her window. The morning mist and fog appeared to be burning off, but sunlight fell through it in a dull haze. It was going to be a warm and humid day.

She wondered how Lhean fared, where he was being held, and if it was true he was going to be moved to the Capital. She gazed at the creased map spread on her lap. Roughly, the Capital was comprised of L'Petrie Province; and the Capital's city, Gossham, had replaced Corsa, her home. It was a Corsa she would not recognize with its many waterways and re-aligned streets, all emanating outward in circles from the city's central point, the emperor's palace. The palace and its grounds were situated on an island in a lake that had not existed in her own time. Lake Scalus was fed by a diverted Grandgent River, now the River Scale, which then emptied into Corsa Harbor, also renamed. It was called the Great Harbor, and of all the changes, she found this the least offensive.

When she had browsed the atlas on previous occasions, it had pained her to look too closely at what once had been her home. Her father's estate was in Corsa's countryside, but if she was measuring the scale right, it appeared to have been swallowed up by Gossham.

Gossham? What kind of name was that? It did not inspire greatness if that was what Amberhill had wanted for his capital city.

She wondered once again what had happened to her father and aunts, to the extended Clan G'ladheon. She had guessed that many of her Rider friends had perished on the field of battle, or when Sacor City and the castle had been demolished by Amberhill's great weapon. But her family? She still believed it was best that she not know, but she couldn't help but wonder. She prayed they had died peacefully of old age despite the turmoil Amberhill's victory must have wrought.

She glanced again at the map. It appeared that the Corsa Road remained, though it was now named the Capital Way. The map did not encompass enough of the surrounding countryside to show the Kingway, but when she flipped it over, there was the wider view. The Kingway had simply been renamed the East-West Road, and the Corsa Road split off where it always had. Names may have changed, but at least the essential layout of some of the roads remained. She would find her way to Gossham.

Someone tapped on her door. She folded up the map and concealed it up her sleeve.

"Yes, come in."

To her surprise, it was the professor who entered. He closed the door behind him. "I wish to apologize for Arhys' abominable behavior," he announced.

"I'm not sure you are the one who should be apologizing." Karigan replied.

"I know, I know. She is a difficult girl. Still, I am not sure what brought on this destructive behavior."

Karigan raised an eyebrow.

"All right," he admitted. "I know that she has been terribly jealous of you since your arrival, but I've had a, hmm, talk with her, and I think she'll behave much better now."

Karigan was, needless to say, skeptical. "What did you tell her?"

"First of all, she is confined to her room without supper."

Karigan did not expect that this was likely to change the girl's attitude anytime soon. "And?"

"And second, I promised to pay her more attention and to buy her some pretty dresses."

Karigan couldn't help herself. She laughed and shook her head. He was hopeless.

"I know. I should be more firm with her." Then he leaned

close to her ear and in an almost inaudible whisper said, "The dresses are a bribe so she won't give away our secret door in the library."

"You can trust her with that?" Karigan whispered back.

"I have to." He shrugged to indicate the futility of it. In his normal voice, he added, "We will also step up her education. She is very sharp for a girl, and I suspect boredom with her studies has allowed for mischief. I also request that you reach out to her, my dear. Become her friend. I think you could be a positive influence on her."

Oh, dear gods. Karigan hardly knew what to do with children under the best of circumstances, much less with such a beastly imp who hated her. Well, she would not be staying around for much longer and would not have to deal with Arhys forever. "I'll think about it," she said.

The professor nodded as if her reply was about what he had expected. He turned to leave, but she tugged on his sleeve.

"The Eletian," she mouthed.

The professor's wolfish eyebrows shadowed his eyes. He shook his head subtly and bent close to whisper in her ear. "I asked. The opposition said no. Too risky. I'm sorry."

"I am sorry as well," she murmured.

"Promise me you will not go after him."

She nodded because that was what was expected of her. He expected compliance of a woman of his time, but she, of course, was not of this time. She did not, however, have to feign looking upset.

"Very well," the professor said aloud. "I've a few matters to settle at the university today. I shall see you again at suppertime. Also, think on Arhys and how you two might make peace."

She did not reply, but glowered toward the window. The professor sighed, then left her, once again closing the door behind him as he retreated into the corridor.

Karigan tugged the map of the Capital out from her sleeve. It disappointed her, angered her even, that the professor and his opposition would do nothing to help Lhean, but she hadn't really expected their aid. Cade's group was right—the profes-

sor and his opposition were a bunch of useless old men.
Would Cade's group help her? She did not know, nor did she
know when she'd see Cade again to ask him. Time was slipping away, and the longer she waited, the less of a chance she
had of reaching Lhean. She had little idea what she'd face if
she tried to enter the Capital by herself, but at least she had
a map to show her the way. She also had the entire day to
plan.

When she thought of time slipping away, Captain Mapstone's riddle came back to her.

> *The scything moon is held captive in the prison of for-*
> *gotten days. Seek it in the den of the three-faced reptile,*
> *for you are the blade of the shadow cast. Beware! The*
> *longer you linger, the faster we spin apart.*

The final line seemed to reinforce the idea that she was
running out of time, that the longer she hesitated to act, the
less likely she was to reach home. And if she succeeded in
reaching home, would she be too late to prevent the fall of
Sacoridia?

Through the rest of the day, Karigan ran through several sce-
narios for finding and rescuing Lhean, but all of them were
incomplete. She knew too little about the outside world and
how she might move safely through it. The professor had
done his job of protecting her all too well.

Her planning alternated with quiet recitations of the captain's riddle as she paced her room. She hoped some inspiration would reveal all to her and somehow tell her both how
to save Lhean and how to get home, but none was forthcoming.

She peered into her shard of the looking mask, shivering
as she remembered the dream of the mirror eyes. The shard
likewise remained elusive. She saw only her reflection.

She decided she must destroy the first message from Captain Mapstone telling her to go to the Heroes Portal. She did
not wish to leave behind any evidence that might lead to the
tombs. At first she wondered how she might destroy it with-

out attracting attention, then an idea set in. She strode down to the privy, locked herself inside, and ripped up the message. She did so with some regret because it was a link to home.

She dropped the shredded pieces into the sitting bowl and pulled the big lever. She watched sadly as the paper whirled out of sight down unknown pipes and into the fathomless depths.

I will see Captain Mapstone soon, and everyone else, too, she thought, more determined than ever. She returned to her room to resume planning. Tonight was as good a time as any to move and she was tired of waiting.

At supper, it was just her and the professor dining on boiled dinner. Or rather, the professor dined. Karigan stared at her portion with lip curled at the stench of cabbage. Why did her final supper have to be this? Luckily there were dinner rolls.

She had hoped Cade would join them, but he rarely ate supper with them, so she was not really expecting him. Had he been there, however, she would have found a way to speak privately with him, told him what she planned to do. Would he have helped her or tried to dissuade her? Perhaps it was better she did not see him, though it gave her pangs of regret.

"You look preoccupied tonight, my dear," the professor said.

Karigan looked up, startled. She must not give away her intent. "I am sorry, Uncle, but I am not fond of boiled dinner. I was wondering if there might be some soup left over from midday."

"Is that all?" He nodded at Grott, indicating the butler should look into the availability of soup. "You look as if you had the weight of the world on your shoulders."

She did rather feel that way, but said, "It's the cabbage. And corned beef." She shuddered.

The professor laughed. "I shall have cook strike it from the menu then. No more boiled dinner for my niece."

No, there certainly would not be. She was not his niece nor was she staying.

"I actually have a piece of pleasant news," the professor said.

She looked up, attentive and hopeful that he'd changed his mind about Lhean.

"Mrs. Downey expressed her desire to me, today, that you meet her son."

"Oh." Karigan tried not to reveal her disappointment.

"Oh?" The professor echoed, raising both eyebrows. "My dear, he is a fine young man."

As the professor began to list the attributes of Mrs. Downey's son, Karigan saw clearly how the professor was trying to integrate her into his world. She was to make friends with Arhys. Boiled dinner was being struck from the menu. She was to be courted by the scions of Mill City's Preferred families. He wanted her to forget where she came from and give up any notion of returning. In fact, he didn't want her just to integrate, he wanted her to conform.

When he finished his litany of praises for the virtuous paragon of masculinity that was Master Downey, Karigan said, "You know, my father tried matching me with appropriate suitors, but it never went well."

The professor froze, then looked this way and that to see who might have overheard. Perhaps she had spoken recklessly, but she was tired of the whole charade, and it wasn't like she had named names. Whatever anyone knew, her fictional father might have tried to arrange a good marriage for Kari Goodgrave before she was put away in the asylum.

"I would be careful of your words, my dear," the professor warned her, giving her a significant look.

Grott re-entered the dining room just then with a steaming bowl of soup, alleviating her need to respond. She waited for the soup to cool, and was glad she'd requested it. It was thick with chicken and vegetables, a good heartening meal for one who did not know how well she would eat after this night.

The professor did not speak while she ate, sunk deeply into his own thoughts, but by the time she was tilting the bowl to get at the last of the broth, he looked up at her, his expression plaintive.

"I just want you to be happy here, my dear."

"I will be happy." *Just not here.* "I am grateful for all you've done for me, Uncle." And she meant it. But did he hear the underlying meaning to her words,? That these were words of farewell? She could not tell.

When she finished, she headed upstairs to await the midnight hour. She was intercepted by Mirriam who squinted at Karigan through her monocle.

"Miss Goodgrave."

"Mirriam." Karigan waited. Mirriam looked like she had something on her mind that needed saying.

"Well, now," the housekeeper said on an exhalation, and much more softly than usual. "If that Tam Ryder of yours decides to go riding at odd hours, you best warn him to take care. He has been seen and not just by Luke."

By the look Mirriam gave her, Karigan gleaned that the housekeeper was referring to herself. Stunned, Karigan blinked rapidly. "I—I will."

"Good." The monocle dropped to the end of its chain, and Mirriam turned to go then paused. Even more quietly she said, "Also, ask Tam to tell Mr. Harlowe to refrain from engaging in further taproom brawls. It is not becoming of a gentleman."

Karigan nodded emphatically, wondering exactly what and how much Mirriam knew, and why she had not alerted the professor to Karigan's late night excursion. It was clear Mirriam was aware of more going on, within and without her household, than was typical, but to what extent it was impossible to say, and to what ends it was impossible to ascertain. Everyone here seemed to have a secret agenda, even the housekeeper. Karigan watched after Mirriam as she made her way down the corridor, then called after her.

"Yes?" Mirriam turned, her usual severe expression on her face.

"Thank you. I just wanted to thank you for everything. And . . . good night."

"Good night, Miss Goodgrave." Mirriam turned to descend the stairs.

When the time came for Lorine to help Karigan prepare for bed, Karigan offered her a heartfelt good night as well, silently wishing the best for the former slave. Karigan had grown almost too comfortable in the professor's house, eating good food and wearing fine dresses. She would miss the professor, Lorine, and Mirriam, and all the others, but not as much as she missed her own home.

She'd grown comfortable, but she'd also become a prisoner. A prisoner of the professor's protection, as well as his time, and of the constraints of the empire. It was time to break bonds of all kinds.

She pulled the bedcovers up to her chin to await the striking of midnight.

ARHYS

Arhys had a room of her own, but it was not as big as Miss Goodgrave's. Arhys had a bed to herself, but it was tiny compared to the one Miss Goodgrave got to sleep in. After the professor made Arhys go to her room, she had wailed and stomped and broken the dolls he had given her. They had real hair and porcelain faces and pretty dresses, but two now had cracked heads, and a ripped-off arm spilled sawdust across the floor. Now she didn't even have her dollies to talk to. They were ruined, and it was all Miss Goodgrave's fault. Miss Goodgrave had made her do it.

She'd also pulled all her dresses out of her wardrobe so that they were strewn about, and she stomped on them. She had swept her pretty toiletries off her dresser. She gouged at the plaster wall with a hair pick. She'd show them. She'd show them all.

The professor had been very stern with her. He'd ordered her to not tell anyone, no one at all, about the secret door that went to secret places. It was very important she keep the secret. He would buy her dresses if she was a good girl and kept it.

She'd promised, but it wasn't fair. She wanted to go to secret places, too. She'd spotted the professor, Miss Goodgrave, and Mr. Harlowe going through the hidden passage in the library. It had been after her bedtime when she wasn't supposed to be up, but sometimes she couldn't sleep and was bored. She'd been in the parlor across from the library at the time, pretending to be taking tea with the important ladies of the city. When she heard footsteps, she turned off her light and hid and watched. She never figured out how they opened the secret door or where they went. What did they do when they got there, wherever *there* was? She wanted to know.

Well, if Miss Goodgrave got to sneak around, so did she. She'd show them. She'd show them all.

She picked among her rumpled dresses and found her coat. She pulled it on, then slipped her feet into her everyday shoes, not the nice shiny ones Mirriam said were only for special occasions. Then Arhys changed her mind and kicked off the old ones. She would wear the nice ones if she wanted to.

The eleven hour bell had rung. It was again past her bedtime, but it had never stopped her before. She crept out of her room, down the stairs, and to the front door. She turned the lock and let herself out.

She stood frozen on the front step. She had never gone out this late on her own. Never. She looked nervously up and down the street. The lamps were bright, but cast shadows against the houses and fences, beneath trees and shrubbery. Anything could hide in those shadows and leap out at her.

But the emperor wouldn't let that happen, would he? That's why there were so many Inspectors out at night, right? To keep away monsters and bad men? Reassured, she set off.

It took her longer than she thought, walking past so many houses with their darkened yards. Her good shoes hurt her feet, and she was sorry she hadn't worn her old pair. Angry, she splashed in a muddy puddle.

It was not until she reached the last house at the end of the street that she finally encountered an Inspector patrolling with his Enforcer. The Enforcer shone dully beneath the light of a streetlamp.

"There, young miss, what are you doing out at this late hour?"

Arhys strode right up to him, faltering only when she neared the Enforcer. The Enforcer tilted its eyepiece so it could look down at her. The lens in its eye whirred as it focused on her.

I am not afraid, she told herself, but the Enforcer was so much bigger close up.

"Say," the Inspector said, "aren't you Arhys? The little girl who works at Professor Josston's?"

She gazed up at the Inspector. He was impressive with his red uniform, shiny buttons, and the weapons on his belt. She recognized him—Inspector Gant. He'd come to the professor's house before.

"Yes, sir," she said as sweetly as she could manage. "There is something I need to tell you. I want to tell you about the professor."

FOUND

Karigan was out of bed before the first strike of the midnight bell faded. When she left her room that final time, she took nothing with her except the map of the Capital, the mirror shard, the bonewood, and a canvas satchel she'd found in the downstairs cloak room. She left behind the comfortable bed, the silly novels Mirriam had given her in her early days here, and a wardrobe filled with skillfully tailored dresses, hats, shoes, and gloves. And veils. Oh, yes, she was certainly leaving behind the veils.

She was well-practiced by now in sneaking around the house at the deepest hours of night, though she had been chagrined to learn that Mirriam and Arhys had both observed her nocturnal activities. She resolved to be extra careful, knowing the professor could also be prowling about on his own business.

Taper in hand, she descended the stairs, and crept into the library. Taking more care than usual, she made sure Arhys was nowhere to be found. Then she went to the dragon on the bookshelf, twisted its tail, and the secret passage opened. When the bookcase swung closed behind her, she finally felt totally committed. She would have to come back to the house one last time, however, because she believed the doors to the old mill were boarded shut and she could not exit through them. Plus, she needed Raven.

She hastily changed from her nightgown into her black swordswoman garb and began the long descent into the underground. This was her first time taking the route on her very own. Well, the first time had been sort of on her own. But she'd followed the professor and Cade, and they'd been awaiting her at the other end. What if the professor was there now? What if he came after her and found her in the old mill? Well, they'd have it out. He could not force her to stay and play his mad niece for the rest of her life. She'd rather live in the tombs.

If need be, she had the skills to extricate herself forcibly from the professor's control, but she'd prefer an amicable parting. He'd been good to her. He had protected her and taken her into his home and his confidence. By sneaking out, she did not have to take the chance of a confrontation of any kind.

The underground was as she remembered—dark and haunting, the light of her taper reflecting on dusty windows. "I will see this the way it's supposed to be when I get home," she said, but her voice sounded tiny, doubtful.

She hurried on past the remains of the Cock and Hen, past the harness shop and all those buildings she had once known above ground and exposed to the sky.

Once she climbed up into the old mill, she had the sense of trespassing. The old building was dark. No one awaited her, no one had accompanied her or given her permission to enter. She felt uncomfortable and very alone as her feet clunked on wrought iron steps. Where once she'd been accustomed to being so often alone as a messenger, she had now become used to being around people in the professor's house and escorted whenever she left. She'd been made too comfortable and protected. Perhaps less confident.

She shook her head. Hadn't she gone to the Heroes Portal by herself last night? But she hadn't had that sense of trespass . . .

She climbed past the yawning doorway of the second floor where Cade had done his weapons practice, honing his skills to become a Black Shield, and where the professor had lovingly preserved his library of damaged books. She did not stop for her destination lay on the third floor.

Once there, with the aid of her taper, she found the lever that illuminated the phosphorene lights. She set the taper aside and quickly oriented herself, striking off to find that one particular aisle that contained her personal belongings. She would not leave them behind—not her brooch, the moonstone, or the feather of the winter owl. Nor would she leave behind her uniform, tattered as it was. These things were *hers*. They allowed her to touch something real from her home.

She found the proper aisle, her steps quickening until they brought her to the table that held her belongings. She immediately pinned the brooch on. She'd forgotten how it felt, that slight weight against her chest. She slipped the moonstone into her trouser pocket. Next she traded the professor's bonewood for her own. She had not appreciated the differences between the two before, for they were subtle. The professor's lacked the black shield emblem on it, of course, and it had the patina and feel of age on it. Hers did not.

She then hesitated, wondering whether or not to take all the mirror shards with her. No, she would keep the one. The rest would remain, an enigma for the professor to ponder. Maybe they'd be forgotten with time, just like much of the rubbish in this room; rubbish the professor considered artifacts.

She carefully rolled the feather of the winter owl in the sleeve of her greatcoat, then stuffed her uniform into her satchel. She decided to leave her infantry boots behind. The muddy soaking they'd received in Blackveil had turned them stiff and hard as they dried in storage. They were cracking and smelled of mildew. She had no oil or time with which to recondition them, so in the future they would stay, one more enigma for the professor.

She turned to leave, and there he was standing in the aisle watching her—the professor. She was so startled she squawked and dropped her satchel. How had he crept up on her like that? She detected his smile beneath his ostentatious mustache and remembered that, like her, he'd had plenty of practice sneaking around at odd hours of the night.

"You—you followed me here?" she asked.

"Yes, of course. I wanted to see what you were up to."

Karigan gestured at her satchel. "As you can see, I am collecting my things."

"I do see, but you know it is safer for all of us if they remain here."

"They can't remain here," Karigan replied.

"Why ever not?"

She strongly suspected he knew the answer. "Because I am not remaining here. I am leaving. I have to."

The professor stepped closer. "You worry about your Eletian friend."

Karigan nodded. "Yes. He, I believe, is my link to finding my way home."

"Oh, my dear, I had so hoped you would settle here, become part of my family." He shook his head sadly. "It has been a joy to have you. You reawakened my passion for learning about the old days, motivated me ever more to bring down the empire."

"I appreciate all you've done for me," Karigan said. She could not allow herself to feel guilty for leaving him. "You took me in, a stranger out of time, and allowed me to heal from my injuries. You've protected me from the empire and made for me a safe haven. But now it is time for me to go."

"You are resolved to do this?"

Karigan nodded. "Yes. I want to put things right in my time so yours never has an emperor the likes of Xandis Pierce Amberhill."

"You believe you can do this?"

"My king—King Zachary—he's a good man, a good ruler, and he will hear what I have to say. If there is a way to prevent the empire from rising, he will find it."

"Well then. I daresay you are resolved."

"I am."

His expression sagged. He looked suddenly older. "Do you think you could spare your uncle a hug before you strike off onto these new adventures?"

Karigan was relieved he had not fought her on this. Not much, at least. He must have seen that he could not contain her forever. He held his arms wide open for that hug. He still smiled, but his eyes looked sad. She had to admit her own eyes were feeling a little moist, too. She walked into his embrace, and he hugged her fiercely.

"I will think of you often," she reassured him.

"I am sorry, my dear, so sorry."

She started to pull away from him, but he shifted and the next thing she knew was a sharp pain stabbing into her upper arm.

"Ow! What?" She shoved him away and staggered. A syringe impaled her arm. She yanked it out and dropped it to the floor, the glass tube cracking. Droplets of clear fluid stained the wooden floor.

What? She'd meant to say it aloud, but her mouth wasn't working right, like in the dream she'd had of mirror eyes.

She wanted the professor to explain. She meant to grab him by the lapels of his tweed coat, but she staggered again, and when she tried to catch herself on a nearby shelf, her hands knocked over a stack of pottery and sent it smashing to the floor.

"Easy," the professor said, reaching out to her. He'd become distorted in her vision, blurry and elongated. "It's just morphia."

Karigan leaned back against the shelving, trying to remain standing, but she sank toward the floor inch by inch.

"I will take good care of you," the professor said, his voice sounding miles away.

She blinked, fighting to stay aware. *Why?* The word rang out in her mind but did not reach her lips. She knew the answer anyway—he could not allow her to leave. She had made the mistake of letting her guard down. She had trusted too much.

She was out before she hit the floor.

The professor grimaced as his shoe crunched on the shards of rare Second Age pottery, but it was a small sacrifice compared to what might happen if he allowed Karigan G'ladheon to leave. She would undoubtedly be captured, and she knew too much. He knelt beside her, relieved to see her breathing normally. The morphia had been left behind by Mender Samuels after Karigan had first arrived with her painful wounds.

She had refused further injections after she regained consciousness, so there had been quite a bit left over.

The professor had not known the correct amount to administer, so he had filled the syringe and injected it all. He
could keep Karigan dosed for a good long time. He would tell
anyone who questioned him about her that she had relapsed
into madness, but he hadn't the heart to send her to the Mill
City Asylum after her terrible experiences in the east.

He knew that those treated with morphia often developed
a deep, addictive yearning for it. He would not have to force
doses on her after a while. Before long, she would be begging
him for it. It was all very simple, but regrettable. Still, it was a
small price to pay for protecting his secrets.

He brushed her hair out of her face. "Indeed, I am very
sorry, my dear. You've a bright spirit, but I've my own home
to look after."

But now he faced a conundrum of practical dimension. He
had to bring her back to the house, but he didn't have the
strength to carry her all the way by himself. He needed Cade.
What would Cade make of this, what he'd done to Karigan?
Cade, he was sure, would see that they had no choice but to
ensconce her at home, keep her weak and unable to act. Bed-
ridden. It would keep the opposition safe—surely Cade
would see that.

As it turned out, he did not have to wait to find out what
Cade would think.

"Professor?"

The professor rose and slowly turned to face his protégé.
Cade stood just paces away. His face was colored with bruises.
So the students had been right about a brawl. But Cade?
Brawling? It had sounded so unlikely.

"Your timing is good," the professor said. "I could use
some assistance."

To his surprise, Cade brushed right by him and knelt beside Karigan. "What happened here?" He patted her cheek,
but she did not respond.

It did not take long for Cade to espy the remains of the
syringe. He picked it up carefully, the long needle pointed
away from him. "What have you done?"

"Listen, Old Button—"

Cade rose in one swift move. Anger suffused his face the likes of which the professor had never seen before. *"What have you done?"*

"It's just morphia," the professor said. "She'll come out of it soon enough. She was trying to leave, Cade."

"How much?"

"What?"

"How much did you give her?"

"Well, er, the whole thing, except for a little that didn't get in before she pulled the needle out."

Cade smashed the glass tube at the professor's feet. The professor stepped back, stunned by Cade's ferocity.

"A full syringe? You old fool, were you trying to kill her?"

The professor hastened back another step, astonished by this side of his student, a side he'd never witnessed before. "She'll be fine. I'm sure of it."

"You had no right."

"I had every right. I could have given her to the Inspectors long ago."

"But you did not because she is an artifact of the old realm."

"I did not because, yes, her presence here is fascinating. I thought perhaps she'd have some knowledge the opposition could use, as well."

"She is a human being," Cade said.

"And so are we all. By not giving her to the Inspectors, I've kept her from harm at great personal risk. And you should know more than most that I've grown very fond of her."

Cade's expression of disgust rocked the professor. No, not just disgust, but something far worse: disappointment. He saw it in Cade's eyes, how he had failed him, his student, his protégé, his young friend. Cade had thought better of him. Thought his professor better than one who would stoop to such a tactic to silence Karigan. The professor saw it now, how he'd acted as thuggishly as one of the emperor's minions. He saw it reflected in Cade's eyes.

Not only have I wronged Karigan, he thought, *but I've be-*

trayed the values I was teaching Cade, that we could be better than the empire. Now he'd lost Cade's respect, the last person he'd ever wanted to hurt. Something withered inside him with the shame.

Cade pointed at him, ready to make another accusation, when he was interrupted by pounding. Pounding that rang all the way up the nearest stairwell. Someone was hammering on the boarded up door that was one of the original entrances to the old mill.

Both men froze, then the professor said, "We've been found."

THE TAILRACE

"Inspectors?" Cade asked anxiously.

The professor did not answer, but ran to the stairwell. In the light that leaked out of the room onto the landing, he spotted the discreet cabinet mounted on the wall. He opened it, and within gleamed the brass eyepiece and hand-crank wheel of a periscope. He'd installed one in each stairwell. He'd had to purchase the parts and build them himself. Buying a finished device would have drawn unwanted imperial scrutiny.

He retracted the eyepiece from the cabinet, and rotated the wheel to extend the scope out of the stairwell tower. The periscopes were placed so he could look right down at the mill entrances. When he peered through the eyepiece, he saw the intruders carried enough light with them to verify his worst fears.

"Professor?" Cade had followed him. "Are they Inspectors?"

The professor nodded. "A fair mob of them." He shook his head. "How could this happen? Everything I've done, everything I've worked for . . ."

"We have to get out of here," Cade said.

"The underground—"

"No," Cade said sharply. "If they know about the mill, they'll be at your house, too. The underground may be compromised, and we'd be trapped."

"Yes, yes, of course. You are right." The professor swept a shaking hand through his hair. He thanked goodness for Cade's calm thinking, for all he could think of was his world coming to complete and utter ruin, that Silk and the empire had won. He had lost everything. Secrets were such fragile things. He led the way back into the artifact room, striding toward the aisle where they'd left Karigan.

"Professor, we need a way out," Cade said, his voice louder.

As if to augment his urgency, the pounding now echoed up the stairwells at both ends of the room. The Inspectors were attacking both entrances. Long ago, the professor had reinforced the doors from inside with steel, but they would not hold up forever under a determined battering from Inspectors.

"Yes," the professor said, approaching the spot where Karigan lay. "All else may be lost, but you will have to protect Arhys."

"I will, but we need a way out. And we're not leaving without Karigan."

"Of course not." Maybe, the professor thought, here was his chance to redeem himself, to regain Cade's respect. "There is a way out, my boy. If there was one lesson I learned years ago from the fire that destroyed the rest of this complex, it was to always ensure there was an extra route of escape. Collect my niece . . ." He sighed. "Collect the *young lady* and follow me. Don't forget her bonewood—she may have need of it when she wakes up."

Cade did so, strapping Karigan's satchel across his shoulder and gathering the bonewood staff. He made lifting Karigan on his shoulder look effortless. The Old Button was strong, very strong.

They hastened to the stairwell and the professor grabbed a taper. They clattered down the stairs as fast as they could go, though Cade followed more carefully with his burdens. The professor paused, holding the light so Cade could see better, and what the professor saw in turn was determination and concentration on Cade's face. His student would need both not only to escape the mill, but also to evade capture once he was on the outside. Poor Karigan hung limply, draped over Cade's shoulder as though dead. The professor was sorry, so sorry for what he had done to her. Cade had awakened him to his terrible error in judgment, but now he would make it up to them both.

When Cade caught up, the professor continued down the spiraling stairs, the battering on the doors growing louder and louder. He kept going past the second floor, and the first, heading down into the low-vaulted brick basement. There the banging on the doors grew muffled.

"I thought we weren't going underground," Cade said.

"Not to *that* underground," the professor replied.

He led Cade past the one trap door that led to their secret passage, and hurried by the flyball governor that had once controlled the volume of water flowing into the mill's turbines. They passed by the first two penstocks and stopped at the third—a huge metal pipe bent like an inverted elbow, fabricated in riveted sections. The penstock had once funneled water from the canal to beneath the floor and into the turbine. The force and pressure of the water carried in by the penstocks forced the turbines to spin-spin-spin, which set the complex network of gears, drive shafts, and pulleys into motion, in turn powering the machines. But alas, this mill had not seen the power of water in many a year. Not since the fire.

Cade looked at him questioningly.

"After the fire," the professor explained, "the penstocks were closed off. The canal authorities did not wish to waste water power on a defunct mill." He pulled a section of the penstock away like a hatch, metal screeching. "Therefore, not only is the penstock dry, but the tailrace tunnel as well. Mostly anyway. Fortunately there have been no floods this spring. The tunnel will take you to the river, where I've hidden a small boat. It may be hard and a little cramped with the young lady slung over your shoulder, but you will manage."

"Aren't you coming?" Cade asked.

"I'll follow you shortly. I have some matters to take care of first. You get Karigan out. Take care of her. When she wakes, tell her how sorry I am, and that I hope she finds her way home."

A furrowed line formed between Cade's eyebrows. "You sound like you aren't coming."

"I'll do my best, Old Button, but we're running out of time."

Inside the rusty walls of the penstock was a step ladder

instead of the turbine shaft that should have been in there. Cade dropped Karigan's satchel and the staff down and they thudded to the bottom. Cade then stepped through the opening into the penstock, balancing himself on the ladder, only his head and shoulders clearing the hatch. Meanwhile, the professor held Karigan. She was rather like an oversized ragdoll, but he was relieved to note she was still breathing normally, if slowly. Briefly her eyes fluttered open—he caught a glint of them in his light, but all too soon they closed again.

"It was an honor getting to know you, my dear," he murmured into her ear. Then he helped Cade maneuver her through the hatch and into the penstock. The professor watched her vanish into the darkness below.

Cade reappeared at the hatch. "I could use a light."

"Yes, of course." The professor passed him the taper. "Know that you were always my best student, Cade."

A smile flickered on the young man's face. "Do what you need to do, then follow after us. We'll wait in the boat."

The professor nodded. "Hurry now!" and he replaced the cover on the hatch to forestall anymore painful leave-taking.

The basement was dark, but he knew his way well. At the base of the stairwell he found and lit another taper and examined the door. It appeared to be buckling, even with the steel reinforcement. The hinges were giving way. He hastened up the stairs to the second floor and threw the lever to illuminate the room. There were barrels he kept near the entryway in which he stored phosphorene to keep the lights functioning, but also it was there in case of an emergency. An emergency like the one he now faced.

He rolled the barrels to the center of the floor and unplugged them. The clear viscous fluid that was phosphorene flowed onto the floor, rather like the molasses he sometimes liked on cornbread. The dry mill floor soaked the phosphorene right up. The fumes drove the professor back.

The barrels of phosphorene were not the only precautions the professor had taken. He had feared this day might come to pass, and so he had planned. He could not allow his precious artifacts to fall into the hands of Ezra Stirling Silk, much less the emperor, so among the shelves on the third floor he had stocked smaller barrels of black powder. Silk may have rounded up most of the blastmen in Mill City, but what he hadn't known was that Bryce Lowell Josston, imperially licensed professor of archeology, was also versed in the art of blasting.

He shook his head sadly and made his way to his big desk. He sat down, and from the drawer removed his pistol and his grandfather's chronosphere. He opened the sphere and watched the little mechanical man inside pick out the time with his walking stick. Half past the morning's first hour. In all the excitement, he had not heard the city bell toll. He snapped the sphere shut and waited.

When the doors finally crashed open—first on one end, followed shortly by the door on the other end—the professor consulted the chronosphere once more. It had taken them approximately ten minutes to break in since he had last checked. That meant his doors had held up remarkably well under the onslaught, and he congratulated himself on their design, which, he hoped, had also provided Cade time to make progress down the tailrace.

Voices and stomping feet echoed up the stairwells, and he simply waited. He listened as they cleared the basement— apparently not finding the hatch in the penstock or the trapdoor to the underground—and moved on to the first floor. There, he knew, they found little more than discarded scraps of machinery.

When they all clambered up to the second floor and swarmed through the doors with arms drawn, the professor stood, picked up his taper which he'd kept burning, but left his pistol on his desk. Each movement was followed by the muzzles of firearms and the lensed eyes of Enforcers.

"Gentlemen," he said as he strode to the center of the room so they could all get a good look at him. "To what do I owe this intrusion of my property?"

"You are under arrest," one of the Inspectors announced. The local commander.

"Whatever for?"

"For suspicion of anti-empire activities."

"That does not sound very specific."

"It does not have to be," the commander replied. "As we all can see, you have been keeping secrets. I'm sure we'll find all the evidence we need in this building." Already there were Inspectors looking over Cade's collection of practice weapons. Enforcers scanned the walls and his bookcases.

One Enforcer tip-tapped toward him and stepped in the phosphorene. It lifted its foot gingerly, like a cat that has stepped in a puddle. It issued a warning *bleep*. Meanwhile, two Inspectors conferred with the commander.

". . . smell of phosphorene," one was saying.

"Gentlemen," the professor announced, and they all looked his way. "I do not think you are going to find anything. Not a thing. Your masters are going to be woefully disappointed." He let the taper tumble from his hand onto the phosphorene soaked floor. Its bulb broke baring the flame. "Oh dear," he said with false contrition. "I seem to have dropped my light."

Flames *whooshed* up from the floor. The professor leaped away from the sudden heat. Men and machines bolted into action, calling for water, to retreat, shouting, *Fire!* as they ran.

The professor backed away from the flames and returned to his desk. He warred with every fiber of his being not to run, to escape to safety, but by sheer will forced himself to sit. Sit at his desk in his precious library of forgotten books. His people would lose all these bridges to the past, all the objects which he, and others before him, had found and lovingly preserved. Better this than what the emperor would do with it all.

The professor coughed on the hot smoke that was quickly filling the room, obscuring the panicked Inspectors and Enforcers from sight. The fire would spread fast, fed not only by old, dry wood soaked in phosphorene, but by the machine oil that had dripped and been absorbed into floorboards over the many decades the mill had been active.

Then there were the barrels of black powder on the third floor.

There was a circularity to it all, he thought. All those slave workers who had perished when the rest of his complex had burned. They had not been able to escape. They'd been chained to their machines. Their deaths were on him, and now they'd have some measure of justice. He hoped they would, at least, forgive him for taking the easy way out, a choice they had not had.

He picked up his pistol and pressed the muzzle to his head.

It was time for others to lead and carry on the opposition. Cade would protect Arhys, he knew. Perhaps Karigan G'ladheon would even reach her own time and change the course of history. A pity he would never find out.

He pulled the trigger.

When the professor had sealed the hatch on the penstock, Cade sensed he would not see his mentor again. Now he crouched at the very bottom of the mill in the tailrace tunnel. The turbine with its rusted vanes and gears had been shifted out of the way at the bottom of the penstock, leaving just enough space to maneuver. How the professor had managed to move the turbine, and secretly, too, he had no idea. In fact, only now did he realize how little he knew about his mentor.

He could not dwell on it. He was on his own, and he had someone else to take care of. Karigan lay on her side on the granite masonry floor of the tailrace, quite oblivious to all that had gone on so far. He hoped the professor had not irreparably harmed her by giving her such a large dose of morphia. Cade did not know how, precisely, it would affect her, for morphia could be unpredictable, but he did know she'd be out for quite some time.

He shone the light of the taper around, surprised to find the subterranean tunnel high enough for him to stand up—so long as he remained in the center of the arching ceiling. He had never been beneath a mill before—tailraces were usually filled with water, except when some repair must be made. He would never have thought of using a tailrace tunnel as a path of escape, but the professor had. He shook his head. The professor's paranoia was well honed.

The tailrace was constructed entirely of granite block masonry. In places he saw where silt had collected, imprinted with the ghost ripples of flowing water and the footprints of large river rats. The tailrace went far beyond the glow of his taper. To reach the river, he'd have to pass not only beneath this mill, but the width of the abandoned courtyard of the complex, and beneath the ruins of yet another mill. If he was going to reach the river anytime soon, he had better get at it. There was no telling what was going on up above.

When he started to lift Karigan, her eyes fluttered open. She squinted at him, unfocused. "Cade?"

"Yes?"

"You have . . ." she began.

"Yes?" he asked, gently shaking her when her eyes started closing again.

She blinked hard. "You have a nose." And just like that, she was out again.

"Glad to hear it," he muttered, and he hoisted her once more over his shoulder. Fortunately she was not heavy. Juggling the staff, the taper, the satchel, and one Green Rider altogether, however, proved more of a challenge, but he managed, moving swiftly down the tunnel. His footsteps echoed loudly around him, and he was pursued by his own shadow. This dank tunnel felt more like a tomb to him than what he had seen beyond the Heroes Portal.

Thinking of the tombs and of the Weapons gave him fresh strength, and he hurried onward. He was one of them now, a Black Shield, and his responsibilities ranged beyond the workings of opposition groups, and even beyond protecting Arhys. While he had been with the Weapons, he'd learned how distorted the world he lived in had become under the emperor. Instead of progressing into a bright future, the descendents of Sacoridia, and all the other nations that now comprised the empire, lived in a repressed gloom. Except for a privileged few. Including the professor.

Cade did not know if it was possible for Karigan to return to her own time and set things right, but he aimed to help her try. This, he believed, was his mandate as a Weapon, above and beyond all others. He did not see himself as abandoning his duty to Arhys by doing so. Not at all. Conversely, he believed helping Karigan would be the ultimate way to protect Arhys. He would help alter his time for the better, to restore Sacoridia to its rightful rule by kings and queens. In this way, he reasoned, he would protect Arhys, give her a world in which she could fulfill her destiny as a princess, out in the open as was proper, not as an exile hidden away lest she be hunted down like an animal should the empire learn of her existence. Nor did he intend to simply abandon Arhys in the here and now to some unknown fate but do whatever was in his power to keep her safe.

As for Karigan, he would personally deliver her to her king if he could. He wanted to see the old realm in all its glory, to see what Sacor City and the castle had really looked like before their destruction—not just some artist's fanciful renderings. He wanted to meet figures out of history—King Zachary and Queen Estora. Would the Weapons of that time accept him? Maybe or maybe not, but if he were *there*, he too could help prevent the rise of the emperor, fight in the past for Arhys and for the people of his present.

And he'd be with Karigan.

The subject of his thoughts shifted on his shoulder.

"Cade?" she said.

He halted. "Karigan? Are you awake?"

"Cade, why is the floor down there?"

He eased her off his shoulder and helped her stand when her knees buckled. Her eyes were open, but again unfocused.

"Where in the hells am I?" she asked in a dazed voice, her gaze wandering.

"Somewhere beneath the old Josston Mills complex."

She squinted at him and reached as though to tweak his nose, but almost put his eye out instead. He grabbed her hand before it could do any damage.

"I think you have six, maybe seven noses."

He patted her cheek to get her attention. "Do you think you can stay upright?"

"I feel all tippy." As if to illustrate, she started to keel over. Cade caught her, and again she was totally out. He hoisted her back over his shoulder and set off once more.

Who would have ever guessed that one day he'd be carrying around an unconscious legend of almost two hundred years ago, in the bowels of an old mill complex? Certainly not he. But he'd come a long way from not believing who she said she was, even when the professor had insisted she spoke the truth. His professor, his mentor who was likely sacrificing himself this night.

Cade could not afford to think about the professor or the life he had left behind. He surged through the tunnel, which sloped gently downward on its way to the river. Nothing would ever be the same again. He could not return to the university to resume his studies. If Inspectors were knocking down the doors of the old mill, they would inevitably go in search of the professor's students for questioning. Cade could not get himself caught—he knew too much.

He slowed when he came to the foundation of the mill across the courtyard. Its turbine must have been salvaged, and the penstock, too, for there was only a gaping hole into the basement above. The scent of old, wet soot mixed with a current of freshening air that circulated from the outlet at the river. Odd light flickered above, and he knew this mill to be a ruin open to the sky. He'd explored the remains of the complex some during daytime hours. The roof and floors had collapsed and only one jagged wall of brick still stood. During his explorations, he'd found soot-blackened manacles still chained to a loom buried beneath a pile of rubble.

The professor should have knocked down the last of the ruins and filled in the foundations. He should have sold off the land, a prime mill location with water rights. But the professor had held on to this one complex, the one that had been ravaged by fire, not so much because of the single remaining building where he could store his collection of artifacts, but because this, all of this, was a monument to his guilt. It forced him to remember. The professor had never said as much, but Cade had been around him enough to know, to pick up on comments and moods. The memory of the fire had driven the professor's support of the opposition.

Cade stepped over debris that had fallen down the penstock hole—blackened bricks, moldering wood, dead leaves. The floor here was damp, weather had found its way through the ruins to this place. He slipped as he hurried on, but was surefooted enough not to tumble and drop Karigan.

At long last he reached the end of the tunnel, the damp air of the river flowing full on through the arched opening of the outlet. Wavelets slurped at the retaining wall that girded the river bank. Crickets chirped in the distance.

The professor's boat was actually stored in the tunnel, covered with a tarp. Cade carefully set Karigan and his other burdens down, and pulled the tarp off the boat. It was a very small row boat. He worked quickly, tossing Karigan's satchel and the staff into it, and pushed it toward the opening. If the river were higher, more level with the tunnel's outlet, he might have put Karigan in the boat, too, but it was not and he did not wish to risk injuring her from too much jostling.

He worked the boat over the edge, bow first into the water. He held onto a line connected to the bow and watched the boat bob on the surface, relieved it did not sink. He turned to gather up Karigan, but she was sitting and staring back up the tunnel, her hand outstretched.

"Karigan?" Cade asked, keeping his voice low. There was no telling how sound would travel on the river.

"He is saying good-bye," she said.

Cade flashed the taper into the darkness thinking perhaps the professor had followed them after all. No one was there. She must be experiencing strange visions from the morphia, like when she'd seen his six—or was it seven?—noses. He'd heard morphia could be like that.

"We are going to get into the boat, very carefully," Cade told her, and he helped her to her feet, draped her arm around his neck, and held her steady.

"Good-bye," Karigan said, glancing once more down the tunnel.

"Who are you saying good-bye to?"

"My uncle."

Waves of foreboding coursed through Cade. They stood now on the very edge of the tailrace tunnel's outlet, and he had to figure out how to get her into the boat without getting them both wet. Karigan started to sag against him and rested her head on his shoulder as she dropped out of consciousness again.

He sighed. "Oh, professor, what have you done?"

The sky lit up reflecting a fiery glow on the river, followed by a thunderous explosion that sent a gust of air and a throaty roar rumbling down the length of the tunnel.

"What in damnation?"

He stood rooted in shock trying to make sense of it, but the roar grew, the wind from the tunnel pushing at his back. He turned, peering down the tunnel with his light, at first uncomprehending. When he registered the wall of water rushing down the tunnel at him, it was already too late to get out of the way.

SWIMMING IN FLAMES

Cade tossed Karigan into the river ahead of him, jumping just as the water slammed into his back.

The cold black river swallowed him. The flow that rushed from the tailrace hammered him beneath the surface. He fought upward in a panic, limbs thrashing against the pounding, lungs aching for air. He hadn't the strength to break the surface beneath the weight and force of all that water pouring down on top of him.

Something pulled steadily at his wrist and started to draw him free of the falling water, and he realized it was the line to the rowboat. He allowed it to pull on him, and he kicked clear of the turbulence, surfacing in calmer water. He gasped and sputtered for air. He'd been so lucky that in the onrush of water he had not been pummeled with loose debris carried down the tailrace. A brick could have ended everything. He could only guess that the explosion he'd heard had broken the sluice gate that damned the intake at the canal, thus loosing the water and sending it cascading down the tunnel.

Karigan! he thought, remembering he was not alone.

The boat was drifting downstream, and he with it. He tread water looking frantically around.

"Karigan?" he called out. No answer. She'd been so drugged. She could have drowned already. He whirled around, searching, searching. Had she, too, got caught in the outflow from the tailrace? Was she still down there, churning in the pounding water? He swam against the current back toward the tailrace, towing the boat behind him.

The fire plumed, brightening the sky and river, and there,

floating just yards away on her back, with arms splayed out, was Karigan, bathed in the reflected firelight as though she drifted in liquid flame.

Cade changed course, keeping an eye on her even as the glow of the fire dimmed. When he reached her, he saw her eyes were open, also glistening with the fire's light.

"Karigan?"

"Fergal?"

"No, no, it's me, Cade."

She blinked, and in a weary voice said, "Why do I always end up in rivers?"

Cade was too relieved to care about her odd comment or wonder who Fergal was. "Can you swim?"

"Of course I can swim."

"Then let's make our way to the far bank." On the far bank, there was no sheer stone retaining wall supporting the tailraces of mills, just the boggy edge of the river. He started to swim away, but she just floated there staring at the sky.

"Karigan?"

"I'm swimming," she said. "Just swimming in flames."

With the reflection, the image was apt. Cade sighed and secured the line of the rowboat around his waist, then he grabbed Karigan by the collar and stroked for the river bank.

"I am swimming faster," Karigan observed. "Swimming in the pretty light."

Cade started to curse the professor for the morphia, but stopped. The professor was gone. He knew it. Like a captain going down with his ship, the professor would have gone up in flames with the mill, sacrificing himself alongside his beloved artifacts, atoning for the slaves who had perished there, sacrificing himself for the good of the opposition. A dead man could not be interrogated.

When finally Cade crawled onto the river bank, he pulled Karigan up beside him and, exhausted, just held her. It was too painful to watch the roiling flames across the river that were the professor's pyre, so he nestled his face in the nape of her neck, where he would not have to see.

*   *   *

Cade rowed down the river, the current helping to carry the small boat along. It had taken him awhile to decide what to do next, to consider the few options available to him. Widow Hettle's house was out—the Inspectors would search for him there, plus, her house was too far from the river. He also thought about the old slave market, but it too, was logistically difficult to get to while carrying an unconscious woman over his shoulder. The Inspectors would be out in force, and he'd be sure to get caught. He needed someplace near the river, someplace where he and Karigan could get dry and warm. One place did come to mind.

The rowing kept his blood flowing, and while the night was not cold, it was cool enough that a person in wet clothes could get chilled. He worried about Karigan, curled in the bottom of the boat, as bouts of chills racked her body even as she lay unconscious.

"Oh, professor," he murmured for the hundredth time, as he hastily blinked away tears and dragged on the oars with more urgency.

He could still see the mill fire up river, lighting the sky, but farther down, the river banks were serene. Silent, dark mills loomed on his left, and the waterfront warehouses, shops, and hovels shouldered together to his right. He tried not to watch the fire glow, but searched instead for a certain dock he wanted, the one that catered to fishermen. Fishing was not a true industry in Mill City, and was illegal without an imperial license, but those who fished surreptitiously were able to supplement their meager larder. Cade did not think there was much caught other than carp—the dams and locks had killed off most everything else.

He was past the dock before he realized he was anywhere near it and plowed the oars in the water to slow his momentum. The dock canted at a precarious angle on its pilings. There was a bait shop directly on shore. Cade worked the bow around, oars groaning, and headed in.

When the hull bumped alongside the dock, Cade nosed the boat in as close to shore as possible. Well past curfew, the shorefront was quiet. He saw no sign of Inspectors, so he tied the boat's line to a cleat and placed the staff and satchel on the dock. Fortunately they had stayed safe in the bottom of the boat where he'd stowed them, even after he and Karigan had ended up in the river. He then tended to transferring her to the dock without tipping the boat over and giving them both another soaking.

She murmured something as he shifted her, but she did not wake up. With a deep breath, he hoisted her onto the dock. His body was beginning to feel the strain of having carried her through the tailrace tunnel, then fighting the outflow in the river that had almost drowned him. He decided to look upon his travails as strength training. Karigan was the perfect weight to challenge him, to help increase his stamina. This was what he told himself, anyway.

He lifted his burdens and hurried ashore.

Cade had never been to Jax's house before, but he knew exactly where it was, one block from the river. It was not the seedy part of town, but it was not one of the better neighborhoods, either. Cade also knew where Thadd and Jonny lived. He'd made a point of learning as much about the rebel leaders as he could.

He strode up to the small cottage with its shutters closed, but he detected light in the cracks. He'd have been surprised if Jax had not been up. The news of the professor's mill fire would have spread quickly among the rebels.

Cade knocked on the door. A moment later, a small panel slid open, and Jax peered out at him.

"Cade? What in damnation are you doing here?"

"Can you let us in?"

"Whose hind end is that sticking out on your shoulder?"

"You met her last night."

Jax grumbled, then opened the door just enough to allow Cade to dash in, then swiftly closed it and drove the bolt home. Cade did not hesitate, but crossed the room to Jax's cot and lay Karigan down on it.

"Is she dead?" Jax demanded.

"No. Just . . . drugged. Morphia. Do you think you could stoke up the heat? We're both wet."

"What did you do, swim here?"

"Something like that."

Jax moved to the small coal stove and opened the grate. Orange flames flickered inside. Cade closed his eyes, not wishing to see flames.

"So, you know your professor's mill is burning," Jax said matter-of-factly, shoveling coal into the stove.

"Yes, and the professor with it."

"You know that for sure?" Jax slammed the grate shut.

"We . . . we were there with him and almost got caught in it ourselves." Jax would have no idea what the professor had stored in the mill. Cade had kept that secret.

Jax squinted hard at him. "The girl is his mad niece, isn't she."

Cade nodded.

"Sounds like you've got some story to tell, but I hope you aren't bringing a load of Inspectors down on me."

"No. No Inspectors. My guess is that they are concentrated at the mill and the professor's house. Look, Jax, I need your help. Everything has unraveled."

"Why should I stick my neck out? I don't need Inspectors looking my way."

"You are a leader of our group," Cade said. "What is our primary goal?"

"To oust the emperor to make life better for everyone. To get rid of slavery at all levels."

"Yes, and the key to all that may be the young woman lying on your bed."

"How could—"

"No time for explanations," Cade said. "I'll tell you what I need you to do. But first, do you have a change of clothes? I'm freezing. Something for Miss Goodgrave, too."

Karigan floated through a strange series of visions with long stretches of darkness between. Her memory was hazy, unreliable. She remembered being at the old mill, the professor hugging her. After that, she had blurred images of Cade staring into her face, saying things to her she could not recall.

There were nightmarish tunnels and water. And now she was on a bed. Not her nice bed back at the professor's but more comfortable than . . . than what? How had she got here? Where was here? She was clammy cold and shivering.

She peered at her surroundings. At first everything was blurry then resolved into multiples. Three or four of the same chair, three or four of the same table, and so forth. The place smelled of sawdust.

Cade was talking to some man. It took too much effort to concentrate on what was being said. It came to her as a jumble, like another language. There were three of the man. She thought she might recognize him, but she couldn't place him just now. And, there was three of Cade. Three of Cade stripping out of his clothes. She watched in fascination as coat and vest came off. Since it was three of everything, it was *coats* and *vests*.

Off came his shirts, and there were the fine shoulders and chest . . . chests . . . she had seen before when he'd been at practice in the mill. Off came his trousers and undergarments. This was a new view, with three of *everything*. She could not say if this was a very nice dream vision or something really happening, but she was quite enjoying it. Cade, she thought, was well proportioned in every way—threefold!

All too soon he started to dress again. He had some final words with the other man, and the man left. Karigan started to slip into oblivion again, until she felt someone's hand on her. She grabbed and caught Cade's wrist. His real wrist, not an illusory one. Cade yelped.

"You're awake," he said a heartbeat later.

"Am I?"

"We need to get you into something dry. Jax pulled out this nightshirt for you."

Karigan blinked trying to see it clearly. Cade reached to start unbuttoning her shirt. She slapped his hand away.

"I can do it." Just speaking took great effort, so she wasn't sure she really could. "Turn around."

Cade obediently crossed the room to the stove, all three of him turning his backs on her. She struggled with buttons, fighting the darkness that tried to reabsorb her. What was wrong with her? She didn't feel hurt or injured, rather the opposite. Just drifty, floaty, sort of happy. She also knew this was somehow all very wrong, and yet it did not perturb her like it should have.

She'd have asked Cade about what was happening, but it was hard when she was concentrating on peeling off wet garb. Once she had succeeded, she pulled on the oversized night-shirt.

"Done," she murmured, the tide of darkness pulling her in.

Cade collected her wet clothes.

"Brooch," she said urgently, reaching after him. She fell out of the bed. "Brooch."

Cade lifted her back into bed, and the last things she remembered was him pinning her brooch to her borrowed nightshirt and drawing a blanket over her. Already drifting away, she wondered if it would have been so bad to let him undress her.

Blurred images of people coming and going, sibilant voices working themselves into her mind, interfered with her rest. At one point, she saw Yates sitting at the foot of her bed drawing. He was clear, unblurred. There was only one of him.

"Why don't you ever show me your pictures?" she asked him.

"Karigan?" It was not Yates who spoke her name, but Cade.

"Yates never shows me what he is drawing," she complained.

Cade drew his eyebrows together, perplexed.

Darkness came again, and when next she was aware, someone's face hovered close to hers, one of the eyes greatly oversized. Karigan shrieked and shrank away.

"Miss Goodgrave," said Mirriam, dropping her monocle, "is that any way to say hello?"

Mirriam? Karigan squinted. The woman was blurred, but at least Karigan was not seeing in threes.

"It is time for you to snap out of it, young lady," Mirriam said. "Time is slipping by and the world will not wait for you to wake up."

LOST IN HISTORY

**"I**t is hard," Karigan said. "Everything is fuzzy." But Mirriam's words about time running out set off a clangor of alarm bells in her mind. Unbidden she saw the captain's script before her eyes: *The longer you linger, the faster we spin apart.*

"We shall start easily, one thing at a time," Mirriam replied. "Try to sit up."

Karigan did so. Her surroundings did not spin so much as lurch. She gripped the side of the bed, feeling like she was going to spill out of it.

"What happened to me? Have I been sick?"

"Not precisely," Mirriam replied. "You received a large dose of morphia."

"How—?" Then Karigan remembered the professor giving her a hug back in the old mill, and the stab of a needle in her arm.

"I believe some poor judgment was involved. How do you feel now?"

"Tired. Like I want to sleep for the rest of my life. Weak. Everything is blurry."

"Not surprising," Mirriam replied. "Morphia is a heavy soporific."

"The professor didn't want me to . . ." Karigan trailed off, not knowing what Mirriam knew.

"Leave?" Mirriam provided. "It appears he feared the consequences of your abrupt departure."

That I'd give the opposition away. But, Karigan thought, there was a more basic fear at work—he feared change. He had spent his adult life preserving what was old, and though she had come from the past, he had feared what she could do to his present. Was that it? He feared any change wrought by her return to her own time?

"Where is he?" Karigan demanded. She would straighten him out, and take him to task for the morphia. She felt that she should be angry, very angry, but the medicine had dulled even that.

"Let us see if we can get your feet on the floor," Mirriam said, pulling the blanket off.

Karigan shivered with the layer of warmth removed, but she obediently swung her legs over the side of the bed, keeping her eyes closed to stave off the terrible swooning sensation when she moved. Closing her eyes was peaceful, and she started drifting, fading.

"Miss Goodgrave!" Mirriam's tart voice was as good as a slap across the face, and Karigan opened her eyes, her surroundings just as much a blur as before.

"Where am I?" The texture of the floor beneath her feet was of rough wood. She appeared to be in a one room cottage, very small, but tidy.

"This is the home of Jaxon Booth, a friend of Mr. Harlowe's. I believe you know him by the name of Jax."

Yes, Karigan thought. *The man in the old slave market.*

"He is a carpenter this side of the river."

River. A flash of memory, of being cold and wet and floating, washed over Karigan. "Mirriam, you have to tell me how I got here and what has happened. Nothing makes sense."

"I am sure it does not. First, try taking a little water, and if that stays down, we shall try some of Mr. Booth's porridge."

Mirriam handed Karigan a tall glass of water—not the fine crystal of the professor's house, but she did not care. She realized she was terribly parched and started drinking it all down.

"Slowly," Mirriam said. "You don't want to bring it back up, do you?"

When Karigan finished, desperate as she was to hear what Mirriam had to tell her about how she had gotten here, she was more desperate to use the privy. Mirriam helped her rise.

"Keep steady on your feet, Miss Goodgrave, for I have not

the strength to pick you up off the floor and no one else is here to help."

Karigan staggered like a drunkard, but did not fall. When presented with a door, she reached for the handle but missed the mark and rapped her knuckles on the wall. Mirriam helped guide her hand on the second try. When she had the door open, she stared. Light filtered through a curtained window and fell upon what was essentially a sitting place with a hole and a lid. No porcelain with fancy decoration, no lever to pull to swirl away the unmentionable in a wash of water.

"Not the professor's house, is it," she murmured.

"This is how most of the empire's citizens live," Mirriam said. "Many not even this well."

Karigan nodded, and was immediately sorry she did so when it sent the room spinning around her. She closed her eyes and held herself steady in the doorway. She did not tell Mirriam that this type of privy was what she'd been accustomed to before coming to the professor's.

She was able to do what she needed without assistance or falling down the hole or taking a nap, though she was powerfully drawn toward sleep. Afterward, Mirriam helped her back to the bed. The blurred vision not only made her balance unwieldy, but also disturbed her stomach, so when Mirriam offered her a simple porridge, she wanted only to decline and curl up in bed.

"If you do not eat," Mirriam told her, "you will only weaken further. Also, I will not tell you how you came to be here, or anything else that may be of interest to you."

Karigan gamely took the bowl of porridge. If it came spewing back up, Mirriam would have only herself to blame.

Mirriam pulled a stool over and waited to ensure Karigan had eaten at least two spoonfuls of porridge before she started.

"I was wondering where to begin," she said, "but I guess beginning at the beginning makes sense. At some point last night—we guess around eleven hour—Arhys snuck out of the house and went to the Inspectors."

Karigan dropped her spoon into the bowl with a clatter. "She *what?*"

"Oh, that spoiled girl. I warned the professor many times he was turning her into a little monster, I did, but he wouldn't listen. He was too soft-hearted, treating her like one of those porcelain dolls he was always giving her. She was apparently so upset at him for her punishment after the atlas incident that she went to the Inspectors and told them the professor had secrets, and secret places into which he could disappear."

"Mirriam . . ." There was no way to ask the housekeeper without being direct, even if it led to revealing some of those very secrets. "How much do *you* know?"

"A good deal and quite a bit more since I've spoken with Mr. Harlowe."

"Do you know why the professor took a special interest in Arhys?"

"Yes. I suspected something of the kind, and Mr. Harlowe confirmed it. He felt he needed to confide in Mr. Booth and me if we were to risk ourselves helping the two of you. Frankly, I was already in deep enough to be hanged without a trial."

"Which opposition group were you, er, involved in?"

"Mr. Harlowe's, of course. Child, the professor's group would not pay me a whit of attention. I am a housekeeper so far beneath their notice that I'm not even on par with being a flea on one of their pedigreed dogs. But the professor trusted me with a few of his secrets. I was something of a confidant. He needed someone in the house he could trust totally."

So, like Cade, she'd been playing both sides. "Did he or Mr. Harlowe tell you about me?" Karigan asked.

Mirriam snorted. "I knew you were no Goodgrave, or any relation of the professor's from the start. I knew he was sheltering you, but I had no idea why. Just another foundling he took in maybe, and you were peculiar enough that I thought you might have actually been from a madhouse."

Karigan raised an eyebrow.

"What Mr. Harlowe told me about you explained the peculiarities, though it has not been so easy an explanation to accept. Yes, I know what the brooch you are wearing means, and that you are from . . . the past."

Karigan's hand flew to her brooch. She'd forgotten it was there. It was comforting to touch its familiar contours.

"Your porridge, Miss Goodgrave," Mirriam reminded her. "It will get cold, and I will tell you no more unless you eat."

Karigan dipped her spoon into the porridge, trying to keep as still as possible to avoid upsetting her stomach even more. She did not know why Mirriam continued to call her Miss Goodgrave when she knew it to be incorrect, but perhaps it was difficult to change old habits.

Mirriam told her how Inspectors had raided the professor's house after Arhys had gone to them.

"Poor old Grott," she said. "You and the professor had already disappeared into the mill, and he would not permit the Inspectors in without the professor's leave. They took him outside and beat him. Beat him horribly. He was an old man, but they had to punish him for standing up to them."

"Is he—?"

Mirriam looked weary and haunted. "They just let him die there in the yard. They would not let us help him."

Karigan set her bowl aside. She hadn't eaten but a few spoonfuls. How could she eat while Mirriam told her such dreadful things? Mirriam did not scold her or stop telling her story. She related how the Inspectors started searching the house, tearing it apart, giving special attention to the library and questioning the staff.

"They took Lorine away."

"Lorine? Why?" Karigan instantly feared for the former slave. What terrible interrogations might the Inspectors put her through?

"They informed us they planned to send Arhys to Goss-ham," Mirriam replied. "We—Mr. Harlowe and I—don't know why, except that it is possible they somehow learned of her lineage. If that is the case, we don't know how. At any rate, they took Lorine to be her governess, someone familiar to care for her and *handle* her. No doubt those Inspectors found Arhys to be, shall we say, *trying.*" At this last she emitted a dark chuckle then added, "They were about to question me when the fire started."

Fire. Karigan racked her brain, trying to remember something about fire. Floating in it. The images were dreamlike, vague. Perhaps they really were from a dream.

"The Inspectors became very distracted and most left," Mirriam said. "I used that distraction to escape."

"Escape?"

"To a safe place, naturally. And this is where your story, and Mr. Harlowe's, and the professor's, come in." Mirriam appeared to know that part of it from Cade, who had found Karigan already unconscious on the mill floor just after the professor had drugged her. "They'd begun to argue," Mirriam said. "Argue about you and what the professor had done, but they were interrupted by another team of Inspectors trying to break in to the mill."

She described how the professor had led Cade to a secret escape route out through the tailrace tunnel. "Mr. Harlowe carried you all the way."

The heat stoked to furnace proportions in Karigan. He'd carried her? All the way? She remembered something of tunnels but nothing of being carried.

"There was a boat stashed at the outlet," Mirriam continued, explaining how they'd been washed into the river when the mill exploded.

"The mill exploded?" Karigan said. "How?"

"The professor, the fool of a man, must have decided his artifacts were too precious to come into the hands of the emperor, so he chose to destroy them first. He lit the mill on fire, and black powder finished it off."

Karigan gaped at Mirriam, unable to believe the professor would do such a thing to the old objects he so loved. "Where is he? The professor? Do the Inspectors have him?" If they did, it would be only a matter of time before they forced him to spill his secrets.

"Oh, dear girl." Mirriam reached for Karigan's hands. "The old fool died in the fire."

"*Gods.*" Karigan reeled, and it wasn't just the result of what the morphia had done to her. Her hands shook, and Mirriam squeezed them.

"Yes, it is a shock."

Of course the professor died in the fire, Karigan thought. He would not have burned his artifacts and then gone on himself. They'd given him meaning, a touchstone to the past. He'd been their guardian, and he had failed.

"Gods," she murmured again.

"He never understood," Mirriam mused, "that we did not need the past for us to create a new, better future. He got lost in the history, I think."

Karigan saw him clearly in her mind, the professor with his wolfish features, wearing his dapper tweed. She remembered him showing her his artifacts, the pride with which he regarded them. She remembered him inundating her with questions about what various objects were for, what they did. He had not really been her uncle, and he'd betrayed her in the end, but she'd grown very fond of him almost as if he really were her uncle. A sometimes distant, mercurial uncle, but he'd protected, sheltered her, even trusted her with many of his secrets. It was hard to balance that with the man who had tried to force her to stay in Mill City against her will. Except . . .

He had redeemed himself, really, by allowing Cade to carry her out so she might survive and try to reach her home. The professor must have known she would try.

But by then, it was, by his own measure, all over.

She tried not to think of what might have become of her if the Inspectors had not come for him, if there'd been no fire. Would she still be his captive? She did not wish to remember him that way.

"Miss Goodgrave?" Mirriam asked in a surprisingly gentle voice.

Karigan sniffed and rubbed away tears. The morphia hadn't cut the pain of his loss.

"Do not grieve overmuch," Mirriam said. "He chose his path, and he took several Inspectors and Enforcers with him in the conflagration. They will not be so easy to replace."

Karigan only half heard, through the combined haze of grief and morphia, Mirriam finish the tale of how Cade had brought her down the river in a rowboat and finally to Jax's place. Her thinking grew ever more cloudy, and when she started to slide away into blissful nothingness, Mirriam shook her.

"Not now. We must ready you for Mr. Harlowe's return."

"Where is he?"

"Preparing to do what the professor never could."

MILL NUMBER FIVE

 ade and Jax entered the silent mill lugging tool boxes, both of them disguised in nondescript work clothes. It was, at least, a disguise for Cade, if not so much for Jax, who was a carpenter. It was odd seeing the two hundred looms still and silent, the metallic exoskeletons of machines in their perfect rows, all threaded, with finished cloth wound around the rollers. No belts and pulleys whirred in endless cycles, no turbine churned in the depths beneath the mill, no slaves tended the machines.

At the far end of the mill floor, however, an argument between two men erupted in the silence. One man, the mill owner, wore a fine-tailored suit, the other, Inspector red. Cade and Jax did not approach, but kept a respectful distance. There was no need to get any closer to an Inspector than was necessary.

"I will not release the rest of my slaves to that excavation," Mr. Greeling, the mill owner shouted. "Three of the mills in this one complex alone are shut down due to Silk's project, and the Water Power Authority is threatening to cut me off altogether if I'm not at full capacity. This is costing hundreds of thousands in losses, do you understand?"

"I'm sorry, Mr. Greeling, but you must release the slaves to us tomorrow, by imperial order." With that, the Inspector turned on his heel and left the mill owner fuming.

Cade and Jax glanced at one another, then walked down between rows of looms. Mr. Greeling turned on them at their approach.

"Yes? What do you want?"

Cade halted in front of him and removed his cap. Recognition flickered on Mr. Greeling's face, and he glanced anxiously around to ensure the Inspector was well gone.

"What do you think you are doing here?" he hissed. "How dare you endanger me like this? And who is this—this other man with you?" Mr. Greeling glared at Jax as if he were the dregs of the Dregs, dragged out of some gutter on the street.

"He is one of us," Cade replied.

"I hardly think so."

"Told you," Jax muttered. "He's just like the rest. Let's go."

"Hold on," Cade said. "Mr. Greeling, we come to you in common purpose. The drilling in the Old City has got to stop. It is time for the empire to see true opposition. We just ask for your help in—"

"What? You want me to help set off little explosives so the Inspectors can arrest everyone in sight?"

Explosions could be useful, Cade thought, but he'd come seeking Mr. Greeling's cooperation in the releasing of slaves. The mill owner, however, appeared to be too worked up to hear his plan.

Mr. Greeling jabbed his finger at Cade. "Your professor talked like that and see what happened to him? And thanks to him, the Inspectors are investigating everyone who associated with him, even the Preferred. The old idiot got himself killed and has now drawn the attention of the empire on me and the others."

"He was no idiot," Cade said quietly, his fingers balling into a fist, which he kept safely at his side. "He envisioned a better life for everyone."

"Oh, yes. He even brought rubbish off the street and into his home so he could play at being the generous father figure, did he not, Mr. Harlowe?"

Cade's fist quivered.

"Made him feel good to do it, as if he were defying the empire. That's why he did it, Harlowe, that's why he took in rubbish like you off the street. Not to help *you,* not to care about *you.* He did it to defy the empire."

With that, the anger bled out of Cade. He relaxed his fingers, opened his hand. "I know."

His words seemed to deflate Mr. Greeling.

"I know," Cade repeated, "and then the fire—the first fire—changed him. But yes, he and his vision are gone. It does not mean his work is done."

"Well, I'm done," Mr. Greeling spat. "I've had enough trouble thanks to your professor and his damned opposition. In fact, I should just call that Inspector back in here to arrest you."

Jax looked fearful, but Cade just shook his head. "You won't do that, of course, since I can tell the Inspectors all about your participation in the opposition and how you supplied the black powder for the little adventure in the Old City. At this point, I have little to lose. But you, Mr. Greeling, have much. What? Four mill complexes, several warehouses, a fine manse, a wife and three children, and of course the mistress you keep down on Calder Avenue."

Mr. Greeling's face turned very red. "How—" He stopped himself. Just glared at Cade with a murderous expression.

"So," Cade said, "I trust you'll keep your mouth shut, or word will get out about your own anti-empire activities. And probably, your wife will hear about your mistress. If that is not enough to keep you quiet, during the deeps of some night, while you sleep in that tower room of yours, associates of my friend here will find you and cut your throat."

"Get out!" Mr. Greeling cried. "Get out!"

Cade shrugged, and he and Jax turned back between the rows of looms. Cade did not hurry his stride though he could feel Mr. Greeling's glare burning into his back.

"Bet that bastard never had anyone talk to him like that before," Jax said.

Cade shrugged. "I am too tired to waste energy on being civil to someone who cannot conduct a simple, courteous conversation."

Jax howled with laughter. Cade smiled.

"Those Preferreds deserve to be brought down a peg," Jax said. "Too complacent, being favored by the empire. And I told you he'd be like the rest. None of them who were part of the professor's group want anything to do with scum like us. Now that the niceties of parties and concerts are over, they just want to go back to making money and lording over the rest of us."

"We are not done here yet," Cade replied, as they started down the stairwell.

He felt very odd, suddenly being the one who decided what was to be done. His dear professor was dead, and now he was wanted by the Inspectors. He was also now, officially, a Weapon. His life had changed dramatically in the last forty-eight hours. No longer could he stand in the professor's shadow and wait for someone else's decisions to be handed down. It was as if he'd been set free, freed to do what needed to be done. To do what should have been done a long time ago.

Cade and Jax crossed the mill complex's courtyard to mill number five. He had someone to see. They got by the guard at the entrance on the pretense they were there to re-hang a door.

"Foreman's waiting for ya on the fourth floor," the guard said.

They climbed up the stair tower, their footfalls drowned out by the clamor of machines in full motion, spinning thread and weaving cloth. Bobbin boys and girls ran past them, up and down the stairs in their bare feet, their arms loaded with either freshly threaded bobbins if they were going up, or empty bobbins if they were going down. They were not chained to machines, but their work was grueling. The children appeared to take no notice of Cade and Jax, their pinched faces expressionless as they hurried to fulfill their tasks and avoid a beating.

Cade scowled as he climbed, helping a girl who tripped reclaim a couple of bobbins she had dropped. There were two brands marking her cheek. She trembled, he presumed in fear, that her delay would incite an overseer to use his whip on her. She did not say a word to him when he handed her one of the bobbins. She simply scrambled up the stairs at an accelerated pace.

Karigan was right, Cade thought. The slaves had more to fight for than anyone. And that was what had brought him to mill number five of the Greeling Textile Company. When the two of them reached the landing on the fourth floor, Cade braced himself before opening the door. When finally he pulled it open, the cacophony almost pushed him back out. In contrast to the silent mill where they'd spoken to Mr. Greeling, mill number five was fully active, shafts and gears and pulleys spinning at full tilt, leather belts singing as they transferred power to the looms.

The greatest clamor came from the looms themselves, with metal tipped shuttles being hammered back and forth, unspooling weft between warp threads, their heddles slamming up and down in alternating patterns. The shuttle moved so fast it was difficult for the eye to follow.

Through the haze of cotton fibers drifting in the light that streamed through the windows, slaves tended their looms. Male and female, young and old, their skin color revealed they'd come from all corners of the empire. Overseers, five of them, moved up and down the aisles of looms. They carried whips short enough not to get entangled in the intricate belt and pulley systems, but of a length vicious enough to inflict real pain. Blood seeped through the shirt of one nearby worker.

Across the room stood the foreman. He waved at Cade and Jax indicating they should join him. They stepped onto the mill floor, the force of the machines making it quake beneath their feet, and walked carefully down the aisle between looms to avoid brushing against any of them. One heard of horrific injuries the machines caused. Cade thought of poor Lorine who'd been partially scalped when her hair got caught in the belting. She hadn't told him why she wore a headscarf all the time, but the professor had.

The foreman was known to Cade, was one of their own, a man who witnessed cruelty inflicted on slaves every day. He awaited them at the door at the opposite end of the mill floor. Even shouting, it was almost impossible to hear over the racket of machinery, so he pointed at the door. Cade and Jax set down their tool boxes, and Jax began to inspect the door and its hinges while Cade carried on a surreptitious "conversation" with the foreman using hand gestures, just as the

slaves did among themselves when overseers were not looking.

The foreman nodded at the nearest loom. It was tended by
a tall man with skin as deeply dark brown as kauv, his hair
graying, his face full of dignified lines. A Tallitrean.

The foreman leaned over and shouted directly into Cade's
ear, "The General!"

Cade nodded. The Tallitrean gave them the barest of
glances to indicate he knew what they were about.

To keep up appearances, Cade helped Jax remove the pins
from the door's hinges and went about the business of re-
hanging it. In between acting as helper, Cade continued his
conversation of hand gestures with the foreman in such a way
that The General could see.

Once the door was rehung, and Jax finished by oiling the
hinges, Cade shouted in the foreman's ear, "Give us twenty-
four hours!"

The foreman made the sign that he understood, then gestured like he was twisting a key in a lock. Cade glanced at The
General and saw the faintest of smiles on the man's lips. Cade
and Jax collected their tools and departed.

Even after they were halfway across the complex courtyard, the machine noise still hammered in Cade's head, the
throb of it only slowly fading.

"We got anyone else to see today?" Jax asked.

Cade shook his head. They'd gone to all the mills he'd
planned on visiting, seeking out members of the professor's
opposition as well as those in their own rebel group. As one,
those in the professor's opposition had refused help, just like
Mr. Greeling. The rebels, however, were eager. Jax, Thadd,
and Jonny had spent a good part of the previous night spreading the word to their people.

Whether their plans heralded a rebellion or simply a diversion, Cade could not say for sure. Hopefully, it was a rebellion that provided the added benefit of a diversion. He did
not wish for anyone to meet with violence or die for the decisions he had made, but he was not naïve.

"How'd you know that hand talk?" Jax asked, waving his
hand through the air to mimic what he'd seen.

"I tutored one of the professor's servants who had been a mill slave," Cade replied. "Lorine. She taught me the basics. It varies a bit from mill to mill, like an accent, but we seemed to understand one another."

"Useful," Jax said.

"I learned it because it seemed interesting at the time," Cade replied. "I never expected it would prove useful. At least, not this much."

After they turned down Canal Street, they were stopped by Inspectors more than once, demanding to know their business and to see their papers. The Inspectors were more numerous and officious than usual, after the mill fire. Cade, of course, had had a false set of papers forged years ago, in case he was exposed or the professor found out.

As they continued on their way, Cade tried not to look at the smoldering ruin across the canal, all that remained of the last Josston mill. The stench of smoke laid low on the ground here. The professor's pyre. No artifacts that were not thick metal could have survived the ferocity of the flames or the explosions. Cade hastened his pace, and Jax hurried after him.

When they reached Jax's house, they found Mirriam putting on water for tea, and Karigan curled up on the bed asleep, but this time attired in her Tam Ryder outfit, which had been retrieved from Professor Josston's stable by Luke.

"So we are putting our faith in this one who always sleeps?" Jax said, and not for the first time. "Some heroic legend *she* is."

"Not her fault," Cade replied.

"No, it is not," Mirriam agreed. "If what you told me about the syringe is correct, the morphia should have laid her out cold for a solid three days, but perhaps she didn't get as much as you thought, or it lost some of its efficacy over time. Miraculously, I got her to stay awake and coherent long enough to tell her what's happened and help her change clothes, but I'm afraid the news about the professor took it right out of her again."

"Are you still planning to leave this afternoon?" Jax asked Cade. "With your sleepy girl, there?"

Cade nodded. "Just as soon as Luke arrives."

Jax shook his head and shuffled to the little kitchen area, reaching for a jar of tea on a shelf. "So, it's all going to happen. At least our end of it."

For better or worse, Cade thought. *For better or worse.*

MILL CITY FAREWELL

Karigan wished people would leave her be and stop patting her face and shaking her. She flung her hand out blindly, hit someone, and was rewarded with an, "Ow!"

She cracked her eyes open, and there was Cade, all three of him, standing over her and rubbing his face. Damnation. She was back to seeing three of everything. "Sorry," she mumbled, and started to drift off again.

"Oh, no you don't," Cade said.

He shook her again and made her sit up. She simply melted back into the mattress.

"Karigan."

His sharp voice jabbed at her. He cradled her face in his hands and forced her to look up at him. *Hims.* "Do you remember what Mirriam told you today?"

Somewhere over Cade's shoulder she perceived the housekeeper standing nearby. Yes. She had spoken with Mirriam—strange stories of tunnels and fire and the river. "I think it was a dream," she murmured.

"No," Cade said. "It was not."

"None of it?" There had been something very sad Mirriam had told her. Karigan hated how sluggish her brain had become. *Must wake up.* But she was stuck in this perpetual fog.

"None of it," Cade replied firmly.

The professor had died, she remembered, and she let out a little cry. "He's gone, isn't he."

"Yes," Cade replied. "And now we must leave."

"Leave?"

"We are going to the Capital so you may rescue the Eletian, and I, Arhys."

"Lhean."

"Yes. We must get you to the wagon. We will help you."

Karigan nodded, which made the room jerk up and down in nauseating waves. She swallowed down the sickness rising in her throat, closed her eyes, and wiped her clammy forehead. "My things?" she asked.

"Your satchel is in a secret compartment in the wagon, along with the bonewood."

"Brooch?"

Cade opened the front of her jacket and guided her hand to where the brooch was pinned on her shirt.

"Your moon crystal is in your pocket."

Touching the brooch centered her. "Good."

Cade helped her rise, and Mirriam supported her on her other side. Jax was there, too, and he frowned at her with a sour expression, made even more sour by seeing him in triplicate. There was another man in the little house with them. He was dressed in a good suit with one of those brimmed bowl hats cocked on his head. A pair of gold specs shone on his face. She gawped at him.

"I don't think she knows me," the man said in a cultured voice she thought she recognized. Different, but . . .

"Luke?" she asked quietly.

He laughed. "Yes, but just as you are to be Tam Ryder, I am now Stanton Mayforte, maker of fine wine. You and Cade are my servants."

It was not easy to make all that work in her muddled mind. "Wine? Making . . . ?"

"As you regain your senses, we shall explain."

They helped her outside, and there was Widow Hettle's mules and wagon, with Raven tied to the back. He whickered in greeting. The wagon was laden with casks. A space just large enough to fit Karigan was left empty in the very back. Before climbing in, she threw herself at Mirriam for an unwieldy hug.

Mirriam returned it awkwardly. "Really, Miss Goodgrave. This demonstration of affection for a mere housekeeper is a little unseemly."

Karigan just squeezed harder. When she staggered back, there were beautiful prismatic droplets glistening on Mirriam's cheeks. Thinking the tears could only be her imagination, Karigan shook her head and instantly regretted the motion, grabbing the tailgate of the wagon before she fell over. Cade placed his hands on her hips and started to lift her.

"Don't carry me! I will not be carried." She struggled wildly.

"I'm just putting you in the wagon," Cade said between gritted teeth.

Before she could protest further, she was in a nest of straw and a blanket was drawn over her, up to her chin.

"I suggest you let her sleep it off as much as is possible," she heard Mirriam say. "That is the only cure. And you should know there will be other ill effects, too, as she comes out of it."

"I suspected as much," Cade replied.

"Some hero you've got there," Jax said.

Karigan had just enough energy left to rise on her elbow and stick her tongue out at him. Then she fell back into her nest, the endless blackness reclaiming her.

Luke, in his gentlemanly attire, rode just ahead of the mules on the professor's gray gelding, Gallant. By sheer luck, Luke had been in the city visiting his family when the Inspectors raided the professor's house. The mill fire, with its explosive component and the pandemonium that followed, had drawn most of the Inspectors away, allowing the servants to disperse, including Luke's loyal stableboys who delivered Raven and Gallant to him.

Cade had known that, like Mirriam, Luke had long been entrusted with some knowledge of the professor's secrets. After all, it was Luke who drove the professor's carriage to most of those parties that were actually opportunities for clandestine meetings. If Luke had not been of like mind in regard to the empire, the professor would never have kept him in his employ. It was natural then that Cade bring Luke into his plan. Cade had intended to play the part of Stanton Mayforte himself, but the others had protested that he might be too recognizable as the professor's protégé. Besides, Luke had said, he knew something about the wine business after having worked at a winery—in the stables of the winery, yes, but, he claimed, one picked up a thing or two just being around it.

In the good suit, acquired from a member of their group who was a tailor, and with hair and sidewhiskers neatly trimmed, Luke was transformed into the business-minded vintner on his way to the Capital in an attempt to win favor with the Adherents in the emperor's inner circle, and thus elevate his position in the world. One would not guess he was, in reality, a stablehand. His disguise would be tested very soon as they headed south and out of the city.

Cade guided the mules, Ted and Ned, through the streets, behind him the Old City with Silk's excavation at its summit. He would not look back. He would not second guess the rebellion he, Jax, and the others were setting in motion. The rebellion would succeed or it would not. The only affair he had settled prior to his departure was to leave enough of his scanty savings with Widow Hettle to cover the mules and wagon. All that mattered now was helping Karigan with whatever she needed to do, and rescuing Arhys. If anyone figured out who that child was, she'd be slain.

They halted at the south gate of Mill City where Inspectors, with their ever-present mechanical companions, checked the papers and cargo of those entering and leaving the city. Many of the travelers drove freight wagons carrying textiles, or bales of cotton and wool. There were plenty of other goods as well, brought from various parts of the empire.

The Great Harbor, which served the Capital, was the major port for shipping. From there, goods could be moved via river, transportation canal, or wagon. Cade had considered using the canal, but then they'd have to interact more with the authorities to load and unload canal boats, go through locks, declare cargo, and generally face additional scrutiny. It was an unsafe option considering that the false bottom of the wagon concealed weapons and Karigan's Green Rider garb.

The average citizens of the empire were not encouraged

to travel, so there were few non-commercial travelers waiting in line, which kept things moving at the checkpoint. When it was Luke's turn, he smiled broadly at the Inspectors.

"Good afternoon, gentlemen," he said with a tip of his hat.

"Papers." The Inspector held out his hand without even an attempt at pleasantries.

"Of course." Luke produced a leather wallet from an inner pocket of his coat and tugged out the papers for Stanton Mayforte, vintner, Harley Dace, servant, and Tam Ryder, servant.

One Inspector gazed at the papers, while a second and his Enforcer approached the wagon to give it a close look. Cade slouched on the bench, hoping his bruised, unshaven face and work clothes served as a good enough disguise. He really hoped that Karigan remained asleep and quiet in the back.

"Where are you going and what is your business?" asked the first Inspector.

"My business should be quite obvious. I am a vintner, and I am taking samples to Gossham so I may become fully licensed." Luke lowered his voice confidentially. "I am seeking an audience with Webster Silk himself."

Was Cade mistaken, or had Luke assumed a very good likeness of the professor's personal charm? It was almost uncanny.

The Inspector, however, appeared unimpressed by Stanton Mayforte's aspirations. Out of the corner of his eye, Cade watched the second Inspector tapping the wine casks, each carefully branded with "Mayforte." The wine had actually come from a tavernkeeper who was one of their own, and the casks re-branded. The Enforcer rose up, extending on its legs to full height, to scan the casks with its eye.

"Where is this other servant of yours?" the first Inspector asked.

"You mean Tam?" Luke glanced over his shoulder. "He got into some of the samples today. He is sleeping it off in the back of the wagon."

"I see him," the second Inspector said. "He's back here. Dead drunk, I'd say."

"I'm not telling you your business, but he sounds like a

poor servant to me," the first Inspector told Luke. "I'm surprised you'd take one so ill-disciplined with you on so important a trip."

Luke chuckled. "Not to worry. I'll skin his hide when he wakes up, though I expect the after-effects of the wine may be its own punishment."

The Inspector actually cracked a smile.

"I don't suppose you gentlemen get any fine wine here at your posting," Luke said. "Harley, grab a cask for our friends here."

Cade shouldered a cask he'd placed by his feet just for this purpose, and climbed off the wagon. Bribes were common enough, and the Inspectors made no protest. Cade set the cask down on the road and returned to his place on the wagon. The first Inspector handed the papers back to Luke and waved them through the gate. Cade snapped the reins, and Ned and Ted came once more to life and plodded forward. When they were through the gate, Cade almost wilted in relief. They had overcome their first major obstacle. He tried not to think of those that lay ahead.

Nor did he look over his shoulder even now, to see Mill City one last time. It was no longer home, and one way or another, he would not be returning.

"Wake up, Tam Ryder," Cade said, shaking Karigan's shoulder. She slept as one dead, and it was unnerving. He shook her again. This time she mumbled something at him and pulled the blanket over her head.

They were stopped at an inn along the East-West Highway. They'd only traveled for a few hours, since they had started late in the day. Cade had already parked the wagon beside those belonging to other travelers in the secure, walled courtyard of the inn. It would be guarded through the night. If the innkeeper could not ensure the security of his guests' goods, he would lose custom fast, especially among the long-haulers who would spread word to their brethren. Even worse, the empire would expel him from his position and keep him from any other with like responsibility. The roadside inns were operated by the empire, which governed the management of each one. The empire did not like to lose money.

Cade had also stabled the mules and horses while Luke negotiated for rooms. There had been some question of exactly what they were going to do with Karigan, since servants generally shared bunkhouses with other servants. It was unlikely her disguise would pass for an entire night in a bunkhouse full of men.

Cade watched Luke step into the courtyard and saunter between wagons with his hat cocked at a jaunty angle, his stylish walking cane swinging at his side. He was certainly playing his role to the hilt.

When he reached their wagons, he peered down at Karigan. "Can't wake up our Tam?"

"Not yet. What of our arrangements?"

"Well, I have a very nicely appointed room in the inn proper—feather bed, plumbing, all the luxuries. You and Tam will retire to bunkhouse three."

"But—" Cade began.

"Not to worry. Once I informed the manager of Tam's fever, he booked the bunkhouse for just you two. He'd rather avoid allowing the contagion to spread to the servants of other guests. I gather it does not make for good advertising for guests to come down sick at one's inn. Also, he accepted an additional fee, of course, for the inconvenience."

"Additional fee? How much?"

"Not to worry, dear fellow." Luke patted Cade's shoulder. Then whispered, "We are well off. The professor kept an emergency stash of funds behind a wall board in the stable. I snuck back for it."

Cade shook his head in disbelief—not at the idea of the hidden funds, but at the fact that, to retrieve them, Luke had managed to sneak behind the backs of the Inspectors keeping watch on the house.

"Bunkhouse three," Luke reminded him. "There'll be food waiting for you. I shall see you in the morning."

Still incredulous, Cade watched after Luke, fully immersed in his role, casually strolling between wagons back toward the inn. He sighed and then turned back to the problem at hand.

"Tam, Tam Ryder." He shook Karigan once more.

She stared at him through squinted eyes. "You've only got one face and a half this time," she said.

"Is that an improvement?"

"Yes."

"Good. We are stopped for the night, and if you don't want me to carry you to our lodging, you need to—"

"No, no carrying." She pushed herself up and paused for a moment with eyes closed. She did allow him to help her off the wagon. She swayed and leaned against it.

"Your cap," Cade said. "You need to fix it."

She patted her head, turned the cap around, and stuffed her braid back beneath it. Cade grabbed a duffle and slung it over his shoulder.

"Can you walk?"

It turned out she needed assistance, so he held on to her arm as she staggered beside him. Others on the inn's grounds gave them a wide berth—Luke's story about his fevered servant must have circulated to the other guests. It was a clever ploy, really. No one would want to get too close to them and ask questions.

When they reached the bunkhouse, a pair of lamps were already lit for them, and a couple bowls of soup and a hard-crusted loaf of bread sat atop the long table. There were six bunks in the little rough-hewn building. Not luxurious by any means, but adequate.

"Are you hungry?" Cade asked.

Karigan frowned. "Are you kidding? Where's the privy?"

He steered her toward the door that led to the closetlike room, and she gained momentum as she went, as though the floor were tilted toward it.

"Do you need—?" Cade began, but she was through the door in an instant, and he heard the sound of retching.

He waited anxiously until the door opened and she stood there wiping her mouth with her sleeve. He stepped forward to help her.

"I don't need help," she said, but she was sliding to the floor.

"Don't worry. I won't carry you." And he proceeded to do

just that, placing her on the closest bunk. She seemed too tired to argue.

"Why did the professor do this to me?" she asked plaintively.

Cade poured water into a cup from a pitcher that sat on a nightstand next to the bunk. He sat beside her and tried to get her to drink. When she pushed it away, he said, "The professor drugged you because you are trouble. Now try some water before you get more sick from the lack of it. It'll help dilute the morphia." He did not know if it was true, but his reasoning persuaded her. When she finished that cup, she asked for another.

He could see in her eyes how much she disliked being in a state that required the help of others. He remembered having overheard Mirriam tell the professor what a difficult patient "Miss Goodgrave" was after Karigan had first arrived. He also remembered his first meeting with Karigan on the dark streets of Mill City when he'd helped her fight off the assailants in the alley and then brought her to the professor's house. He'd been astonished by the amount of fight in her then, and even more so after he'd learned the extent of her injuries.

Even so, it had still taken him a long time to accept what she, a mere female, was capable of. If he'd known at their first meeting, he would have been far more careful. As it was, he'd only gotten the better of her because of the chloroform he'd used to knock her out. Likewise the professor must have realized that the only way to control her was to dose her with morphia. Unfortunately, he'd used a rather large dose.

"More water?" Cade asked when she drained her second cup.

"A little."

This time he handed her the pitcher. If it was difficult for her to accept help, he'd let her try to help herself. He grimaced at how her hands shook, the water slopping over the cup. When she thrust the pitcher back at him, he was almost splashed, too. When he looked at her, though, there was some of that old fire in her eyes and less despair.

The cup clunked on the nightstand as she set it aside. Then she flung herself at him, throwing her arms around him.

"Thank you," she said. "Thank you for helping."

With her embrace clamping his arms to his sides, and her cheek pressed against his chest, he didn't quite know what to do or what to say. Here he had just decided that she was averse to help, and now she was thanking him for it? Maybe it was the morphia confusing her.

"For helping?" he asked.

She pushed away back into her pillow. "For—for not being like the professor. For helping me go after Lhean."

Then Cade understood, and he nodded to himself. That was the sort of problem for which she could accept help, because it was coming to the aid of someone else. The rest, he thought, was the same. She would not thank him for helping *her.* He wondered if the people who knew her in her own time had to often grapple with her stubborn nature.

He smiled at the thought that he might be able to ask them himself.

SILK

Ezra Stirling Silk turned up the light of the lamp beside his armchair and enlarged the image he was gazing at with a magnifying glass.

Was it his imagination, or were Miss Goodgrave's features beginning to define themselves? With his poor sight, it was difficult to say, but her head looked less transparent, and he could almost make out her features. Had something happened with the image trapping process that her face was only now quickening?

The rest of the picture remained as before, her body well defined in its dress, the backdrop, too. He gazed hard at her shoulder, but the ghostly hand resting on it seemed to have faded into almost nothing.

He turned the lamp down to lowest glow which left his sitting room dark. He removed his specs and rubbed his eyes. Night time was so much easier on them. Day time and intense light left them aching.

It was relatively quiet in the cabin of this, his private packet boat, on the Imperial Canal. He heard the chug up ahead with its pulsing steam engines and the rhythmic plash of its paddle wheels. Attached directly behind the chug was a packet boat for servants and personnel. Next in line was his packet, which housed a couple of his body servants, with a cabin set aside for the child and her governess in the forward section. In the middle, between his quarters and those of the servants, lay the kitchen and dining room.

It was an extraordinary luxury having his own private packet boat. Public boats squeezed up to a hundred ordinary citizens per load, and they were nowhere as graciously outfit-

ted with mahogany and teak and gleaming brass embellishments. Velvet drapes crumpled from ceiling to floor over
portholes, rich carpeting underfoot. The furnishings, art, and
details were as fine as any room in his house in Gossham, just
on a smaller scale.

The chug did not pull just two packets, however, but a
third, as well, a freight barge coupled to the stern of his own
boat. The barge carried his horses and carriage, luggage, the
exhibits he'd displayed at his dinner party, various pieces of
equipment, and most importantly, a circus wagon garishly
painted with lions. It contained the Eletian.

Canal travel was very easy going, and Silk did not even feel
the motion of his boat gliding through the mirror-still water.
Much more soothing than by carriage, even on the empire's
well-maintained roads. That was not to say he felt nothing, did
not sense the water beneath the boat's hull, not so very far
from his feet. Only some layers of wood and carpet separated
them. The closer they drew to Gossham, the stronger the sensation would grow, like a tingling beneath his feet. A feather
touch on his flesh. Before the accident that had injured his
eyes, he had never sensed the etherea, even in the heart of
Gossham, but ever since, he could. Even this far out. Most of
the etherea remained locked up in Gossham, less so in the
outer regions of the Capital. A small amount leaked out so he
felt it even here. He wondered if the Eletian could, too.

They had gotten nothing out of the Eletian, nothing about
how he'd come to be here, or why. He ate little of the food
they gave him and looked unwell. Silk hoped the creature
stayed alive long enough to be presented to the emperor.
He'd hated to leave his drilling project in the Old City when
it was making such good progress, but he didn't want the Eletian to die on him before he reached Gossham. He hoped the
emperor would be fully awake by the time they arrived at the
palace, but Silk had not had any updates from his father stating what stage the emperor was in.

In an effort to preserve the Eletian, he'd chosen not to use
more forceful means to make the creature speak. He needed
his gift to be as whole as possible. Plus, the most skilled tor-
turers were in Gossham, his father among them. Except for

one. After the opposition blasted the road to the drill site, the elder Silk had assigned Mr. Starling to Mill City to interrogate suspects, and it turned out to have been a wise decision, for he was on hand to contend with the city's latest excitement.

The shrill steam whistle broke into the meditative silence. They were heading under a bridge. Silk gazed at the gently arched ceiling until he heard the tell-tale thunk on the roof. Good, a messenger from Mill City. It was an easy jump from any canal bridge to a packet boat's roof. He put his specs back on and waited.

Shortly, Mr. Howser escorted the messenger down, an Inspector with his red uniform made dusty by the road. Silk did not *see* the dust, rather he smelled it, along with the stench of sweat and horse.

"Report," Silk said. He did not turn up the light.

The man recounted the casualties of the mill fire. Six Inspectors dead, four Enforcers destroyed, and of course Bryce Lowell Josston. Once Silk's very close friend and his adversary.

"You found no other remains?"

"Not so far," the Inspector replied. "It will take time to sift through the ruins. They're still smoldering."

"And you are taking care to look for . . . evidence?"

"Yes, sir. But if I may say so, the fire and explosions did a very thorough job in destroying anything useful."

Silk did not doubt it. If the professor had been storing illegally obtained artifacts and secrets, he'd find a way to destroy them totally if need be.

"So," he continued, "no sign of additional bodies so far, which means Mr. Harlowe and Miss Goodgrave may still be alive."

"I have more news on that front, sir."

Silk raised an eyebrow. "Indeed?"

As the Inspector told his tale, Silk was pleased to note Mr. Starling had been doing his job and doing it well. When the Inspector finished, Silk mulled over everything for a moment, issued instructions to both the Inspector and Mr. Howser. "Do we come to a bridge soon?" he asked.

"Gracy Bridge," Mr. Howser replied. "It's one of the ones where we've posted relays."

"Good." Silk consulted his chronosphere, its display glowing with ethereal light. "If you disembark at Gracy Bridge, Inspector, you'll be able to send my instructions back to Mill City to your commander and Mr. Starling. Remind the messengers to ride hard. They must reach the city as soon as possible."

He dismissed the men and was left once again with his ruminations. He steepled his fingers before him thinking that Cade Harlowe had made a grave error if he thought he could pick up where Bryce Lowell Josston had left off and lead Mill City in an uprising. With its network of informants and spies, the empire could not be duped so easily. It would soon be in hand.

And, oh yes, he would let Cade Harlowe and his companions come directly to him. Directly, and without hindrance. With that comforting thought, he once again picked up the odd portrait of Miss Kari Goodgrave and turned up the light. Was she one of Harlowe's companions, perhaps disguised? Or had she perished in the mill fire? He possessed no evidence either way, but his gut feeling was that she had not died.

Who was she, really? he wondered. He'd sent a request to the asylum in her home town for information on her, but even in this modern age, it still took much time to traverse the land with messages. The emperor's artificers were working on devices that would permit rapid communication that did not require the physical travel of a human being. That day could not come soon enough.

Odd how these captured images made the subjects look less alive, deadened, Silk thought. So still, trapped in a moment of time. No wonder there was such good business in death portraiture. If well staged, you could barely tell the difference between the living and a cadaver.

He tilted the portrait trying to divine new details, but none were forthcoming. He rather suspected Kari Goodgrave had never been in that asylum, and it was unlikely she was even related to Josston. This much he had suspected from the very beginning, knowing Josston's proclivities.

On impulse, he stood and took the portrait with him through the dining room, forward to the much smaller sitting room near the bow and the cabins of his servants and "guests." The child and her governess were reading to each other from one of the books borrowed from the boat's library. They looked up at his entrance.

The governess hastily veiled her face and stood. Even through the veil she could not look at him, and she nervously pressed her skirts smooth, gazing at the floor. What was her name? Morine? Lorine? He had learned she'd been a slave the professor had rescued and freed. Admirable, Silk thought, but pointless. There were always more slaves to take this one's place.

In contrast, the child, Arhys, stared openly at him. Bold, that one, a street brat the professor had also taken in, and spoiled. Silk learned quickly that it only took promises and bribes to make her behave.

"Lorine," Silk said, using a gentle tone. He knew doing so would be more effective with this nervous woman than bullying her. "Do you happen to know the person in this portrait?"

He showed it to her, and she looked hard at it, but she shook her head. "I'm sorry, but the lady's face is too faded out."

The child looked too, and her reaction was almost immediate. "I know her! That's Miss Goodgrave. I hate her." Lorine placed her hand on the child's shoulder as if to quell her outburst.

"Lorine?" Silk said. "Your young charge appears to recognize the person in this image. Are you sure you can't tell?"

"It could be Miss Goodgrave, sir, but it's just not clear enough to say."

Silk nodded. Most likely the truth. While he knew who had sat for the portrait, the child, at least, confirmed that the image was becoming more visible and it wasn't just his imagination. He had questioned the two about Miss Goodgrave, but they'd only told him what he'd already heard.

"I want a portrait of me!" Arhys declared.

"And you shall have it." *And much more,* Silk thought.

Arhys twirled and clapped. "You are much nicer than the professor!"

"Then you shall not be dismayed to hear that your professor is dead."

Lorine stumbled back raising her hand to her mouth. Arhys watched her uncertainly. Silk turned on his heel, not interested in witnessing the wailing of females that was likely to begin as soon as his words sank in.

Now that he knew the portrait was becoming more identifiable, another impulse led him to leave the comfort of the cabin for the outside world. He stepped out on deck and paused to take in the air, which was moist and heavy. A mist drifted up from the smooth water of the canal, hazing the running lights of the boats. The thrum and splish-splash of the chug were louder outside. The still water carried snippets of conversation back to him. Frogs chorused along the banks. Others on duty outside cursed as they were bitten by insects, but the biters never seemed to bother Silk.

He made his way back to the stern. The freight barge floated quietly behind, though the coupling that joined it to his packet squeaked intermittently. The circus wagon, a rectangular shadow in the night, was tied down to the barge's deck. Guards and boatmen moved about in the light of deck lamps, the mist swirling around them. Mostly he saw just pinpoints of light and silhouettes. Unlike boatmen who agilely leaped from the stern of one boat to the bow of the next, Silk required a more cautious course.

"Boatman," he called to the nearest man on watch.

"Yessir?" The fellow was little more than a boy.

"I require the bridge and a light."

The boy sprang into action, lifting the wooden arch bridge and securely setting it from the stern of the packet to the bow of the freighter. Another boatman on the freighter helped place it. Bridges were generally for the use of ladies and the elderly, but Silk felt no shame in using one himself. After all, he was a gentleman, and an important one. He did not have to prove his manliness.

He accepted a lantern as he stepped up onto the bridge. It was wide enough to make the crossing comfortable. Once on the other side, he went straight for the circus trailer and slid open a viewing panel on the near end. He focused the light of the lantern so it shone into the depths of the wagon.

The Eletian sat cross-legged on straw in the middle of the wagon, his eyes open and unblinking, his stillness uncanny. Silk did not know if it was simply a trancelike state the creature went into, or more like a torpor. He had shed most of his armor, which Silk had carefully packed away for later study. The underlayer of black cloth was stiff with the dried membrane that had clung between the armor and the Eletian's flesh. The cloth itself was tattered, looked moth-eaten. The Eletian appeared to be deteriorating day by day, his aura diminishing.

Still, he was beautiful, the aural light still radiating from him. Perhaps it was dimmer, less vibrant, but it was still ethereal, the embodiment of magic.

"Eletian," Silk said. The creature did not stir.

"Eletian!" Still nothing.

"Allow me to give it a try, sir," said one of the boatmen. Without awaiting permission, he walked down the length of the wagon and battered its wooden side with a club. The drubbing echoed up and down the canal. It was enough to rouse the dead.

"Stop," Silk ordered. He'd punish the boatman for his insubordination, but the tactic appeared to work. The Eletian's eyes focused. His aura became . . . more contained.

"Eletian," Silk said, "look at this picture. Do you know the person in it?" He held the portrait up for the Eletian to see.

The Eletian gave no hint he understood, but his gaze shifted subtly, narrowing in on the picture. Outwardly he showed no sign of recognition, but in Silk's vision, his aura pulsed, almost urgently.

"You do know her," Silk murmured. The Eletian's sight had to be extraordinarily sharp to see the image from that distance. "Who is she?"

The Eletian, of course, did not answer.

"You may be interested to know she died in a fire last night." Whether or not it was true, it had been worth saying for the effect on the Eletian was startling. His gaze dropped and his aura either faded out or turned to some dark shade that Silk could not discern. Otherwise, there was once again no real outward sign the creature had heard a word Silk said.

Silk nodded to himself and closed the panel. That would give the Eletian something to mull over. So, the Eletian knew Miss Goodgrave. Could it be that she, like the Eletian, was out of step with time? He'd known there was something special, different about her from the beginning—the uncanny glimpse he'd had of dark wings about her. When they found her, and he still felt strongly she had not perished in the fire, he would have many questions for her. Many, indeed. No wonder the professor had laid claim to her.

As the banks of the canal slipped by, it also occurred to Silk that she would make an excellent additional gift to the emperor. Silk's immortality was all but assured.

THE BELLS OF MILL CITY

Karigan snarled and batted away the dark hands of the shadow beast that reached for her. She kicked and heard a very human grunt.

"Stop!" The shadow beast sounded like Cade. Was it a deception, or . . . ?

"Wake up," he told her.

She opened crusty eyes, shivering as a layer of sweat cooled on her skin. Cade stood nearby, only a little blurry.

"You've been having nightmares," he said.

Yes, nightmares.

Wan daylight pooled in from unshuttered windows. Karigan's head pounded dully, and she felt as unrested as though she'd been fighting monsters all night.

"Too much morphia can do that," Cade said. "Give you bad dreams." She noticed he kept his distance.

"How are you doing otherwise?" he asked. "We'll be meeting Luke soon to head out."

"Don't know yet."

"Well, uh, Luke brought you an extra set of clothes from his son if you want a change."

Karigan got up and staggered around the bunkhouse, bumping into beds and chairs as she readied herself for the day. Her head felt full of a pea soup fog, and she trembled from weakness. Cade looked like he wanted to offer his help, but to his credit he did not. Still, he watched her with an uncomfortable vigilance, and it was a relief when she made it into the privy and slammed the door behind her.

Afterward, Cade convinced her to eat some porridge and

drink water before they left, but she managed only a little. When they met Luke by the wagon, he said to her, "You look terrible." Then he added in a whisper, "All the better for our ruse, eh?"

Karigan ignored him and patted Raven, then climbed up into her place on the wagon. Already her fresh change of clothes was sodden with sweat. She could not stop shaking. She closed her eyes and napped fitfully as the wagon rumbled along the road. Sometimes she awakened to see the jagged rooflines of some town, its chimneys reaching for the heavens and soiling the sky with black smoke. Now and then they passed beneath a tall statue of the emperor, Amberhill in some heroic posture gazing into the distance.

After a time, their road paralleled a canal wide enough for odd, tubby boats to travel two abreast. They were propelled by what looked like mill wheels, starboard and port, and she wondered what everyone back home would make of it all. When she told them of her adventures and all she'd seen, would they believe any of it?

Now and then she became aware of the wagon stopping and of Luke being questioned. He always answered with cheerful aplomb and a level of charm she had never known he possessed. Papers were demanded, bribes given and received. Karigan once opened her eyes to find a man in Inspector red peering down at her, the eye lens of his Enforcer whirring at her. She had to clamp down a scream. Maybe it was all a nightmare. Maybe this whole future world was some sort of dream. She must still be in Blackveil. Surely she must, but the dream kept going on and on.

Cade woke her at midday, and she was sorry because she'd finally fallen into a more restful, dreamless sleep.

"It is time for a break," Cade said, leaning against the tailgate of the wagon. Raven stood next to him and both watched her.

"Where are we?"

"Roadside tavern in Appleton."

The name meant nothing to her. They were pulled to the side of the road with a couple of other wagons, next to a clapboard house with a sign that simply said, "Tavern." Across the road, beyond a copse of trees, a canal gleamed. No boats passed by at the moment.

"Luke said he'd send out some food," Cade continued. "I think he is enjoying his role a little too well."

And no wonder, Karigan thought. His "servants" must wait outside for him while he took his time and dined in the comfort of the tavern. In the meantime, Karigan drank some water and stumbled her way to the privy, this time a simple shack that almost made her ill with the stench and flies.

The short walk back exhausted her. How was she to be of any help to Lhean, or herself for that matter, in this condition? She managed to climb up into the wagon without help, but just barely. She rubbed perspiration off her forehead.

Cade took little heed of her. He gazed toward the canal, but more into space than at anything in particular. When a bell rang a little ways back down the road toward the village, he tilted his head. The bell rang only once—the first hour of the afternoon. Cade then paced, not seeming to know what to do with himself. His agitation caused Raven to paw and side-step. Karigan spoke softly to the stallion to comfort him.

She asked Cade, "What's wrong? Raven can tell something is bothering you, and it's upsetting him."

He paused and looked at her, his face ashen. "Whatever happens in Mill City from this hour forth is my responsibility."

She stared at him. "What do you mean?"

"The rebellion has begun."

Mirriam and Jax sat in silence at the table in Jax's small cottage, taking tea. The sand in the hourglass trickled out, and Jax turned it over, starting the countdown of another hour.

They waited anxiously, straining to hear, but the city bells did not ring.

They stared at the hourglass transfixed as if willing the bells to ring, but they did not. Jax's tea cooled untouched.

Finally, Mirriam could no longer help herself. "Is your hourglass accurate?"

"Very," was Jax's gruff response.

If the bell did not ring, the slaves would not be let out of quarters to return to the mills. If the slaves were not let out, then they could not do their part. Carefully selected members of the rebel group, mill workers who had access to both slaves and keys, were to unlock the manacles. The slaves would then make a bid for freedom as they wished.

Slaves running free would force the Inspectors to run after them and meanwhile the rebels were supposed to take over key imperial holdings — Inspector stations, the city gates, the office of the city master, and the armory. The rebels would hold and defend Mill City in the face of whatever the emperor sent their way. All to buy Cade and Karigan time, all their hopes pinned on what a Green Rider out of the past could do.

A Green Rider addled by morphia, Mirriam reminded herself.

As the top half of the hourglass drained itself of sand, the two of them stared at it. Still, no bells rang. Jax did not bother to flip the glass. He slowly moved his gaze to Mirriam, eyes full of fear.

"If the bells are not ringing," he began.

"Then they have learned of our plan," Mirriam finished.

She had hardly finished speaking when the door crashed in. Inspectors swarmed the cottage, muzzles of weapons leveled at her and Jax.

They had failed.

In the dark, stifling slave quarters that belonged to the Greeling Textile Mill, the restlessness of the slaves indicated knowledge that something was amiss. They sat on rough benches, their meager midday rations long gone. It was far past time for the bell to ring that was supposed to send them back to work.

The General watched the foreman from the corner of his eye. The man paced in nervous circles near the entrance to the long, squat building. Once or twice he paused to stare at The General, then continued his pacing. The General sat hunched on his bench as if nothing unusual was going on. If the bells were being withheld, then the Inspectors had to know something was afoot. A clever tactic, that, preventing a rebellion by withholding time.

The General watched as some sort of decision registered on the foreman's face. He strode forward and pressed his hand on the bench beside The General. When he removed it, a key remained. So, he wanted to go forward with or without the bells. The General did not protest, and took the key. Meanwhile, the foreman caught the attention of the overseers so they would not observe The General unlocking his leg irons and passing on the key. The building murmur of the slaves, however, as the key was passed round, was enough to catch their attention. When they advanced with their whips poised, a dozen slaves sprang on them, beating them as only those would who have been held in chains and were mistreated and worked unto death. The overseers fell beneath the pummeling and did not rise again.

The slaves were quiet. They were not accustomed to being allowed to raise their voices, not even at the triumph of having their leg irons off. Not even when avenging themselves by beating the overseers. But The General saw the expressions on their faces, the young and the old, the light and the dark. It was an expression they had rarely known: hope.

The sudden booting open of the door and its rebounding smash into the wall, however, quickly smothered their hope and shocked them all into stillness. Inspectors poured into the building, guns drawn. They'd been so close, The General thought, but the plan had indeed failed. He guessed that the other slave quarters involved had been raided as well.

He stood, faced the Inspectors. He had this one moment of freedom, a moment of freedom to attack his enemy as he had once done on the battlefield. He picked up his leg irons, but he would never be chained again. Other slaves, sensing what he was about, did the same.

When he and the others rushed the Inspectors swinging their chains, it was into the fire and blue smoke of the guns.

THE BUTTON THIEF

 **B**efore Luke returned from the tavern and they set off again, Cade explained to Karigan in low tones how he'd hoped to create a diversion for them by causing trouble in Mill City. The crux of his plan was the freeing of as many slaves as possible. Without an orderly work force, not only would industry come to a halt, but so would Silk's drilling project in the Old City. The Inspectors would scramble to round up escaped slaves while being harried by armed rebels.

"If the rebels take the Inspector stations, armory, gates, and city master's office, they will have control of the city," he told her. Of course, it would mean troops would have to be sent out from the Capital to regain control, leaving the Capital, he hoped, less secure.

Karigan rubbed her eyes. Even with her thought processes so muddy, she could see this was not going to end well. "You expect your rebels to hold the city?"

"No. That is not their purpose. They are to hold it as long as they can. Long enough to divert troops from the Capital to make our entrance into Gossham easier."

She stared at him. "All of this so we can . . . ? You're putting all those people at risk for us?"

Cade nodded.

"Oh, Cade." She closed her eyes and slid back into her straw nest in the wagon.

"Arhys is the last heir," he said tersely, leaning over the tailgate, "and if you can find your way home, you can change everything."

Such a great burden, she thought. "What if we fail?"

"Perhaps Mill City's efforts won't have been in vain. Perhaps the uprising there will foment others throughout the empire. No matter how the Adherents try to suppress the news of the rebellion, it will get out one way or another."

And the empire would make an example of Mill City, Karigan thought. She had wanted to find a way home so she could *be home,* with the side benefit of being able to inform the king of Amberhill's treachery, and thus avert this future. It had all been very personal. But now, all those people relying on so slim a hope added a weight she was not sure she could bear.

The rest of the afternoon went by in a fog for Karigan. Luke riding ahead, Cade driving the wagon, and she in the very back bouncing along in the straw. Every now and then Raven would poke his nose over the tailgate as if to reassure himself she was still alive.

She'd gone from craving only sleep, to still being exhausted but too agitated to truly rest. If she could have more morphia, maybe she could be at peace again. She tried not to think about it. She faded in and out, waking in a cold sweat, head aching. Unbidden, there would be Raven looking at her. She raised a trembling hand to stroke his nose.

She drifted in and out of awareness, glimpsing the tall, hard buildings of towns, inhaling air that tasted like dirt and rotten eggs. She came to once when the wagon abruptly stopped.

"Papers," an authoritative voice ordered up ahead, followed by Luke's chipper tones. A checkpoint. Again, she tried not to cringe when an Inspector and Enforcer came back to look at her.

"What is wrong with you?" the Inspector demanded.

She wiped sweat from her forehead. She did not have to answer for Luke reined Gallant around and said, "Don't get too close. Tam there has a fever."

The Inspector stepped back. "You should not be transporting sick people around the empire."

"He came down with it along the way. I've been keeping him away from people." There was a pause before Luke continued, "Say, Inspector, I don't suppose you and your men get to taste very much good wine here. I wonder if you might care for a sample?"

Luke drew off the Inspector with that, but the Enforcer paused, its eye focusing an intense moment on her face until the mechanical belched a puff of steam from its stack and click-clacked away.

After they were cleared and underway once again, the haze moved back into Karigan's mind until Cade paused in the shade of trees in a stretch of countryside to rest the mules, the sun glancing off the silent canal beside them.

"—too easy," Cade was telling Luke.

"Too easy? You want them to search the wagon?" Luke countered. "Interrogate us?"

"Of course not. I just can't get over the feeling it should be harder for us to get through those checkpoints."

"Neither of us have done much traveling," Luke said. "Maybe the empire just wants us to think it's hard so everyone will stay put. Not to mention I am a very convincing wine merchant, if I say so myself." The last was said with a certain dash of pride.

"It is a sheer tragedy the scouts for the Imperial Players overlooked you."

"Gah! And waste my talent in propaganda pageants? No, this is much more the thing—the theater of life!"

"Yes, and it is well done," Cade admitted.

"Applause. Where is my applause?"

Luke's question was followed by Cade's desultory clapping. Karigan peered ahead just in time to see Luke bow with a flourish.

That evening they stopped at another inn, and in an arrangement like the previous night's, Karigan and Cade had an entire bunkhouse to themselves. Karigan dove for one of the beds and wrapped herself in a blanket, still shaking.

"You need to try to eat," Cade said. "Luke had some soup sent over." He lifted the lid on a tureen and sniffed. "Chicken. Again."

It appeared that Luke's solution to Karigan's affliction was soup at almost every meal. She had to admit that while her stomach wasn't interested in anything at all, chicken soup was the least offensive offering she could think of. She forced herself to rise and join Cade at the table. He ladled them both bowls of soup, a good thing, too, with her hands so shaky. As it was, it mostly splashed out of her spoon before she could bring it to her lips. She all but tossed the spoon down in frustration.

Cade watched her. "It will pass," he assured her. "The shakes and so forth. It means the morphia is wearing off." To his credit, he did not offer to feed her like a baby.

"Keep trying," he said quietly. "You need to keep your strength up."

"Right," she said, "because all the people in Mill City are depending on me."

"Not just you. The decision was mine, and they actually agreed to go along with it."

"Mirriam, Jax, and the others."

"Yes. Many others. If it . . . if we fail, then the responsibility is mine." He stared into his bowl of soup as if trying to scry some secret message. He chuckled.

Karigan gazed at him, startled. "What's so funny?"

"Who knew this would be my fate?" he replied. "I started out among the Dregs, stealing to get by. I never expected . . . I never expected to come by such responsibility. I never expected the professor to die, leaving me to make the decisions."

"Cade," she said, "the professor wasn't making decisions. Not the difficult ones, anyway. He was just maintaining the opposition's usual state of affairs. Keeping safe."

She was intrigued by the tiny glimpse into Cade's past. So, he'd been a street thief when he was a boy. She wanted to ask more, but a heavy oppression seemed to have settled on him.

In the course of eating her supper, she ended up with more soup on herself than in her belly, so she did her best to clean up and get ready for bed. Cade remained at the table, chin on his fist as he stared into space. That was her last vision as she drifted into an uneasy sleep: he sitting there in the golden lamp glow.

She dreamed she was on a message errand, but could not

find her way. Too many trails cut through the woods, and she
could not remember which way to go. Sometimes she rode
Condor, sometimes it was Raven, and once it was a great
black stallion with rippling muscles and the universe shining
in his eyes.

She awoke with a gasp, only to find the lamp at a very low
glow, and Cade staring out a window into the night. She rose
on her elbow, wiped perspiration from her forehead.

"You're still up."

He stiffened at the sound of her voice and turned around.
"Can't sleep."

The window was open and she heard the chirps of crickets.
Sultry air rolled in, and she was racked by chills despite the
warmth of the night.

"Are you thinking about Mill City?"

The floor creaked as Cade crossed it to sit on the bed next
to hers. "Mill City, and other things. But those are for me to
worry about. You should get back to sleep so you can get
better."

"What is the hour?"

He shrugged. "I've lost track."

She leaned back into her pillow and closed her eyes. She
did not think it would be so easy to fall back asleep. "Were
you really a thief when you were young?"

"It's true."

"How did you become a student then?"

Cade laughed quietly. "I tried stealing from the professor."

Karigan rolled over onto her side to face him, quite awake
now. "You did?"

He nodded.

"I take it he caught you."

Cade laughed again. "He did, indeed."

"Well?" she said.

"Well what?"

"How did it happen? You can't expect me to fall asleep
now with just that little morsel of information."

He stared at her, looked poised to say something, then
shook his head as if he changed his mind.

"Please?" she said in a wheedling tone. "I won't sleep till

you tell me." She could not guess what he was thinking, but his gaze became particularly intense. Then he relaxed.

"All right," he said. "You must promise me you'll try to sleep after."

"I will."

"All right." He cleared his throat, then, "Yes, I tried to steal from the professor. He was doing an excavation in the Old City, and I thought he must have been digging up great treasure. As a boy living off trash in the street, I loved to imagine the idea of buried treasure. I saw enough Dregs earn some coins on the black market for pieces of junk they scrounged in the Old City, so I imagined I could be rich. I didn't understand back then that you couldn't be rich unless the empire allowed it."

Karigan wondered what her father would make of that. In this Sacoridia, he'd never be allowed to become the success-ful merchant he was and would have been relegated to a life of fishing until the end of his days.

"So, I saw the professor set up his excavation, letting oth-ers do the digging, and I thought, why do all the work myself? I'd let them dig up the treasure, and then I'd just steal it."

"Clever," Karigan said.

"Lazy," he replied.

"So what happened? How'd he catch you?"

"I thought I was being real careful and hid out among the ruins in a place where I could watch the excavation. When they all seemed focused on what was in the hole and were paying their tent of artifacts no heed at all, I snuck into it to find treasure."

"Did you?"

"The professor considered it treasure—ceramic shards, pieces of rusted metal, broken glass—heaps of stuff that looked like the rubbish I saw on the streets every day, yet these were carefully arranged and labeled. I did see some shiny objects that looked like gold coins to me, and I scooped them up. I was about to put them in my pocket when the pro-fessor walked in. 'Dear boy,' he said, 'what do you want with those old buttons?'"

"Old buttons? Is this when you got your nickname?"

Cade nodded. "Yes. I'd tried to steal old buttons. Old brass buttons not worth much of anything to anyone but the professor, not even on the black market."

"What happened then?"

"He offered me some of his midday meal. I remember it well—cold fried chicken, an apple, and fresh bread that was not moldy or hard. It was ordinary fare to the professor, but to me, it was a feast of dreams. After that, he said that if I was interested in old buttons, he would pay me if I helped with the digging, and he'd also bring food. I went every day, of course, and our relationship developed from there, I becoming his student, and he my mentor."

Cade stretched out on his bed, lying on his back with his hands beneath his head. "The professor became the father I'd never had."

Karigan watched him, waiting for more, but soon his chest rose and fell in a slow and steady rhythm, the tension in his body relaxing. He'd fallen asleep, finally, an expression of peace on his face. She hoped his good memories of the professor lingered into his dreams.

As her own eyes started to close, it occurred to her she'd been born around two hundred years ahead of Cade. She smiled to herself thinking she didn't feel that old. Did Cade, she wondered, like "older" women?

THE MEMORY OF
HOOFBEATS

When she drifted to sleep once more, she dreamed she gazed down at Cade from atop a stone horse. He wore Weapon black, sword and pistol girded at his side. She tried to speak to him, to reach for him, but she, too, was made of stone.

Despite this and other disturbing dreams, she felt noticeably better the next day, much more herself. As she rode in the back of the wagon, she did not drift in a haze, and the shakes had ceased.

Cade informed her they were traveling along the Capital Way, but she saw little that reminded her of the old Corsa Road, as it had once been named. The farm fields and woods she had known were transformed into towns both small and large. They were all gray granite and brick red, the people as somber as those in Mill City.

Raven, in contrast, seeming to have noticed her improvement, pranced and cavorted behind the wagon. He looked like he wanted a good long run, but she wasn't ready to sit a saddle, nor did she think Luke or Cade would allow her to take Raven for a ride in this unknown region. She was, however, tiring of being an invalid and, like Raven, craved a good cross-country gallop.

The canal never strayed far from the road, and the farther south they traveled, the busier it became with the odd wheel-sided boats pulling others laden with everything from passengers to livestock. At midday they pulled up at a roadside tavern next to a set of locks. As usual, Cade and Karigan were left outside to wait while Luke swaggered his way into the tavern to dine.

"I hope he brings me something different than soup," Karigan said.

"You're hungry?"

"Yes," she said, surprised to realize it was true.

"Good, you're getting better." The relief in his voice was palpable.

While they waited, they watched a pair of young men tend the locks, raising the water level between the gates so boats could continue from one elevation of the canal to the next. Cade tensed as two of the paddle boats, positioned side by side and each towing two packets filled with armed men in gray uniforms, came into view on the rising water.

"Who are they?" Karigan asked.

"Infantry of the imperial army."

"Heading to Mill City?"

"That would be my guess."

They watched as the boats, once at the proper level, chugged up the canal. Cade paced, keeping an eye on the locks, but when the lock keepers returned to their little gatehouse to take their ease, he appeared even more anxious.

"What is it?" Karigan asked.

"There should have been more."

"More?" She tried to keep her voice low. "There were a lot of soldiers on those boats."

"Not enough for a siege," he replied.

She understood. If Mill City was not to be held under siege, it must mean his people had failed to take the city.

"They didn't have an equipment barge or anything," Cade said. "I'm thinking those troops are just for show, to help keep order in the city—to supplement the Inspector force, not to battle to regain control of it."

Cade fell into a pensive silence, but even with his dire conclusions, Karigan could think only of her growling stomach. When Luke finally returned bearing their midday meals, she could have kissed him—instead of soup, he'd brought her a meat pie. She was so hungry she dug right in and missed Cade's and Luke's low but emphatic discussion, until she heard Luke say, "You spent too much time around the professor. His paranoia has rubbed off on you. You don't even know if those soldiers were headed to Mill City."

Which would be worse, she thought, because that meant Cade's rebellion hadn't gone off at all.

"Look," Luke said, "we have no way of knowing what's going on. You know how the Inspectors can suppress the spread of news. I've been keeping my ears and eyes open at our stops, but I haven't picked up anything of interest yet."

"I can't help but worry," Cade replied.

"Yes, that is the lot of those who would lead," Luke said, "and while it is commendable, a good leader must also move forward. There is nothing we can do for our friends in Mill City, except fulfill our end of the plan. Or at least try."

Cade's shoulders sagged. "You are right."

Luke smiled and clapped him on the back. "Good man." Turning to Karigan, he asked, "How was your meat pie, young Tam?"

With some surprise, Karigan realized she had devoured the whole thing, even the burned pie crust edges. "Er, good." She'd eaten so fast she couldn't even remember tasting it.

"I'm glad to see your appetite improving. Harley, you best eat, too. We've a long haul ahead of us this afternoon."

Karigan's full belly and the warm afternoon left her drowsy, and she nodded off as the wagon gently swayed. As she drifted, she heard hoofbeats. Hoofbeats thrumming through her, making her heart hammer in rhythm. It was not the slow plod of the mules she heard but the rhythm of a messenger horse cantering. Raven whinnied, and she came to herself with a start, glancing about with bleary eyes. Oddly, she still heard the hooves. She had not been dreaming or imagining them.

In fact, they grew louder.

She sat up in time to see horse and rider pass by. The rider did not wear messenger green, but Inspector red. Still, she knew that intent look on the man's face as he cantered by, and his sure, competent seat, and she knew a horse in good enough form to run long and hard. Even in this time and place, with all she knew turned upside down, she could pick out a fellow messenger. She reached beneath her jacket and caressed her brooch, feeling more homesick than ever.

The hoofbeats ebbed as the messenger put distance between them, but she remained so stirred by his passing that by the time they reached their inn for the night, she practically jumped out of the wagon and nearly fell into a pile of manure. She saved herself by grabbing the tailgate.

Cade came around back. "Here now, what are you doing?"

Luke had already gone to the inn to secure their rooms for the night. She clamped her hands on Cade's arm.

"I need my things," she said.

"Your things?"

"The hidden things," she whispered.

He looked uneasy. "You mean your, um, walking cane?"

"No, not that. The satchel."

"I don't know if it's a good idea to—"

"Please," she said. "It's important." She did not explain it was probably only important to her.

He gazed hard at her, then nodded. "All right, after supper, when it's a little darker. Now remember, you're supposed to be sick, so no more leaping out of wagons."

She nodded, and when she realized she was still hanging onto his arm, she reluctantly let go. Luke returned with their bunk assignment and wished them a good night. Karigan wondered how much extra Luke was paying out to ensure their privacy and if they'd have enough to reach Gossham, but neither he nor Cade seemed concerned. The professor's stash in the stable must have been considerable. She shrugged and decided that since they were not worried, she wouldn't be.

"I should probably pretend to be holding you up, like the other nights," Cade told her.

She raised her eyebrows. *Pretend?* Despite her leap from the wagon, she still felt weak enough that she would not have to pretend. Yet this time, when he wrapped his arm around her to support her, and hers settled around his waist, it felt different. She was more conscious of their bodies touching, their hips bumping as they walked. She bowed her head so none could read her face, see her blush.

When they reached the bunkhouse, they stood inside, arm in arm for a lingering moment until Cade cleared his throat and pulled away from her. As though there had been no closeness, they began what had become a routine of settling in and sitting down to supper, this time with a platter of pork roast and potatoes.

Karigan was pleased once again to have solid food and made admirable inroads on her meal. She was quickly full, however.

"So, what happens when we reach Gossham?" she asked Cade. She'd been too deep in the fog of the morphia to worry about it before now.

"Luke has a letter of introduction from the city master of Mill City to be presented to Webster Silk. Forged, of course."

"Dr. Silk's father," Karigan said.

Cade nodded. "It should get us into the palace, and that is, invariably, where they are taking the Eletian. Of Arhys, I'm less certain. It depends how much Silk suspects, if anything. Perhaps he is simply amused by her."

"Amused?" Karigan couldn't imagine anyone being amused by that girl, but she made no joke of it for the lines of concern were deeply graven on Cade's face.

"Just like the professor, Silk is a collector, and he will be intrigued by anything that was once the professor's. He will want to know why the professor found her interesting enough to shelter her."

"Lorine, too," Karigan said.

"Perhaps. And you. Especially you."

"All of us. We were all collected by the professor."

"I'll be of less interest," Cade replied. "Silk already knows my story."

"That you were a button thief?"

Cade nodded and smiled. "Yes."

An uneasy silence fell between them. The very air felt charged. Did he feel it, too? She wished to shatter that silence, say something—anything at all—but she couldn't seem to put two thoughts together, and she had never been like some girls to whom inane chatter came easily. When Cade cleared his throat, she jumped.

"I was wondering," he began.

"Yes?" she asked too eagerly.

He couldn't quite look at her. "I mean, I know little of your life back . . . Well, back at your home. I know it's the circumstances. It was not appropriate for me to ask when you were Miss Goodgrave, and so much has happened since."

"What do you want to know?" She wondered if he were about to quiz her about her time like the professor once had. Did he want to know about society and customs, or religion and law? All those ordinary details that had brought life to the objects in the professor's collection.

"What I'm asking . . ." There was a slight tremble to his voice. "I mean . . ."

Now she was worried. He shouldn't have such trouble asking about what was, to him, history. Something in particular was on his mind. He looked at everything in the bunkhouse but her.

"What is it? I won't bite your head off whatever it is—I swear."

Quite suddenly he grinned. "You do? You swear?"

"I do."

He nodded. "It is not the easiest thing to ask, but here it is. Back in your home, do you have a suitor?"

"A what?" she asked faintly.

"You know, is someone waiting for you? A man who is special?"

Karigan's fork clattered on her on her plate and she sat back in her chair, gazing at him in astonishment.

"I—I want to go back with you," he said, "and I need to know the lay of the land, so to speak."

A *suitor?* A wave of warmth rolled over her. Yes, once before he had expressed a desire to accompany her back in time. She had not known if he'd spoken in whimsy, until now. And now he watched her intently, waiting for an answer.

"What about Arhys?"

"I will attempt to help her as I can, but if you—we—make it back to your time, we can change the present, and she will not need me. All will be as it should, and there will be plenty of Weapons to protect her.

"So, do you have a suitor?"

"Um . . ." She swallowed hard. It was plain he had given this some thought. "My father tried to marry me off."

Cade dismissed that with a wave of his hand. "But is there anyone special? A man in your life, one whose arms you will return to?"

She bit her bottom lip and looked away. "There is no guarantee I'll find a way home, even if we free Lhean and don't get killed in the process."

"That's not what I asked."

There was a man back in her Sacor City. Did he wait for her, or had he forgotten her already? He'd have married Estora by now if their timelines were running parallel. Day of Aeryon had come and gone—not that they called the Longest Day that here.

"Karigan," Cade said softly. He reached across the table, placed his fingers under her chin, and gently steered her gaze back toward him. "I need to know."

King Zachary might await her as a king awaits a missing messenger, but he was not hers to claim. He had his queen, and Karigan was no more than his servant. She would not return to be held in his arms. She pulled up the barriers inside because it was a loss to accept it, to know it. She allowed nothing to show outwardly. There was just the scalding pain of emptiness inside.

"No, there is no one," she told Cade.

He searched her eyes with an intense gaze, then nodded and stood a little too abruptly. "Good. I will go now."

"Go?" she asked, perplexed by his sudden change in course. "Where are you going?"

"The wagon. You wanted your things, didn't you?"

She nodded and sagged in her chair, exhausted. She'd been feeling better, but now the day was catching up with her. That's what she told herself at least. She pushed her plate aside and pillowed her head on her arms on the table. She'd known there was that something between them, but when he'd declared his intent to be a celibate Weapon, she'd set aside—or tried to, at least—any expectation that their attraction would progress. She was well practiced in this setting-aside thing, first with Alton, then with King Zachary.

Did Cade expect to forego being a Weapon, if they made it to her time? Otherwise, why ask her the "suitor" question. He didn't want to go to the past, give up all he knew, just for her, did he? Surely not. She must pose the question to him, make sure that she wouldn't have to carry that added responsibility on her shoulders, as well. It was comforting, however, to think she would not be going home alone.

The next thing she knew, Cade was shaking her awake again. She'd dozed off.

"Careful," he told her when she went to rub her eyes. He grabbed her wrist.

"What?" Upon examination, she saw that her hand was covered in mushed up potatoes and butter. Not only had she fallen asleep at the table, but her hand had ended up on her plate.

Cade set the satchel on one of the bunks, and after Karigan cleaned her hands, she wasted no time in digging into it.

"One of the guards saw me shifting the casks around and asked me what I was up to."

"What did you tell him?"

"Told him I was redistributing the weight to make it easier on the mules. I then had to listen to him complain about all his aching joints and bodily functions before he finally moved on and left me alone. Thankfully he did not offer to help."

Karigan set aside uniform pieces while Cade watched on in interest. While she sought the shard of the looking mask rolled up somewhere in her greatcoat, he examined her uniform trousers with its rent pant leg and dark, crusted stains. When she found the shard, she held it up in triumph, then perceived Cade's gaze on her as his hand hovered over the tattered trousers.

"You really are . . ." He faltered.

"What?" Karigan asked.

"A Green Rider."

Karigan raised an eyebrow. "I thought we'd already been over this."

"I know, I know." He raked his hand through his hair. "I've seen your uniform before . . . even on you, though I didn't know what it was at the time. But . . . seeing it here, now, with you, it's more real." The awe in his voice was the same as she'd heard when she'd shown him her ability with the staff, back in the old mill. He took the sleeve of her greatcoat, touching the winged horse in gold thread as if he'd never seen embroidery before.

He'd been to the tombs, had even seen her brooch, and now he was impressed by her simple uniform?

"It has truly sunk in," he said to himself, shaking his head. "Tell me, what was it like? Going into Blackveil?"

"I already told you and the professor about it."

"You gave us the story but not the details. What was it *really* like?"

Karigan sat on the bunk. "Very unpleasant." A bit of white caught her eye among the folds of her greatcoat, and she pulled out the feather of the winter owl. She twirled it before her eyes and shuddered with memory.

When Cade gave her a plaintive look, she told him about the wet and chill, the depressing murk, and how everything in the forest possessed an awareness, a hidden intelligence that seemed to watch them at all times. She told him how they lost their first companion to a flock of murderous hummingbirds like the ones Dr. Silk had exhibited at his dinner party, and how they lost their second companion to a tree root come to life like a massive tentacle. She described ruins, poisonous vegetation, and strange creatures, explaining in more detail this time much of what had passed at Castle Argenthyne, including the death of their Eletian leader, Graelalea. She stroked the feather. It had proven resilient, remained uncrushed and unbroken despite all it had been through, including being rolled up in her greatcoat and stashed in a satchel.

"And then I came here," she concluded. "Well, to Mill City." She yawned. She had told him more, but not everything, by far. How could she convey the desperation she had felt when she and a blind Yates had become separated from the rest of the group? She did not tell him of Estora's betrayal, of how the king's betrothed had sent a Coutre forester with the expedition to murder her.

No, Karigan could not believe it of Estora, but those were his instructions, why he'd been sent, and he claimed to be doing it at Estora's behest, so what was Karigan to think?

Cade, who now sat opposite her on an adjacent bunk, looked overwhelmed. "I did not know the depth of your travails. I'm sorry I asked you to relive it all."

Karigan nodded, actually relieved to have spoken of it. She had not realized how the memories had eaten at her like acid. Normally she would have reported to the captain right away upon her return to Sacor City, and that would have helped, but she'd never made it back to Sacor City. At least, not her Sacor City. She set the feather aside. *Enmorial,* Graelalea had called it, memory.

"And those shards of mirror were pieces of the looking mask?" Cade asked.

Karigan nodded, the piece glinting in the lamplight.

"Gossham will be nothing to you after all that," Cade said.

She thought he meant it as humor, but she hoped he was right. Not for the first time, however, she felt she'd rather face Blackveil than this empire.

A MOTE OF SILVER
IN HER EYE

"So why did you hold onto that one piece of broken mirror?" Cade asked.

Karigan explained to him how she'd seen images of her own time, of her friends and the king, by gazing into it.

"May I see it?" Cade asked. She passed it to him, and he looked closely at it and into it, turning it over on his hand. "I did look at these shards after your arrival, but aside from their being double-sided and curved, neither the professor nor I observed anything extraordinary about them." He handed it back to her.

"Most of the time I see nothing in it," she said, "but my own reflection."

She sat cross-legged on her bunk, and even now saw a fragment of that reflection, her own tired eyes with dark rings beneath them. Cade moved so he could gaze over her shoulder. He was near enough that she could feel the warmth of his body.

"Why did you want it tonight?" He asked. "What do you expect to see?"

His question made her feel a little guilty. She'd heard hoofbeats—the hoofbeats of an imperial messenger riding by, but nevertheless, hoofbeats. It had stirred her up inside and left her yearning for home and, well, to once more hear the Rider call and answer it. Otherwise, there was no other practical reason to seek a vision in the shard. Previous visions had done little more than connect her with home, but provided no hints about how to return or how to contend with Amberhill and his empire.

531

Belatedly she realized how much she had endangered Cade and their mission by sending him out to rifle through the secret compartment of their wagon. What if that guard had been more cautious? What if Cade had been caught? She gazed at her uniform spread out on the bed. What if someone barged in right now and saw it?

She closed her eyes, flooded with guilt, and berated herself for her selfishness. She could not even blame the morphia. "I don't know if I'll see anything," she said. "It doesn't work on demand, but I just felt a need to look."

Cade's reflection in the shard nodded gravely and he did not question her reasoning. He trusted her, she realized, now feeling doubly guilty.

She gazed into the shard, all too conscious of Cade's closeness. If a vision was revealed to her, would they both see it? A long stretch of time passed—she did not know how much—when Cade finally gave up. She felt him draw away, heard the floorboards creak as he moved about, his yawn and the cracking of joints as he stretched. A bunkbed groaned as he lay down, and the groan was soon followed by deep, regular breaths and light snoring.

Perhaps because Karigan no longer felt under the scrutiny of another, she relaxed, and the mirror shard's surface rippled like the surface of a lake. The vision came, at first in muted tones and indiscernible shapes, but then focused to reveal King Zachary astride a heavy warhorse she had not seen before, a tabard of black and silver over his armor. His helm was tucked beneath one arm, and he raised his sword high with the other. The banners of Sacoridia snapped behind him in a strong breeze. She had an impression of many soldiers before him, her perspective as if she were among them, and by the way he rode up and down the line, he appeared to be rallying his troops.

Where was this? Was he about to go into battle? Had war with Second Empire progressed so much since she'd been gone? She could not see the force with the king or how they were arrayed. She could not see the enemy. She wished she could hear what he was saying. He sat his horse with calm assurance, his face determined, so earnest, so much the man she knew. Unlike many who led, he would personally fight for his own country like the warrior kings of old. She knew this about him. He would not hide behind the ranks, but stand before them, and great fear grew in her, not just for the safety of her king, but for the man.

The image moved and blurred as if time itself passed before her eyes, and solidified once more into a confusing mass of steel clashing, blood smearing across shields and armor. In the center of it all she saw him, missing both his horse and his helm, his sword hacking, sweeping, thrusting. The elegance of the swordmaster's technique became exquisite butchery in the reality of battle. Graceful, deft, merciless.

An enemy broke through those who guarded him. Karigan emitted a strangled cry as a sword descended toward Zachary's unprotected head.

No! she cried within, unable to speak aloud. *No!* She wanted to press through the shard, be there to protect him, but she was helpless. She could not pass.

Before the sword fell, the scene clouded up and vanished.

No! Tears splattered on the surface of the mirror shard. What had happened? Her insides felt flayed apart with fear, grief. She willed the shard to show her more, to show the outcome. She had to know if Zachary lived, if he was all right. At first there was nothing, then the mirror shimmered and thrust her through images so quickly that she had only impressions streaming before her eyes, of people and places she could not identify. It was like flipping the pages of a book to get to the end.

Finally the motion ceased, but all she saw at first was vibrant color, like paints running together. The images then resolved into geometric patterns, like pieces of stained glass bound together with lead. It took her a moment to realize that was exactly what she was seeing.

Please show me that he is all right.

Her point of view pulled out so that the dome of the First Rider opened up like an umbrella above her. She could not tell how, but three figures appeared to hover in the air within the dome, silhouetted by the lights that shone behind the glass to illuminate it.

She recognized Captain Mapstone's slight form in between two men. With a quickening of her pulse, she also recognized the shape of Zachary, his broad shoulders and the posture of a warrior. *Thank the gods,* she said over and over in her mind. *Thank the gods.* He was alive. He was all right. The mirror had moved her ahead in time. Yet doubt gnawed at her. Was it truly so? Did the shard necessarily show her scenes in their correct sequence? The mirror man who had given her the looking mask had been a trickster. Was the shard playing tricks on her now? No. She must believe the sequence was correct. Zachary had to be all right. He had to have survived that battle.

Then she remembered that he must have, only to die in the final battle before Sacor City. She recalled the account in the diary of Seften, which the professor had shown her. King Zachary rode out to support his troops, only to be overcome by Amberhill's great weapon. Even remembering this, however, was a relief. She had time, time to get back to him, time to change outcomes.

Unless time was really speeding away from her.

The other man with the king and captain appeared to be gesturing at the glass. There was something familiar about him and about the way he moved, but she could not place him. Her eyes were drawn to the king, anyway. He, like the captain, gazed where the unknown man pointed. She could not see much of the king's face, his expression, only the hint of colored light shining on his hair and glancing off his cheek.

Have you forgotten me? she wondered.

Had they all resigned themselves to the fact she was never returning from Blackveil? That she was dead? But the captain had left that odd message, passed down through generations of chief caretakers in the tombs. The captain, at least, must have had some hope, some idea, that Karigan might return. If only she could pass through the mirror shard itself and be there. If only a whisper from her lips would reach their ears. Zachary's ears.

There is no one, she had told Cade. Truth or lie? Perhaps only Captain Mapstone's ability could tell her for sure. When—*if*—she reached home, she'd be tested when once again in Zachary's presence. It was too easy now with her so far away to believe one thing or another. She knew, rationally, that he and she could not be together, but what had to be did not necessarily govern how she felt deep within.

Was she being fair to Cade who had expressed his desire to travel back with her, to be with her? One thing she was glad of was that he slept and did not witness her reaction to seeing Zachary. Her feelings about the two men twisted up inside her, so she tried to do what she was getting so very good at and locked away her feelings, her uncertainties. It was the safest course. To set aside the issue, to mute her feelings, not think about it, go on with life. At the moment, that meant trying to absorb this gift, this vision of home she had been granted, and puzzling over what it was about the stained glass that was so interesting.

"What are you looking at?" she murmured. It was vexing to not be able to hear what they were discussing.

She brought the shard close to her face, but it was a mistake, for when she did so, the mirror flashed intensely into her right eye with a sharp, searing pain. She cried out and dropped the shard on the bed, and clapped her hand over her eye.

"Wha—what is it?" Cade was up immediately, came over to her.

"My eye! The shard flashed and—"

"Let me see." He carefully pried her hand away from it. "You must have gotten something in it."

She blinked against the sting, but it was quickly dissipating. Cade placed his hand against her temple to lift her eyelid, and she squirmed.

"Hold still," he commanded. She did her best as he peered into her eye.

"I don't see anything." He let her go. "How does it feel now?"

Karigan blinked rapidly, but the sting had faded. There was an afterflash, like a mote of silver in her eye. "It's all right. I'm sorry I woke you."

"What happened?"

She explained her vision, and she could tell he was still struggling with the whole idea that it was real, but he did not interrupt her. She told him about the flash of light, as he sat wearily on his bed.

"I—I don't understand how that little piece of mirror did all that," Cade said. "Magic is all but a myth, except to the Adherents and the most Preferred."

"To be honest," Karigan replied, smiling but exhausted from all the visions the shard had put her through, "I don't understand it much myself. The looking mask was an object of unknown power—the fact that I'm here proves it, and even its broken remnants retain a certain amount of power." She picked up the shard once more. It showed her no new images, but counter-reflected in her right eye, turning her iris silver. She blinked, and the illusion was gone.

All at once her reserve of energy drained away. The morphia was not entirely done with her yet, and her exertions left her shaking. She lay down, right across her Rider uniform, and slid quickly into a deep slumber, never knowing that Cade carefully pried the mirror shard from her fingers and placed it on the table next to her bed, and covered her with a blanket.

"Good night, Green Rider," he whispered, and he kissed her forehead.

In the present: Captain Mapstone

"So as you can see," Master Goodgrave explained, pointing at the glass, "we have cleaned the entire panel, and it has clarified some of the details with remarkable results."

It was, Laren thought, astonishing to be so high up above the floor of the records room on the scaffolding of the glass craftsmen, virtually surrounded by the intense colors of the stained glass dome. Lit from behind by lanterns, it was breathtaking, really, the subtle shades and details that had come to life with cleaning. She wondered what it had been like, before the dome had been built over, when bright sunlight shone through the glass. She could only imagine that it was brilliant, and the clouds and changes of weather only lent drama and movement to the scenes.

By Zachary's stillness, she could sense that he, too, was overwhelmed by this new view of the dome.

Master Goodgrave and his helpers had only just finished their meticulous cleaning of the panel that depicted the triumph of the First Rider after the Long War. She saw ripples in banners and cloaks she had not noticed before, the emerald of the First Rider's eyes, and the gleam of sunlight on armor and swords. The cleaning had added depth and dimension to the scene. And there was more . . .

"We had taken these to be horsemen in the distance," Master Goodgrave was saying, "but we thought it odd they were slightly out of proportion when the rest of the scene was so masterfully crafted. As we cleaned, we realized they weren't horsemen at all."

Laren gasped when she saw what he was talking about. No, those were not men at all, nor were those horses. They were p'ehdrose, part man, part moose. The size of the moose bodies compared to horses would account for the odd proportions the glass craftsmen had perceived.

Zachary laughed softly behind her. "There you are, Captain, your mystery solved. The fourth member of the League."

She groaned. P'ehdrose? They were more myth than fact. They certainly had not been seen in modern times. If they had ever existed, they were quite extinct. Had they once existed? The legend was that the horn now in her keeping had once belonged to Lil Ambrioth, and it had been given to her by a p'ehdrose. So, why wasn't there more proof of their existence from that long ago time?

Zachary placed his hand on her shoulder. "In solving one mystery, it appears you've opened another."

"The only mystery is why I pinned my hopes on a fourth member of the League to help us when no one has ever claimed that part in history in the first place."

"Perhaps they had their reasons," Zachary replied.

"They must have died out by the end of the war."

"Perhaps, or they went into hiding when the Scourge began. Keep in mind that the Eletians had become no more than legend until just a few short years ago."

"You're not saying there could still be p'ehdrose out there, are you?"

Zachary shrugged. "There have been stranger things."

A pause in their conversation allowed Master Goodgrave to start rattling off the techniques he and his assistants had used to clean the glass. Laren did not listen, but wondered about Zachary's words. It was true, the Eletians had receded into myth until they chose to reveal themselves and become part of the world again. The Scourge had been a terrible time after the Long War, a reaction of hate toward magic after all the terrible uses Mornhavon the Black had made of it. There'd been no distinction of good users from evil. To those who wanted to suppress magic, it was all corrupt. Even the Green Riders had been forced to hide their brooches—with spells, ironically—to preserve them.

Could it be the p'ehdrose had hidden themselves to avoid persecution? Any documentation of their existence could have been destroyed during the Scourge, along with any other objects or writings that had anything to do with the p'ehdrose.

Master Goodgrave cleared his throat and was about to resume his lecture, when they were buffeted by a cry come from some far distance, a cry of pain that made Laren's brooch pulse against her chest. She staggered and grabbed a railing. A great gust swirled up from below blowing documents in a vortex. The one cry was followed by the hushed echo of ghostly voices, and Laren glimpsed ragged, transparent forms flying around them. The scaffolding swayed and groaned.

"Hold on," Zachary said.

She was already holding the railing with a deathly grip that left her knuckles white, but he wrapped his arm around her as if it would be enough to protect her from the structure's collapse.

"Your Majesty?" the Weapon, Travis, called from below.

"We're all right," Zachary replied.

He could speak for himself, Laren thought, but the phantom wind had ceased and the scaffolding was already settling.

Master Goodgrave scratched his head. "Well, the scream

was new. The spirits have been quiet of late, so I certainly was not expecting such an outburst." His complexion was decidedly pasty, and beads of sweat dribbled down his cheek.

"Felt like it came across all the layers of the world." Laren shuddered as her ability whispered a faint, *True,* and her brooch punctuated it with a twinge. She did not particularly like it when her ability cast random judgments. She also did not like the implication of its confirming that the voice had come through the layers of the world.

"Voice sounded familiar." Zachary spoke so faintly, Laren was not sure she actually heard him. He looked thoughtful as he gazed off into space.

She would question him, but later. The sway of the scaffolding had made her more than a little queasy, and she wanted off as soon as possible. "I think it time we climbed down. Your Majesty?" She valiantly gestured at the ladder indicating Zachary should descend first.

"After you, Captain. I insist."

He did not have to insist, or even ask twice. She got the feeling he regarded the whole climbing of the scaffolding as a great game, like when he'd climbed trees as a boy. He appeared unfazed by the ghostly display and shifting scaffolding. As she made her way down, she overheard him instructing Master Goodgrave to inspect the structure to ensure its safety before it was used again.

When they were both on ground level, with the solid stone floor beneath their feet, Laren and the king headed for the door. Zachary glanced back over his shoulder, and she followed his gaze to see Master Goodgrave's assistants already scrambling to check the stability of the scaffolding. The dome still shone with brilliant light down into the room.

"Do not tell my wife the queen about this," he said. "She worries about me enough as it is."

"She isn't the only one," Laren muttered.

He heard her and scowled, slowing his stride as they made their way down the corridor. An almost healed scar cut down from the edge of his scalp through his eyebrow. He'd received the wound in a skirmish with Second Empire on the northern border.

"You think a king should not rally his troops in battle?" he demanded. "Why should I send them into a battle I'm not willing to fight myself?"

"There is a difference between rallying the troops and almost getting oneself killed on the front line."

"I tried leading from behind. I did not like it."

She halted.

"Captain?" He paused, and behind them Travis took up a watchful posture at a respectful distance.

She had been through this with him on more than one occasion, as had his other advisors. He knew that he put others at risk when he rode to the front line, and was a distraction to those who must not only fight, but protect him. He'd heard and understood that if they lost him, so much else would be lost. He countered, however, that so much was gained by his being present for the troops, lifting their spirits, leading by example, just as had the kings of old.

While this was all true, Laren knew there was more to it. She knew he was testing himself, proving he was whole and not afraid to face death after the assassin's arrow had almost taken his life. He needed to prove he commanded his own destiny, that no one else held that power over him.

Compelling as that was, Laren knew it was not the only reason. When it had become clear that Karigan was not returning from Blackveil, he'd decided to travel to the north to observe the troops, only to get himself caught up in the fighting. She'd heard the reports of his courage and fighting skill, and of how resounding a victory it had been.

Despite their defeat, Second Empire had to be salivating for another opportunity to face Sacoridia's king on the battlefield, to take him down. All arrows would be aimed at him. All swords would be harrowing the field of battle to reach him.

"Laren," he said, "you have that look."

"Look? What look?"

"That pensive look you get when you have something unpleasant to tell me. You might as well get on with it."

If this had not been so serious a subject, she might have been amused. "All right," she said. "Karigan and the others did not go into Blackveil just so you could get your head lopped off in a minor skirmish."

He did not reply, but his eyes blazed.

"Furthermore, she would not have wanted you in harm's way." Laren could've heard a feather alight on the floor, the corridor had grown so silent. "Zachary, she is gone, but she'd want you to live on. She loved Sacoridia, and she loved you, and not just as her king."

He looked away from her then. She could not imagine the intolerable weight of the crown he wore, all that it represented.

"I do not . . ." he began then shook his head. "She is resilient. I cannot accept she is gone."

"Then," Laren said, "why try to get yourself killed off before she comes back?" Because, she told herself, as much as he could not accept that Karigan was gone, he knew deep inside that she was.

He'd rallied after the visit of Somial, the Eletian, but nothing had come of the messages she'd entrusted to Agemon in the tombs, and she didn't think anything ever would.

She sighed, watching Zachary stride down the corridor, Travis trailing after him. The only thing that would keep her king safely behind the line of skirmish was winter's onset. It would soon be upon them, and she hoped that by spring he would come to his senses.

DANCING AROUND

"I would kill for a long soak in a hot bath," Karigan said the next morning over porridge. She had undone her braid for the first time in days and spent a good amount of time trying to work a comb through her hair, only to have to rebraid it again so it would fit neatly beneath Tam Ryder's cap. She had caught Cade sneaking glances at her as she worked on it. He'd got that look on his face, the intense one.

"I'm not sure a scruffy servant boy like Tam Ryder is supposed to be the bathing type," Cade replied.

"Hmph. Harley Dace could stand a good washing, too. And a shave."

Cade fingered his beard growth. "Part of my disguise."

She reached across the table and stroked his chin. "Prickly. It does kind of suit you."

He opened his mouth as if to protest, then shut it. She chuckled. She was feeling much more herself. No blurred vision, no headache, no weakness, and she was fully awake. However, she still had to pretend sickness when they left the bunkhouse, she leaning against Cade, and he holding her closer than ever. He had stashed the satchel with her uniform in it in the secret compartment of the wagon soon after she woke up. She had fallen asleep right on top of it.

For the first time, Karigan felt well enough to sit up front with Cade on the bench while he drove the mules, Luke jogging ahead on Gallant, as usual. Raven signaled his disapproval of this change with whinnies. Luke rode back to check on the stallion, then urged Gallant up beside them.

"What's wrong with him?" Karigan asked.

"At a guess, I'd say he's jealous," Luke replied.

"Jealous? Of what?"

"Cade, here." Luke smiled and urged Gallant ahead.

Cade and Karigan exchanged glances, both hastily looking away.

There was no sign announcing they had entered the outer reaches of the Capital, except having to pass through yet another checkpoint. Something changed in the air, however, and Karigan realized there were no tall chimneys spewing smoke. It smelled cleaner. There were no signs of industry as there had been elsewhere. They passed through neighborhoods of tiny whitewashed houses. The grass looked greener, the trees taller and fuller, farm fields neat and filled with crops.

Ditches, irrigation ditches, she thought, angled off from the canal, reflecting clouds.

Cade, who observed her interest, said, "Workers who serve the important people of the Capital live in its outer districts. That's what I've heard, anyway."

It made sense to Karigan, after all she had learned about this world, that the elite would wish to remain segregated from the laboring classes. It did look, however, like these servants lived better than those packed into the cities and the grim little villages they'd passed through.

They rode in companionable silence. Karigan watched boats chug by on the canal and studied the foot and wagon traffic they met on the road. This had been L'Petrie Province once, but she did not recognize it—maybe some landforms in the distance looked the same, but overall it was as though the land had been remade, and she might as well have been traveling in a different country altogether. She supposed that really, she was.

She tried not to think about what had happened to her home, the G'ladheon estate. It must no longer exist, certainly not in a form she would recognize.

"You seem a little sad," Cade said.

"The Capital is basically the province I grew up in," she replied.

"Ah. Not much like you remember it then."

She shook her head. It was not, she reflected, as much a

shock as having seen the ruin of Sacor City for the first time. Between that experience and the map of the Capital she'd taken from the professor's atlas, she'd been expecting change. She was not shocked, but it was still painful.

Their travel that day was uneventful, and when they stopped for the night, the grounds of the roadside inn Luke chose were better-kept than the others they had stayed at, with trimmed hedgerows and colorful flowerbeds. When Karigan and Cade received their bunkhouse assignment from Luke, they made their way to the building where they'd be spending the night. Even the bunkhouses, where lowly servants stayed, had window boxes full of flowers, the siding looking like it had received a fresh whitewashing.

Once they stepped inside, however, they discovered the bunkhouse was not unoccupied. A man snored away on one of the beds, and two burly, tough-looking drovers sat at the table playing cards. Karigan and Cade stared. The card players stared back. A fourth man suddenly emerged from the privy, entirely unclothed and hairy enough to be mistaken for a bear. Karigan bit her lip to suppress a gasp of laughter.

Cade slowly backed her out of the bunkhouse. "There must be some mistake," he told her. "Wait here, and I'll be right back."

Karigan sat on a bench outside the bunkhouse. From the outside, it had looked so promising and pleasant, a fine respite for the two of them. What would they do now? Would they have to find another inn? She couldn't stay in the bunkhouse with those other men—she'd be found out. Even worse was imagining not being alone with Cade.

Soon, Luke, Cade, and a short man she took to be the innkeeper trooped out of the main building.

"... highly contagious," Luke was saying. "I have paid you good money to reserve the *entire* bunkhouse."

Karigan slumped in a sickly manner in an effort to corroborate Luke's words.

"Yes, Mr. Mayforte," the innkeeper said, "but it would be some trouble to remove those drovers. I know them. They are a tough lot." He paused as if thinking the matter over. "There might be another possibility."

"Yes?" Luke asked.

"A guest cottage, rather more exclusive and usually reserved for the Preferred."

"How much?" Luke asked in a resigned voice.

The innkeeper named his price in imperial terms Karigan was unfamiliar with, not having been allowed to handle currency. But from Cade's gasp, she guessed it was an exorbitant sum.

He turned to Luke. "Sir, we can try someplace else."

"Just a moment, Harley. Innkeeper, you promised me that bunkhouse, and have now gone back on your word. It is on you to make good."

The innkeeper scratched his chin, named another price, and after some haggling an agreement was reached, followed by the clinking of coins as they passed from Luke's hand to the innkeeper's. Cade was given the key to the cottage, and he lifted Karigan into his arms. With the audience present, she dared not protest. She could feel his silent laughter through his chest. Only when they reached the little cottage, without their audience, did he set her down. She poked him in the ribs, eliciting a chuckle.

Though the bunkhouse had looked nice, the cottage had a sweet demeanor, set in the midst of gardens smelling of sea roses and honeysuckle. Intricately carved gingerbread curled beneath the eaves. Inside it was light and airy. There were two beds, larger than the usual bunks, and thicker looking, with down quilts. There were even rugs on the floor and curtains pulled aside from the windows. Upon further investigation, she discovered an actual bathing room with running water. It was not as ostentatious as the one at the professor's house, but it possessed all the plumbing and mechanics with which she had become familiar, and, most importantly, an enormous tub. What had initially appeared to be bad luck with their bunkhouse, had turned into something far better. She could barely contain herself and came bouncing out into the main room.

"You *are* feeling better," Cade said.

"I shall have a hot bath tonight," she informed him.

"Good. Now you won't have to kill anyone." She must

have given him a quizzical look because he added, "Last night you said you would kill for a hot bath."

"I will if anyone gets in my way." She gave him a playful pat on his cheek.

The bath was as blissful as she could have wished. She washed away days of travel and illness, scrubbed her skin with a lavender-scented soap, and washed her hair. She settled into languor as she soaked, steam billowing up from the water, and thought about how perfect a setting this cottage was. A setting for her and Cade.

They had been dancing around each other for so long now, and it left her confused. He'd declared his celibacy as a Weapon, yet seemed to signal the opposite by expressing his desire to travel back in time with her, presumably to be with her, and asking if she had a suitor back home, so he could "know the lay of the land." In other words, he wanted to find out what competition he might have to face for her attentions.

So which was it? she wondered. He could not have it both ways. Was he celibate or not? If the latter, she could not imagine wanting to share her most intimate self with anyone else but Cade.

Well, there *was* one other, but he was so far away and so inaccessible even when within physical reach. He could not be hers. Cade could.

Except for the fact he was a Weapon. She slapped the water in aggravation. Why was she always reaching for the impossible?

Would he consider breaking his declaration of chastity to . . . to be with her? No matter what she might wish, she could not, would not, ask it of him. She respected him too much, admired the honor of all Black Shields. He would have to make the decision on his own.

She shifted in the tub, sending wavelets rippling across the surface of the water and against her skin. If, by chance, he had a change of heart, she was ready, a conclusion she'd come to only recently. After years of internalizing the teachings of her four strong-willed and conservative aunts who ensured she knew, in no uncertain terms, that an unmarried woman bedding a man was unacceptable, her expedition to Blackveil had given her occasion to reassess her beliefs. On the eve of entering the forest, lonely and realizing she might never return from her perilous mission, she had desired nothing more than the comforting touch of another. As fate would have it, she'd begun her journey without it.

In addition to her aunts espousing their morals as they raised her, she'd grown up wanting to emulate her parents, thinking it honorable to wait for that one true heart mate, only to find out her father had consorted with prostitutes. Not necessarily while he was married, but it had still dashed her illusions about his perfect love for her mother.

Could Cade be her heart mate? She did not know, but thought she'd like to find out.

As for honor? She had challenged that notion, as well. Some of her friends among the Green Riders had placed no restrictions on their personal lives, and were they any less honorable for seeking human companionship during respites in their otherwise hazardous lives? No. They were the most courageous, honorable people she knew. They were the ones to emulate, though, being particular in her attachments, she could not give so freely of herself as some of them.

Karigan was an adult now. She did not have to answer to her father, her aunts, or anyone. She'd watch out for her own honor.

She soaked till she wrinkled and the water cooled. She pulled the plug and, as the water drained from the tub, she felt as though the last of the morphia whirled away with it. She was once more whole and herself and ready to take on anything life flung at her.

Wearing only one of her oversized shirts, she peered out of the bathing room. She did not see Cade anywhere, so she entered the main room, sat on her bed, and engaged in battle with the tangles in her hair.

Before she'd gotten far, the door opened, and Cade stepped across the threshold. He smiled easily. "What have you done with Tam Ryder?"

"Uh . . ." Karigan blushed, wanting to cover her legs. Accidentally she yanked on the comb. "Ow! Damnation."

Cade latched the door shut and strode over to her. "Here, let me help."

She let him take the comb from her hand, and he started working it through her hair.

"Whoever you are," he said, "you smell much nicer than Tam."

Heat flamed in Karigan's cheeks. She tried to tug the shirt farther down her legs, which only made the collar gap in front. She pressed it back into place. Had she really smelled so bad before her bath?

Cade was tender in his ministrations, and as the tangles came apart, the stroking of the comb became soothing, made the rest of her relax. If she'd been a cat, she would have started purring. He stroked her hair with his hands, then draped it all over one of her shoulders and leaned down to kiss her bare neck. Surprised, she stiffened, and he stepped back, no longer touching her.

"I'm—I'm sorry," he said. "That was forward of me."

Forward? After all their dancing around? She turned to face him. "Don't apologize. It wasn't . . . forward. It just startled me. I thought as a Weapon you wouldn't be interested in—" she gestured ineffectually at the air.

"Er, interacting with women?"

"That's one way to phrase it."

"I learned a few things talking with Joff and the others at the Heroes Portal." He looked away bashfully. "It appears I misinterpreted the codes of conduct of the Black Shields as passed down to me by the professor."

"Oh, really?" she asked, her interest piqued.

"Yes, pertaining to, um . . ."

"Interactions with women?" she provided.

He nodded. "Celibacy. It—it is not a requirement, as I had thought. However, marriage is not permitted until retirement. Abstaining is an individual choice. Some Weapons are very strict in practice, others are not."

"And what is your preference on the matter?"

His answer was to sit beside her and take her into his arms and kiss her, a long, sound kiss that left no room for misinterpretation.

For her, it was as though everything that had held them apart—propriety, immediate danger, her illness—was finally melting away. There were now no barriers between them, and Karigan, who had so assiduously set aside her feelings for others and denied her own needs so often, found that she was hungry, hungry for the touch of another, and not just anyone, but Cade.

Cade, however, was apparently still struggling between desire and propriety, for he pulled away. "I—I am not being a gentleman. It is not acceptable for me to—"

"I do not want a gentleman. I want Cade."

"But—"

She laid her fingers across his lips and smiled. The cottage darkened as dusk settled in. Neither of them moved to light a lamp. "I can't help but think," she said, lowering her hand to twine her fingers with Cade's, "that it was no mistake we met and have been brought together through time. What are the chances?"

"Fate?" he asked.

She shrugged. "Fate, destiny, the gods? Take your pick. Maybe it's pure coincidence. I do not know. What I do know is that you are here, and so am I. It seems to me that between all that has happened and all that is to come, it would be wise to make the best use of our time."

"Are you sure?" Cade asked.

"Let me show you," she replied.

STARLING

Karigan was determined to show Cade all she had set aside. *No more holding back.* She shook with suppressed excitement as she kissed him.

Cade, perhaps surprised by her ardor, responded a heart-beat behind her, but quickly adjusted, drawing her close into his arms. Her hands fell upon the muscles of his chest, and she was filled with the desire to get under his shirt.

As she attempted to do just that, amid a flurry of kissing and nervous laughter, they rolled right off the bed and hit the floor with a thunk. Barely distracted, they rose up, still kissing and touching, and entangled in Cade's suspenders. Karigan growled in frustration, wishing she had a knife on hand to cut them away, and his trousers, too. In retrospect, she guessed Cade would have been alarmed by her using a knife near that region of his body. Her persistence paid off, however, and soon his suspenders, along with his trousers, lay crumpled on the floor beside their bed. What she had once seen of him in threes while in the grip of the morphia, she discovered was just as impressive singularly.

Cade was more patient than she, opening her shirt one button at a time at a leisurely pace, kissing her exposed flesh as he went, his lips lingering. The wait was excruciating, and she wanted to tear her shirt off for him, but in the end, when it did finally fall away, the wait proved worthwhile as his mouth and hands found her breasts. She blazed within.

He paused, pulled away from her just the slightest bit, but it felt like a gulf as wide as the ocean.

"Don't stop," Karigan said.

"But . . ." He blushed. It was interesting to observe that not only his face reddened, but so did parts of his body usually concealed by his clothes. "I have never . . . I never, um . . ."

"Me either, but I'm sure we'll figure it out."

"This is your . . . first, too?"

"Yes."

"Oh! Maybe we shouldn't—"

"Are you afraid I will sully your honor?" Karigan asked, eyebrow raised.

"What? No! But you . . . Yours . . ."

"I thought we'd settled this."

"That was before I knew—"

"That I was some chaste maiden with her virtue at stake?" Karigan smiled, amused by Cade's renewed blushing and that he hadn't realized it was her first time, too. "Look, Cade, I love that you are concerned. I know it's because you care about me, but this is my life, my body. I am of age to choose what I do with both. At this moment, I choose this. With you."

"You are certain?"

She kissed him deeply enough to show him how certain she was. As her hands and mouth traversed his body on new adventures, he did not ask any more questions.

They were awkward at times, shyly hesitant, but they learned by experimentation how to give pleasure to one another, their touches quickly growing more confident. Karigan delighted in the myriad textures that were Cade, the hairs of his chest, the sleekness of long muscles. She inhaled his musky scent spiced with a bouquet of sweet hay, sawdust, and horse. His hands brushing over her skin made her shiver.

Their breaths and heartbeats quickened, his complementing hers, their warm flesh pressed together, hands clasped. As the cottage fell into the dark of full night, Karigan was finally able to reveal herself wholly. For once she did not have to be someone else, not a Green Rider, not Miss Goodgrave, nor a merchant's daughter. She came to him as herself, unmasked, and thinking only of him as she did so. She met him as he met her, open and joyful, and discovering a peace she had not known before.

In their joining, it did not matter where she was or when.

The world and its layers, with all its problems, became unimportant and vanished from thought.

They slept entwined, in the aftermath of their lovemaking, or at least Cade did, his deep breaths warm on the back of her neck. Karigan rested in a state of contentment she could not recall experiencing before. She marveled over how it felt to be enfolded by him. Their bodies fit together so very perfectly as if one had been made especially to match the other. She did not want this moment to end. If only it could be captured for all time, but that made her think of a picture made by image trapping, and it was a disturbing notion when all else had been so wonderful. She'd rather think about Cade coming home with her so every night could be this way. Except, of course, when she was away on message errands. But he'd be there when she returned. She sighed.

She felt unchanged, yet not the same, as though she'd finally crossed a threshold she'd long hovered over. Had her being with Cade this night finally made her a true adult? No. Many other situations had forced her into adulthood before now. She'd grown up abruptly, irretrievably, the first time she had killed a man. There'd been no going back after that. Even so, she could not help feeling she'd taken another long stride away from childhood. It did not sadden her. On the contrary, she felt alive and excited for the future. She hoped it was the same for Cade.

The moon glimmered through the window and across the floorboards, outlining the shapes of chairs, the footboard of their bed, and the fine hairs of Cade's arm, which was wrapped around her. There was a flutter of movement beside the bed, and at first she thought it was a speck of dust reflecting the moonlight, or the wings of a moth, but gradually a figure resolved in her vision. She took a sharp breath and quivered. Cade, who even in sleep must have been so attuned to her, murmured into her hair and held onto her more snugly.

A ghostly Yates looked down at her. His sketchbook was closed for a change and tucked beneath his arm. A forelock of hair, like filaments of moonlight, spilled across his brow. At first his expression remained impassive as always, so unlike

Yates in life, his eyes blank as though he did not see her at all. Then there was the slightest upturn to his mouth and a wink.

Now *that* was Yates.

He turned away and strode across the room on silent feet and paused by the window. He blended into the moonlight. Then stepped through the wall.

As much as Karigan did not wish to leave Cade's warmth, she disentangled herself from him, and taking a blanket from the other bed, wrapped it around herself and crossed over to the window. She peered out and saw Yates there in the inn's yard, gazing back at her. He raised his sketchbook and fanned the pages. He faded away, laughing, until there was nothing but the night. What drawings did his sketchbook contain? Perhaps she would never find out, but why would he keep appearing to her with it in his hands?

She heard the creak of floorboards behind her, and realized her absence in bed had roused Cade. He crossed over to her, and she admired how the moonlight limned the contours of his body. He glanced out the window.

"Something wrong?" he asked.

She shook her head.

He caressed her hair away from her face and gave her the whisper of a kiss, then he gathered her into his arms and carried her back to bed. She did not protest the carrying, and when once more they made love, it was with no awkwardness or hesitation, only lingering delight in the glow of the moon.

In the morning, Karigan felt weightless, that if unanchored she'd drift among the clouds. Yes, there was a certain soreness from the night's activity, but it was a minor distraction. It had not been easy for her and Cade to part and ready themselves for the day and the ordinary world beyond their little cottage. Cade was solicitous, pulling a chair out for her at breakfast, gazing at her with longing. She must look much the same. She could not help but gaze back at him. They needed few words, only fingers entwined together on the table and knees touching beneath.

Later, Karigan waited beside the wagon with the mules and Gallant while Cade fetched Raven from the stable. She tried to slouch against the wagon to look sick, but she could only guess she was radiating the complete opposite. Repeatedly she had to wipe a silly grin off her face.

When Cade returned without Raven and there was a troubled expression on his face, Karigan straightened up. "What's wrong?"

"Your horse almost took a hunk out of my arm." He showed her his ripped sleeve. Immediately she was at his side, examining him for a wound, but thankfully found none. "He smells you on me," Cade said in a low voice. "I'm sure of it. I think you should try to get him."

She nodded and, adjusting her cap, set off for the stable. Fortunately no one else was about, so she would have no audience. Raven gave a high-pitched whinny when he saw her, then lifted his nose into the air, curling back his lip to take in her scent. This was followed by a round of more whinnies, kicking at his stall, and his making a general ruckus. Karigan approached ever more cautiously.

Cade, she saw, had managed to attach a lead rope to the stallion's halter. Raven whipped it around as he tossed his head and circled.

"Calm down," she said. "You might hurt yourself."

This was answered by another ear-splitting whinny and a half-rear.

"*Stop.*"

He did not. She waited for him to settle down before she attempted to approach him again. When she opened the stall door, he lunged at her. She backed out swiftly and slammed the door shut.

"Listen," she told the stallion in low, heated tones, "you are a horse. I am not. So whatever possessive nonsense you are feeling has got to stop. It has got to stop, or I am leaving you here."

Her words were followed by another whinny and a crack at the wall from a hoof. Karigan turned her back on him. She *would* leave him behind if she had to. Their mission was too imperative. She noted silence behind her. When she started to walk away, there was another whinny, but this one was quieter, held a querying note to it.

She paused and turned. Raven stared at her over the stall door, ears attentive.

"Are you going to behave?" she asked.

His ears flicked as he received her words. He blew through his nose. She approached again, and when he did not act up, she reached in to stroke his neck.

"Go easy on Cade," she told the horse. "He's a good man and, well, I love him and you should, too." She almost choked when she realized what she'd just said. Did she truly love Cade? Some words had flowed out during their coupling, but she had thought it was just a result of being in the moment. As she stood there considering it all, she decided there was a very good chance that she in fact really did love him. It left her giddy and off balance.

Raven nuzzled her belly, seeking attention, and she gave it to him, stroking him and running a brush over his hide. She checked his hooves, and after giving him a hug around his neck, she led him from the stable.

Cade and Luke stood waiting as she entered the courtyard. Cade's face shone with relief as she led the now well-behaved stallion to the wagon and hitched him to it. Then she joined Cade up on the driver's bench. Luke, now astride Gallant, looked them over closely.

He muttered something under his breath, then said aloud, "Try not to be so obvious. Not decent for a pair of lads."

Karigan and Cade exchanged glances. Then burst out laughing. He could tell.

"Two lads in—" she started to say, reaching for Cade's hand. Before she realized what was happening, Luke's whip ripped through the space between them and slashed the back of her hand.

"Ow! Damnation!" Karigan retracted her hand and held it close. Cade stood, crackling like the manifestation of a storm.

"Sit down," Luke commanded, his voice harsh. Cade did not. "You must not even joke about it. You, Cade, as well as anyone, know why."

A tense moment passed before Cade nodded and sat. He left a large space between him and Karigan. It felt like a hundred miles. Luke grunted and reined Gallant around, and rode out of the courtyard. Cade didn't follow.

"Let me see your hand," he said.

Karigan, who had been too stunned to react, held her hand out. The flesh had been torn open and bled. It stung fiercely. Cade took a clean handkerchief from his pocket and bound it around her hand.

"Luke is right," he said quietly. "We cannot forget where we are. We cannot joke about such things."

"But—"

His voice dropped even more. "I do not know how it is in your time, but men loving one another is not tolerated here. They are publicly stoned to death."

"But that's monstrous," Karigan said, thinking of family friends back home, and of a Green Rider or two.

Cade nodded. "It's the empire." After he finished bandaging her hand, he squeezed her wrist, but that was the only affection he dared show her.

Karigan held her stinging hand protectively to her once again. What hate, she wondered, had Amberhill held for Sacoridia and its people that he'd gone to such extremes? He had never struck her as so destructive, so monstrous. She'd known him as an annoying aristocrat too full of himself and his own good looks, yes, but she'd never have guessed to what extent he'd go to attain power and keep it. There was more to him than she could ever have supposed.

Her thoughts did not linger long on Amberhill, however. It was terribly distracting to sit next to Cade like this and not be allowed to touch him. She recalled moments from their night together, and when she realized she was smiling so hard, she cleared her throat and did her best not to smile. Maybe passersby would assume the wine merchant's servant boy was simple, but she preferred not to invite speculation of any kind.

When they paused at midday, and Luke left them to dine in a roadside tavern, Cade went to the kitchen, and returned shortly with meatrolls, a pitcher of water, cups, and bandages. He tended her wounded hand, tearing away the crusted handkerchief, and washed the wound with water from the pitcher. She hissed at the sting. From his pocket, he produced a small tub of salve.

"The headwoman in the kitchen was very helpful," he said, and he slathered some of the herby smelling ointment on the back of Karigan's hand. "Luke overreacted."

"I'm not so sure," she replied.

Cade raised an eyebrow. "No?"

"We're in the Capital, Cade, and that makes everything more dangerous. He was right to correct me. Us. We can't make mistakes like that—too much is riding on our being successful."

He nodded his acceptance and tied off her bandage. "I didn't like him hurting you."

"I didn't either, and I bet he feels bad about it. We see him acting his part, but he's got a family back in Mill City that he must worry about, with the uprising and all, and who knows what it's really like when he goes into those taverns pretending to be someone he is not. It must be exhausting."

"You're right," Cade replied, and he led her to the shade beneath a maple with their meatrolls and water. "But if he ever raises a whip at you again, I will tear it out of his hands and use it on him."

The fierceness of Cade's expression made him look hawklike just then, and she did not envy anyone who got in his way.

When Luke stepped into the darkness of the tavern after the bright sunlight outside, he paused a moment to allow his eyes to adjust. The common room was very quiet, almost sleepy, with few patrons eating their meals.

A man approached and introduced himself as the tavern keeper. "You are Mr. Mayforte?"

Luke nodded.

"Ah, then you are invited to our private dining room."

Luke's spirits, already wearied by having to play this part and worrying about his family, not to mention feeling despicable after having lashed Karigan with his whip, sank to a new low. His overseer was checking up on him. He had no choice but to follow the tavern keeper into the small dining room with seating for four. Only one man, however, awaited him: an Inquisitor named Mr. Starling. The man sat there with his napkin tucked into his already straining collar as he cut into a hunk of beef.

"Ah, Mr. Mayforte," the man said. "Please join me."

Luke sat across the table from him, but did not speak, not even in greeting. A servant brought in a steaming plate of food for him and then left, closing the door to ensure privacy.

"Please, eat," said Mr. Starling. "The beef is especially fine today."

Luke did not, but the Inquisitor sawed into his own, unperturbed. He was stout with wobbly rolls of fat beneath his chin, and he wore an expensive, well-cut suit, with a spray of flowers tucked into his lapel. Sweat gleamed on his forehead as he worked on his food. Mr. Starling played the part of a buffoon so others would underestimate him. Luke knew that one should never underestimate an Inquisitor.

Starling, with his talent as a spy and interrogator, had been provided by Webster Silk for his son's use in Mill City, or so Luke was told. The elder Silk had ultimate authority over the Inquisitors. He trained many of them himself.

Luke first met Mr. Starling the morning after the mill fire. He hadn't gone into hiding and had been easily found at home. Mr. Starling greeted him by having the bodies of Luke's stable lads dumped at his feet. Then he was questioned. He closed his eyes, trembling at the memory, a trickle of sweat slithering down his own forehead. There had been no reason to kill the lads, and that was precisely the point. Mr. Starling wanted Luke to understand that if he could easily kill the lads for no particular reason, it was best to cooperate and not give him a reason to do worse.

When Mr. Starling tucked away all that was on his plate, he slurped down a glass of wine and belched. He dabbed his mouth almost daintily with his napkin. His fingers were tiny, round sausages.

"Your journey goes well?" he asked.

"Yes," Luke replied.

"Good, good. And your companions have not guessed?"

"No. They are bes—" Luke clamped his mouth shut. Starling did not need that particular piece of information.

"Besotted? Is that what you were going to say? They are besotted with one another?"

Luke did not reply. He did not have to. Starling had only managed to get it out of him a couple nights ago that Tam Ryder was not a he. There had been threats, and Starling was well-trained in the detection of lies and evasions. Luke was an ordinary stablehand. What was he compared to an Inquisitor of the empire?

"Well, well," Mr. Starling said. "That is very interesting, indeed. Could be useful. He is taking care of her in her illness, then? Yes, well, not so uncommon for a frail girl to fall in love with her caretaker, eh?"

Luke cursed himself for his slip. He'd seen the bond growing between Karigan and Cade well before their journey had begun. Allowing them to have a bunkhouse of their own each night had only encouraged them, but what choice had he?

"My master was terribly delighted by the news that your servant boy was really the girl. Very delighted. He just wants you to keep traveling as you have been. We will take care of the rest. Have you found out any new details about the girl?"

"Just what the professor told me. Miss Goodgrave has been too sick to tell me anything. Besides, I thought asking questions was your specialty."

Mr. Starling quivered, setting his jowls a-jiggle. "Yes, yes, of course it is, and I would not want an amateur to tip them off by asking questions indiscriminately."

Luke exhaled in relief. He'd managed to not reveal Karigan's true identity. Let them believe Cade was the catalyst for the rebels, and that Karigan was really the professor's frail, mad niece. This little he could do. So very little, but it was something.

"My family," Luke said. "What of my family?"

"Your son still has his other fingers, if that is what worries you. No, I do not have any new ones to show you." Mr. Starling paused thoughtfully. "Must be hard for a farrier to work without all his fingers. In any case, if you continue to cooperate, he'll keep what's left, and he and the rest of your family will remain safe. Can't say the same for the rest of your associates in Mill City, however."

Luke bowed his head. He didn't want to know the particulars. He could guess.

"That's right," Mr. Starling continued. "Justice will be meted out. All have been caught, and the feeble rebellion squashed."

Was it true? Luke wondered. Had everyone been caught?

"Carry on, Mr. Mayforte," the Inquisitor said.

Luke hesitated. "You will go easy on them—Cade and Miss Goodgrave, won't you?"

"Go easy on them?" Mr. Starling guffawed, his oversized belly heaving. "Harlowe has fomented rebellion. I can see you are fond of him, but he is a traitor to the empire. There is no way we can go *easy* on him. What a terribly funny notion."

Mr. Starling's laughter increased Luke's misery, but back in Mill City, with the corpses of his lads at his feet, he'd been given an ultimatum: if he did not deliver Cade to Dr. Silk in Gossham, his wife, his daughters, his son, would all be imprisoned, and probably worse. Luke did not care what happened to himself, but when it came to preserving Cade or his family, his family came first. He'd been made to tell Starling about the planned rebellion, but so far his betrayal had kept his family safe. Under house arrest, yes, but safe.

"What about Miss Goodgrave?"

Mr. Starling shrugged. "None of my business. Dr. Silk is interested in her, that's all I know. You are excused."

As Luke left, the Inquisitor reached across the table for his cold, uneaten meal.

A PASSING STORM

Even though Karigan had to pretend that she was a boy and there was nothing between her and Cade, she enjoyed sitting beneath the maple with him, her back against the tree trunk. He lay on the shady grass with his hands behind his head, gazing at the interwoven branches above, or perhaps daydreaming, or maybe counting leaves. Their silence was comfortable, more comfortable, actually, than it had ever been before.

The stuttered call of a white-throated sparrow rang out from a grove of evergreens across the canal. Bees droned among the summer flowers in the meadow beside the tavern. It was all very pleasant in the Capital. Those who never left it would have a difficult time comprehending grim places like Mill City. Everything was much more vibrant here, perhaps because it wasn't all paved over and built up with brick, with tall chimneys belching smoke into the sky. There was supposed to be etherea in the Capital, or Gossham, at least. Could that have anything to do with it? Karigan supposed another answer might be that the elite of the Capital did not wish to have to see, on a daily basis, the blight imposed on the lesser classes in other parts of the empire.

Luke stepped out of the doorway of the tavern. As he approached, she noticed his stride lacked some of its usual swagger. She nudged Cade with her foot.

"Luke's coming."

Cade sat up, brushing off stray bits of grass.

When Luke reached them, he said in a very low voice, "Tam needs to be sick. Do you understand? Play sick, and you'll ride in the back of the wagon as before."

Karigan wondered if Luke saw this as a more effective way of keeping people from speculating about the affection between the two "lads," but Cade, his voice very low as well, asked, "Spies?"

"We must not forget the emperor's eyes are everywhere," Luke replied.

"Is there a specific threat?"

"Only if you do not do as I say."

Cade nodded, and Karigan pretended weakness and allowed him to help her rise and make her way to the wagon. It was hard not to smile, and she was pleased by his touch, tense though it was in the wake of Luke's warning. He lifted her into her old spot in the back of the wagon, and Raven whickered his approval. He nosed her over the tailgate.

Karigan settled into the straw as the mules hauled the wagon down the drive. She looked back at the tavern, where on the front step, watching after them, stood a portly gentleman in a dark suit. Eyes of the emperor? No wonder Luke had grown tense about their behavior and appearances earlier—he knew they were likely to be watched.

The villages they passed through remained pastoral, but grew in size and population as they traveled. Each, like the towns and cities outside the Capital, had a statue of Amberhill the emperor gazing over his realm. Often he was depicted in a heroic stance, but there were variations, such as the one the wagon now rolled beneath. It showed him standing tall with his hands placed on the shoulders of a boy and a girl. To show his compassion? Or his ownership of *all* the people? In the next village, his statue held a book. Whether to show he was a scholar, or holding the laws of the empire in his hands, she did not know. The facial expression on each statue, however, looked very much the same—a distant, stern version of the Amberhill she'd once known.

Another detail she noticed as they traveled was the increasing number of irrigation canals snaking through the land. Water flowed over beds of granite blocks, well-made smaller versions of the Imperial Canal. They even meandered through villages. Small bridges allowed traffic to cross in several places. Karigan began to wonder if they were actually for irrigation at all, and if not, what were they for? Riding in the rear of the wagon, she was not able to ask Cade. She would try to remember later.

The Imperial Canal skirted around the villages, but the road always rejoined it. Canal traffic grew steadier the deeper they got into the Capital, and though she saw many Inspectors patrolling the streets with their mechanicals, there were no more checkpoints than before. She sank back into the straw and gazed at the clouds above. As the afternoon wore on, they grew thicker, tinged with gray. She could smell rain in the air. Yes, it would rain tonight, but there was something else, a briny tang mixed with it. They were nearing the coast, and Corsa. No—not Corsa, but Gossham. Her Corsa was gone.

That evening, as the first few drops of an incoming storm plunked down on their heads, they had to try a few different inns before they found one with space, much less an entire bunkhouse that Luke could reserve for the night. Karigan pretended sickness as usual, with Cade supporting her all the way. Once securely in the bunkhouse, they were immediately in one another's arms, kissing like long lost lovers separated by continents and the passing of years, instead of only by the length of a wagon and the passing of a day.

Cade pulled away.

"What is it?" Karigan asked.

"I just want to check in with Luke for a minute. I'll be right back."

Before Karigan could question him, he was gone. She decided then to make use of the bath tub with which this bunkhouse was equipped. Even after she finished, however, Cade had not returned. She paced for a while, sampling spoonfuls of the stew that had been left for them. Hers was lukewarm, and Cade's would be cold before he returned. She had too much restive energy to sit still, so she occupied herself by working through swordfighting forms. She had no sword or staff, not even a broomstick to work with, but it felt good to go through the motions anyway.

She was in the middle of Aspen Leaf when Cade finally returned. She froze.

"Don't stop," he said, closing the door quietly behind him.

She continued the series of forms she had begun, and became more than mildly distracted when he came up behind her and wrapped his arms around her, his hands resting on her belly.

"Don't stop," he murmured into her ear when she hesitated.

Thunder clapped and rain thrummed on the roof. With Cade folded around her, moving through the steps and patterns of the forms with her, the techniques of the swordmaster truly became a dance. His hands roved down her arms, along her waist and hips, and lower, till she could hardly bear it, aching with need.

Using steps all his own, he led her into a different form of the dance, the storm their orchestra.

Karigan lay contentedly in Cade's arms once again as rain still pattered on the roof. The bunkhouse interior sprang into relief with flashes of lightning, rumbles of thunder delayed by distance. Cade's thumb rubbed a scar beneath her ribs, an old sword wound given her during Prince Amilton's attempted coup of King Zachary's throne.

"What did you and Luke need to talk about?" she asked.

"Hmm?"

"Earlier. You said you had to talk to Luke."

"Oh." He shifted position, making their narrow bed creak. "Tomorrow we reach Gossham, and I wanted to go over our approach."

So soon, Karigan thought with dismay. She did not feel prepared. What would they be walking into?

"When we reach the inner city, Luke will find us accommodations and send his letter from Mill City's master ahead to Webster Silk."

"And then?"

"And then we wait for a response. Hopefully an invitation to the palace."

An invitation, she hoped, that would allow her to rescue Lhean. And wring Amberhill's neck in the process.

"We may not have more than another night together, if even that," Cade said quietly.

Karigan took the hint and, banishing all else from her mind, gave Cade her full attention.

They did not sleep after, but as rainwater dripped from the eaves of the roof in the wake of the storm, they talked into the early morning hours, Cade asking her about her life back home, and she telling him about the Green Riders, her father, and her aunts.

"Your aunts sound fearsome," he said.

Karigan chuckled. "Individually they can be intimidating. As a group, yes, fearsome is an apt description."

"Now I know where you get it from," Cade said. "You are like all four of your aunts in one."

"Hey!" She poked him in the ribs, and his laughter shook their little bed.

"They'll love you," she said. *As I do.* Or, at least, she thought they would. He wasn't the heir of a major merchant clan they'd been angling for, not even of a minor one, but once they met him, she knew they'd love him before long. In fact, she thought they'd just be relieved she'd finally found someone.

"Tell me about King Zachary," Cade said. "He must have been a very great man."

"He *is*," Karigan said, her voice trembling. She swallowed hard. It did not feel right to speak of Zachary while she lay in Cade's arms. Made her feel . . . guilty? "He's a good king. He loves his land and its people."

"But not all love him back," Cade prompted.

She bit her lip. The question came so close to—other things. "No." She had to force herself to speak. "Not Second Empire, nor those who desire no king at all, and there are those who bridle at peace and live just for war. They do not get it under King Zachary."

"The responsibility cannot be easy. Do you know him personally? You must have some contact . . ."

Karigan didn't answer immediately. She wanted to get up, pace, pour a glass of water. Anything but talk about this. But if she did not answer his innocent questions about King Zachary, what would he think? "Yes. Occasionally a Rider will receive messages directly from him, or report immediately to him following an errand, depending on the nature of the message."

Cade must have heard something in her voice, or maybe felt her tense beside him, because, much to her relief, he started asking about the Weapons.

"I really don't know too much of their ways," Karigan said. "They are secretive. They receive most of their training at a place called the Forge—it's a keep on an island that is kind of the home of the Black Shields." Then she frowned thinking that if Cade pursued being a Weapon in her time, he'd probably be sent off to the Forge to train and prove himself. How long of a separation would that be? The idea of any time apart disturbed her.

When did this happen, she wondered, that she could not imagine her life without Cade? She had done all right on her own for so long. She'd been independent.

But yes, lonely.

Cade, she did not think, was the sort of man to stifle her, to demand she give up her independent ways. He certainly would have no say over her duties as a Green Rider. It was odd to realize, however, that returning home without him was a bleak picture she did not wish to contemplate. Even if it meant the occasional separation as they pursued their individual duties.

Yes, she thought, resting her head on his shoulder, there might be periodic lapses of loneliness, but better that than not having him at all.

AWAKENING

Webster Silk, attired in a long coat of mink, stood attentively in the icy chamber, his breaths fogging the air before him. On the bier lay the emperor, his head upon a pillow, a red velvet cover drawn up to his chest. He looked like one of the kings of old upon a sarcophagus with his pale marble face. But the emperor was not dead, and was in fact on the verge of awakening after only eight years of rest. The change in routine was disturbing, and there was no telling what state the emperor would be in when he woke.

In fact, they never knew. Sometimes he was confused but affable, sometimes demanding, often violent. They kept his chamber cold so he would not burn from rage, and several slave girls, bred for comeliness, stood ready in a nearby chamber should he need to slake any thirsts upon rising, carnal or cruel.

The only other allowed into the chamber was the emperor's own Eternal Guardian, brought with him from the old days and armored in blood-red steel and leather, his face masked by a helm. Copper tubing protruded from the helm's bevor and snaked back to a breathing apparatus, a pump, and the pair of cylinders he wore on his back. It hissed and sighed as air was pumped into his lungs. In some ways, his appearance reminded Webster of a sea creature with a carapace, or a segmented insect, inhuman and dangerous. Few had seen the Guardian's true visage.

He was a tall, silent, and forbidding presence, and he carried only a longsword—no firearms. He had been made immortal by the emperor, just as Webster Silk had been, but the

Guardian had been by the emperor's side from the beginning, before Webster had even been born. As much as the Guardian watched the emperor, Webster watched the Guardian.

The awakening was imminent. Webster could tell by the subtly warmer hue in the emperor's cheeks. Webster's own body was taut in anticipation. Did the emperor's shortened sleep period mean he'd be awake an extra two years? Did it mean a permanent alteration in the cycle, or would all go back to normal after this one time? These were important things to know, for the emperor's periods of awakening sometimes turned bloody and caused turmoil across the empire.

The awakenings, of course, interfered with Webster's own workings. It was he who had shaped the empire, solidified its power. It was he who put laws and policies in place. What better way to fulfill his existence than by steering the fortunes of a great empire? It was not so easy to occupy one's time when one had all of eternity.

He rarely took credit for his successes, and few knew the true extent of his authority. He did all he did in the emperor's name, but took great pleasure in being the true strength behind the throne. His work was not a complete secret, of course. The Adherents knew.

It was a fine thing to deploy the governing power of the emperor, yet not have the responsibility of being the emperor.

The emperor's lips moved as though he tried to speak. His eyelids parted to slits and revealed the whites of his eyes. Not long now.

Eternal life had also brought Webster a stillness. Where once he would have lost patience and been annoyed with waiting, it now bothered him little. He had time. Few could afford patience the way he could, and it was just another way in which he wielded power over others.

"Mead," the emperor murmured, eyes still not quite open. "No, a good burning whisky."

If the emperor was awakening thinking of libations, it might not go so badly this time. Webster went to the door to tell the guard on duty to fetch a variety of liquors for the emperor to choose from. Sometimes the emperor would argue with himself at length over such choices.

As Webster moved back toward the emperor's bier, he felt the gaze of the Eternal Guardian follow him, burning into him. The Guardian, too, was patient. How else could he stand sentry over the emperor's body day in and day out? Over centuries?

The door guard returned with a tray of bottles and glasses, casting nervous glances toward the emperor. "You can go," Webster said, taking the tray and placing it on a table next to the emperor's bier.

"I remember a particular year of fine Rhovan wine," the emperor said in a dreamy voice. "You could almost taste the dew on the ripening grapes." He licked his lips.

Rhovanny was no more, but slaves now worked the rows of grape vines and made the wine. Webster eyed the tray and there was a bottle from the lake country, a pleasant, fruity white that usually pleased the emperor. He poured some into a glass and held it ready.

The emperor's slow awakening was usually over like the snap of fingers. This time was no different. The emperor inhaled sharply and sat straight up. "Lady Alger's diamond necklace," he announced.

"What about it, Your Eminence?"

"She was so delightful I forgot about it and left it behind on her dressing table. Could have bought back most of my estate with that one piece alone."

"Of course, Your Eminence." The emperor sometimes fancied he'd been an infamous thief at one time.

"Webster, is that you?" the emperor asked, as if only just realizing he was not alone. "What do you have there?"

"Some wine, Your Eminence. I've no doubt you are thirsty after your long sleep."

"My long sleep . . ." The emperor took the glass absently and sipped. Then he spat a mouthful to the floor and tossed the glass across the room. It shattered near the Eternal Guardian's feet. The Guardian did not flinch.

"I am sorry the wine did not please you," Webster said.

"I forget where I am," the emperor replied. "I forget how the years pass. That wine is nothing like the Rhovan. It gets worse every time. It tastes like soot."

"I am sure we've older vintages you would find more palatable."

"Don't bother." The emperor eyed the bottles, slowly sitting up and swinging his legs over the side of the bier. "Pour me some brandy."

As Webster obeyed, the emperor stretched as though he'd taken only a nap. None of them—not Webster, the Adherents, the menders, or even the emperor himself—knew why there were these long sleep intervals, except to guess that they helped preserve the emperor's body from the extreme powers it housed.

It also preserved, Webster reflected, the empire from its emperor.

He handed the emperor his drink, and this time, the first sip was met with a sigh of satisfaction.

"So, Webster, tell me what has passed in the last ten years since I fell asleep."

"It has been only eight years this time, Your Eminence."

The emperor scratched his head. "Eight years? The shadows were restless, gnawing at my dreams, their bright eyes burning into me. That's what woke me." Darkness clouded in his eyes, and Webster braced himself. "Something has changed in the fabric of the world." He stood, set his glass aside, and paced, unweakened by his lengthy sleep. "Something is out of order. Something has interfered." He sniffed the air. "I smell an old god. An old god prying into affairs where it has no business."

"But you are god," Webster said.

"I am."

Webster could not bear holding the emperor's gaze of blue-black edged with flame.

"There were other gods before I defeated all," the emperor said. "This one smells of rotting corpses, and I hear its tattered wings whispering upon the currents of the heavens."

Before the emperor's rise, the Sacoridians had worshipped seemingly hundreds of gods. This one sounded like the death god. Webster's son, Ezra, would know. Ezra was very keen on the history. To Webster, the old gods were superstitious nonsense.

The emperor paused in front of the Eternal Guardian and tapped on his breast plate. "How are you, my statue friend?"

The Guardian inclined his head in a bow, leather and steel creaking. If he spoke, Webster did not hear it. Just as the Guardian's face remained hidden, so did his thoughts. He shared few words with others.

"Do you remember the old gods?" the emperor asked.

The Guardian tilted his head non-committedly.

The emperor slapped the Guardian's breastplate in a careless, friendly way, the coal-fire gone from his eyes. "They don't make warriors like they used to. A true warrior is more lively, more drunk, more merry, more lusty." He barked a laugh.

Webster, accustomed to the emperor's abrupt mood swings, asked, "Do you wish to hear the news of the past eight years, Your Eminence?"

"Bah. I guess not. It can wait. I've got appetites, my lad." He grabbed a bottle off the tray and drank from it. Amber liquid dribbled down his chin and stained his silk sleeping shirt. After several gulps, he wiped his mouth with his sleeve. "You've got some female flesh for me?"

"Yes, Your Eminence."

Webster ordered the door guard to send the girls in, and when he saw the emperor happily occupied, he left the room closing the door behind him. In a matter of minutes, the emperor had gone from affable to dark, and from dark to coarse. He wondered if this last mood would persist, or if they'd be cleaning corpses out of the emperor's chamber when he finished.

The moods of the emperor, his personalities, were distinct, but Webster could explain it no better than he could the emperor's sleep patterns. He had heard of people who exhibited more than one personality, had even examined a few over the years, but this was very different, as if the emperor was inhabited by three different personalities, rather than that they originated from within him.

Webster had once questioned the witch about it. All she had said was, "Two I love, one I do not."

Always cryptic was Yolandhe, no matter how they tortured her, but he got the impression that if they loosed her, she would kill the three despite her love of the two, because of her hatred for the one. In fact, when the emperor rose to power, she had turned on him, but was captured before she could harm him. The emperor must never learn she still lived, for he would go to her. Webster could not imagine the destruction and chaos that would ensue. It would unmake the empire. He had put too much of his soul into it for that to happen, and he was prepared to hold Yolandhe prisoner for all eternity if need be.

GOSSHAM

In the morning, while Cade made use of the tub, Karigan readied herself for the day, dressing once more in the rumpled clothes that had belonged to Luke's son, the farrier. When she checked her pocket to ensure her moonstone was where she always kept it, it lit up.

"What?"

When she drew the moonstone out, it shone with a wavering glow. The whole room did not fill with silver moonlight, but the moonstone was brighter than the feeble glimmer it had emitted since her arrival in Mill City. It must be true that the closer they got to Gossham, the more etherea was present.

She replaced the moonstone in her pocket and decided to try another experiment. She reached for her brooch where it was pinned to her shirt, and wished herself to fade out. Like the moonstone, she wavered, flickered in and out. Cade, who had just stepped out of the bathing room, gasped behind her. Before she could explain, a fierce pain rammed through her head like a spike. She let go, fell to her knees, and vomited.

In a moment, Cade was crouched beside her with only a towel wrapped around his waist. He touched her arm as if to ensure she was real.

"Karigan?"

When she finished another round of retching, she wiped her mouth with her sleeve. A dull pounding in her skull replaced the sharp pain of before.

"You—you were there, then only half there," Cade said, sounding worried. "You came and went."

"Etherea. My Rider magic," she said wearily. "The empire's etherea." Not only had she tried to use her ability where the etherea was weak, but it was, as the professor had once explained, etherea pulled from Blackveil. It was "filtered" he'd told her, but she had the feeling it was not enough to purify it. It was not etherea in its natural form. It was tainted.

When she sighed, Cade sat there on the floor and drew her onto his lap. He pressed her head against his chest and stroked her hair. There she rested with her eyes closed, the thump of his heart soothing away the pounding in her head.

"My Green Rider," Cade murmured, "you are full of surprises."

"I surprise myself sometimes," Karigan admitted with a smile. "But it worked, sort of. I still have my ability." Though she had not reacted well to its use, the fact that it was still there was an enormous relief and gave her hope she could once again cross thresholds, return to her own time with both Cade and Lhean.

"You are light as a feather," Cade said, shifting her on his lap, "and sometimes I think fragile as well, until I remember how well you can beat me in a bout of swordplay. And then I see you demonstrate an amazing power. I have never seen anyone fade out like that, not ever. Not even remotely."

She understood. She'd grown accustomed to having that ability and living in a world where magic still existed, even if only in a much diluted form compared to what had once been known.

"We are apt to see etherea wasted on meaningless diversions when we reach Gossham," Cade said. "But your ability, that is something wondrous."

She did not bother to tell him how minor it really was. She was just glad it hadn't spooked him, caused him to see her as something other than human. It was not every person who would react in such a positive way to someone who could do something so very strange.

"I suppose we should get going," Karigan said with regret. As much as she enjoyed sitting in Cade's lap, she didn't think Luke would appreciate having to wait around for them. Sorely tempted as she was to whip off Cade's towel, she restrained herself and rose. Evening would be soon enough, and she'd probably be feeling better by then, as well. Besides, she did not think he'd find her vomit breath particularly alluring.

The road grew continually busier as they traveled deeper into the Capital. There was less cropland and more habitation. Karigan saw nothing like the rectangular brick buildings of Mill City, but edifices of granite with masterfully carved embellishments around windows and doors. The finery worn by the people was more colorful, and she saw that, like at Dr. Silk's dinner party, the women of the Capital wore their veils stylishly short, or perhaps provocatively short, depending on one's point of view. Many were followed by unveiled slaves, who appeared better dressed and fed than their counterparts in Mill City, although just as many of their faces were marred with brands. Well fed or not, they were still slaves.

The irrigation ditches widened into transportation canals with breadth enough to permit small boats, but too narrow for the wheel-sided chugs. One man poling a flat boat full of flowers beneath an arched stone bridge looked like a whimsical painting. Many rowed ladies from one landing to another.

Sometime after midday, Karigan surmised that they'd reached the entrance to Gossham proper when they were stuck in a long line of travelers waiting to be cleared by Inspectors. A pair of enormous bronze statues loomed overhead—surprisingly, not of Amberhill the emperor but of horses. One held its head tossed back in defiance, and the other stood with head bowed, its neck elegantly arched.

"Just like you," she told Raven. He bowed his head at her words as if to imitate the one statue.

When they got closer to the Gossham city entrance, she saw that from the bases of the statues, walls ran off in both directions. As she recalled from the atlas map, the wall was a horseshoe around Gossham, with few entrances, open only at the shore of the Great Harbor. Once they entered the city, it would be difficult to exit.

It turned out that they very well might not even make it

inside. Karigan craned her neck when she realized Luke was being questioned hard by an Inspector whose Enforcer emitted an angry red glow. Luke tried to appear as affable as usual, but she could see his act was showing signs of strain and that the Inspector was having none of it.

"We will have a thorough look through your cargo and your wagon. All travelers from Mill City are suspect."

That was interesting, Karigan thought. If all travelers from Mill City were suspect, did that mean the uprising had met with some success after all? Did the Inspectors fear insurgents entering the city to commit some form of mischief? That would be the opposite effect Cade had intended, making Gossham *more* watchful, endangering their rescue mission before it had really begun.

"I am but a simple merchant of wine," Luke protested, "with a letter of introduction to Webster Silk himself."

At that point, another Inspector joined the first and whispered into his ear, then pointed at a sheaf of papers in his hand.

The first Inspector gazed up at Luke with keen eyes. "Mayforte, isn't it?"

Luke nodded.

"Your papers are in order. You may proceed."

Luke tipped his hat, and the wagon jolted forward. What had made the Inspector relent? Karigan wondered. Why did he allow them to pass without looking through their cargo? She did not like it. Remembering she was supposed to be sick, she sank back into the straw, and just in time, as she came beneath the eye of an Enforcer keeping close scrutiny of the wagon and its occupants.

She did not breathe freely again till they passed under the shadow of the horse statues and through the gates. Finally, they had entered the imperial city of Gossham.

Within the walls of the city there were more branching canals, and it was clear that they, too, were streets of sorts, with boats conveying goods and passengers. Many houses and businesses fronted the canals, not the paved streets. The interweaving of roadways and bridges and waterways must appear, from a bird's vantage, like a sort of weird lace.

Business looked brisk in most shops and at the booths of street vendors. Children ran alongside adults in grassy parks and played with toy sailboats in fountains along the way. Some of the founts made impossible ephemeral shapes sculpted of water that plumed into the air—horses, dragons, and giant fishes—and made a pleasing, chiming sound as prismatic droplets rained back into their basins. Was this etherea at work, or some mechanical innovation denied the less fortunate regions of the empire?

Karigan glanced at Raven to see how he fared with all the activity. He looked around, ears flickering and tail swishing. He did not appear alarmed but definitely attentive. She noticed he received the occasional admiring gazes from those they passed. She could not swear to it, but Raven seemed to know he had an audience and tossed his long mane and made his gait high-stepping and showy. When they stopped at an intersection to allow other traffic to proceed, a man actually asked Luke if the stallion was for sale.

"He is a gift for the emperor," Luke said. "Not for sale."

Karigan started, for this was the first she'd heard of it. Surely Luke was saying it just to put the man off. She had not thought about what would become of the horse when she went home. Could she take him with her, along with Cade and Lhean?

"He is a fine specimen," the man said, "and of course the emperor loves his horses."

"Enough to have named the city after his favorite, I hear," Luke replied.

Amberhill named his capital city after a horse? Karigan had thought the name "Gossham" odd. She shook her head. The Serpentine Empire's fearsome leader could be so brutal to his own people, and at the same time so—so whimsical?

Finally it was their turn to enter the intersection, and Luke bade farewell to the man with whom he'd been chatting. Further surprises along their route included a drawbridge over one of the canals that lifted by itself to allow a boater to pass, buildings taller than any of those in Mill City, and a mechanical that looked like a modified Enforcer, playing sequences of musical notes that emitted from its central orb. Then wonder of all wonders, a little metal dog danced and flipped to the music. The adults and children who gathered around appeared delighted, but though Karigan liked the dog, she found the music tinny and unpleasant, not at all like the melodious, natural sounds her minstrel friend, Estral, could create.

As they progressed, the city sloped down toward the harbor. It heartened Karigan to look upon the blue of the ocean with gulls wheeling in the sky and the harbor dotted with so many boats, though few had sails, but instead, stacks billowing smoke. Less heartening was a missing landmark at the entrance of the harbor. The abandoned keep of Mordivelleo L'Petrie, a clan chief of old, had been replaced by a colossus of a statue.

"Amberhill," she murmured.

She could not see its face for it looked out across the ocean, but she assumed it was Amberhill, carved of stone and seated in a throne chair. It reminded her that in this time, there was only one history, and it belonged to the empire.

Something else in the harbor caught her eye, as well: a small island, really too small to be an island. It was more of a rocky ledge with dead trees on it. She could not remember it being there. She'd grown up in Corsa, so she should have known all the islands and ledges in the harbor. Then she recalled how the land around Sacor City had changed, with a river created and redirected to flow past what was now Mill City. Then she pictured the ruins of Sacor City itself. Amberhill's great weapon had unleashed unimaginable forces that had not only brought an entire city down, but had also caused changes in the landscape. Why not in the seascape?

She could no longer look at her home harbor so changed, so she looked ahead into the city. Rising above even the tall buildings of Gossham were the sky-touching spires that could only belong to the emperor's palace. Before she could see more than the spires, however, Luke turned down a narrow side lane.

The lodging he found for them that evening was not the typical traveler's inn to which she'd become accustomed. It was a rambling old house that looked like it might have survived from her own time or earlier, with newer wings added on. It was nice to know that not everything in Corsa had been demolished. It was fronted on one side by a canal, with a smaller entrance from the lane. The sign on the place named it Laughing Gull House.

The horses and wagon were led off to the attached carriage house and stable. When Luke finished conferring with the inn-keeper, he led Karigan and Cade to an entrance on one of the wings where he'd reserved them a suite of rooms. There was a large master bedroom, a sitting room with fireplace, a bathing room, and a very small servants room. Whether they wanted intimacy that night or not, that's what they were going to get regardless. The rooms were not luxurious but had an austere tidiness that she appreciated, the low timbered ceiling, leaded windows, and a slanting floor with wide, painted boards. It reminded her of home. In a place where even the land had been dramatically altered, it was no small thing.

"Nice place," Cade said. "Different, anyway."

"There are many inns in Gossham," Luke said. He stood by the fireplace surveying the sitting room and nodding with approval. "This was recommended to me by the keeper of the last inn we stayed at. He said it would be the proper place for a gentleman like Stanton Mayforte to stay when on business in Gossham. Not too lowly and not extravagant."

"And what business does Stanton Mayforte have at this moment?" Cade asked.

Karigan was wondering the same thing, since it was not too late in the afternoon.

"I think," Luke said, "it is time for Stanton Mayforte to send his letter to Webster Silk at the palace. So I shall be off to find a courier, and perhaps to hear what news of the city there is."

"Be careful," Cade said. He looked as if he wanted to say more but did not.

Luke nodded and, walking cane swinging at his side, he headed for the door. Before stepping out, he told them, "Probably best if you two stay inside. I do not doubt you'll find some way to occupy yourselves before my return." With that, he was gone, Karigan choking on laughter.

"Well," Cade said, "the empire may not like two lads being together, but coming from Mr. Mayforte it almost sounded like an order. Speaking of which, let me see your hand."

Karigan sat on a window seat looking out over the canal while Cade re-dressed the wound Luke's whip had left on the back of her hand. It was an angry red, swollen and bruised, but the salve Cade had acquired the previous day seemed to be helping. She watched boat traffic on the canal as he bandaged it back up.

"That should do it," he said, patting her knee, then taking to a rocking chair nearby.

"Cade," she said, watching through the window as a man rowed by with a spotted dog at the prow of his boat, "what was it you were going to tell Luke?"

"Hmm?"

"Just before he left. You seemed to have more you wanted to say."

"Oh, well, I'm just worried, after what he said about spies yesterday, and then the odd change-about by the Inspectors at the city gates today. But Luke knows how to be careful."

"Yes, the Inspectors' behavior troubled me, too."

They stared at one another for a moment, then Cade shrugged. "It could be the Inspectors are truly suspicious of anyone out of Mill City, or . . ."

"Or?"

Cade's expression darkened. "Or, we've been found out."

That had been Karigan's line of thought too, but she hadn't wanted to admit it.

"What do we do?"

The floorboards groaned as Cade slowly rocked back and forth. He rubbed his chin as though deep in thought. "I don't know," he said. "They haven't come and arrested us—not yet, anyway. I suppose we just keep going forward."

Karigan did not like it, going blindly forward, but hadn't that been her whole experience in this world, thus far? She did not know its ways or even its geography. The professor and Cade had been her guides, but now the professor was gone, and Cade was as much in a different world as she.

She stood, stretched, and started pacing across the uneven

floor. Cade sank into his own thoughts, his eyes half closed, his chair rocking back and forth in a slow, rhythmic pace. Having no plan was no plan at all, but what could she do? She could head out, get a feel for Gossham, or at least get a look at the palace's exterior. She could watch and listen, same as Luke. He'd told them to stay put, and she could see the wisdom in that. If she got caught, it was all over. And her chances of getting caught? Well, if there were spies keeping watch on their little group, chances were pretty good. They'd wonder why Stanton Mayforte's sick servant was up and about prowling the streets.

"Damnation," she muttered.

"What's wrong?" Cade asked.

"I am tired of hiding. I want my sword. We might as well go up to the front door of the palace and knock on it for all the good this waiting around is doing us."

"That would be one approach," Cade said, "but I don't think it would accomplish what you hope."

"I know, I know." Karigan flung her arm out in frustration. "I feel like I want to do *something*."

Cade raised his eyebrows and looked like he had a suggestion, then clamped his mouth shut. Instead, he rose and strode over to her. He wrapped his arms around her and rubbed her back. "Let's see what news Luke brings back."

She was too wound up to feel comforted, but said, "All right, all right. I just hope he returns soon."

A couple hours passed, and just as their supper was being delivered to their doorstep, Luke grabbed the tray from the startled servant, stepped inside, and booted the door shut behind him. After he set the tray on the table in their sitting room, he lifted the lid off the pot of the main course and an offensive odor wafted out. "Oh, my favorite," he said. "Boiled dinner."

Karigan groaned.

"How was the city?" Cade asked.

Luke straightened. "Very interesting as a matter of fact. I have some unexpected news. The city is abuzz with rumor."

Karigan and Cade glanced at one another.

"Well?" Cade asked.

"From what I was able to pick up," Luke replied, "the emperor has awakened early."

A WAKING DREAM

"The emperor has awakened?" Cade demanded, aghast. "Early?"

Luke nodded and began to dish himself some boiled dinner. "That's the rumor going around. Or it may be he hasn't awakened quite yet, but the palace is making ready."

The professor had told Karigan that the emperor—Amberhill—slept at intervals of ten years. He had not known the reasons for such extraordinary sleep periods, but he'd told her that the emperor's wakeful periods were to be feared. Even so, she was just as glad. Trying to get answers out of a sleeping Amberhill would not have yielded much satisfaction.

"But rumors," Cade said.

Luke dropped into a chair at the table, ready to dig into his meal. "Rumors with an element of truth. Certain foods known to be the emperor's favorites have been ordered into the palace kitchens, there's been extra activity in the emperor's quarters, extra attention paid to his horses, and certain officials have attempted to flee the city . . . There are enough servants, and others who work in the palace, to note changes in its daily routines, and of course they mix with people in the city and the word spreads." He took a bite of corned beef. "Mmm. Just like my wife's."

In that moment, he looked forlorn and suddenly much older. *He must miss her very much,* Karigan thought. He had spoken little of his family on their journey, but perhaps it was his way of coping with the separation.

Karigan and Cade joined him at the table, Karigan picking at potatoes and trying not to be repulsed by the cabbage.

Luke told them of his outing, of having sent his letter off to Webster Silk, and then of lingering in an open air market and a tavern to hear the news of the city.

"It sounds as if the Eletian is definitely at the palace," he told them. "People described a closed circus wagon with lions painted on it, making its way through the city and to the palace just a couple of days ago."

Karigan nodded. "He was kept in one like that at Dr. Silk's party."

"Yes, well, there was much speculation over what was to be done with the Eletian. One gent referred to him as 'a priceless treasure.'"

Karigan hoped that Cade was right about Dr. Silk's being a collector. It might prevent harm from coming to Lhean, at least for a while.

"There was nothing about Arhys and Lorine?" Cade asked.

Luke shook his head. "They would seem to be inconsequential in comparison."

"That's good," Cade said. "It means they've not discovered Arhys' secret."

"Overall, I'd say the mood of the city is edgy," Luke continued. "People are trying to go about their daily routines, but it's as if they know a storm is brewing."

"To be expected if the emperor is indeed awakening." Cade shook his head. "And why early?"

As the two men mused over the possibilities, Karigan investigated the contents of a crock that had arrived with the boiled dinner, to see if it was anything more palatable. It was a steaming blueberry crumble and now it was her turn to think of home. Her Aunt Stace made wonderful crumbles during summer when the low lying bushes around the G'ladheon estate were filled with tiny blueberries. Picking the wild ones had been a nuisance until Aunt Stace acquired a hand rake like those used by growers out on the cultivated barrens. Not to mention, more blueberries usually ended up in Karigan's mouth than in her bucket when she "helped."

Hastily she scooped a heaping mound of the crumble into a bowl and drowned it in the heavy cream that came with it.

"Hey!" Cade said. "You hardly left any for us."

"You can have my share of the boiled dinner."

Luke chuckled, and Cade glowered.

While the crumble was wonderful, it could never be as good as Aunt Stace's, but at least it was made in Corsa, even if Corsa was now called Gossham.

"Yes, I thought it was peculiar, too," Luke was saying when Cade brought up the Inspectors at the gates. "Word must have passed from checkpoint to checkpoint that a wine merchant from Mill City, named Mayforte, was headed for Gossham."

"But why would that make them decide *not* to search the wagon?" Cade asked.

Luke shrugged and poured himself tea. "I haven't the faintest. It could be a trap, as you proposed, but like you also said, why not just arrest us? This has been a dangerous endeavor from the outset, and almost anything could go wrong. That forged letter of introduction from Mill City's master? It's well done, but what if they detect it's a forgery? We are done for."

"So what do we do?"

"I do not think there is much else we can do, but keep playing the game. If Webster Silk invites us to the palace, we go and have a look around. If he does not invite us, we find another way."

Later, after Luke retired for the night to his comparatively spacious bedroom, Karigan sat once more on the window seat watching moonlight glimmer on the canal. They had gotten nowhere with the planning. It was all or nothing, and Cade had agreed that if invited into the palace, they would use it for scouting purposes, no more. It was not at all satisfying.

She could not see the moon itself from where she was, but it was nearing full. Thinking of the moon reminded her of the first phrase in the Captain's riddle: *The scything moon is held captive in the prison of forgotten days.* Karigan felt imprisoned like the scything moon.

"Should we get invited into the palace," Karigan said, "I want to make sure my ability is still working."

"Are you going to do that fading thing?" There was an apprehensive edge to Cade's voice.

She nodded. "First I need to check something else." She

peeled back her jacket and revealed her Rider brooch. To her, it looked the same as always, but could Cade still see it? "Is my brooch still there?" she asked him.

He squinted, moved closer. "No. It's gone. What happened to it?"

She grinned. "Oh, it's there."

"Then why can't I see it?"

She explained the spell that concealed it, and how long ago the brooches had been saved by being hidden in plain sight.

"Remarkable," Cade said. "So it's the etherea of Gossham at work."

"Yes. And, by way of testing it further . . ." She took the moonstone from her pocket, and the room flooded with liquid silver light. She extinguished it quickly.

"I have never . . ." Cade said, blinking. "So much brighter than phosphorene. It's truly a silver moonbeam?"

Karigan nodded. It had emitted a much stronger glow than in the morning, and yet . . . It appeared to her as . . . muddy compared to what she remembered it being like back home, where it had been almost painfully clear and crystalline.

"Now to try my ability. Let's turn down the lamps." When Cade cast her a querying glance, she explained, "My fading is more complete in dim light."

When the light was lowered, Cade asked, "You aren't going to vomit again, are you?"

"Hope not. If I do, I'll try not to do it on you."

"Promise?"

"Yep."

"Thank you."

Karigan, standing where moonlight puddled on the floor through the window, took a deep breath, then reached for her brooch. When she touched it, she knew she'd faded because her vision turned gray, and even the glow of the lamps became cold. And then, of course, there was Cade's expression indicating her success, one of awe maybe mixed with a little fear. Fear for her? Fear of her ability? Fear *of her*?

"I can see through you," Cade said. "You are like a ghost."

Which she had used to great effect in the past. She stepped

out of the moonlight and into the shadows, and his hiss of surprise told her she had faded completely from sight.

"Karigan?" he asked. "Are you still there?"

She walked toward him as quietly as she could and rose on her toes to kiss his cheek. He jumped back, startled.

She released the fading, and that was when the headache struck. It was not, perhaps, as fierce as the last time, but it staggered her, and she had to fight with her rebellious stomach to retain its contents. After all, she'd made Cade a promise . . .

He steadied her and led her to a chair—not the rocking chair, thankfully, which would have only aggravated the nausea. She massaged her temples.

"Perhaps you shouldn't use your ability if it makes you ill," Cade said.

"The headache will go away. Always get it." But not usually this bad. In addition to the headache, she felt raw, like her heart had pumped sand instead of blood through her arteries.

Back in her own time there were Eletians who believed the D'Yer Wall should fall so that the etherea trapped in Blackveil could replenish the lands. If this was what it was like, she was pretty sure the Eletians would be sorry, unless they were better able to endure the taint. They were beings of magic, and she could not believe Blackveil's influence on them would have a positive outcome. Would they listen to her if she told them? It was difficult to say.

When she saw the worry on Cade's face, she straightened and smiled, though the movement jarred the hammering in her head anew. "It works," she said, "and I can use it if need be. If there are enough shadows, anyway."

Cade shook his head. He had seen her ability and could not argue about its usefulness. Nor would she allow his concern to override her decision to use it, should the necessity arise. When Karigan announced she was ready to retire for the night, Cade claimed weariness and suggested they actually try to just sleep so they were able to face whatever the following day would bring. She did not believe him for an instant, guessing that he had perceived her own weariness and was making an excuse to ensure she got some sleep. She was grateful. Just that small use of her ability had tired her out.

They did not exactly sleep apart, however. When she dropped into one of the narrow beds in the servants room, Cade pushed the other beside hers, and in this way they were together, but with a comfortable space around them for sleeping. Before Cade even got into bed, she'd drifted off into a deep sleep.

At some point during the night she had one of those dreams where it was hard to tell if she was really awake or just dreaming. In it, she was sitting up against the headboard, soft moonlight working patterns across the floor. Cade was buried beneath his blanket beside her. Across her lap lay a piece of paper with a drawing on it. It was a well done rendering of the inside of a building, or at least a section of a building. She knew, without knowing how she knew, that this was the interior of the palace.

The drawing appeared to be of some great hall with a fountain in its center featuring a winged dragon rearing back, water flowing forth from its mouth. To either side of the fountain were colonnaded corridors.

Cade rustled beside her and sat up, but it was not Cade. Yates, his ghost, sat beside her. An otherworldly cold drafted off him and against her skin. It was as though he were an open door through the veil of death.

Yates. She mouthed his name, not sure if she mumbled it into her pillow, or if she was actually sitting up speaking it, or if she had uttered it at all.

His translucent hand hovered over the paper. He had finally revealed one of his drawings to her. He pointed at the corridor to the left of the fountain, and once again, with unfounded assurance, she knew it led to *the prison of forgotten days.*

In the morning, Karigan arose foggy and out of sorts, like she'd been at the Cock and Hen all night imbibing too much. Unfortunately, when she shook off the initial layer of fog, she remembered she hadn't been anywhere, or anywhen, near the Cock and Hen. She dressed and found Cade and Luke already at breakfast.

"Started without me?"

Cade glanced over his shoulder at her. "We couldn't let

the flatcakes get cold. Besides, you were restless last night. I thought it better to let you sleep."

She dropped into a chair beside him, and he passed her a cup of hot tea and a blueberry muffin. The muffin brightened her mood.

"I think I dreamed a lot," she said. She grasped at fleeting images as she tried to remember the dreams. Had Yates been in one of them?

"I never remember mine," Cade said.

"Well," Luke told Karigan as he buttered a muffin, "while you were dreaming the morning away, Cade and I have been discussing possible strategies should we hear back from the palace."

Karigan raised an eyebrow. "Oh?" She wondered if Cade had told Luke what he had witnessed of her ability.

"Luke thinks you should remain behind," Cade said, "so that if things go wrong, at least one of us can try to flee."

"And what did you say to that?" she asked him.

Cade smiled. "I told him that he'd better give you a good dose of morphia if he expects you to stay put."

Karigan conjured up the sweetest smile she could summon. "And the one who came anywhere near me with a dose of morphia would find himself—"

She was interrupted by a knock on the door. At first they just looked at one another, then she scrambled out of the sitting room and back to the bedroom to hide, half eaten muffin in hand. She left the door open just a crack so she could see and hear.

Luke opened the front door. The person on the other side did not step in, so she could not see him, but he said, "Mr. Mayforte? I am a courier from the palace. The Honorable Webster Silk extends his welcome to you on your visit to Gossham, and he has sent you this message."

Luke received an envelope, and closed the door after the courier.

"Well?" Cade asked.

Karigan slipped out of the bedroom as Luke opened the letter and briefly read the contents. "We've been invited to the palace," he said. "We are to arrive at four hour."

GATES AND WALLS

It took a moment to sink in: they'd been invited to the palace.

"That was quick," Cade said.

"Yes," Luke replied, still staring at the paper in his hands. "I had heard Webster Silk wasn't one to waste time, but I didn't think . . . not so soon." He handed the message to Cade, who in turn passed it to Karigan. It was brief: *Mr. Mayforte, four hour.* At the bottom was the official seal of Webster Silk, Adherent Minister of the Interior.

"Not one to waste words, either," Karigan remarked.

They convened once more at the table to resume their conversation that had been interrupted by the courier.

"I *am* going with you," Karigan said before either of the men could speak.

"I think she should," Cade said over Luke's protest. "She has as much at stake here as we do, and is a fierce opponent in a fight. I should know." Then he gazed at Karigan. "And she won the esteem of her king for unimaginable deeds. If any of us is more suited to go, I can't think of a better person than Karigan."

Karigan smiled at him and affectionately nudged his leg under the table. He did not mention her special ability, so perhaps he'd said nothing of it to Luke earlier. She was just as glad. She was too accustomed to keeping quiet on the subject.

Luke, clearly outnumbered, nodded. "All right, but I suggest she stay with the wagon when it's time to enter the palace. Now don't you glare at me, young lady. We've gone to great lengths to shield your identity, including putting forth the story of your illness. Webster Silk will have heard of it I've no doubt, and it is best not to tip him off that it was all a fabrication."

"But maybe I—Tam—has recovered!"

Luke stared hard at her. "Also, by not meeting with Silk, you have less of a chance of being questioned, and you are not very convincing as a boy when you speak."

"It would give you a chance to get a good look at the palace grounds while we're inside," Cade mused. "Watch the guards and so forth."

"You are also our secret asset," Luke said. "They don't know who or what you are. If anything should go wrong, you can flee on that stallion of yours."

"You aren't giving him to the emperor?" Karigan asked.

"Of course not. I'm giving the emperor nothing."

"All right," Karigan said. "I'll do this your way, but I will act on my own if I must."

She also wanted access to her bonewood staff, but both Cade and Luke opposed the idea saying it was too risky to take their weapons out of hiding. They were apt to be detected before reaching the palace.

"If it is true the emperor has awakened," Cade said, "they will be extra alert. Mind, I would feel better if I could have a Cobalt with me, myself."

There was little more they could do than speculate on what they might face at the palace, and when they ran out of guesses, Luke stood and scratched his chin.

"Think I could stand to get a proper shave in town," he said. "I have to look my best for our meeting with Silk. I'll get my boots shined, too, while I'm at it."

With that, Luke left them. This time Karigan and Cade decided to make good use of their time alone. There was an urgency to their lovemaking that made them both fierce, more forceful. They did not need words to know that if things did not go well at the palace, this could very well be their last time together.

A teardrop formed at the corner of Karigan's eye and glided down her cheek.

"Have I hurt you?" Cade asked.

"No."

He kissed her cheek, then her lips, and she tasted the salt of her own tears.

On the way to the palace, the physical separation between them—he up front driving the wagon, and she in the rear—was painful. At the height of their coupling, they had clung to one another, unwilling to let the moment pass. Every contact with Cade renewed her and renewed her determination. She would find a way home, and she would take Cade with her. After all the darkness she'd faced as a Green Rider, his presence was a parting of the clouds.

This time she hadn't even Raven to comfort her. Instead, Gallant was hitched to the back of the wagon and Luke rode Raven up front. Luke had asked Cade to tack up Raven, saying that if Karigan must escape quickly, it was best if the stallion was saddled and ready to go. Luke was an expert horseman, so he was able to hold in the spirited stallion who'd gone too many days without being ridden. Karigan, along with everything else she was feeling, was a little jealous.

It was not long before the buildings and the commotion of the city fell away, and they found themselves on the shore of a lake—Lake Scalus, Karigan remembered from the atlas—and in its center lay an island upon which sat the palace of the Serpentine Empire. The palace was a collection of spires and copper roofs partially hidden behind a curtain wall, upon which guards patrolled. To reach the island, they would have to cross first one narrow bridge to a smaller island with a guard house, and then a second. The designers had created a city and palace that could be easily defended but not easily escaped.

A grassy, parklike sward made up the shoreline that circled the lake, but few made use of it, even on so fine an afternoon as this. Perhaps being exposed to the palace and under the scrutiny of so many guards made the folk of Gossham too uneasy to walk along the shore. It certainly made Karigan uneasy.

They stopped at the checkpoint at the first bridge, the flag of the dragon sigil flapping restlessly in the lake breeze over the guardhouse. Luke passed their papers, including the invitation from Webster Silk, to the Inspectors to examine. His conversational chatter with the Inspectors was much more subdued than usual, and considering the gravity of what lay ahead, it was not surprising.

It did not take long for the Inspectors to verify the papers and open the gate to the bridge. Luke and Raven led the way, with Cade snapping the reins to get the mules moving again. Karigan closed her eyes and tried to make herself small as she came under the eyestalks of a pair of Enforcers.

Hooves clacked on the stone treadway of the bridge, and water plashed against the piers. The lake air was fresh, and Karigan took a deep breath, finally opening her eyes. A sailing vessel came into view, triangular sails bent as it heeled with the wind. It was too far distant to make out the people on board, but its prow was the silhouette of a dragon's head.

The bridge was surprisingly long, but when they finally reached the second checkpoint on the small island, they were allowed to proceed as before. Karigan kept watching the sailboat carving through the surface of the lake until it disappeared from sight beyond the main island. She then tried to focus on ducks paddling near the bridge in a V-formation and a dragonfly hovering over her knee, but it was not enough to quell her rising uneasiness.

They reached the island and were ushered through the heavily fortified gate of the curtain wall. When she saw all the armed Inspectors and soldiers, and no few Enforcers, she realized that Luke's plan that she flee in case of trouble was unlikely to meet with success. Before they left the inn, Luke had mentioned how fast Raven was—much faster than Gallant, he assured her—but a bullet was even faster. She must remember she could not outride the weaponry of this time.

She would never reach the curtain wall gate, much less pass through it.

As the gate closed behind them, her entire body tensed. Had Luke had any idea of the palace's fortifications? If it wasn't already a trap, it could effectively become one.

Cade halted the wagon in a grand courtyard of fountains and flowering plants. Wide steps led up to the ornate entrance of the palace, the door adorned with carvings in an odd combination of dragons, horses, and . . . lemon trees?

A gentleman approached Luke. "Mr. Mayforte?"

"Yes," Luke replied.

"I am Mr. Jones, Minister Silk's secretary. On the minister's behalf I bid you welcome. I'll escort you to his office so you may meet with him."

Luke nodded and dismounted. "Tam? Come here, lad."

It took Karigan a moment to remember she was Tam. She climbed out of the back of the wagon, not sure if she was supposed to pretend illness or not.

As she approached cautiously, Luke explained to Mr. Jones, "My stallion is temperamental, and Tam here is the only one who can handle him besides me, so I'll leave the lad out here with the wagon and the beasts."

The secretary made some appreciative remarks about Raven's conformation as Luke passed the reins to Karigan. His hands, she noted, were trembling. Meanwhile, Cade had climbed down from the wagon with one of the small casks of wine on his shoulder. He'd pulled his cap down low over his eyes.

"This way if you would, Mr. Mayforte," the secretary said.

"One moment," Luke replied. "I've final instructions for Tam." He strode over to her and said in a low voice, "I did not know there would be so many gates and walls. I'm sorry." Then more loudly, in a scolding voice, he said, "And no more sampling of the wares."

And that was all. He joined the secretary, initiating pleasant chatter about the weather and the beauty of the courtyard.

Cade brushed by her and whispered, "I love you," before hastening away to fall in behind Luke.

No, no, no! She wanted to run after him and grab his arm, prevent him from entering the palace, but she stood rooted, knowing that any such move would be seen as belligerent by all the men carrying firearms in and around the courtyard. The game must go on, regardless. They had all agreed. She clenched Raven's reins in her hands, a scream welling up inside her as Cade climbed the steps, entered the palace, and the big doors closed after him.

She forced the scream back down and doubled over in something like physical pain. Raven lipped her ear, and she eased, slowly stood upright once again and breathed. She placed her hand on the stallion's neck to steady herself and stood resolute once more.

She would not abandon Cade no matter what it took. They would leave the palace together or not at all.

When the doors shut behind him, Cade paused and, briefly, closed his eyes. It was like the door slamming on a crypt. A large extravagant crypt, he realized, as he took in the marble colonnades, the fabulous paintings on the ceiling, and the gold chandeliers. He hurried after Luke and Mr. Jones, aware of guards' watching him. The wine sloshed in the cask on his shoulder as he strode along. He tried to keep an eye open for palace details, how it was defended, any sign of Arhys and Lorine, or maybe something of the Eletian, but the halls were hushed, and all he could think about was Karigan left behind in the courtyard all alone.

She is more than capable of taking care of herself, he kept reminding himself, but it didn't help. How had it happened? How had he fallen so hard for her when he'd already prepared himself for the celibate life of a Weapon? He hoped that she would forgive him the lie if she ever found out about it, that there was, in fact, no choice. The professor had been correct in his teaching that Weapons must be celibate. Cade had given all that up, however, for something greater.

He had told her he loved her. He'd said those words before, but he thought they would have more meaning when not spoken in the midst of passion. He never found such words easy to say aloud, and he thought it was probably the same for her. At least he'd spoken the words in case events went poorly here, and if they didn't? Then she knew his true feelings.

He frowned. He appreciated Luke's attempt to give her a way out. She had the stallion, but not even that high-tempered beast would be able to scale the curtain wall's gate.

They came to a large circular room with a dome ceiling, filled with the sound of splashing water and, oddly, the echoing laughter of children. A veritable grotto of ferns hung down from the ceiling, and a very natural-looking waterfall cascaded into a large basin with mossy boulders where children played with toy boats. Luke must have been just as startled as he to see it, for he halted.

"Marvelous, isn't it?" Mr. Jones asked.

The water reflected shimmering light on the walls, columns, and the part of the domed ceiling that was not grotto. The children were up to their elbows in water, half-drenched, pushing their boats around and splashing their friends. Beyond the fountain, in contrast, sat veiled governesses like a row of mute statues.

"The emperor has fond memories of playing with boats in fountains when he was a boy," Mr. Jones explained, "so he had this one made for the palace children."

"How extraordinary," Luke murmured, and Cade agreed, especially when one knew of how blood-thirsty the emperor could be. A place for children to play?

On impulse, Cade gazed at the children, both boys and girls, searching. Searching for one little girl. And there she was, with her golden hair, pushing a boy away from a boat.

"This is *my* boat now. Go away!"

Cade would recognize that voice anywhere. He almost dropped his cask to run to her, to grab her and make his escape.

"Harley?"

Cade ignored Luke, glancing at the governesses. Was Lorine among them? How could he tell, with their veils? The veils. One was longer than the others, like those worn in Mill City.

"Harley." This time Luke's voice was sharp, and he tugged on Cade's arm. "We must not keep the minister waiting."

Cade stared at Luke, trying to make sure he understood Arhys was there. Luke stared back just as hard and gave him a subtle shake of his head, and mouthed, *Later.*

Cade reluctantly followed behind Luke. He glanced over his shoulder once more and saw a dripping Arhys show Lo-

rine her boat. He also saw in the shadows beyond, the gleam
of Enforcers alongside red-coated Inspectors. Perhaps Luke
was right to draw him away, that this was not the time to
make an unconsidered, foolish move, but would he be able to
find Arhys again at some later time? Would they even be able
to gain access to the palace again?

One thing at a time, Harlowe, he told himself. There were
enough immediate problems to contend with, like meeting
Webster Silk, that he didn't need to invite more trouble.

It turned out that Webster Silk's chambers were not too
far from where the children played in the fountain. The room
Mr. Jones brought them to was less an office than an opulent
drawing room, a place for gentlemen of means to relax and
sip brandy, or, perhaps, try some of Stanton Mayforte's wine.
A palace guard was posted outside the door, and another
within. Also within waited three men, one of whom was Dr.
Ezra Stirling Silk, wearing his characteristic dark specs. Cade
tried to shift the cask to obscure his face. Dr. Silk would undoubtedly recognize him, even disguised as he was.

"Your visitor, Minister," the secretary said. "Mr. Stanton
Mayforte."

"Thank you, Jones," said the youngest looking of the trio.
With a start, Cade realized this was Webster Silk, and he saw
the resemblance to Dr. Silk. This couldn't be right. Webster
was supposed to be the father, but he looked much younger
than Ezra. Cade knew Webster had lived an unnatural number of years, but looking so youthful, as well?

Mr. Jones bowed and withdrew from the room, closing the
door behind him. Silence settled among the men.

Until Dr. Silk asked Luke, "So where is the third member
of your party?"

"Tending the horses," Luke replied.

Cade twitched. Why would Dr. Silk care about a lowly servant boy?

The third man in the room, a portly gentleman, said,
"Luke, dear fellow, you aren't trying to protect her, are you?"

Cade felt the blood drain from his head. They knew Luke.
They knew Tam was a "her."

Trap.

"She'd have been suspicious if I asked her to come in," Luke said. "We'd been playing she's ill all along."

"You didn't want to give our scheme away," said the portly man. "Very commendable."

"You can put the cask down, Mr. Harlowe," Dr. Silk said.

Cade did not move, glimpsed the advance of the guard from the corner of his eye. Sensed another who must have lain hidden coming up behind him.

"You are under arrest, Mr. Harlowe, for traitorous actions against the empire and fomenting unrest."

Cade took a breath, did not reply. He heaved the cask at the first guard and spun to meet the second with a fist to the man's jaw. Both guards went down, just like that. He tensed to spring out the door. He would run, grab Arhys, go to Karigan.

"Well done, Mr. Harlowe," the portly man exclaimed. "But far, far too late."

Cade whipped around just in time to see the fire flash from the muzzle of a gun. White hot pain bore through the tissue of his shoulder and shattered bone, as the impact threw him to the floor.

STARLING AND SILK

Cade could not recall hitting the floor, but there he lay, writhing in agony as though a molten spike had been pounded into his shoulder and left there to burn. The slightest movement turned his vision white.

"Cade?" It was Luke kneeling beside him. "I'm sorry, lad, I'm so sorry."

"Now none of that, Luke," said the portly man. He held his pistol at his side, the muzzle still issuing smoke.

"I did not expect a mess in my office, Mr. Starling." Through the pain, Cade recognized Webster Silk's voice. "There are other ways he could have been subdued."

"I'm very sorry, Minister," said Mr. Starling. "I am too fond of my firearms."

A glance revealed to Cade that the room was now filled with booted feet. The gunshot must have drawn additional guards. The wine cask had rolled away, and the man he'd knocked over with it had either recovered or been removed. He touched his shoulder, and his fingers came away bloody.

"You set us up," he said to Luke between gritted teeth.

"I had no choice." Luke bowed his head.

"There are always choices." Mr. Starling stepped forward and hovered over the two of them. "Mr. Harlowe, you and I are going to spend some time together getting to know one another. You see, we have many questions about your role in the uprising in Mill City, among other things, and my job is to extract the answers to those questions from you."

Inquisitor, Cade thought, losing hope even as blood leaked out of him.

"And don't worry about your wound over much," Mr. Starling said. "You are in Gossham, and we have very good menders who will heal you. I do so like beginning my work with a fresh canvas." His smile was anticipatory, grotesque.

"Do not hurt her," Cade whispered as the edges of his vision darkened.

"Her? You can't mean your lady dressed as a stable lad, can you? Or, perhaps the little girl from your old professor's house? Well, we shall talk more about them later. Both of them. For now, my guards will take you to my place of business."

Cade barely held back a howl when two guards lifted him to his feet. He kicked out, but one of the guards slammed his fist into Cade's wound. His legs buckled beneath him, and in the twilight of consciousness, he heard Luke's voice.

"I've done what you wanted. What of my son? My family?"

"You will be delighted to know," Mr. Starling replied, "that we haven't taken any more of your son's fingers. However, there is a price every conspirator must pay for betraying the emperor."

"I don't care. Kill me. As long as they're all right, I don't care."

"Very noble sentiments," Mr. Starling said. "Very noble, indeed, but I'm afraid you misunderstand."

Through the haze of pain, Cade saw Mr. Starling signal a guard over, who bore a wooden coffer. Mr. Starling lifted the lid so Luke could view what lay within. Cade strained to see, and when he did, he was so revolted he thrashed in the grip of his captors. A man's head . . .

Nightmare, he thought. It was all a nightmare.

Luke staggered back, his body convulsing. "No, no. Not my son." Then he lunged at Mr. Starling, a rising cry of grief and rage issuing from his mouth, his hands reaching out like claws. The report of shots battered Cade's ears, and the next thing he knew, Luke lay sprawled on the floor in a widening puddle of blood. Mr. Starling, wreathed in gunsmoke, stood over Luke's body shaking his head.

"A pity," the Inquisitor said, clucking his tongue. "A pity I never got to tell him what we did to his wife and daughters."

The guards jostled Cade from the room, smoke burning his eyes.

Karigan waited. No one gave her a second look as they passed by. No one questioned her presence. It must mean that all was going well in the palace. Luke and Cade were playing their parts, so she must play hers no matter how marginal it felt. It was difficult to note anything exceptional here in the courtyard, but if she started exploring, she would be noticed, and by the look of the guards, they were apt to kill on the slightest provocation and not worry about a reason.

She brushed flies away from Raven's eyes, and on inspiration, started walking him in circles. *I can do this.* One of the duties of a Green Rider was scouting. This should be second nature to her, but standing right beneath the nose of the enemy, on his own ground, and against weapons she had never before faced, was daunting. Walking Raven in circles, she hoped, would be construed as keeping her master's fine beast limber. She would gradually widen the circle to see what she could—

"Now there is a first-rate horse, Admiral," a man said, breaking into her thoughts. "Boy, trot him. Let me see him move."

Though startled, Karigan had the presence of mind to keep playing her role and obeyed at once. She did not dare look directly at the man, but a sideways glance revealed he wore a suit and was accompanied by several people. Some scout she was—she hadn't noticed their approach. She ran alongside Raven so she could show off his stride at a trot. Always a performer, he arched his neck and gave her his fancy high-stepping gait, which made him look like he was trotting on air. The man and his attendants were a blur as she ran by.

After several circles, the man called for her to halt, and he came forward to inspect Raven more closely. Karigan kept her head bowed as a meek servant would. Raven side-stepped and snorted when the man reached out to touch him.

"Shhh . . ." was all she dared tell Raven. He tensed, but did not act out.

The man ran his hands up and down Raven's legs and along his back. It was as he stroked Raven's neck that light glanced off his ruby ring and into her eye. She couldn't help but stare as the ring went back and forth in a mesmerizing fashion with the stroking. She had seen it before. It had belonged to Lord Amberhill.

"Give me a yacht or ship any day," said a man in a fancy white military uniform. "Horses? Too unpredictable."

"But, Admiral, I know our little lake is predictable, but you cannot tell me the sea is. It is the never knowing what to expect that I find so challenging and intriguing."

"Yes, Your Eminence."

"Boy," said Xandis Pierce Amberhill, emperor of the Serpentine Empire, "to whom does this horse belong?"

Karigan stood frozen. She held her gaze to the ground and fought the urge to scream at him and demand why he had done what he had done, why he had destroyed the realm of his birth, how he'd become such a monster. She fought for control, dared not speak knowing it would give her away immediately, and more importantly, endanger Cade and Luke. A guard in leather and light armor, enameled in red, closed in. Armor? Here? It was the first she had seen, and she assumed it was ornamental since the projectiles of firearms could punch through it, rendering it useless. It was not entirely like the armor she was accustomed to seeing back home, but had gears and pivots at the joints, and copper tubes fed from narrow cylinders behind the shoulders into the bevor concealing his lower face.

"Idiot," the admiral said. "Your emperor has asked you a simple question. Now answer."

She pointed at her throat to indicate a problem with speaking, and then in a harsh whisper, said, "Mr. Mayforte." Then remembered to add a quick, "Your Eminence," and bob her head.

"Mayforte?" Amberhill asked. "Do we know a Mayforte?"

"A vintner, apparently, Your Eminence," said another man who was gazing at the casks in the wagon.

Amberhill suddenly turned his attention to the palace entrance as he sighted someone or something. "Webster, my friend," he called out. "You missed a fine sail on the lake. Now come take a look at this horse. It is owned by a vintner named Mayforte."

Webster could only be Webster Silk, Karigan thought. If the Adherent was here, did that mean his meeting with Cade and Luke was over? If so, where were they? A furtive glance revealed only one man standing on the palace steps.

There was the tap of shoes on stone as Webster Silk approached. "I am sorry I missed the outing, Your Eminence, but I just met with the Mayforte fellow."

The guard in red armor edged closer. He wore a long-sword girded at his side, but no gun. She felt his gaze on her and saw him blink through the eye slits of his visor.

"What is the horse's name, boy?" Amberhill asked.

"Raven," she replied in her harsh whisper.

"Good name. I make him mine. I'm sure your master won't mind indulging me. If he does? Well, doesn't matter. The horse is mine."

This was too much. He sounded very much like Arhys, of all people, greedy and spoiled. Karigan did not know how much longer she could contain herself.

"No," Webster Silk said. His closeness behind her made her jump. "Mayforte will not mind. He is quite dead."

"Dead?" Karigan cried.

"And," Webster Silk continued in his calm, matter-of-fact voice, "this lad is not who *she* pretends to be." He removed her cap. Her braid fell down and thumped her between the shoulders. She felt naked before all those eyes staring at her. And shocked. Shocked by what Silk had said about Luke. A storm brewed within her for she knew Cade could have only met the same fate. Amberhill had caused the destruction of her home and betrayed the people she loved, and now this.

She stared brazenly at him now that she was revealed, the pressure of the storm building to an explosive level. Amberhill looked almost exactly as she remembered him, the black hair tied back, the light gray eyes, the well-structured face. The same, but different in some indefinable way.

"You killed them," she said, her voice a low threat. "You killed them all." Raven echoed her with a shrill whinny.

"What are you talking about?" He gazed blankly at her.

"You've destroyed Sacoridia and everything. Why? Why did you do it?"

He tilted his head as if he did not understand her. "Sacoridia?" He sounded it out as if speaking a foreign word for the first time.

"Yes, Sacoridia!"

"That is quite enough," the admiral said.

Someone else shouted, "Control that horse!"

Karigan was only peripherally aware of Raven, snorting aggressively, ears flattening. At some point she had dropped his reins and held her hands in fists before her. Her entire being was focused on Amberhill even as men closed in around her, their guns glinting in their hands. They would not dare fire them as long as she stood so close to their emperor, would they?

Memory or recognition registered in Amberhill's eyes. "Yes, a long time ago. I remember there was a war. And I remember you. You are the vanishing lady, are you not?" Then his eyes began to cloud over, grow smoky, almost black. His face rippled with change. He sneered at her in a way she had never seen before. Not on *his* face. "Galadheon, I know you." His voice had changed also. It did not sound like him, but she was too angry, too overwrought, to see what was right before her. Cade was probably dead. Amberhill had killed Zachary, destroyed her home. She would avenge them all, but before she could speak or throttle the life out of him, a red armored hand swept down and struck her collar bone. The next thing she knew she was down hard on her knees in front of Amberhill, nerves ringing, too stunned to think clearly. She shook her head, but it only made her more woozy.

Someone barked orders and rough hands grabbed her arms. She was dragged, pushed, and shoved, up the palace steps. Though the blow had not knocked her out, it left her so dazed that the passage through the palace was a blur of white marble. She lost track of time and distance until finally she was flung into a room. The motion jolted her collar bone, and she cried out at the sudden pain. Her vision blackened.

"Miss Goodgrave?" asked a familiar, if anxious, voice drawing her back.

This time gentler hands helped her up so that she sat on a chair or sofa. Voices ebbed and flowed. Karigan wanted to retreat to the darkness, but the world was just too bright.

Someone placed his hands on either side of her face. She was so muddled. Her head felt fluttery light and tingly. Then the pain slowly eased, eventually fading altogether. Slowly her senses sharpened, and a man in blue robes stepped back from her.

"Miss Goodgrave?" Lorine. It was Lorine.

"Who—who is this man?" Karigan asked.

"A mender," Lorine replied. "His name is Marcus. You were hit very hard, and he healed you with—"

"I am a true healer," the man said. "I can channel etherea through my hands to heal. The blow cracked your collar bone, but I knitted it back together."

It all started to come back to Karigan. The courtyard, the confrontation with Amberhill. She tried to rise, but the world started to fade out again.

"Easy," the mender said, pushing her back into her seat. "You can undo all the good work I've done if you don't take care. Perhaps you would like some water?"

Lorine appeared before Karigan and pressed a glass into her hand. When she lifted it to drink, her hand dragged on something and there was the clink of metal. Her other hand, she realized. Her wrists were manacled. When had those been put on?

Prisoner.

She drank deeply trying to gather her wits, and when she paused, she eyed Lorine who looked none the worse for her time at the palace. She wore no restraints, no manacles.

"Lorine," she asked, "you are all right?"

"Yes, miss. We have not been harmed."

"Arhys is . . . ?"

Lorine nodded. "She is having lessons with some of the palace children right now."

"Let me see into your eyes," the mender told Karigan. She saw a brand on his forearm and realized he was a slave.

A pinpoint of light formed magically between the tips of his thumb and forefinger, and he aimed it into her eyes. "Easy," he said in a soothing voice. "The light will not hurt you. I just need to see how your eyes react to it."

She did not feel threatened by him, so she obeyed, and he grunted with approval at what he saw.

"All is well," he told her. "I will leave word with the guards that they are to inform me if you should become ill, but I do not think there will be a problem." With that, he collected a case that must hold his instruments and let himself out of the room. Beyond the door, she saw a flicker of red that must be guards.

She felt for her brooch. It was there, hidden by its spell. Next, she checked her pocket. Her moonstone was missing. She'd been searched. She gazed about. The room she occupied was well-furnished. She sat upon a plush sofa. There was art on the walls, and doors leading to other rooms. If not for the knowledge of where she truly was, she would have guessed she was in some country manse. If not for the manacles on her wrists, she might have found it comfortable.

Lorine sat down beside her. "Oh, Miss Goodgrave! How did you come to be here? Did Dr. Silk bring you, or that horrid Mr. Starling?"

"No. I came with . . ." And when she remembered Luke was dead and probably Cade, too, she could speak no more.

DR. SILK'S EYES

"Miss Goodgrave?" Lorine shook Karigan's arm. Chains clinked. "Miss Goodgrave, please, what is it?"

Karigan barely heard her. Her vision had narrowed, grown dark. She could not grasp the loss.

"I—I came with Luke and Cade," she said finally. It was too much to tell Lorine everything, all the events that had led to her being there. "Luke is dead and . . ."

Lorine clapped her hands to her mouth and paled. Karigan had not been the only one who loved Cade.

"Nooo!" Lorine wailed. "It can't be true—it can't!"

While Lorine was able to express her grief, Karigan could not seem to. She was broken, unable to speak, act.

The door to the room opened, and a pair of guards barged in. Even distraught, Lorine had the presence of mind to veil her face. Karigan had no veil, nor did she care. The guards roughly pulled her to her feet and without another word, pushed her out of the room. The door was slammed behind her, cutting off Lorine's sobs.

The details of the corridors the guards dragged Karigan down were lost to her. She did not see others who passed by. She was trapped inside herself. She thought they passed a fountain with the statue of a dragon in it, and only noticed because it reminded her of something, but she let it go. Nothing else mattered.

Eventually they entered a darkened room, and the guards forced her into a chair. It was unmistakably an office with bookcases and a massive desk, and sitting on the other side of that desk was Dr. Silk gazing at her through those specs of his. She should want to kill him, she thought, for any part he might have played in Cade's death, but it was hard enough just to sit upright and not fold into a fetal position. She was cold ashes, not fire.

Dr. Silk waved the guards out and then stared at her, alternately gazing at something lying on his desk.

"You are she," he said at last.

Karigan stirred. "What?"

"You are Miss Goodgrave," he said, "or whatever your real name may be. Do you remember the image-trapper at my dinner party?" He lifted a framed picture, tilting it so she could see. "The image of you is still oddly transparent, but less so now."

Karigan blinked, focused. It was her in black and white and layers of gray. Her posture was stiff and unnatural, the expression on her face dead of emotion. She could have been looking in a mirror, for the image reflected how she felt at this very moment. But Dr. Silk was right—she could see the backdrop through her face as though she had used her fading ability at the time of the image-trapping. *Cade is gone.* The thought had nothing to do with the picture or Dr. Silk sitting there on the other side of the desk. It came unbidden.

Dr. Silk set the portrait aside and folded his black-gloved hands on the desk. "What is your real name?"

"Does it matter?" Nothing mattered, not with Cade gone.

"It does to me. That you acknowledge you are not a Goodgrave is a positive beginning."

"Ask your emperor. He knows who I am." She glanced listlessly at his shelves. They were much neater than the professor's had been, but there were similar artifacts; a rusted helmet, a skull, rolled maps.

"The emperor is currently indisposed." A muscle twitched in his cheek.

"Seeing me was too much for Amberhill, was it?"

It was difficult to gauge Silk's expression with those specs concealing his eyes, but she saw him start in surprise. "My dear," he said, "it would be wise of you to use care when speaking of the emperor."

Karigan shrugged.

"Now, you can keep your name to yourself," Dr. Silk said, "but in time we'll have it from Mr. Harlowe."

Karigan jerked upright. Her mouth dropped open, but once again she could not speak.

Dr. Silk leaned forward to study her. "You thought he was dead, didn't you."

Her heart pounded. Her head pounded. "He's—alive?" She hated revealing herself this way to this man, but she could not help it.

Dr. Silk leaned back into his chair, a slight smile on his lips. "For now. I cannot say the same for Josston's old carriage driver, however. My dear, now that you know Mr. Harlowe is alive, your answering of questions could make things much easier on him. You see, he is with an Inquisitor. Inquisitors are not gentle questioners, and they will use whatever methods they require to extract the information they seek. It can go badly for the one being questioned. Do you understand?"

Karigan licked her lips and nodded. Oh, yes, she understood. They were torturing Cade.

"Good. I had hoped you would cooperate, which would only lighten the burden on Mr. Harlowe."

"I want to see him," she said. "Prove to me he is alive, or I won't answer any questions."

"I am afraid you are not in a position to make demands. You will have to take me at my word. If you choose not to cooperate, we will get the answers out of Mr. Harlowe, and I guarantee he won't find it a pleasant experience."

Karigan considered her circumstances, the manacles on her wrists. She could leap across the desk and throttle Dr. Silk, manacles or no. He would not be expecting it, not from a female. But that wouldn't help Cade, nor would she be able to overcome every guard in the palace. No doubt they would execute Cade as soon as they got whatever information they wanted from him. He had betrayed the empire. He had started an uprising in Mill City. They would make an example of him.

The only course she saw was to make an ally of Dr. Silk. There was no reason to hide her identity or where she was from, not anymore. She would gain his confidence and maybe make things easier on Cade. She would buy time to figure out what to do. She took a deep breath trying to gather her composure. "I assume you are a man of some influence in the empire," Karigan said.

Dr. Silk preened. "I do have some influence. My father is second in power to the emperor. It is not openly acknowledged; it is understood in the emperor's inner circle."

"And you are an archeologist? Like the professor?"

He frowned. "I oversee all archeology throughout the empire. The professor was merely one of many who answer to me. I am the emperor's special consul on antiquities and true history."

Here was a man, Karigan thought, who was obscured by his father's shadow, who wanted to be regarded as important on his own merit. "We both know," she said, "that the empire's true history is, in fact, false."

"Those words are heresy." But Dr. Silk was not angered by her statement. He looked intrigued. "What makes you believe such a thing?"

"Did you know I was born here?" Karigan asked. "Right in this very area, which was once known as Corsa, the province of L'Petrie. You see, I was born over two hundred years ago." Dr Silk was a rapt listener. "I attended school in Selium, and then I went to Sacor City to serve King Zachary Hillander. You want to know my name? In my time, I am known as Rider Sir Karigan G'ladheon, a Green Rider of His Majesty's Messenger Service."

Dr. Silk paled, looked shaken. He gripped the armrests of his chair. She had caught him off guard. He must not have expected her to be so forthright, or maybe it had something to do with the information itself. She smiled to herself. Instead of feeling like she had given away a part of herself, announcing her name and title made her feel more powerful. She no longer had to hide.

"Well," Dr. Silk said, visibly trying to regain equanimity, "that would certainly explain a few things."

Karigan relaxed in her chair, her shackled hands resting on her lap. She had him now. If he was anything like the professor, he'd be overcome by his curiosity of the past. He would not even realize she had taken control of the situation.

"I have so many questions that I hardly know where to start," Dr. Silk said, the eagerness in his voice confirming her thoughts.

"I would be happy to answer your questions," Karigan replied. "There is no reason for me not to, except for the matter of Cade Harlowe."

"I told you—"

"Hear me out, please. You told me you are a man of influence, and I'd wager you can influence how Mr. Harlowe is treated."

"He is your lover," Dr. Silk said with distaste. "Do not try to deny it."

Imperial spies must have found out about it somehow. She tried to suppress a shudder of revulsion. "All right, I won't deny it." Her easy admission once again appeared to surprise him. The next part was not as easy to say. "We both know that Mr. Harlowe will be executed." Not if she could help it, of course. "I will answer your questions, but I expect to have your personal assurance of his well being until . . . his execution."

"Well—"

"Furthermore, I will want to see him one last time." Before Dr. Silk could interrupt, she hastily continued, "I know you said I wouldn't be able to see him, but I have something to offer in exchange."

"Oh?" He could not seem to help himself but look intrigued. "And what would that be?"

"You know that Green Riders have special abilities, do you not?"

"Yes, I have heard this. The foundation stud of our enslaved true healers was a Green Rider, from before the emperor conquered your Sacoridia. We have carefully bred the line to maintain and enhance the healing ability."

It was her turn to be shocked. He couldn't mean Ben Simeon, could he? The only Green Rider known to fear horses? Poor Ben, enslaved and bred to produce more healers? She'd been cold ashes before when she thought Cade already dead, but now there were embers glowing within. They threatened to flare, but she subdued them. She needed Dr. Silk.

"You will tell me of your ability?" Dr. Silk asked eagerly.

"I will *show* you," she said. "If you personally ensure I can see Mr. Harlowe."

"I am a man of influence as you say, but alas, even my influence goes only so far. My father would not permit it. Besides, I could always use Mr. Harlowe's welfare as leverage to force you to show me your ability."

"My ability cannot be coerced. If I feel I am being threatened, or Mr. Harlowe is being used as leverage, it will not work." It was pretty much a lie, and he'd probably see right through it, but she had to try. "Would your father necessarily have to know about my seeing Cade? It could be between you and me."

He said nothing, weighing her words, no doubt.

"Look," she continued, "we both want something, and we can both make it work to our mutual benefit."

Dr. Silk laughed. It was a scratchy sound. "You did say you were born to merchants, did you not?"

"The very best."

"Very well." She could tell he was trying to sound indifferent, but she could hear the underlying eagerness in his voice. "As long as you remain cooperative and answer my questions, as well as show me your ability, I will find a way to let you see your lover. You will just have to trust me to keep my end of this . . . bargain."

She nodded. "I will accept your word, on your honor, as you will have to accept mine."

"Agreed."

Karigan gave him the traditional merchant bow to seal it. "I am at your service."

Dr. Silk nodded gravely in return. "Then let us begin with questions, shall we? About your ability—"

"Not until I see Cade."

"That will take time to arrange."

Karigan shrugged. "I will not show you, or talk about it, till I see him." She imagined Dr. Silk glaring at her from behind his specs as the silence lengthened between them. She did not capitulate.

As though they had not spoken of her ability or Cade, he

folded his hands upon the desk once again and began to speak. "I have a number of questions, which you have agreed to answer. As improbable as it sounds, the fact that a person from so long ago is sitting before me now, there is precedent for it. One only has to look to the emperor or my father for that. But unlike either of them, if you are who you say you are, I gather you have not been living among us for these two centuries but are only recently arrived. And if that is, in fact, the case, how is it you came to be here?"

The questioning, and her answering, were both very like what it had been with the professor. Dr. Silk listened avidly to the story of her journey into Blackveil.

"Some of the materials we've found and preserved make mention of a Green Rider named Karigan G'ladheon, and that she vanished into Blackveil and never returned," he said.

Karigan had no idea what documents and artifacts he might have access to, so she could only shrug and continue, telling him of the looking mask, how she smashed it, and—

"You *smashed* it? An artifact of such amazing power?" He looked like he wanted to reach across the desk and shake her for her stupidity. The professor had not responded this way when he'd heard about the looking mask. "Why? Why did you give up such an opportunity? To hold the balance of the world in your hands?"

She shuddered. "I did not want the responsibility." It had not been her place. It was the responsibility of the gods to wield such power, not some small, fallible mortal. She also had not wanted to be held captive by the power, forever separated from her world, her friends and family, to be its guardian. Is that why the mirror man had tried passing the mask on to her? Had he tired of his guardianship?

Dr. Silk shook his head, clearly aghast over the choice she had made. Men like him could never understand. They did not care about the responsibility, only the wielding of power over others, only power for power's sake, so they could stand over other men and not be the one at the bottom of the heap, who is looked down upon by those above.

"Also," she said, "breaking the mask prevented Mornhavon the Black from possessing it." As bad as the empire was, she believed the world would be in far more dire straits had Mornhavon controlled the mask.

Dr. Silk looked thoughtful, but he gestured that she should go on with her tale, and so she recounted how she'd ended up as part of a circus performance in the current time period.

"Ah, so you were the ambulatory corpse Rudman Hadley complained so bitterly about," Dr. Silk mused. "I don't know why it upset him so much when it increased ticket sales thereafter. Well, that's one mystery solved. In an effort to solve the mystery of you, I've my experts going over some very interesting items we've found in the secret compartments of your wagon. My experts will judge their authenticity, but I suspect they will corroborate your tale. I must admit, I have had questions about you for a while." He leaned on his forearms on the desk. "You see, my eyes are not very good with ordinary sight. You probably find my office to be dark. My eyes are sensitive to light, even with my lenses." He tapped the rim of his specs. "It was an accident some time ago, with an etherea engine. It altered my sight. Do you want to know what I see when I look at you?"

Fascinated despite herself, she nodded.

Dr. Silk removed his specs. He gazed at her with nacreous eyes that gleamed in the low light. His pupils were tiny and gray, his eyelashes stark white. Karigan, who had seen many extraordinary things in her life, was not repulsed or taken aback but more curious.

He looked mildly disappointed by her lack of reaction. "I learned the hard way not to look directly into an etherea engine when one threatens to implode, which happens occasionally," he said, "though I've never heard of anyone else being thus afflicted in such accidents. However, I believe . . . my altered sight is, in a way, a gift, for all that it pains me, and makes everyday vision different. For instance, here is what I see when I look at you. I see an aura of green clouding around you, and dark wings. Tell me, do you know what it means?"

DARK WINGS

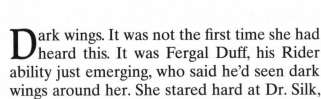

Dark wings. It was not the first time she had heard this. It was Fergal Duff, his Rider ability just emerging, who said he'd seen dark wings around her. She stared hard at Dr. Silk, his eyes agleam with pearlescent fire. Fergal was able to sometimes see auras around other magic users. What Dr. Silk had seen sounded very much like that. Could this accident of his have brought out the same sort of ability as Fergal's? In her own time, might he have heard the Rider call? No, she thought. He was not Rider material.

"Well?" he asked. "Have you nothing to say?"

She shook her head. "No. I—I don't know why you would see such a thing. I don't know what it means."

He appraised her a moment more with those disconcerting eyes of his before replacing his specs. "I believe you. It is how I see people—the aural energy around them. Sometimes there are patterns, but yours is different. It is why I first took an interest in Professor Josston's supposed niece. You are . . . different. Josston was clever to come up with the story that you'd been in an asylum. How better to explain you? Here we have taken you prisoner, you were struck hard by the emperor's Eternal Guardian, which was surely painful, you are in manacles, and yet you have not shed a single tear or begged to be let go. You bargained on behalf of Mr. Harlowe, not yourself. Most females would be making unseemly caterwauling nuisances of themselves in the same situation. You have exhibited no such normal female behavior, and you show no sign of shame at baring your face before strangers. I do not think you are mad, and these factors combined with the story of your arrival and the questions you have answered, lead me to surmise you are who you claim to be." He paused then went on. "You mentioned you traveled into Blackveil with Eletians. We found on your person a small round crystal we associate with Eletians."

"Yes. It was my mother's, and it was only recently passed to me."

"Your mother was an Eletian?"

"No. She was befriended by one who gave her the crystal." Although Karigan had come to question how much she really knew about either of her parents, she was firm on at least that point: Her mother had not been Eletian.

"How did it come about, this friendship between your mother and an Eletian? At that time, Eletians were not prone to making appearances outside their forest."

"I don't know exactly." That much was true, she thought. Somehow Laurelyn had sought out her mother and found her, but Karigan did not feel she needed to bring Laurelyn into this discussion with Dr. Silk. "My mother died when I was little, and I only found out about all this toward the end of winter. *My* winter."

"So what are they used for, these crystals?"

"The Eletians, on the expedition, used them as a light source, like in the legends about how they collected silver moonbeams. Have you heard those?"

"Yes, yes, of course. But we can't make the ones in our possession light up."

"You have some?"

"Several, obtained from captives during the war."

There was too much Karigan had failed to learn about the empire's rise. Had the Eletians fought alongside the Sacoridians? Had the entire population been annihilated? What had become of them?

"I think they light up just for Eletians." Some instinct prevented Karigan from admitting that she could illuminate her own with a touch. The less he thought she knew, the better.

"Magic?" Dr. Silk murmured.

Karigan shrugged. "Even in my time, we find Eletians to be very cryptic."

Dr. Silk chuckled. "Can't argue with that. This line of questioning is, of course, leading somewhere." He stood unexpectedly and came around the desk. "Come with me, Miss G'ladheon."

"*Rider* G'ladheon," Karigan corrected. "Or Sir Karigan."

"Come along." Dr. Silk acted as though he hadn't heard. "We haven't all day."

She held her tongue and followed him into a corridor. Accompanied by the guards who had brought her, they set off into the depths of the palace. This time she paid attention—not so much to the ornamentation, unless it provided a convenient landmark—but to their various turnings through the hushed corridors. When they came upon the fountain of the dragon this time, she stumbled to a halt and remembered. She remembered a dream that might have been more than a dream. Just like in the drawing shown her by the ghostly Yates, there were corridors to either side of the fountain. Yates had pointed to the one on the left. It led to the prison of forgotten days. She knew it with that inexplicable sense of knowing. Would Dr. Silk take her there? The scything moon was held captive there, whatever that meant.

For that matter, the riddle had gone on, telling her to *seek it in the den of the three-faced reptile.* Well, she was in Amberhill's den, but she didn't get the reference to three—

"Miss G'ladheon?" Dr. Silk glanced back at her in annoyance. A guard shoved her forward, and they were off once again.

"*Rider* G'ladheon," Karigan muttered.

They did not enter the passage to the left of the fountain, as she had hoped, but they took the one right after it. Close, but not close enough. Some ways down the corridor, a guard unlocked a stout door and opened it for them. She followed Dr. Silk into a chamber quietly lit. At first all she made out were stacks of wooden crates, then tables and cabinets draped in sheets. Dusty, odd-shaped glassware and copper tubes glinted on shelves. In the very back of the chamber was a darkened cell.

"This is the emperor's old laboratory where he once studied Eletians," Dr. Silk explained. "As you can see, it has not been used in some time since there have been no specimens to study until now."

Lhean.

"At my dinner party, you saw the one I captured. You knew him, didn't you? He came with you through time. He was on the Blackveil expedition. It is the only explanation."

Karigan had been peering into the distant darkness of the cell, but now she turned to Dr. Silk. "He didn't tell you?"

"He won't speak most of the time, and when he does, it is Eltish gibberish. I'd ask my father to pry information from him, but I want him to be pristine when I officially present him to the emperor."

Karigan shuddered at the word "pristine."

"So, was the Eletian you saw at my party one of your companions?"

"Yes."

He looked jubilant. "Then let us reunite you. Perhaps he will deign to speak if he sees you."

He led the way between crates and tables to the back of the room to the cell. He raised a lever in the wall and a ceiling fixture threw cold light into the cell. There, behind steel bars, on a scattering of straw strewn on the floor, sat Lhean, legs crossed, hands on his knees, eyes closed as though he slept in the awkward position. Nothing of his armor remained, just the black clothlike membrane clinging to his skin, stiff-looking with dried ichor. His face was thin and pale, the radiance she associated with Eletians faded or absent altogether. He appeared not to sense their arrival.

"He has spent most of his time in these trances to evade interacting with us," Dr. Silk said.

More like he's trying to preserve himself, Karigan thought. He appeared barely to breathe.

"Make him talk," Dr. Silk ordered her.

"*Make* him?"

"Or our agreement is off, and I'll find ways to make you reveal your ability."

"I told you—"

"That it can't be coerced. I grant it may make it more difficult, but I don't believe you for one moment. I am humoring you, Miss G'ladheon, because it's easier. Unless you humor me, your situation, and Mr. Harlowe's, will only grow more difficult."

So he would use Cade as leverage after all, to manipulate her. She could not say she was surprised. His honorable word was not worth much, and better she learn it now rather than later.

"Remember, if you please me," Dr. Silk said, "I have the influence to make the coming days easier on Mr. Harlowe."

His lack of honor did not defeat her. After all, she'd come to Gossham wanting to find Lhean, and here Dr. Silk had delivered her right to him. The rescuing part, however, was going to be harder, much harder, especially since the list now included Cade, Lorine, and Arhys. Not to mention herself. In the meantime, she must keep Dr. Silk happy.

She sighed. "I can guarantee nothing, but I will try."

"That is all I ask."

She pressed right up against the bars of the cage, her manacles ringing against the steel. "Lhean?" she said.

"Is that the creature's name?" Dr. Silk asked, excitement behind his words.

She ignored him. "Lhean, it's me, Karigan. Er, the Galadheon."

Slowly his eyes opened, and they were the startling blue she remembered.

"*A mien,* Galadheon." Then he rattled off a whole stream of words in Eletian.

"What did he say?" Dr. Silk asked.

"I—I don't speak Eletian," Karigan replied, but she had gotten the impression that Lhean had insulted the company she kept. "Lhean, could you speak in the common, please? Dr. Silk knows how we came to be here in his time."

Lhean deigned to gaze at Dr. Silk with a baleful glare and then spat more Eletian at him. The language was always lyrical, more music than mere words that made the glassware on the shelves chime, but even Dr. Silk could not possibly mistake the strains of venom in Lhean's speech. The effort appeared to tax him, and he struggled to remain sitting up.

"Lhean?"

"This place," he said, finally speaking in the common, "is killing me."

Karigan turned to Dr. Silk. "Have you not been caring for him? Have you been offering him any food and water?"

"We have, but he refuses food." Dr. Silk shrugged. "He has taken some water."

"Lhean," Karigan said, "what can we do to help you?"

"Take me home."

It was so plaintively said, and expressed all that Karigan felt as well. "I do not know the way."

Dr. Silk chuckled. "We would not let you go even if you did."

"This place is poison," Lhean said.

"The etherea? It is . . ." She recollected the way it had been explained to her. "It is from Blackveil, filtered."

"The air, the land, everything," Lhean replied. "The mechanicals destroy etherea."

"That's not true," Dr. Silk said. "There is plenty of—"

"Not outside this place," Lhean snapped. "It is dead. And what you have here, poison."

Lhean was just stating fact, Karigan knew, but she could sense anger building in Dr. Silk. She did not know what would happen if Dr. Silk erupted in fury. He may wish to keep Lhean "pristine" for the emperor, but that would not necessarily forestall some rash act.

"Chocolate," she interjected. Both Dr. Silk and Lhean glanced at her in surprise. "Chocolate," she repeated. "It . . . it has some sustaining quality for Eletians."

Dr. Silk raised an eyebrow but did not argue. When he turned to order his guards to locate some chocolate, Karigan whispered so very low she herself could not hear it, knowing how keen Eletian hearing was. "I will try to find a way home," she said. "I will need your help."

Lhean nodded his understanding and touched his chest in the spot where the winged horse brooch rested on hers. "Thresholds," he whispered, but said no more as Dr. Silk turned his attention back to them.

In short order, several varieties of chocolate were brought in on a rolling tray and presented to Lhean—fudge, solid bars of dark chocolate, truffles, lighter chocolates oozing with cordial, chocolate molded into soldiers, turtles, and gold-dusted leaves. There was even a pitcher of warm, thick sipping chocolate and a tiny mug to drink it from. All of this, but no Dragon Droppings. Lhean chose the solid bar of dark chocolate. The scent of all of it concentrated right in front of Karigan almost made her swoon, and she realized they had probably passed suppertime quite a while ago. She was starving. Dr. Silk did not invite her to try any of the chocolate.

Lhean was delicate in his eating, and Dr. Silk watched closely. "Yes," he murmured. "I can see it helps. There is improvement in the colors around you."

Lhean glanced sharply at him but said nothing.

"What prizes you both are," Dr. Silk said, "and the emperor will reward me greatly." He left instructions with the guards that the Eletian should be given chocolate whenever he desired, or any other food at his request, then with a gesture, his other guards grabbed Karigan and dragged her away.

She got in one last glimpse of Lhean who had risen to his feet to watch after her. *Thresholds,* he had said. He must believe she had the power to take them home. As she was jerked and jostled out into the corridor, she wished fervently he was right, but at the moment, her hope was flagging.

"I am done with you for now," Dr. Silk told her, "and must attend to other matters."

He simply discarded her and went on his way, leaving her with the guards who shoved her in the opposite direction. He'd better be keeping his word, she thought, and use his influence to help Cade, but he'd already shown himself to be untrustworthy. If he did not keep his word, she would show him no mercy.

POTENTIAL

The bluish haze was peaceful and healing. Cade felt as though he were floating, and the encounter in Webster Silk's chambers only a nightmare. No gun, no wound. Unless he were dead, and this was what death was: all this peaceful floating.

A stab into his shoulder made him cry out, pain spidering along every nerve, the peace shattered. Cade realized he hadn't had nightmares, he was living one.

"That's right, Mr. Harlowe, let's wake up."

Cade shook his head. His vision was blurry at first, but then resolved into sharp, harsh lines. The portly man from Silk's office, Mr. Starling, loomed in front of him, suitcoat off, sleeves rolled up. He wore an apron and gloves. The gloves glinted with metal knuckles. Mr. Starling seated himself before Cade. He appeared to have a plate of cakes and a teapot on a table beside him, along with a tray of shiny and sharp implements. Just beyond him stood a young man in blue robes.

Cade tried to move, but his wrists and ankles were cuffed to a chair, which, he discerned, was bolted to the floor. A single lamp hung overhead. There were no windows, and the rest of the Inquisitor's room was left to the shadows and imagination.

"Very good," Mr. Starling said. "Glad to have you back with us. It took a while, I must say, but Marcus here has brought you back." He indicated the young man in robes. "He is not just a mender, Mr. Harlowe, but a true healer, and he stopped your bleeding and healed your shoulder."

Like a viper, faster than could be believed of so stout a

man, Starling's hand struck out and jabbed where Cade had been shot. Once again the shocking pain burned through Cade's body, and he cried out and jerked involuntarily. "Well, mostly healed," Starling amended. "We didn't remove the bullet. It makes for a very immediate point of contact, don't you agree?" Without waiting for a reply, he popped a teacake into his mouth and chewed vigorously. "Must keep my strength up." He patted his lips with a napkin and cleared his throat. "Now Marcus here is very good at fixing any damage I may inflict upon your body, but as I told you earlier, it is only so I can hurt you some more. Do you understand?"

When Cade did not respond, Mr. Starling sighed, then struck again, this time pinching the flesh around Cade's wound and twisting it. Cade started to fade out from the pain.

"Do you understand?" Starling repeated.

Cade nodded.

"Soon I will have you saying, 'Yes, Mr. Starling. Whatever you say, Mr. Starling.' But, a nod will do for now." The man chuckled, causing his belly to shake. "I could take you to a point where you beg me to hurt you. That you tell me you love me. I know it seems inconceivable now, but I am a master of my art. Isn't it so, Marcus?"

"Yes, Mr. Starling."

"See?" the Inquisitor asked, his voice full of mirth. "Even Marcus knows. He has seen me at work often enough. He has even been privileged to have experienced my touch first hand. You should be honored as well, Mr. Harlowe, that my superiors thought you important enough to leave you in my care. We are not here, however, just because I take great pleasure in my art, but for the glory of emperor and empire. The emperor requires that you answer certain questions about your traitorous actions in Mill City, and your purpose in coming to Gossham. That's a rather brazen move, coming to the emperor's very door, and I can't believe you've done so just to recover some bratty child and her governess."

Cade thought of Luke's betrayal. "Didn't Luke tell you everything?"

"He told us you intended to bring the uprising to Gossham, and yes, to rescue Professor Josston's favorite little servant, but not why. Was she just some urchin plucked off the street to be raised by your generous mentor? Well, we shall have answers. Indeed, we shall. And I will tell you what, Mr. Harlowe: the more forthcoming you are, the easier it will go on you." Starling popped another teacake into his mouth. Powdered sugar dusted his lips and the front of his apron.

"You are just going to kill me anyway."

"True, true, but there is a difference between going to one's death easily and without pain, and going to death after feeling as if all your bones were broken and rearranged, tendons severed, flesh grated, and parts of your body immolated and carved off. Trust me, I do know how to keep you alive and alert during these procedures. I also have a colleague who enjoys overseeing a good castration. Now mind, Marcus is good at what he does, but regrowing body parts does not work well. We've tried. The results are, well, grotesque. Intriguing for us, but not so much for the recipient.

"So, shall we begin? You do realize your little rebellion has failed, do you not? We know who a number of your accomplices are in Mill City, and they are being questioned, as well. However, I want names. Names of all your conspirators, including those who collaborated with Professor Josston."

Cade thought of Jax and Mirriam and all the others, and wondered if they'd been found and arrested, or worse. It was all on him, the failure of the rebellion and whatever happened to the folk of Mill City. All his fault. He must not give up names of his accomplices in case they'd managed to remain undetected. It sounded noble as he thought about it, the protecting of his comrades, but the fact of the matter was that as a student of archeology, he had never faced anything like this before, and none of the professor's training had prepared him to resist an Inquisitor. Back in the early days, when he'd been brought into the fold of the opposition by the professor, all such notions of personal sacrifice had been romantic and far off rather than anything real. He hadn't considered what it actually felt like to be shot or tortured. A true Weapon, he knew, one who had been through all the proper conditioning, would know how to withstand torture.

Worse than worrying about what might happen to himself

was what might happen to all those connected to him, especially Karigan. What did they plan for her?

"Mr. Harlowe," the Inquisitor said in a voice of warning, "I am waiting. The names."

"I don't know any."

Starling sighed dramatically and glanced over his shoulder. "Marcus, it appears we're going to have to do this the hard way." He turned his piercing eyes back on Cade. "Are you sure this is how you want it to be, young man? If not, give me the names."

"I have no names to give you."

Starling rose and paced in a slow amble before Cade, his hands clasped behind his back. Cade glanced apprehensively at the tray of sharp tools, wondering what was coming. It appeared not much as Starling continued to pace and mutter to himself. Cade settled in and waited, his thoughts once again turning to Karigan and what would become of her. He had led her into this trap. He—

Starling turned on his heel, pummeling Cade across the face, not once, not twice, but time and again, back and forth so hard Cade thought his head would snap off his neck. The metal studs embedded in the knuckles of Starling's gloves raked his cheeks open. He was so stunned by the ferocity of the attack he couldn't even seem to cry out.

It stopped. Cade struggled to catch his breath. Inhaled blood. He wanted to touch his face, for surely his flesh had been shredded to ribbons.

"That, Mr. Harlowe," Starling said, "was just me warming up."

Cade blinked, trying to clear his vision. Starling stood before him, hands on hips, his apron and sleeves sprayed with blood.

"I must admit some sentimentality for the old methods," Starling said. "Some of my colleagues, well, they'll use a mechanical to do the work, which is very precise, but lacking in artistry. Or, they'll have an assistant exert themselves. Me? Well, this is my art, and I like doing it myself. No surrogates. I like the old tools, too." He flexed his hands in the stained gloves. "Now, Mr. Harlowe, would you care to give me those names before I begin to work on you in earnest? If you do, Marcus will heal up what I've done so far, and we'll get you some water or tea, anything you like. What do you say?"

It sounded so very reasonable. Just give the man a few names and avoid more beating. Maybe Cade could give him false names. He suspected, however, that Starling would know he was lying. Starling would know and punish him for the lie.

"I can see you are thinking it over, Mr. Harlowe. You are an intelligent man. A scholar even. By all accounts you did very well at university. The records show you succeeded at the uppermost levels in your courses and fieldwork."

They had looked at his school records? Cade despaired of getting any lies past the Inquisitor.

"Perhaps some of your classmates were conspirators," Starling continued. "Or maybe some of your other professors. You can give me names, and there will be no reason to further—"

He was interrupted by knocking, and a door creaked open somewhere behind Cade. It shed thin illumination across the floor.

"Yes? What is it?" Starling demanded. "Can't you see I'm with a subject?"

"Sorry, sir," came a reply from the direction of the light. "Dr. Silk would like a word with you."

Starling's surprise was obvious. "Dr. Silk? What does *he* want?"

"I don't know, sir, but he's outside waiting and quite insistent."

"All right, all right. One moment." The door closed, and Starling grumbled. "In the name of the empire. No one interrupts one of my sessions. Ever. Not even Dr. Silk. But alas, I must obey." It was said as if he expected Cade to sympathize with him. "Butler!" he cried as he strode across the floor.

A mechanical apparatus rolled over on a trio of cast iron wheels. Instead of a spherical body like an Enforcer, its mechanisms, the whirring gears, wheels, belts and pulleys, were exposed. Cade had never seen the internal workings of an Enforcer, though he, Jax, and the others had dreamed of capturing one to learn what they could about the devices, but they'd scrapped one plan after another as too dangerous. The Enforcers and Starling's "butler" were different, but they must be similar in essential ways. There was, however, no steamworks. Here in Gossham, a city brimming with etherea, the mechanicals would not require steam. Etherea engines were enough to power them, unlike mechanicals located in other parts of the empire.

Cade had never seen an etherea engine, so he could only guess that it had to do with what looked like an ordinary jug in the center of all the workings filled with muddy fluid, which was circulated through a snarl of piping, to various parts of the apparatus, with a pump that gasped and wheezed like a sickly old man.

Besides the wheels, the mechanical had a pair of appendages that scissored out toward Starling. Each had a claw on its end. Starling extended his hands and the claws tugged off his gloves. The mechanical butler then rolled away back into the darkness and out of sight.

Starling turned once more to Cade. "You must excuse this interruption, Mr. Harlowe, inconvenient as it is, but perhaps it will give you the opportunity to reflect and consider your options." Then he turned to the mender. "And you, Marcus, are not to touch him. Understood? I will know if you do anything."

"Yes, sir."

Starling grunted, then left them, the door creaking open again and closing. Cade sat back, closed his eyes. The very air ate at the slashed skin of his face. His head still rang from the blows, and this was, Starling had said, only his warm-up.

"Mr. Harlowe?" His name was spoken barely above a whisper. He opened his eyes to see the mender hovering closer. "I am sorry," he said.

"For what?" Cade's voice was muffled by swollen lips.

"I—I am not allowed to heal you."

"Not your fault."

"It is the reason for my existence," Marcus replied. "I mean, what all true healers were born for before the empire. We can't tolerate the torture of others, but we of the palace, we are slaves born into it, made to heal the damage of torture so more pain can be inflicted. It goes against everything we stand for. But the consequences of disobeying . . ."

"I understand," Cade said. "It is another evil among many."

Marcus glanced furtively toward the door, then took a hesitant step closer. "Mr. Harlowe, I have seen the lady that came with you. I healed her fractured collar bone—"

Cade started. "Fractured collar bone?" He fought his restraints, but to no avail.

"Please listen. Time is short. I healed her, and she was well when I left her. Please believe me. She is well."

Cade nodded. He knew personally what Marcus could do.

"I can sometimes see into a person I'm working on," Marcus continued. "I can learn things about them. I saw she has some minor ability with etherea. I couldn't discern exactly what, except that it is there. If my masters learn of this, they will use it, as we menders are used. Used and bred to produce more with powers that can be harnessed. The emperor is very keen on his breeding programs, whether it is his horses or his slaves."

Battered as Cade was, the insinuation was clear. He clenched his hands, nails biting into his palms. He had led Karigan into this. He wanted to howl his frustration, his utter helplessness.

Marcus was not done. "When we produce children, they are taken from us. If they have the ability with etherea, they are raised here at the palace. Some are menders, others have an affinity for working with etherea engines. Those children without abilities are entered into the general slave population or otherwise discarded."

Otherwise discarded? It was, for Cade, yet another example of why he'd chosen to oppose the empire, but the reasons kept getting worse and worse.

"I tell you this," Marcus said, "because besides your lady's health and ability, there was more I observed. I could sense a seed, a new potential, seeming to quicken within her, and if I am not mistaken, it is of your making."

Cade stilled, working out the mender's words until he was

sure he understood. He nearly roared out a response, but Marcus was quick and slapped him across his raw cheek. The pain sobered Cade. He saw how unhappy Marcus looked.

"I will tell no one," the mender said. "This has gone on for too many generations, the stealing and enslavement of our children."

Cade jammed his eyes shut. Tears stung his scored cheeks, but inside, his agony and joy was over the potential that Karigan could be carrying.

THE SCENT OF
HOPELESSNESS

The door opened and closed, and Starling appeared once again in their circle of light. He gazed appraisingly down at Cade.

"Well, well, well. It appears, Mr. Harlowe, a change of tactics is in order." He came close, leaned over Cade, and whispered in his ear, "Do not forget that I always get what I wish, no matter the method."

Then he straightened and backed away. "Marcus, heal the damage to Mr. Harlowe's face." Then he turned away and called, "Butler! I need my coat."

When Marcus stood before him, Cade tried to read the mender's expression to see if he knew what was going on, but all he saw was consternation. Was Starling merely planning to keep him guessing and confused, or had Dr. Silk issued some new directive, and if so, why?

Marcus placed his hands to either side of Cade's face, not touching his ravaged cheeks but close enough to feel their heat. Marcus closed his eyes and a soothing haze of blue suffused Cade's mind, and once again he felt as though he were floating. Was this the healing? Had Marcus been right about Karigan? The shiver of joy, counterbalanced by dread, passed through him once more. Could he trust the mender's word, or was it merely an act, some ploy of Starling's to manipulate his emotions? In the empire, it was never easy to know who to trust, but the mender had seemed so earnest. As the pain receded from his wounds, he was willing to give Marcus the benefit of the doubt, which brought back the joy and dread.

He dared not dream of what could be, or even try to imagine the worst. Doing so could only induce madness. He must narrow his vision and find a way to free himself and Karigan. So long had he prepared to be a Weapon, he had never paused to consider the idea of fatherhood. Now, everything had changed.

Starling dismissed Marcus and, in turn, ushered in a pair of guards. They unlocked Cade from his chair, made him stand, and manacled his wrists behind his back. Starling had said there was to be a change of tactics. What came next?

Starling did not explain, just hummed a jaunty tune as Cade was pushed through the chamber. Cade caught glimpses of machines and chains and sharp objects waiting in the shadows. What methods could be worse than these devices of torture?

He was taken into a corridor. This was not one of the magnificent colonnaded halls he'd seen before, but a dimly lit narrow corridor of stone blocks. They stopped at an open door that led into a small, closet-sized room. Cade noted the levers inside, and realized that it must be a lift. He'd heard about them certainly. They were of particular use in the empire's mines, but there were none he knew of in Mill City.

"Step inside," Starling said.

When Cade proved too hesitant, he was shoved in. Were they going to use the lift to torture him? Apparently not, for the guards stepped right in with him, followed by Starling, who had resumed humming. He closed the lift's door and manipulated the levers. The car bounced, then descended.

Cade had never before felt anything quite like the downward motion, like a very slow, controlled fall. The whine of cables guided through the pulley system told the story of their descent as much as the motion. When the car came to rest, Starling did not immediately open the door but turned to Cade.

"Mr. Harlowe, I am to understand that you and the lady who arrived with you were far more than just traveling companions. Now don't glare at me in that fashion, though it does confirm for me your protective feelings for her."

Had Luke informed his imperial contacts about them? He clenched his hands behind his back, wishing he could beat them into Starling's fleshy jowls.

"In fact," Starling continued, "I am to understand the young lady has quite the unusual background. Professor Josston had claimed her as his niece, but it was all to protect her true identity."

"I don't know what you are talking about."

Starling laughed. "Of course you do. She has given her real name and story to Dr. Silk."

Given? Cade wondered with alarm. If they had done anything to her . . . He strained against his manacles.

Starling gloated at Cade's distress for a moment, then continued on. "But right now, none of that concerns me. What does interest me is this—what shall we call it?—this romance? This love between the two of you, so very like those silly girl novels my fourteen-year-old daughter loves to read. What, you are shocked I have a daughter? A beast like me? Two sons and three daughters, Mr. Harlowe. I cherish my children.

"In any case, this romance, this love between you and Miss G'ladheon, it is so very useful."

"There is nothing—" Cade began.

"You are quite welcome to waste your breath as much as you wish, but I know the truth. Now, I am going to show you someone we've kept down here beneath the palace for a very long time. I am accustomed to her appearance, but you may find it—no. Dear me, but I don't want to spoil the surprise for you. When you do look upon her, I want you to imagine your Miss G'ladheon in her place. Strange name, G'ladheon. I can't even begin to imagine its origins."

With that, Starling opened the door. The guards that greeted them were not the usual palace guards. These wore uniforms of scarlet, their faces concealed by sinister masks. Cade was shoved out of the lift into a corridor of stone. It was damp, and he slipped. The bare phosphorene bulbs did little to illuminate the space. Cade imagined they were very deep in the earth. A powerful force even deeper vibrated the floor beneath his feet in a regular cadence—the distant roar of water and turbines. He'd been in enough mills to recognize the sounds. Why turbines beneath the palace? He supposed he would never know, and it did not matter. He had more pressing concerns.

They approached a steel door at the end of the corridor, and as one of the guards in scarlet started turning keys in a series of locks, Starling said, "This is a sight few have ever seen. Mainly just the members of the Scarlet Guard, Minister Silk, and myself. The Scarlet Guard, by the way, is under a strict oath of secrecy about what it is that is kept here. Yes, this is indeed a rare privilege, Mr. Harlowe."

When the final lock released, the door was slowly drawn open. Cade was not prepared for the foul stench that flowed out from within, and he turned his face away. A taper was brought in to illuminate the cell.

"Behold the witch, Yolandhe," Starling said.

Witch? Cade looked, and the creature he saw, molded out of flesh and shadows, did not appear human to him, not even living, with her mutilated body, the masses of snarls that had once been a head of hair. She hadn't even eyes—just depressed eyelids over the sockets. At first he could not discern what was wrong with her mouth, maybe because his mind could not, did not wish, to grasp it. Her lips were sewn shut with large, crude stitches.

How could they do this to any living being? The obvious torment scarred upon her body, chaining her spread-eagle to augment her vulnerability, the tines of a metal collar digging into her neck.

Cade looked at Starling who appeared affable as ever and started humming again.

"Monsters," Cade spat. "You are monsters."

Starling stopped humming. "So judgmental are we, Mr. Harlowe? You don't know who she is or what she is capable of. She is here for a reason, but for now I want you to look at *her*, not me." He gripped Cade's chin with fingers like iron and turned his head to force him to look.

"Now, Mr. Harlowe, I want you to think of your love, your Miss G'ladheon, in the witch's place. The torment, the torture, every conceivable indignity could all await her here. The members of the Scarlet Guard are eager for a new prisoner, fresh flesh upon which to sate their pleasure and carve their initials."

Cade struggled fruitlessly against those who held him.

"Women are much stronger than men, you know," Starling continued matter-of-factly. "At least when it comes to pain. A man would never survive childbirth." He chuckled. "The witch here, she has endured for a very long time. She is extremely strong and has never been entirely broken. From all accounts, your Miss G'ladheon looks to be the strong type. The guards like them strong, for it prolongs their sport.

"But you being a man who loves her, you will want to spare her the pain, the degradation, the violation. Am I right?"

"If you touch her—"

"You will do what, exactly?" Starling asked.

Cade trembled with rage.

"Yeees," Starling said, and released Cade's chin. "It appears I was right."

Cade wanted to look away again, but something about the witch caught his attention. Her head was slightly cocked as though she listened. He had not been able to tell if she were even conscious.

"No one deserves this," Cade said.

"You are being judgmental again regarding a case about which you know nothing. But for her imprisonment the empire stands."

Cade regarded her with renewed interest. This poor wretch? This woman? She could bring down the empire? Was it his imagination, or did the corners of her mouth twitch, forming a ghastly smile?

"All you need to know," Starling said, "is that if you do not answer my questions, this is the fate that awaits your lady."

Cade strained against those who held him, wanting nothing more than to lash out.

"Yes, yes," Starling murmured. "Your impulse to protect what is yours is strong. Remember this vision of the witch, and remember your duty as a man."

Cade wanted to scream at Starling how he planned to kill him, but it never passed his lips because a ripple of calm, like a soft ocean current, soothed his mind.

Patience.

Cade looked wildly about, but no one appeared to have

spoken. The witch hung in her chains like a perverse marionette. They slammed the door closed, sealing her away, cutting off his view of her.

As he was escorted back down the corridor, he asked, "Why is her mouth sewn shut?"

Starling smiled. "A precaution only. You see, one of my predecessors, or perhaps Minister Silk himself, wrecked her voice long ago. It held power, her voice, and by wrecking it, we diminished her, but there is still some, hmmm, persuasiveness, shall we say? in her voice. We could have removed it entirely, but we need her to speak on occasion. With a newcomer such as yourself, we deemed it necessary to prevent her from speaking. As diminished as her power is, there is still something there. Her tongue is most vile, in any case, and it is a relief not to have to listen to her."

As Cade was pushed into the lift and the pulleys began winding it upward, he realized he had learned something valuable: that this woman, this Yolandhe, was still some danger to the empire, which was why they kept her prisoner in such a state. He also learned that Starling and his masters wanted information from him badly enough that they were willing to show the witch, their secret prisoner, to him.

Would they do to Karigan what they had done to Yolandhe? He did not doubt they wouldn't hesitate if they thought it would fulfill some purpose. And the potential within Karigan—what would happen if it came to fruition? What would it to do to his—to *their*—child? The genteel society he'd known in the professor's house and at the university was a façade only. The emperor's men knew no bounds when it came to cruelty and crossing the lines of human decency.

"Yes, I can see you are thinking it over," Starling said. "The Scarlet Guard are eager to meet your Miss G'ladheon."

If Starling wished to enflame Cade's emotions, he was succeeding. Cade could not help but see Karigan's face in place of Yolandhe's, her lips sewn shut, the body he'd touched so tenderly mutilated by the hands of monsters. He tried to force the image from his mind. He could not let it happen. But even if he did all that Starling wished, what would guarantee Karigan's safety? Maybe they'd go ahead and do to her whatever they wished, even if he gave them every single name of the leaders of the opposition. Luke's betrayal had done nothing to save his family. He shuddered, remembering the head of Luke's son in the coffer.

What of my *child?*

Misinterpreting Cade's shudder, Starling smiled. "One does not soon forget the sight of the witch."

Cade didn't reply. He knew he could not allow them to harm Karigan. But if giving up names was no guarantee, how could he rescue her? He was guarded and in chains. He could not even help himself.

Starling leered at him as if he could scent hopelessness.

THE PRISON OF
FORGOTTEN DAYS

Karigan was unceremoniously tossed into Lorine's chambers, and she sprawled across the floor. A pair of slippered feet hurried over to her.

"Miss Goodgrave!" Lorine was in a sleeping gown and robe. She helped Karigan rise to her feet. "Are you well? I didn't know what to think when those brutes dragged you away."

"I'm hungry, mainly," Karigan said.

"What are they thinking?" Lorine fretted. "Manacles and no food. If Mirriam were here, she'd tell them a thing or two."

Karigan agreed and slumped wearily onto the sofa. Lorine's eyes, she noted, were red-rimmed and puffy. She must have been weeping for Cade. Before Karigan could tell her anything, a look of resolve set in Lorine's features, and she hurried off to what must be her bedchamber. Moments later, she returned with a veil covering her face. She strode to the door without a faltering step, and swung it open.

"Miss Goodgrave has had no supper," she informed the guards. "You should be ashamed of yourselves for her poor care on your watch. You must have something brought for her right away."

Karigan thought Lorine did as well as Mirriam ever could. When Lorine rejoined her on the sofa and pushed the veil back, it looked as though the effort had cost her.

"I believe some of Arhys' willfulness has rubbed off on me," she said.

"In a good way," Karigan reassured her. "Perhaps you can convince them to remove my manacles."

"Oh no! I didn't even think!"

Karigan had only been jesting, believing it was beyond anyone's power but Dr. Silk's to have them removed. "Speaking of Arhys, where is she?"

"In bed. I haven't had the heart to tell her about Mr. Harlowe."

"About Mr. Harlowe," Karigan said, "he is not dead after all. I fear I jumped to that conclusion when I heard about Luke."

"Oh!" Lorine placed her hand over her mouth and paled. "You are sure?"

"As sure as I can be without actually seeing him. It does not mean he is out of danger, however."

"Thank all that is good that he still lives," Lorine whispered.

"I don't know for how long," Karigan murmured. "He is being . . . questioned."

"It is all too much. All of this."

"Yes," Karigan replied. "Yes, it is." She glanced about the room wondering if there were listeners, or even watchers. She decided she could assume nothing. "Lorine, I am feeling chill. Do you suppose we could have a fire?"

Lorine gave her an odd look at the change of subject. Karigan tried to convey in her return gaze that it was more than a simple request to start a fire in the fireplace.

Lorine nodded. "Yes, Miss Goodgrave, I'll see to it."

While Lorine worked on starting a fire, Karigan hunted for writing materials. On a table, she found Arhys' lesson books and a sheaf of plain paper where the girl had practiced her figures and handwriting. Karigan took the paper and a graphite stick, cleverly encased in a cylinder of wood, to the sofa. Just as Lorine got a blaze going, the guards returned with a tray for Karigan. Lorine gave a good accounting of herself trying to convince them to free Karigan of the manacles, but they refused. Mirriam, however, would have been proud of Lorine's tenacity.

They'd brought Karigan chicken soup and tea, and she thought sadly of poor Luke who'd so often had soup brought to her while she was under the influence of morphia. It was tepid and not so easy to spoon into her mouth with her wrists bound, but it was tasty. When she scraped the bottom of the bowl, she asked Lorine, "Do you like to play games?"

"What?"

"See here," Karigan replied, and she wrote on the paper: *Pretend we are playing a game.* "Bridge and Rabbit," she said aloud. "Do you know that one?" It had been a common children's game in Karigan's time.

"Yes," Lorine said, still obviously perplexed. "Arhys and I play it sometimes."

"Oh, good," Karigan said. She wrote: *We are all in danger. They will want to know more about Arhys.*

Lorine took the graphite. *Why?*

"Bridge," Karigan said, as if they were really playing the game. She decided that Lorine was better off not knowing that Arhys was the last heir of the old realm. *Because they are evil and cruel,* she wrote, *and Arhys was the professor's favorite. You need to tell me about the palace, what is where, schedules, anything you can think of. Remember, we are playing the game.*

"Rabbit," Lorine said faintly. She proceeded to draw a map of what she knew of the palace. It was only a small part of the main palace building, which was not surprising. Her movements were relegated to whatever Arhys was involved in from day to day. There were classrooms, the play yard, and little else but the corridors. Fountains were located at major junctions in corridors. Lorine marked the "grotto fountain," the "horse fountain," and the "fountain with the trout in it." Also, she noted the dragon fountain Karigan had seen.

"Rabbit," Karigan said, and so they went back and forth asking and answering questions. *The next thing I'm going to ask will sound very strange,* Karigan wrote. *First, though, you should know my name is not Kari Goodgrave.* In as few words as possible, Karigan tried to explain who she was, when and where she was from, and what help she needed from Lorine. "Bridge," she said before handing the paper and graphite back to Lorine.

The paper trembled in Lorine's hand. *How do I know you're not just as mad as Professor Josston said?*

"Faith," Karigan replied aloud. Then she wrote, *The professor believed me, and so does Mr. Harlowe. Mr. Harlowe's life depends on your help.*

Lorine nodded.

Good, Karigan thought. Lorine would do this for Cade.

"Rabbit," Karigan said. "I win." Then she crumpled the papers they had used and threw them into the dwindling fire.

The two stood and gazed at one another for several seconds before Lorine, sounding like a not-so-good actor in a play, stiffly asked, "Are you ready to retire for the night, Miss Goodgrave?"

Karigan, who was anything but, replied, "Yes."

Lorine nodded and set about dousing their lamps one by one until there were only the tongues of flame in the fireplace casting illumination into the room. She then flicked her hand in a gesture that seemed to ask Karigan if she was ready.

Karigan nodded, and faded out. Lorine gasped and wavered on her feet. Karigan had told her what to expect, but as usual, actually seeing it was a different story. If nothing else, Lorine probably now believed that Karigan was who she claimed to be.

Lorine steadied herself, then veiled her face and collected Karigan's supper tray. She opened the door to the corridor, Karigan creeping behind her, holding her breath.

"Here, gentlemen," Lorine told the guards. "Thank you for arranging to bring Miss Goodgrave her supper."

As one of the guards reached for the tray, she dropped it. Crockery smashed and metal clattered, and Karigan used the moment to slip out, tucking her manacles to her belly to muffle any clinking of chains. She hastened down the corridor, glancing over her shoulder to see Lorine and the guards on their knees picking up pieces of broken crockery.

"I am *so* sorry," Lorine told the guards.

How Karigan was going to get back in, she did not know. Perhaps she would not need to, but it was probably too much to hope for. Tonight she was scouting. If opportunities for more than simple scouting presented themselves, she would pursue them.

The corridors, as she hoped, were dimmed for night time,

and very quiet. Still, she kept as close to the shadows as she could, concealing herself behind columns if she saw anyone coming her way. In the low light, her fading was good. In the shadows, it was better.

This outing of hers reminded her of the times she had tried to sneak around the professor's house, but back then she hadn't her ability to aid her. The brilliant white marble and gold fixtures of the palace were gray in her vision. It was muddier than normal, which she attributed to the tainted etherea. She hoped she could endure any pain and sickness it caused her.

She retraced her steps to the dragon fountain, the water still burbling away as it had earlier. However, instead of taking the corridor that led to Lhean's cell, she went down the one to the immediate left of the fountain, the one the ghost of Yates had indicated would lead to *the prison of forgotten days.*

Karigan did not hesitate. This side passage was even less illuminated. The corridor was lined with doors. How would she know which one led to the prison of forgotten days?

In her gray vision, she discerned the figure of a man some distance ahead of her. He opened one of the doors and disappeared into a room. Karigan hurried down the corridor, halting when she arrived at the door. Actually, it was a pair of doors with columns to either side and frosted windows with "Imperial Museum" etched into them. She almost laughed despite herself. What else could a museum be but a prison of forgotten days?

Would identifying the scything moon prove as simple? There was only one way to find out. One of the doors stood ajar, and she slipped into the museum. It, too, was dimly lit. Perhaps the man who had come in ahead of her was Dr. Silk, who preferred darkness. The low light was good for her ability, but might Dr. Silk still be able to see her "aura" even if she was faded out? She could overpower him, she was sure, if she had to, but she needed him. He was her connection to Cade.

The exhibits in the hall made strange lumps and forms in the half-light. It glinted off display cases, metallic objects, and glass eyes. A statue of Amberhill in luminescent marble stood near the entrance. It was closer to life-sized than the others she had seen. She wove her way past cases of arrowheads and daggers, of baskets and pots, while dead creatures watched her progress from their mounts.

One such creature stood near the rear of the room, part moose, part human, a p'ehdrose. This one was female and had to be the mate of Ghallos, the taxidermied specimen she'd seen at Dr. Silk's dinner party. Her name had been Edessa. Like Ghallos, the human part of her flesh had been poorly preserved. It was leathery and puckered. A length of cloth draped across her front looked like it was just thrown there to protect the modesty of visitors by concealing her breasts.

Karigan did not linger, but passed into another exhibit hall, this one with a lofty ceiling and an aviary type of cage through which Dr. Silk was peering. She hid behind a case of pinned insects and watched.

"Did you get fed tonight, my pretty little jewels?" he asked.

It was too dark to see, but the unmistakable whir of hummingbird wings told Karigan what the aviary held. She frowned.

"Indeed, we fed them tonight, Dr. Silk," said a new man, striding toward the aviary from even deeper in the museum. "A nice fat hog."

"Excellent. I see that Ghallos isn't back on exhibit yet."

"We've been going over him, sir," the man replied, "ensuring all is well after his long journey. We're putting him back in place tonight."

"That is acceptable. I have come to do some research in the library."

"Very good, sir. If there's anything you need, we'll be here working on Ghallos. Just let us know."

Wonderful, Karigan thought. More people to watch out for.

Dr. Silk and the museum workman parted, walking in opposite directions. Dr. Silk went to a door just beyond the aviary and unlocked it. Inside he turned on the light. Karigan moved carefully, just beyond the light that spilled across the floor. Within the library she espied shelves and shelves of books. She wondered if this library contained, as the professor's had, the ragged, abused, and nearly destroyed tomes from her own time and farther into the past.

She skittered forward when the workman opened a door of his own and more light poured out, almost merging across the exhibit hall with light from the library. She continued to the back of the chamber and passed beneath an elaborate arch into another vast space. She stepped aside at the entryway and paused to lean across the wall and rest. Dare she drop her fading? She was exhausted, and her head pounded. She needed to rest, or she wouldn't make it back to Lorine's rooms. She sank to the floor, hugged her knees to her chest, and dropped the fading.

The head pain and nausea were not nearly as bad as the last time she had tried, maybe because there was so much more etherea in the palace proper. Still, it was bad enough. She kept her eyes closed willing the discomfort to pass, but keeping her ears alert for the tiniest noise that would indicate someone was coming her way. All she heard, however, were the distant sounds and voices of the workmen.

When the worst of her head pain eased, she opened her eyes, and her sight was no longer occluded by the graying of her ability. When her eyes once again adjusted to the dark, she realized she'd found the scything moon.

THE SCYTHING MOON

 The obsidian floor glimmered like black ice beneath the glass ceiling of the exhibit hall, which was more like an observatory open to the night sky. Karigan ran her hand across the smooth floor beside her. It was not layered with dust, not like the last time she had set foot on it.

Four winged figures carved of stone stood upon pedestals, with wings spread as though ready to fly. They were arranged, Karigan was certain, to designate the four cardinal directions, and even though she could not see their faces well in the dark, she knew they were Eletian, for she had stood among them before.

She rose and walked across not just a floor, but across a universe of stars and worlds, a celestial map embedded into the obsidian with quartz and flaring silver. There were subtle tints of blues and greens and rose in the quartz, and spider-fine lines showing the paths of heavenly bodies. Characters in luminous Eletian script rippled at intervals along the lines. When she reached the very center of the room, she stood upon a full moon of quartz, and arrayed around it were smaller representations of the moon in its various phases. They shone with a subtle gleam, picking up the barest glint of starlight through the glass ceiling. She had stood here before, in another time. No, this was not Castle Argenthyne in the heart of Blackveil Forest, but somehow the floor and statues had been removed from the chamber of the moondial in Castle Argenthyne and meticulously reassembled, here in the emperor's palace in Gossham.

Karigan knelt before the phases of the moon. She had

called these structures "moondials" because they were like sundials, where a shadow pointed to the time of day. Only with Eletian moondials, it was more. A properly aligned shadow cast by moonlight could take one to a "piece of time," a time preserved at a particular phase of the moon. Karigan had experienced this power in Blackveil, first outside the ruined village of Telavalieth, then in Castle Argenthyne. At the castle, the legendary queen, Laurelyn, had preserved a piece of time preceding the invasion of Mornhavon the Black. For a thousand years it protected those of her people who "slept" in a grove of vast trees in retreat from the burden of eternal life. Karigan, using her ability not only to fade, but also to cross thresholds between the layers of the world, had led the Sleepers from Laurelyn's refuge to the safety of Eletia's distant past.

As she stood on the full moon, the gentle light of the quartz glowing about her ankles, she reflected that Captain Mapstone's riddle had been correct, that she would find the scything moon held captive in the prison of forgotten days. Not only that, but she was sure this would be her way home. Why else had she been sent that message from almost two centuries ago, other than to guide her home?

Problem was, which of the crescent moons of the moondial was the correct "scything moon?" One of them had to preserve a piece of time from her own timeline. She refused to believe otherwise. Could she cross thresholds without Laurelyn's help? Or without the light of her moonstone?

One thing at a time, she thought. She'd have to bring Lhean here for he would know more, know if using the moondial was even possible.

Chattering voices and a screeching sound made her freeze, then tip-toe to the arched entry. Gazing out into the hall of the hummingbirds, light flowed across the floor from an open door revealing several men attempting to push an enormous something across the hall.

Ghallos, she realized.

They appeared to be stuck.

"I am telling you, this axel is broken," one of the men said. It led to an argument about the wheeled platform and the p'ehdrose not moving at all.

Uh oh, Karigan thought. She was going to be trapped here for a while. There was a chance she could get by the men while faded out, but she decided to wait, weighing in on the side of caution. If this went on very long, however, she would not reach Lhean this night.

While the workmen bickered, she decided to explore the moondial room further, for there were display cases to look in. It was difficult to make out details in the dark, but there was just enough ambient light to pick out weapons—some Eletian arrows, an ax, knives, and a saber. Though she could not see it well, she was certain the saber was her own, returned to its display case after its showing in Mill City. She glanced back at the ax. Could it be Lynx's throwing ax? Had Dr. Silk acquired all the gear she and her companions had left behind in Castle Argenthyne?

There were other items in the case, bulky artifacts that might have been their packs, and smaller items, their contents. It felt strange that people could spend time gazing at her personal items, such as her comb and brush. But how many visitors actually came to this museum? Surely none from outside the palace. She had a feeling that Dr. Silk had created this place more for his personal gratification than as a museum where people could come to appreciate the past.

In a separate display case, the contents appeared to draw starlight to themselves, and Karigan knew immediately they were moonstones. Hundreds of them filling the entire case. Dr. Silk had said earlier that they'd acquired moonstones in war from Eletian captives. She thought about all the lives those moonstones represented. Amberhill may have defeated them in battle, but any survivors must have perished from the loss of etherea and what had become of the lands with the use of machines. Lhean had said even the air was poison.

When she finished trying to view the contents of the display cases, she checked on the workers in the main exhibit hall, but it appeared they had not progressed far in their repairs of Ghallos' cart, so she returned to her sitting spot and settled in to wait.

The use of her ability combined with the trials of the day left her exhausted, and she dozed. She dreamed—at least she thought she dreamed—that a ghostly Yates sat beside her on the floor. Translucent and silent as always, he revealed to her another drawing. It was a sketch of the room she now sat in. Only, in the sketch, Laurelyn stood in the middle of the room on the full moon. Yates had captured her ephemeral beauty well, which could not have been at all easy, especially with only ink scratchings and no paint to bring her to life in color.

When Karigan had last seen Laurelyn, after having led the Sleepers to Eletia, the queen of Argenthyne had bade her farewell; after protecting her Sleepers for a thousand years, she had expended her life's energies and passed on to wherever Eletians passed on. It had been a bittersweet parting knowing that such a legend would never again be present in Karigan's world. And yet, here was this sketch of Laurelyn made by a mortal's ghost—all of which, she decided, was a dream.

When the sketch came to life, the scratchy lines wiggling and moving, Karigan knew it was, most certainly, a dream.

In the drawing, the winged statues rotated and the shading shifted, as though a new source of light had been introduced from above, like the moonlight in the chamber of the moondial in Castle Argenthyne. Laurelyn strode forward, the ink moving with and around her, holding her form together. She halted, and Karigan heard Laurelyn's voice in her mind: *I leave a final gift for Kariny's daughter, the ice-glazed moon.* Then in her arms she cradled a crescent moon, a scything moon.

After that, it was all gone, the drawing, the presence of Yates, and when she blinked her eyes open, she realized she'd been asleep and was now lying on her side on the cool floor. The sky above the glass ceiling was beginning to lighten with gray tones. *Five hells,* she thought.

They were heading toward dawn. She had to get moving before the palace woke up. She put the peculiar dream/not-dream to the back of her mind and climbed to her feet. Peering through the arched entrance, she found the main hall, though light still filtered out from the room of the workmen.

She took a deep breath, faded out, and left behind the Eletian moondial. As she passed through the main hall by the aviary of the hummingbirds, she noted a bar of light beneath the closed door of the library. Dr. Silk must still be working on his research.

She hurried along the palace corridors, weaving among the shadows. Fortunately all was still very quiet. She halted when she neared Lorine's door and hid behind a column, wondering how she was going to get past the two guards. She smiled at the irony—they were guarding the door to prevent her escape, not her re-entry.

As she stood there in indecision, she sensed another walking down the corridor. To her surprise, it was the forbidding red-armored guard of Amberhill's who had struck her so hard the previous day. In her grayed vision, the red of his armor looked like dried blood. She licked her lips and remained as still as possible.

He stopped. He came to a halt abreast of her. Karigan held her breath. He did not move, only his cloak rustling as it settled around him. The apparatus on his back emitted a rhythmic *hiss-sigh*. *Hiss-sigh*. Even the two guards at the door watched him apprehensively.

What had Dr. Silk called this man? The Eternal Guardian? Did that mean he'd live endlessly like Amberhill? It was difficult to get a sense of anything about the man with the helm and visor hiding his face. Was he even a man? What else could he be? A mechanical?

His head slowly rotated in her direction, then stopped short of looking straight at her. He remained in that position for what felt like forever.

Hiss-sigh. Hiss-sigh.

With a suddenness that almost made her gasp, he strode forward once again. Karigan felt as if released from a spell, and took another deep breath, then watched with surprise as he halted in front of the guards, who looked ready to melt into their boots. If the Eternal Guardian spoke, she could not hear him, but he made a beckoning gesture and the guards replied, "Yes, sir," in unison. To her happy disbelief, they followed the Eternal Guardian and left the door unguarded.

Karigan did not pause to analyze her good fortune. She was not going to ask questions. Instead, she hurried across the corridor and, ensuring no one was around to observe her, she opened the door and entered. Once on the other side, she leaned her back against the door and released the fading.

Lorine had left a single lamp at low glow. If there were watchers, she hoped they had not observed her coming and going. If so, she was sure to find out about it. She made her way to the sofa and lay down. It was not the most comfortable of beds, but she was exhausted, and it wasn't long before she slept.

"What is *she* doing here?"

The child's voice blared at Karigan like a trumpet. She groaned. Hadn't she just closed her eyes? She covered her face with her hands, smacking her chin with the forgotten manacles. While she tried to regain her bearings, there was surprising silence from Arhys. Then: "Why are you wearing those?"

Through bleary eyes, she saw Arhys pointing at the manacles.

"Arhys," Lorine said sharply. "Come to breakfast. Do not bother Miss Goodgrave."

Arhys looked more curious than petulant, and when she turned to obey Lorine, she asked, "But why is she here?"

"Hush now. You have lessons in one hour, so you'd best attend to your breakfast."

Karigan tried to shake the cobwebs out of her head. She felt like she had a hangover, but it was from using her ability, not from drink. How unfair to suffer without even the enjoyment of a good bitter ale as its cause. She sat there dazed and unmoving until Lorine brought her a blessed cup of tea and pressed it into her hands.

"You slept as one dead," Lorine said, concern in her eyes. "Even the arrival of breakfast didn't wake you. Can I bring you anything?"

"Give me a few minutes," Karigan replied.

Lorine left her alone while she sipped her tea and came slowly back to life. At least, she thought, Cade would have been pleased she hadn't vomited. In the background, Arhys complained about her eggs and toast, and chattered on about which dress she should wear that day. When Karigan finished her cup of tea, she joined Lorine and Arhys at the table.

"What are you doing here?" Arhys demanded. "And why are you dressed so funny?"

Karigan glanced down at her bedraggled clothes, the cast-offs of Luke's son. She thought about the various answers she could give the girl, but decided there was no point in hiding the truth.

"I am a prisoner of Dr. Silk's. So is Mr. Harlowe, and whether you realize it or not, so are you and Lorine."

"Am not," Arhys replied. "Dr. Silk is nice. He gives me pretty dresses—prettier than the ones the professor gave me."

Karigan restrained an impulse to reach across the table and slap the girl, but she was, after all, a child, who could not possibly understand all the machinations going on around her. And there was something else. As unpleasant as it was to contemplate, Arhys was, in a sense, and in this time and place, Karigan's sovereign, and not only would it be treasonous to harm her royal person, but it would be against everything Karigan believed and stood for. Not that she would tell Arhys any of this, of course.

"The professor is dead because of Dr. Silk," Karigan said. "Did you know that? And Luke, too."

Lorine gave her a warning look.

"No! Nonono!" Arhys got up from her chair and stamped. "Dr. Silk is nice." And she ran off to her room and slammed the door behind her.

"Was that necessary?" Lorine asked quietly.

"I don't know," Karigan admitted. Having grown up without any siblings, and with few friends at school, she found children perplexing and did not know exactly how to talk to them. She did know it rubbed her the wrong way to have Arhys dismiss two good men who had tried to protect her and died for it. It was not an auspicious start for a queen who might one day have the power of life and death over thousands. "I don't know," Karigan said again. "But I don't think it helps anything, hiding what her new champion, Dr. Silk, is capable of. As much as she has gained from his benevolence, she has lost far more."

Lorine gave Karigan a sidelong look, perhaps guessing that there was more to Arhys than having been the professor's favorite. "You may not see it, but she mourns the professor every day. Dr. Silk has been trying to take his place, but he hasn't the warmth. His smiles are not real, and I think Arhys sees that. I should go check on her."

She watched after Lorine as she went to Arhys' room. The last thing Karigan had wanted to do was alienate an ally. She would try to be more delicate with Arhys next time, but her patience was in short supply at the moment. She shrugged and helped herself to some eggs and toast.

A few minutes later, a knock came on the door, and two guards entered, one bearing a couple of boxes.

"You," the first guard said, pointing at Karigan. "Come here."

She chafed at being ordered about, but she set her fork down and obeyed.

"Hands out," the guard said when she reached him.

To her surprise, he took out a key and unlocked her manacles. Grateful, she rubbed her wrists. Meanwhile, the second guard set the boxes down on the sofa.

"Dr. Silk says you are to wear what is in the boxes," the guard said. "We will be back for you in an hour." With that, they left, and she looked down at the boxes, speculatively.

"What is it?" Lorine asked, poking her head out from Arhys' room.

Karigan lifted the lid off the top box, and smiled.

THE MANY FAILURES
OF CADE

After seeing the witch, Cade had been taken up a couple floors in the lift and placed in a box of a cell with a solid steel door and no way to look out at anything. There was a metal bench affixed to the wall, no mattress, blankets, or pillow. Bright light poured down on him from a fixture in the ceiling secured behind a grill.

"Remember what you saw," Starling said before leaving, "and how it could become the fate of your lady."

They'd unshackled his wrists, but Starling was gone before Cade could attempt to leap past the guards and throttle him. He paced in the tiny chamber, imagining how he'd bash Starling's head to a pulp against the stone wall if ever given half a chance. That image alternated with that of the tortured witch wearing Karigan's face.

He paced until exhaustion forced him to sink onto the bench. Though his wounds had been healed, his body had undergone great trauma, and he felt it. His shoulder throbbed, and he gingerly touched the place the bullet had entered, the cloth around it stiffened by dry blood. He did not know how many meals he had missed, but his mouth was dry and his lips chapped. With no natural light to inform him, he'd lost track of time. No one extinguished the light above.

Everything had gone wrong. He'd been a fool to think they could enter the heart of the empire—the emperor's palace itself—and not get caught. It did not matter what happened to him, but now Karigan would pay the price for his idiocy, as likely would Arhys and Lorine. He'd failed as a

Weapon, a rebel, and a man. He had failed in every way, and it was the worst, most helpless feeling.

He covered his face with his hands, continuing to blame himself, when a voice, remembered or actual, once more spoke into his mind: *Patience.*

The witch, he was sure of it. Did this mean all was not lost, that his plight was not as hopeless as it seemed? Or was he just deluding himself?

Cade curled up on the icy steel bunk, recriminations and hope cycling through his thoughts, his eyes closed against the light, though it was so bright it leaked through his eyelids. He did not expect to sleep in such uncomfortable circumstances, but so fatigued by his ordeal was he, that he began to drift off.

An explosive noise made him leap from a dead sleep to standing in a mere moment, his heart raging against his ribcage. He had no idea what the sound was or where it had come from, but he guessed it was for one purpose only: to torment him, to deny him even the escape of sleep. Without it, he'd be ever more likely to falter and give them the information they wanted. It would weaken him.

He sat once more on the bench and tried to relax. Every time his eyelids drooped, he shook himself awake, his mind and body now anticipating the shocking noise at any moment. When once he drifted off, it did come again, closer, louder. His reaction this time included a shout that was one part shock and one part frustration. He kicked the wall and yelled, then stumbled back to his bench.

He tried to figure out how they spied on him. He scanned the walls, ceiling, and even the floor for a peephole, but saw nothing. This was Gossham, he remembered, the emperor's palace, where they did not need peepholes. Magic would allow them to view him.

Cade rubbed his eyes and settled in for the duration. Only now, the noise came at unexpected intervals, even when he hadn't fallen asleep. Otherwise, his existence in his small cell passed like a lifetime. It could have been a matter of a few hours, or an entire night, or more. He had no idea. He was almost grateful when Starling returned.

The door to the cell creaked open and a guard brought in

a table and chair, wiping them down while a second guard stood watch over Cade with his hand on his holstered gun. The first guard left, while the second remained.

When Starling entered, he filled much of the room with his buoyant presence as much as with his stout figure. "Well, well, Mr. Harlowe. How are we doing?"

Cade noted he had not made mention of the time of day or night. His answer to the question was, *Miserably,* which he of course did not speak aloud. A headache from lack of sleep and food plagued him, and his entire body ached. But he would admit none of it.

Starling made a great show of seating himself, then unpacking a basket of food. There was cold chicken and biscuits, and pungent sharp cheese, a plump peach, and a slab of butter cream pie, with a mug of ale to wash it all down. Cade's stomach grumbled, and he salivated. He tried not to look as Starling worked his way through his food, but the aromas were too pronounced. This was a different sort of torture.

"My wife," Starling said between mouthfuls, "does not think they feed me adequately here at the palace. She packs me a basket every day so I may keep up my strength. She is a very good cook."

He made it all the worse by smacking his lips and licking the tips of his fingers. Cade's stomach growled loudly.

Starling patted his lips with a napkin and said, "I trust you had some time to consider our previous conversation, as well as our visit with the witch."

Cade said nothing.

"Still silent, eh?" He took an object out of his pocket. It dangled at the end of a long chain and flickered in the light. "I was wondering if perhaps you recognized this object."

Cade recoiled—Mirriam's monocle, or one like it. The lens was cracked. He'd expected Starling to begin baiting him by using Karigan in some way, not Mirriam. He'd tried to steel himself against any threats to Karigan, but this he had not been prepared for.

"I see by your reaction," Starling said, "that you do, or think you do. This was taken from your old professor's housekeeper, who we know to be a member of your band opposing the emperor. She and others, of course, have been questioned by my fellow Inquisitors. Your conspirators are a tough lot, I hear. Quite surprising for a domestic, a carpenter, and assorted mill workers. I'd be quite interested to know the names of others, especially those of higher classes who might have been involved."

Cade couldn't have cared less about men like Mr. Greeling, the mill owner who had refused to help the cause, but what he hated more was telling Starling anything at all. He could only guess what Mirriam and the others had suffered at the hands of Starling's colleagues.

"One thing you will learn about me, Mr. Harlowe, is that I am extremely patient. So what was Professor Josston's interest in the little girl, Arhys?"

Cade started, taken aback by the abrupt change in topic, and silently cursed himself for reacting. If he'd had a proper sleep, he'd have guarded himself better. This was, of course, the sort of thing Starling wanted.

"She is here in the palace," Starling said, "but of course you know that. It is one of the reasons you are here, isn't it? What is so important about one little girl that you endangered yourself so extravagantly to come here and attempt her rescue?"

Starling kept on in this manner for some time. No attempt was made to physically torture Cade. He kept his lips clamped shut and continued to resist answering any questions. Starling's equanimity did not falter, and Cade guessed the two of them followed some time-proven pattern familiar to the Inquisitor, who would eventually wear Cade down no matter what the technique used. He certainly lacked no confidence that this would be the case.

"Well, this has been quite a diversion," Starling said. He made a production out of repacking his basket and offering the guard an uneaten muffin. Cade was offered nothing.

The guard opened the door for Starling, but he paused. "By the way, Mr. Harlowe, I understand your lady is being taken to the emperor shortly. As I noted before, she has a most fascinating background. I should like to know Dr. Silk's method for having made her so forthcoming so quickly, or perhaps she is simply weaker than I thought."

Cade fought outrage to retain calm. So, Starling had finally "attacked." Cade would not give him the satisfaction of a response.

"You do not fool me, Mr. Harlowe," Starling said in a low, studied voice. "I know how to read a person. I must, in this line of work. You've stiffened all up, your chin squared. The rage floods your eyes, reddens your face."

The more Cade tried to relax, the more he tensed.

"Yes," Starling said, "you want to know what the emperor wants with your lady, don't you, but you are trying very hard not to speak."

Cade also wanted to break all the teeth in Starling's grinning face.

"Believe me, I understand your concern," Starling continued. "If our positions were reversed, and it was my dear wife going to the emperor? I would want to know why, too." He shook his head and proceeded once more toward the door.

Cade thought he'd explode. He fought with himself, but lost. "Wait."

Starling halted and turned. "Yes?"

Cade hated himself for breaking his silence, but he had to know. "What—what does the emperor want with her?"

Starling smiled slowly. "So now you speak. I thought perhaps you had lost your tongue."

"What does the emperor want with her?"

"You expect me to answer your questions when you have answered none of mine?" Starling clucked his tongue. "I am sorry, Mr. Harlowe, but it does not work that way." He turned to leave, then paused once more. "Just hope that while your lady is in the presence of His Eminence, that he is in one of his better moods. He does often become quite . . . volatile. In the meantime, if you should like to talk and answer some of my questions, just let your guards know, and they will send for me." His eyes glinted with amusement as he turned away.

Then he was gone, and the guard slammed the cell door shut. The lock was secured with a series of clicks, and Cade was left to himself. He lunged about the cell in frustration. What had Silk done to get information out of Karigan? She was not weak-minded. What would happen when she went before the emperor? What would happen to *her?*

Me. They have used me, Cade thought. They had gotten her to talk using his own welfare as leverage. He was sure of it. Why else was he still in one piece, much less alive?

His guilt renewed, he sank back onto his bench, shaking his head. Starling had won this encounter. He had baited Cade and gotten him to speak. Cade added it to the litany of failures he repeated in his mind.

DRAGON TIME

Karigan pulled the supple boot on. It was close in make to her Rider boots, but the leather was too glossy and lacked wear. The stitching of the sole and seams were too perfect, and she supposed if the mechanicals of this time could weave cloth, they could also make boots.

The empire may have made the boots, but the uniform was hers, meticulously cleaned and mended. If one did not look closely, it appeared as whole as if it had not seen duty in Blackveil Forest and then been brought forward a couple of centuries into the future. Unfortunately, Dr. Silk had not seen fit to return to her the bonewood, the feather of the winter owl, the mirror shard, or most important, her moonstone. She could only guess they were locked away for further study.

She did not understand Dr. Silk's motive in giving her her uniform to wear, but it only made her feel more herself and ready to stand up to the empire, ready to face whatever came her way.

When she stood, attired as a Green Rider ought to be, Lorine's expression was a mix of respect and consternation, but Arhys' reaction proved humbling—she laughed.

"You look very funny," Arhys said. "Funnier than when you were dressed like a boy."

"Hush, Arhys," Lorine said. "Miss Goodgrave—I mean, Rider G'ladheon, is of a different time. Things were different back then, and so was the style of dress."

Arhys laughed again. "That is no dress!" She herself wore a lovely dress with layers of skirts that were frilled with ribbons. No doubt it was a gift from Dr. Silk.

Karigan smiled, amused by Arhys' reaction. Since Silk knew all about Karigan's identity, there was no longer any reason to hide it, so she and Lorine had tried to explain her origins to the girl, who had been naturally curious about the uniform. Arhys, however, was predictably unimpressed. When told Karigan had been a king's messenger, she declared, "There has never been a king. Only the emperor." Ironic, coming from the sole heir of that king's bloodline. But what Arhys believed to be true, might help keep her alive for the time being.

After what Karigan assumed to be the passage of an hour's time, a pair of guards appeared at the door to escort her away. They did not manacle her but regarded her and her uniform with disgust in their eyes.

"Where are we going?" she asked.

They did not answer, but pushed her along whether or not she kept up her pace. She thought maybe they were taking her to Dr. Silk's office again, but they struck off down a grand corridor of marble and gold, frescos and statues. Oddly, a channel of water originating from a fountain flowed beside them, along the corridor, over a pebbled bottom. Trout darted from shadow to shadow. With all the fountains, and the palace located on an island in a lake, not to mention all the canals in Gossham, it became apparent to her that someone was obsessed with water.

Having grown up on the coast, Karigan was fond of water herself, but she could never have imagined using it to such a degree for transportation, commerce, and decoration. She supposed it was one detail of many that she would never understand about the empire, though she did find the fountains and this indoor stream pleasant, under otherwise unpleasant circumstances.

The corridor only became richer, grander, and busier as they went on, the ceilings higher, the art more vibrant. They came to a great golden door with images of dragons, horses, and lemon trees shining in relief, much like the doors at the palace's main entrance. Dr. Silk waited there with his aide, Mr. Howser. He surveyed her through his dark specs, and she wondered what his nacreous eyes took in. Did her aura show the same shade of green as her uniform?

"Well, well, well," he said. Excitement made his voice and movements sharp. "A living breathing artifact of an earlier time."

Karigan scowled. She had not liked such inferences from the professor, and she liked them less from Silk.

"What is going on?" she demanded. "I take it there is a throne room on the other side of this door?"

"Correct. I am going to officially present you to the emperor and his inner circle. Sadly, since he has seen you already, the element of surprise is lacking, but the uniform should make an impact."

Ah, Karigan thought. *That's why he wanted me to have it.*

"My dear Miss G'ladheon," he said, "between acquiring you and the Eletian, and giving you to the emperor, my status in the empire will rise immeasurably. No doubt I shall be granted great Preference, perhaps even exceed my father's."

"Have you given the Eletian to the emperor already?"

"Oh, no, no. He is not presentable yet, and it does not hurt to wait a day or two. It will only prolong and reinforce the emperor's pleasure at receiving my gifts."

Karigan was relieved Lhean had not been "given" yet, whatever the giving might entail. It could not be good in any case. As for herself, she detested being regarded as a commodity to be given and received.

"Now let me have a look at you to make sure all is correct." Silk circled around her, gazing up and down, brushing nonexistent lint off her sleeve. Karigan crossed her arms, feeling even more like a commodity, livestock that has been brushed before being presented at auction. She was relieved he didn't check her teeth.

When he finished his inspection, he stood before her. "Do not speak unless directly addressed. Remember, the welfare of Mr. Harlowe is riding on your good behavior."

Karigan bristled. "*Your* welfare depends on my seeing him well and healthy."

Silk looked amused. "If I were you, Miss G'ladheon, I would focus more on your performance than on absurd threats. Look around you, and perhaps you will recall your situation."

The corridor was populated by a large number of guards who wore no-nonsense expressions on their faces and were armed with guns. They looked well-trained and disciplined.

Silk grabbed her wrist with his unnatural hand, concealed in its black leather glove, and squeezed bones and tissue that had healed not so long ago in the refuge of the professor's house. The even, mechanical pressure of his grip strained her wrist, threatening to re-break it. Her knees buckled, and she sank to the floor, tears slipping down her cheeks. She gasped in pain.

"Remember," Silk said, towering over her, "who is master here."

The next thing she knew, he had released the pressure and was helping her rise. He offered her a handkerchief, which she refused, holding her throbbing wrist to her body.

"Now we do not wish to go before the emperor with any signs of distress, do we?" Silk reached to dab her tears himself, but she jerked away.

"Miss G'ladheon," he said sternly, "have you not yet learned your lesson?"

"You won't ruin your gift for the emperor."

He raised his eyebrows. "I won't? I always do what is necessary. It would be unfortunate to damage you, of course, but there is always the Eletian to please His Eminence."

But, he did not attempt to minister to her again. She used her sleeve to wipe the tears, and she glared at Silk.

He leaned down and said in a low voice, "In the history we do not speak of, it is said the Green Riders were stubborn, very difficult to track down and kill. Intractable under torture, causing them unnecessary grief. There is no sense for you to make matters more difficult on yourself, though I see the Green Rider character runs true."

Karigan clenched her fists, forced herself to remain calm no matter what he said about killing and torturing Green Riders, her friends, no matter her desire to lunge at him and rip his throat out. *Patience,* she told herself. Silk would pay. She was going to get Cade and herself, and Lhean, too, home, and she would make sure Lord Amberhill never came to power. The future of her land and others would never have to know the iron-handed rule of the emperor and his cronies.

The gold door opened. Cold air pushed into the corridor, and a man in a fur coat and hat stepped out. "Dr. Silk, we are ready for you now." His face barely poked out from the fluffy fur, and it would have been funny except for the circumstances.

"Remember," Silk told Karigan, "no reason to make matters worse for yourself."

He was right, she decided. After all, he was nothing compared to Amberhill, and she must not waste her energy on him. She obediently walked through the doorway and into the throne room just a few paces behind him, Mr. Howser following.

She was startled by how frigid the room was and looked around in amazement at the crystalline frost that coated the floor, the walls and columns. Icicles hung from chandeliers and the frames of paintings. They grew from the ceiling like stalactites. The stream they had followed in the corridor continued into the throne room, but was sealed in black ice. A fountain's water had frozen in motion creating an otherworldly sculpture of ice. Why was the room kept so cold?

They walked atop a runner that prevented them from slipping on the floor. At the far end of the room sat several men, each attired in varying styles of fur and hats, some with muffs to cover their ears. The guards who stood vigil in the room were also garbed warmly. The only two men who were not dressed for the cold were Lord Amberhill, sitting relaxed in a well-cut suit, and the Eternal Guardian in his light armor and leather.

Silk paused, and she halted obediently behind him. A scraping noise grated through the room and the floor vibrated as a section of it retracted, breaking away a layer of ice.

"Right on time, Silk," one of the fur-wearing men called out.

A mechanical dragon the size of a horse reared out of the opening on a platform, the floor trembling with the grinding of gears underneath. The platform was encircled by numerals, just like the professor's chronosphere but on a much larger scale, and the inlaid ivory all scored with scratches. Was this a giant chronosphere?

"I do like to make a point of being punctual," Dr. Silk said.

The dragon lifted its head, the sound of mechanisms ticking inside it. Its eyes flashed red, and it unfurled its wings with an ingenious belt and pulley system, the membranes between the wing fingers fashioned of chain mesh that sounded like rain as they moved. The dragon's tail lashed with articulated metal plates, and it swiveled its head. Karigan jumped when it roared and spouted flame, steam hissing through its nostrils.

"Don't worry," Silk said. "It won't hurt you. It's just a time piece."

Just a time piece? Even if its movements were not terribly lifelike, it was cunningly crafted. To pick out the time, the dragon scratched the numbers with a forefoot, roared and spouted flame once more, and withdrew into the floor. It was certainly a dramatic device for keeping track of time.

They proceeded toward the throne till they were abreast of the seated men in their furs, about a dozen of them. Amberhill's inner circle, his Adherents.

"Bow to the emperor," Silk said, doing so himself.

When Karigan didn't immediately obey, Mr. Howser shoved her to the floor, so that she lay sprawled before the throne. She rose on her elbows, but Howser's foot to her back pushed her back down.

She recoiled when she saw what she thought was her own reflection in the floor, peering back up at her, was actually a man entombed in ice. A rotund little man with specs askew, an expression of shock frozen on his face. When a pair of shiny black shoes came within inches of Karigan's nose, she glanced up at Amberhill looming over her.

"Do not be concerned," he said, indicating the man in the ice with a nod of his head. "That's just Yap."

THE THREE-FACED REPTILE

"Yap?" she asked.

From nearby, Silk hissed to silence her, but Amberhill seemed undisturbed by her speaking out of turn.

"Yes. He was . . ." Amberhill paused as if trying to remember. "A servant. Friend. My conscience. My enemy." His voice changed as he spoke, uncertain, then wistful, then angry. "I keep him here because he reminds me . . ." His shoes retreated. "Rise," he ordered.

Karigan scrambled to her feet and sidled away from the poor man trapped in ice beneath the floor.

"So, Doctor," Amberhill said, "you have brought me one of your relics of the past."

"Yes, Your Eminence, a Green Rider."

"I know what she is." Amberhill's voice slithered out as he stared at her with darkened eyes. "I defeated your king, Green Rider. What do you think of that? And I defeated more. This continent is mine. All of it. Did you know that?"

Karigan was well aware of what he had done, but she knew better than to answer.

"How do we know she is of another time?" asked one of the Adherents. "Besides the distasteful display of her face and the wearing of trousers."

"It is actually quite fas—" Dr. Silk began, but Amberhill cut him off.

"I knew her before. Back in the early days before I came into my power. A messenger of Zachary's court lost in Blackveil, or so it was thought." The intensity of his expression

663

turned to one of befuddlement and he shook his head. "The disappearing lady. How did you come to be here?"

Dr. Silk answered for Karigan, explaining what she had admitted to him the previous day, while Amberhill paced muttering harshly about the interference of old gods. Karigan did not remember the Lord Amberhill of old being so erratic. In fact, she remembered him being intensely single-minded. He looked the same as she remembered, but he had changed. He was . . . a different man.

"Unbelievable," the Adherent said when Silk finished his account, but none of them appeared shocked or, really, all that impressed. Having an emperor around for almost two centuries must have inured them to such an oddity.

"But very true." Karigan recognized Silk's father as he stepped forward. "Congratulations, my son, on your find. Well done."

Dr. Silk looked stunned to hear such praise from his father.

"Not to mention, as I hear," said another of the men, "co-ordinating the quashing of a rebellion in Mill City." There was applause muffled by gloves and mittens. Dr. Silk nodded in acknowledgment.

Amberhill paid Silk scant attention, which couldn't have pleased Silk since it was the emperor's approval he desired above all else. Instead, Amberhill gazed at Karigan and she crossed her arms, chilled by the cold room and his regard. She could almost see some decision spinning in his mind, his lips moving with unheard words.

When the applause faded away, he spoke. "All I see is this useless, weak girl. No, no, a Green Rider. I've known her. They are not weak, I assure you. You did not know my Hilda. She makes this one look a scrawny infant."

He was having a conversation with himself, was the only way Karigan could describe it. Who was Hilda? The Adherents looked on as if they were accustomed to their emperor's digressions.

"Or Yolandhe. There was no one like Yolandhe, was there, Webster."

"No, Your Eminence," the elder Silk replied. There was

something false about his answer, made to please the emperor only.

Then Amberhill's more serpentlike voice hissed out: "The Green Rider is the blood of the betrayer, an old enemy, and avatar of a dead god."

Avatar of a dead god? It sounded impressive, but she didn't understand.

"You mean the stallion I saw that night in Teligmar was real?" Amberhill asked himself in surprise. The dark look in his eyes returned, and he nodded to himself.

It dawned on Karigan then that she was not dealing with Lord Xandis Pierce Amberhill alone. This was him, but not entirely. There was an aspect of his personality that was too familiar, one she had known intimately. The only one who would call her, "betrayer."

Mornhavon. She shivered, and this time it had nothing to do with the cold of the room.

"The Green Rider recognizes me," he whispered. Then he added, with a moderation of his voice, "But not all of me."

Mornhavon inhabited Amberhill's body, but there were nuances, words, traits, that did not fit either of them. Could it be there was a third personality, as well? *The three-faced reptile.* She recalled the riddle from Captain Mapstone. Karigan had found the scything moon in the prison of forgotten days, located within the den—or palace—of the three-faced reptile. The dragon symbol of the empire must represent the "reptile" part of the riddle.

Learning the meaning of this part of the riddle did little to reassure her. She'd seen Mornhavon inhabit the bodies of others before, including her own. The last had been poor Yates. It explained much about what Amberhill had done to his country, but who was the third aspect of his personality, and how and when had this all come about?

"You are our great and mighty emperor," Webster Silk said, "and that is what she recognizes."

Amberhill smiled. Or was it Mornhavon? "Yes, I've destroyed the world and the people she knew." A blank look, the fluttering of his eyes, then a painful whisper, "I'm sorry."

"There is nothing to be sorry about, Your Eminence,"

Webster Silk said hastily. He placed a hand on the emperor's arm, probably the only person who dared touch him. He led Amberhill back toward his throne chair. "You have created a great empire. We are strong."

"Yes, yes, of course I have." Amberhill sat, looking baffled for a moment. "We are strong, aren't we?" he asked the elder Silk, with uncertainty in his voice.

"Very strong."

Mornhavon, Karigan thought, was not fully potent. He must fight for dominance over the other two personalities. Mornhavon by himself would have been pure malevolence. In this state, he was . . . diluted. Was there a way to get through to Amberhill? To help him dominate? Or a way to get through to that other unknown personality? If Mornhavon felt threatened, compromised, he might flee to another body, one of the Silks, possibly. Not at all a comforting thought. Yet, he remained with Amberhill. Why would he?

"I am bored," Amberhill said, though Karigan did not think it was Amberhill or Mornhavon who spoke this time. She noticed the Adherents shifting nervously. Dr. Silk darted a glance at her. It was apparently not good to let the emperor get bored.

His gaze was leveled right at her. "Very bored."

At that moment, the Eternal Guardian, who had remained still as a statue until now, leaned toward Amberhill and spoke too low for her to make out words. Amberhill nodded, and the Guardian then spoke to one of the nearby guards. The guard hastened from the throne room.

"We shall have a contest," Amberhill boomed, "and we will see what this weak girl is capable of. Wagers, gentlemen?"

A contest? What kind of contest? she wondered, biting her bottom lip. She forced herself to stand tall, fought anxiety. Did not want them to see her fear.

The Adherents talked among themselves, making wagers, while Dr. Silk visibly fretted beside her. "This is not what I intended," he said.

His words did not help. Any confidence Karigan's uniform had brought her was waning, sapped by the cold, and Mornhavon's presence, and now the threat of this contest. How did she ever get to be in this place? Well, she knew, but still . . .

Amberhill did not participate in the wagering. Instead, he seemed to derive pleasure from her uncertainty and fear, and fed off it.

The guard that had been sent away returned quickly, and what he carried with him took her by surprise.

"What?" Dr. Silk said. "We can't use that, it's a valuable artifact."

"And your Green Rider is not?" Amberhill asked. "It all belongs to me anyway, and I can use it as I wish."

Dr. Silk bowed. "Of course, Your Eminence. I forget myself."

"Do not do so again."

"I won't, Your Eminence."

What the guard carried in was Karigan's bonewood staff, and a second staff of a lighter wood.

"It will be a contest of the Eternal Guardian against the Green Rider," Amberhill announced. "With staves. But not to the death, as our living artifact may have other, future value."

Karigan had no idea what "future value" she might represent to him, and she didn't want to know, but she was glad to find out this was not to be a fight to the death. Still, though she had fought and trained with Weapons, she had no idea what the Eternal Guardian was capable of, or even if he was human.

The bonewood was brought to Karigan, and the guard told her, "Any use of this for anything other than your contest with the Eternal Guardian, and you will be shot. We will have guns trained on you at all times. Do you understand?"

Karigan nodded and took the bonewood into hands stiff with cold. The wood warmed, seemed to hum in her grip. Despite the circumstances, it was good to have a familiar object to hold. It had been her companion all the way through Blackveil. It was solid, reliable, and deadly. If not for all the guards with their guns, she bet she could take on almost anyone in this throne room.

"Don't get too damaged," Dr. Silk warned her, before clearing out of the way to give room for the bout.

"Thank you for your concern," she mumbled.

The Eternal Guardian stood before her. Though he was no taller than an ordinary man, his bearing made him seem a giant. He did not remove helm or armor, but he'd handed his swordbelt over to one of the other guards. Karigan wondered only briefly why he did not carry a gun, like all the others.

"Where is *my* armor?" she asked. "It hardly seems fair not to have any."

He did not answer, there was only the *hiss-sigh* of the mechanism on his back. She knew this contest was not about fairness, anyway. He raised his staff at the starting position and waited. If they did not mean for her to get killed in this bout, they meant to be entertained by the spectacle of the big, strong Guardian fighting the weak female from the past, who had the temerity not to wear a veil. Well, entertain them she would. Let them see she could wield a staff.

She flexed her hands around the staff and stepped up to the Guardian. His eyes flickered as he blinked behind his visor. They touched off and began.

The Guardian did not hesitate. He did not take time to size her up. He simply attacked. Karigan barely deflected the blow to her mid-section and found herself desperately parrying a series of sophisticated moves. She was cold, stiff, slow. The icy floor caused her to slip and slide when she tried to maneuver away from the attack. The Guardian appeared to have no problem with his footing. He was like a stout tree rooted in the floor, she a pebble skittering across ice.

Meanwhile, the Adherents jeered and laughed at her, calling her names and using words they, as proper gentlemen, would probably never use in the presence of their wives or daughters, or in polite society, but she was not part of their polite society. To them, she was not even a person. She was a captive, in their minds a slave.

She took a glancing blow to the hip and slid away, steam puffing from her mouth. For all that the Guardian's moves were swift and well-executed, they were familiar to her. She willed herself to recall her training, and to allow it to overtake her. She must incorporate the uncertain footing into her fight, find her center, use it to her advantage. It was not easy, for the Guardian was relentless. He pounded on her bonewood, numbing her hands, the wrist that Silk had clenched so hard aching. But she was warming up.

Soon she found a rhythm, a desperate rhythm, but one she could work with. Still, she had to be ready when the Guardian made an unexpected move. Just as she had tried to teach Cade in swordplay, she must not become lulled by that rhythm.

The constant din of colliding staves filled the room, the raucous shouts of the Adherents falling into the background. The Guardian's staff smashed into a mass of icicles hanging from a chandelier. Shards of ice pelted Karigan, bit into her hands and cheeks, but she managed to block another numbing blow.

She used the slick floor to move quickly out of the way, sliding here, then there. The Guardian's armor slowed him down only a little. She skated among columns, using them as shields. She knocked a phosphorene sconce off the wall, a ball of flame hissing to the floor, a burning tail sizzling behind it in an arc.

When Karigan engaged in yet another punishing series of forms, she thought, *I am a king's messenger. I have lived through worse. This is nothing.* Even if the Guardian defeated her, humiliated her, she could live with it. With that in mind, she decided to make a move that would likely be her last, but which was better than breaking a leg, or worse, her head, on the slippery floor. It was a move that was not part of any proper form, one that only the desperate and untrained would attempt. She took her staff by the end and swung it like an ax, bearing down on the Guardian's. Wood splintered like a crack of thunder. Not hers, but his, for she wielded bonewood, which was the strongest of them all. She jerked her staff back, its hooked metal handle catching his staff and pulling it apart into two pieces that clattered onto the floor.

At first all she heard was her own hard breaths. Then Amberhill's laugh. The Adherents had fallen silent in astonishment.

She could not tell what the Guardian felt because of the visor and bevor concealing his face, but he blinked rapidly and gazed at his empty hands.

Then he stared directly at her. She cocked her head. Was there something familiar about his eyes?

"Well done, Rider," he said in a low, harsh whisper.

The voice . . . No, she didn't think she knew it, but because she was distracted and mulling over it, she did not see him move before he backhanded her across the face.

THE ETERNAL GUARDIAN

The blow sent Karigan careening, and she landed on her knee, heart hammering from shock, and face stinging. She shook her head and touched her cheek, and opened and closed her mouth to make sure her jaw worked properly. Fortunately the Guardian's armored gauntlet had not broken or dislocated it.

She rose unsteadily to find that Dr. Silk had confiscated her staff, which had dropped from her hand when she'd been hit, and the Eternal Guardian was returning to his post beside the throne chair. Coins clinked from hand to hand as the losers of the wager paid up.

A thunderous boom shattered the quieter noises, and everyone looked up.

"What now?" Dr. Silk muttered. His moment of triumph clearly was not going the way he had hoped.

BOOM! The throne room door shuddered. Guards scrambled toward the entrance. Were they under attack? *BOOM!* The door cracked, and then another impact slammed it open. A high-pitched whinny resounded down the length of the throne room.

"Oh, no," Karigan said when she realized what was going on. A familiar stallion reared in the doorway. "No, no, no."

She set off for the doorway at a run, her feet slipping as she went. She paid the Adherents and the emperor no mind. No one tried to stop her; they must have all been distracted by Raven's intrusion. Her only thought was to reach him and calm him before anyone else could harm him. How had he even gotten into the palace?

"Raven!" she cried.

He had most certainly sensed her distress and was coming to her aid. Green Rider horses bonded strongly with their Riders, and he being the headstrong and willful creature he was, had come for her.

It was difficult to see exactly what was happening in the confusion of the doorway, but she saw a guard nearby raising and aiming his firearm.

"No!" She leaped toward him, grabbing the gun, holding on despite the pain that seared her hands just by being in contact with the weapon. She knocked it out of the guardsman's hand, and it slammed to the floor, steel striking icy marble.

Despite her efforts, the unmistakable report of gunfire exploded in the entryway. Before she could even break away from the guard she wrestled, there was more shooting, and Raven's screaming. Desperation made her strong, and she pushed the guard away in time to turn and see Raven stagger.

"No!"

His knees buckled as she ran toward him, and he crumpled to the floor.

She slid to his side. "No," she whispered, frantically patting his neck. Blood pooled beneath him, and his legs jerked and trembled.

"Don't leave me! Please . . ."

But the light in his intelligent eyes faded, and after he heaved a final breath, his whole body went limp, his tongue lolling out between lax jaws. He was gone.

Karigan rested her forehead on his already cooling neck, all the strength and life gone from it. Some essential element of her soul had been stripped out leaving her drained, abandoned. By having saved him from the meat market in Mill City, she had still brought him to his death.

"Old Samson," said his former owner, Dr. Silk. He shook his head. "So he meets his end after all." He nudged one of Raven's huge hoofs with his toe. "He will be dog meat and glue now."

Karigan stood unsteadily, rage washing over her. She was ready to unleash it on Dr. Silk. She forgot where she was and all who depended on her. She could only think of murdering Silk.

He must have seen it in her eyes, for he took a step back. "Mr. Howser?"

The man moved toward Karigan, and she was ready and willing to take him down, too, if he got in the way.

Oddly, it was the presence of the emperor that calmed her. She had been unaware of his approach. Amberhill was just suddenly there, kneeling at Raven's head. He placed his hand between the stallion's ears in a sort of benediction. "He reminded me so much of my Goss." He shook his head sadly. This was not Mornhavon, but Amberhill.

"Why did he do it?" someone asked.

"That horse was always wild," Silk said. "Insane."

"He was a Green Rider horse," Amberhill said. "He came to defend his Rider."

Silk stared aghast. The others who crowded around looked on uncomprehending.

"This noble horse will not be made into glue or dog meat," Amberhill told Silk reproachfully. "He will be interred in the great pasture with my other beloved steeds."

"A Green Rider horse?" Silk asked himself in disbelief. He must have regretted not knowing he'd had such an "artifact" right in front of him the whole time.

Amberhill rose and demanded, "Who shot my horse?" Heat rolled off him like palpable waves of anger.

Two guards fell to their knees right away, heads bowed. One said, "We feared—"

A flare of heat shut the man up. Ice melted beneath Amberhill's feet, and vapor rose up around him like a shroud. Even amidst her loss, Karigan remembered how Yates seemed to burn up when Mornhavon occupied his body. Was the throne room kept cold in an attempt to prevent the emperor from burning up?

He strode to the guard who had spoken and held out his hand. The guard did not hesitate, but unsheathed his gun and handed it over to the emperor, head still bowed. Too shocked by the loss of Raven to understand what was happening, Karigan reeled when Amberhill fired the weapon and much of the guard's head blew off in pieces.

By the time the second guard was executed, the Eternal Guardian was dragging Karigan from the throne room, its gold door battered by the impressions of horse hooves.

Karigan did not resist, too depleted by all that had happened. She stumbled alongside the Eternal Guardian, his steely grip on her arm the only thing keeping her upright. The passing corridors were a blur, and it was with some surprise when they entered the suite of rooms she shared with Lorine and Arhys.

The Guardian released her, and she collapsed onto the sofa, placing her head in her hands. There were no tears yet. It had not sunk in. She was just intolerably empty, wanted nothing more than to be in Cade's arms. She was barely aware of the Guardian moving through the rooms, looking through doors, moving objects. There were no sounds or indication of Lorine and Arhys being home.

When the Guardian, that fearsome presence in leather and red armor, stood but inches in front of her he could no longer be ignored. "They cannot see or hear, at least for the moment," he said in his wreck of a voice.

She was so dazed she had little idea what he was talking about.

He took her chin in the same hand that had struck her. She flinched.

"I am sorry about that," he said, "but I had to make it look good after the disgrace of losing. I used a weaker staff on purpose."

Look good? Weaker staff?

He tilted her chin up so he could study her face. "I cannot believe it," he murmured. "After all these years. It is actually you. After Dr. Silk found your belongings in Blackveil, I thought you had vanished utterly, never to be seen again."

Karigan jerked her chin out of his grasp. He did not reach for her again. Instead, he knelt before her. He twitched his head, and wheels and gears on the sides of his helm were set in motion. Ticking and whining, they lifted the visor and lowered the bevor. The *hiss-sigh* of his cylinder apparatus ceased. She looked upon a visage as wrecked as his voice, the features of his face fused together by scars and melted flesh. The extent of the scarring was horrific, beyond even what her friend Mara had sustained when Rider barracks burned down. It was like looking at a face of clay slapped together by a child. She wanted to look away but could not. There was something in his eyes, something about the way he had fought and held himself. Something about his stoic attitude.

"Do you know me?" he asked, his breaths a terrible wheezing sound. "I am much changed."

She squinted, tried to fill in spaces where eyebrows might be, the original shape of his nose. How could it be? It was impossible. Just as impossible as it was for her to be here. "Fastion?" she whispered.

He nodded.

"How?" How was he right here before her, a Weapon of King Zachary's court? One whom she considered a friend, as much as one could call a Weapon a friend. He was of the past, should have died long ago.

Then she launched from the sofa and battered his breastplate. "You betrayed him!" she cried. "Zachary! All of us! *Traitor!*"

He simply shrugged her off him, his strength undiminished by time or injury.

"Shh," he said quietly. "There are still guards posted outside, and I've much to tell you before the emperor misses me. Will you hear me out?"

She wanted to hurl more accusations at him, lay blame on him for all that had become of Sacoridia and all the losses—the professor, those left behind in Mill City, Luke, now Raven. She also wanted to throw her arms around him and weep. Here he was, someone from her own time, though so disfigured she hardly recognized him. She did neither.

"You had better talk fast," she told him, not imparting what she might do to him if he didn't. She wanted him to give her reason to trust him, she wanted to believe there were good reasons for his being the emperor's Eternal Guardian.

Fastion, still on his knees, simply nodded and began. "During the final battle with the hosts of Blackveil and Second Empire upon us, it was my duty to help Queen Estora and the prince escape into the tombs. Lord Amberhill had already turned on us. When I put her into the care of the tomb Weapons, I returned above so I might aid in the defense of the castle. King Zachary had ridden out onto the field of battle and may have already been slain by then. I don't know."

She had already known this outcome for Zachary, but hearing it again on top of everything else caused an intake of breath that sounded like a soft cry.

"I fought at the castle gates," Fastion continued, "but all I remember of it was fire, fire and burning." He closed his eyes. "The burning. I should have been dead, but Lord Amberhill rescued me."

"Why?" Karigan demanded. "If he had turned, you were his enemy."

"It is something I often question myself, but I believe it was because I had saved him earlier. Something I have spent so many years regretting." Fastion paused to take some rasping breaths. "He had returned from voyages in the east changed, but remained essentially himself and not threatening. He promised the king he'd help turn the tide of war in favor of the Sacoridians. It was sometime after I had rescued him that he changed yet again." Fastion's expression darkened.

"Mornhavon," Karigan said.

"Yes. Somehow the dark one insinuated himself into Lord Amberhill's being. The part that was still Lord Amberhill rescued me. The part of him that was Mornhavon healed me, gave me eternal life. I think it amuses Mornhavon to have one of Zachary's Weapons now guarding him. I also believe that the part that is still Lord Amberhill wishes for me to ensure he does not fall."

"He wants to be emperor forever."

"No. I think he wishes he could end his life, but killing his body would only make things worse."

Karigan nodded in understanding. "Mornhavon would find a new host before the body expired."

"And that new host would probably be Webster Silk, who is a cruel man. It is his policies that have made this empire what it is. Imagine him and Mornhavon bound together, without the moderating influence of Lord Amberhill, or the third personality."

So she'd been right. There was a third.

"A sea king of old," Fastion continued, "with access to destructive forces Mornhavon covets. It is my thought that Mornhavon has never abandoned Lord Amberhill's body for Silk's of his own volition because of that power. It brought Sacoridia and the free lands to ruin. It—"

A knocking on the door interrupted him. "Guardian?" one of the soldiers posted outside called. "Is all well?"

"I must go," Fastion said. "Know that I serve the emperor because I do not wish for worse upon these lands and its people."

"I need to go home," Karigan said, "to tell the king, to change things."

"I know."

The soldiers knocked again. "Guardian?"

"Silence!" Fastion barked. The knocking stopped. Fastion stood, twitched his head, and the visor and bevor closed off his face once again. The *hiss-sigh* resumed its regular rhythm. "If anyone can do it, you can. You and the Eletian. You are not here by accident, this I believe. I will help as I can, but we must speak no more at this time."

When she began to protest, he waved her to silence and became the forbidding presence she had known before. He moved quickly through the rooms, undoing whatever he had done to block the watchers.

He paused a moment before leaving and said, "Very good bout today, but you lost focus in the end. A mistake. Drent would not have approved."

She touched her tender cheek, and he was out the door. She was still stunned and bereft, but he had kindled a new flame that shone in the dark. She'd found an unexpected ally, and perhaps she would reach home after all.

BARGAINS

Overcome and exhausted, Karigan curled up on the sofa hugging a pillow to her, finally able to give in to her grief for Raven and for everything else that had gone wrong. Now she had an idea of how her fellow Rider, Ty Newland, had felt when his beloved Flicker perished a few years back during a groundmite attack on Lady Penburn's delegation in the northern wilds.

Yes, she now knew how he felt, but he had carried on. He had turned around after Flicker's death and mounted another horse, Crane, whose Rider had been slain in the same battle. Ty had turned around and taken another Rider's horse and ridden to Sacor City to tell the king of the attack.

Karigan had no idea how Ty grieved on his way to Sacor City, but she knew it had not crippled him, had not slowed him down. He'd carried on and done his duty. She rubbed her face. When she was a Rider-in-training, Ty had mentored her, and now it seemed he was once again setting an example for her but across the expanse of time.

She would do her duty, too. It did not mean she did not grieve, but she would honor Raven by carrying on. Although His Majesty's Messenger Service did not exist in this era, Raven had been a true Green Rider horse, and he'd understand. She reminded herself that if she was able to get home, she might help change outcomes so that another version of Raven might live a long, healthy life.

Yes, she thought, her resolve building. *I am not going home just for myself, but for so many others.*

With that, peace descended on her and, exhausted by so much emotional turmoil, she slept.

Only to be abruptly awakened sometime later by meaty hands grabbing her and yanking her off the sofa. She was dragged stumbling and confused out into the corridor by guards and Dr. Silk's man, Mr. Howser. Dr. Silk himself awaited her there, his hands clasped behind his back.

"Today did not go quite as planned," he said. "There were distractions."

"Not my fault," Karigan muttered.

"No, perhaps not. The emperor is mercurial of temperament. I am told he is currently overseeing the burial of that horse. So, while he is busy, I have decided we each live up to our ends of the bargain we made."

Karigan shook herself fully awake. "You are taking me to see Cade?"

"Yes. Which means you will show me the workings of your magic."

It also meant, Karigan knew, that they must be done with Cade, that they would execute him soon.

She was ushered through several corridors, and along the way, she asked, "Then what happens?"

Silk shrugged. "That is up to the emperor. Maybe he'll lend you to the circus as part of the sideshow, or you'll become part of the imperial breeding program."

Karigan's eyes widened at that. "Breeding . . . ?"

"If your magic is of any interest, the emperor may want to try to reproduce it."

Oh, yes, she would show them her ability and much more, and there would be no circus side show, no . . . no breeding program. This empire was beyond revolting, beyond monstrous. She tried to devise a plan, but it all depended on where they were taking her. Even if she escaped with Cade, could they reach Lhean and the museum? And once they reached the museum, could they activate the moondial? She had no idea. And when she, Silk, and Howser stuffed themselves into a closetlike room that moved, her doubts grew. Silk called it a "lift," but the sensation she felt fluttering in her stomach registered only that they went down.

When it stopped, and Howser opened the doors, they filed out into a corridor that was utilitarian, somber in its gray

stone walls and gloomy lighting, in deep contrast to the corridors above. Was this a prison level? She had tried to memorize every turn they'd taken before entering the lift, and
then carefully observed how Howser controlled the mechanisms. Her confidence was slipping by the moment.

They did not walk far before they came to a door with
guards in the otherwise abandoned corridor.

"Mr. Starling is expecting me," Silk told them.

The guards let them in, and the first thing Karigan saw was
Cade sitting in a chair, his front covered in old blood, his face
haggard. It took all her willpower not to run to him. Instead,
she surveyed the room, which had the same utilitarian look
as the corridor. She made note of where the lever for the
overhead light was located. A stout, pig-eyed man stood
nearby, watching her curiously. In contrast to the setting, he
wore a red carnation in his lapel. This, she deduced, was Mr.
Starling. There were no other guards in the room. The main
threat was Howser.

"Karigan?" Cade stood unsteadily.

Karigan looked to make sure her going to him would
cause no other threat to arise. She was acutely aware of the
three men watching her and Cade, Silk absently adjusting
the cuff of the glove that concealed his mechanical hand. She
walked to Cade slowly, fighting the urge to run to him, not
willing to give Silk the satisfaction of witnessing her desperate need to be with Cade. When she reached him, she
halted, searching his eyes, desiring to throw her arms
around him. Instead, she tentatively pressed her hand
against his chest, reassured by its steady rise and fall and
his warmth against her palm.

"Are you all right?" she asked.

"I am now," he said. "You?" He lightly stroked her cheek
where the Eternal Guardian had struck her. It must have
bruised. It did feel stiff and swollen.

"I'm fine."

Silk cleared his throat. "You can see, Miss G'ladheon, that
we've not abused Mr. Harlowe."

She glowered. The dried blood on Cade's front did not
make him look unabused.

"It is your turn," Silk continued, "to come good on our bargain."

Cade held on to her. "What bargain? What's he talking about?"

"It's all right," she said. Then she leaned forward as though to kiss him and whispered, "Trust me."

No longer caring what Silk saw, she brushed her lips against Cade's, hoping there would be time for more later. Either that, or there would be no later, but she refused to accept such an outcome. She pulled from his grasp, strode away, and stood before Silk. Howser remained by the door, unfortunately very near the lever that controlled the light. She gave Mr. Starling a sideways glance.

"I did not realize we would have an audience," she said.

"Irrelevant," Silk replied. "You did not forbid it as part of our bargain."

"Fine." Behind her, she felt Cade closing the space between them.

"Mr. Harlowe," Mr. Starling said, "you would do well to remain near your chair."

Karigan tried to block Cade from her mind and focus on what she needed to do. "You do realize that Rider abilities are not very powerful," she said.

"Yes, yes," Silk replied, his voice tinged with impatience. "Let us see yours."

Karigan took a calming breath. "Very well." Silk looked on in anticipation, leaning forward and adjusting his specs on his nose. She touched her brooch—the one element Silk had apparently not known about Rider abilities, or he would have taken it from her right from the start.

She faded. She did not wait to see their reactions, for in the light, she was transparent, but not fully vanished. She used the moment of surprise to sprint toward the doorway, toward the lever for the light. She rammed her shoulder into Howser. It was like hitting a granite boulder, but he stumbled back a step and out of the way, and she grasped the lever and shoved it down. The room fell into darkness.

At first there was just silence, except for the sound of breathing, perhaps her own. She dropped the fading since she

did not need it now. In the dark, they couldn't see her faded
or not. Unfortunately, it also meant she couldn't see them
either. Well, she had not expected to come up with the perfect
plan on the spur of the moment. She edged away from the
lever, hoping she didn't knock into anyone.

"Miss G'ladheon," Silk said, "there is no need for dramat-
ics. Mr. Howser, turn the light back on."

"Of course, sir."

Damnation, Karigan thought. She listened for his movements, and when she heard his footsteps, she rushed him,
hands outstretched. When she ran into him, she pushed him,
and he cursed. She felt currents of air as he flailed after her.

"Mr. Howser?" Silk inquired.

"Trying, sir."

Karigan punched blindly toward his voice and must have
hit him in the gut for he emitted an *oof.* She kicked and hit,
and he swore, unable to get his hands on her.

She registered another scuffle breaking out in the room.
Cade must have engaged Starling. In another instant, something like a log knocked Karigan off her feet, and she rolled
onto the hard floor, shaking her head to clear it. Not a log, she
decided. Howser's arm.

"Stop at once!" Silk cried, his voice pitched higher. "It will
get you nowhere." She sensed he had not moved from where
she had last seen him, which was probably wise in the dark.

A gun blasted so close to Karigan's ear she was partially
deafened. The muzzle flash caught the room in a brief, bright
staccato stillness. Another shot rang out, and glass shattered
and rained to the floor—Howser had shot out the light fixture.

"Idiot!" Silk cried. "Put that thing away—you'll kill one
of us!"

The door opened and dim light from the corridor came in,
along with the two guards. Karigan faded again, their odds
worsening with reinforcements. Now, however, she could see
them, but they could not see her.

Silk whirled toward the two newcomers. "Get her!"

"Get who?" one of the guards asked.

Karigan smiled and lunged, pushing the guard into

Howser. The two went down. The other guard gaped. Silk and Starling might have been prepared for a show of magic from Karigan, but the guards were not.

"What's in here with us?" the second guard demanded, aiming his gun this way and that, attempting to track her.

Karigan stilled, realizing that though she was invisible, her movements could give her away just as Howser's had in the dark. As stealthily as she could, she crept up on the guard and wrenched his wrist back. He cried out, and the gun clattered to the floor. She kicked it away. The guard grabbed after her, but she moved swiftly enough that he caught only air. She snatched a clublike weapon from his belt as she went, and clouted him over the head with it. He sank to the floor and moaned.

She discerned Howser and the other guard clambering over one another to regain their feet. Karigan kicked and pounded them with the club to make that as difficult as possible, but the guard broke away, ran out the door, and did not return. He would probably rouse the entire palace.

Howser regained his gun and started shooting at random, bullets sparking on stone.

"Idiot!" Silk cried. "Stop firing!"

Howser must have hoped he'd hit her by chance, she an invisible target. Karigan crouched, ears ringing from the din, and inhaling acrid smoke. The guard she'd knocked on the head attempted to climb to his feet, but one of Howser's bullets hit him in the chest and propelled him backward onto the floor. He did not rise again.

The next shot that blasted through the room was not one of Howser's. This time it was Silk's. He held a small pistol in his hand that glimmered silver in the dim light. Howser dropped his own gun and keeled over, hitting the floor with a fleshy thud.

"I told him to stop," Silk said.

Cade and Starling still wrestled on the floor. Karigan started toward them so she might help Cade.

"Miss G'ladheon," Silk said, "I can't see you precisely, but there is a certain darkness in my vision, deeper than shadow, that appears to be you. I can shoot that shadow as easily as I shot Mr. Howser, who was, until now, a most sensible and reliable member of my staff. I can also shoot Mr. Harlowe." He strode over to Cade and Starling and kicked them. "Do you hear me? I will shoot everyone if need be."

The two men parted, breathing heavily. Starling's carnation lay crushed on the floor. Gun smoke wafted in the air. Although the fading wore oppressively on Karigan, she did not drop it.

"Now, Miss G'ladheon, I surmise the guard who got away will return with reinforcements, and the entire palace will be alerted to you. There is no escape, no matter how impressive your ability with the etherea. Why not make things easier on yourself and Mr. Harlowe by reappearing and giving yourself up?"

"Don't do it," Cade said.

Starling punched him in the shoulder, and Cade cried out in pain, much more than the blow should have warranted. Once again, Karigan prepared to rush to his aid when a hulking figure arrived, silhouetted in the doorway and wreathed in smoke.

"Ah," Silk said. "Finally, our reinforcements have arrived."

THE KING'S MAN

Karigan rotated the club in her grip and turned to face the new threat.

"Welcome, Guardian," Silk said. "A couple of my prisoners have gotten unruly, and your aid is most welcome."

She let out a relieved breath, but Fastion's countenance in his inhuman armor, and his general forbidding presence, left her uncertain, wary. Was he truly on her side, or had his earlier words been an act to win her trust, even in the face of his betrayal of king and country?

He said nothing, did not move, which reassured her not at all. Then he stepped into the chamber. He crossed the floor to Silk, wrenched the gun out of his hand, and tossed it aside.

Even as Silk sputtered in shock, Karigan took another easing breath. She dropped her fading, staggering from all that its use had taken out of her.

"How dare you?" Silk shouted at Fastion.

Ignoring him, Fastion tossed an object to Karigan, which she caught deftly. Her bonewood! She shook it from cane length to staff length and discarded the club.

"You are the emperor's man!" Silk said. "As am I!"

Still, Fastion said nothing, so Karigan spoke. "The Eternal Guardian is an old friend of mine."

"What is this you say?" Silk looked desperately between Karigan and Fastion.

"I am the king's man," Fastion said finally in his harsh voice.

Starling chuckled. "Oh, my. And here I feared this would be just another dull day."

"You're a traitor, is what you are," Silk told Fastion.

"He is anything but," Karigan said.

"Do you wish me to kill them?" Fastion asked, drawing his sword.

She did, and it was immensely satisfying to see Silk and Starling quail at the suggestion, but she said, "Wait. They might be useful."

She went to the doorway and peered out. The crumpled body of the guard who'd tried to escape lay on the floor. His unfortunate encounter with the Guardian had prevented him from sending reinforcements as Silk had hoped. Still, there was no telling who had heard all the gunshots, although at the moment, it appeared they hadn't drawn anyone. Perhaps they were far enough underground that the noise had not penetrated other levels.

Cade moved to Karigan's side. "You know the Eternal Guardian?" he whispered.

"Old Granite Face? We go back a long way." She turned and studied Cade anew. In the light from the corridor she observed darkened rings beneath his eyes, and fresh blood trickling from his nose. He looked bent with exhaustion. She felt exhausted herself. They would have to hold each other up.

"What now?" Cade asked.

"Yes, what now?" Starling echoed. "I am most entertained. Please don't disappoint me."

Karigan felt Cade stiffen beside her.

"We go get Lhean," Karigan said. "Then go to the museum."

Cade's eyes were full of questions. "The museum?"

"Our way out."

She could tell he wanted to ask more, but Fastion interrupted. "Time is slipping by."

"There is someone else who needs help," Cade said.

"Arhys?"

"No. I mean, yes. I need to help Arhys and Lorine, too, but there is a woman being held captive here. They call her a witch. We need to help her."

Fastion turned his head sharply to look at Cade, as if surprised.

Starling laughed, but Silk looked horrified. Based on Silk's reaction, Karigan thought Cade's statement must have merit. However, it complicated an already complicated rescue and escape.

"I cannot imagine what you will come up with next," Starling said.

"I wouldn't laugh if I were you," Cade said, "since Rider G'ladheon thinks she has a use for you, but I would just as soon the Guardian run you through with his sword. If you ever want to see your wife again, and eat her good cooking, you will shut your mouth and do anything we say."

"My wife, Mr. Harlowe? What wife?"

Cade faltered beside Karigan. "But . . . she cooks for you. And your daughters."

Starling laughed mirthfully. "What makes you think it was true? My word, how naïve you are. I do have a very good cook—that much is true."

Cade's eyebrows narrowed in consternation.

"Cade?" Karigan asked.

He shook his head. "He's right," Cade muttered. "I am naïve."

"You believe it is important to rescue this witch?" Karigan asked him.

"She has been tortured. Horribly. I—I sense it would be best to free her. Not just humane, but there is something else. I don't know how to explain it."

Karigan glanced at Silk who appeared to be struggling with himself as if gauging whether or not to protest. He actually looked frightened, and that in itself was telling.

"Fastion?" she asked. "What do you think?"

The other men looked confused. Apparently they'd never heard the Eternal Guardian's name before.

"Something of this witch is known to me, though I had thought her dead long ago. The emperor thinks her dead, too. Yes, she should be released, though I cannot say what the result will be."

Silk paled, and even Starling looked none too happy. So, they'd been keeping a secret from Amberhill. There wasn't time to discover the reason behind the witch's captivity, or why she was hidden from Amberhill in his very own palace, but it was enough to convince Karigan.

She and Cade stepped out into the corridor to hammer out the details of their plan, the dead guard their only witness. Fastion stood in the doorway, where he could hear, but also keep watch on Silk and Starling.

"All right," she said in a low voice, "I think we need to split up and—"

"No!" Cade protested.

"It will be more efficient," she said. "We'll meet up in the museum."

Karigan quickly told them her plan. Cade, using Starling, would go for the witch. "Fastion should go with you."

"But—"

"If there is any trouble, he will handle it."

"But—"

"You said there were guards down there."

"Yes, special guards. Different than the palace guards."

"Fastion is a special guard, too. They can't very well disregard the emperor's own Eternal Guardian."

"It is true," Fastion said. "They will answer to me."

"But what about you?"

"Oh, I think I can manage Dr. Silk." She purposely spoke loudly enough for her voice to carry into the room.

"Is that so?" Silk asked. "And how will you manage me?"

Karigan slipped past Fastion to re-enter the room. She smiled as she faced Silk. "Did you see me fight the Eternal Guardian in the throne room?"

Silk nodded.

"I am good with a staff if I say so myself."

"Why not a gun?"

She would not admit that she couldn't handle one. "Because," she said, displaying the bonewood, "this is so much more personal, don't you think?"

"I must say, Silk," said Mr. Starling, "I am rather liking your girl there. Yes, indeed, I like the way she thinks."

Karigan did not want to believe there could be anything about her *he* could like, but just now she had to be ruthless. If she wanted to go home, this was what she had to do.

She took a few steps toward Silk. "I will be with you all the way, in the shadows, a ghost that haunts you, the constant whisper of footsteps behind you. If you do anything I do not like, I will strike. Do you understand?"

"She is a swordmaster initiate in her own time," Fastion said. "I think you know what that means."

There was a downturn of Silk's mouth. "I know my history."

"Good," Karigan said. "Then we will go to where Lhean is being held."

They all walked out into the corridor to the lift's doors. Fastion worked the levers to bring the car to their current level. When it arrived, Karigan said, "Cade, Fastion, you take Starling and go first."

"Rider," Fastion said, "I will show you how to operate the lift first. After we descend, I will send it back to you."

Fastion showed her the settings she needed. It did not look much more complicated than operating the plumbing mechanisms in the professor's house. When she was sure she understood and memorized what Fastion showed her, she stepped out of the car. Cade looked like he wanted to speak with her but held back. She understood, for she felt the same.

"Time," Fastion reminded them, pushing Starling into the lift.

"Karigan—" Cade began.

"I will see you in the museum," she told him firmly, and turned away. She *would* see him. She refused to believe otherwise.

She felt Cade pause before he moved to enter the lift. Then she heard the doors close, and it was just her and Dr. Silk.

"It is madness, you know," he said, "to think you can get away with this."

"Then I am mad," Karigan replied, smiling without humor. "Madder than the professor ever claimed when I was Kari Goodgrave."

The silence in the lift wore on Cade as they descended, the Eternal Guardian at the controls, and the Inquisitor, Starling, uncharacteristically sunk into himself.

Cade had hated parting from Karigan after only just being reunited with her, but she was right: it was more efficient for them to split up. Still, he worried about her traveling the palace alone with Silk. He supposed he had learned enough about her that Silk was the one who ought to be concerned. It also occurred to him that if his part of the escape failed, she would not be caught in it and would still have a chance of getting home.

He did not want to fail, however. He wanted to go back with her to see how the world had been, how it should be. And he could be with her.

He patted the weight in his pocket. He'd recovered Silk's pistol before leaving the room above. It was a gentleman's piece, filigreed silver with an ivory handle, and only three chambers with two shots left. Cade had thought such pistols more ornamental than practical, but this one had proven deadly. Still, he missed his trusty, blue-handled Cobalt-Masters revolvers. They'd been confiscated with everything else when he was taken prisoner.

When the lift came to a stop, Starling asked, "So, what is your plan?" When Cade just stared, Starling continued, "Surely you have a plan. You don't just wander out onto this level and expect the Scarlet Guard to accept it, do you?"

"It will be like when you brought me down here before," Cade said. "I am your prisoner. You are going to show me the witch again."

"I suppose you could do worse but not much. They are not expecting us. No appointment has been made. It is irregular. And so is having the Guardian with us."

Cade recognized that Starling was trying to sow doubt, though his observations were likely correct. There was nothing to be done about it.

"They will not question my presence," the Guardian said.

"Not aloud," Starling replied.

"They will not question my presence," the Guardian repeated, "and you will not give them reason."

Aside from Karigan, Cade did not think he could have better help than the Guardian. It was hard to remember at times he was a human being beneath the armor. He had a name. Karigan had called him "Fastion."

"I will open the doors, and we will step out," the Guardian said. "Then I will return the lift to Rider G'ladheon."

The corridor was as gloomy and disheartening as Cade remembered, the turbines still churning away somewhere below them, the lighting dull. Four members of the Scarlet Guard awaited them.

"What is your business here?" one of the guards demanded.

When Starling did not reply immediately, the Guardian placed his armored hand on the Inquisitor's shoulder.

"I am bringing this prisoner to see the witch once again. He needs further convincing."

"You did not make an appointment," the guard replied.

"I will remind you," Starling said, almost sounding indignant, "that mine is an art, and art rarely recognizes the constraint of appointments."

"Very well." The guard did not sound happy, but he made no further protests. He and his compatriots glanced at the Eternal Guardian as he turned to send the lift back to Karigan, but as he said, they asked no questions.

Instead, two of the guards roughly grabbed Cade and dragged him down the corridor, through the antechamber, and to the cell door. A third grabbed a taper so they could see in the cell, and the fourth started the complicated process of unlocking all the locks. Cade glanced over his shoulder. Starling watched the proceedings with an unreadable expression. The Eternal Guardian returned to Starling's side, his hand resting lightly on the hilt of his sword. The Guardian did not carry firearms, Cade reminded himself, but the Scarlet Guard did, and the two shots he had left on Silk's pistol were not going to be enough if they had to fight their way out.

It then occurred to him they were not going to get the witch out without a fight.

A stench seeping out into the corridor announced the opening of the cell door. The light of the taper revealed the painful sight of the witch chained just the same as Cade had seen her before, her flesh naked beneath layers of grime, old blood, and scars, and her lips sewn shut. Though he'd been expecting the sight, he still quailed from it. How could her guards be considered human?

"Now what?" Starling asked him. "There she is, now what?"

The four guards glanced at one another as if wondering if this was part of the Inquisitor's technique. A smile strained against the stitches that held the witch's lips closed.

It was the Eternal Guardian who answered. "Unchain her."

Hands went to guns, but before the weapons could be drawn and fired, the Guardian's sword hummed through the air in a blur. The guards were felled as wheat to a scythe, the Guardian's blade shearing through flesh and bone as though they were nothing. His swordwork was spare and clean and astonishing. Cade looked down at the bodies in disbelief. The blood on the Guardian's sword matched their uniforms.

The tip of the Guardian's sword went to Starling's throat. "Unchain her."

Starling's nose flared as if taking in the scent of blood. Without protest, he knelt beside one of the bodies to remove the key ring from a dead hand. Cade fetched a fresh taper to replace the one that had fallen with its guard, so they could once again see into the cell.

As Starling tried different keys in different locks of the witch's chains, Cade sensed something new in her demeanor—not gratitude, not hope, not even triumph or anger, but *power.*

A DARKNESS IN HER MIND

The lift returned and after Karigan opened the doors, she ordered, "Get in."

To her surprise, Silk obeyed without hesitation or argument. She followed in after him, closed the doors, and stepped up to the controls, recalling what Fastion had shown her. It was then she perceived, on the periphery of her vision, Dr. Silk's mechanical hand striking down at her. She pivoted and blocked it with her staff. It clattered hard against the bonewood. For good measure, she brought the metal handle around and smashed his hand. His fingers jerked, spasmed, and curled. Tiny arcs of fire flared through his glove and sputtered across his knuckles. There was the smell of burning and melting.

Silk did not cry out in pain, but stared in disbelief at the smoke wisping up from his hand. "You broke it," he said. "It does not work anymore." He launched himself at her again. She sidestepped and tripped him. His fall caused the lift to bounce and shudder on its cables, and his specs skittered across the floor. She scooped them up.

"Not much of a fighter, are you?" she said. "Are you sorry you killed Mr. Howser now?"

He squinted up at her, raised his dysfunctional, still smoking hand to shield his eyes from the lift's light. "My specs!"

She dangled them in front of his face, yanking them back when he tried to snatch them. "You get these back when we reach the palace floor. In the meantime, I suggest you behave. Otherwise, I will find a way to do this without you."

His mouth became a grim line as he took her meaning, and he climbed unsteadily to his feet. Karigan dropped his specs into the pocket of her greatcoat and started the lift. It jerked upward, numbers ticking by in a small panel indicating floors. This, she thought, was a vast improvement over stairs, which could become tiresome, particularly in the castle, but she would take all the stairs in the world over a lift any day just to be home.

When the word "Main" rolled up into the panel, she applied the brake. The car screeched to a halt and shook so hard that she and Silk almost fell.

"It would seem I need practice," she muttered. Silk just glared at her. She glared back at him. "We are going to Lhean. If you deviate from our course, or try to alert others to your predicament, it will go badly for you."

"It could go badly for you, too."

"I can hide in the shadows."

He held his broken hand to him like an injured wing and seethed. The hand had finally stopped smoking, which was a good thing, as it would have provoked unwanted questions.

"Now we will proceed calmly," she told him. "You will act like there is nothing amiss." She returned his specs to him, which he took with his left hand. As he put them back on, Karigan hoped it was the last time she had to see his nacreous eyes. "A false move, and they will think a ghost has killed you."

"The emperor was right to conquer the lands and put females in their rightful place," he muttered.

"You are welcome to your opinion," Karigan replied. She had no interest in arguing just now.

"It is not an opinion, it is the natural order of the world."

She ground her teeth. He was not making it easy to avoid an argument. She faded out and slid the doors open. When Silk did not move, she shoved him out of the lift into the marble and gilt surroundings of the palace. Karigan surveyed the corridor. Fortunately, the massive columns she had seen in almost every corridor, and other architectural embellishments, provided plenty of concealment and shadows.

Silk paused just outside the lift, peering around, either looking for aid or searching for her.

"I am right behind you," she murmured. "Now go." She jabbed the small of his back with the bonewood.

Silk made some inarticulate noise and set off, but he'd not gone more than a few paces when a messenger hurried up to him. Karigan waited in the shadow of the nearest column.

"Dr. Silk," the messenger said. "I have been searching all over for you. This missive came in for you from Mill City."

The messenger handed a folded piece of paper over to Silk, and Karigan tensed, watchful lest Silk attempt to betray her, but he simply took the letter and stared at the envelope. The messenger bowed and trotted off.

By the time Karigan reached his side, Silk had opened the message and scanned the contents. He tilted his head back in laughter.

"You think you are so clever," he said, presumably to Karigan.

She snatched the message from his hand. His gasp reassured her he hadn't anticipated that. "I'll remind you to keep quiet," she warned him. Fortunately the corridor remained empty.

The message was from a Heward Moody, Imperial Engineer. Among the various lines scrawled across the paper, one stood out: *As you desired, the drill has breached what we believe to be the royal tombs.*

"No matter what you do here today," Silk said, "I have succeeded."

The faces of Chelsa, chief caretaker of the tombs, and the tomb Weapons, flashed through Karigan's mind as she reread Heward Moody's message, that the drill had broken through to the tombs. What did this mean for them? How would they defend the tombs? Certainly Silk would not anticipate anyone living down there, much less a dedicated defense.

She stuffed the message into her pocket. She would not enlighten him, but she could not help saying, "I would not be so pleased if I were you. The tombs are not so easily taken."

The truth was she had no doubt the Weapons would put up a fight, but they'd never withstand the full might of the empire. The tombs had been the last bastion of the home she knew, and now they, too, would fall.

"Keep moving," she said, prodding him firmly with her staff but not hard enough to hurt him — though it was tempting to injure one of his kidneys by shoving harder in just the right place. Injuring him would prove . . . satisfying. She returned to the shadows, darkness fringing her thoughts. For all the harm he had caused her and her friends, would anyone blame her for hurting him? Killing him?

No, she thought, as she glided from the shadow of one column to the next. *Insufficient. He deserves torture. Drawn out and excruciating torture.*

The darkness in her mind grew as she traveled abreast of Silk. Every so often someone would pass in the corridor. Some greeted Silk, others did not. Some actually seemed to go out of their way to keep their distance from him.

Karigan tried to focus on remaining silent and faded. The use of her ability weighed on her, wearied her, steeped her mind in the darkness.

A man walking from the opposite direction actually stopped to speak to Silk. Silk engaged in the conversation. Karigan listened closely to them, but the topic appeared to be bureaucratic in nature.

"I am preparing form 2018A for acquisition of archival storage cabinets as you requested," the man was saying.

Silk affected keen interest, eagerly asking about forms this and that, and debating the dimensions of cabinets. The other man, encouraged by Silk's interest, eagerly supplied the dimensions and made recommendations for additional cabinets.

What if, Karigan wondered, Silk alerted the man to his predicament? She would kill both of them. A quick glance along the corridor showed only one or two other souls anywhere nearby. She would kill them all. It would be so easy to dart out of the shadows and take them by surprise. She was beginning to like this ruthless thing.

It was clear that Silk was stretching the conversation beyond its natural conclusion. He was trying to buy time, or possibly communicate to the man that he was in trouble. The man was so flattered by the attention of such an important personage that he seemed oblivious to Silk's need for rescue and eagerly carried on the conversation.

Down the corridor a door opened, and another man poked

his head out. "Tomkins! There you are, you laggard. Back to work now!"

Silk's companion, Tomkins, grimaced. "I am sorry, sir, but duty calls." He bowed and added, "It is an honor to know of your interest in the procurement of the cabinets." He bowed again and left.

Silk watched after him with hunched shoulders, then continued forward at a reluctant pace on the course Karigan had set for him. He peered about as if looking for someone else to converse with.

It would not do.

When Karigan found an empty side corridor, she grabbed Silk and dragged him into it and snatched his specs off his face. He squinted and shielded his eyes even in the muted lighting.

"Give them back," he said.

"You will not stop to talk to anyone," she said. "If you do, I'll break your specs."

"I have other pairs, elsewhere," he said.

She did not care. "Then I will break your eyes." The idea grew on her as she stared into his eyes, of popping them, making them bleed . . .

"Your aura has browned," he said.

"No more conversation," she told him.

"I can't help it if someone stops me."

"You are Dr. Silk, son of the Adherent, Webster Silk. You are too important to talk to some low level bureaucrat. You are too busy. Dr. Silk would not pay the slightest attention to someone so lowly."

"But—"

"You will do as any man of your rank would do."

"Which is what, precisely?"

"Move on, dismiss them. Just act the way you normally would."

"You are fortunate it is after hours," he said, "or these corridors would be busier." His broken mechanical hand twitched as if he were trying to make it work. No doubt he wished to strangle her.

She smiled. *Just try it. Just give me an excuse.*

"If I don't have my specs, people will notice."

"And I won't hesitate to break them if need be."

"Oh, I believe you, Miss G'ladheon, but you must know this can't end well for you."

"No. I don't know that," she replied. "In any case, I've nothing to lose if I fail."

Silk did not have an answer for that.

"And it is *Rider* G'ladheon," she reminded him. "Do not forget it."

She gave him his specs back, and they set off once again. Karigan flitted from column to column, relishing the dark that no longer hung on the fringes of her mind but ate inward. Using her ability became an ever increasing burden, her head hurting from its use, but she embraced the pain. It would get her through this, and it was balanced by the unburdening of her usual restraint against violence. She distracted herself from the pain by imagining how she'd rip Silk's eyes out.

A small voice within her tried to shout, *This isn't me!* But it was smothered by the darkness and the intoxication of being free to do anything she felt necessary.

The etherea is tainted, her inner voice protested, but she dismissed it the way Silk would a petty bureaucrat.

UNLEASHING THE WITCH

As chains and manacles fell away from the witch, including the tiny spiked ones that ringed each finger, she stood taller, not slack, not weak. She did not check the injuries of her body as anyone else would. She did not weep or even cry out in relief. She did tug loose the threads that stitched her mouth shut. Tugged, and pulled them out.

Starling knelt at her feet, which were impaled with stakes bolted in the floor. He looked up at the Guardian. "Now what?"

"Pull the bolts." It was not the Guardian who spoke, but the witch in her broken voice.

Starling had to pry beneath her feet to pull out the bolts that held the stakes in place. Though Cade had not eaten in who-knew-how-long, his gut churned as he took in the black crust of blood surrounding the stakes on her feet, and imagined the damage done to bone and tissue. This could have been Karigan's lot if Starling was to be believed.

Starling, whose line of work would have accustomed him to all sorts of torture and gore, did not even flinch as he pried the bolts out. When he finished, he once more gazed at the Guardian.

And again, it was not the Guardian who spoke, but the witch. "Draw the spikes out."

"Do you really want me to do this?" Starling asked the Guardian. "Do you know what might happen if she is released? Once she leaves this cell, there is no controlling her."

Was Starling just trying to manipulate their doubts again? Cade glanced anxiously at the Guardian, but there was no way to read his expression through his visor.

"Draw the spikes out," the Guardian said.

Starling shook his head but obeyed. He pulled the heavy metal stakes up, revealing how they tapered to a point and had pierced holes through the witch's feet. They were crusted and flaked with blood and flesh. Cade pivoted around to dry heave, but he heard not a single cry from the witch. When he gathered himself and turned to look again, Starling had moved away, and the witch was taking her first tentative steps out of her cell. Cade extended his hand to help her, but she brushed him away. Her steps were small and mincing, shaky, but her expression showed no pain. With each step she grew steadier, and did Cade's eyes deceive him, or did her wounds and mutilations look less . . . intense? She left footprints of blood behind her, but that was because she had stepped through the puddles of blood left by the dead guards.

She paused and pressed her hand to one of the damp walls, then withdrew it and touched her lips. Dabbed her palm with her tongue. Cade moved to her side. "Would you like water? I am sure we can find—"

"Oh," she said, "there will be enough water."

Cade did not know what to make of her response, but was it his imagination or had the turbines changed rhythm down below—quickened? He could no longer see any stitch marks around her mouth. The copious scarring of her body shimmered beneath the grime on her skin. Grime that sloughed away with each moment that passed.

Cade placed Silk's pistol in his waistband and removed his jacket. He draped it over the witch's shoulders. She nodded to him and drew it close.

Just then, the lift arrived at the other end of the corridor.

"Trouble," the Guardian said, his sword held at the ready.

Starling laughed. "Your sword won't help you this time, Guardian. They'll come out shooting."

Cade grasped his pistol and aimed it toward the lift. How accurate was it? How many would be in the lift? He had only the two shots. He licked his lips and watched as the doors opened.

Four members of the Scarlet Guard filed into the corridor. They did not come out shooting as Starling predicted. They were probably here just to change shift with their fellows. It did not take them long, however, to assess what lay before them and draw their guns. Cade perceived Starling diving to the floor to their rear, taking cover in the antechamber of the cell behind some bodies. The Guardian was already charging down the corridor, sword raised. The man was a maniac, if man he truly was beneath armor and leather. He did not slow down even as the guards pulled their first shots. Cade fired and missed. He had one more shot, had to make it good.

Before the Guardian could reach the enemy, before Cade could pull the trigger again, there was a change in the air. Cade's ears plugged up from the pressure. A sharp wind whistled past him. At the other end of the corridor, it threw the guards backward. They slammed into the wall and floor and lost their guns.

The witch wove air with her hands, the bloody darkened wounds from the finger manacles now looking like simple ring bands.

The Guardian halted his charge to plaster himself against the wall while the wind roared past him. It ripped the weapons out of the hands of the guards, stripped them of their uniforms. They screamed. The wind began to strip them of something other than cloth. Their flesh.

Once again, Cade averted his gaze, and it was some time before the wind stopped and the screaming died. The witch just stood there, her arms limp at her sides, facing a scene at which Cade dared not look. Starling was right about what they had unleashed.

The Guardian returned and said. "We must go and meet Rider G'ladheon."

"Yes," Cade said faintly. For Karigan, he would brave the mess at the other end of the corridor.

Back in the antechamber, Starling climbed to his feet. Too late, Cade spotted the flash of metal, a gun he'd retrieved from one of the bodies. He fired. The Guardian's body jerked backward, but he did not fall. Cade could not seem to raise his pistol fast enough, and Starling fired again. This time the Guardian staggered.

The witch whirled and wind ripped down the corridor. It

lifted Starling off his feet and hurled him into her old cell. The door slammed shut after him, and locks clicked and closed seemingly of their own volition. A moment of silence was followed by muffled banging on the door.

Cade helped the Guardian sink to the floor. One bullet had penetrated plate armor over his chest, the second his gut.

"Lie quietly," Cade said. "I will stop the bleeding."

He cast about for something he could use as bandages when the Guardian gripped his wrist. As wounded as he was, he was still strong.

"No need," he gasped.

"But—"

"Death is honor."

Cade knew that phrase. "That is the motto of the Black Shields."

The Guardian's eyes flickered beyond the eye holes of his visor. "You . . . you know it?"

Cade nodded. "I was training. In secret. To be . . . I had hoped to become a—a Weapon."

"I was King Zachary's Weapon. And the queen's." The Guardian's words grew faint. "Proud."

Cade bowed his head, realizing there was little he could do to help him. A true Weapon, dying right in front of him.

"Tell . . . tell Rider G'ladheon. Tell her I died well."

"I will," Cade said, even as the Guardian's grip slackened on his wrist. The sound of the pump apparatus that fed air to the Guardian from the cylinders on his back sputtered to silence.

"Unneeded," the witch said.

Cade had almost forgotten her presence. "What?"

"Unneeded," she repeated. "This dying."

"Of course it's unneeded!" Cade snapped.

But she disregarded him and knelt beside the Guardian. She laid her hands over his wounds. When she withdrew them, a bullet lay on each palm. Cade's mouth dropped open. Blood no longer flowed from the wounds, and the Guardian's grip strengthened on his wrist. The breathing apparatus wheezed back to life.

"Thank you, Yolandhe," the Guardian said.

"You freed me."

The Guardian refused help and rose under his own power, showing no sign he'd been dealt mortal wounds just minutes ago. Cade had been magically healed himself, but it still amazed him. Dead. The Guardian should have been dead . . .

The three of them made their way toward the lift and the gore splattered across it. Cade's feet slapped in puddles that had not been there before. Water seeped between the stones of the wall and dripped from the ceiling. Back in the cell, Starling still banged on the door and yelled for them to release him.

By the time they reached the lift, there was no mistaking that the drubbing of the turbines had increased. Now they pounded like a rapid heartbeat, the shuddering floor sending ripples across the surface of the water that was now ankle deep.

"It's flooding," Cade murmured. That it was the witch's doing, he had no doubt.

"Yes," said the witch, Yolandhe.

Cade followed the Guardian into the lift, Yolandhe serenely stepping in after him. Before the Guardian slid the doors closed, the last thing Cade saw was the corridor rapidly filling with water. It now poured down the walls and out of the ceiling, sounding like a storm, the turbines the thunder. Even over the clamor, Cade could hear Starling still yelling and pounding on the steel door of his cell.

Yolandhe did not speak as the lift ascended. She tilted her face up as if gazing at the ceiling, though she had no eyes. To Cade, the farther the lift carried them from the prison level, the less gaunt she appeared, the more power she emanated. It made his skin prickle.

"I have to reach Arhys and Lorine," he told the Guardian. "They are not safe here."

"The little girl and her governess? I assume one of them is more important than she seems. Dr. Silk was very interested in the little girl, and you were training as a Weapon."

Cade glanced anxiously at Yolandhe, but he sensed that to her, they might as well not exist. He wondered what went through her mind, or was she simply insane from all the years of abuse and captivity?

As for the Guardian? Karigan trusted him. He had helped them escape. He'd been a Black Shield, and his skill with a sword down below had been the stuff of legend, but it was not so easy for Cade to give up Arhys' secret, a secret he had guarded for so long.

"Is there some way you can prove to me you are still a Black Shield?" he asked. "Some way to show me you are loyal to the kings and queens of the old realm?"

The Guardian undid a couple of buckles and moved a portion of his breast plate aside. He removed a brooch or badge from his leather undercoat and displayed it on his palm. It was a piece of bonewood like Karigan's staff, and shaped into a plain black shield.

"I have worn this over my heart since before Sacoridia ever fell. I have worn it every day even as the Eternal Guardian."

Cade knew of these badges. The professor had told him about them, and how all the Weapons from the period of the fall wore them. He'd actually seen them worn by the tomb Weapons. They represented unwavering loyalty and duty to their country and their order.

"You must have guessed who Arhys is," Cade said.

"I have."

"What does it mean to you?" Cade asked carefully.

"It means I would protect her as I would King Zachary, Queen Estora, and their son." The Guardian pinned the badge back on and replaced the section of breastplate that concealed it. Then he turned his attention to the lift's controls.

They arranged that Cade would once again play the prisoner, the Guardian his captor. The Guardian would escort Cade through the palace. As for Yolandhe, when they all exited the lift, she wandered off in her own direction.

When Cade made to go after her, the Guardian grabbed his arm. "No. Her fate is her own."

"But . . ." he began, then watched her go. She walked without shame of her nudity beneath his jacket, and not at all disoriented by her lack of sight. She appeared to know exactly where she was headed. Her fingers danced as if she felt her way along the currents and eddies of air that streamed through the corridor. What would happen when she encountered others?

The memory of gore strewn across the prison level below gave him some idea.

The Guardian was right—they had freed her, and now her fate was her own. Whatever it was, Cade wished her well, and hoped that her release would distract the palace guards away from his own mission.

The Guardian steered Cade through the palace corridors. They were fairly quiet, so he guessed it was evening. The only unusual thing he noticed along the way was that the various fountains were spilling over and were erratic in their displays. Water trickled from a fish's mouth one moment, then spurted with great force the next. Harried slaves worked to mop up the puddles forming around the fountains, but could not keep up.

"Which way to Arhys and Lorine?" Cade asked.

"Do not worry about them," the Guardian replied. "I will help them. I will lead them out of the palace and protect them. You will help Rider G'ladheon."

Cade did not argue. Could not, for now Arhys would have a true Weapon to protect her. They halted near the dragon fountain. Water was slopping over its sides as well, but the slaves had not gotten to it yet. They must have been overwhelmed elsewhere.

"I will leave you here," the Guardian said, then told him how to reach the museum. "I will go to the princess and her governess now, before the whole palace is aroused."

They clasped one another's wrists in a warrior's leave-taking. "My thanks," Cade said.

"Just see that Rider G'ladheon succeeds."

Cade nodded, but the Guardian was already away, trotting back down the way they had come. Cade moved quickly, too, choosing the corridor that would lead to the museum. Perhaps it was his exhaustion from captivity, but from the moment he had left Karigan to go to Yolandhe's cell, it had seemed he moved in a dream. A dream of witches and blood and legendary warriors.

INTERLUDE

As Yolandhe the sea witch, unfettered after her long imprisonment, passed through the grand corridors of the palace, the turbines far below spun out of control with the force of water. Fountains overflowed, pipes burst, and the stream flowing toward the throne room rushed. The very foundation of the palace trembled. Outside, waves swelled on the lake that surrounded its island as though driven by a storm. The surfaces of the ordinarily mirrorlike canals throughout Gossham and beyond, roared like swollen rivers, causing barges and smaller boats to buck and capsize.

All the way to Mill City currents ran wild and high. The Amber River threatened to pour over its banks. It churned into Mill City's canal system. The strong currents led the mills to shut down their turbines to protect their machines from the unprecedented force of the water. Those who oversaw the locks and dams feared they would not hold and the city would flood.

Standing in the execution yard of Mill City's prison, Mirriam, former head housekeeper for Professor Bryce Lowell Josston, and conspirator against the empire, stood against a wall blindfolded and with her hands tied behind her back. The yard smelled of blood, expelled bowels, and gunsmoke, but even as the commander prepared to order his squad to fire, a sniff of the air made her think of spring rains. The damp, clean smell was pleasant, brought her some measure of peace. She wondered if it was going to storm, but she would never know, for the order rang out and the last she knew was thunder and smoke.

Up in the Old City, where the best engineered drill in the whole empire chewed through the remains of the old realm's castle and deep into the royal tombs, the drill's maker, Heward Moody, oblivious to the threat of flooding down in Mill City, worked the steam engine that powered the drill at its utmost efficiency, while slaves, under the watchful gazes of overseers and archeologists, sorted through the tailings for artifacts. The bits and pieces of jewelry, ceramics, gold, and bone were well and good, but the ultimate prize would require the exploration of the realm beneath. Once Moody deemed they had drilled deep enough, the archeologists would go below to search for the dragonfly device Dr. Silk so coveted.

Dust fogged the corridors in the sacred depths of the royal tombs. The Weapon, Joff, pursued Chelsa past recumbent kings and queens, princes and princesses, the treasures that had been interred with them in death flashing in the light of his taper. Joff found himself lagging behind more than once, for Chelsa ran like a woman possessed, her gray robes flapping behind her. He had tried to reason with her, then argue against her heading into the sections of the tombs compromised by the accursed drill, but she had not heeded him, and only replied with, "I must try. All my research has led to this."

There had been cave-ins where the drill ground through bedrock and corridors. It had desecrated many of the dead, who had been so diligently tended by caretakers, and protected by Weapons, for so many centuries. But they, the tomb

Weapons, had been unable to protect the tombs from Dr. Ezra Stirling Silk's drill.

As if the drill was not threat enough, Serena had reported sudden flooding in the lowest levels of the tombs.

The Weapons had evacuated all the living inhabitants to the Village, for safety's sake. The dead were left to fend for themselves, their halls left unlit for the first time in recorded history.

The Weapons had a strategy in place against those who would invade the tombs, but they were too few against the power of the empire. Plans had been made to move everyone out of the Village if it proved no longer safe, with the aid of helpers who lived in the outer world. This would go against everything caretaker society believed in. It was taboo for them to see the living sun. Joff did not believe many of them would make the transition well.

The dust grew heavier the closer they got to the area where the drill drove into the earth. The ground beneath and above them vibrated with its power. Chelsa finally halted at a passage mostly blocked by rubble. Joff raised his taper observing all the cracks in the ceiling, walls, and floor. Chelsa surveyed the damage, too, and he hoped she would see reason.

"I think I can climb over the rock slide and fit through the hole near the ceiling."

No, she had not seen reason. "Chelsa, please. This could all collapse at any time. You are doing your people no favors by endangering yourself." As if to augment his words, silt showered down on them.

She rubbed grit out of her eyes. "Joff, I have to. This could end everything—the empire's power, everything."

"Then let me go."

"I don't think you'll fit through that hole. Besides, I have to see the artifact for myself to know if it is the correct one."

She was right on both counts, but he was not sure the artifact, this dragonfly device, was worth it. For all they knew, its power to turn away the emperor's great weapon was legend only. It could have simply been a metaphor, and victory against the sea kings, in those long ago days, achieved by more conventional means. Chelsa had acknowledged this argument earlier, but was not dissuaded. In fact, she was already climbing up the rubble, loose rocks clattering down the pile, seeking the hole that would allow her entrance to the burial wing of the Sealender kings.

LAURELYN'S GIFT

Karigan trudged on in her cloud of darkness. Silk appeared to be obeying her by making only perfunctory responses, if any, to those who greeted him in the corridor. He walked on with his shoulders slumped and head bowed.

She herself had almost walked right into a palace guard. She'd been between shadows and only half-faded. The guard's shock gave her enough time to knock him over the head with her staff. It had been most satisfying, but she had to make Silk help her stash him away where he would not be found immediately. They tied him up and gagged him in a store room, and left him hidden behind stacks of broken chairs.

Had she hurt him worse than a bump to his head? A part of her hoped so. It also served to remind Silk that she knew how to use her weapon, and that she would not hesitate to do so.

So fogged and exhausted by using her ability for so long was she, that it was with some surprise she realized they had reached the grotto fountain. Only a few children played with boats in the water, their governesses looking on. She did not espy Arhys or Lorine. She wasn't sure what she'd do if she did, as they complicated matters.

As for complications, the lighting around the fountain was generally dim, but she would have to cross spaces without concealing shadows. Silk forged on, oblivious to her dilemma, and she could not let him get too far ahead of her. There was nothing for it but to go.

She almost tripped over a boy who froze and stared wide-eyed at her. The taint of darkness rippled through her, took hold like a fever. She raised her staff. She would bludgeon him, and then he would not be able to tell anyone about her. The staff descended, the boy did not move. The urge to kill drove the staff down, but she pulled it away just in time, stumbling back.

Kill a child? She was going to kill a child? No, no, that was not her, but the darkness rode heavily on her shoulders.

The boy unfroze. "Nanny! Nanny!" he cried. "I seen a real ghost!"

Karigan did not wait to hear the governess' reply, but ran. She ran as fast as she could to the nearest shadow and after Silk. She ran feeling sick because she'd almost killed that boy, and a part of her still hungered to do so.

This is not me, she told herself. *But it is me, nonetheless.*

Before they reached the chamber where Lhean was being held, Karigan grabbed Silk by the collar and hauled him aside to give him instructions. When he nodded in understanding, she dropped her fading. The burden of it evaporated so abruptly that she would have fallen to her knees but for her staff. She wished she could lay her head down on a cool pillow and close her eyes.

"It weakens you."

"What?" She straightened. Silk was staring at her. Her face looked pale reflected in the blackness of his specs.

"Using the etherea weakens you," he said.

"Don't count on it." She pushed him along before he could say more. Unfortunately, what he'd observed was true. She shook her staff to cane length—at least she would look like she needed it.

When they reached the door to the laboratory room, Silk told the guard, "I have brought Miss G'ladheon back to speak with the Eletian."

"Yes, sir," the guard said. He eyed her bonewood, but since Silk made no issue of it, he did not question it. Karigan pretended to limp to reinforce the idea that it—and she— were harmless.

The guard opened the door, and Karigan followed Silk in. There was no second guard. Either Lhean was not deemed enough of a threat to require one, or the second guard had stepped away. In his cell in the back of the room, Lhean certainly did not appear to be a threat. He sat in his position of meditation, as she had seen before, appearing perfectly oblivious to the world.

Silk, in contrast, glanced sharply about, as if looking for a weapon or help. At this point he was supposed to request the keys from the guard. Instead, he ordered, "Guard! Take her!"

Karigan figured Silk would at some point attempt to take advantage, so she wasn't entirely caught unawares. In the moment it took the guard to digest Silk's order, she had shaken the bonewood back to staff length and was charging him.

His eyes widened as she came at him. He tried to tug his gun out of its sheath. She was tired of guns. They were noisy, nasty weapons. She was tired of being a target and more than willing to do some honest fighting.

The guard backed into a cabinet and the odd-shaped glassware within—cylinders, small pot-bellied pitchers, and tubes—clinked. He finally cleared his gun, but she was already on him. She struck the gun out of his hand, and he howled. She went for his head, but he ducked and the handle of her staff smashed through the glass door of the cabinet, shattering the contents. Broken glass spilled onto the floor.

The darkness and rage had diminished when she dropped the fading, but not entirely, and now it burned again, a fever. She whirled and tripped the guard with the bonewood as he tried to run after his gun. He skittered across broken glass, but did not fall.

Gun? Try this!

As he struggled to get his legs under him again and escape her, she struck him across the back. He dropped to his knees and tried to crawl away. She struck again. And again.

Even after he stopped moving, she pounded him with the bonewood. A part of her recognized this was not honorable, it was not how one used a fighting staff, but she did not stop.

She would have pulverized him but for a quiet voice that intruded on her mind. "Galadheon."

She stopped, backed away from the prone guard, both satisfied and appalled.

"Galadheon," came the quiet voice once again.

She turned and saw Lhean pressed up against the bars of his cell.

"Lhean!"

"The Silk has fled."

Karigan glanced around. Sure enough, while she'd been so occupied with battling the guard, Silk managed to escape.

"Damnation."

She charged out into the corridor, but he was nowhere to be seen. In no time he'd have all of the palace down on them.

Back in the laboratory chamber, she said, "We've got to get out of here."

She returned to the guard to retrieve his key ring. Her hand trembled as she reached to pull it off his belt. She could not tell if he was dead or alive, nor did she check. She saw she had beaten him beyond reason, beyond need. Why couldn't it have been Silk?

She shook herself and ran to Lhean's cell, trying different keys in the lock.

"The etherea here is not good," he said as she worked. "It has poisoned you."

Karigan thought that was all very interesting, but she was more intent on finding the right key. When one fit the lock and clicked it open, she wasted no time and threw the door open. Lhean emerged looking better than he had when she'd last seen him. The chocolate must have done him some good.

She was ready to run. They had to make for the museum before Silk's alarm sent hordes of guards after them, but Lhean caught her arm, anchored her.

"We've got to—" she began.

He placed his hand on her brow. "The taint has filled your being with darkness."

"That's fine, but—"

"Shhh. Peace, Galadheon."

His touch lightened her, lifted some of the darkness that had been eating at her, soothed her. She thought of the shade beneath the greenery of the summer forest. A quiet breeze, a stream trickling nearby.

He removed his hand. "Now we go," he said.

She nodded. "Now we go."

Karigan and Lhean ran through corridors, she holding on to him to keep them both faded. Somehow his presence, being in contact with him, helped stave off the darkness of before, made her lighter and less weary.

They paused by the dragon fountain, surprised to see it overflowing and no one tending it.

"Odd," she murmured, stepping around puddles. "I wouldn't expect such a failure in the palace."

"It's not a failure," Lhean said, gazing at the erratically flowing fountain. "Something has been unleashed."

"Something has been unleashed? What is it?"

"A power. I have sensed that this empire circulates its etherea through its water systems. These fountains, the lake, the canals in the city, and perhaps to a smaller degree the areas beyond. It is concentrated, however, within the city."

That explained all the fountains and canals, but she had no time to admire the concept, for she detected the onrush of booted feet pounding marble floors in their direction.

They pelted down the corridor, sliding to a stop at the museum doors. She tried the handles.

"Locked," she muttered.

Just then she perceived a shadow emerging from another doorway, and she whirled, raising her staff to strike.

"Karigan?" a familiar and very welcome voice queried.

"Cade!" She dropped her fading. "You made it."

"Yes, I—"

"We have to get in—stand back." She smashed the handle of the bonewood through the glass, then reached inside to jigger the lock. By the time she tripped it and pulled the door open, their pursuers had entered the corridor.

"In!" she cried, pushing Cade into the museum after Lhean.

She slammed the door shut and bolted it, not that it would thwart anyone for long.

"We've got to barricade these doors."

Cade was already pushing a display cabinet across the floor. Lhean joined in to help, Karigan adding her strength. It effectively blocked the door. They pushed another display case in front of the cabinet.

"Lhean, the moondial is—" she began, but he was already running toward the back of the museum.

As a final measure, Karigan and Cade rolled Ghallos the p'ehdrose across the floor to supplement the barricade.

As they worked, Karigan asked, "Where's Fastion? And your witch?"

"They went their own way," Cade replied and then explained.

When he finished, she nodded. Arhys and Lorine would be in excellent hands with Fastion. As for the witch? Who knew?

Just as soon as they pushed Ghallos in place, the enemy began banging on the doors. Karigan and Cade glanced at one another, and then ran for the back of the museum. When Cade vanished from her side, she paused to look back and saw him removing a longsword from a display. He grinned at her and saluted. At the sound of breaking glass, they picked up their pace past exhibits, past the entrance to the museum library, and past the aviary of the hummingbirds.

When they ran beneath the arch into the room of the moondial, Cade halted, a look of wonder on his face. Wan moonlight gleamed down through the dome of glass and across the obsidian floor. The four winged statues gazed pensively into the dark corners of the chamber. It was indeed a wondrous sight, but the lead seams that held pieces of the glass dome in place cast shadows across the entire room like a net that trapped them.

Karigan did not pause but dashed past Lhean who was studying the moondial. In the captain's riddle, she was to seek the scything moon. She hoped Lhean knew which of the crescents was the scything moon. She halted at the display case that held her saber. She broke the glass and lifted out the weapon that was as familiar to her as an old, broken-in pair of boots. She swept the blade through the air, joyful to have an old friend in hand once again.

A screech and crash, and shouting at the museum entrance, brought her back to the present. Cade was already trying to push a display case beneath the arch, but the span was too wide—they'd never be able to block it adequately.

"Lhean?" she asked anxiously.

"It is a puzzle," he said, his voice and demeanor strangely calm. His gaze followed the phases of the moon laid out on the floor. "I cannot read what pieces of time these lead to. It may be that their having been moved from Castle Argenthyne disrupted—"

A sense of discord rippled across Karigan's flesh, raising the hairs on her arms, like a god's hand sweeping across her mortal soul.

"Lhean?"

"Yes, I felt it." He was now kneeling by the moon phases, hovering over one of the crescent moons. He remained unperturbed by that strange sensation, as well as by the commotion at the museum entrance. "Whatever was unleashed earlier is expressing its—*her*self."

"You must find us a piece of time," she said. "They're going to be on us any minute."

"I know." He remained impossibly serene.

Karigan trotted to where Cade was moving another case and helped. They exchanged worried smiles.

"Is the Eletian going to find our way out?" Cade asked.

Karigan wished she could be as calm as Lhean. "I don't know. I really don't." She glanced back at Lhean, kneeling on the floor. Beside him stood the ghostly figure of Yates, gazing back at her. The residue of dream came back to her, of when she was last in this room. "Laurelyn!"

"What is it?" Cade asked.

"A gift—the ice-glazed moon!" she cried at Lhean. "The ice-glazed moon!"

"An elder name," he said. Beside him, the ghost of Yates faded away.

"Do you know it?"

She did not hear his response for there was another great crash near the entrance. She peered through the gloom to see that the enemy had toppled Ghallos and were leaping over him.

"Do not break anything else," came Silk's anxious voice. "Just get the prisoners!"

Cade had a gun, which he aimed out into the museum. The silver of the weapon flared, hurting her eyes. He'd leaned his longsword against their barricade, close at hand.

"About half a dozen of them," he said, "plus Silk and a pair of Enforcers."

Not good odds. "I'm going out there," she said.

"What? No!"

Shots rang out as Silk's men ran toward their end of the museum. Karigan faded out and climbed over the barricade. When she landed lightly on the other side, bullets whizzed by her. She crouched to make herself as small a target as possible. They might not be able to see her, but she understood that even wild shots could hit a mark.

Her saber in one hand and the bonewood in the other, she ran toward the enemy. So only six men and two Enforcers, which meant that although these were not good odds, the emperor's guards did not rate them so great a threat that more had been sent. The first man she encountered, she tripped with the bonewood, and his cry caught the attention of the others. They swung their weapons around in her direction.

Uh oh. Silk must have informed them of her ability.

A shot rang out from behind her and one of the men dropped. She glanced back and saw Cade toss his gun aside and pick up his sword. She ran to the next closest guard, and her sword, like a song in her hand, took him down. The remaining men shouted in confusion, but were more disciplined in their shooting than Mr. Howser had been. They did not take down any of their own.

Karigan's blade passed through the rib cage of another guard. As he slid off her sword, the lights were thrown on, and she found herself surrounded and very visible. Cade had also climbed over the barricade, his ancient sword held in a position of readiness, a hard gleam in his eyes she had never seen before. He was prepared to die in this fight. She could sense it. She knew it.

"We can see you, Miss G'ladheon," Silk called out from his location near the light lever.

Guns and the eyestalks of the Enforcers, were aimed at her and Cade. She dropped her fading. It would not aid her now. Though her sword and staff were useless against the firepower of the empire, she did not lower them.

Acceptance descended on her. Like Cade, she realized this was the end. She wasn't going home, it was going to end right here. A bead of sweat trickled down her temple as she stared into the barrel of the nearest gun. She would, she decided, die fighting.

One of the Enforcers sprang over bodies and landed in front of her. It opened a hatch and ejected a net. The weight of it threw her down.

Damnation! She frantically tried to pull it off, but every movement just entangled her further. The mechanical held Cade off with one of its legs, using it like a sword to parry his blows.

"Hold fire," Silk ordered as his men advanced. "We'll take them alive if we can."

Cade's longsword clattered against the Enforcer's leg even as the mechanical dragged Karigan closer. She poked the bonewood through the net and whacked it against the central orb with a resounding *clang.* The mechanical paused, swiveled its eyestalk toward her, and appeared to be opening another hatch.

With a grunt, Karigan smashed the eyestalk, shattering glass and denting metal. It dangled from its socket by wires that sparked. The mechanical squealed and whirled around, skittering erratically and dragging Karigan on the floor in circles at a breakneck speed.

"Cade!" she cried.

Her blind Enforcer ran into display cases and grew more erratic by the moment, bowling into the guards and bouncing off the other Enforcer, which went flailing across the room. Glass and wood and plaster smashed around Karigan until Cade shoved his sword between the mechanical's legs and tripped it. It heaved over, splitting its central orb along a previously invisible seam. Dark viscous fluid and tubing, like entrails, gushed out onto the floor into a boiling, hissing puddle.

At that moment, another wave of discord passed over and through Karigan. The ground shook and articles fell off shelves and smashed to the floor. The guards who remained standing paused in consternation. The remaining Enforcer, already unbalanced by its collision with its companion, staggered. The quaking undermined the last of its stability, and it tripped over its own spindly legs. It keeled over, its legs scurrying in the air like a dying insect.

"What in the name of—?" Silk cried.

Even if Karigan had wanted to give him an answer, she didn't have one.

YOLANDHE UNLEASHED

If anyone tried to stop Yolandhe, she simply shoved them aside with a thrust of air. If they actually threatened her with a weapon, their landing was messier than that of others. She had, in fact, left a trail of bodies from the lift all the way to the emperor's throne room.

The emperor was not present in the icy throne room when she arrived, but Webster Silk was. He'd known she was coming so he met her with a small army. They were nothing to her. She flung them and their spider-legged mechanicals away with a gesture, like the felling of a forest, leaving only one tree standing. The others were meaningless to her, but not Webster Silk, not the man who had imprisoned and tormented her, the first to carve his initials on her body. Those scars now blazed with furious light. The power filled her, and even without eyes, she could see.

He tried to shoot her with one of his fire weapons. She melted it in his hand. He screamed and tried to shake off the molten metal. His cries were music to her. Next she stripped off his clothing with a mere thought, first the fur coat, then his suit, and finally his small clothes, revealing flesh and a manhood shriveled by cold and fear.

"Do you wish to romance me, Webster Ezmund Silk?" Her voice rang out more sweetly than it had since he had crushed her vocal chords.

"Please . . ." he said, shaking.

Beautiful music.

"Do you remember how you shackled me? I will shackle you now."

She drew on her powers and melted ice from the ceiling. She reshaped the melt water and froze it into an icicle-pronged noose around his neck. He fought to break it off, but it might as well have been made of steel. Blood trickled from his neck onto his chest.

"Webster Ezmund Silk, you were the first to show me your love." She pointed to his initials across her breasts. She would not sully herself by touching him, so instead, she hurled her memories of the violations, the degradations, the torture, into his mind so he experienced them as she had. His body thrashed and pleas spilled from his mouth in incoherent sobs, a grand symphony.

It was still not enough.

She slashed her hands through the air, and he howled. With every gesture she sliced his skin open, writing her own name upon his flesh in the characters of a long lost language that once belonged to the goddesses of the sea. Blood pooled around his feet. She covered him in her name.

"Webster Ezmund Silk, no sea witch am I, but a goddess of elder days. Older than old, yes? You played at an eternal life, but you will not know immortality."

He sobbed.

"I am Yolandhe. Look upon me. You did not make me, but you reshaped me."

She forced him to look, to look at the river of power flowing through her. She drew on the etherea that was so rich within these upper levels of the palace, as though trying to quench a deep thirst.

When she was sure he had seen her, she with her scars blazing triumphantly, she slashed out his eyes. She admired her handiwork, satisfied. She did no more and dismissed his existence from her mind. He was no longer of any consequence to her, for she sensed the arrival of her beloved. Anticipation sent shockwaves of power through the palace, through the water-borne systems of etherea. The very ground shuddered.

Her beloved strode toward her, giving Webster Silk, writhing in his collar of ice, a sidelong glance, but that was all. His eyes were wide, and all for her.

"Is it really you?" he murmured more to himself than to her. "You are so very bright."

"Yes, my love."

"They told me you'd died. That you'd perished in the war. All my fault."

"No, my love, I was entrapped. Held prisoner beneath the earth, but now I have emerged."

He reached for her, trembling. His third aspect, the corrupt, vile one, attempted to assert control. His gray eyes clouded, darkened in a storm.

"It is time," she said, "to lance the poison in you."

His body convulsed then steadied. His eyes were completely black. "You are too late, Yolandhe. All is mine."

"We shall see."

She warmed the room so that ice drip-drip-dripped into a crescendo of rain and steam rose up from the floor. Webster Silk's noose melted and broke. He fell to the ground, an icicle driven through his throat.

The vile one laughed as water streamed down his face. "You believe warming the room will cause me to burn up?"

She froze the water around him so he became encased in ice, but he just cracked it off with a shrug.

"Feeble elemental magic," he scoffed. "Is that all you can conjure? Minor entertainments?"

"Entertainments, perhaps, while I drown your empire."

"You cannot. You are not capable."

"Oh, but you have concentrated so much etherea here, and I had so much time to consider you."

His eyes briefly lost focus as his awareness traveled the empire, witnessing the raging seas tossing up against coastal cities, including Gossham. He took in rivers bursting their banks and flooding fields, villages, and cities. He perceived the turbines beneath the palace, mere man-made machines of steel, disintegrating from the forces she threw at them.

"Why would you do this?" he demanded.

"If I kill your empire, I kill you. It is those you rule who give you power. I will cleanse the world, renew it."

He burned with anger. Yolandhe knew he struggled to retain his composure, for if he scorched his current body, he no longer had Webster Silk in reserve to contain him. Should he try to use her body, he would find it inhospitable, to say the least.

He lashed at her with oily, black, slithering strands of power, but she was prepared, and it sizzled against her shield of water and air. He was ancient and mighty, but she was more ancient still, a goddess rooted in the earth, the ocean, the sky. He may be a deep dark force that fouled the world, but her power had become terrible, as well, after absorbing so much tainted etherea. Terrible, yes, but she'd use hers to purge the empire from existence. She regretted the loss of life, but with time, the forests would grow back, the rivers would run their natural courses, and etherea would be free of corruption.

She teased him with feints and parries of her own elemental magic—a sharp wind, mini-waterspouts that skittered across the floor—teasing him, distracting him, while thick, dark clouds rumbled across his lands. Lightning touched off fires in valuable tracts of forest, while ocean waves ate off the coastline. She sought to keep the vile one occupied so maybe her beloved could surface and re-exert some control. He smashed the ceiling with more strands of power, blasting plaster and stone that collapsed around her. She showered him with sharp needles of water that turned into a hissing steam when they hit him. The stream that had meandered through the throne room overflowed and trout flopped across the floor. One slapped his foot.

It was at that moment it happened: the gray returned to his eyes in some small measure, and her beloved, the warrior sea king and the nobleman thief combined, loosed his own power. Yes. Together they would cleanse the world.

In the harbor, an island awakened, a huge barnacle-clad head of a sea dragon reared up and out of the surf, shaking off kelp and rockweed, revealing the iridescent scales of its hide. Fishing boats capsized and men fell screaming into the sea. In the lake that surrounded the palace, the little island next to it shifted, shaking off small trees and moss that had grown along its spine. In the Great Mounds, where a Green Rider out of time had observed something out of place, one of the mounds uncoiled and shook the dirt of its burrow off its back. It unfolded membranous wings and roared into the evening sky.

Across the empire, the strategically hidden beasts had lain in wait for almost two centuries, slumbering the years away until the one who commanded them called them in need.

They attacked the empire. Their fiery breaths flared in the night sky. They glided over fields, scorching them. They burned down towns. Taloned feet the size of small cottages tore down mills and imperial government buildings.

The Eternal Guardian, with a complaining Arhys sitting in the saddle in front of him, whipped his horse across the bridge from the palace toward Gossham. Lorine frantically held onto the mane of her horse as she tried to keep up without falling, her veil peeled away from a face tight with fear. They galloped through spray that lashed over the bridge from the stormy lake. Droplets sparkled in a rainbow haze beneath the lamps that lit the way. Pursuit was just lengths behind, a dozen horsemen armed with guns.

Fastion had ordered Lorine and Arhys not to look back. He told Arhys to close her eyes before he slaughtered the guards at the gates and checkpoints with his sword. But as they neared the mainland, a great presence hovered over them. Fastion looked up, and what he saw brought back his memories of being engulfed in the burn of dragon breath during the fall of Sacor City. His emperor's great weapon had been released.

The dragon of the lake was silvery like a fish as lamplight glanced off its belly, its true size hidden by night, its sinuous tail a rudder that steered it through the sky. It circled over the bridge. Arhys started screaming hysterically. She had looked. Lorine stared ahead with an expression of determination.

Gunfire rang out, but their pursuers aimed not at the fleeing trio, but at the dragon, which backwinged as if taken aback, but not for long. It roared in rage and plunged down at the men. Fastion had no need of looking back when, over Arhys' cries, the crashing of waves, and the roar of the dragon, he heard the screams of men.

Forward. They could only go forward. He lashed his horse onto shore, not slackening speed for the panicked folk of Goss-ham who ran in a confusion of light and dark, into their path. Fastion's first duty was to the little girl struggling and shrieking in the saddle before him. He never saw the palace tremble from the magical battle that racked it from within and the great turbines breaking apart from beneath. When those forces un-dermined the palace's foundation, he did not witness the col-lapse of one of the towers. He did not look back to see what was left of the bridge or the men who had pursued them.

Forward. Duty. He kept faith in Rider G'ladheon, but just in case, the little girl he protected may very well be all that was left of their future. If anyone survived what was being unleashed, anyway, for there to be a future.

The dragon from the Great Mounds soared through the dim sky above, its scales luminescing in moonlight as it attacked the engineers, archeologists, overseers, and slaves operating the drill in the Old City. Heward Moody was killed by a single slash of talons, his steam engine knocked apart by another. Steam scalded the dragon. It bellowed in pain and pumped its wings, lifting it vertically into the sky. From a generous elevation, it stooped into a dive, preparing to obliterate any thing and any human left standing at the drill site.

Below, in the tombs, the dust circulated in ever-thickening clouds, and more rubble collapsed from the ceiling and walls.

"Chelsa!" Joff cried.

"Give me a moment," came her muffled reply from the other side of the cave-in.

Joff could not know of the dragon attack above, he only knew the danger underground, and when he no longer heard the chew of the drill, and yet the tombs still shook, his fear mounted.

The last thing he expected to hear from Chelsa was laughter. Not hysterical laughter, but the hearty laughter of someone who had been told a good joke.

"Chelsa?"

"Joff," she called. "I have found it, the antidote to the emperor's weapon, and—"

He never heard more for layers of bedrock and earth, weakened first by the destruction of the castle and Sacor City one hundred and eighty-six years ago, and then by the drill, collapsed. Dirt and rock and tombs crashed down atop Chelsa and Joff. Chelsa's people would never know of her discovery and how close she came to averting the destruction wrought by the emperor's dragons.

THE BLADE OF THE
SHADOW CAST

It was no longer just a sense of discord Karigan felt from beneath the net that still trapped her, but the palace shuddering. Wall-mounted artifacts crashed to the floor. Cabinets and display cases toppled over. Above the din, she heard Dr. Silk cry out in dismay as he attempted to rescue teetering urns and busts. The lights blinked and the walls around them groaned.

The remaining guards retreated as a heavy scrolled cornice smashed to the floor around them. They ran for the museum entrance.

"No-no-no!" Silk cried.

Cade leaped to Karigan's side and hacked through the net. They pulled severed strands apart until she was able to slip free, even as a heavily framed painting crashed to splinters beside her.

Karigan prepared to go after Silk, but Cade caught her arm and pulled her back as more ceiling and a portion of wall caved in before them. Cade guided her through a haze of dust to the room of the moondial.

She coughed and waved dust out of her face. "Silk," she said.

"Forget him."

The room of the moondial remained strangely serene, Lhean gazing at the phases of the moon. A few panes of glass from the dome had shattered on the floor, but there was little other obvious damage.

"Lhean?"

"Galadheon," he said. "You are the blade of the shadow cast."

The riddle! How did Lhean know the line?

His eyes were fathomless as he gazed at her. "The threads of time are in flux," he said, as if knowing her thoughts.

Eletians did not necessarily perceive time in the same linear fashion as mortals. If time was in flux, that was good, wasn't it? They were already changing this future.

"What does he mean," Cade asked, "that you are the blade of the shadow cast?"

A growing rumble and more quaking caused a couple more glass panels to crash to the floor. The four statues of the cardinal directions swayed on their pedestals.

"I am the gnomon," Karigan said faintly, "just like in Castle Argenthyne."

Lhean nodded. He held his hand out to her, and she walked toward him as if in a dream, Cade close behind her. Lhean centered her on the full moon.

"Stand close," Lhean told Cade.

"What—what now?" Cade asked as the world shook itself around them.

"Yes, what now? I haven't my moonstone—it's what cast my shadow in Castle Argenthyne."

Before Lhean could answer her, a drone filled the air.

Ezra Stirling Silk shook himself out of the pile of rubble and dust that had collapsed on him. He felt around for his specs, but could not find them. The ancient urn he'd been trying to protect was in pieces beneath him, and indistinguishable from the ruin that surrounded him. His museum . . . The artifacts he had so lovingly collected. He rubbed his temple. It throbbed terribly. He must have been knocked unconscious for a little while. Where were his guards? His prisoners? The sputtering light seared into his sensitive eyes and revealed in brief flashes the catastrophic damage to his museum.

Above the sounds of destruction, he heard a familiar drone. The drone of hummingbird wings.

He squinted in the direction of the aviary. Support beams had dropped from the ceiling and broken through the cage and mesh.

The drone increased in volume, the sound of furious hummingbird wings working. Had they been fed today?

He glanced here and there, the flashing light burning his eyes, making it more difficult than usual to see. Wings buzzed past his ears. He scrambled to dislodge himself from the rubble so he might escape, but no sooner had he regained his feet than he lost his balance and fell to his side. He twisted to look up, and for a moment, the light dimmed to almost dark, and he saw their auras aglow, a great cloud of blood-red hovering over him, the whir of their wings nearly deafening.

When the cloud plunged down on him, he could only scream.

Karigan swatted at hummingbirds with the flat of her sword-blade. Cade pulled one out that had lodged in his arm. Lhean struck and caught one out of mid-air, but others circled around and hovered over them. Karigan's leg buckled when a beak impaled her behind her knee. She cried out in pain and yanked the bird out, its feathers greasy with her own blood. She staggered to her feet and tried to brush several off Cade.

"*Vien a muna'riel!*" Lhean suddenly shouted.

The shock of silver light spread to every corner of the chamber and sent the hummingbirds spiraling away through dust and debris into the other exhibition hall.

The three stood there silently, breathing hard, and blinking in the intense light.

"How did you—?" Karigan began.

"I remembered how in Blackveil, Telagioth commanded the lumeni along the Lighted Path to illuminate," Lhean replied.

"It scared the birds off," Cade said. "The light."

Karigan squinted toward the display case that held Silk's collection of moonstones, but it was too bright to look at directly. Was hers, she wondered again, among them, or locked away in Silk's office, or . . . ?

"Do you not see, Galadheon?" Lhean asked. "We've our silver moonlight to reach a piece of time. You but need to lead us across the liminal line."

Could it be true? Was this enough to send them home to their own time?

She glanced at Cade. "Do you really want to do this—go to my Sacoridia?"

"More than anything."

Karigan smiled, but tried to contain her excitement. After all, this might not work, and she'd be stuck here for the rest of her life. The rumbling and shaking of the palace made her think that the rest of her life might not be that long.

Lhean re-positioned her so now, with the brilliant silver light of the moonstones knifing past them, her shadow crossed the phase she assumed to be the ice-glazed moon. The three of them linked arms, Karigan in the middle.

"Call upon your ability," Lhean said, "so we may cross the threshold."

Karigan took a deep breath, and even as the palace was racked by more quaking and glass panels shattered on the floor around them, she grasped her brooch and faded. All went gray. Along with the noise of destruction, she heard the grinding of the winged statues rotating until they gazed down upon her, Cade, and Lhean.

The crossing of this threshold stretched her, threatened to tear her apart. To one side, the side Lhean clung to, she sensed a summer night's breath of air, fresh and alive and familiar— home! To her other side, Cade's side, was a maelstrom, devastation, the future she was attempting to escape.

Lhean hauled on her, but she could not move. She was anchored. Her sword slipped from her grip and arrowed back into the future. Her bonewood vanished, too, but into the past. Cade's hold on her threatened to yank her arm out of its socket. He was wavery in her vision and was in danger of being sucked into chaos like her sword had been.

No! She tried pulling harder on him, but she only edged closer toward chaos herself.

"Galadheon!" Lhean pulled back on her, her shoulders being wrenched out by opposing forces.

"Karigan!" Cade shouted, his voice distant. "You must go home."

"Not without you! I will not leave you!"

"I am holding you back—I am not allowed to cross."

"No! I won't—"

"Karigan," he said, "I love you." He let her go. He fell back into the maelstrom and vanished.

"Nooo!" she wailed and reached after him, but Lhean held on to her. "Let me go! Let me go!"

"No, Galadheon. He would no longer remember you."

Lhean drew her back toward the familiar, the chirruping of crickets, the embrace of a summer evening, a cobblestone street underfoot, a familiar series of rooflines: the city that was no longer Gossham, but Corsa. Home. She breathed deep of it.

But before she could even drop her fading, she was grabbed again, torn from Lhean's grasp, from her world, and hurled into the heavens, among the stars, the planets, undulating masses of celestial clouds. She spun out of control, catching glimpses of tiny silver shards that glinted in starlight and pursued her like a comet's tail.

Why? What had it all been for?

The spinning eased, and as she traveled, she thought she saw a crystalline staircase, a lone warrior standing on the landing, with her sword at rest. Forms vast and filmy moved about the heavens—celestial hunting dogs, great eagles, winged horses. Gods strode across the stars.

She plunged. She was falling, falling, the silver shards changing course to follow as though she and they were inextricably linked. She remembered the silent laughter of the mirror man. She'd been presented three masks, had been forced to choose. She had rejected the three and chosen his. He had called her bluff.

She fell at a great velocity, stars streaking by. The sound of immense wings sweeping the air came to her, and *he* caught her once again, Westrion, the Birdman, god of death. He cradled her to his chest as he had before, slowing her descent. The mirror shards slowed with them.

"Why?" she asked him. "Why do you do this to me?"

His raptor's visage remained impassive as one word thundered in her mind: *AVATAR*. Then he flung her away, and she hurtled from the heavens and into the world.

THE LONGEST NIGHT

It was the winter solstice. Night of Aeryc. Despite the lively music echoing through the banquet hall, and festive boughs of evergreens adorning the rafters and great hearth, the mood was subdued among the guests who feasted with King Zachary and Queen Estora.

Laren had eaten earlier with her Riders, a far more merry bunch than this lot, playing jokes on one another, singing, exchanging gifts, and dancing to simple tunes played on flute, fiddle, and drum. She could have ordered one of her Riders to attend the king this night, but they deserved a holiday, a little time off, and it was no hardship for her. She stood near the entrance to the banquet hall with a dozen or so attendants of various kinds, secretaries, aides, servants, all keeping watchful gazes on their masters and mistresses.

Outside a snowstorm lashed at the windows, which would no doubt put a damper on the midnight candle walk along the streets of Sacor City. Lights to illuminate the Longest Night. The view of the candlelit streets, from the castle walls and battlements, was a sight to see, but tonight those candles would not stay lit in such high winds. Anyone going out was apt to get frostbitten for their trouble. No, it was best to stay in and sip the traditional mulled wine, and nibble on sugary pastries, and place the lighted candles in windows.

She yawned, looking over the king and queen's guests—local aristocrats and high-ranking officials mainly, some of the queen's kin over-wintering in the city, and just a few lord- and lady-governors. The same winter weather that quelled battles with Second Empire also made ordinary travel difficult.

731

They sat at three long tables laden with holiday specialties. A fish chowder had just been served. King and queen sat at the head table, presiding with quiet dignity over the dinner.

Laren yawned again, earning a raised eyebrow from the Weapon, Fastion, who stood opposite her across the hall. It was the short days and long nights this time of year that got to her. They always made her sleepy. And it was just too . . . quiet. Not a bad thing, she supposed, especially with Queen Estora in her gravid condition. First pregnancies, so early on, could be precarious.

A mild commotion broke out at the entryway, and Laren perked up. She glanced at Zachary to ensure he did not need her, and went to the doorway where guards and the Weapon Donal were holding back a trio of cloaked travelers. Not just any travelers, she realized, but Eletians. Immediately she recognized their leader, Somial, and the two who had accompanied him before.

Somial's eyes lit up when he saw her. "Ah. Captain Mapstone, it is well to see you."

"We were not expecting you. The king is — "

"With deference to your gracious king," Somial replied with a bow of his head, "we are not here for him."

"Then what brings you? What do you wish of us?" Did he have another puzzling message for her to take down to the tombs?

"Merely to observe."

"To observe? To observe what?"

Somial pointed back into the banquet hall. At first she did not notice anything unusual. Had the Eletians come to observe the humdrum rituals of nobles at their meal?

Then the lamplight wavered. The fire in the great hearth roared up the chimney and threw off a shower of sparks. Tapestries fluttered along the walls and the air compressed in her ears. This was no ordinary draft.

The guests looked around as their cloaks and skirts rippled around them. The usually stationary Weapons cast suspiciously about trying to identify the source of the disturbance.

Then the air fractured and disgorged something— *someone*—out of nothing on a frigid current, as frigid as the starry depths of the heavens themselves. He, no she, flew by in a blur, landing unceremoniously on the center table with such force that she slid down its length, smashing a bowl of late harvest apples, sending goblets of wine splashing on guests. Baskets of bread flew into the air along with utensils and crockery. Hot fish chowder landed on Lord Mirwell's lap, and among the cries of shock and consternation of the guests, his shrieks were the most piercing.

Behind trailed a line of silvery shimmering . . . somethings. Laren could not seem to work her limbs or even her jaw. It was Karigan. This much she knew. Even if she couldn't see her Rider's face, only one person could make such an entrance.

Zachary, who must have realized the same, stood. The Weapons ran toward the table. While Karigan moved swiftly, the motion around her was stretched out, took too long to happen. Karigan's slide finally halted and she sat up, shaking her head as though dazed. The shimmering silver particles followed her down the table. She flung her arm up to protect her face as they impacted her. Her cry rang out clear and shrill through the hall.

Even as time slowed the reaction of those around her, Karigan climbed to her feet, her hand over her eye, crimson trickling between her fingers. Her uniform blossomed with blood where silver was embedded in her flesh. She started running back down the table, and her boots, or what Laren had thought were boots, disintegrated off her feet and vanished. Her trousers frayed apart on one leg.

"No!" Karigan cried out. "Let me go back! I must go back for him!"

When she reached the end of the table, she leaped without hesitation as if expecting the frigid air currents to carry her back from whence she came.

It was Somial's companion, Enver, who was quick enough to catch her as she plummeted.

Normal time resumed and the banquet hall was chaos, with screams of alarm and dismay echoing off the vaulted ceiling. Weapons and guards swarmed Enver and Karigan.

Laren shook herself out of the spell that had befallen her.

"To the mending wing," she ordered Fastion and Donal. "Get her to the mending wing!"

She would leave others to sort out the disruption in the banquet hall. She was about to run after the Weapons and the struggling Karigan who yelled at them to let her "go back," when Zachary grabbed her arm. His eyes were wild. He was in shock. They all were.

"That is Karigan," he said.

"Yes."

"She came back. I knew she would. We must—"

Just then, a cry, a different cry from all the others, ripped through the hall. Queen Estora was doubled over in her chair. More Weapons and her maid came running.

Oh, no, Laren thought. Zachary hesitated, looked torn. "Your place is with your wife and the child she bears," she said. "Go to her now and get the castellan to calm your guests. I will report to you on Karigan's condition just as soon as I can."

"Yes." This time he did not hesitate but strode directly toward Estora, issuing orders as he went.

Laren ran out into the corridor both elated by Karigan's return, and sorely worried for Estora.

Karigan still struggled and fought against the Weapons who carried her away. All the way to the mending wing, she pleaded with them to let her "go back."

Go back where? Where had she been all this time? She had entered Blackveil nine months past and vanished. How had she arrived in such . . . in such a fashion? The Eletians followed along in silence, revealing nothing. How had they known when and where to "observe" Karigan's arrival?

Laren chose not to summon any of her Riders, not even Connly, Mara, or Elgin, in order to prevent an onrush of Karigan's concerned friends to the mending wing. Word would reach them soon enough. Ben, her Rider-mender, was here on duty. She grabbed him and pointed ahead to where Fastion and Donal tried to restrain Karigan so that Master Mender Vanlynn could look her over. Despite Vanlynn's soothing tones, she could not calm Karigan.

When Ben saw who needed his help, his mouth dropped

open and he paled as though . . . as though he was looking at a ghost. Laren knew the feeling.

"Quiet her, lad," Vanlynn ordered him. "We can't help her while she struggles in this manner. She's near crazed."

Ben had learned a new facet of his special mending ability in the fall, and he used it now. He touched his finger to Karigan's forehead, and she slumped in the arms of the Weapons. Ben's touch would allow her to rest peacefully for a time, giving the menders an opportunity to examine and treat her. Perhaps when she woke, she'd be more herself.

Vanlynn hobbled over to Laren, leaning on her stick. The elder woman had come out of retirement to replace the former master mender.

"One of yours, eh?" Vanlynn said.

"Yes. She is—"

"I know who she is. My assistants will see to her. Meanwhile, I've been summoned to the queen's quarters, and Ben with me. Your Rider will have to wait. Why they can't bring the queen here is beyond me. Lord-Governor Mirwell will have to wait, too. He is apparently demanding my presence to treat the scalding of his nether parts. Ben!"

"Yes, Master Vanlynn." He had a mender's satchel over his shoulder. He glanced back with regret to where Karigan was being moved into a room. "I've got to go," he told Laren.

"I know. The queen needs you."

He nodded and hurried after his chief. His *other* chief.

Laren found a chair in a waiting alcove and sank into it. She had a feeling that the Longest Night was going to indeed be long. Elated, shocked, concerned—she did not know how to feel.

The Eletians followed her into the alcove, and she noticed Fastion and Donal taking watchful positions in the corridor outside. She was not sure whether it was because they were concerned about Karigan, or the manner of her return, or about the Eletians. Probably all of it.

"We shall keep vigil with you," Somial announced.

"We have prepared ourselves," Enver added.

"Prepared?" Laren asked incredulously. "Prepared for what?"

Enver, his face serious, removed a parcel from his pack. Laren saw a familiar sigil stamped on it. "Dragon Droppings," Enver said, "from the master of chocolate."

Laren thought perhaps it was time to make the candy-maker, Master Gruntler, an ambassador to Eletia.

Somial seated himself in the only other chair in the alcove, his two companions gracefully lowering themselves to the floor to sit cross-legged.

"What do you know of this?" Laren asked.

"Less than you may imagine," he replied.

"Your less is more than my nothing."

He conceded her point with a bow of his head. "As you may recall, one of our own, Lhean, who accompanied the expedition into Blackveil, never returned, as the Galadheon had not."

"Of course." It had been assumed, at least by the Sacoridians, that the two had perished in Blackveil.

"Lhean returned to us late this summer. He arrived in your city of Corsa."

"Corsa? Where did he arrive from?"

"A piece of time almost two centuries hence. He had been held captive by the people of that time. There were no other Eletians, no Eletia."

Laren shuddered from a sudden chill. "No Eletia?"

"A bleak thread of our story. Alas, Lhean could tell us little of that world, for not only was he a captive, but he mostly remained in . . . hmmm, you might call it torpor? to preserve himself. He did say he hid for a time among the ruins of this castle and city before he was captured."

Laren was gripped by a sensation greater than a chill. It was colder, darker, the frigid exhalation of death.

"We believe Karigan will be able to explain much more," Somial said, "for she was there, as well."

Of course she was, Laren thought. It would not be the first time Karigan had surpassed the boundaries of time.

"Why didn't you come to us when Lhean returned?" And why hadn't Lhean and Karigan arrived together? So many questions.

"He returned weakened and disoriented," Somial replied.

"And Prince Jametari had his own reasons, which he need not explain to his subjects."

Laren narrowed her eyes. Eletian games.

A mender leaned into the alcove. "Captain? Your Rider is resting. We—" The mender faltered when she realized the others there were Eletians, not everyday visitors to the mending wing.

"Go on," Laren said.

"We, uh, have checked her over, and aside from bruises and lacerations, her main injuries appear to be from broken mirror shards. We picked most of them out, though the one in her eye . . . it is difficult, so we are awaiting the return of Master Vanlynn and Ben."

"Her eye? Will she—"

"I do not know, Captain. We'll keep you informed. In the meantime, you may sit with her if you like."

When Laren turned her gaze back to Somial, he had closed his eyes as though asleep. His companions spoke softly to one another in Eletian and shared Dragon Droppings.

She stood and headed toward the room where they were keeping Karigan. Broken mirror shards. Lynx, who had also been on the expedition into Blackveil and returned, had told how Karigan had received a looking mask in the midst of Castle Argenthyne and destroyed it to deny Mornhavon the Black its power. Where else could the mirror shards have come from?

Only Karigan could provide answers, but when Laren cracked the door open to look in on her Rider resting in the dimly lit room, she suspected it would be some while before they got any.

INK AND MEMORY

Laren half-dozed in the chair next to Karigan's bed, startled awake every few minutes by Karigan's muttering and tossing. She had decided to sit with Karigan in case her Rider awoke, or said anything of where she'd been all this time, but all she heard was a name repeated: *Cade, Cade, Cade . . .*

Karigan was under the influence of Ben's sleeping touch, but it was not enough to give her peace, and the menders were reluctant to supplement it with some other additional soporific, fearing the combination would damage her in some way. Laren wished Ben and Vanlynn would return. She wished she'd hear news of Estora.

Laren herself had finally sent word to Connly down in the Rider wing about Karigan's arrival. She very much wanted to send the news to Karigan's father. From all accounts, hearing of his daughter's death had been crushing, and rumors reached her of the merchant chief neglecting his business interests in his grief. He needed to know, but not before Laren could ensure Karigan was well, that she'd come back to them whole, nor could she send anyone out with a message while the storm raged.

Karigan tossed again and muttered some words that sounded like, "Let me go back."

"Go back where, Karigan?" Laren asked quietly. "Who is Cade?"

Her questions were only met with silence as Karigan quieted beneath her covers. Her right eye was bandaged, and having few details on the injury, Laren hoped her Rider did not lose her eye or her sight. It would not be an easy transi-

738

tion for her, as it had not been for others Laren knew. She was aware of plenty of one-eyed soldiers who remained in uniform, on active duty, undeterred by their losses. Karigan likely would have no choice in the matter. If she still heard the call, she would remain a Rider. If her brooch abandoned her, she would leave the messenger service. Whatever happened, Laren was grateful to have her back alive.

She nodded off in her chair again and was not sure if she was dreaming or actually seeing the Eletian, Somial, standing over Karigan's bed, his hands hovering over her sleeping form. Laren heard a wisp of soothing song, which almost lulled her into a deep slumber. Instead, she fought it, shaking herself into a groggy but awake state. She half-rose from her chair.

"What are you doing?" she demanded of Somial. If he harmed Karigan in some way, she would stop at nothing to defend her Rider.

"She was restless, her mind filled with urgency," he replied softly. He turned his gaze at her, the dim lamplight odd in his eyes. "I have sung to her of peace. She rests quietly now."

Laren scrutinized Karigan. Indeed, she slept tranquilly, her chest rising and falling with deep, regular breaths. "Is that all you did?" she asked, still suspicious.

"I sense in her an absence of . . ." He touched his belly. "There was a potential there that she carried, but even the faintest memory of it ever having existed has fallen to ashes."

"A potential? In her? Oh!" Laren fought to shake off the persistent grogginess. "She was carrying a—?"

"Not precisely. The potential was there, the very earliest germination of a seed. The potential became unmade with her return. That which has yet to come to pass, cannot exist before its time."

It was a challenge for Laren's sleepy mind to work it out, but she thought she understood. Karigan had traveled before to the time of the First Rider, about one thousand years ago, and returned to the present with a knife of that era in pristine condition. Objects of the past, objects that existed previously, could come forward. Those yet to be created could not come to the past.

"Her return." Somial sounded uncertain. "It is difficult to know its sway, if any, on the course of events."

"Course of events?"

"There are many threads to the future, Captain, and clear to no one, not even Eletians. There are just too many variations." With that, Somial departed, his feet silent on the stone floor.

He left Laren much to think about, not the least of which that Karigan had been, potentially, pregnant. A curious thing that, since female Riders did not become pregnant. Oh, they could after their brooches abandoned them, and they went on with their lives in the outside world. And some bore children before they were even called into the messenger service, though it was rare. But never while they were Riders. The belief that had come down the generations was that after the time of the First Rider, some magic had been instilled in the brooches to prevent pregnancy as a practicality.

Had Karigan been in a time and place that lacked magic?

She would not know until Karigan told her tale, but she had no doubt it would include heartbreak, and that this "Cade" had played a crucial part.

Morning light woke Laren again. She yawned and stretched muscles cramped by a night spent in a chair. She realized with a start that Karigan was no longer beneath the rumpled covers of her bed, but standing at the window peering through the frosty panes, her breaths fogging the glass.

"Karigan?" Laren rose, took a step forward.

Without turning, her Rider said, "How can it be winter? It was just summer."

Before Laren could speak, the door opened, and Vanlynn entered. "Good morning," the master mender said.

Karigan turned, the bandage over her eye once again taking Laren aback. Of course, Karigan would not know Vanlynn. "This is Master Mender Vanlynn," Laren said, "who has taken over for Destarion."

"We have already met," Vanlynn said, "while you slept in your chair, Captain. It did not seem necessary to wake you."

"Not necessary?" Laren demanded.

"No. Your Rider has had a cup of broth, and now I'd like to examine her."

"But—"

"Please, Captain, if you would step outside. I will report to you when I'm done."

Laren obeyed. Vanlynn was a bulwark of a mender and would not be countermanded, especially not in her own mending wing. It did not make Laren any less irritated.

Her irritation was somewhat ameliorated by an apprentice mender who brought tea and biscuits to the waiting alcove. Neither Fastion nor Donal remained. Either they'd been ordered out of the mending wing or had returned to their scheduled duties. Her Riders remained absent, as she requested. There was little to tell them anyway. Ben was nowhere to be seen, and she wondered if he was still with Estora, and how Estora fared as well as the child she carried. There were no Eletians in sight. Perhaps Fastion and Donal had escorted them away.

When Vanlynn eventually emerged from Karigan's chamber, the master mender settled in a chair across from Laren. Tea was brought for her, too, and Laren noticed for the first time how tired the mender's eyes looked. She must have had a long night. Being the master could not be an easy duty for one of her years.

Vanlynn told her that Karigan was in good form. She'd an old broken wrist and lacerations that had healed well some time ago. The newer lacerations from the mirror shards, she thought, should heal without problem.

"The only question is the eye," Vanlynn said. "We removed a piece of mirror from it, but some particle remains. It irritates her, but she will not lose her eye."

"What of her sight?" Laren asked.

Vanlynn sipped tea before answering. "I am unsure. I'd like to have Ben look at it after he recovers from his work with the queen."

There was more that Vanlynn was not saying, but before Laren could pursue it, Vanlynn continued, "I would say right now the most difficult thing for your Rider is what's going on in here." She tapped her temple. "She is disoriented, and from what the Eletian said, it's not at all surprising."

"You spoke with the Eletian?" Laren demanded. That would teach her to doze off.

"Of course. He told me about your Rider's travel to a future time." Vanlynn said it like it was an everyday occurrence. "In any case, whatever befell her there occupies her a great deal. She will not speak to me of it as she does not know me. It will be up to her friends to draw her out, to listen. But for now, let her rest. She's been through unknown trauma."

At that, Vanlynn set her teacup aside and stood, abruptly ending the interview.

"What of the queen?" Laren asked before the mender could get away.

Vanlynn grinned. "The queen and the babies she carries are, thanks in no small part to Ben, just fine."

"Babies?"

"Twins, Captain. She's going to have twins."

Mara Brennyn headed toward the mending wing, assigned to keep an eye on Karigan for the time being. The captain wanted her to have a friend there to talk with, to be comforted as needed. Mara was one of Karigan's best friends and agreed gladly to go. When Mara had been healing for so long from her burns, Karigan had been a frequent visitor, offering company and cheer. Now Mara would reciprocate.

She left the Rider wing abuzz with promises to bring greetings and well wishes from many of her fellow Riders. After Karigan had been declared dead four months ago, a new Rider had been given her room, so now the Riders threw their energy into clearing out the cobwebs from another chamber. Garth, back from the D'Yer Wall for a time, had taken charge, hunting for furnishings in obscure storerooms of the castle. Mara was all too glad to escape the dust and labor.

The news that Queen Estora was expecting twins was like adding cream on the pudding. They all deserved some good news.

Speaking of good news, Mara decided, as she wove her

way through corridors busy with holiday revelers, that she
would not tell Karigan the news of battles, of Riders who had
died, about Estral Andovian's loss of speech, or that Estral's
father, the Golden Guardian of Selium, was missing. No, that
sort of news could wait. Unless Karigan specifically asked, of
course. Mara would not lie to her.

When she reached the mending wing, she found its halls
filled with the scent of healing herbs and the atmosphere
hushed. It was something of a sanctuary, although, when she
was here for so long while being treated for her burns, she'd
thought of it more as a prison.

"Are you looking for Rider G'ladheon?" an apprentice
asked.

"Yes," Mara replied.

"Fifth door on the right."

"Thank you. How is she doing?"

"I believe she is doing well. Earlier, she requested a pen,
ink, and paper."

That was good, Mara thought. She wasn't exactly sure
what she'd find when she saw Karigan, but requesting writing
implements sounded ordinary and reassuring. Perhaps she
wanted to write to her father.

But when she entered Karigan's room, she saw how very
wrong she was. The papers were scattered around, dark with
ink. Apparently the paper had not been enough, for Karigan
had written on her arm, her nightgown, the bed sheets, and
was adding words to the wall.

"Karigan?" Mara said from the doorway. "What are you—?"

Karigan turned. The bandage over her eye was disconcerting, though not as disconcerting as seeing her covered in her
own writing.

"Mara?" Karigan hurried over and halted, her one eye
darting about. She raised an ink-stained hand to touch Mara's
face—the side scarred by flame.

"What are you doing?" Mara asked. She needed to get a
mender in here. Her friend had gone mad.

"Burned face," Karigan murmured. "Fastion. Fastion had
a burned face." She hurried back to the wall to write on it
some more.

Mara followed her. Much of it was ordinary writing—lists, names, places, but a certain amount was garbled with odd symbols, almost as if from some unknown language.

"Karigan, what is all of this?"

"*Enmorial.* Memory, before it all fades. Before it's unmade." She scribbled on the wall and snapped the nib. "Damnation."

That sounded more like Karigan, but then she started pacing in a circle. "Cade, Cade, Cade," she muttered.

Mara did not know whether to shake Karigan or slap her. She was about to fetch a mender when Karigan halted and looked up. "I need to tell them!"

Before Mara could stop her, Karigan ran, ran right past her and down the corridor, ink-blotched nightgown fluttering around her.

THE TALE IS TOLD

 Mara tore after Karigan, who ran like a berserker through the mending wing corridors. The poor menders did not understand what was happening fast enough to stop her. She ran out of the mending wing into the throngs of cheery revelers who laughed and pointed at her as someone who had been celebrating too much. She shoved aside anyone who got in her way, causing some angry words.

Down stairs, across corridors, along side halls Karigan flew. When Mara realized where she was going, she put on a new burst of speed, but could not catch up. When Karigan reached the doors to the throne room, the guards were too astonished and slow to react. The Weapons, in contrast, merely watched as Karigan bolted through the entryway.

Curious.

The guards blocked Mara, however. "That is Rider G'ladheon," she gasped. "Needs help."

"Clearly," one of the guards said acerbically, and let her through.

The throne room was occupied by the king and his advisors, meeting with the lord-governors gathered for the holiday—except for Timas Mirwell who was, she'd heard, sequestered in his rooms recovering from scalding burns.

Everyone glanced up as Karigan burst in among them. Thankfully, the captain was present. The lord-governors exclaimed at the interruption of the obviously mad woman running amok in the throne room. Karigan dropped to her knees before the daïs, and King Zachary rose, his mouth open, but was unable to speak.

Mara skidded to a halt behind Karigan, panting hard. For someone who had been through who-knew-what and had just run pretty much the length of the castle, Karigan did not seem to be out of breath.

"What is this?" demanded Castellan Javian. He was a severe man with steel gray hair, and his manner was as sharp as his voice, a deep contrast to his predecessor, Sperren.

"Karigan? Rider G'ladheon?" the king asked, still incredulous. He stepped down the daïs to help her rise. "Last I heard you were resting."

"I must tell you, before I forget."

"Karigan—" the captain began, concern clear on her face. "Maybe you should rest some more. You can talk to us later."

"*No!* Now, before I forget."

Before Javian could register a protest, the king stayed him with a look. "Castellan, please adjourn the meeting for me."

"Yes, sire."

The lord-governors were ushered out, while Mara explained to the captain what had transpired. A robe was sent for, to cloak Karigan, who still did not appear to be cognizant of the irregularity of her appearance, especially in front of her king and other important personages.

When the lord-governors were gone, Karigan looked at Javian and Colin Dovekey's replacement, Tallman.

"I don't know these men," she said. "I don't want them here."

"Of all the impudent—" Javian began.

"Easy, Castellan," Tallman said. "Sir Karigan's reputation precedes her."

"Gentlemen?" the king said. "If you would?"

Tallman bowed. "As you wish, Majesty."

He started down the runner, gesturing for the sputtering Javian to follow. It was an indication of how much the king valued Karigan that he did as she wished. Mara had been around long enough to suspect there was more going on between king and Rider. Nothing illicit—that sort of thing never remained a secret—but something deeper. Karigan had never opened up to her about it, and Mara respected that silence.

Mara was not asked to leave, so she stood some paces behind Karigan to listen, and to help if needed. The Weapons, as usual, stood along the length of the throne room. Their presence did not appear to perturb Karigan.

A chair was brought for her, but she disregarded it, instead pacing in circles as Mara had seen before.

"Cade, Cade, Cade . . ."

The king glanced at Captain Mapstone, and she back at him, both clearly unsettled. When the robe arrived, Karigan allowed it to be placed over her shoulders. She had to be freezing with all the bitter drafts from the storm that still howled outside and the cold stone beneath her bare feet, but she didn't show it.

"Karigan," the captain said, "you wished to speak with us?"

Karigan halted and looked up. "Yes, before it all becomes a forgotten dream." Without waiting for further prompting, she began with Blackveil, describing events that paralleled what Lynx had described of the expedition. She spoke of smashing the looking mask. The rest was new to them, how she was transported to a future version of their world. "I ended up in a circus," she said. "That is, stuck in a sarcophagus in the circus."

The king and captain exchanged incredulous looks, as they would often do over the next couple of hours. Karigan told a halting, but astonishing, tale. She paused to recollect missing memories. She pounded her forehead with the heel of her palm as if to shake them loose. She consulted the scrawlings on her arm and nightgown, and muttered she should have brought her papers with her.

Despite the disjointed unfolding of the tale, it depicted a chilling picture of their future. Mara shuddered when Karigan described the ruins of Sacor City and the castle. She went on, trying to explain the machines and weapons of that time, but when she did so, nonsense came out of her mouth, like some other language, like the unreadable scrawlings on the wall Mara had seen.

When the king and captain merely looked on in confusion with eyebrows raised, Karigan said, "You think I'm insane, don't you? That I've turned mad after what I've been through."

"No, Karigan," the king said quietly. "We do not think that.

We are just having trouble understanding what you describe. Try again. It may be that knowing about these weapons, if we can replicate them, will give us an advantage over our enemies."

She tried again and again. The nonsense flowed like a fluent foreign language, sometimes interspersed with words of the common tongue like "horrible," "loud," and "smoke." She grew frustrated when they did not understand.

"You told us," the king said, maintaining his reasonable, calm tone, as if Karigan did not look and sound mad, "that the god Westrion intervened to take you forward in time. Is it not possible the gods are intervening again, preventing us from knowing certain details of the future? A future in which they were discarded?"

Karigan exhaled a long breath. "Yes. Yes, of course. That's it. I was prevented from handling—"

And whatever it was that she hadn't been allowed to handle came out as another garbled word. Now relieved, she dropped into the chair.

"What will be, will be," she said passing her hand over her eyes.

The points she obviously wished to convey were that the king's cousin, Lord Amberhill, would use some powerful weapon to betray his king and country, to become emperor, and that there was possibly an artifact in the tombs called the "dragonfly device" that might help stave off Amberhill's weapon. Karigan, apparently, never saw Amberhill's weapon, only its cataclysmic aftermath. Nor did she know what the dragonfly device was, except that it might be found in the tombs.

At one point, she turned to Captain Mapstone. "You gave me riddles."

The captain nodded slowly. "Yes, but the riddles came from Prince Jametari. Somial brought them and instructed me to leave them for you in the tombs." Her face fell. "I never thought . . . I never thought they'd lead to your return."

"I had help." Karigan spoke of Lhean, a dream of Laurelyn, of Fastion who had somehow survived all those years into the future, and of Cade Harlowe. But she was circumspect when she spoke of Cade, hiding details, while still making him an important part of the tale.

When she came to the end, her head rested in her hands as though it hurt. "He was torn from me," she murmured. "Torn from me."

He had been more than just an ally in Karigan's quest to escape the horrific future. Much more. Mara could tell the captain saw it, too, and although it was often difficult to read the king, Mara was pretty sure he saw it as well. How could he not?

Oh, Karigan. She attracted trouble enough for ten Riders, and after all the things she had seen and done, she did not, Mara believed, deserve heartbreak, too.

The king knelt before Karigan's chair. "You came back to us. To me. I never doubted."

Karigan said nothing. Mara could not see her expression from behind.

The king called on a couple of his Weapons to escort Karigan back to the mending wing. At the captain's nod, Mara followed. She would stay with her friend, and explain to the master mender why her patient had written all over the walls.

As she made her way toward the doors, she overheard the king tell the captain, "She has done enough. More than enough for this realm. I will not have her ride into danger like that again. I won't have it."

As Mara left the throne room, she wondered if King Zachary ever argued so forcefully on behalf of any of his other Riders. She did not think so. Karigan wasn't just another Rider to him.

MEMORIES FADING

Karigan was moved to a new room in the mending wing with a whole stack of paper, should she feel inclined to use ink again. In the meantime, clerks were dispatched by the king to transcribe her notes off the walls, bed sheets, and nightgown in her old room. She even let them copy the writing on her arm before she washed it off.

Despite the stack of paper, she still wrote one word on her arm: *Cade,* and wore it beneath the sleeve of the new uniform Mara had brought her, her old uniform pieces having been redistributed to new Riders upon her presumed death.

The captain checked on her in the evening. "We'll send word of your return to your father once the weather clears," she said, then asked questions to clarify aspects of Karigan's experiences. Already, Karigan had forgotten much.

"Dr. Silk?" She pondered the name and felt a sense of unease about it, but she lacked even the basic knowledge of who he had been. It frustrated her unto tears, but Captain Mapstone promised her a transcript of her notes. What made it worse was that the memories were so dreamlike that Karigan questioned ever having been in the future at all.

It was the Eletians who helped.

The next morning, Somial arrived with his companions. "Do you remember me, youngling?"

"Somial! I could never forget!" Then she realized she could. *Cade, Cade, Cade . . .*

Somial smiled and introduced his companions, Idris and Enver.

"How do you do?" Enver asked, offering his hand.

She took it, bemused. "Er, fine. And yourself?"

"Very well, thank you."

She might have pondered his very un-Eletianlike greeting, and the fact he did not look entirely Eletian, but she nearly leaped on what he carried with him.

"My staff!"

Enver presented it to her with a bow. She took it eagerly. "Where was it?" She wasn't really sure she had known it was missing in the first place, at least not like her saber, which she'd lost in Castle Argenthyne in Blackveil.

"It came back with Lhean," Somial replied, "when he returned from the future time."

That's right, Karigan thought, forcing herself to remember. Lhean had been there with her. Somial had just now confirmed that she had gone forward in time and that it wasn't a dream. *I've not gone mad.*

"Lhean—is he well?"

"Yes. He arrived ahead of you, at the end of summer."

She scratched her head, wondering how he had arrived so much sooner, then remembered Westrion. Westrion snatching her from Lhean's side, flinging her through the heavens. "I would not have made it home without Lhean," she said. Though she could not quite remember how it had all transpired, she was certain it was true.

"Nor he, you," Somial replied. He leaned toward her more closely, peering at her. "I can sense the distance traveled upon you, youngling. Laurelyn and her moons have faded from the world, but stars shine upon your brow. Such travel is difficult enough for an eternally-lived one such as Lhean and can only be more disorienting for a mortal. And yet . . ."

Mesmerized by his voice and intensity, Karigan had to shake herself as if waking from a dream. "I—I *am* disoriented. Or, at least, I'm forgetting everything."

"That is because, by returning, you have changed the threads proceeding forward. What you experienced will never happen. Therefore, your memories of events that never happened are fading and will cease to exist."

She thought this might be so, had prayed it was the reason for her loss of memory. "But those things did happen."

"Yes," Somial replied. "They did. Your captain is ensuring that what you have managed to remember is recorded."

He spoke of the other Eletian members of the Blackveil expedition. Ealdaen and Telagioth were also well, but all of Eletia still mourned Hana, Solan, and Graelalea.

"I lost the feather Graelalea gave me," Karigan said sadly. "If I still had it, I might remember everything."

"Even a feather of the winter owl has its limitations," Somial replied, "but Graelalea's gift was well given. That you no longer have it means it was not meant to be."

Karigan rubbed at her bandaged eye. It itched and prickled. Even Ben, using his ability of true healing, had been unable to relieve it.

"Does your eye pain you?" Somial asked.

"It feels irritated most of the time."

"May I see?"

"I don't know . . ." Even the menders who tended it did not care to look too closely. She did not know what they were keeping from her, and she wasn't sure she wanted to know. In any case, the new master mender had firmly told her to keep the bandage in place, and insinuated Karigan would find herself in considerable trouble otherwise.

"You may recall I am something of a mender among my people," Somial said.

Karigan smiled, remembering his care for her in a forest glade, in what felt like a whole different lifetime. "All right."

She sat upon her bed and let him remove the bandage. As before, everything seen from that eye was a watery blur. She could not focus. This time, however, it was darker. She did not consider this a positive development.

"*Mirare.*" Somial's voice was soft, but sounded surprised. He murmured more in Eletian, his words soothing, so she did not require translation. But *Mirare?* She wondered if it was an Eletian expression of some sort.

Somial gently shifted her head this way and that so he could peer into her eye. Just his touch diminished the irritation, but did not improve her sight. He eased the bandage back over her eye.

"I am afraid I can do no more than has been done already," he said. His expression was unreadable. Then he added in what sounded like prophecy: "What sight you lose, others may gain."

He would explain no further, and she was not reassured. Not one bit.

"We must take leave of you now," Somial said. "Lhean and the others will be most pleased to hear of your return."

Enver stuck his hand out again. She clasped it, and he shook with enthusiasm. "It was an honor to meet you."

Karigan raised an eyebrow, never having encountered an Eletian who would ever admit as much. As far as she could tell, they mostly considered mortals inferior. As if to prove the point, Idris gave her only a cool, enigmatic smile in farewell.

She watched after them as they glided their way from her room and down the corridor. She noted that Enver was huskier than any other Eletian she had met, his stride just slightly less graceful than that of his companions. He was different, more earthly, not entirely Eletian.

She watched until they were out of sight. Watching with only one eye took some getting used to, more effort. She often misjudged the distance of objects, like when she reached for a glass of water and missed. She'd bruised her shoulder on door frames more than once. The loss of peripheral vision on her right side caused her to be startled by people approaching her from certain angles. Vanlynn assured her that, for the most part, she would quickly adjust, her good eye compensating for the bad. If her bad eye did not heal, and her vision did not return, she would have to learn new fighting techniques. Arms Master Drent would be overjoyed and merciless, but she knew that enduring his training would turn her blind eye into an asset.

As time went on, Karigan gathered details from Mara and Captain Mapstone about what had passed while she'd been away. Because the king and Estora had been betrothed well before she'd gone into Blackveil, the marriage between the two was not a surprise, and she'd long considered it inevitable. It still pinched her on the inside, and yet, not as hard as it

might because of Cade. She couldn't quite remember what
had been between her and Cade, but intuition, a certain sense
of longing, the creeping grief that caught her unawares and
made her tear up without warning, told her it had been significant.

As for the wedding of the king and Estora, the captain had
been judicious about what details she gave Karigan. Mara
had not been as careful, and it sounded to Karigan like a
deathbed wedding. That certain of the king's advisors were
gone due to their complicity in arranging it, only enhanced
the impression. That the king had almost died shook her. She
still loved him no matter who he had married. Couldn't help
it. She would've taken that arrow for him if she could, and not
just out of duty.

She also heard about the stepped up aggression by Second
Empire. But not all the news was grim. Ben, for instance, was
actually learning to ride. It turned out that Robin, the horse
who had tormented him so, had actually been choosing Ben
as his Rider. The two had finally come to an accord, and Ben's
confidence around horses had risen substantially, though he
was unlikely to ever be sent out on message errands. He was
too important an asset as a true healer to leave castle grounds,
especially with Estora expecting.

Karigan's thoughts returned to Cade. She walked in circles
in her room, gazing at his name inked on her arm. *Dark hair.
He had dark hair.* Winter light pouring through the small window scoured the flesh of her arm of color. "Dark hair," she
muttered. "But brown or black?"

She became aware of Mara then, standing in the doorway.
Her friend had that worried look on her face, which she
quickly concealed with a smile. Karigan had seen this with
the captain, and Ben, too, trying to hide their concern from
her. She pulled her sleeve down.

"Just for a moment there," Mara said, "the way the light
was coming in, you were all silvery green."

Karigan glanced out the snowy window in surprise. It was
better than hearing, *The way you pace in circles and mutter to
yourself looks insane.*

"Anyway," Mara continued, dissipating the odd moment,

"I come with good news. Garth has proclaimed your new room in the Rider wing ready, and Master Vanlynn has given you leave to, well, leave. The mending wing, that is."

"Finally!"

The only possessions Karigan had to take with her were the clothes she wore and the bonewood. Mara, noticing, spoke about going shopping down in the city for any extras Karigan might require. If she hadn't needed even the most basic things, because she'd been declared dead and her possessions had been returned to her father, it would have been an ordinary conversation. Even so, Mara still managed to get her excited about the prospect of a shopping trip, and they discussed which stores to visit in very much the same manner as they would have before Karigan had ever gone off to Blackveil.

As they approached the Rider wing, Mara said, "Most everyone is at lessons or doing chores."

It was more likely Captain Mapstone did not wish Karigan to be overwhelmed by curious Riders. She was under the impression she was considered a bit fragile.

MEOW!

Karigan glanced down, and there was Ghost Kitty rubbing against her legs, leaving a trail of white and gray fur on her trousers. She picked him up, and he butted his head against her chin. She laughed.

"The menders had to keep shooing him from the mending wing," Mara explained. "He knew you were back. Condor has been just as ridiculous, jumping the pasture fence and trying to run into the castle."

Karigan froze with Ghost Kitty purring in her arms. *Condor!* But what she saw in her mind was a bay stallion rearing in the palace. Palace? There had been a palace. And a horse. But she could not recall the horse's name or why she thought of him.

Mara, mistaking her reaction, said, "Don't worry, we'll go see Condor next. And all the others."

"All the others?"

"The horses Damian Frost brought while you were in Blackveil."

"Oh!" She couldn't wait to go see them all, especially Condor.

Ghost Kitty leaped out of her arms and trotted ahead of them into the Rider wing. Karigan passed familiar doors, including the one to her old room. She peered into the common room with its big table, which looked just the same as she remembered. That not everything had changed was very comforting.

Mara took her all the way down the corridor and around a corner. This was an ancient section of castle they were re-inhabiting, the ceilings lower and stonework cruder, the air currents smelling of must, and the dark corners full of secrets.

"Sorry to say," Mara said, "but we ran out of rooms on the main corridor, which is a good thing if you think about it."

It was. It meant more Riders had answered the call. Riders she had yet to meet. For all that it was good, the old corridors made Karigan uneasy. They were restless with whispers and creaking and shifting shadows.

Mara stopped at the first door. Lamps were lit on either side of it and across the hall to fight off the gloom. Beyond the pool of light lay a wall of dark.

"Anyway," Mara said, "you are the first to have a room down this way, so the whole corridor is yours until we get more green Greenies."

"All mine," Karigan said with trepidation. It was going to be a little too quiet, or perhaps un-quiet?

Ghost Kitty scratched the thick-timbered door.

"Go on in," Mara said.

Karigan did and found a large chamber—large, anyway, compared to the other rooms of the Rider wing. There were support pillars of carved wood, four arrow slit windows with drapes pulled aside, and an actual hearth.

"Fastion thinks this could have been a meeting room or common room at one time," Mara said.

Fastion liked investigating the more ancient parts of the castle.

Karigan's friends had gone to some lengths to make the room comfortable. It was impossible not to miss the large bed with a gaudy gilt headboard elaborately carved with unicorns and a young girl sitting by the bank of a stream. Garth, Mara had told her, had been particularly pleased when he found that piece.

"Ah," Karigan replied, trying not to burst out laughing.

They'd found her a wardrobe almost as large as her old one. Someone had built bookshelves.

Mara, following Karigan's gaze, said, "New Rider built those. He was apprenticed to a carpenter when he was called. Your friends chipped in for some books, which I took the liberty of picking out for you."

Karigan went to the shelves and looked through the books. Some were brand new, novels she hadn't read. Others were used, including *The Journeys of Gilan Wylloland*. It was dog-eared but clearly well-loved by its previous owner, and the illustrations were as vibrant as ever.

They'd also found her a plain, but serviceable vanity. Mara had purchased some small necessities for her, like a comb and brush, and a hand mirror.

"Extra uniforms are in the wardrobe," Mara said, "and the quartermaster said to just ask if you had any needs."

Karigan took it all in, then flung her arms around Mara. "Thank you."

"You like it then?" a voice boomed from the doorway. It was Garth.

Karigan hugged him in turn, and he being the bear of a man he was, lifted her off her feet and practically crushed her in his arms.

"I almost wasn't here to see you," he said after gently setting her back on the floor. "I was due to leave for the wall on the solstice, but all the snow came. Now when I go to the wall, I can tell them all the good news. Not that Connly hasn't already done so."

Garth and other Rider friends of hers, had been assigned to the towers of the D'Yer Wall. Connly could communicate with Trace Burns in Tower of the Ice with his mind. Trace could then convey the news to the others. Distance did not matter with such an ability.

"How do you like the bed?" Garth asked.

"It's um . . ."

"She's stunned," Mara provided.

"Yes, stunned," Karigan echoed.

Garth beamed.

They talked away, Karigan catching up on the doings of her friends, the romances, the feuds between the tower mages, the parties. Meanwhile, Ghost Kitty watched them with disinterest from the bed, busily licking his paw.

They spent time in lighthearted conversation until Garth said in more sober tones, "In the fall, the reconstruction at the breach was knocked down again. Something came in from Blackveil, and left nothing behind but a bit of grubby yarn."

Karigan stilled. *Grandmother.* It had to be.

"Let's not worry Karigan with the wall," Mara said. The significant way she looked at Garth made Karigan think they were under orders to keep her from worrying about anything at all.

Garth hunched his shoulders and sank his hands into his pockets.

"In fact," Mara said, "I think it's time to go see Condor."

"Excuse me." Ben poked his head through the doorway.

Maybe, just maybe, Karigan thought, her new room wouldn't be so quiet after all, if she was already receiving visitors.

"Before you go," Ben continued, "I just need to take a look at Karigan's eye."

Garth and Mara waited out in the corridor while Ben had Karigan sit in a chair beside the vanity and undid her bandage. He bit his lip while he examined her eye. It seemed to her he looked at it while trying not to look *into* it.

"I will get more ointment for the irritation. Can you see any more than you did?"

"Less," she said, realizing her sight had gone darker than even when Somial had looked at it.

Ben chewed on his lip again. "I don't know, Karigan. I've tried everything. The particle appears to be . . . It appears to be permanent. Forcing it out would certainly damage your eye beyond repair and ruin your vision for good. It's like it's clawed its way in there, so I'm not sure we could even force it out. It seems, well, it seems determined to stay lodged in there."

He did not meet her gaze as he spoke. She guessed it was less the news he delivered than what her eye looked like, which was odd for a mender. Menders looked at *everything*.

She reached for the mirror. He grabbed her wrist.

"I want to see it," she said.

"I think it's better if you waited—"

"*Now*. I want to see it *now*. Everyone is tip-toeing around me, and I want to find out why."

"You're sure?" Ben asked.

"Yes."

He released her wrist, and took a step back as if to absolve himself of any fault she might hurl his way. When she finally looked into the mirror, she saw that this could not be his fault. None of it. This went far beyond Ben.

MIRROR SIGHT

The mirror reflected her eye. Her eye reflected the mirror back and the image within it, unto infinity. Her eye, her entire eye, had turned silver, the silver of a mirror. No wonder Ben, and even Somial, had had a difficult time looking at it.

The mirror man, it seemed, had the final say, had called her bluff one last time. This she could not shatter like the looking mask, or even give away. It was a part of her.

"Karigan?" Ben asked. "Are you all right?"

"No," she replied, "but yes." Ben had, she thought, matured a great deal since her departure for Blackveil.

"Somial called you *Mirare*," Ben said.

Karigan glanced sharply at him. "I remember him using that word."

"He said there were once people who could see far, as he put it. The *Mirari*. They wore the looking masks in ancient times. He thought perhaps your ability to cross thresholds was somehow aligned with the mirror sight."

As usual, everyone had been talking about her to everyone else, but avoided speaking to her directly. It no longer annoyed her that much. She understood how difficult it would be for them to broach the subject with her.

"I've tried not to look you directly in your eye," Ben said, "because I saw images once, confusing images, some not pleasant."

"Just like a looking mask," Karigan murmured.

Ben nodded, and she lowered the mirror. It was then she realized the vision in her silver eye had gone black. Black and deep and . . . She saw stars. Their light stabbed into her eye, into her head, like a thousand needles. She cried out and closed her eyes, and the pain ebbed.

"Karigan?"

"Would you put the bandage back over my eye?"

He did so. This way no one would have to see the oddness of her eye, and it stopped the pain.

"Let me know if there is anything I can do for you," Ben said. "Master Vanlynn has made the captain and king aware of your condition. I think the captain wanted to tell you herself, but you wanted to look . . ."

"It's all right," Karigan told him. "I'm glad to know."

He left then, and Mara and Garth returned. She hated the pity on their faces. It would take her a while to adjust to this "condition," as Ben called it. The anger had yet to surface. Maybe she was in shock, numbed of emotion. When the anger did surface, she was reserving it for the mirror man and the gods.

"Shall we go see Condor?" Mara asked, a little too brightly.

They bundled up for the trek outdoors. Garth hung back saying he had work to do elsewhere. Outside, the storm had settled to large fluffy flurries dropping in lazy swirls. The castle groundskeepers had worked long, hard hours to keep the stairs and paths shoveled. Some of the snow piles were as high as their shoulders. They had to trudge through deep snow to reach the pasture. Karigan didn't mind—the winter air was clean, refreshing, lifted some of the care from her— and there were all the horses, the new ones and the old ones— snuffling through the snow for some tidbit of grass beneath.

One horse's head went up high. He issued a shrill whinny and galloped toward them. Karigan stepped between the fence rails to get at him. When he reached her, he nuzzled her shoulder, her hair. She wrapped her arms around his neck. Mirror eye be damned. She pressed her face into his chestnut hide, all warm and furry with his winter coat. As long as he was there, everything would be all right.

"He missed you," Mara said. "Was off his feed and moping, but as soon as you came back, he started eating regular. He's a changed horse."

"I missed him, too," Karigan said. All the way through Blackveil she had. She assumed she had missed him in the future, as well. A Rider should never be separated from her horse.

She clapped his neck and tugged on his ear. He turned on his haunches and ran off bucking, which got some of the other horses playing. He cantered around, coming back to her more than once, as if to make sure she was really there.

"I am sorry I missed Damian Frost," Karigan said wistfully, as she returned to Mara at the fence.

"I enjoyed meeting him. He actually brought more horses than we requested. He said he knew we'd need them. Horsemaster Riggs is working on gentling the unclaimed ones, and we all take turns exercising them and helping in the stable. The stable is, by the way, filling up just like the Rider wing."

It gladdened Karigan that the messenger service was on its way to reaching its full strength, but she also wondered if it was the will of higher powers that Sacoridia be prepared for greater conflict.

After a while, Mara excused herself to attend to duties. Karigan lingered at the pasture watching the horses. It was comforting to see them play, or just dig for grass beneath the snow. Condor periodically returned to her to be scritched, and she stayed until she could no longer feel her toes or the tips of her fingers.

Karigan's first night in her new room proved restless. Halfremembered images of people and places and nightmarish mechanicals reeled through her mind. When she awakened in the morning, her bed clothes were twisted in knots, and she felt spent, as though she'd been running all night, not sleeping.

Shortly after breakfast, a Green Foot runner found her in the common room and delivered a message directing her to attend Captain Mapstone in the records room. The records room resided in another old section of the castle. Karigan checked that her uniform was neat and proper, and she set off.

When she reached the records room, she found it busier than ever. Workers appeared to be disassembling scaffolding from beneath the stained glass dome. Dakrias Brown, the chief administrator, noticed her right off and came over to greet her.

"So good to see you, Sir Karigan," he told her. "You were missed." In a whisper, he added, "And not just by the living."

Mara had alluded to the disruption at the memorial circle they'd held for Karigan. Karigan wished she could have been there to see it.

"They," and Dakrias pointed vaguely in the air, "calmed right down when you returned."

"What is with all the scaffolding?" she asked.

"A special cleaning of the glass," Dakrias said. "Here, let me introduce you to the glass master, Master Goodgrave."

Karigan almost missed a step behind Dakrias as she followed him. *Goodgrave.* The name was familiar. She had been called "Goodgrave" in the future, though she'd forgotten why.

She shook hands with the master, distracted by a familiarity about him, his bushy side whiskers and almost wolfish features, while he explained the meticulous cleaning he and his workers had given the glass.

"A masterpiece this dome is," he said. "Few samples of such proficiency have survived time. I believe your captain is planning a ceremony to reveal it anew in its full splendor."

"Indeed I am, Master Goodgrave."

They turned to find the captain striding toward them with a sheaf of papers tucked under her arm.

"But I thought," she added, "I'd give Karigan a little preview. She helped, after all, to bring it back to light in the first place."

"Well then, now is a good time," Master Goodgrave said, "with us being finished and the scaffolding coming down."

"Fastion is above," the captain said.

A lantern backlit the glass above, and rippled across scenes in a blur of fabulous color as it moved along. Then it paused and more lights were lit, illuminating the panel of the First Rider riding in victory after the Long War. The colors were stunning, so bright, and the images so crisp.

"Not bad, eh?" Master Goodgrave said, face shining with pride.

"It's beautiful," Karigan replied.

"We discovered," the captain said, "that the three-fold leaf meant to symbolize the League that brought down Mornhavon was actually a four-fold leaf."

"Four?" Karigan asked. "There was another ally?"

"Apparently. If you look behind the First Rider, you see what we always thought were horsemen in the far distance, but they aren't. They're p'ehdrose."

The image in glass was far above, but Karigan could see it now, the many p'ehdrose. The dirt had obscured that detail.

"If only they were more than legend," the captain said. "We could probably use some help against Second Empire."

"They're real," Karigan said.

"What did you say?"

"The p'ehdrose. I saw stuffed and mounted specimens in the Imperial Museum."

She and the captain stared at one another in shocked silence, Karigan for remembering such a detail, and the captain for hearing that p'ehdrose were not mere legend.

"That is . . . very interesting," the captain said. She glanced up at the glass, and Karigan could almost see the wheels of speculation churning in her mind.

Master Goodgrave, meanwhile, left them so he could bark orders at his workers as the last piece of scaffolding came down. "Move along, Harland, I have no use for laggards."

Karigan stepped back, stunned. For a moment she thought he'd said "Harlowe."

Cade, Cade, Cade . . .

She had not allowed herself to wonder if, in the future reshaped by her coming home, Cade would still exist. She tried to ignore it, but whether he existed in the future or not, it felt to her like he had died. Maybe she should just let his memory go and forget the little she remembered of him, like so many other details. But no, he was not just a detail. He had been important to her. She was sure she had loved him. She hoped he would exist in the future, that she had not ruined that possibility, and that his world would be a better place than the one she had left.

"I asked you here not just to see the glass," Captain Mapstone said, "but to give you this."

"This" was a sheaf of papers, and with a glance Karigan realized it was the transcript of her notes. As she looked through the pages, she found an addendum of the captain's own memory of what Karigan had told her and the king about her experiences.

"I know you've been having a hard time with recall," the captain said, "so I wanted to make sure you had this to refer to. It isn't quite fair to go through what you did and not remember it."

"Thank you," Karigan replied. "There are people I met, and even if their futures have changed, and they never exist now, they still deserve to be remembered."

The captain nodded. "Yes, and in that way they are given life. Speaking of which, now that the storm has died down, I am sending Ty with the news of your return to your father. If you would like to add a note, which I recommend, you should have it ready by early tomorrow morning."

"I will."

"Good. If you need to talk about anything at all, you know you may speak freely to me. I know you left behind people important to you in that future. Also, what has happened to your eye, it can't be easy."

"I would like to set up sessions with Drent," Karigan replied.

The captain showed her surprise. "So soon?"

"I have got to learn to fight with this." She touched the bandage over her eye. She did not add that the physical exertion would help her cope with the rest.

"Very well, I'll inform Drent. But remember, Karigan, you do not have to carry everything alone. Your Rider family will help."

As much as Karigan knew her Rider family would help, she spent the rest of the afternoon in the solitude of her room away from the new Riders who stared at her and whispered behind her back. It was difficult being looked upon as strange, and as a stranger, by her own. They'd no doubt heard stories about her past adventures that made her seem even more outlandish. Other. They would, Mara reassured her, get over it with time.

Karigan read through the transcript. It was disjointed, sometimes providing only the name of a person or place. Dakrias had given her a fresh pile of paper, pen, and ink, and now she made notes on her notes, adding more if she saw a flash of a face, or recalled even the most innocuous of details. Bad air, she remembered. The air had been bad in Mill City.

There was mention of time, one of the most valuable pieces of information she had recalled. If events continued in a certain way, they had roughly two years to deal with Amberhill to prevent the fall of Sacoridia and the rise of the Serpentine Empire. Would her coming home already have altered the timeline, or would it march on largely unchanged, the fall of Sacoridia inevitable? How would the king and his advisors use the information she had brought them?

She did not have the answers, and for once was relieved to let others take responsibility for them. At least for now.

She continued looking over the transcript, lingering on names. Sadly, she could barely remember the people except for what was written: *Mirriam, head housekeeper. Lorine, former slave and maid. Professor Josston—uncle?*

Then there was Cade. She had the briefest of flashes, and they were like smoke, impossible to grasp and hold onto. She wrote his name in big letters across a sheet of paper. She had his name. At least she had that much.

She set aside her notes and began her letter to her father and aunts. A brief "everything is fine" would not pass muster, not this time. She started and stopped, started and stopped. How did one explain to a worried parent about Blackveil and the future? How was she supposed to break it to her father she wasn't dead? Such news would bring its own shock.

Dear Father,
   Contrary to what you may have heard, I am alive and well.

Then what?

She welcomed the interruption of a knock on her door.

"Come in," she called, and pushed away from her vanity,

which had served as a desk. Garth, apparently, was still searching for a suitable desk for her.

She had expected a Rider, but the man in her doorway was not that. She stood and bowed. "Your Majesty."

He took one hesitant step into her room. A pair of Weapons lingered in the corridor.

"Hello, Karigan." Not Rider G'ladheon, not Sir Karigan.

To her, his face had grown more careworn. She now saw a scar across his eyebrow. Mara said he'd led forays against Second Empire. He was more careful in his movements, and thinner than she recalled. The assassin's arrow with its poison had taken its toll on him.

His near death, his marriage to Estora . . . Karigan did not know how she would have handled it all had she been here and not in Blackveil. Perhaps the gods dealt in backward mercies after all.

"The queen wished me to deliver her fondest greetings."

It had been explained to Karigan that the forester of Coutre—sent with the expedition into Blackveil with orders to murder her—had not, in fact, been sent by Estora but by her cousin, the misguided Lord Richmont Spane. He'd wanted nothing and no one to interfere with his cousin's betrothal to the king.

"How is the queen?" Karigan asked.

"Resting in bed as ordered by Master Vanlynn. We are expecting twins." Like a force he could not control, he smiled, a light shining in his eyes.

"I heard," she said. "Congratulations."

It was odd, but in her notes, Karigan had seen a reference to Estora having had only one child. All had changed, unless one of the babies did not make it. Karigan said nothing about it, but it must have occurred to Zachary as well. "Please return my greetings to the queen."

Their conversation was stilted, had an unreality to it.

"I will. I have advised Captain Mapstone that you are to take as much time as you need to recover."

"I hope to be back on duty as soon as possible."

He raised his eyebrows. "Truly? After all you've been through? Your eye?"

"Yes." She needed to work, to keep her mind occupied. She was not sure how long she could stand to remain in the castle with him married to Estora and all the anticipation of the babies. She needed to move on. She did not want to sit around and stew over what was or might have been. She'd become stuck, unable to function. She wasn't sure, but she didn't think Cade Harlowe would want that for her.

Cade, Cade, Cade . . .

The king studied her for some moments. She could tell there was much he wished to say, but prudence prevented him.

"I do not know why fate has chosen to put you through so much," he said finally. "I would change it all if I could."

"I know." She glanced down at the toes of her boots. "But I would not want to change all of it."

His eyebrows lifted in surprise. "No?"

"Cade." His name slipped from her tongue when she had not meant to speak it aloud. Hastily she added, "The people. I don't remember much, but . . . I'd not have met them had I not gone forward in time." Despite the little she remembered, she felt certain that her time with Cade had been profound, complete in a way that her connection with Zachary never would be. Never could be. She'd always known it to be impossible to have such with him, and it only intensified her sense of loss. Her loss of both men. Maybe Zachary was right to think it better if none of it had happened.

"This Cade, he was—?"

"No! I don't—" she began harshly. When she saw his stung expression, she took a breath and said in a softer tone, "I mean, I don't remember. Not much. But he was important. To me."

Various emotions flickered across his features. She could see him wondering about Cade, a hint of jealousy perhaps? He quickly masked it and settled on concern once again, and reached for her as though to comfort her, but she stepped back, away from his touch, and his hand fell to his side. His forehead crinkled, and once again he looked hurt. How easy it would be to go to him, to be folded in the strength of his arms, to feel his heartbeat against her. She wanted nothing more than to be comforted by him, but too much had happened. It was impossible, too dangerous. She'd already lost too much.

The king nodded in acceptance. "I think you know how I feel, in any case. About you."

Karigan looked away. Found she could not reply. After a painful moment passed, that felt so much longer, he pulled an envelope from his pocket. He held it out to her.

"I—I did not read this," he said. "I refused to believe you were gone. I think I would have *known*."

It took Karigan a moment to realize what it was, but once she saw her own handwriting on it and the green wax seal, there was no mistake. It was the letter she had written to be given to him in the event she did not return from Blackveil. It let him know her heart, all the things she could never say to him while she lived. She did not know whether to feel relieved he had not read it, or disappointed. Relieved because then all she held inside would have been exposed in no uncertain terms. Disappointed for the same reason. It was for the best, she supposed. She did not need that letter adding fuel to the longing between them.

He cleared his throat and said more brusquely, "I've something else for you. Ellen?" The Weapon stepped in briefly to hand him a rolled up paper tied with a ribbon. "A very strange thing. The journal that Rider Cardell took into Blackveil was being catalogued to be filed with other records. His drawings are very good, and I am sure the images and maps he drew will be helpful in the future." He paused, but very briefly. "The odd thing was, a picture we had somehow missed earlier came to light, tucked into the back of the journal. Apparently Rider Cardell wanted you to have it."

He passed her the rolled paper, and she held it with trepidation. What in the world had Yates drawn that he wanted her to see?

Preoccupied by the rolled paper in her hands, Karigan barely noticed King Zachary receding from her chamber. She did not see how his gaze lingered on her, his expression wistful and suffused with regret and his own loss. She did not register the door closing silently and soundly behind him.

She moved to her chair and undid the ribbon. She was glad she was sitting because when the paper unrolled, she saw the gift for what it was, a gift from the spirit of Yates Cardell. He'd be smiling right now, she knew he would.

At the very top of the page was written, *For Karigan.* Drawn in ink were portraits of people, people she'd met in the future. Even without their names labeled, she knew them like a shockwave: Mirriam looking stern as always and peering through a monocle. Lorine and Arhys holding hands as they walked down a cobbled street. Professor Josston looking magnificent in his evening clothes. Luke with his hand on Raven's neck.

Drawn in the center of the page was a portrait of Cade, a bemused smile on his face as if he was telling her she could never possibly forget him. At that moment, she remembered everything they'd been through together, and everything they had meant to each other. *Everything.*

Thanks to Yates, Cade would live in her memory and she would never forget. Not ever.

AUTHOR'S NOTE:

On Inspiration and the Real Mill City

Art is the handmaid of human good.

—Motto of the City of Lowell, Massachusetts

I shifted the lever into place to engage the flywheel of the 1901 Model E Draper Power Loom with the whirring belt hanging down from the spinning ceiling shaft. The loom surged to life, slamming the shuttle containing the bobbin of weft yarn back and forth. While the bobbin unspooled and laid down the weft, heddles threaded with warp yarn rose and plunged, rose and plunged, in their own mechanical rhythm. Beaters rammed the lines of weft and warp together into a tight weave. It was the spring of 1989, and I was a ranger at Lowell National Historical Park, located about twenty miles north of Boston, Massachusetts. I was leading a tour through the park's Suffolk Mill Exhibit and demonstrating the manufacture of cloth as it had been done on a mass scale in the 19th and 20th centuries—with water power.

1901 Draper Power Loom located in the Suffolk Mills. Author photo.

About two hundred years ago, entrepreneurs arrived on the banks of the Merrimack River to exploit its strong currents. As brick mill complexes transformed a farm village into an industrial center, Irish immigrants dug out canals that would deliver water to the breast wheels, and later, the turbines, used to power all the machines involved in the cloth-making process, from carding and spinning, to weaving and finishing. The Suffolk began producing cotton cloth in 1832.

A shuttle with bobbin and thread that would have been used in a loom.
Quarter indicates scale. Shuttles could be deadly missiles for mill
laborers if they skipped their tracks at speeds of up to 200 miles per hour.
Author photo.

Lowell was one of the first planned cities of the American Industrial Revolution, conceived as a sort of experimental urban utopia, a sight some European visitors considered as worthy of being seen as Niagara Falls. Its fortunes rose and fell over the years, and the vision of utopia quickly tarnished. With its rich history, mills, canals, and machines, Lowell inspired aspects of *Mirror Sight*'s "Mill City." In fact, Lowell was often referred to as "the Mill City" at the height of its influence.

During my demonstration in the Suffolk Mill, my tour group witnessed how the kinetic energy of water, fed into a turbine beneath the mill via a canal, transferred power to a system of gears, belts, pulleys, and shafts, all the way to the loom. As the loom worked, they felt the vibration of the wooden floor beneath their feet, heard the clamor of all the moving mechanisms, smelled and tasted the metallic tang of machine oil thick in the air. I asked them to imagine two hundred of those looms on just one mill floor (there were five floors) all running at the same time. It would have been deafening. In fact, many mill workers suffered hearing loss, among other more gruesome injuries, in the line of work. The mills had been developed in an era when there was little or no consideration for worker safety, and all the moving machine parts were left exposed with no protective casings to prevent mishaps. Today, visitors to Lowell National Historical Park can get an even better sense of what an active mill floor was once like by exploring the Boott Cotton Mills Museum.

As a ranger at the park, I was required to learn all about Lowell's stories in order to interpret its history to visitors and students. I learned about water power, and those who came to Lowell to labor in the mills. I learned about the owners and managers of textile companies. I had to know the technology behind the machines and weaving. My learning was hands-on—I got to clamber through old gate houses, their gate hoisting mechanisms shrouded in cobwebs. I explored the back sides of mill complexes where tailraces had once spilled expended water back into the river. I stood on expansive, empty mill floors where machines once hummed and clamored.

*Water power! Pawtucket Falls on the Merrimack River, Lowell,
Massachusetts. Author photo.*

Lowell's bricks and cobbles and canals, its multifaceted
stories, have lingered with me all these years, but for all of
Lowell's inspiration, it is important to remember that *Mirror
Sight* is a work of fiction and Mill City is not meant to be a
replica of Lowell. Any inaccuracies concerning the workings
of textile mills or the machines within are either the result of
artistic license or my own error.

It was a privilege to experience Lowell's myriad stories
and pass them on, and the National Park Service will continue to protect and preserve this important piece of American history for future generations. I am grateful for it all,
especially the inspiration.

I encourage interested readers to discover more about Lowell
and other sites of industrial history by visiting Lowell National
Historical Park's website at www.nps.gov/lowe. The park itself
provides many exhibits and tours that offer a vivid exploration
of Lowell's past and present, and is well worth an on-site visit.

Empty mill floor, Boott Cotton Mills #6 in 1988. Author photo.

Urban ranger. The author standing before the Boott Cotton Mills complex in 1989. The torn up parking lot is now a grassy sward known as Boarding House Park. Visitors can get a real feel for a 19th century working cotton mill by touring the Boott Cotton Mills Museum at Lowell National Historical Park. Photo by Karen Sweeny-Justice.

Kristen Britain is the author of the best selling Green Rider series. She lives in an adobe house in the high desert of the American Southwest beneath the big sky, and among lizards and hummingbirds and tumbleweeds.

For my dear Schoodic Peninsula Writers East,
who helped make this a better book
(and kept me sane during its writing):

Annaliese Jakimides

Elizabeth Noyes (Peninsulan emeritus)

Melinda "MelBob" Rice

Brian Dyer Stewart

Cynthia Underwood Thayer

***

I love you guys!